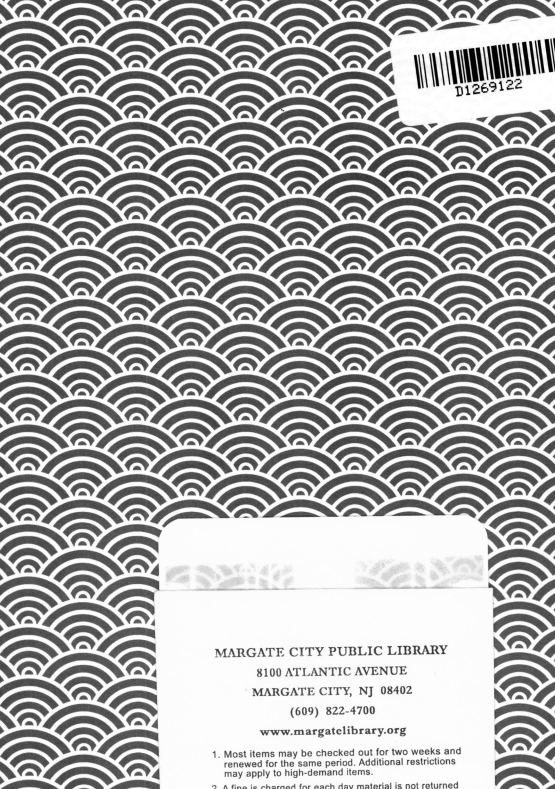

image® comics presents

Wayward

DELUXE BOOK ONE

Created by
Jim Zub &
Steve Cummings

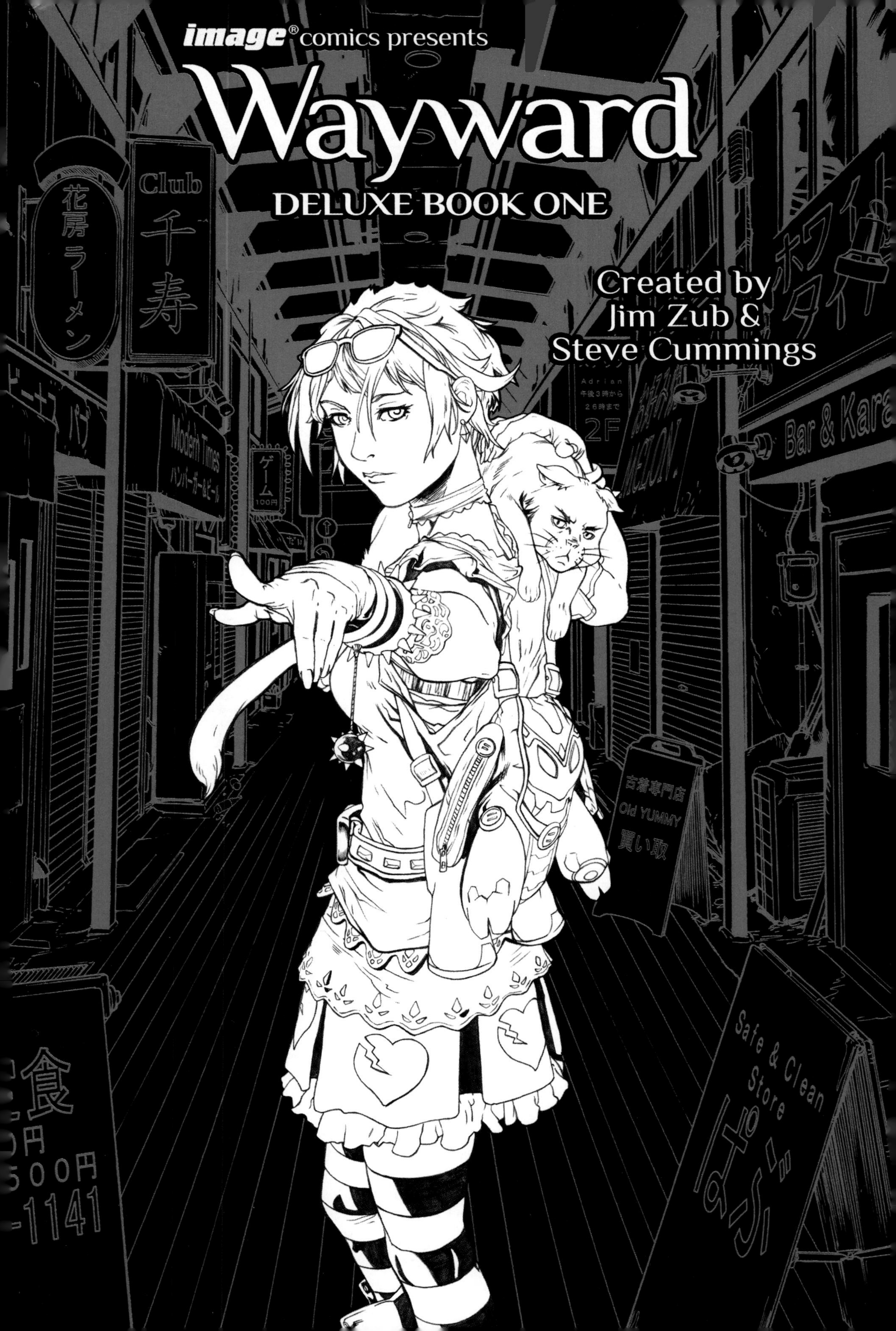

花房ラーメン
Club
千寿
Modern Times
ハンバーガー&ビール
ゲーム
100円
Adrian
午後3時から
26時まで
2F
古着専門店
Old YUMMY
買い取
Safe & Clean
Store

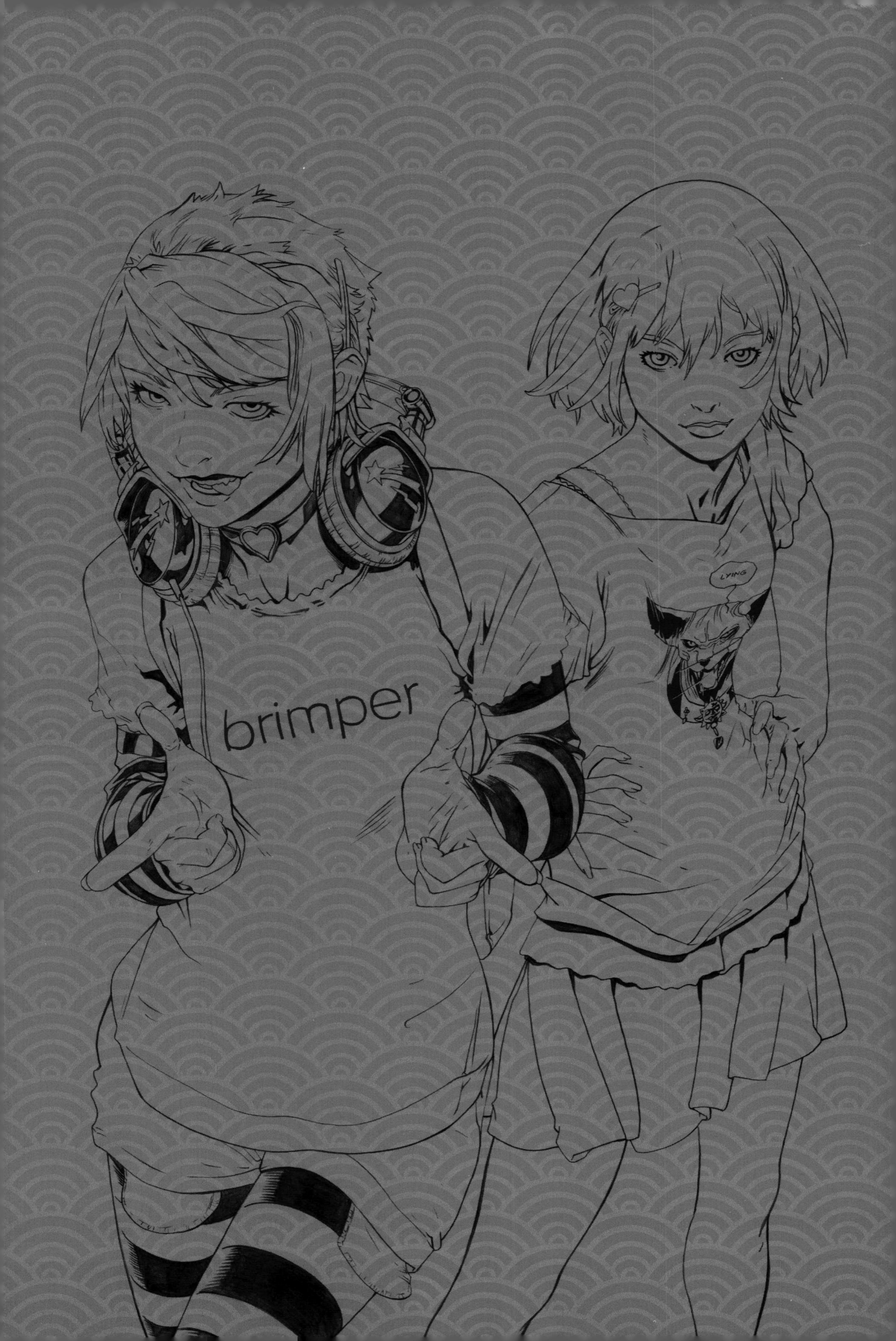
brimper
LYING

story
Jim Zub

line art
Steve Cummings

color art
Tamra Bonvillain
Ross A. Campbell
Josh Perez
John Rauch
Jim Zub

color flats
Ludwig Olimba

letters
Marshall Dillon

back matter
Zack Davisson

copy edits
Stacy King

IMAGE COMICS, INC.
Robert Kirkman – Chief Operating Officer
Erik Larsen – Chief Financial Officer
Todd McFarlane – President
Marc Silvestri – Chief Executive Officer
Jim Valentino – Vice-President

Eric Stephenson – Publisher
Corey Murphy – Director of Sales
Jeremy Sullivan – Director of Digital Sales
Kat Salazar – Director of PR & Marketing
Emily Miller – Director of Operations
Branwyn Bigglestone – Senior Accounts Manager
Sarah Mello – Accounts Manager
Drew Gill – Art Director
Jonathan Chan – Production Manager
Meredith Wallace – Print Manager
Randy Okamura – Marketing Production Designer
David Brothers – Branding Manager
Ally Power – Content Manager
Addison Duke – Production Artist
Vincent Kukua – Production Artist
Sasha Head – Production Artist
Tricia Ramos – Production Artist
Emilio Bautista – Digital Sales Associate
Chloe Ramos-Peterson – Administrative Assistant
IMAGECOMICS.COM

WAYWARD, DELUXE BOOK ONE . ISBN: 978-1-63215-473-6.
First Printing. October 2015. Published by Image Comics, Inc.
Office of publication: 2001 Center Street, 6th Floor, Berkeley,
CA 94704. Copyright © 2015 Jim Zub and Steve Cummings. All
rights reserved. Originally published in single magazine form
as WAYWARD #1-10. WAYWARD™ (including all prominent
characters featured herein), its logo and all character likenesses
are trademarks of Jim Zub and Steve Cummings, unless
otherwise noted. Image Comics® and its logos are registered
trademarks of Image Comics, Inc. No part of this publication may
be reproduced or transmitted, in any form or by any means (except
for short excerpts for review purposes) without the
express written permission of Image Comics, Inc. All names, characters,
events and locales in this publication are entirely fictional.
Any resemblance to actual persons (living or dead), events or places,
without satiric intent, is coincidental. PRINTED IN CANADA.

For international rights contact: foreignlicensing@imagecomics.com.

special thanks
Erik Ko
Brandon Seifert
Charles Soule
Eric Stephenson
Adam Warren

Chapter One

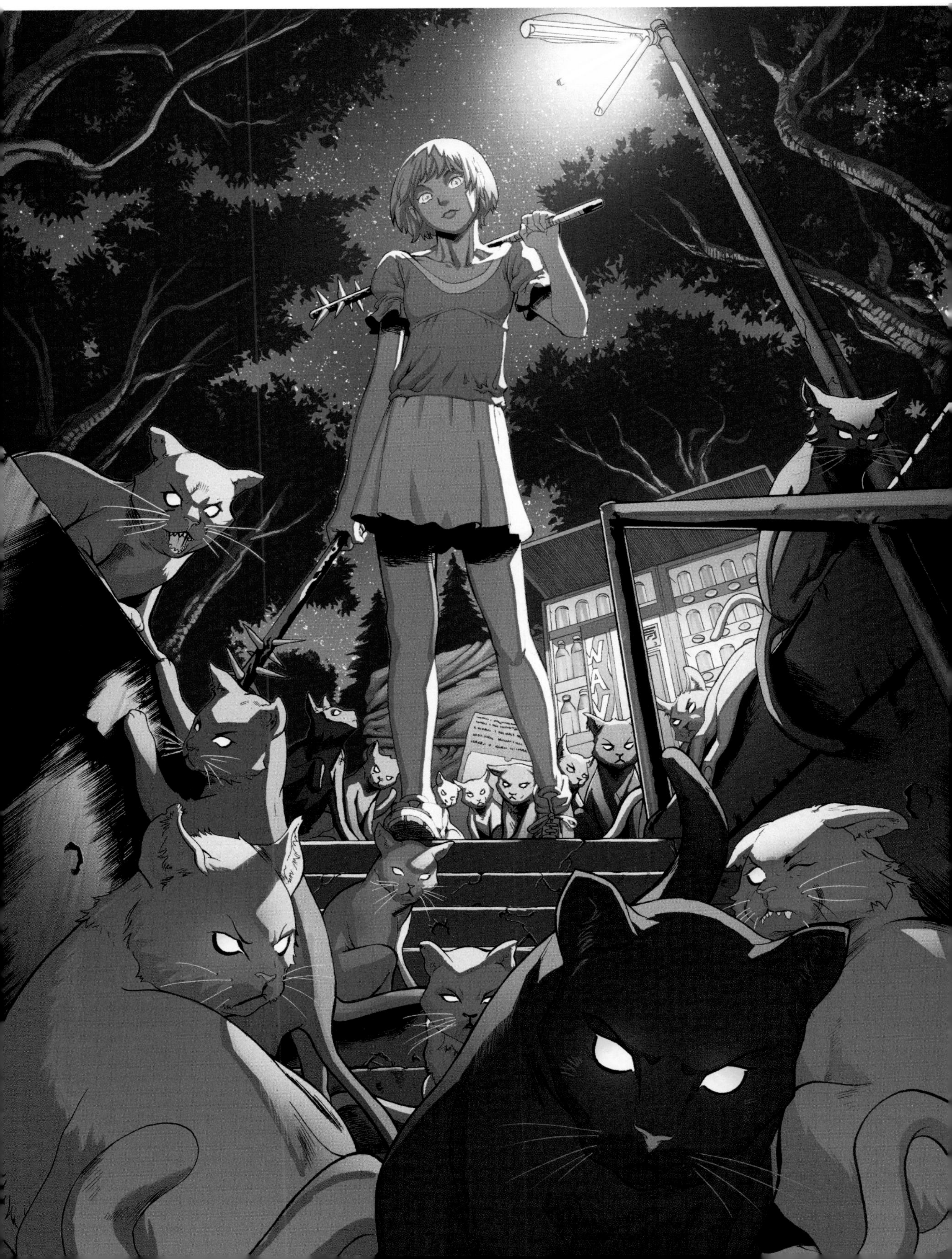

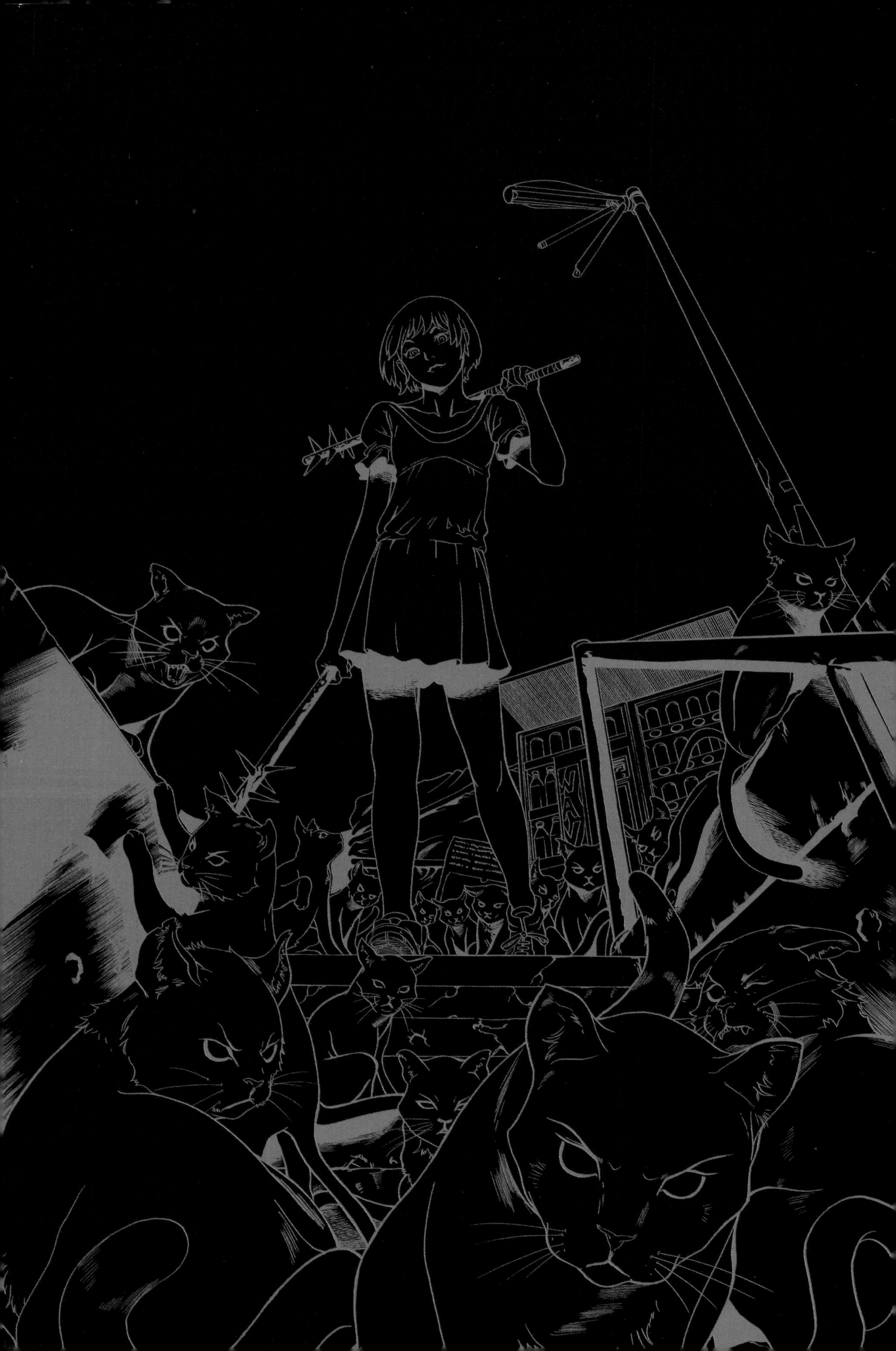

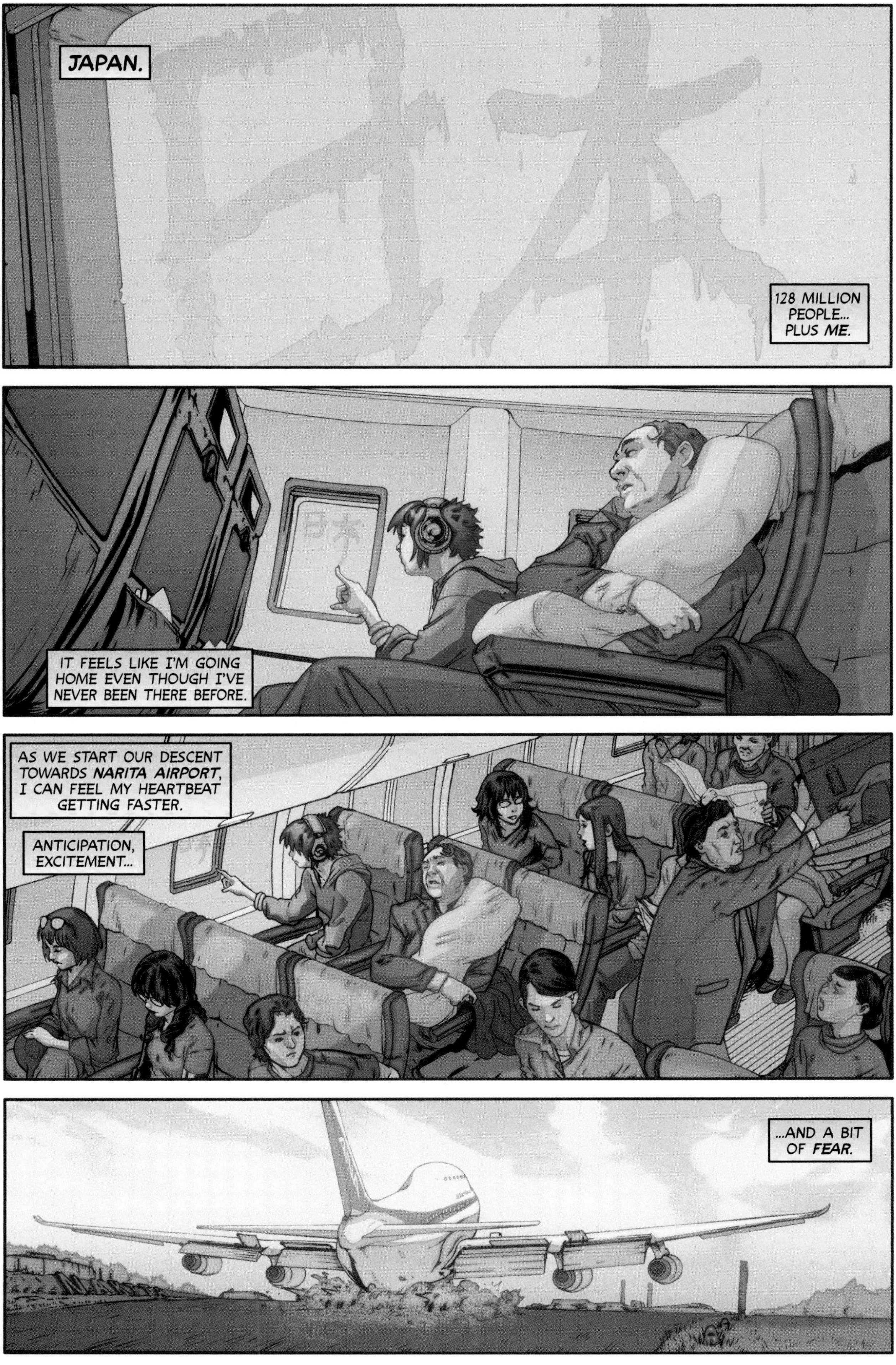
JAPAN.
日本
128 MILLION PEOPLE... PLUS *ME*.
IT FEELS LIKE I'M GOING HOME EVEN THOUGH I'VE NEVER BEEN THERE BEFORE.
AS WE START OUR DESCENT TOWARDS *NARITA AIRPORT*, I CAN FEEL MY HEARTBEAT GETTING FASTER.
ANTICIPATION, EXCITEMENT...
...AND A BIT OF *FEAR*.

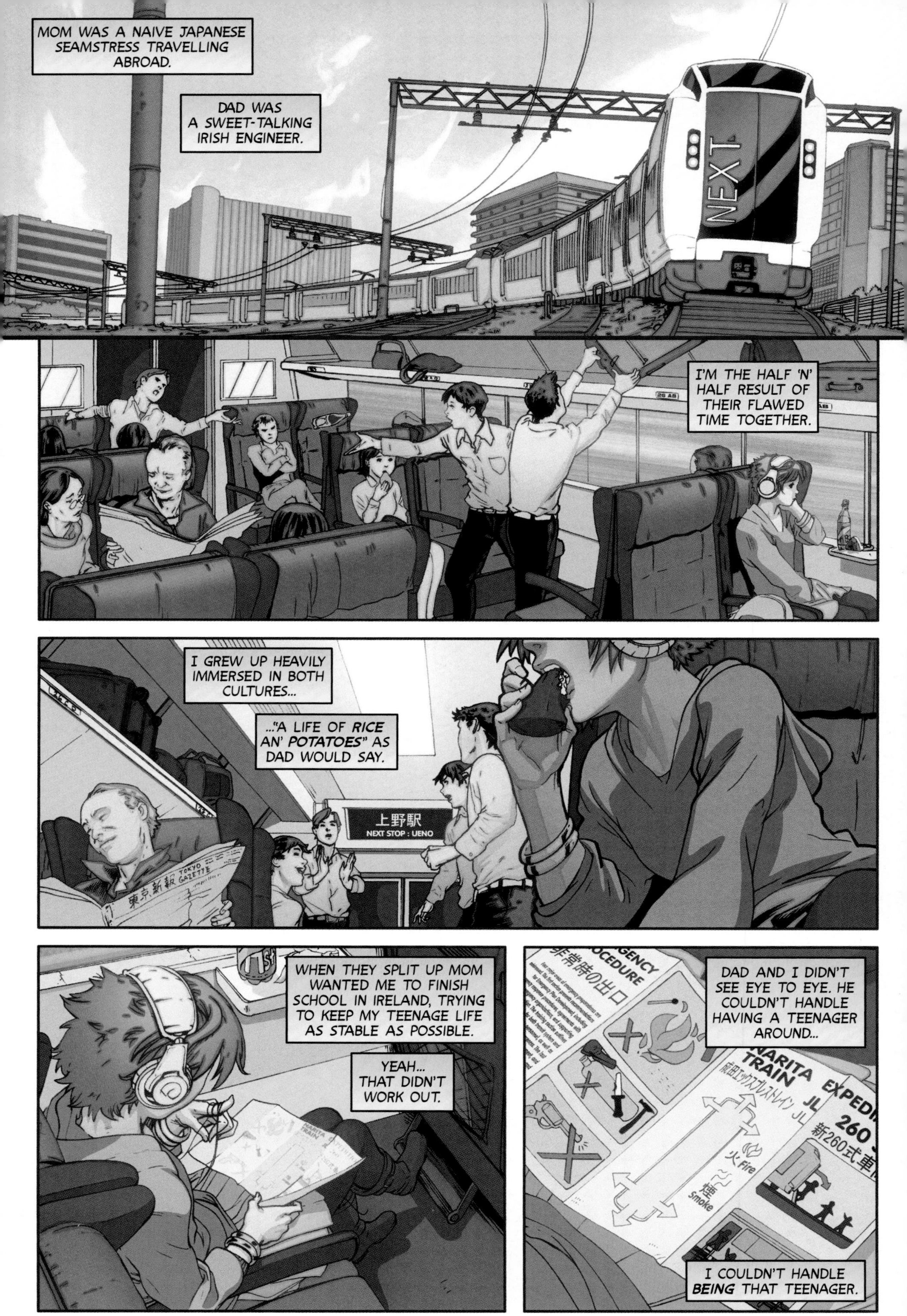
MOM WAS A NAIVE JAPANESE SEAMSTRESS TRAVELLING ABROAD.
DAD WAS A SWEET-TALKING IRISH ENGINEER.
NEXT
I'M THE HALF 'N' HALF RESULT OF THEIR FLAWED TIME TOGETHER.
I GREW UP HEAVILY IMMERSED IN BOTH CULTURES...
..."A LIFE OF *RICE* AN' *POTATOES*" AS DAD WOULD SAY.
上野駅
NEXT STOP : UENO
東京新報 TOKYO GAZETTE
WHEN THEY SPLIT UP MOM WANTED ME TO FINISH SCHOOL IN IRELAND, TRYING TO KEEP MY TEENAGE LIFE AS STABLE AS POSSIBLE.
YEAH... THAT DIDN'T WORK OUT.
DAD AND I DIDN'T SEE EYE TO EYE. HE COULDN'T HANDLE HAVING A TEENAGER AROUND...
非常時の出口
NARITA TRAIN
火 Fire
煙 Smoke
I COULDN'T HANDLE *BEING* THAT TEENAGER.

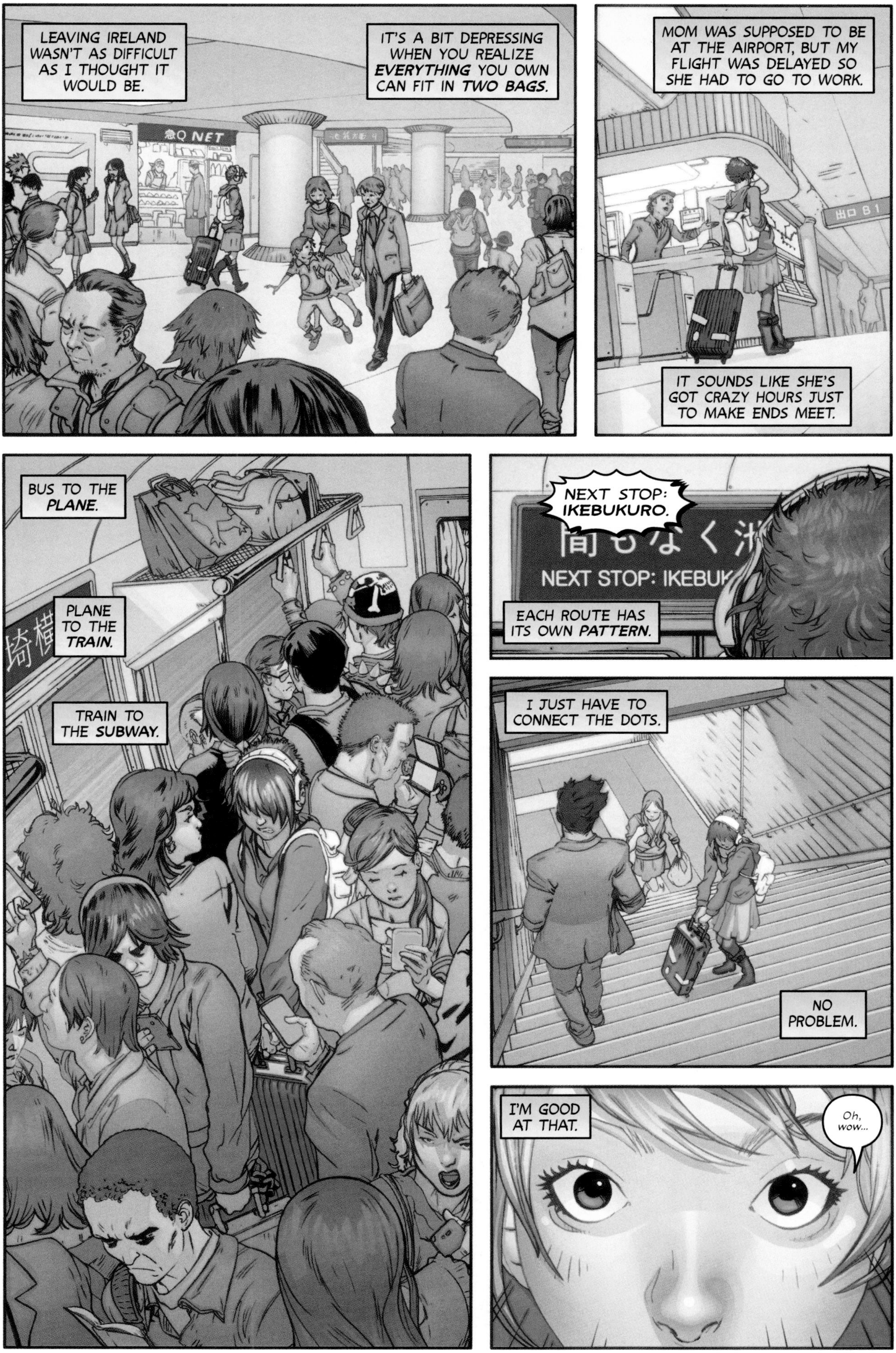

LEAVING IRELAND WASN'T AS DIFFICULT AS I THOUGHT IT WOULD BE.
IT'S A BIT DEPRESSING WHEN YOU REALIZE *EVERYTHING* YOU OWN CAN FIT IN *TWO BAGS*.
急Q NET
MOM WAS SUPPOSED TO BE AT THE AIRPORT, BUT MY FLIGHT WAS DELAYED SO SHE HAD TO GO TO WORK.
出口 B1
IT SOUNDS LIKE SHE'S GOT CRAZY HOURS JUST TO MAKE ENDS MEET.
BUS TO THE *PLANE*.
PLANE TO THE *TRAIN*.
TRAIN TO THE *SUBWAY*.
NEXT STOP: **IKEBUKURO.**
NEXT STOP: IKEBUK
EACH ROUTE HAS ITS OWN *PATTERN*.
I JUST HAVE TO CONNECT THE DOTS.
NO PROBLEM.
I'M GOOD AT THAT.
Oh, wow...

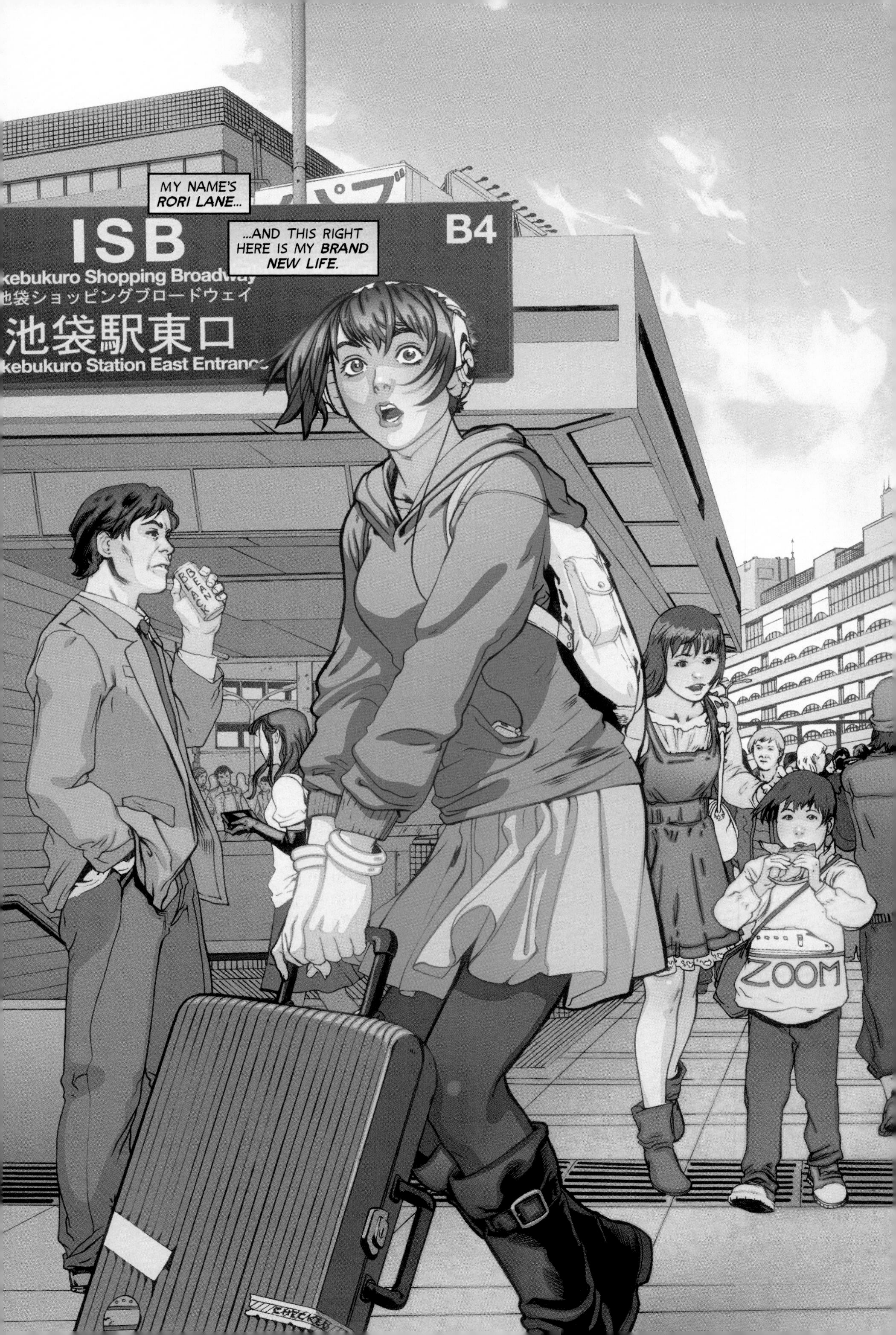
MY NAME'S RORI LANE...
ISB
B4
...AND THIS RIGHT HERE IS MY BRAND NEW LIFE.
kebukuro Shopping Broadway
池袋ショッピングブロードウェイ
池袋駅東口
kebukuro Station East Entrance
BEAN BLACK
ZOOM
CHECKED

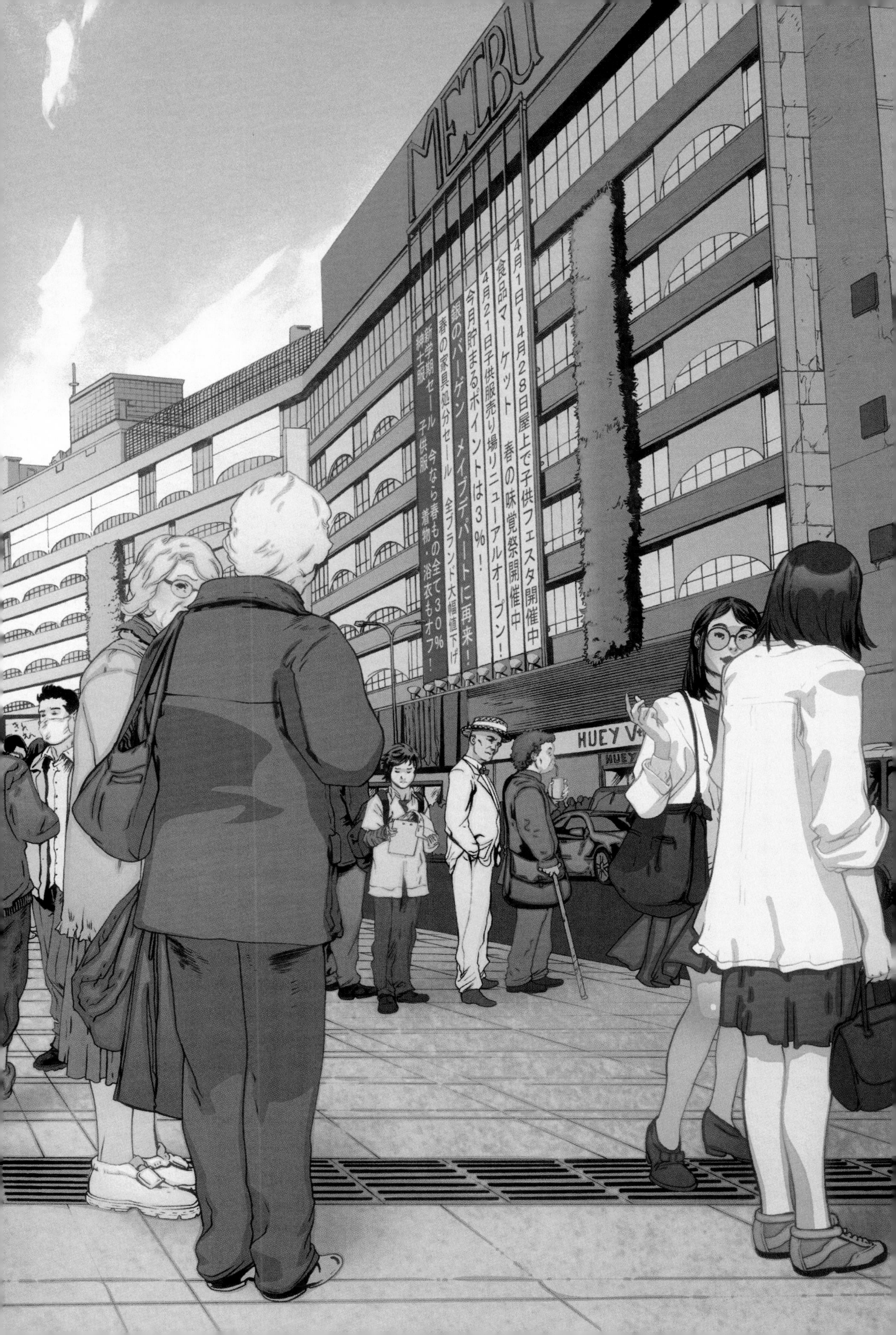
METBU
4月1日〜4月28日屋上で子供フェスタ開催中
食品マーケット　春の味覚祭開催中
4月21日子供服売り場リニューアルオープン！
今月貯まるポイントは3%！
銀のバーゲン　メイプデパートに再来！
春の家具処分セール　全ブランド大幅値下げ
新学期セール　今なら春もの全て30%
紳士服　子供服　着物・浴衣もオフ！
HUEY

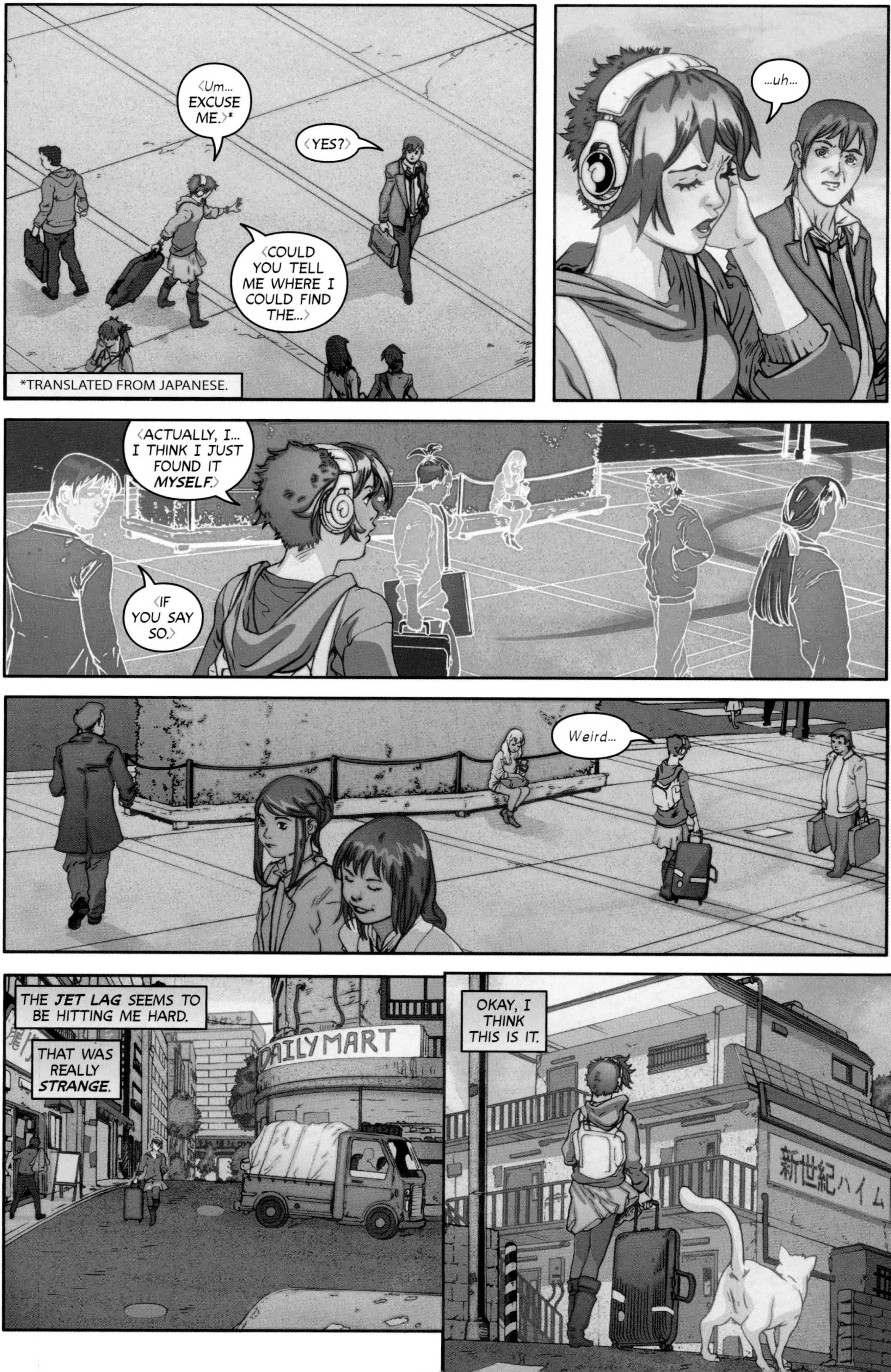

‹Um... EXCUSE ME.›*
‹YES?›
‹COULD YOU TELL ME WHERE I COULD FIND THE...›
*TRANSLATED FROM JAPANESE.
...uh...
‹ACTUALLY, I... I THINK I JUST FOUND IT *MYSELF.*›
‹IF YOU SAY SO.›
Weird...
THE *JET LAG* SEEMS TO BE HITTING ME HARD.
THAT WAS REALLY *STRANGE.*
DAILY MART
OKAY, I THINK THIS IS IT.
新世紀ハイム

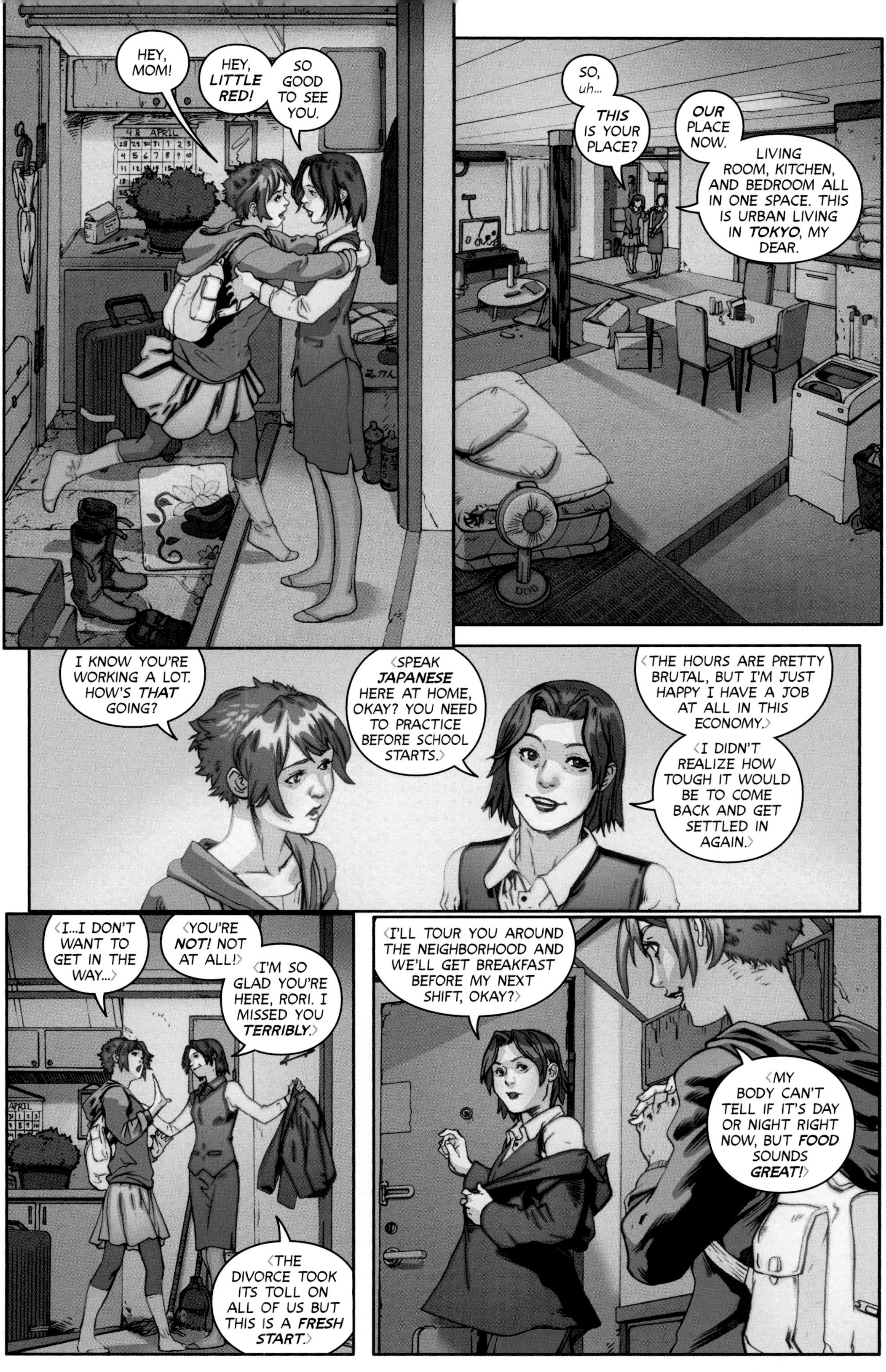
HEY, MOM!
HEY, LITTLE RED!
SO GOOD TO SEE YOU.
SO, uh... THIS IS YOUR PLACE?
OUR PLACE NOW.
LIVING ROOM, KITCHEN, AND BEDROOM ALL IN ONE SPACE. THIS IS URBAN LIVING IN TOKYO, MY DEAR.
I KNOW YOU'RE WORKING A LOT. HOW'S THAT GOING?
〈SPEAK JAPANESE HERE AT HOME, OKAY? YOU NEED TO PRACTICE BEFORE SCHOOL STARTS.〉
〈THE HOURS ARE PRETTY BRUTAL, BUT I'M JUST HAPPY I HAVE A JOB AT ALL IN THIS ECONOMY.〉
〈I DIDN'T REALIZE HOW TOUGH IT WOULD BE TO COME BACK AND GET SETTLED IN AGAIN.〉
〈I...I DON'T WANT TO GET IN THE WAY...〉
〈YOU'RE NOT! NOT AT ALL!〉
〈I'M SO GLAD YOU'RE HERE, RORI. I MISSED YOU TERRIBLY.〉
〈THE DIVORCE TOOK ITS TOLL ON ALL OF US BUT THIS IS A FRESH START.〉
〈I'LL TOUR YOU AROUND THE NEIGHBORHOOD AND WE'LL GET BREAKFAST BEFORE MY NEXT SHIFT, OKAY?〉
〈MY BODY CAN'T TELL IF IT'S DAY OR NIGHT RIGHT NOW, BUT FOOD SOUNDS GREAT!〉

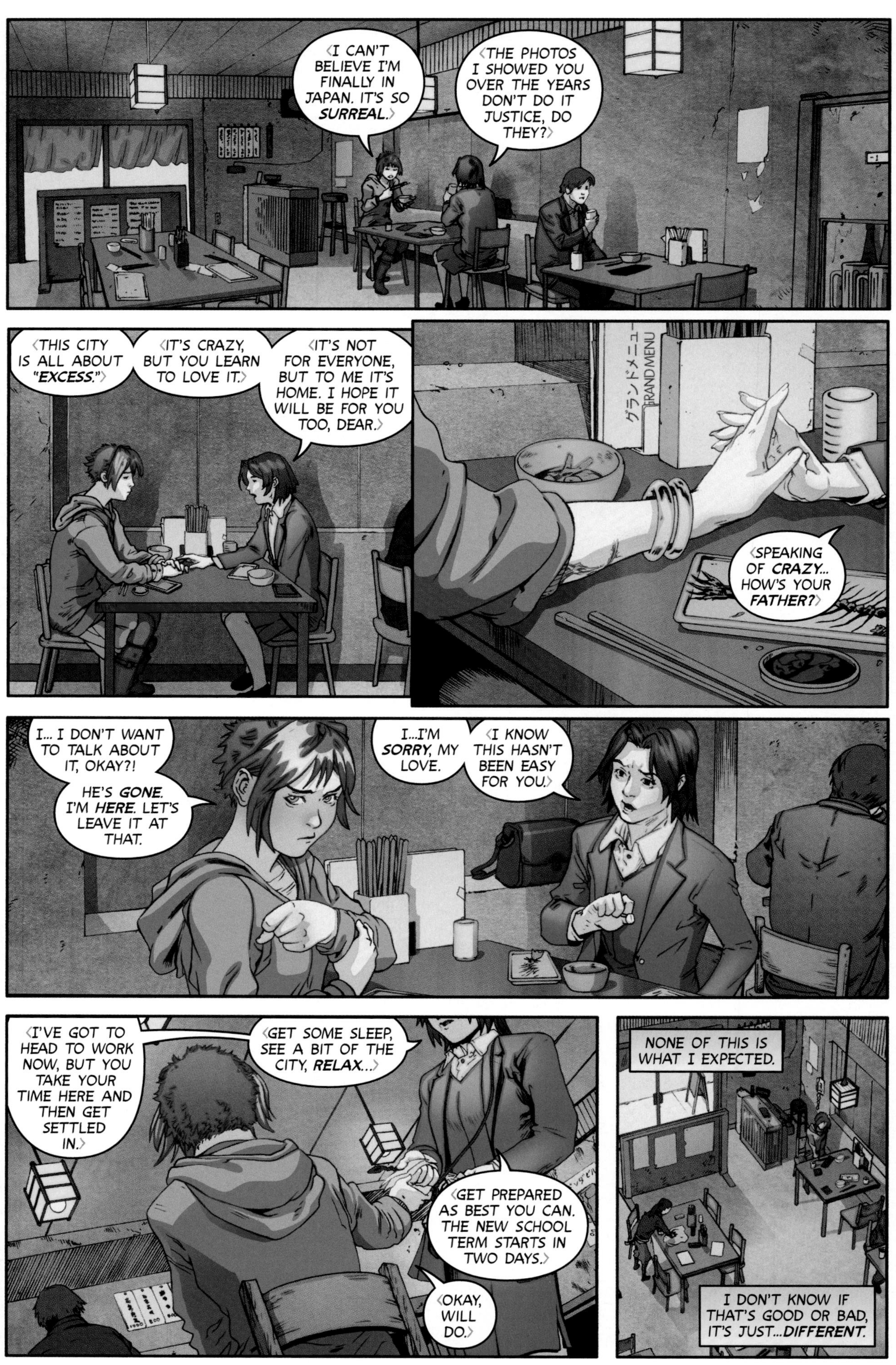

〈I CAN'T BELIEVE I'M FINALLY IN JAPAN. IT'S SO **SURREAL.**〉
〈THE PHOTOS I SHOWED YOU OVER THE YEARS DON'T DO IT JUSTICE, DO THEY?〉
〈THIS CITY IS ALL ABOUT "**EXCESS.**"〉
〈IT'S CRAZY, BUT YOU LEARN TO LOVE IT.〉
〈IT'S NOT FOR EVERYONE, BUT TO ME IT'S HOME. I HOPE IT WILL BE FOR YOU TOO, DEAR.〉
グランドメニュー GRAND MENU
〈SPEAKING OF **CRAZY**... HOW'S YOUR **FATHER?**〉
I... I DON'T WANT TO TALK ABOUT IT, OKAY?!
HE'S **GONE**. I'M **HERE**. LET'S LEAVE IT AT THAT.
I...I'M **SORRY**, MY LOVE.
〈I KNOW THIS HASN'T BEEN EASY FOR YOU.〉
〈I'VE GOT TO HEAD TO WORK NOW, BUT YOU TAKE YOUR TIME HERE AND THEN GET SETTLED IN.〉
〈GET SOME SLEEP, SEE A BIT OF THE CITY, **RELAX**...〉
〈GET PREPARED AS BEST YOU CAN. THE NEW SCHOOL TERM STARTS IN TWO DAYS.〉
〈OKAY, WILL DO.〉
NONE OF THIS IS WHAT I EXPECTED.
I DON'T KNOW IF THAT'S GOOD OR BAD, IT'S JUST...**DIFFERENT**.

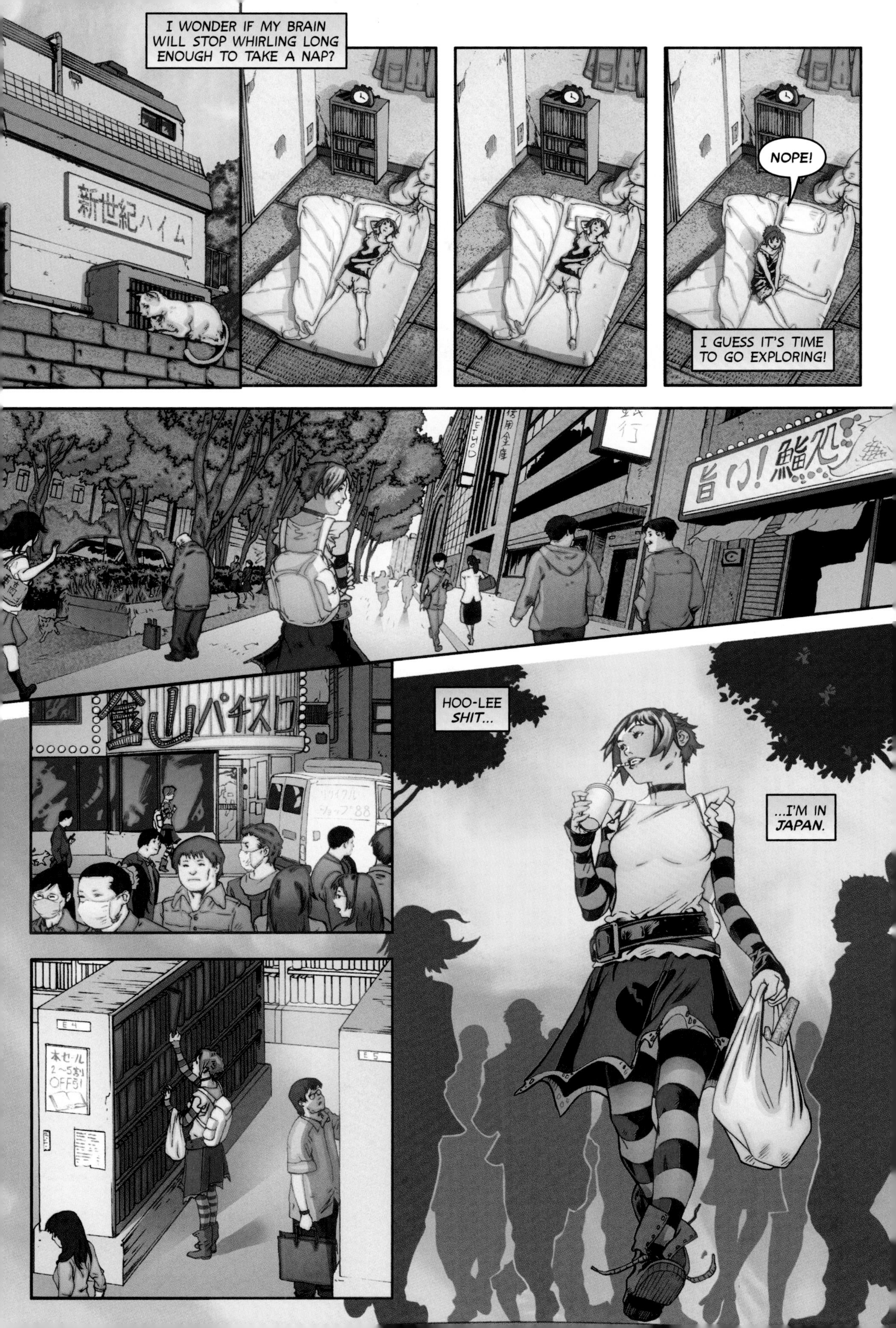
I WONDER IF MY BRAIN WILL STOP WHIRLING LONG ENOUGH TO TAKE A NAP?
新世紀ハイム
NOPE!
I GUESS IT'S TIME TO GO EXPLORING!
HOO-LEE SHIT...
...I'M IN JAPAN.

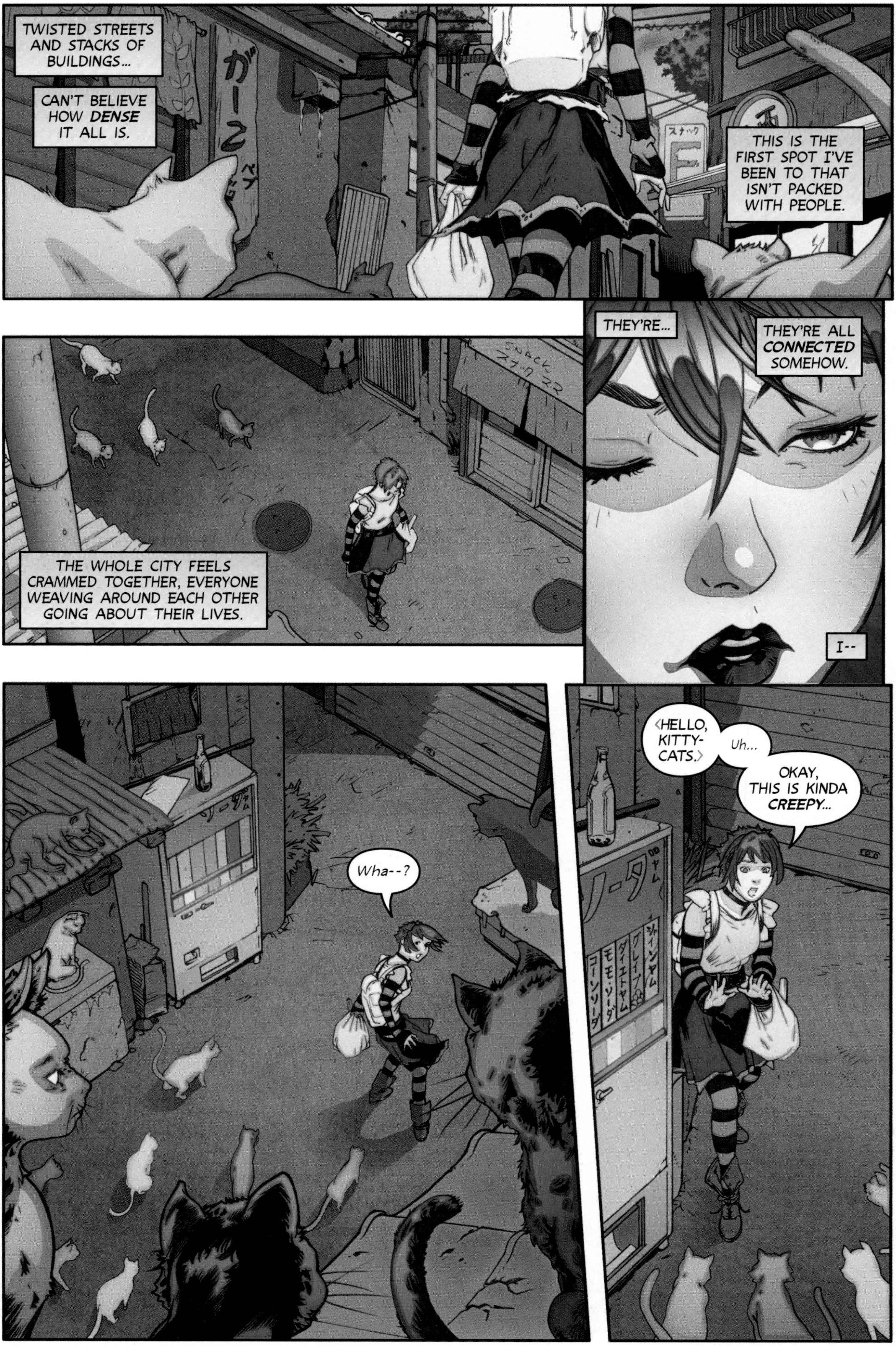
TWISTED STREETS AND STACKS OF BUILDINGS...
CAN'T BELIEVE HOW ***DENSE*** IT ALL IS.
THIS IS THE FIRST SPOT I'VE BEEN TO THAT ISN'T PACKED WITH PEOPLE.
SNACK
THE WHOLE CITY FEELS CRAMMED TOGETHER, EVERYONE WEAVING AROUND EACH OTHER GOING ABOUT THEIR LIVES.
THEY'RE...
THEY'RE ALL ***CONNECTED*** SOMEHOW.
I--
Wha--?
‹HELLO, KITTY-CATS.›
Uh...
OKAY, THIS IS KINDA ***CREEPY***...

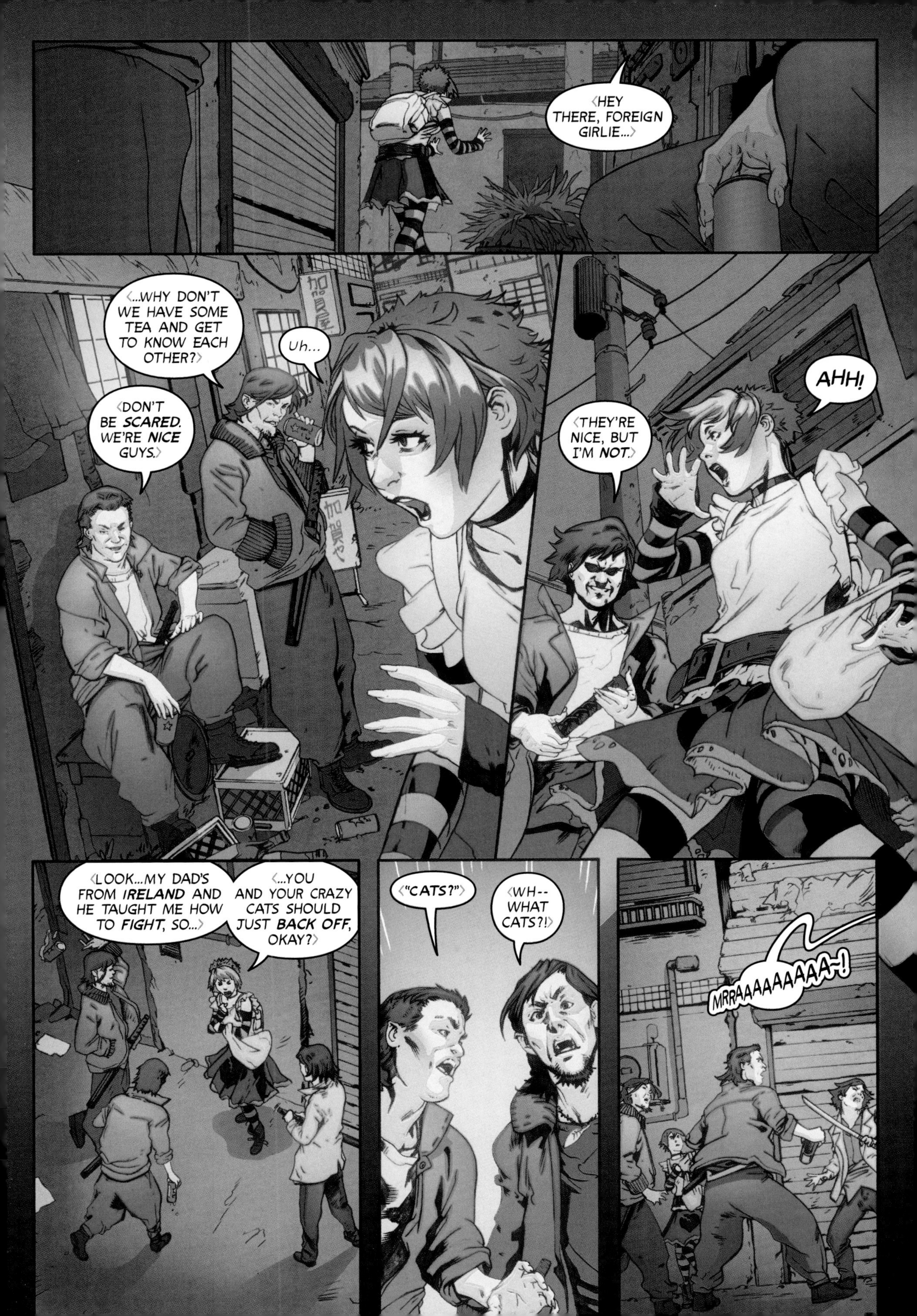
‹HEY THERE, FOREIGN GIRLIE...›
加賀屋
‹...WHY DON'T WE HAVE SOME TEA AND GET TO KNOW EACH OTHER?›
Uh...
‹DON'T BE SCARED. WE'RE NICE GUYS.›
加賀や
‹THEY'RE NICE, BUT I'M NOT.›
AHH!
‹LOOK...MY DAD'S FROM IRELAND AND HE TAUGHT ME HOW TO FIGHT, SO...›
‹...YOU AND YOUR CRAZY CATS SHOULD JUST BACK OFF, OKAY?›
‹"CATS?"›
‹WH-- WHAT CATS?!›
MRRAAAAAAAAAA-!

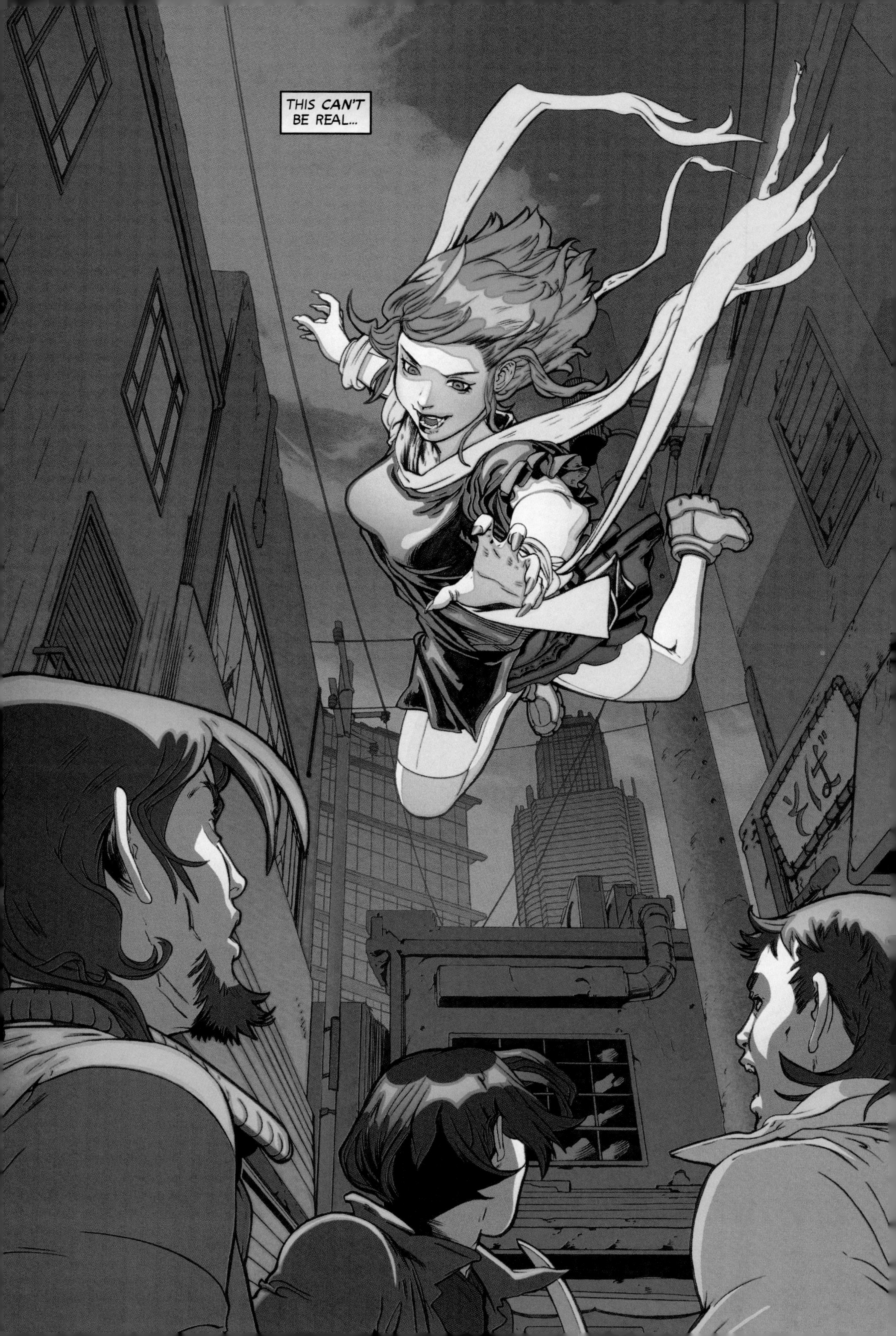
THIS CAN'T BE REAL...
そば

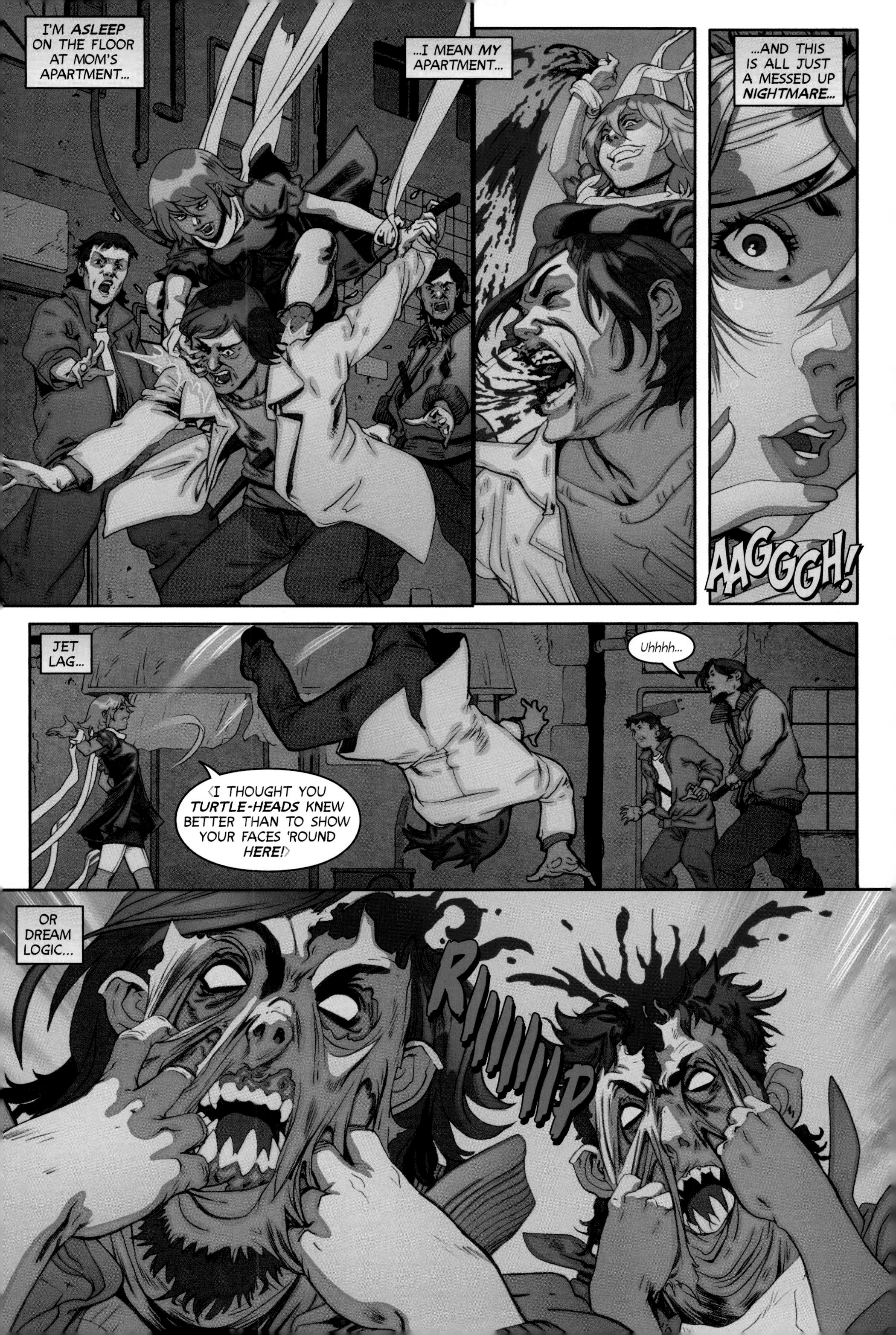
I'M ASLEEP ON THE FLOOR AT MOM'S APARTMENT...
...I MEAN MY APARTMENT...
...AND THIS IS ALL JUST A MESSED UP NIGHTMARE...
AAGGGH!
JET LAG...
<I THOUGHT YOU TURTLE-HEADS KNEW BETTER THAN TO SHOW YOUR FACES 'ROUND HERE!>
Uhhhh...
OR DREAM LOGIC...
RIIIIIIIP

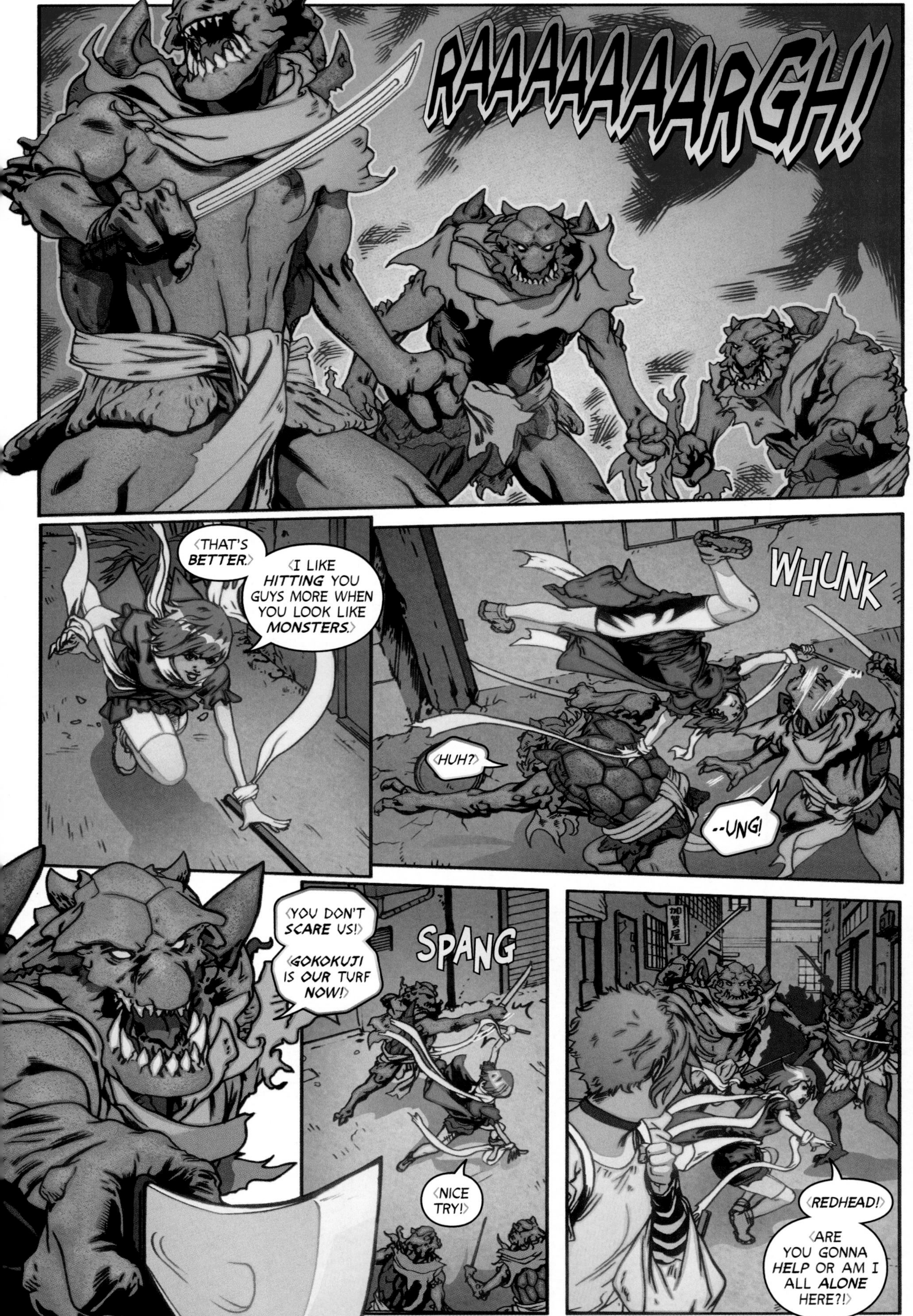
RAAAAAAARGH!
⟨THAT'S **BETTER.**⟩
⟨I LIKE **HITTING** YOU GUYS MORE WHEN YOU LOOK LIKE **MONSTERS.**⟩
WHUNK
⟨HUH?⟩
--UNG!
⟨YOU DON'T **SCARE** US!⟩
⟨**GOKOKUJI** IS **OUR** TURF **NOW!**⟩
SPANG
⟨NICE TRY!⟩
加賀屋
⟨**REDHEAD!**⟩
⟨ARE YOU GONNA **HELP** OR AM I ALL **ALONE** HERE?!⟩

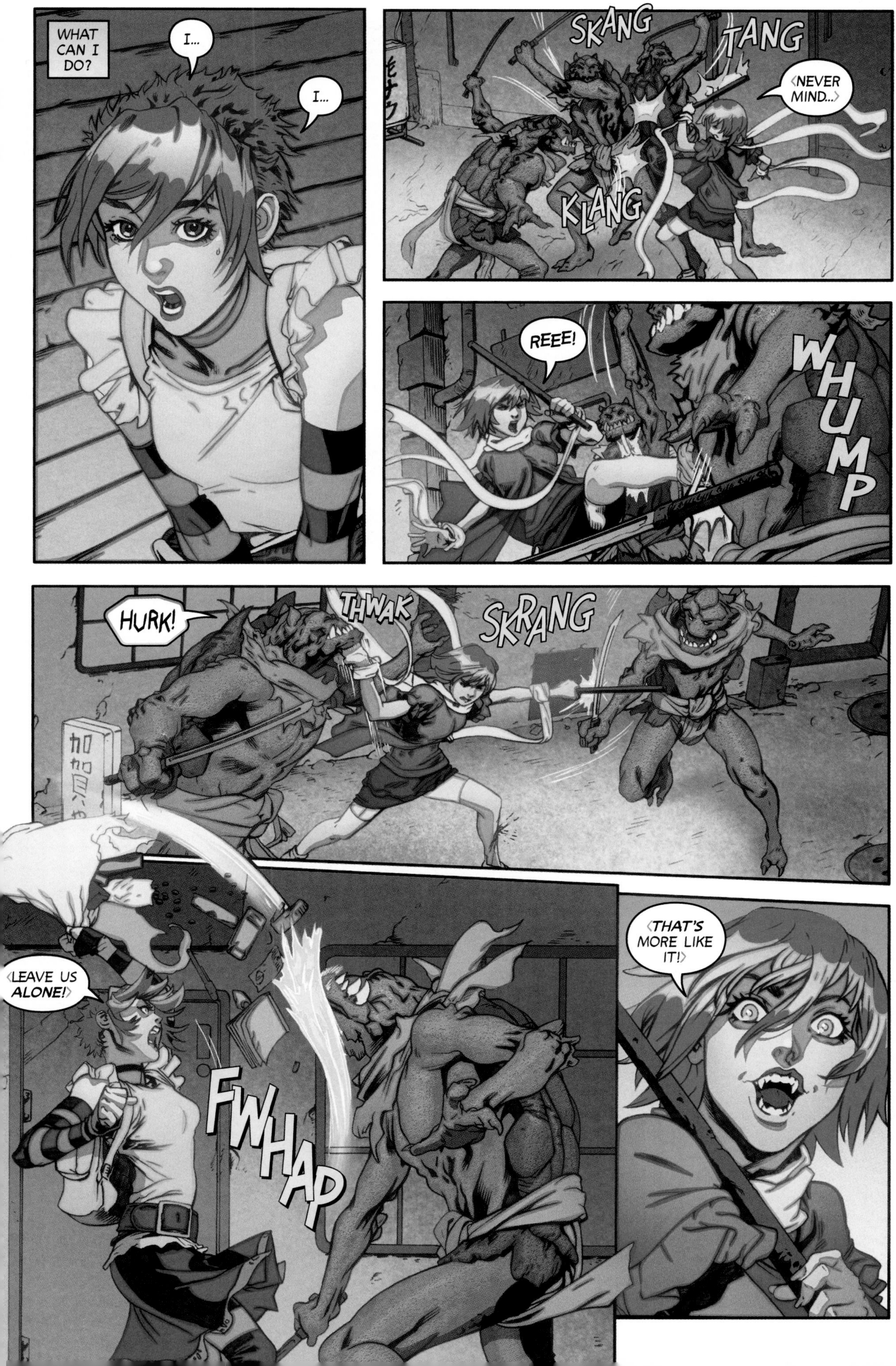

WHAT CAN I DO?
I...
I...
SKANG
TANG
‹NEVER MIND...›
KLANG
REEE!
WHUMP
HURK!
THWAK
SKRANG
‹LEAVE US ALONE!›
FWHAP
‹THAT'S MORE LIKE IT!›

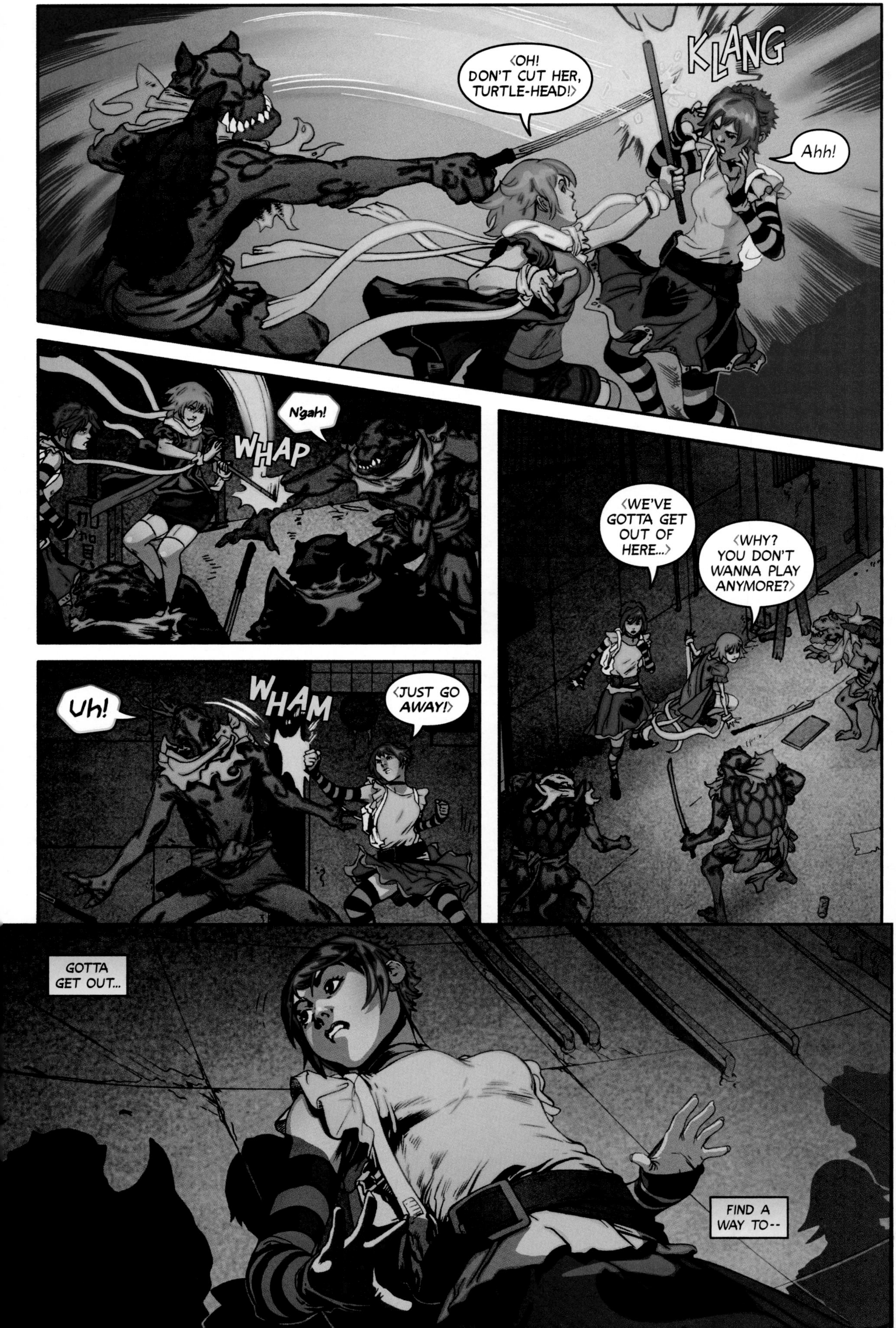
‹OH! DON'T CUT HER, TURTLE-HEAD!›
KLANG
Ahh!
N'gah!
WHAP
Uh!
WHAM
‹JUST GO AWAY!›
‹WE'VE GOTTA GET OUT OF HERE...›
‹WHY? YOU DON'T WANNA PLAY ANYMORE?›
GOTTA GET OUT...
FIND A WAY TO--

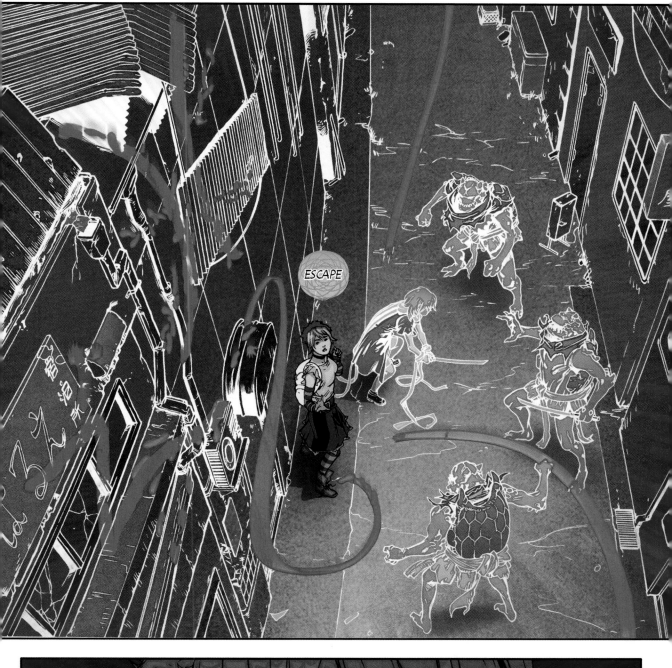

ESCAPE

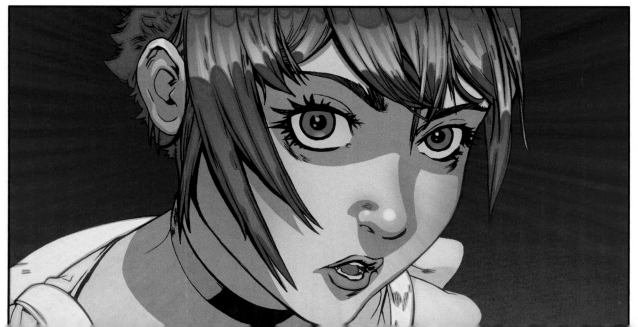

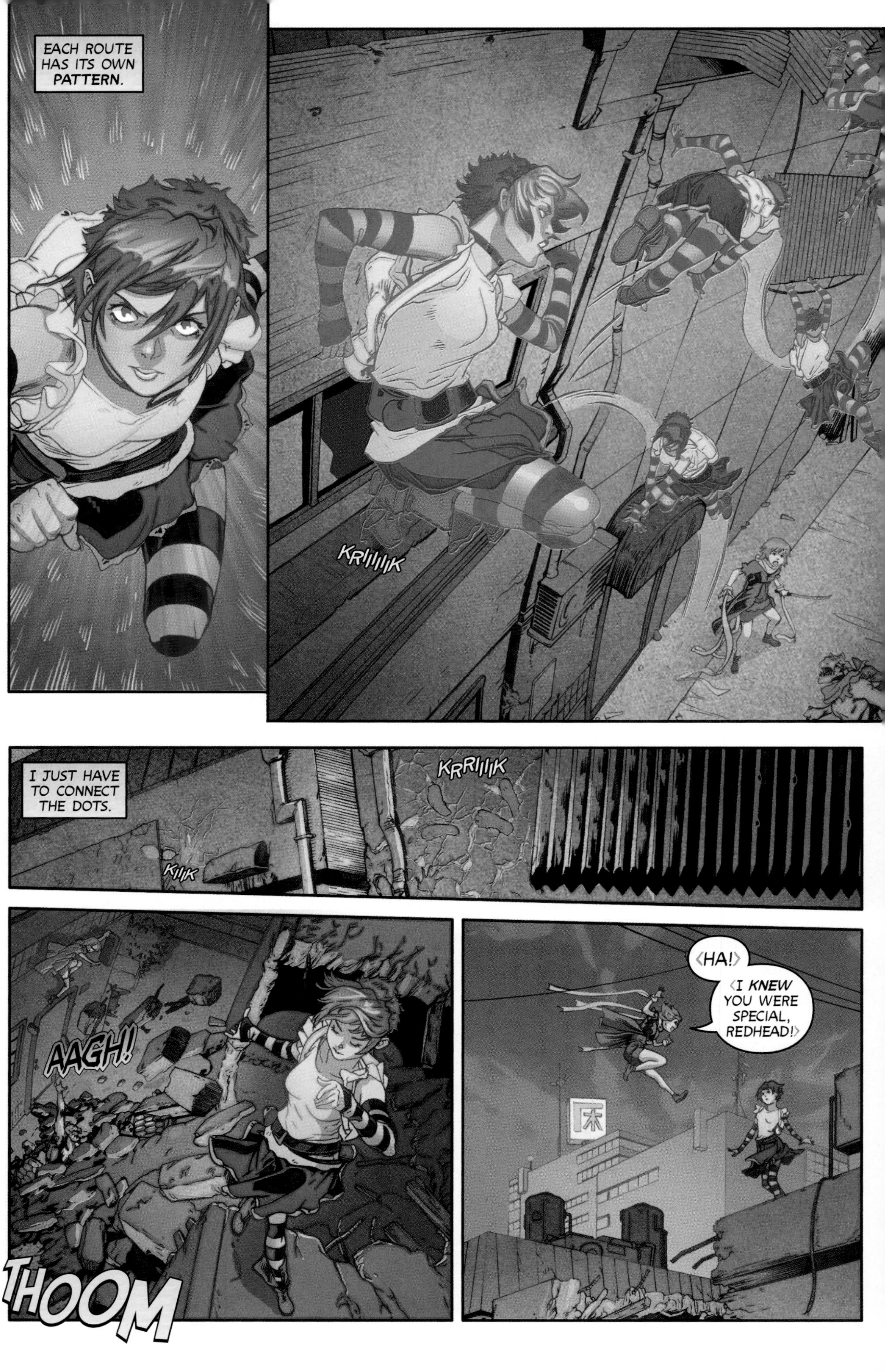
EACH ROUTE HAS ITS OWN PATTERN.
KRIIIIK
I JUST HAVE TO CONNECT THE DOTS.
KIIIK
KRRIIIK
AAGH!
THOOM
‹HA!›
‹I KNEW YOU WERE SPECIAL, REDHEAD!›

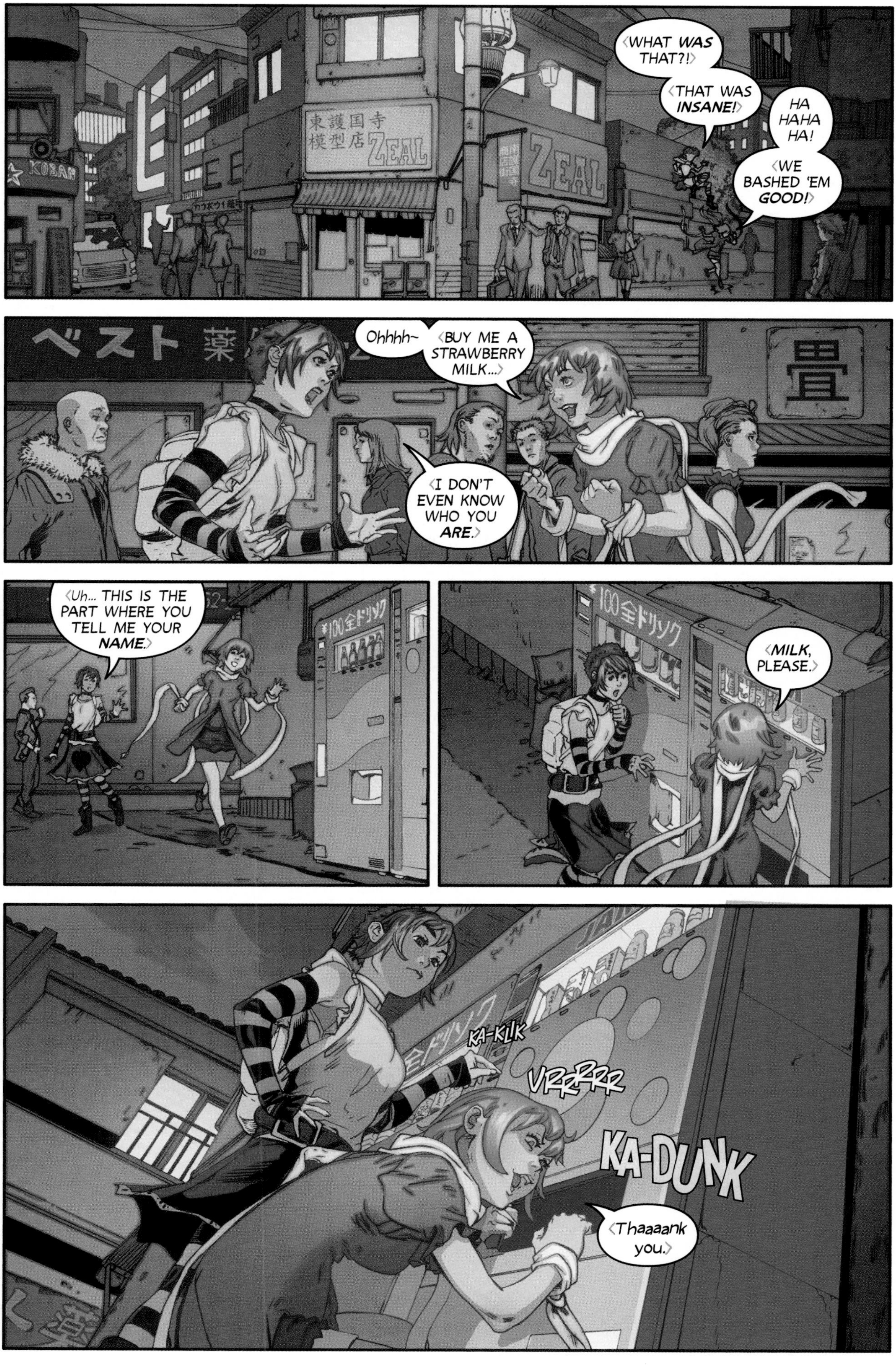

⟨WHAT WAS THAT?!⟩
⟨THAT WAS INSANE!⟩
HA HAHA HA!
⟨WE BASHED 'EM GOOD!⟩
Ohhhh~
⟨BUY ME A STRAWBERRY MILK...⟩
⟨I DON'T EVEN KNOW WHO YOU ARE.⟩
⟨Uh... THIS IS THE PART WHERE YOU TELL ME YOUR NAME.⟩
⟨MILK, PLEASE.⟩
KA-KLIK
VRRRRR
KA-DUNK
⟨Thaaaank you.⟩

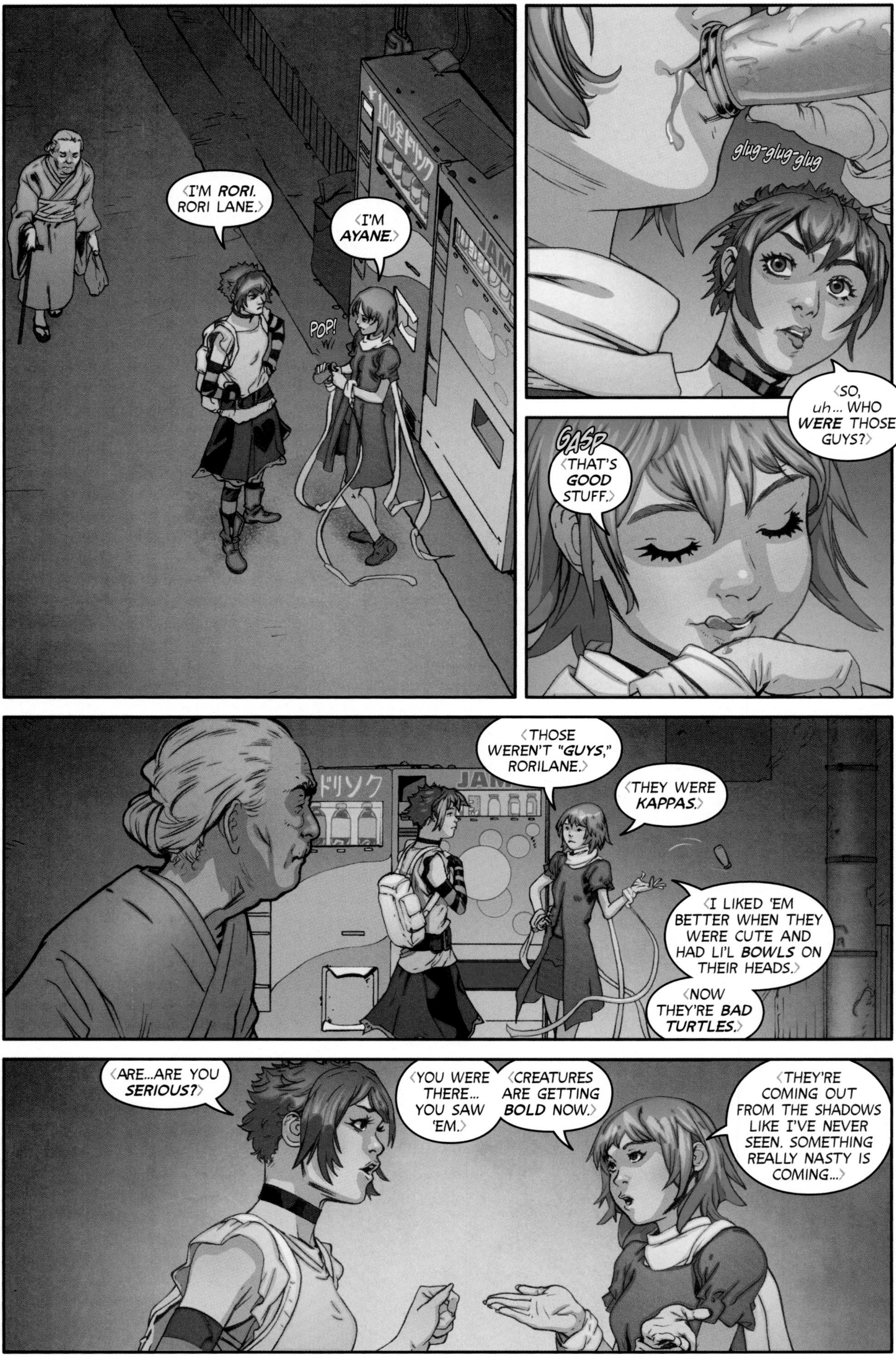

‹I'M *RORI.* RORI LANE.›
‹I'M *AYANE.*›
POP!
glug-glug-glug
‹SO, *uh*... WHO *WERE* THOSE GUYS?›
GASP
‹THAT'S *GOOD* STUFF.›
‹THOSE WEREN'T "*GUYS*," RORILANE.›
‹THEY WERE *KAPPAS.*›
‹I LIKED 'EM BETTER WHEN THEY WERE CUTE AND HAD LI'L *BOWLS* ON THEIR HEADS.›
‹NOW THEY'RE *BAD TURTLES.*›
‹ARE...ARE YOU *SERIOUS?*›
‹YOU WERE THERE... YOU SAW 'EM.›
‹CREATURES ARE GETTING *BOLD* NOW.›
‹THEY'RE COMING OUT FROM THE SHADOWS LIKE I'VE NEVER SEEN. SOMETHING REALLY NASTY IS COMING...›

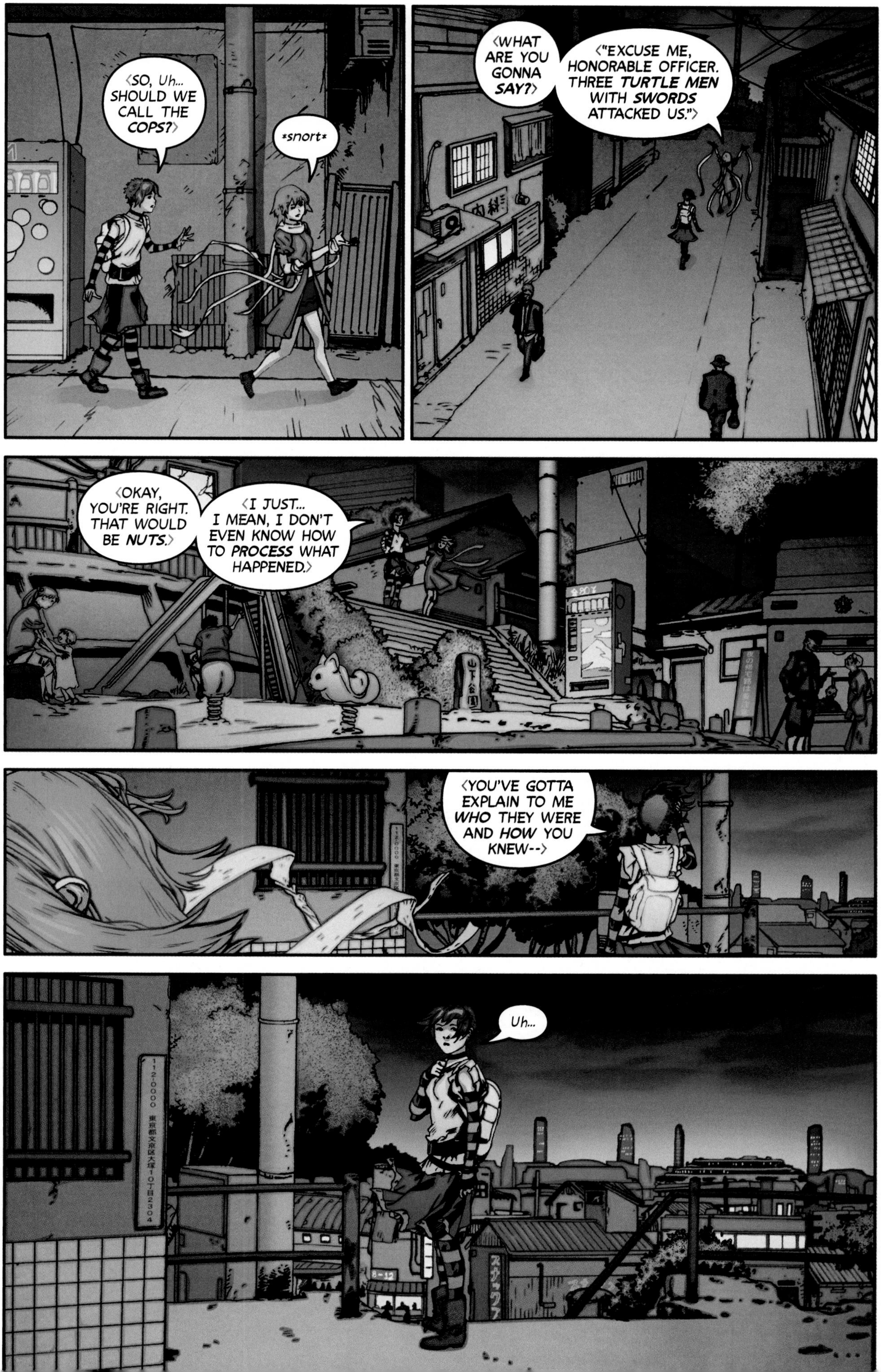
<SO, Uh... SHOULD WE CALL THE COPS?>
snort
<WHAT ARE YOU GONNA SAY?>
<"EXCUSE ME, HONORABLE OFFICER. THREE TURTLE MEN WITH SWORDS ATTACKED US.">
<OKAY, YOU'RE RIGHT. THAT WOULD BE NUTS.>
<I JUST... I MEAN, I DON'T EVEN KNOW HOW TO PROCESS WHAT HAPPENED.>
<YOU'VE GOTTA EXPLAIN TO ME WHO THEY WERE AND HOW YOU KNEW-->
Uh...

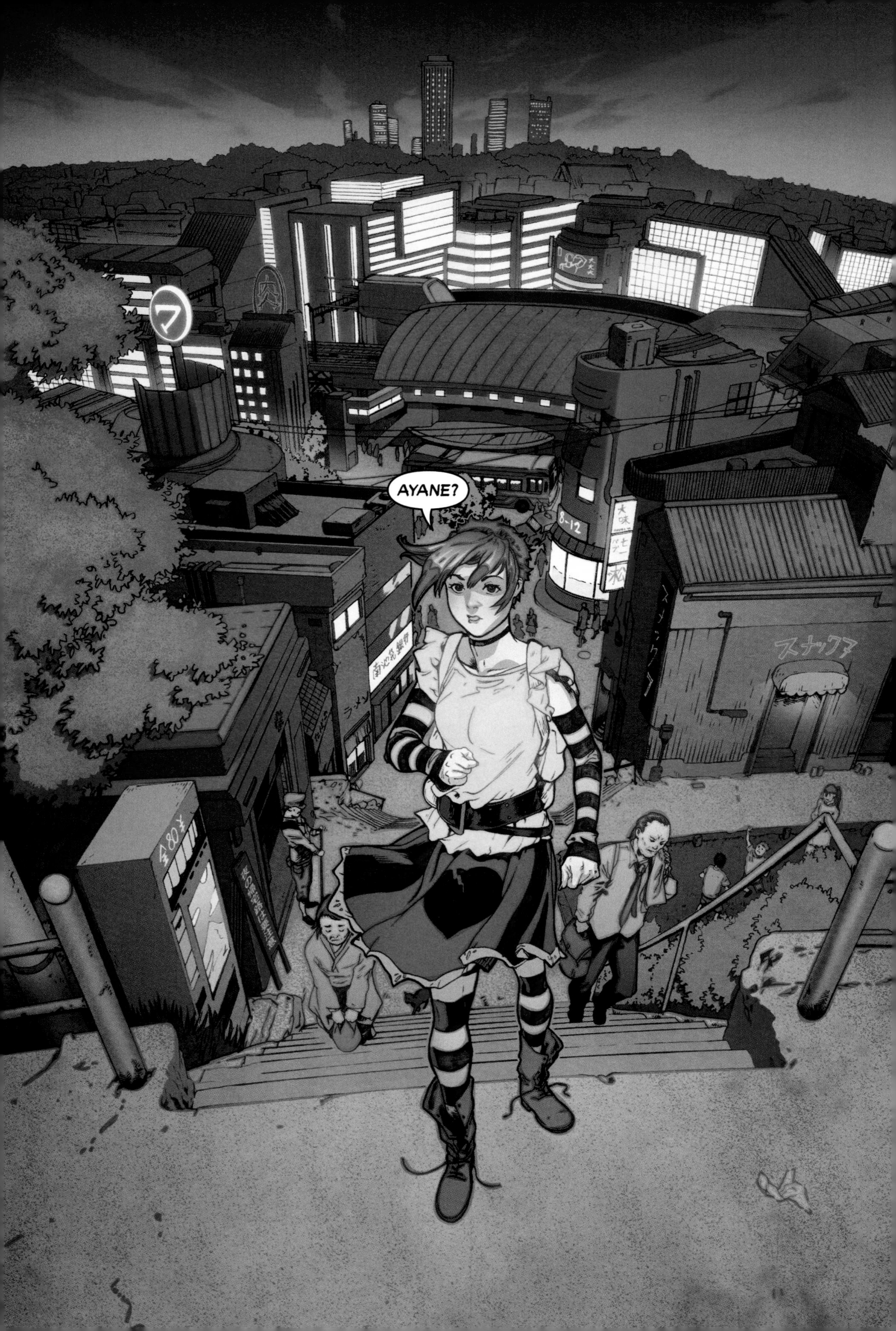
AYANE?
8-12

Chapter Two

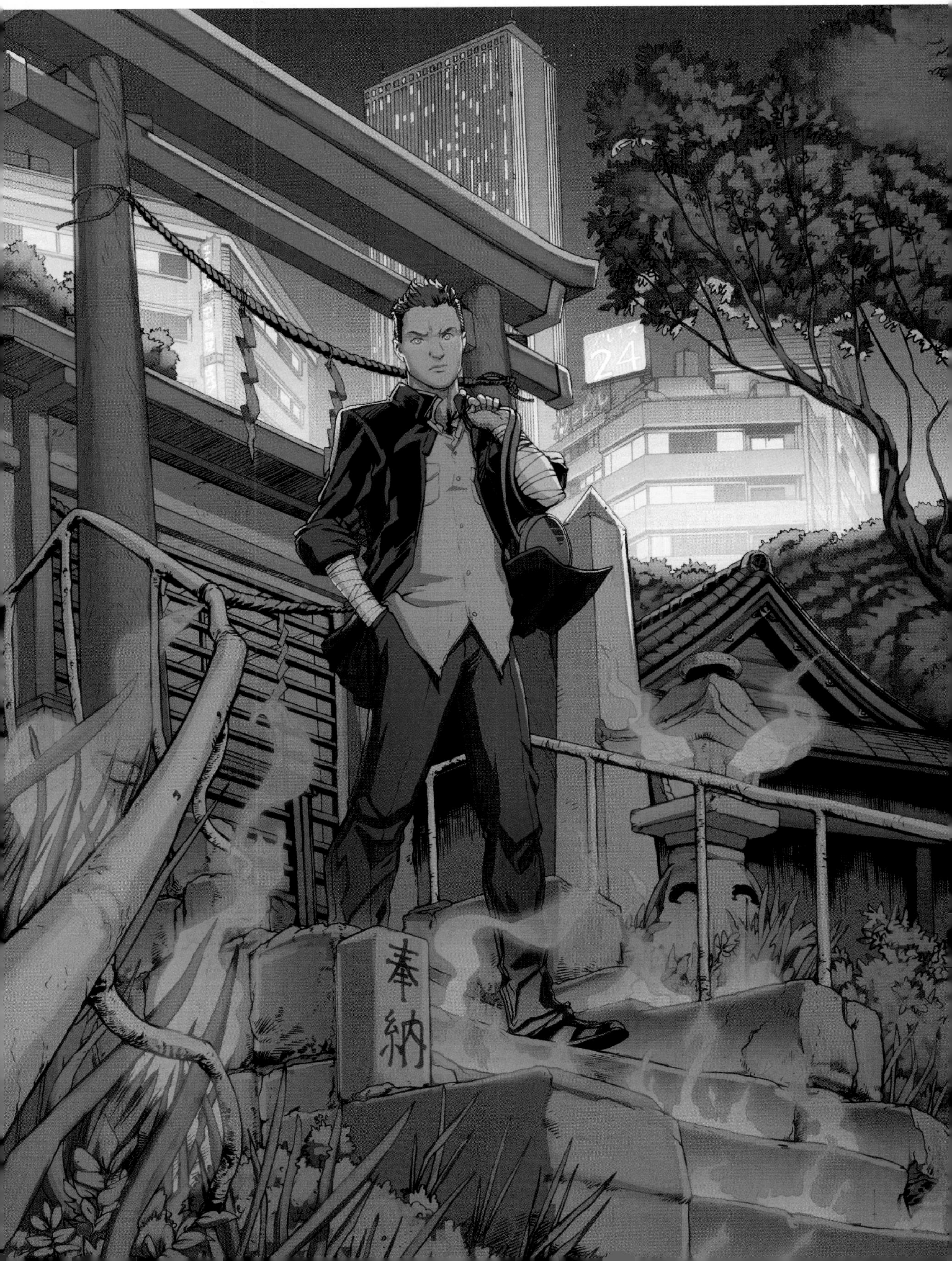
24
奉納

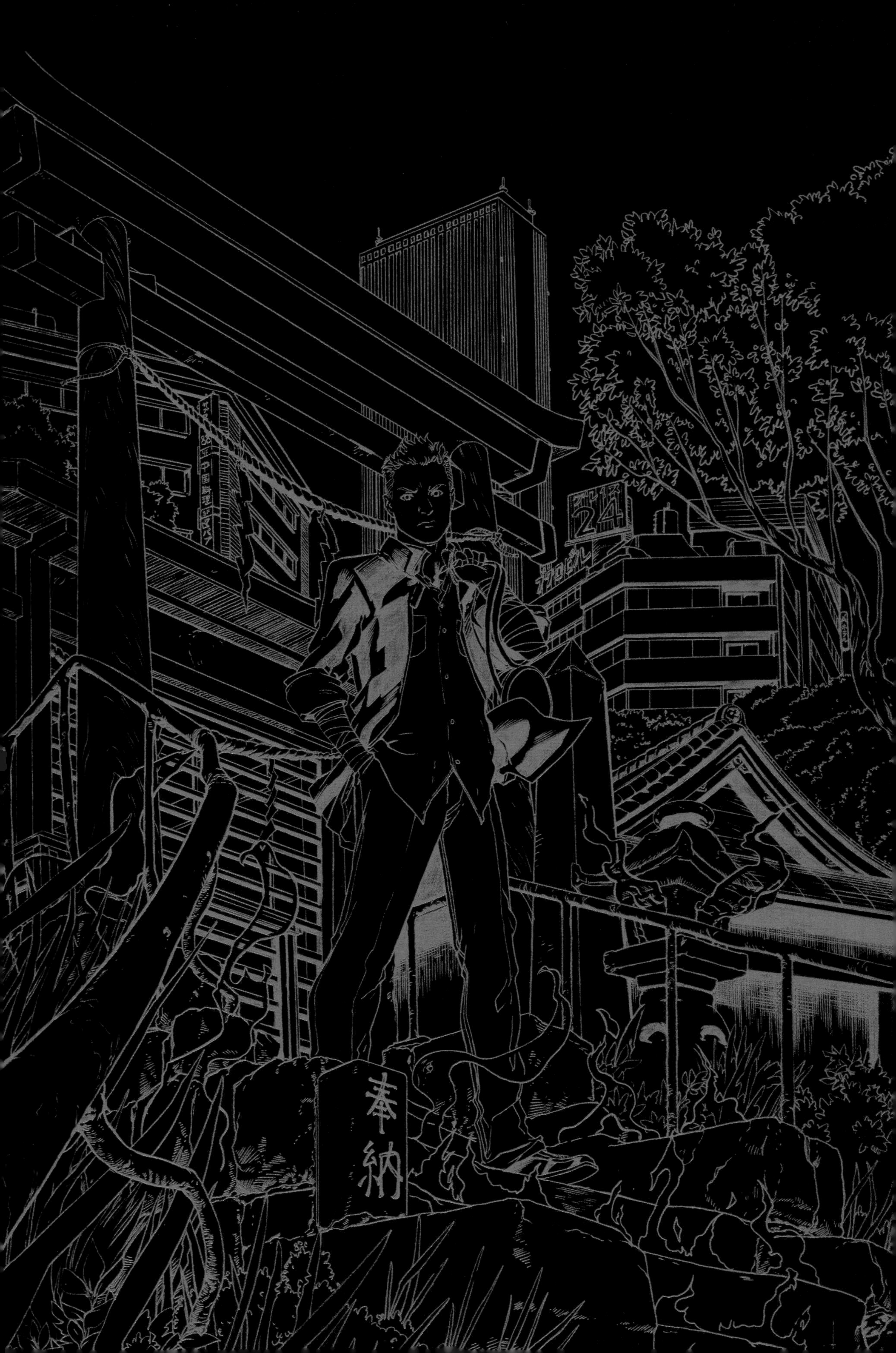
24
奉納

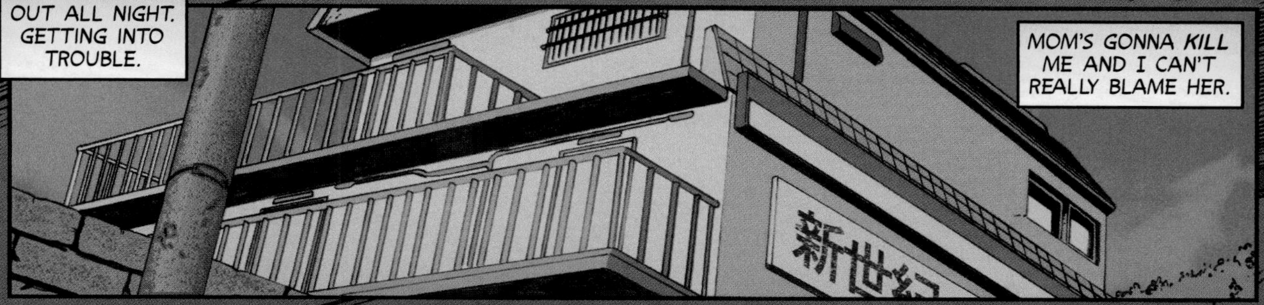
OUT ALL NIGHT. GETTING INTO TROUBLE.
MOM'S GONNA *KILL* ME AND I CAN'T REALLY BLAME HER.
新世紀

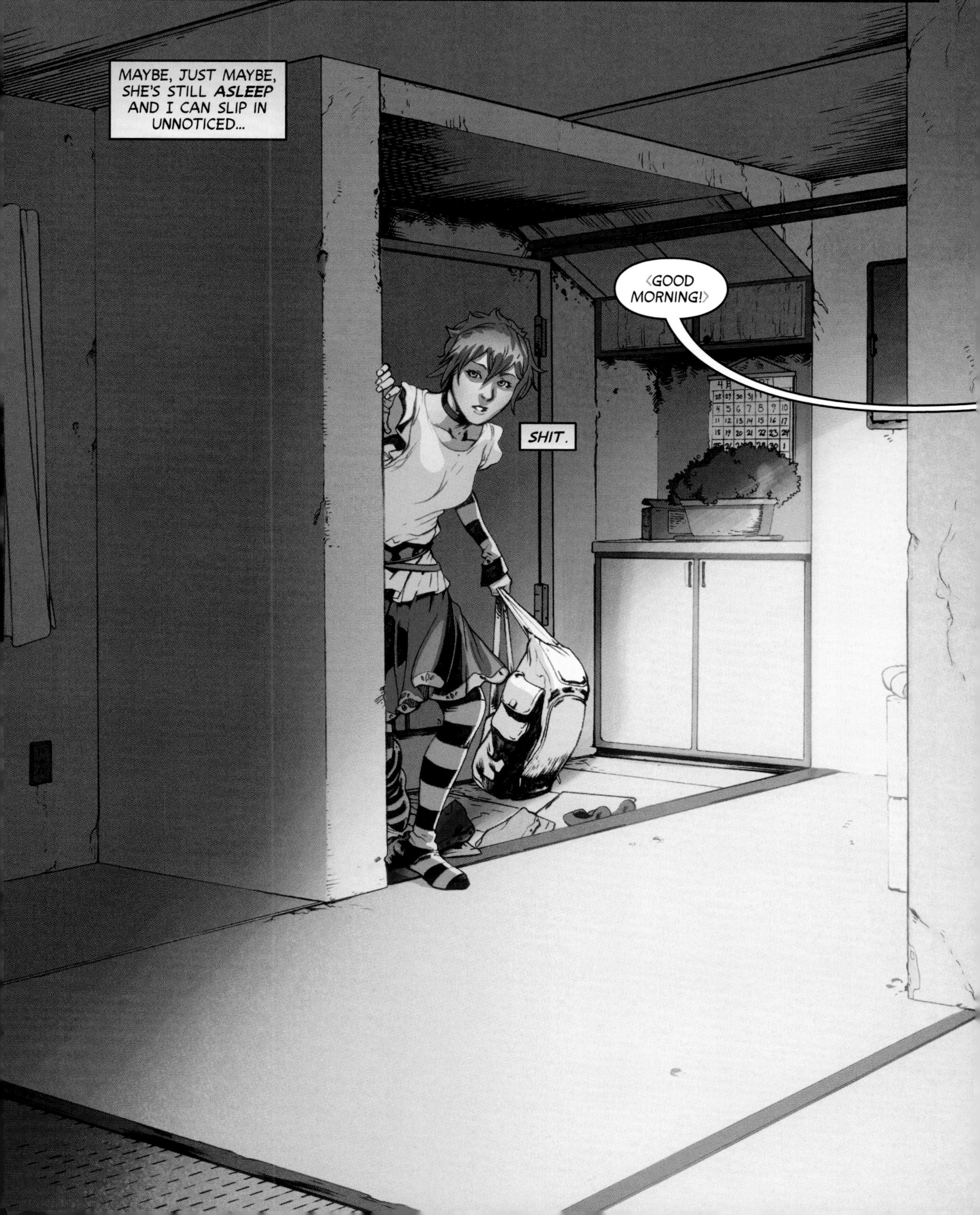
MAYBE, JUST MAYBE, SHE'S STILL *ASLEEP* AND I CAN SLIP IN UNNOTICED...
‹GOOD MORNING!›
SHIT.

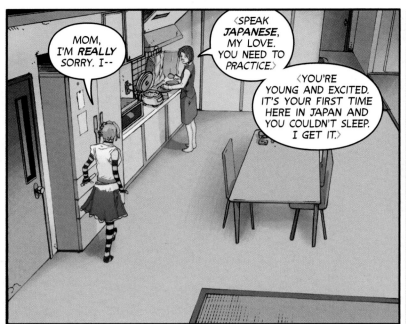

MOM, I'M *REALLY* SORRY. I--

⟨SPEAK *JAPANESE*, MY LOVE. YOU NEED TO *PRACTICE*.⟩

⟨YOU'RE YOUNG AND EXCITED. IT'S YOUR FIRST TIME HERE IN JAPAN AND YOU COULDN'T SLEEP. I GET IT.⟩

⟨YOU... YOU'RE *NOT* MAD?⟩

⟨I WAS AT FIRST, BUT I GOT OVER IT.⟩

⟨TOKYO'S A VERY *SAFE* CITY, DEAR. I KNEW YOU WEREN'T IN ANY *DANGER*.⟩

MONSTERS WITH SWORDS... A *WARRIOR-GIRL* WHO SAVED MY LIFE... *VISIONS*... WEIRD *POWERS*.

NOPE. NO DANGER AT *ALL*.

⟨I'M REALLY *SORRY* IF I MADE YOU WORRY.⟩

⟨WHAT I'M WORRIED ABOUT IS YOU *MESSING UP* YOUR INTERNAL CLOCK WITH *JET LAG* SO CLOSE TO THE START OF THE SCHOOL SEMESTER!⟩

⟨I BOUGHT YOU A *PHONE* SO YOU CAN CALL AND LET ME KNOW YOU'RE OUT, OKAY?⟩

YEAH...

SHE'S ACTUALLY BEING *TOO* NICE. IT'S *STRANGE*.

⟨I'VE GOTTA GO. *EARLY* SHIFT AGAIN.⟩

⟨WILL YOU BE HOME FOR *DINNER* TONIGHT?⟩

⟨YES, *ABSOLUTELY*!⟩

⟨GOOD.⟩

⟨I DON'T WANT TOKYO TO GET *ALL* OF YOU SO SOON.⟩

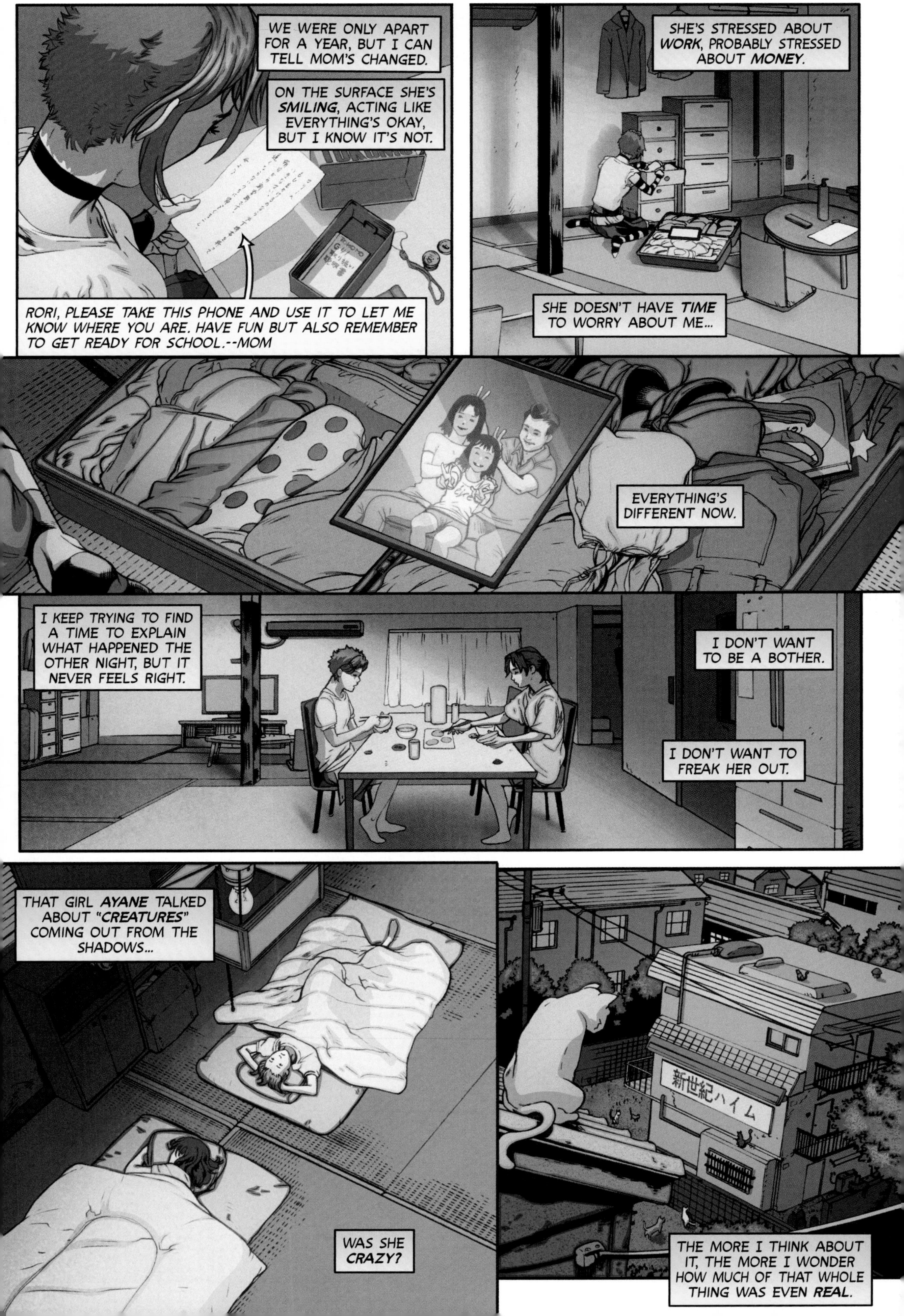
WE WERE ONLY APART FOR A YEAR, BUT I CAN TELL MOM'S CHANGED.
ON THE SURFACE SHE'S *SMILING*, ACTING LIKE EVERYTHING'S OKAY, BUT I KNOW IT'S NOT.
RORI, PLEASE TAKE THIS PHONE AND USE IT TO LET ME KNOW WHERE YOU ARE. HAVE FUN BUT ALSO REMEMBER TO GET READY FOR SCHOOL.--MOM
SHE'S STRESSED ABOUT *WORK*, PROBABLY STRESSED ABOUT *MONEY*.
SHE DOESN'T HAVE *TIME* TO WORRY ABOUT ME...
EVERYTHING'S DIFFERENT NOW.
I KEEP TRYING TO FIND A TIME TO EXPLAIN WHAT HAPPENED THE OTHER NIGHT, BUT IT NEVER FEELS RIGHT.
I DON'T WANT TO BE A BOTHER.
I DON'T WANT TO FREAK HER OUT.
THAT GIRL *AYANE* TALKED ABOUT "*CREATURES*" COMING OUT FROM THE SHADOWS...
WAS SHE *CRAZY?*
新世紀ハイム
THE MORE I THINK ABOUT IT, THE MORE I WONDER HOW MUCH OF THAT WHOLE THING WAS EVEN *REAL*.

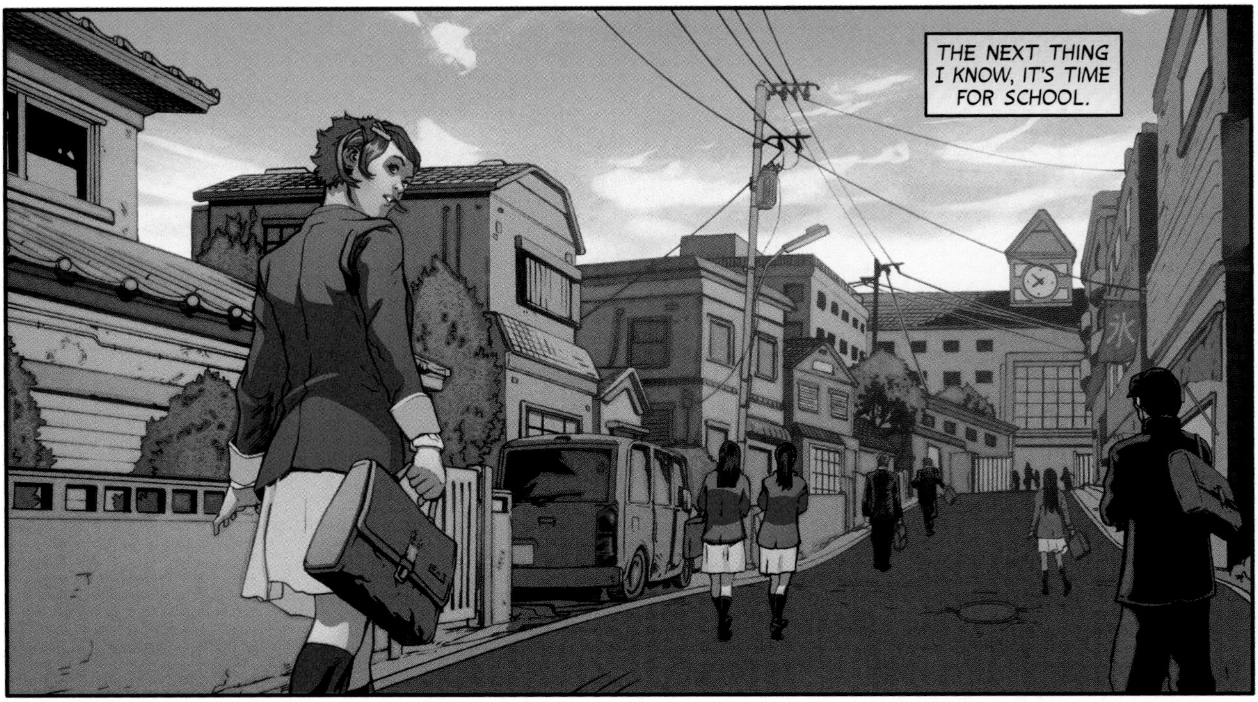
THE NEXT THING I KNOW, IT'S TIME FOR SCHOOL.

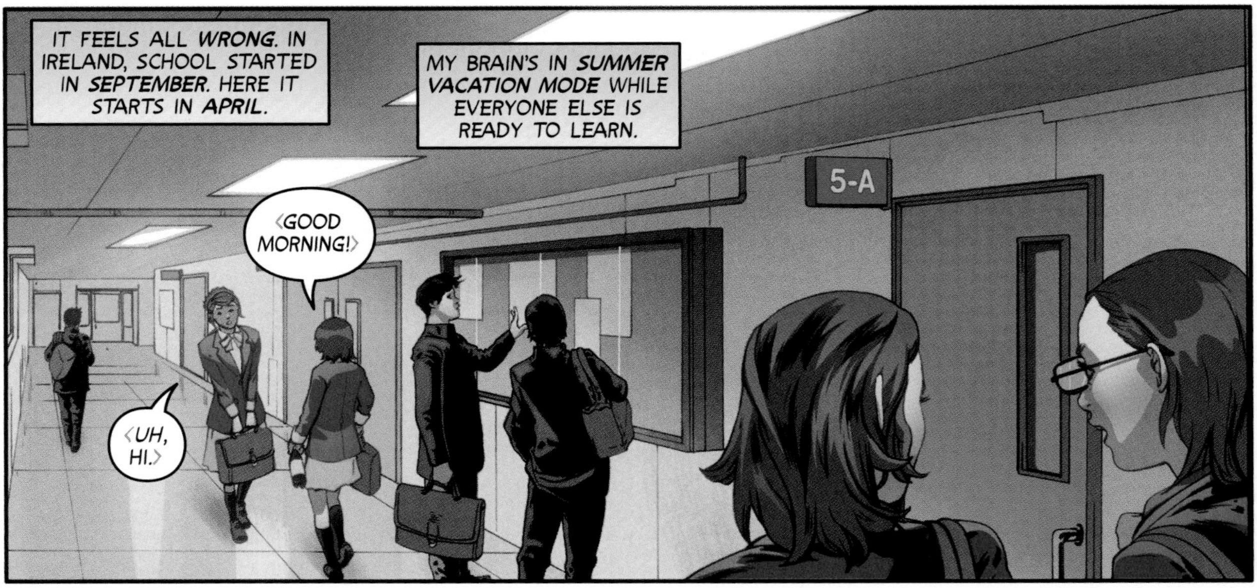
IT FEELS ALL *WRONG*. IN IRELAND, SCHOOL STARTED IN *SEPTEMBER*. HERE IT STARTS IN *APRIL*.
MY BRAIN'S IN *SUMMER VACATION MODE* WHILE EVERYONE ELSE IS READY TO LEARN.
5-A
‹GOOD MORNING!›
‹UH, HI.›

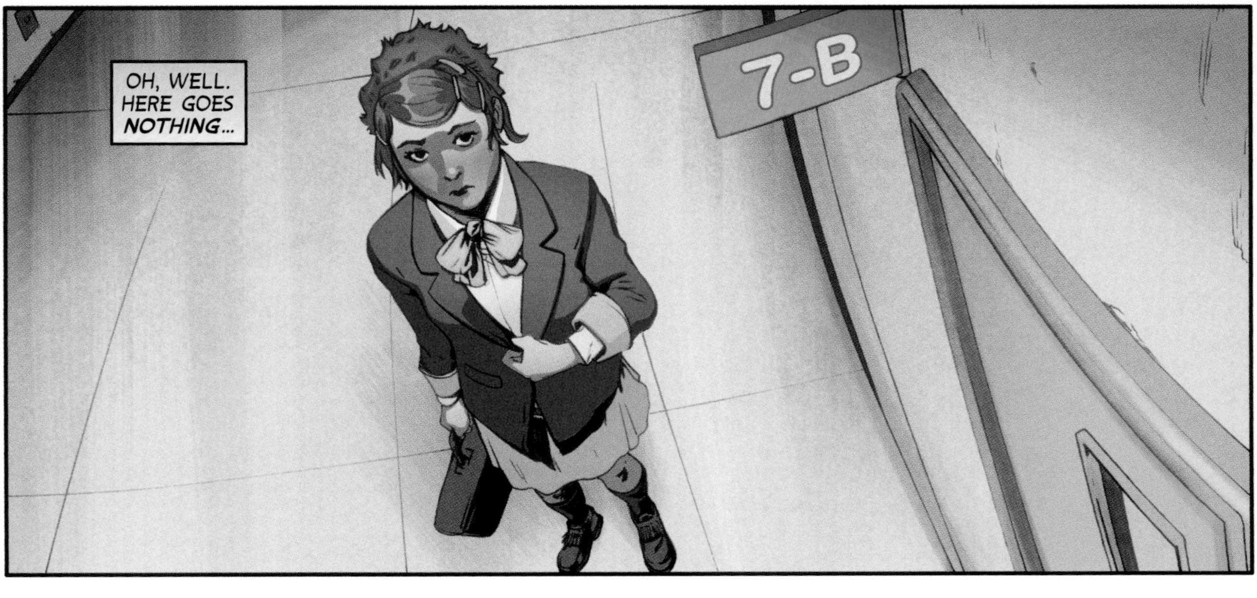
OH, WELL. HERE GOES *NOTHING*...
7-B

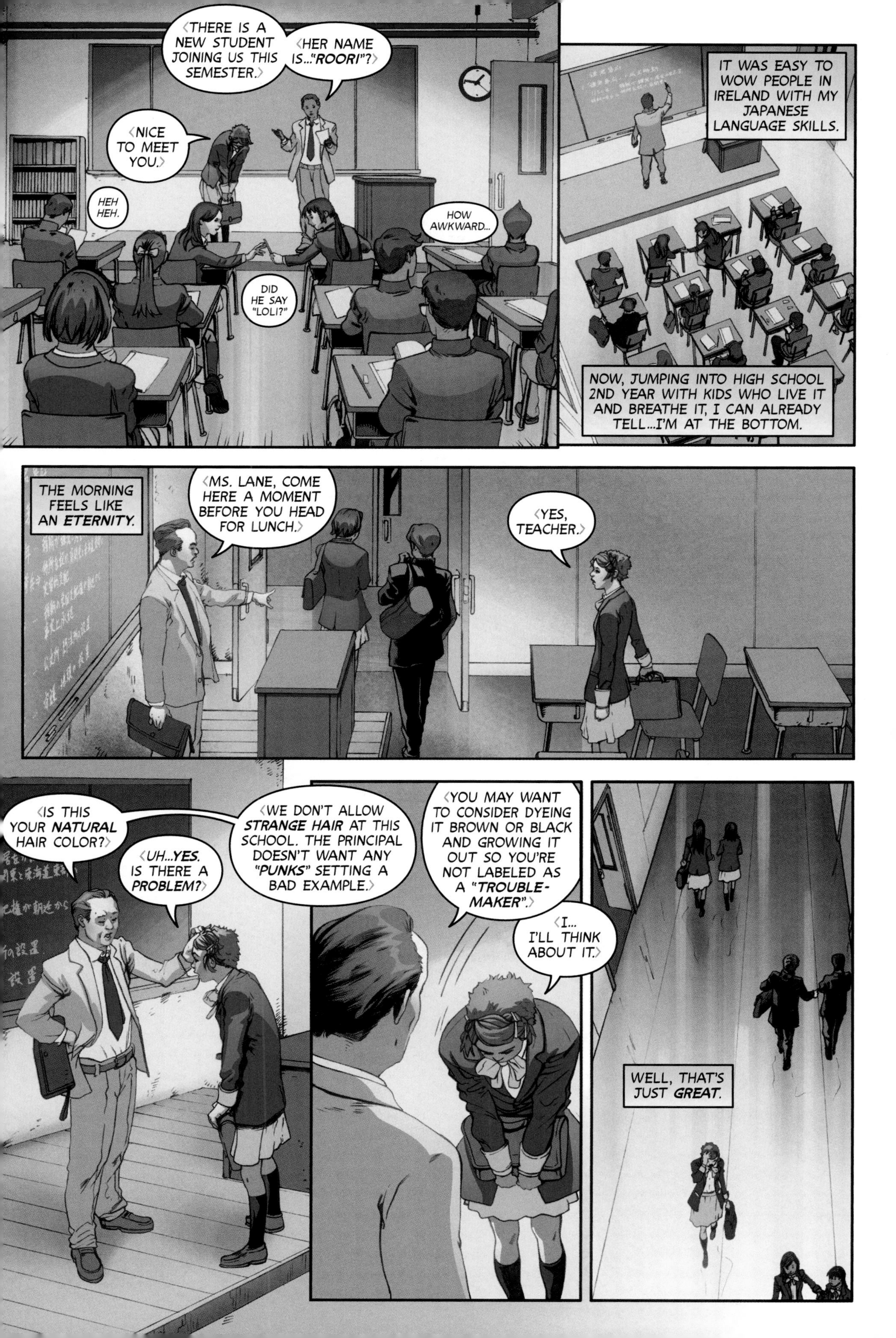

‹THERE IS A NEW STUDENT JOINING US THIS SEMESTER.›
‹HER NAME IS..."ROORI"?›
‹NICE TO MEET YOU.›
HEH HEH.
HOW AWKWARD...
DID HE SAY "LOLI?"
IT WAS EASY TO WOW PEOPLE IN IRELAND WITH MY JAPANESE LANGUAGE SKILLS.
NOW, JUMPING INTO HIGH SCHOOL 2ND YEAR WITH KIDS WHO LIVE IT AND BREATHE IT, I CAN ALREADY TELL...I'M AT THE BOTTOM.
THE MORNING FEELS LIKE AN ETERNITY.
‹MS. LANE, COME HERE A MOMENT BEFORE YOU HEAD FOR LUNCH.›
‹YES, TEACHER.›
‹IS THIS YOUR NATURAL HAIR COLOR?›
‹UH...YES. IS THERE A PROBLEM?›
‹WE DON'T ALLOW STRANGE HAIR AT THIS SCHOOL. THE PRINCIPAL DOESN'T WANT ANY "PUNKS" SETTING A BAD EXAMPLE.›
‹YOU MAY WANT TO CONSIDER DYEING IT BROWN OR BLACK AND GROWING IT OUT SO YOU'RE NOT LABELED AS A "TROUBLE-MAKER".›
‹I... I'LL THINK ABOUT IT.›
WELL, THAT'S JUST GREAT.

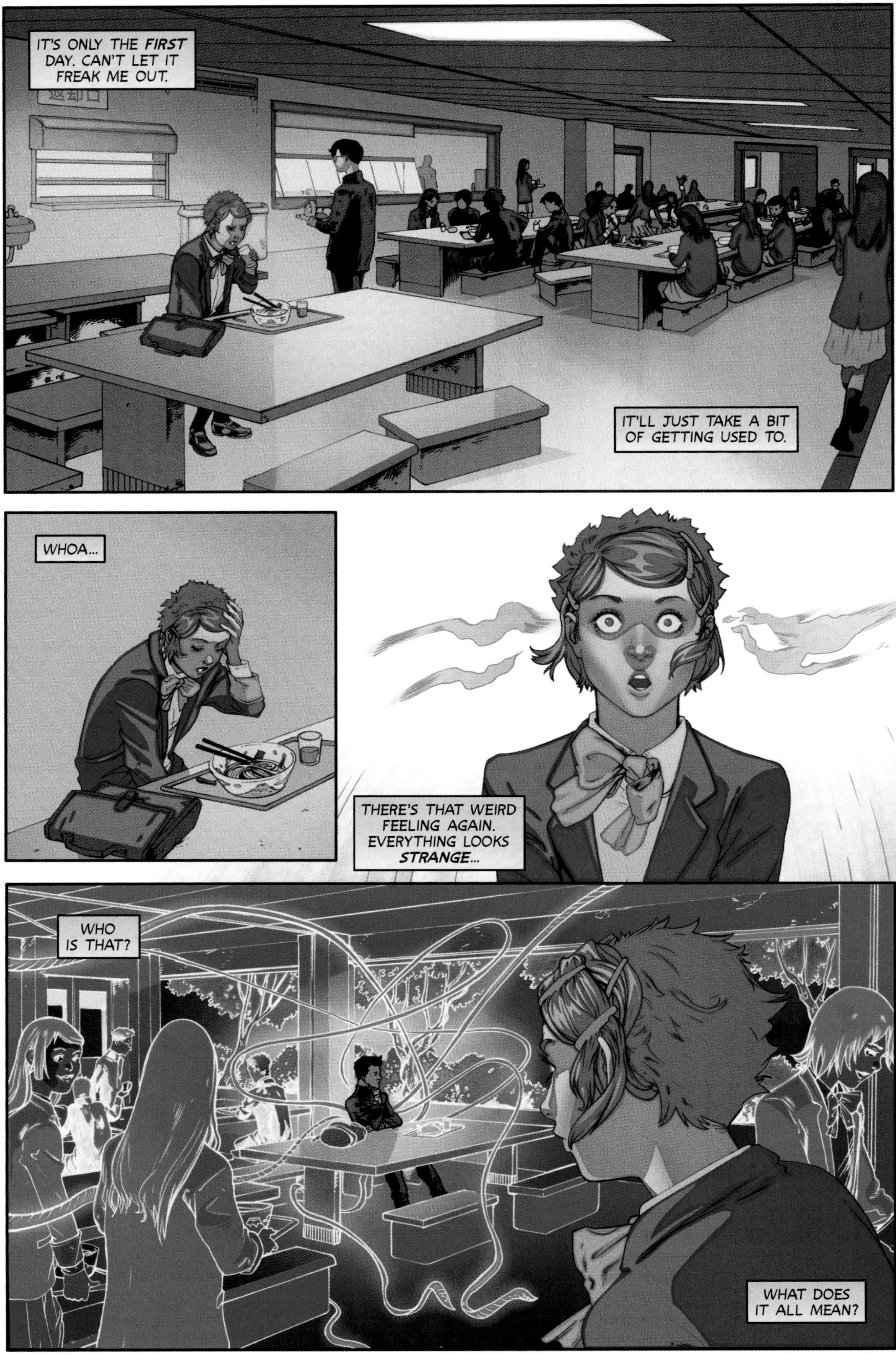
IT'S ONLY THE *FIRST* DAY. CAN'T LET IT FREAK ME OUT.
返却口
IT'LL JUST TAKE A BIT OF GETTING USED TO.
WHOA...
THERE'S THAT WEIRD FEELING AGAIN. EVERYTHING LOOKS ***STRANGE***...
WHO IS THAT?
WHAT DOES IT ALL MEAN?

SHOULD I *INTRODUCE* MYSELF?

MAYBE HE'S *TROUBLE.*

IT LOOKS LIKE HE GETS IN FIGHTS.

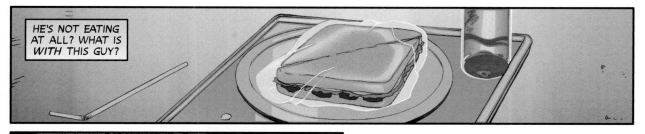

HE'S NOT EATING AT ALL? WHAT IS *WITH* THIS GUY?

DID HE SEE ME?

OH, *SHIT!* HERE HE COMES!

DON'T LOOK, DON'T LOOK, *DON'T LOOK!*

~whew~

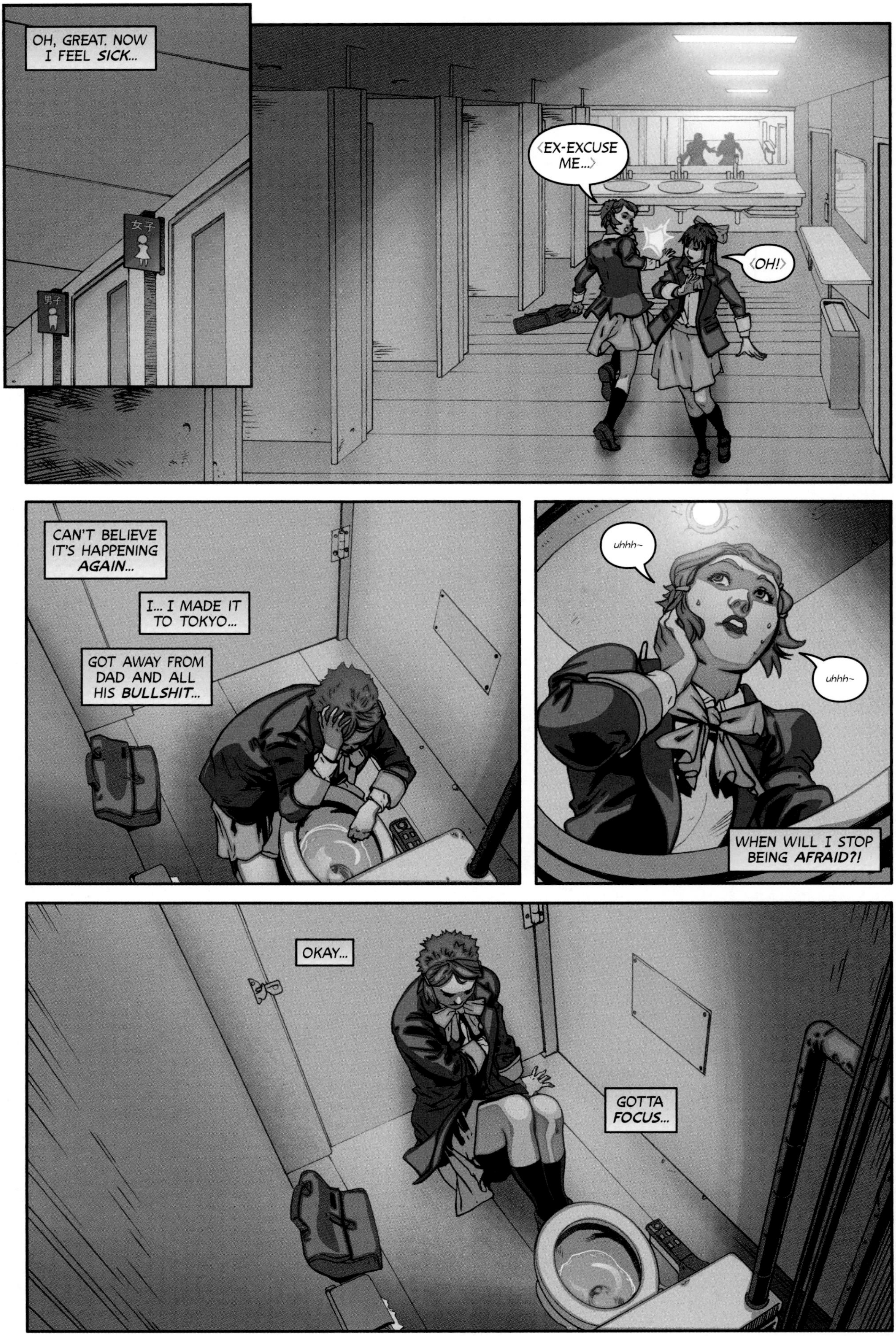
OH, GREAT. NOW I FEEL *SICK*...
女子
男子
‹EX-EXCUSE ME...›
‹OH!›
CAN'T BELIEVE IT'S HAPPENING *AGAIN*...
I... I MADE IT TO TOKYO...
GOT AWAY FROM DAD AND ALL HIS *BULLSHIT*...
uhhh~
uhhh~
WHEN WILL I STOP BEING *AFRAID?!*
OKAY...
GOTTA *FOCUS*...

...FOCUS ON SOMETHING *REAL*.

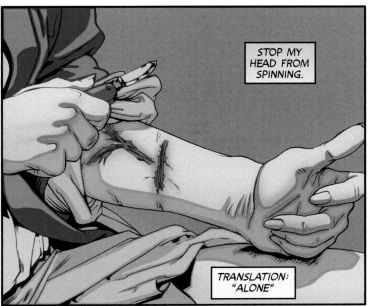

STOP MY HEAD FROM SPINNING.

TRANSLATION: "ALONE"

MAKE MY MARK...

Nnng~

...AND GET THROUGH ANOTHER DAY.

MY LITTLE CURSE.

YOU'RE A REAL PIECE OF *WORK*, RORI LANE.

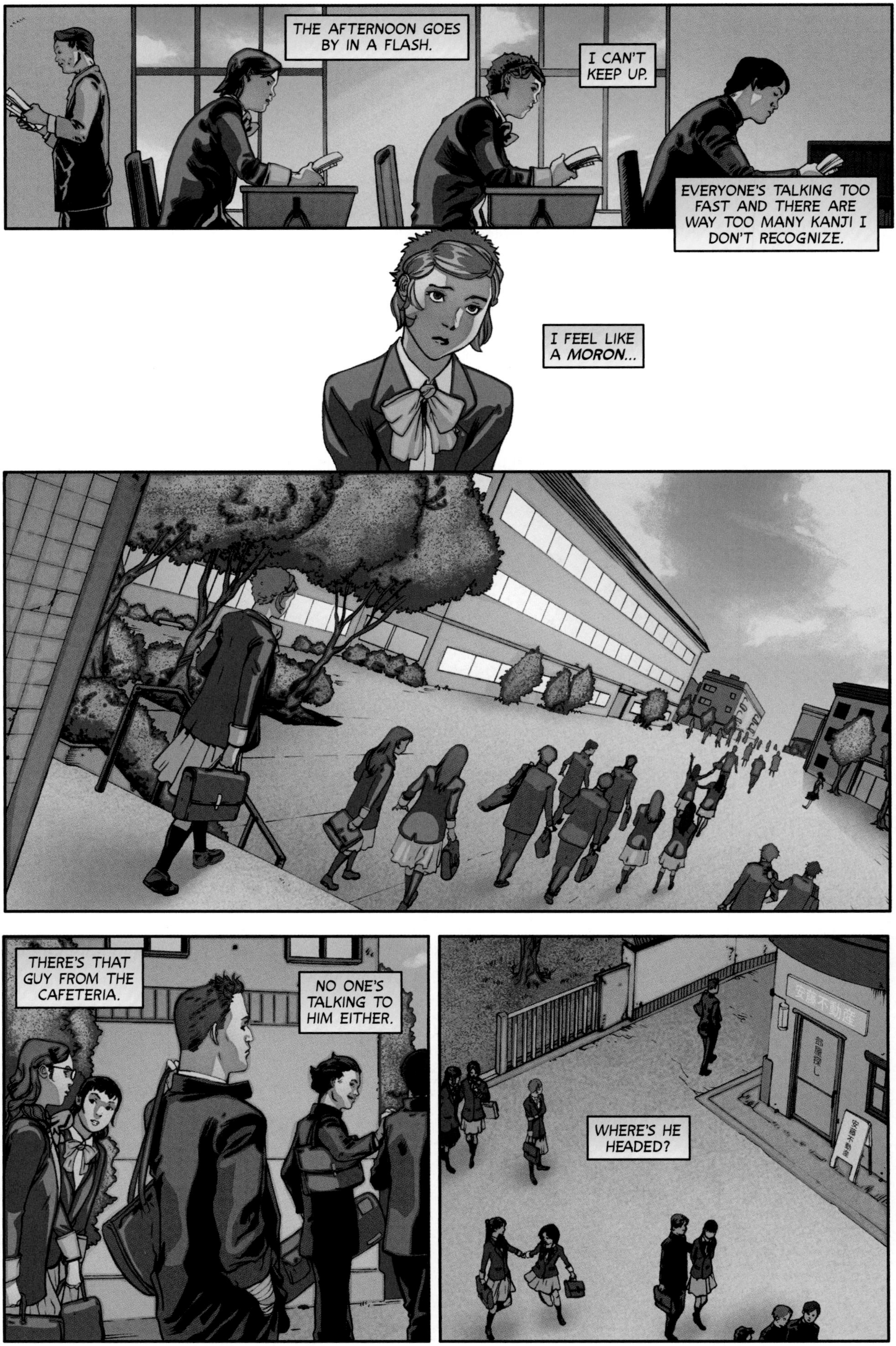
THE AFTERNOON GOES BY IN A FLASH.
I CAN'T KEEP UP.
EVERYONE'S TALKING TOO FAST AND THERE ARE WAY TOO MANY KANJI I DON'T RECOGNIZE.
I FEEL LIKE A *MORON*...
THERE'S THAT GUY FROM THE CAFETERIA.
NO ONE'S TALKING TO HIM EITHER.
WHERE'S HE HEADED?

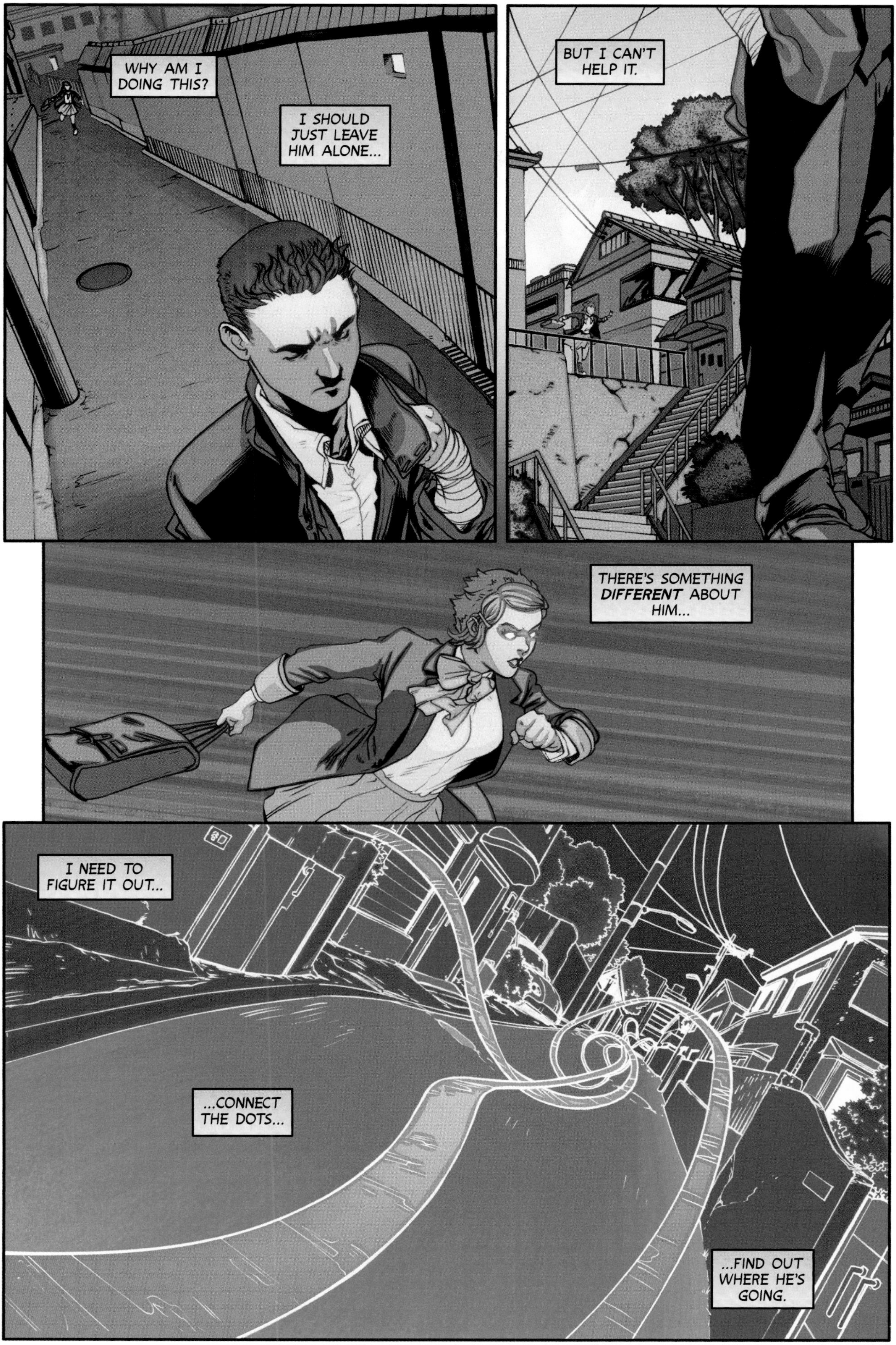
WHY AM I DOING THIS?
I SHOULD JUST LEAVE HIM ALONE...
BUT I CAN'T HELP IT.
THERE'S SOMETHING *DIFFERENT* ABOUT HIM...
I NEED TO FIGURE IT OUT...
...CONNECT THE DOTS...
...FIND OUT WHERE HE'S GOING.

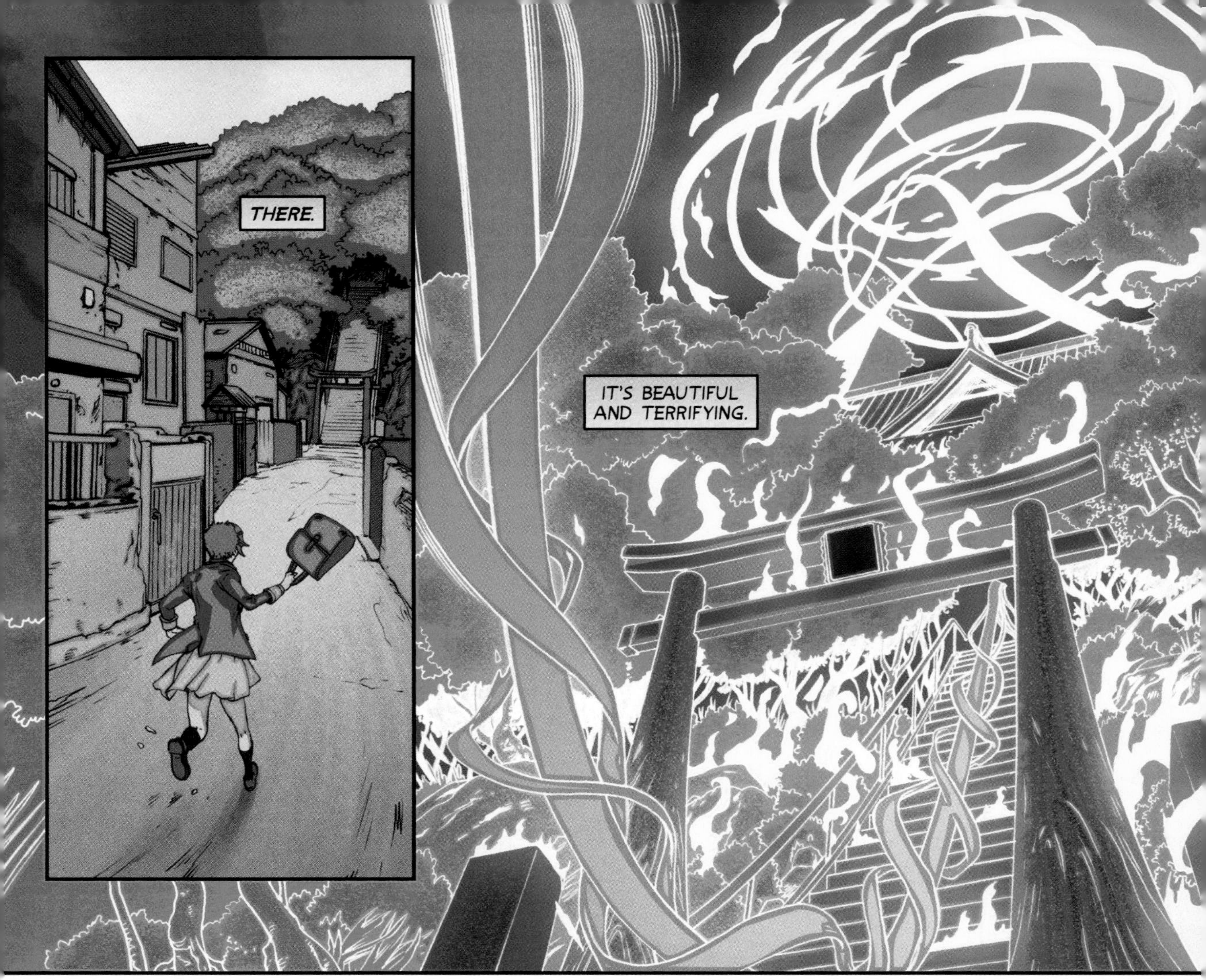
THERE.
IT'S BEAUTIFUL AND TERRIFYING.
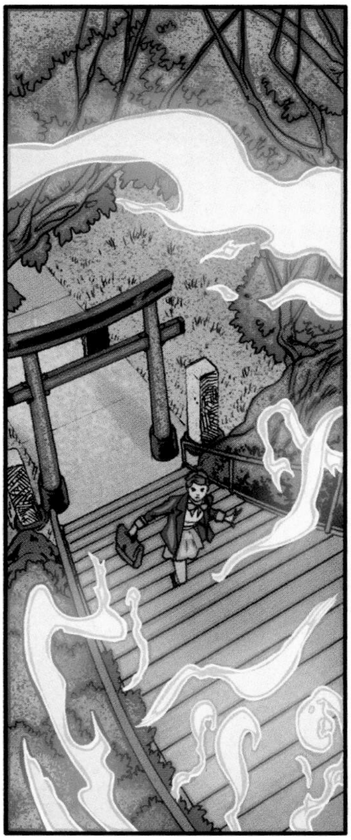
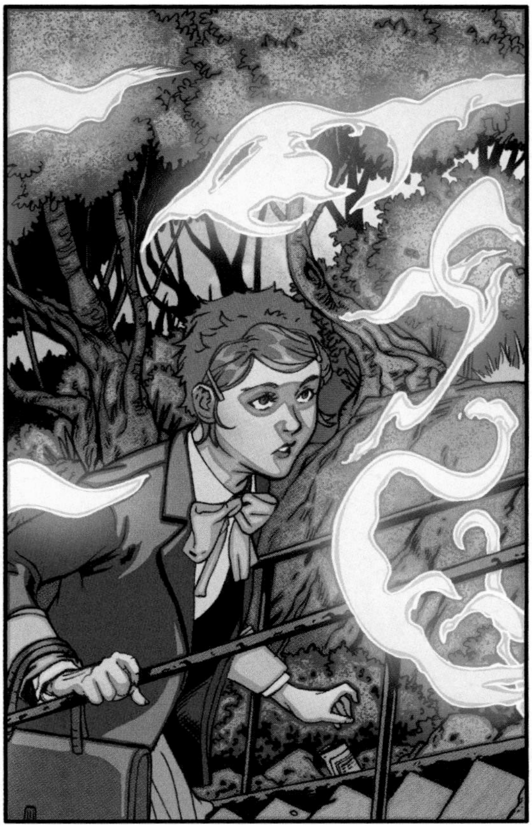
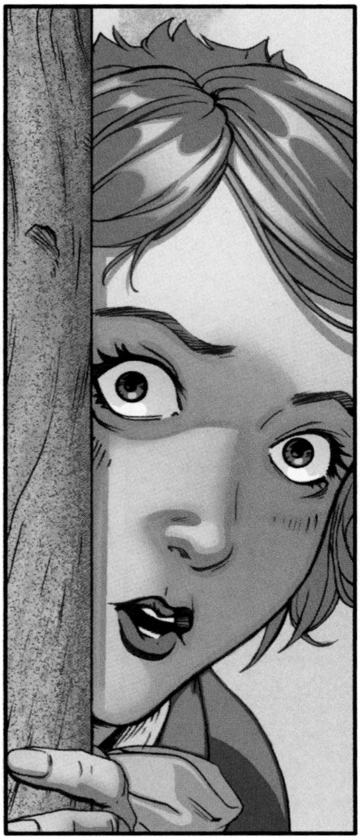

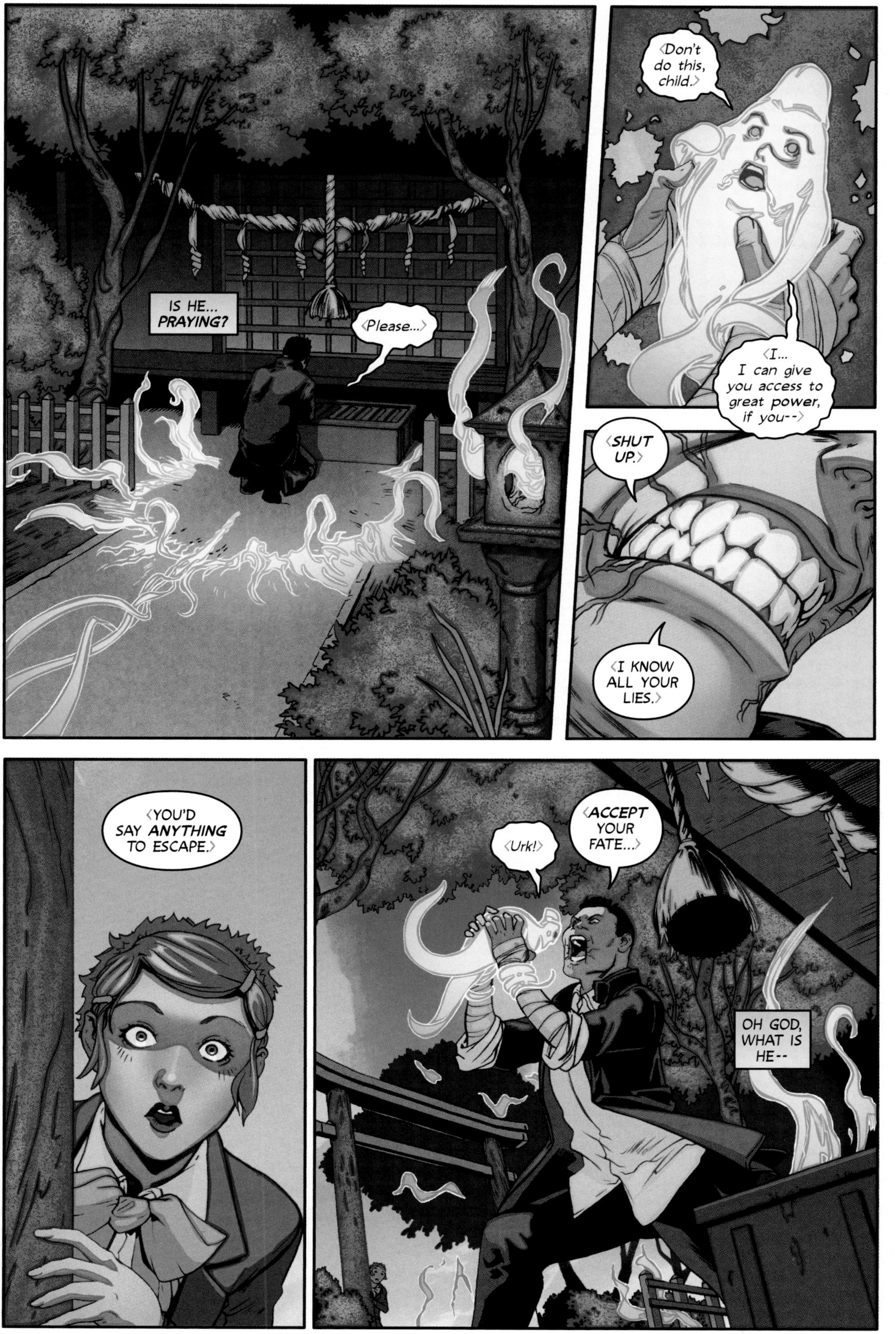
IS HE... **PRAYING?**
⟨Please...⟩
⟨Don't do this, child.⟩
⟨I... I can give you access to great power, if you--⟩
⟨**SHUT** UP.⟩
⟨I KNOW ALL YOUR LIES.⟩
⟨YOU'D SAY **ANYTHING** TO ESCAPE.⟩
⟨Urk!⟩
⟨**ACCEPT** YOUR FATE...⟩
OH GOD, WHAT IS HE--

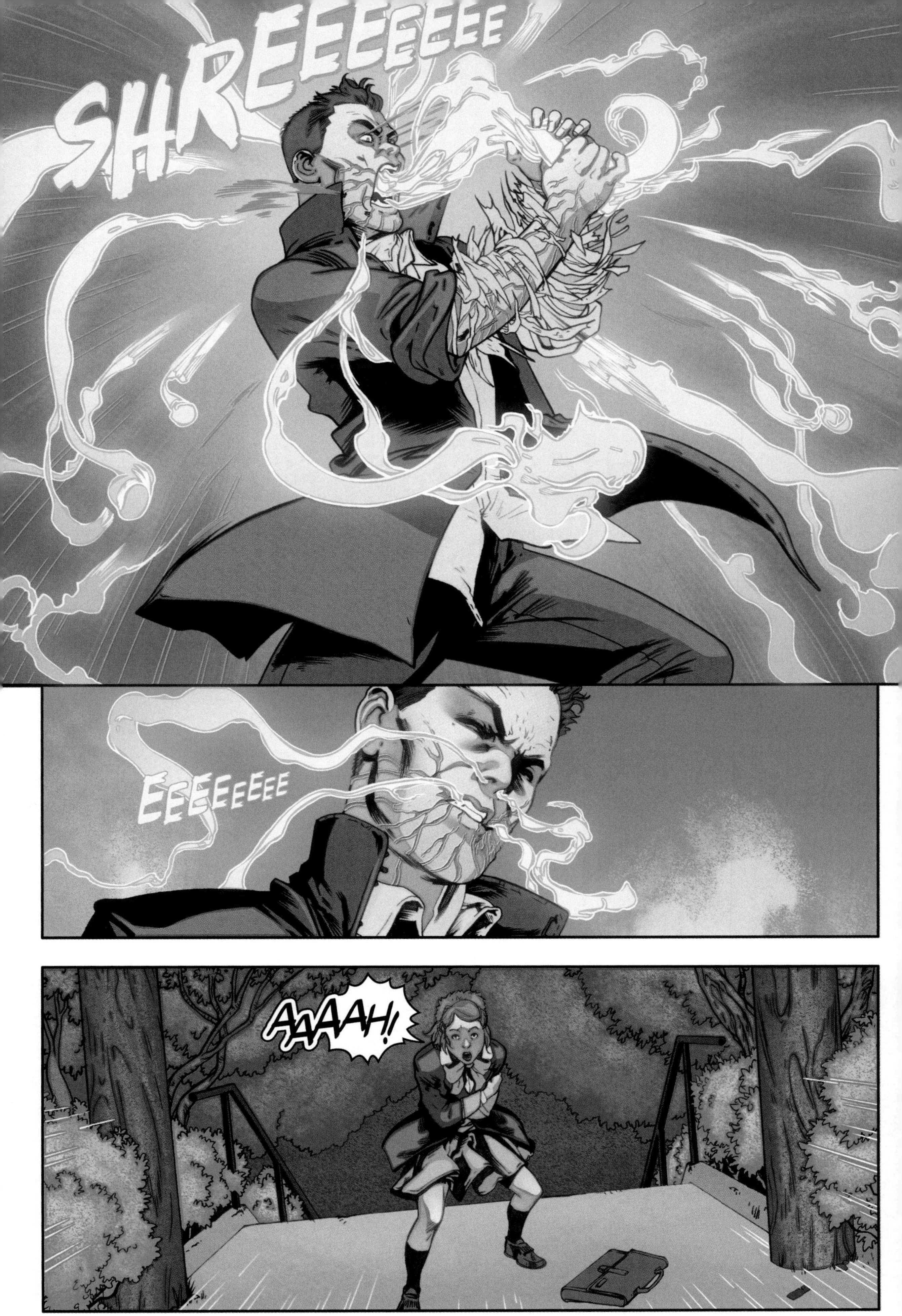
SHREEEEEEEE
EEEEEEEE
AAAAH!

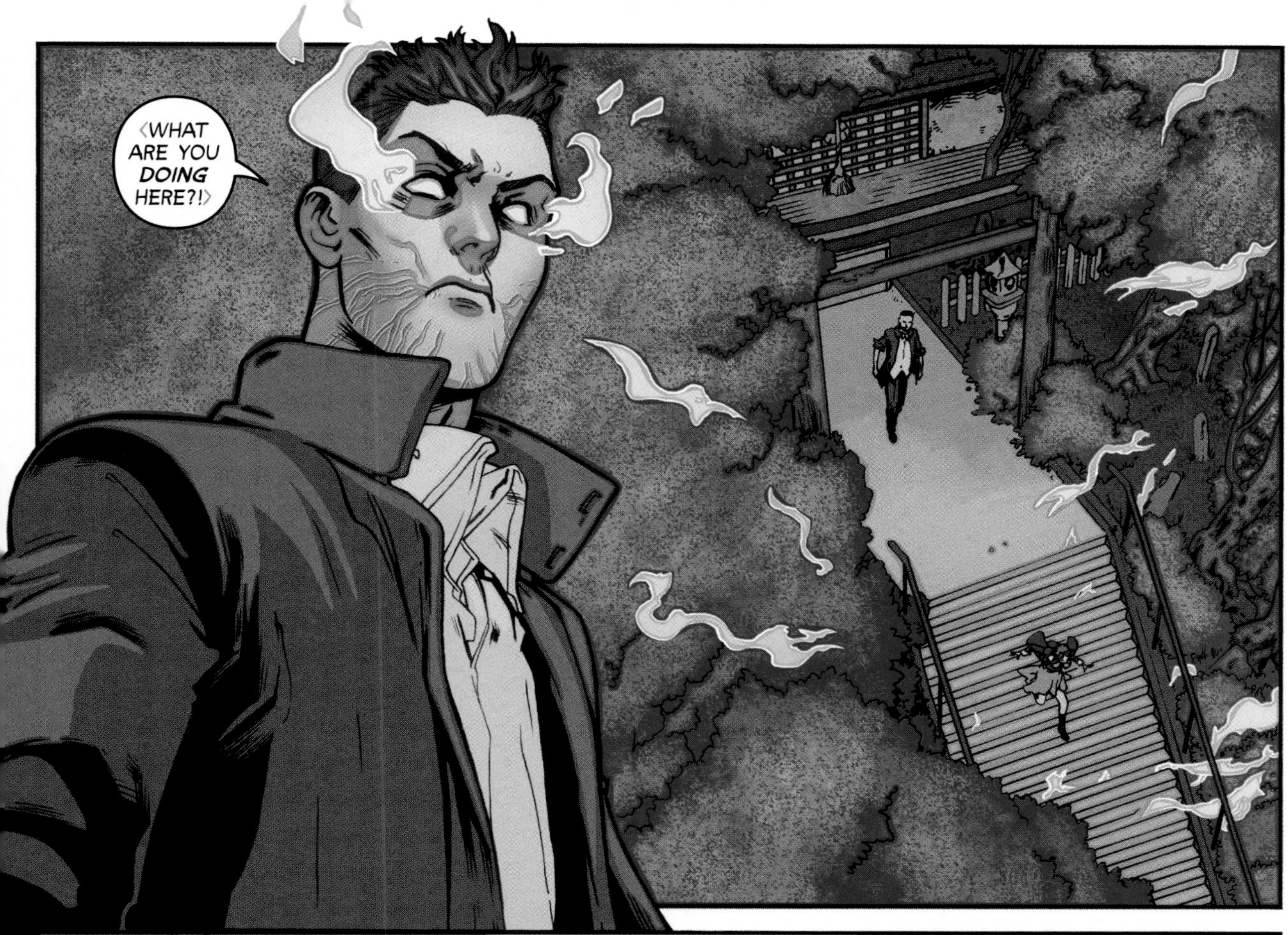
‹WHAT ARE YOU *DOING* HERE?!›

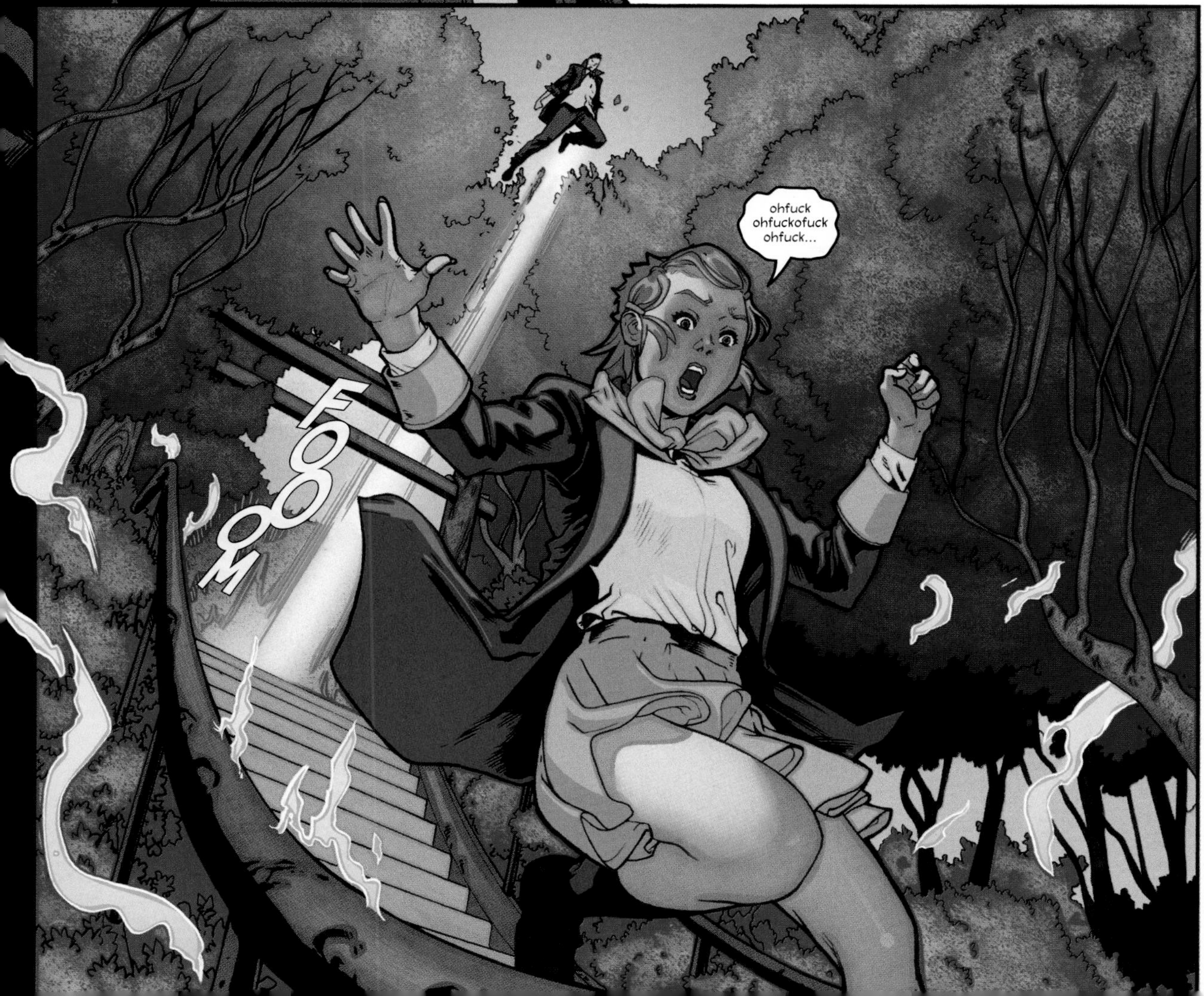
ohfuck ohfuckofuck ohfuck...
FOOOOM

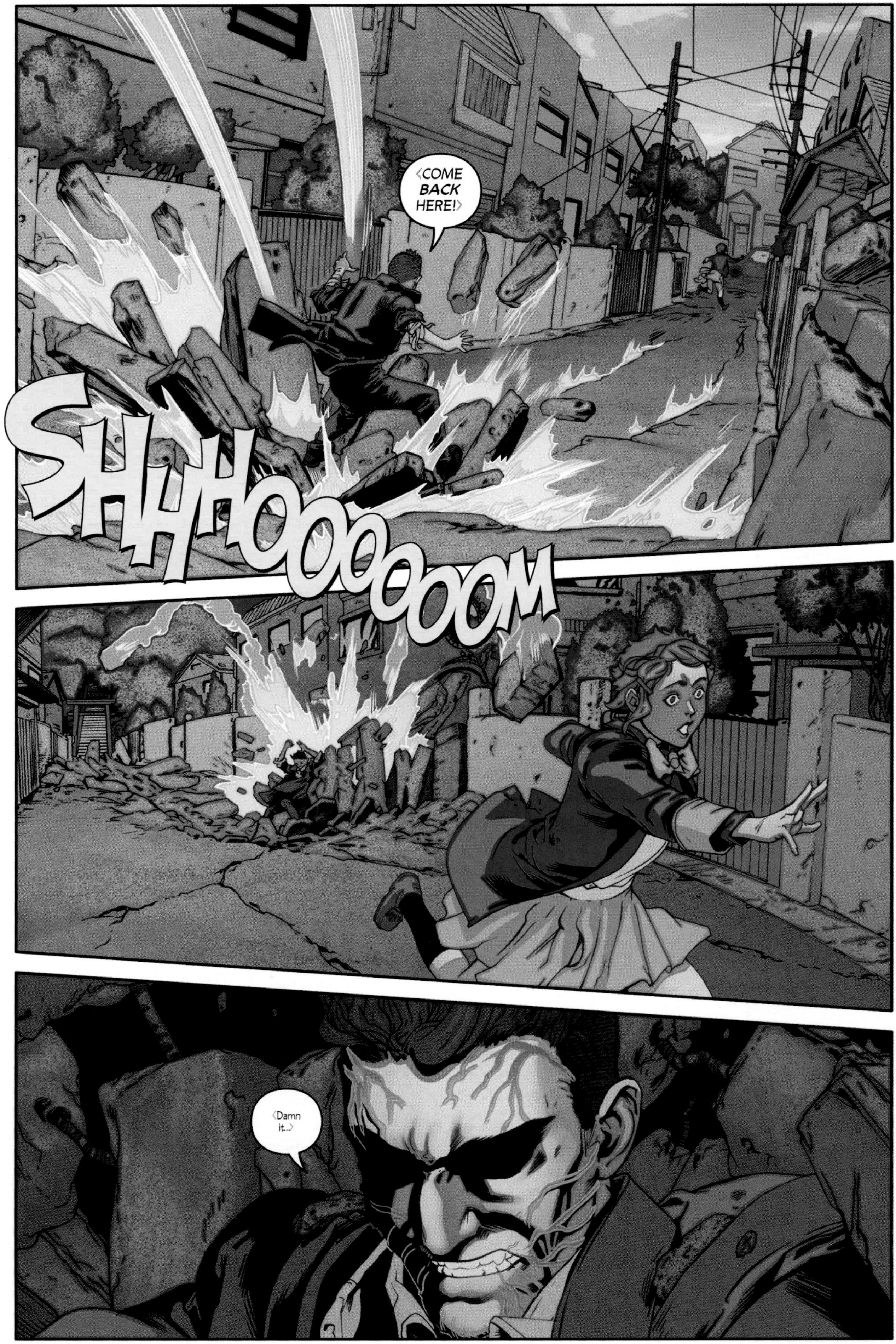
‹COME BACK HERE!›
SHHHOOOOOOOM
‹Damn it...›

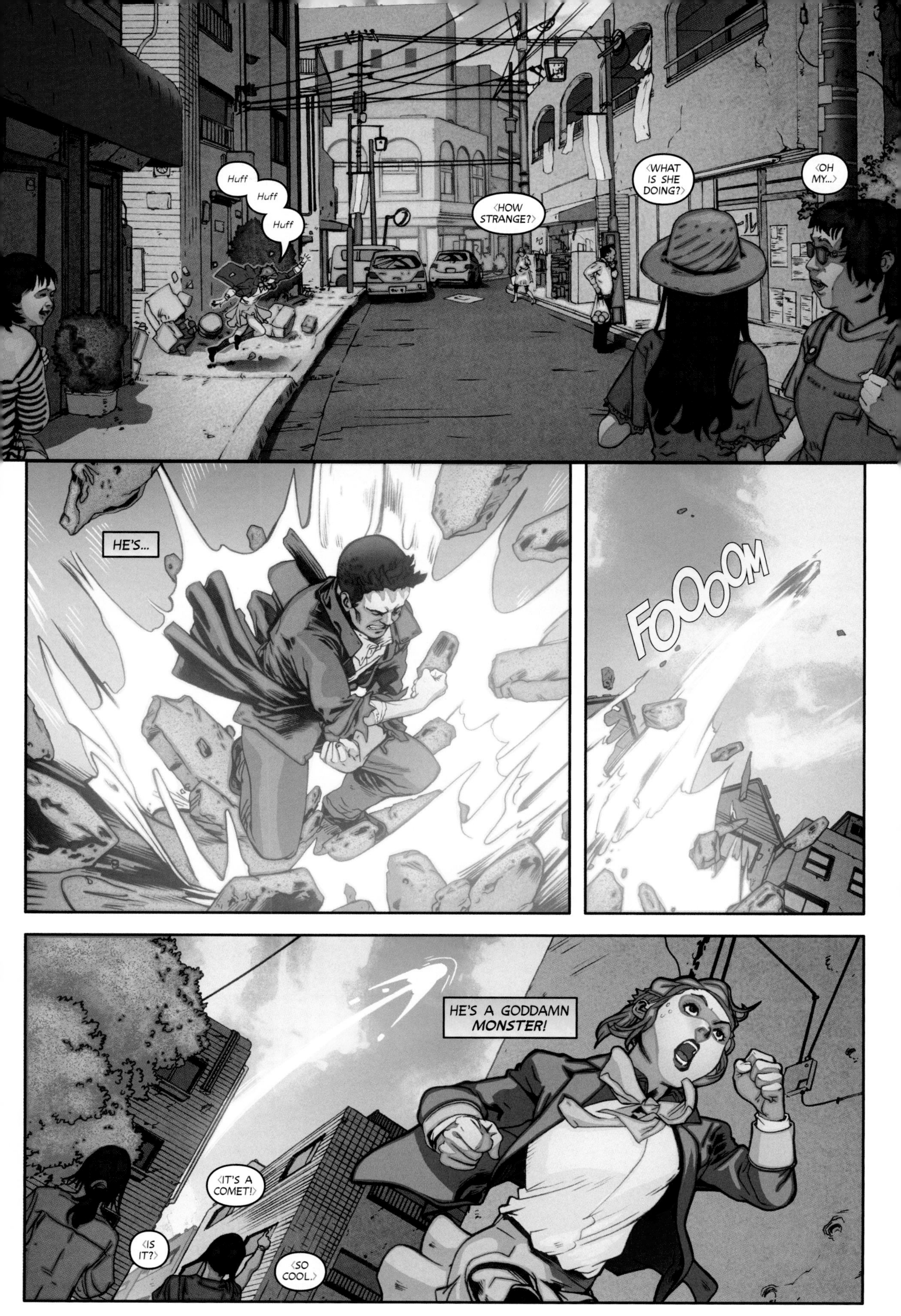
Huff
Huff
Huff
〈HOW STRANGE?〉
〈WHAT IS SHE DOING?〉
〈OH MY...〉
HE'S...
FOOOOOM
HE'S A GODDAMN MONSTER!
〈IT'S A COMET!〉
〈IS IT?〉
〈SO COOL.〉

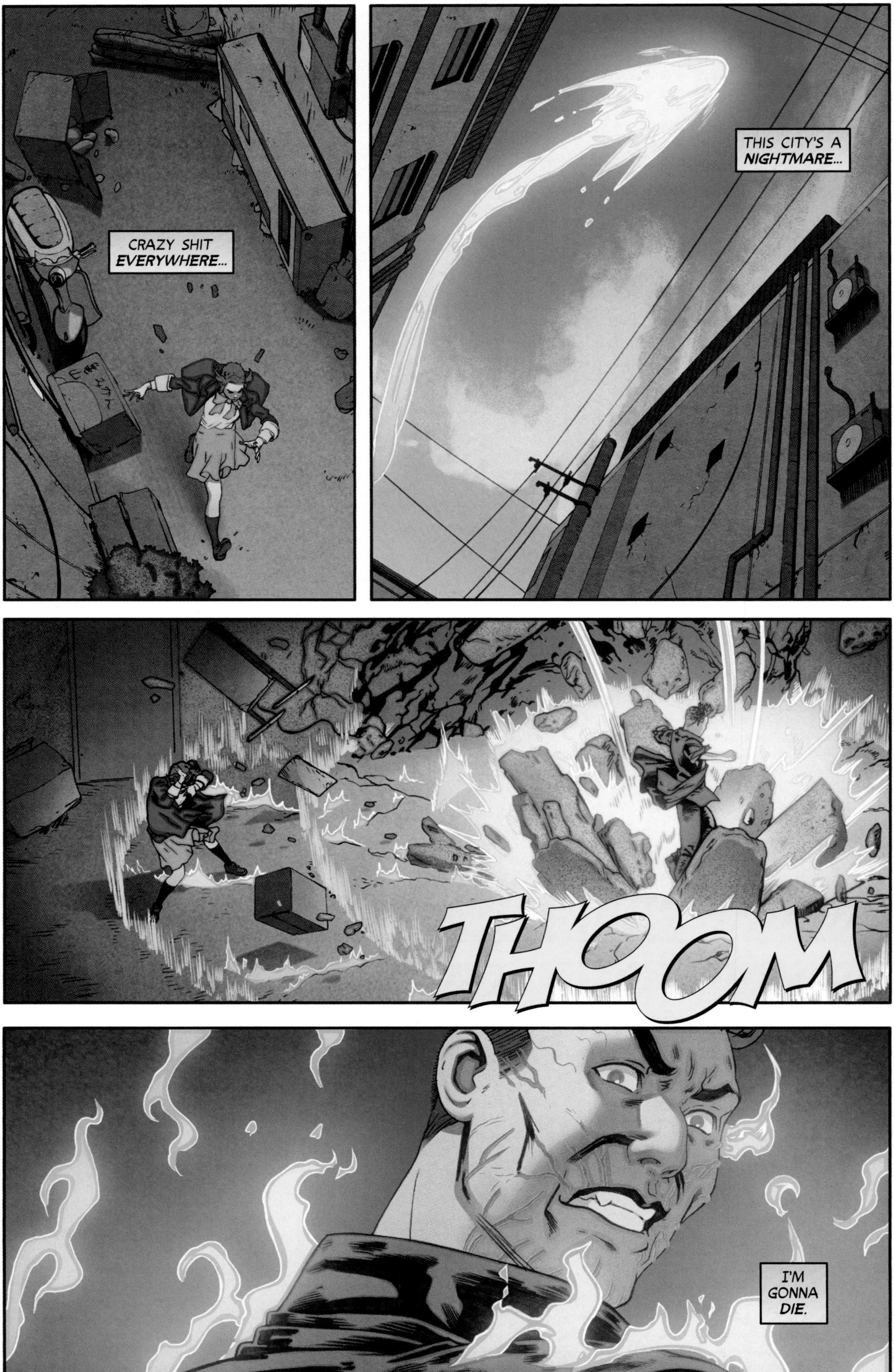
CRAZY SHIT EVERYWHERE...
THIS CITY'S A NIGHTMARE...
THOOM
I'M GONNA DIE.

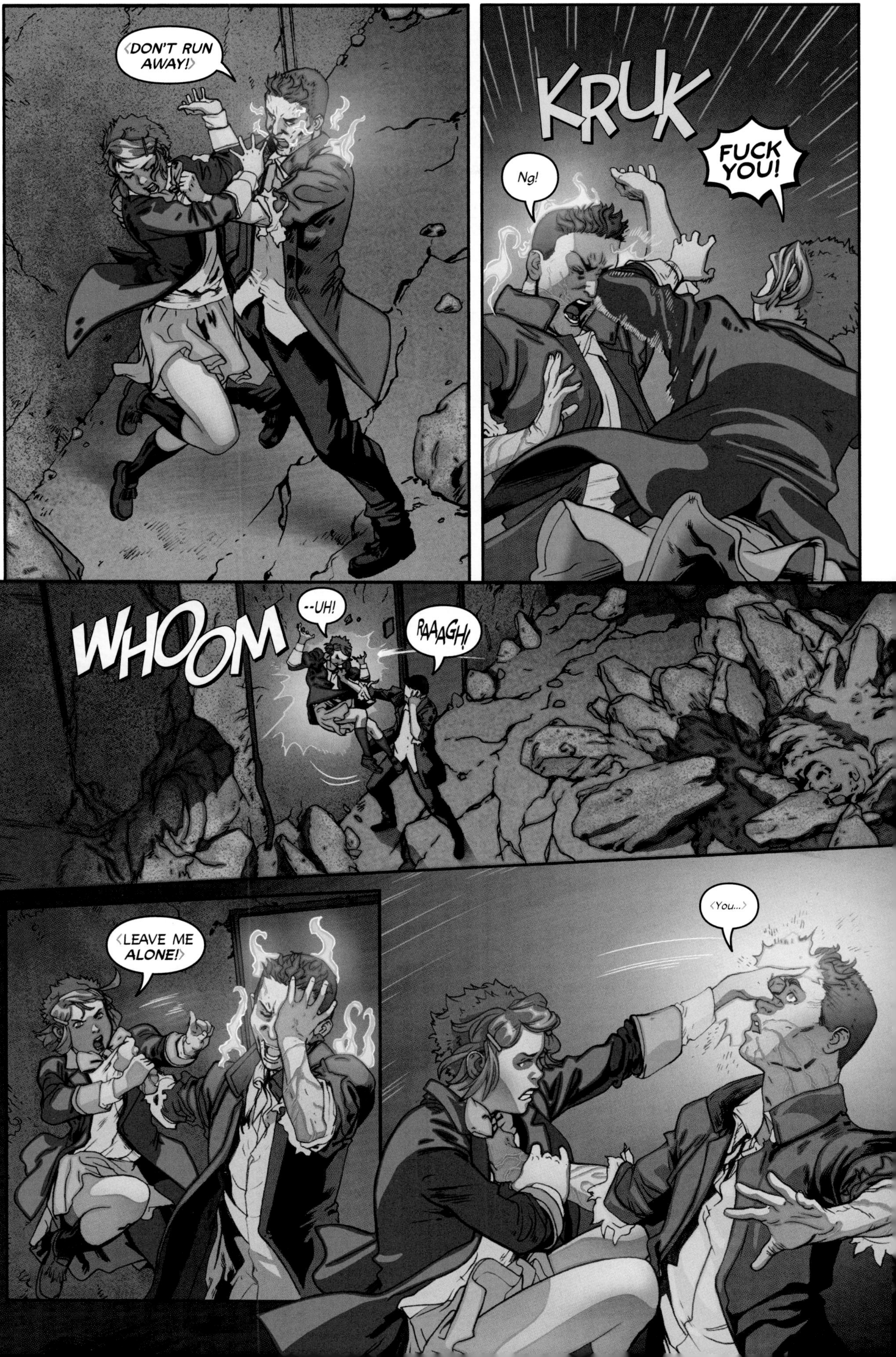
‹DON'T RUN AWAY!›
KRUK
Ng!
FUCK YOU!
WHOOM
--UH!
RAAAGH!
‹LEAVE ME ALONE!›
‹You...›

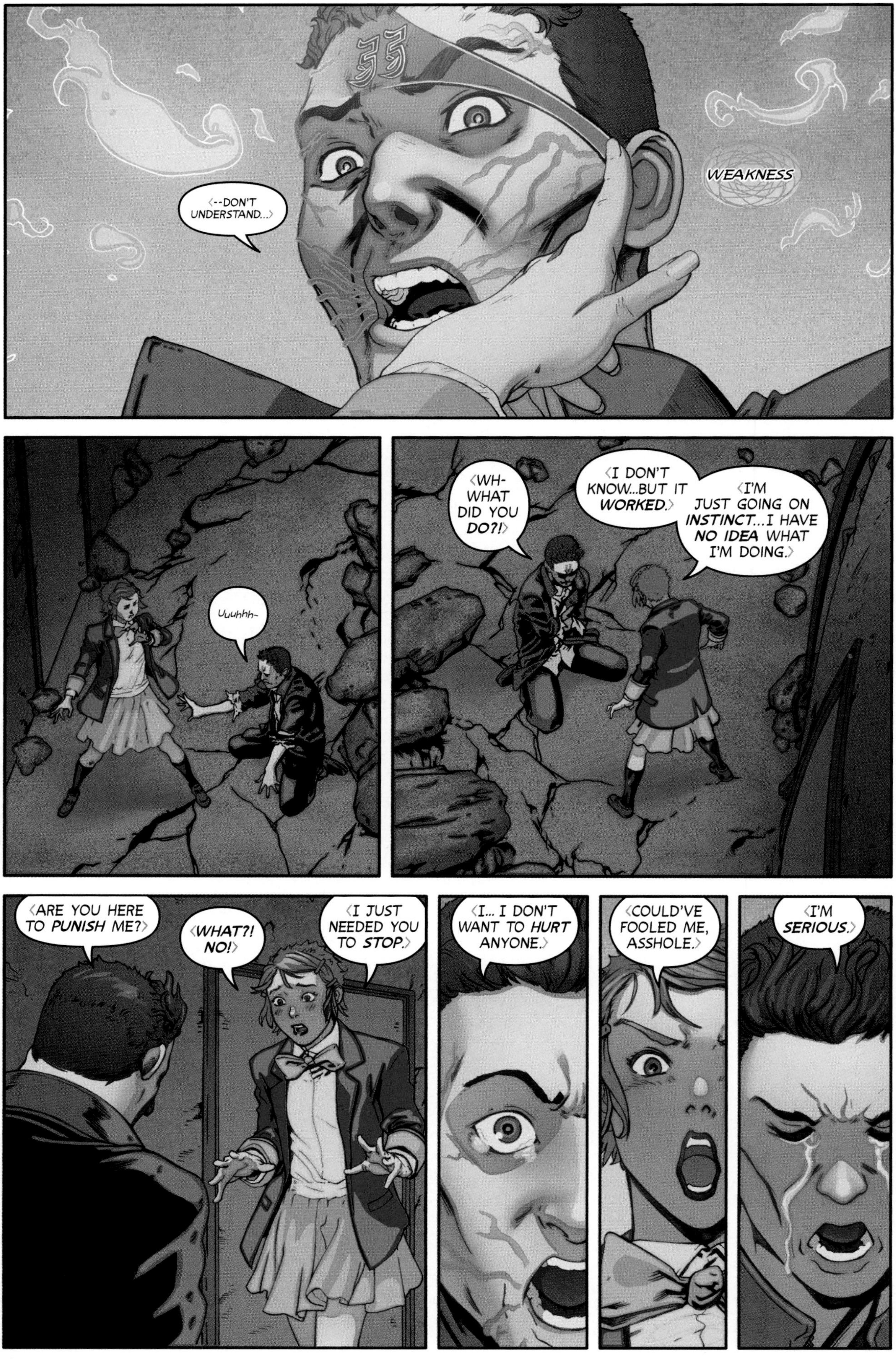
⟨--DON'T UNDERSTAND...⟩
WEAKNESS
Uuuhhh-
⟨WH-WHAT DID YOU DO?!⟩
⟨I DON'T KNOW...BUT IT WORKED.⟩
⟨I'M JUST GOING ON INSTINCT...I HAVE NO IDEA WHAT I'M DOING.⟩
⟨ARE YOU HERE TO PUNISH ME?⟩
⟨WHAT?! NO!⟩
⟨I JUST NEEDED YOU TO STOP.⟩
⟨I... I DON'T WANT TO HURT ANYONE.⟩
⟨COULD'VE FOOLED ME, ASSHOLE.⟩
⟨I'M SERIOUS.⟩

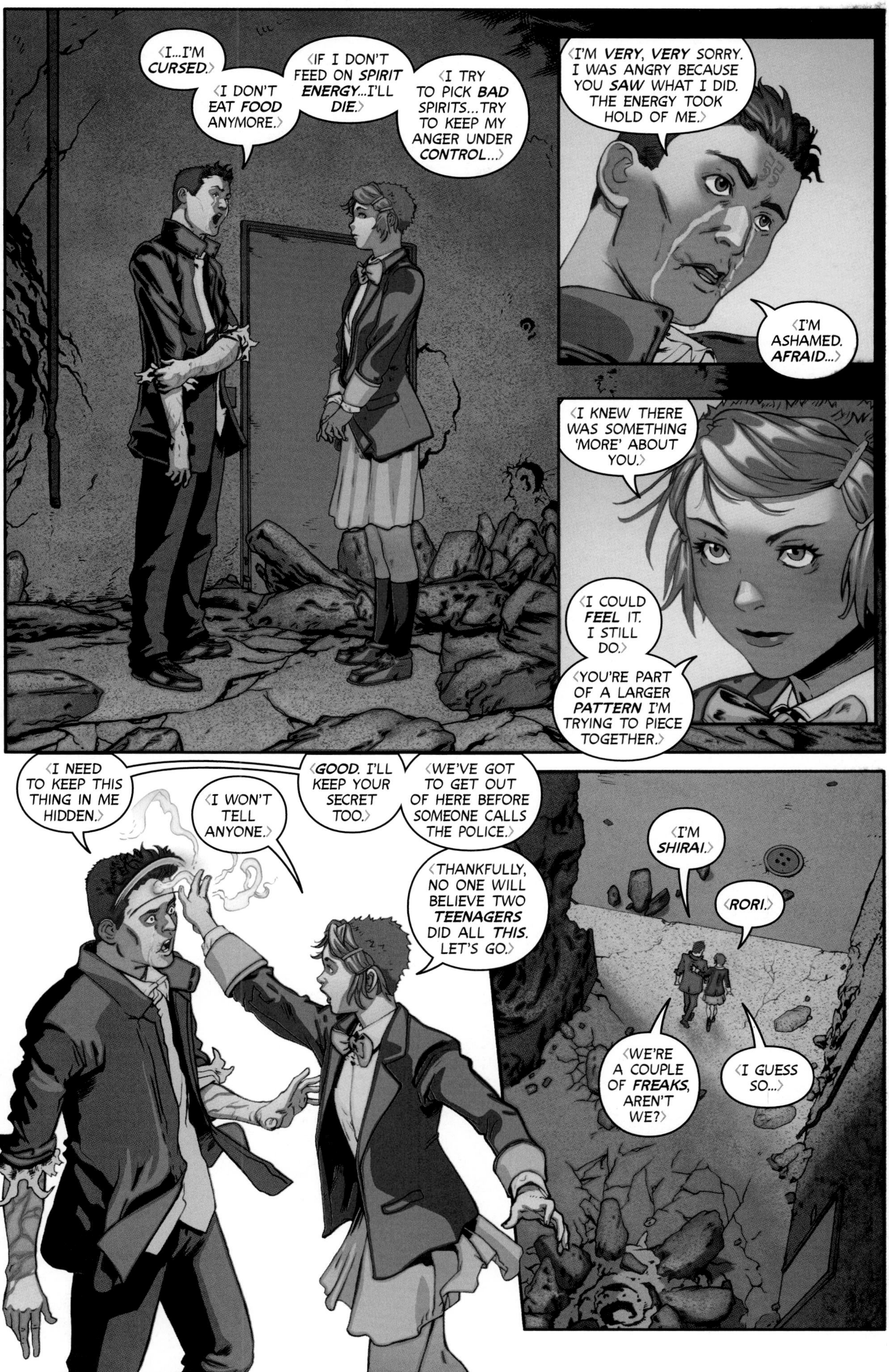
⟨I...I'M CURSED.⟩
⟨I DON'T EAT FOOD ANYMORE.⟩
⟨IF I DON'T FEED ON SPIRIT ENERGY...I'LL DIE.⟩
⟨I TRY TO PICK BAD SPIRITS...TRY TO KEEP MY ANGER UNDER CONTROL...⟩
⟨I'M VERY, VERY SORRY. I WAS ANGRY BECAUSE YOU SAW WHAT I DID. THE ENERGY TOOK HOLD OF ME.⟩
⟨I'M ASHAMED. AFRAID...⟩
⟨I KNEW THERE WAS SOMETHING 'MORE' ABOUT YOU.⟩
⟨I COULD FEEL IT. I STILL DO.⟩
⟨YOU'RE PART OF A LARGER PATTERN I'M TRYING TO PIECE TOGETHER.⟩
⟨I NEED TO KEEP THIS THING IN ME HIDDEN.⟩
⟨I WON'T TELL ANYONE.⟩
⟨GOOD. I'LL KEEP YOUR SECRET TOO.⟩
⟨WE'VE GOT TO GET OUT OF HERE BEFORE SOMEONE CALLS THE POLICE.⟩
⟨THANKFULLY, NO ONE WILL BELIEVE TWO TEENAGERS DID ALL THIS. LET'S GO.⟩
⟨I'M SHIRAI.⟩
⟨RORI.⟩
⟨WE'RE A COUPLE OF FREAKS, AREN'T WE?⟩
⟨I GUESS SO...⟩

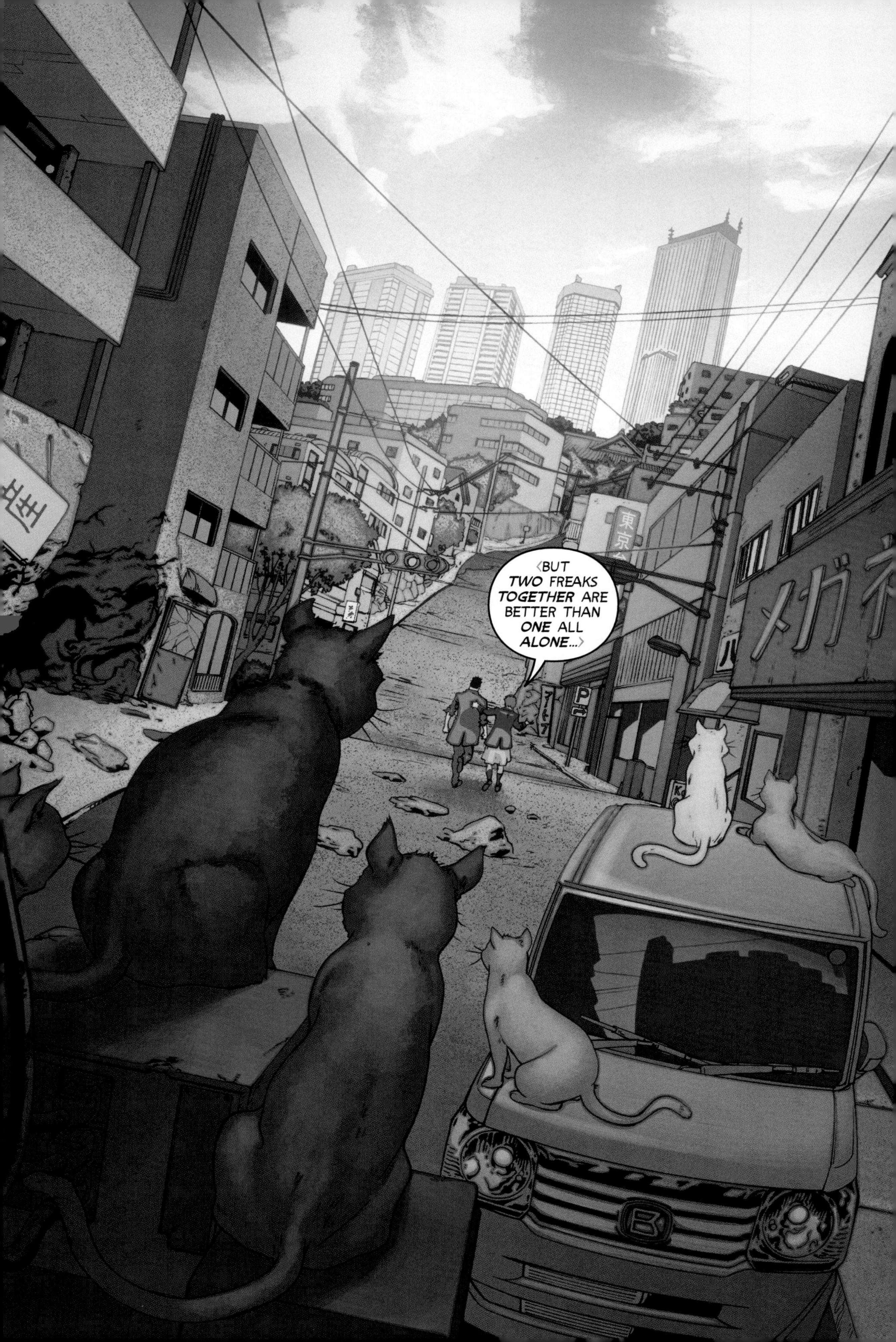
〈BUT TWO FREAKS TOGETHER ARE BETTER THAN ONE ALL ALONE...〉

Chapter Three

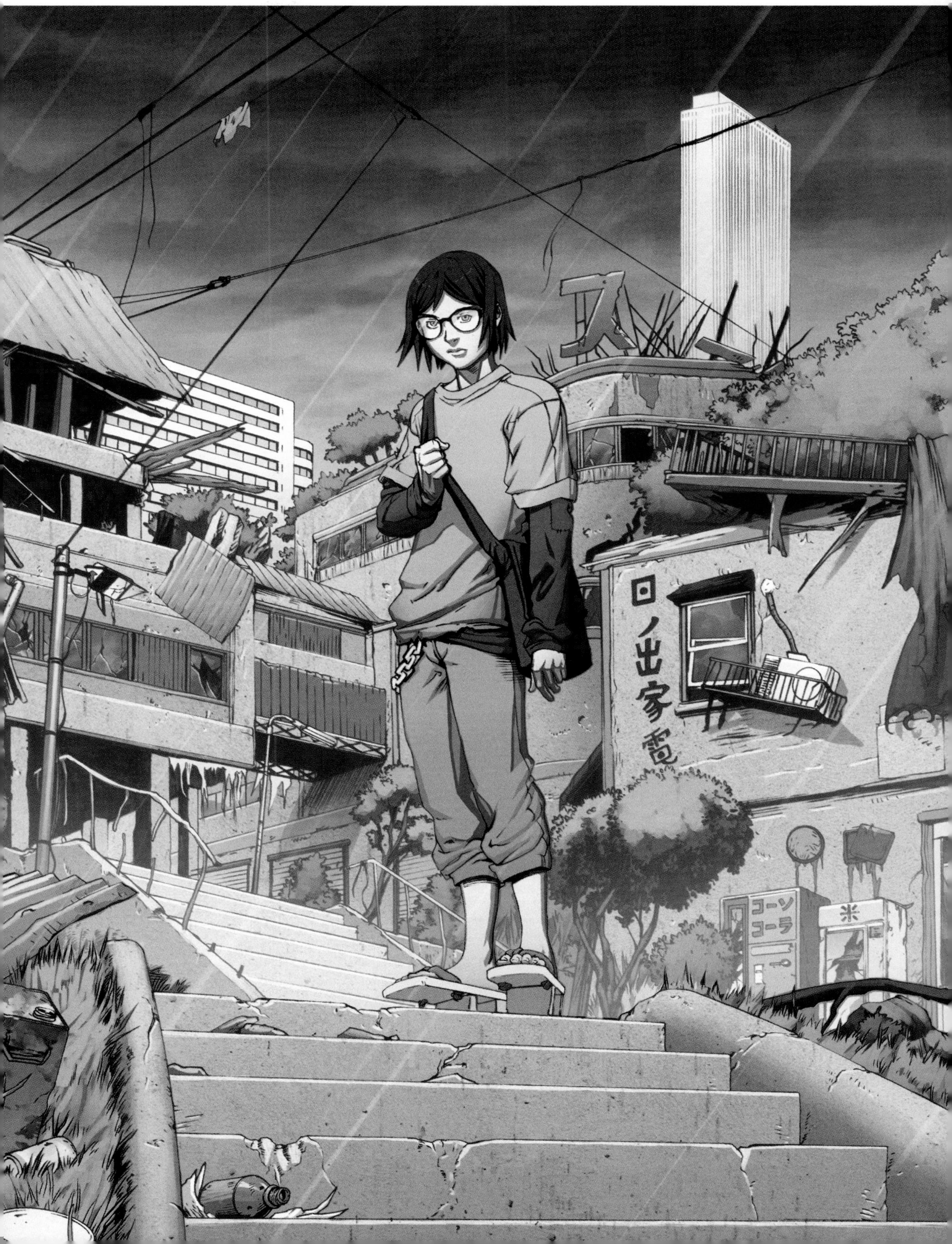
ロノ出家電
コーソ
コーラ

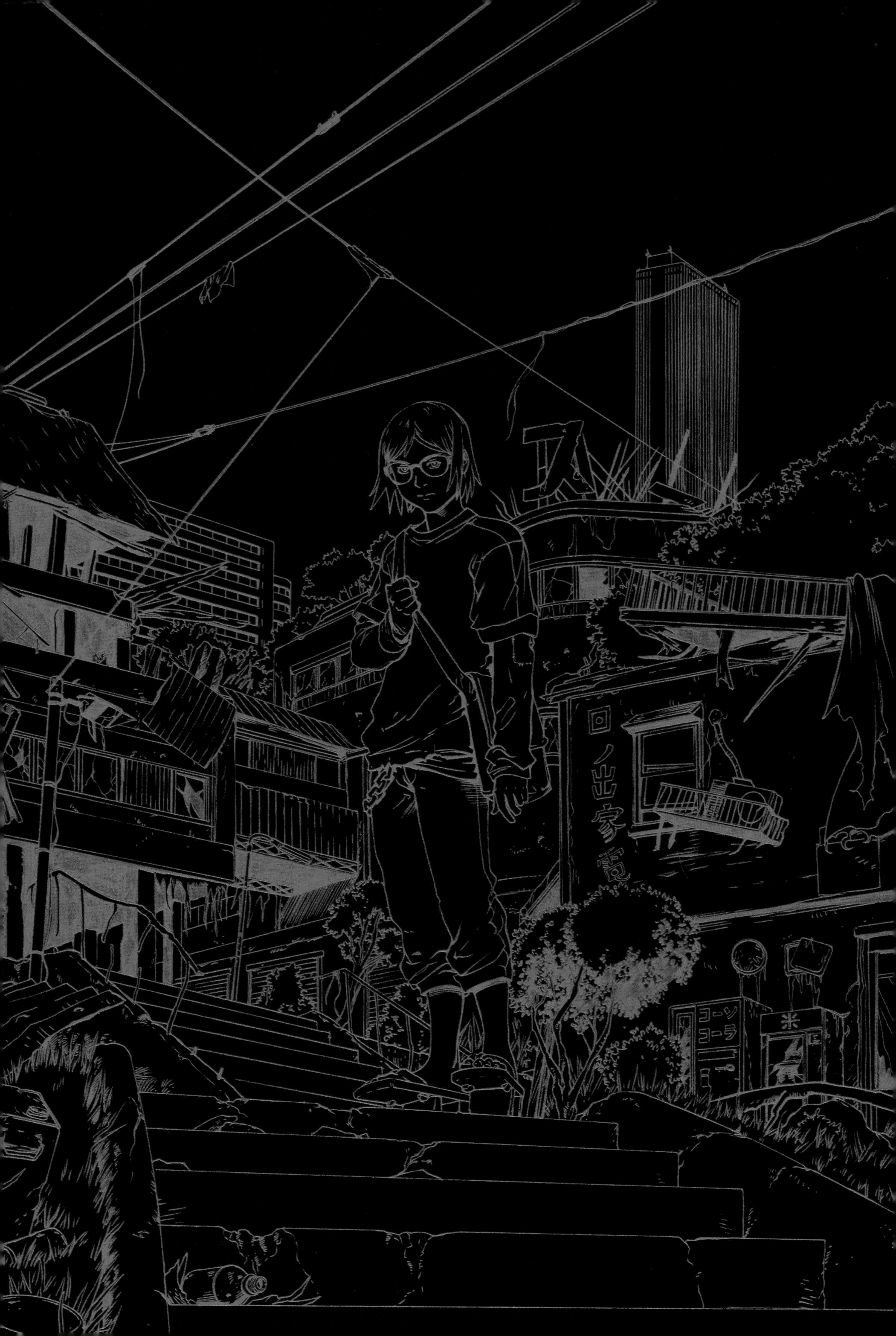

回ノ出家電
コーソ
コーラ
米

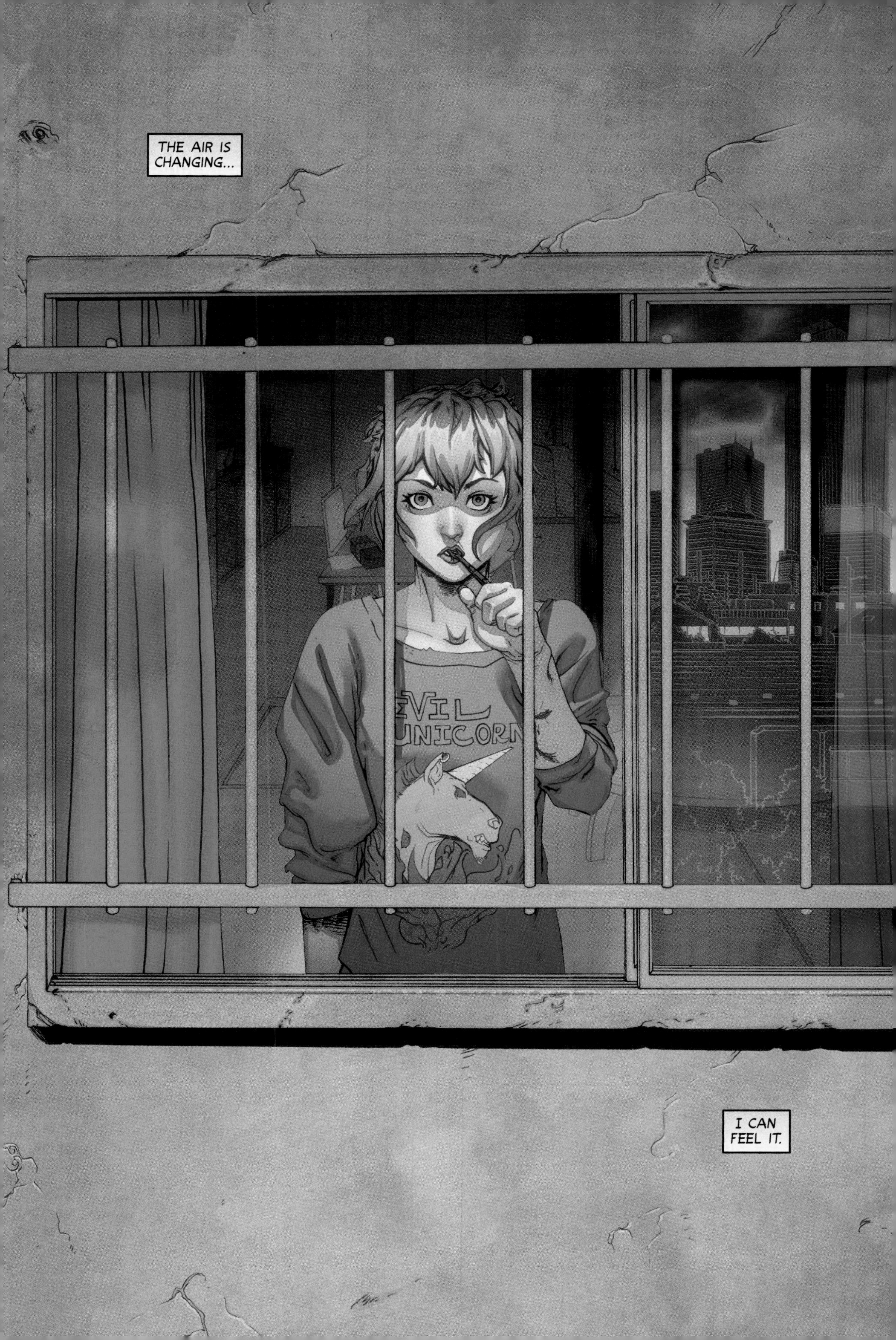
THE AIR IS CHANGING...
EVIL UNICORN
I CAN FEEL IT.

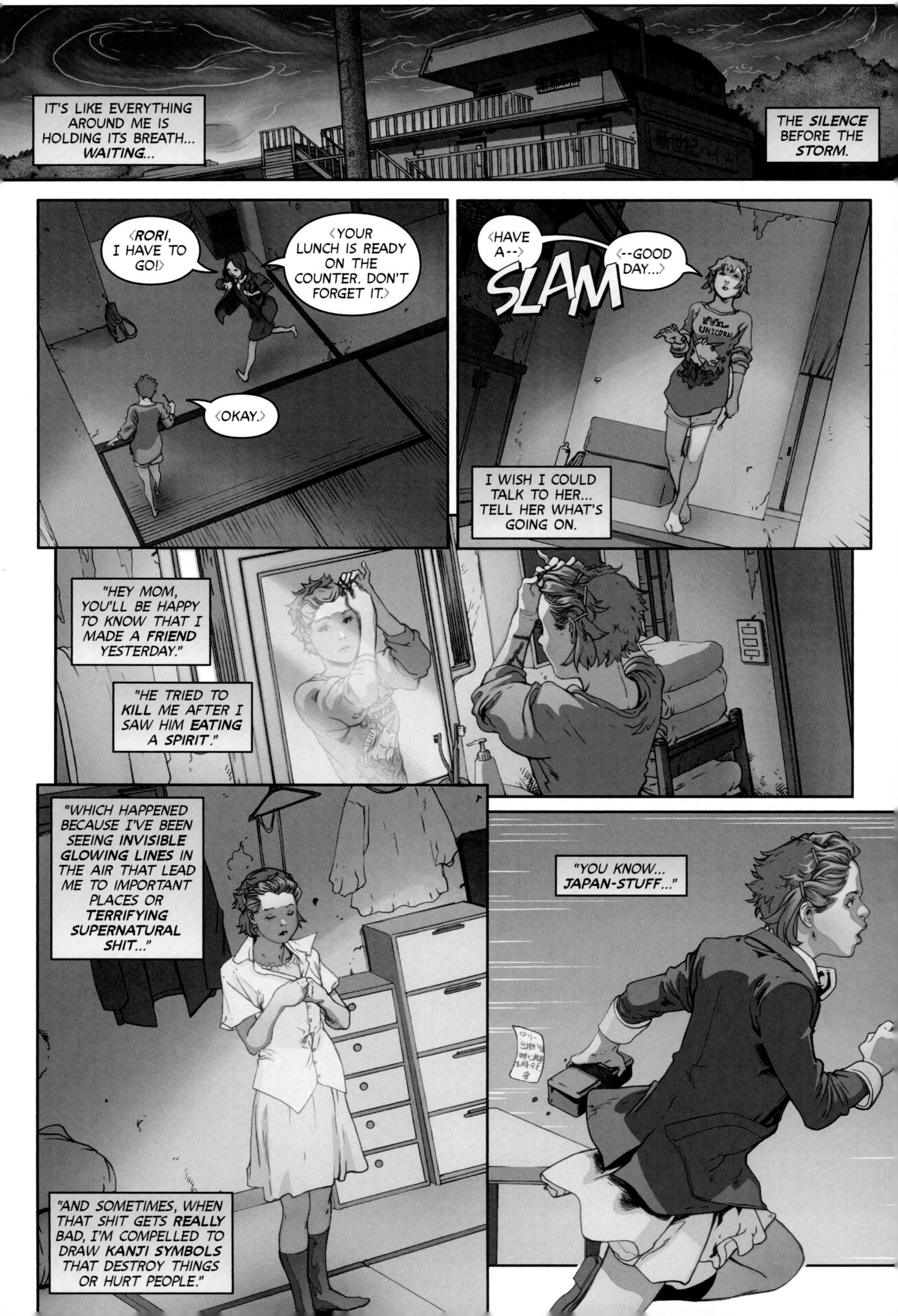
IT'S LIKE EVERYTHING AROUND ME IS HOLDING ITS BREATH... WAITING...
THE SILENCE BEFORE THE STORM.
‹RORI, I HAVE TO GO!›
‹YOUR LUNCH IS READY ON THE COUNTER. DON'T FORGET IT.›
‹OKAY.›
‹HAVE A--›
SLAM
‹--GOOD DAY...›
I WISH I COULD TALK TO HER... TELL HER WHAT'S GOING ON.
"HEY MOM, YOU'LL BE HAPPY TO KNOW THAT I MADE A FRIEND YESTERDAY."
"HE TRIED TO KILL ME AFTER I SAW HIM EATING A SPIRIT."
"WHICH HAPPENED BECAUSE I'VE BEEN SEEING INVISIBLE GLOWING LINES IN THE AIR THAT LEAD ME TO IMPORTANT PLACES OR TERRIFYING SUPERNATURAL SHIT..."
"AND SOMETIMES, WHEN THAT SHIT GETS REALLY BAD, I'M COMPELLED TO DRAW KANJI SYMBOLS THAT DESTROY THINGS OR HURT PEOPLE."
"YOU KNOW... JAPAN-STUFF..."

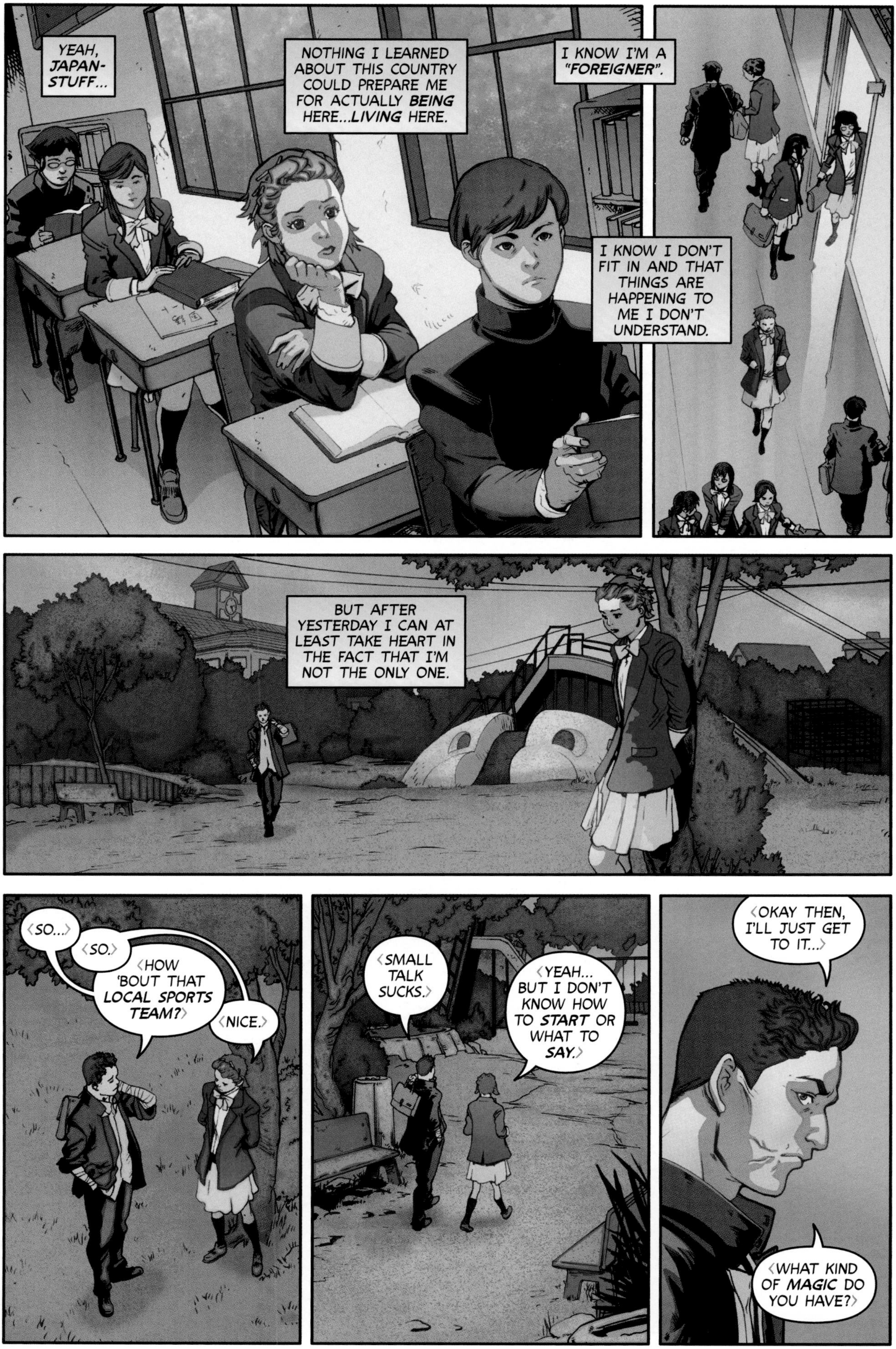
YEAH, JAPAN-STUFF...
NOTHING I LEARNED ABOUT THIS COUNTRY COULD PREPARE ME FOR ACTUALLY BEING HERE...LIVING HERE.
I KNOW I'M A "FOREIGNER".
I KNOW I DON'T FIT IN AND THAT THINGS ARE HAPPENING TO ME I DON'T UNDERSTAND.
BUT AFTER YESTERDAY I CAN AT LEAST TAKE HEART IN THE FACT THAT I'M NOT THE ONLY ONE.
〈SO...〉
〈SO.〉
〈HOW 'BOUT THAT LOCAL SPORTS TEAM?〉
〈NICE.〉
〈SMALL TALK SUCKS.〉
〈YEAH... BUT I DON'T KNOW HOW TO START OR WHAT TO SAY.〉
〈OKAY THEN, I'LL JUST GET TO IT...〉
〈WHAT KIND OF MAGIC DO YOU HAVE?〉

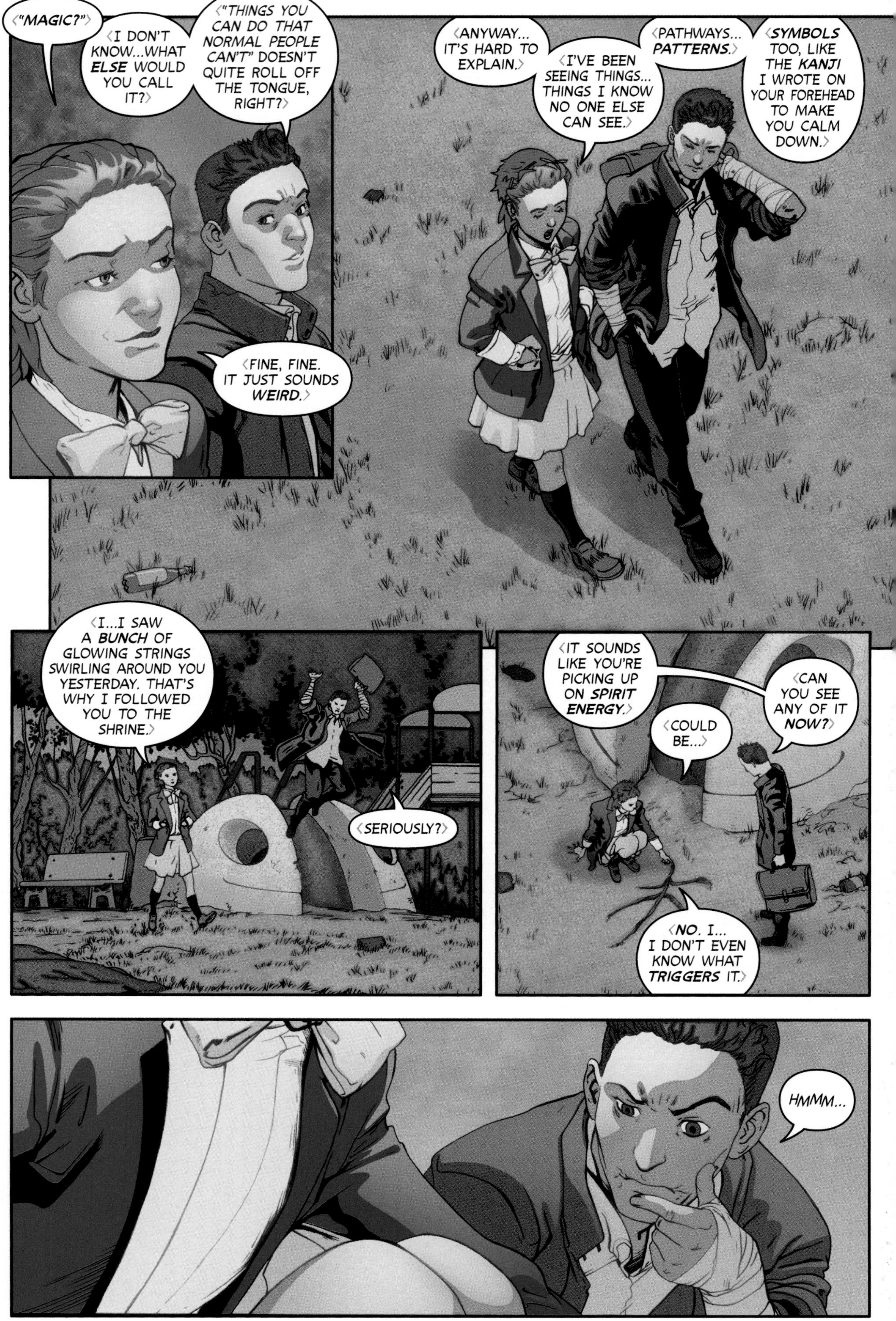

<"MAGIC?">
<I DON'T KNOW...WHAT ELSE WOULD YOU CALL IT?>
<"THINGS YOU CAN DO THAT NORMAL PEOPLE CAN'T" DOESN'T QUITE ROLL OFF THE TONGUE, RIGHT?>
<FINE, FINE. IT JUST SOUNDS WEIRD.>
<ANYWAY... IT'S HARD TO EXPLAIN.>
<I'VE BEEN SEEING THINGS... THINGS I KNOW NO ONE ELSE CAN SEE.>
<PATHWAYS... PATTERNS.>
<SYMBOLS TOO, LIKE THE KANJI I WROTE ON YOUR FOREHEAD TO MAKE YOU CALM DOWN.>
<I...I SAW A BUNCH OF GLOWING STRINGS SWIRLING AROUND YOU YESTERDAY. THAT'S WHY I FOLLOWED YOU TO THE SHRINE.>
<SERIOUSLY?>
<IT SOUNDS LIKE YOU'RE PICKING UP ON SPIRIT ENERGY.>
<COULD BE...>
<CAN YOU SEE ANY OF IT NOW?>
<NO. I... I DON'T EVEN KNOW WHAT TRIGGERS IT.>
HMMM...

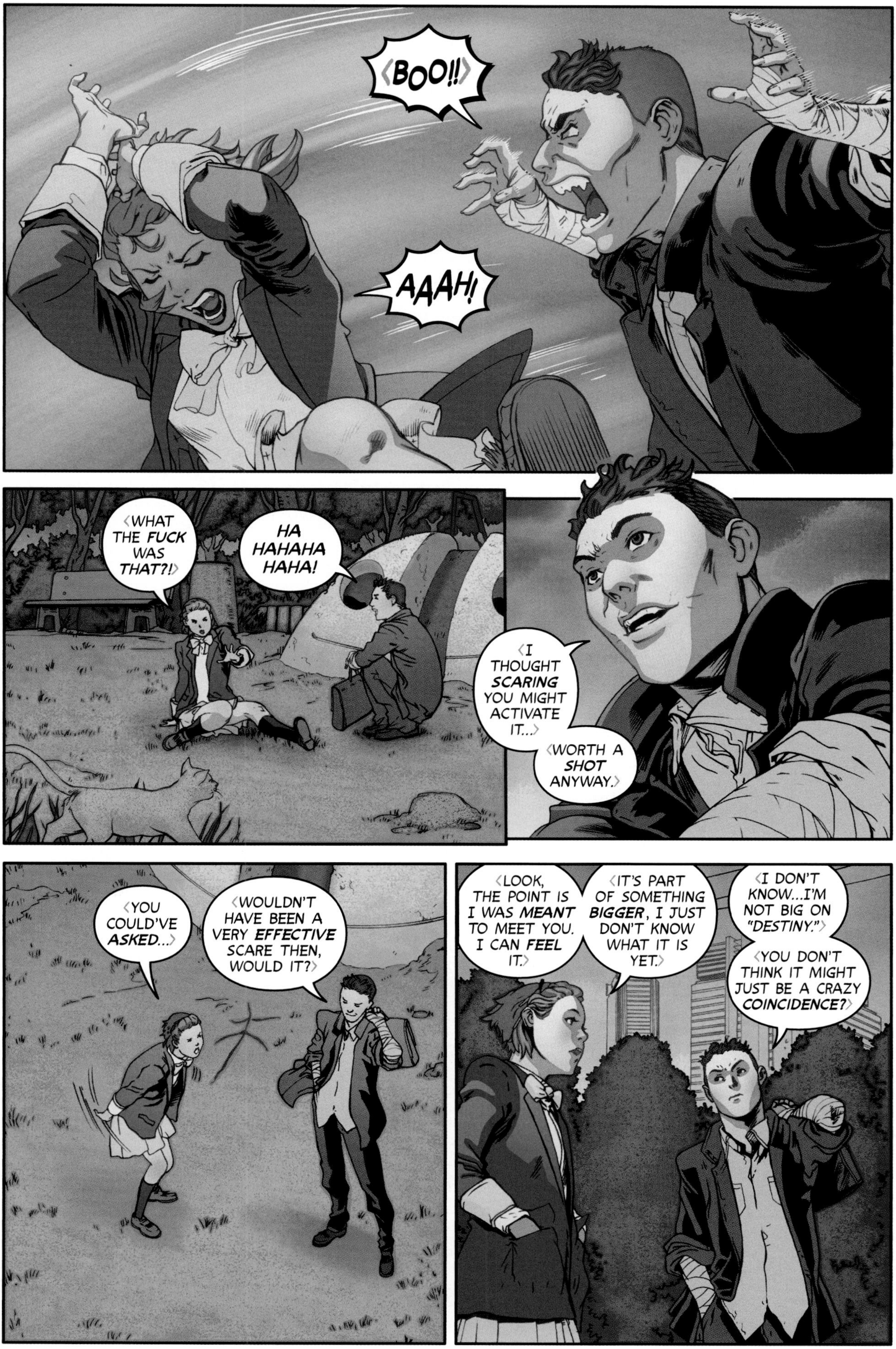

⟨BOO!!⟩
AAAH!
⟨WHAT THE FUCK WAS THAT?!⟩
HA HAHAHA HAHA!
⟨I THOUGHT SCARING YOU MIGHT ACTIVATE IT...⟩
⟨WORTH A SHOT ANYWAY.⟩
⟨YOU COULD'VE ASKED...⟩
⟨WOULDN'T HAVE BEEN A VERY EFFECTIVE SCARE THEN, WOULD IT?⟩
⟨LOOK, THE POINT IS I WAS MEANT TO MEET YOU. I CAN FEEL IT.⟩
⟨IT'S PART OF SOMETHING BIGGER, I JUST DON'T KNOW WHAT IT IS YET.⟩
⟨I DON'T KNOW...I'M NOT BIG ON "DESTINY."⟩
⟨YOU DON'T THINK IT MIGHT JUST BE A CRAZY COINCIDENCE?⟩

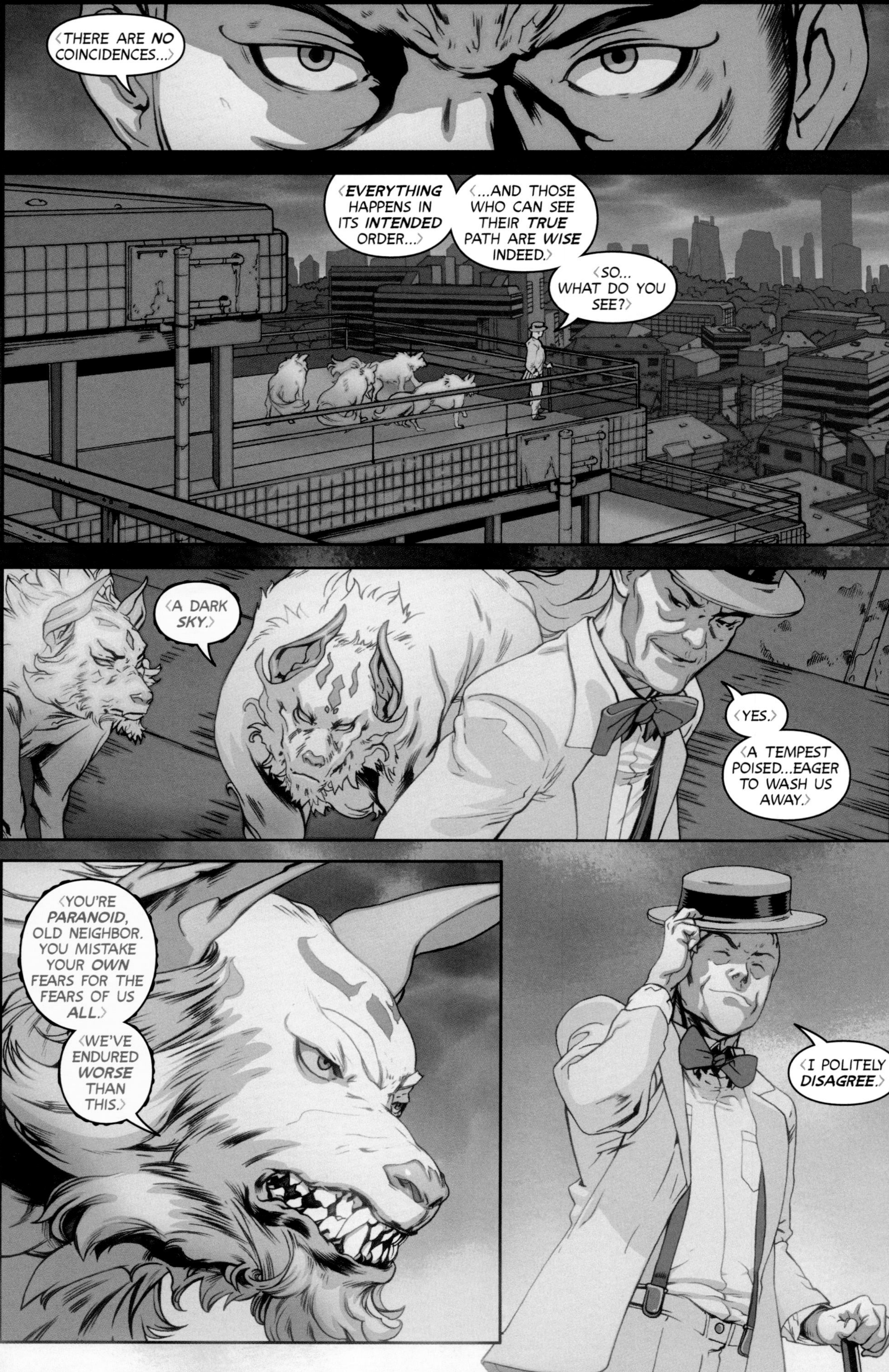
<THERE ARE NO COINCIDENCES...>
<EVERYTHING HAPPENS IN ITS INTENDED ORDER...>
<...AND THOSE WHO CAN SEE THEIR TRUE PATH ARE WISE INDEED.>
<SO... WHAT DO YOU SEE?>
<A DARK SKY.>
<YES.>
<A TEMPEST POISED...EAGER TO WASH US AWAY.>
<YOU'RE PARANOID, OLD NEIGHBOR. YOU MISTAKE YOUR OWN FEARS FOR THE FEARS OF US ALL.>
<WE'VE ENDURED WORSE THAN THIS.>
<I POLITELY DISAGREE.>

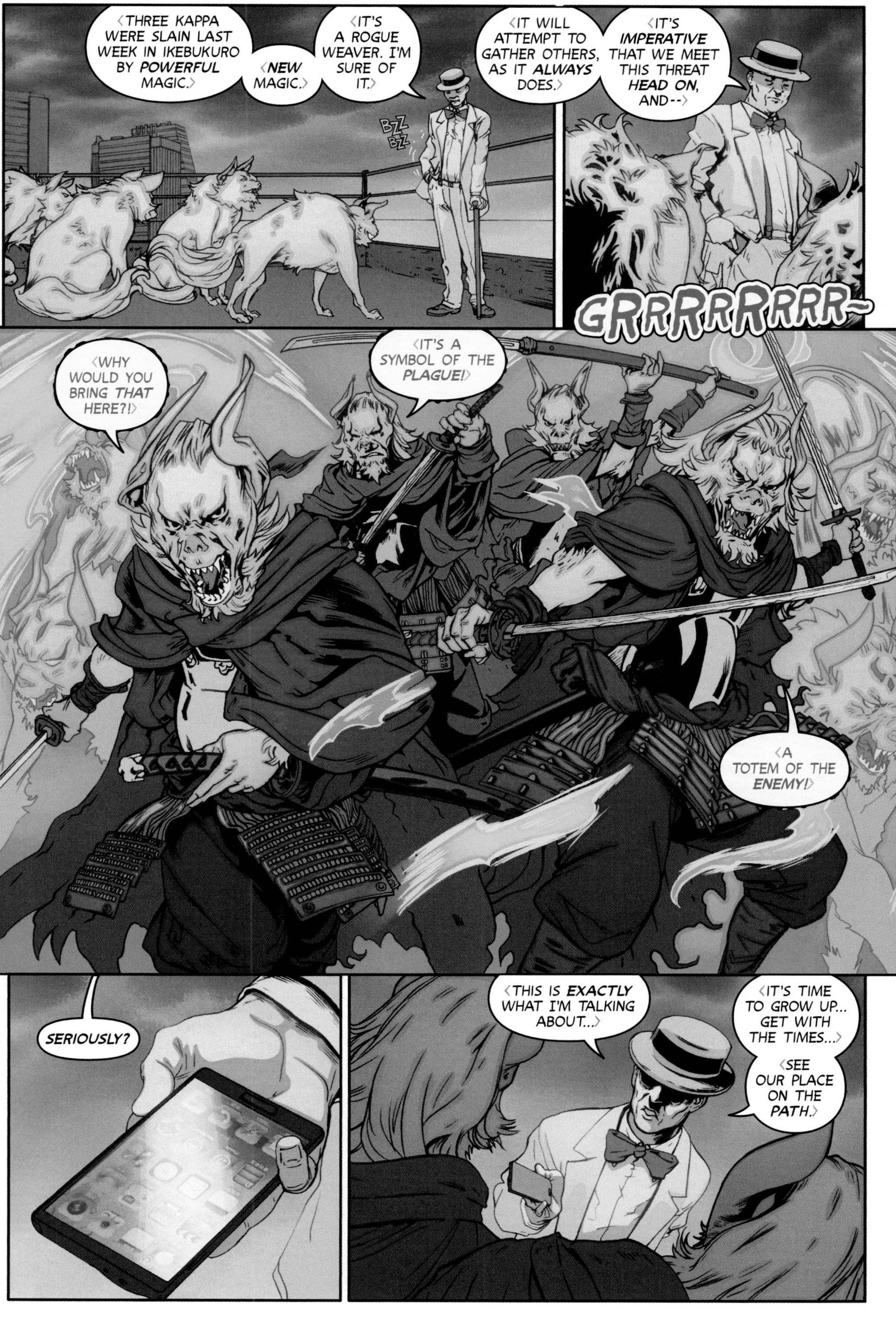

〈THREE KAPPA WERE SLAIN LAST WEEK IN IKEBUKURO BY POWERFUL MAGIC.〉
〈NEW MAGIC.〉
〈IT'S A ROGUE WEAVER. I'M SURE OF IT.〉
BZZ BZZ
〈IT WILL ATTEMPT TO GATHER OTHERS, AS IT ALWAYS DOES.〉
〈IT'S IMPERATIVE THAT WE MEET THIS THREAT HEAD ON, AND--〉
GRRRRRRRR~
〈WHY WOULD YOU BRING THAT HERE?!〉
〈IT'S A SYMBOL OF THE PLAGUE!〉
〈A TOTEM OF THE ENEMY!〉
SERIOUSLY?
〈THIS IS EXACTLY WHAT I'M TALKING ABOUT...〉
〈IT'S TIME TO GROW UP... GET WITH THE TIMES...〉
〈SEE OUR PLACE ON THE PATH.〉

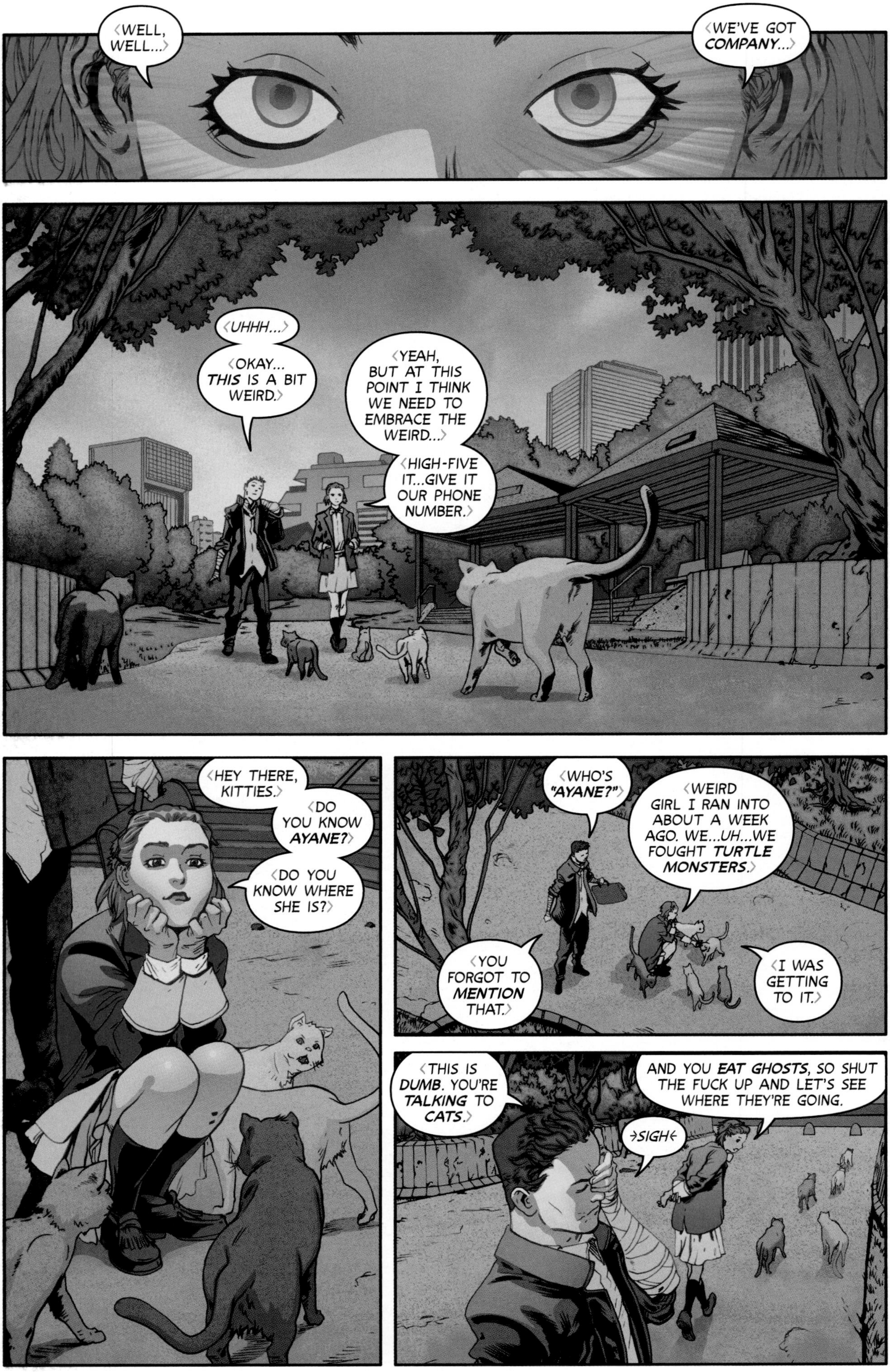

‹WELL, WELL...›
‹WE'VE GOT COMPANY...›
‹UHHH...›
‹OKAY... THIS IS A BIT WEIRD.›
‹YEAH, BUT AT THIS POINT I THINK WE NEED TO EMBRACE THE WEIRD...›
‹HIGH-FIVE IT...GIVE IT OUR PHONE NUMBER.›
‹HEY THERE, KITTIES.›
‹DO YOU KNOW AYANE?›
‹DO YOU KNOW WHERE SHE IS?›
‹WHO'S "AYANE?"›
‹WEIRD GIRL I RAN INTO ABOUT A WEEK AGO. WE...UH...WE FOUGHT TURTLE MONSTERS.›
‹YOU FORGOT TO MENTION THAT.›
‹I WAS GETTING TO IT.›
‹THIS IS DUMB. YOU'RE TALKING TO CATS.›
AND YOU EAT GHOSTS, SO SHUT THE FUCK UP AND LET'S SEE WHERE THEY'RE GOING.
›SIGH‹

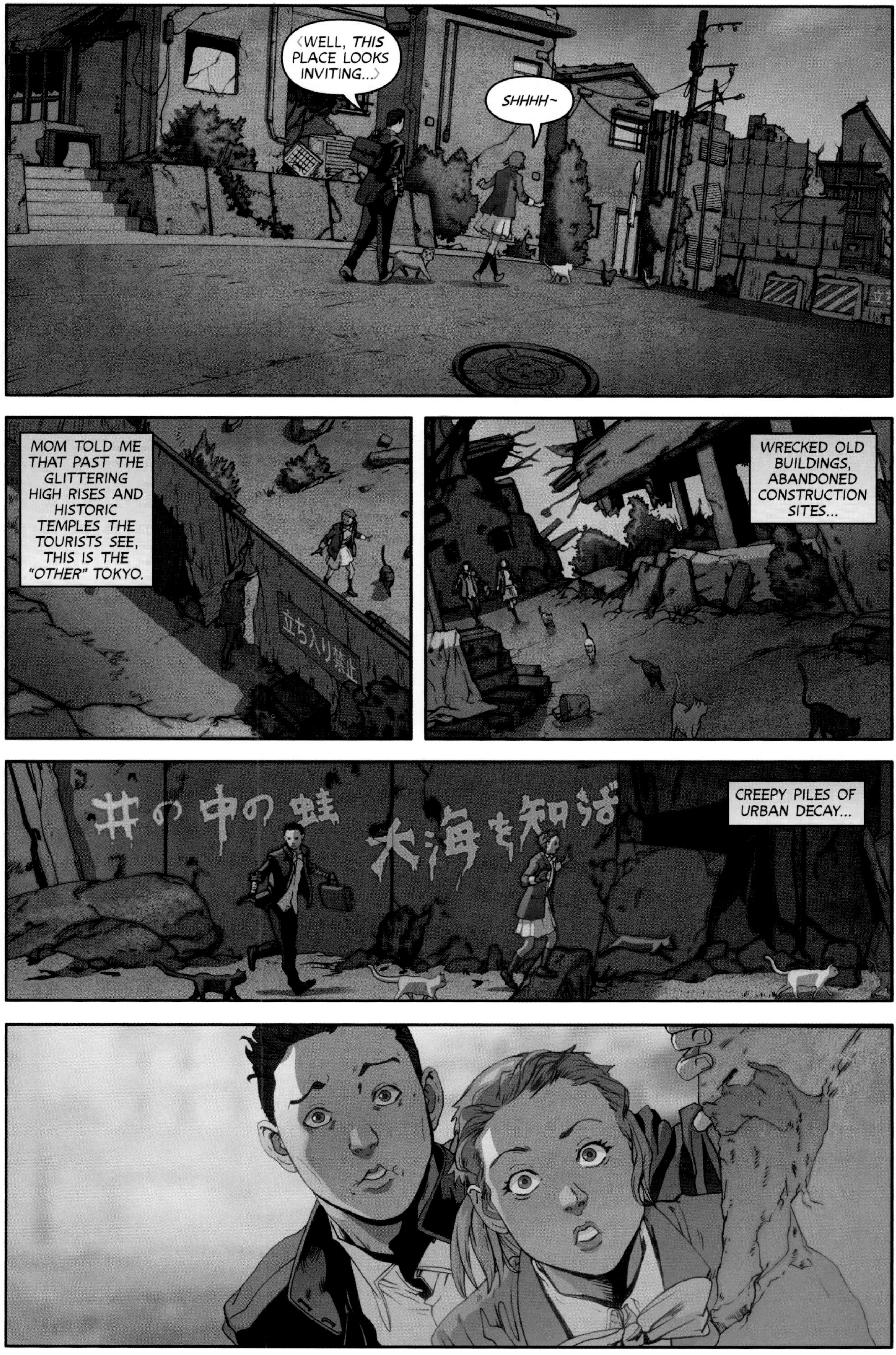

<WELL, *THIS* PLACE LOOKS INVITING...>
SHHHH~
MOM TOLD ME THAT PAST THE GLITTERING HIGH RISES AND HISTORIC TEMPLES THE TOURISTS SEE, THIS IS THE *"OTHER"* TOKYO.
立ち入り禁止
WRECKED OLD BUILDINGS, ABANDONED CONSTRUCTION SITES...
井の中の蛙 大海を知らず
CREEPY PILES OF URBAN DECAY...

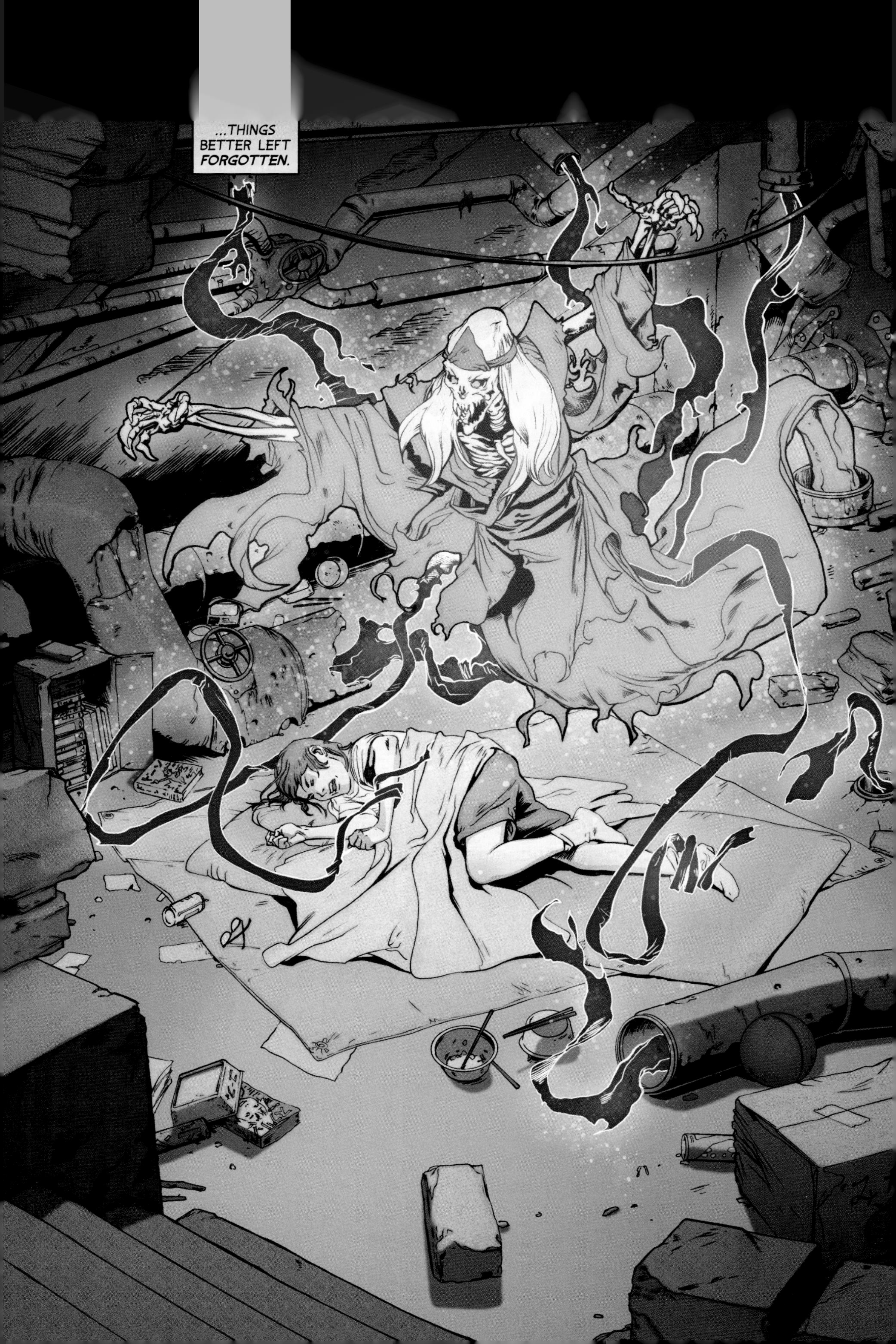
...THINGS BETTER LEFT *FORGOTTEN.*

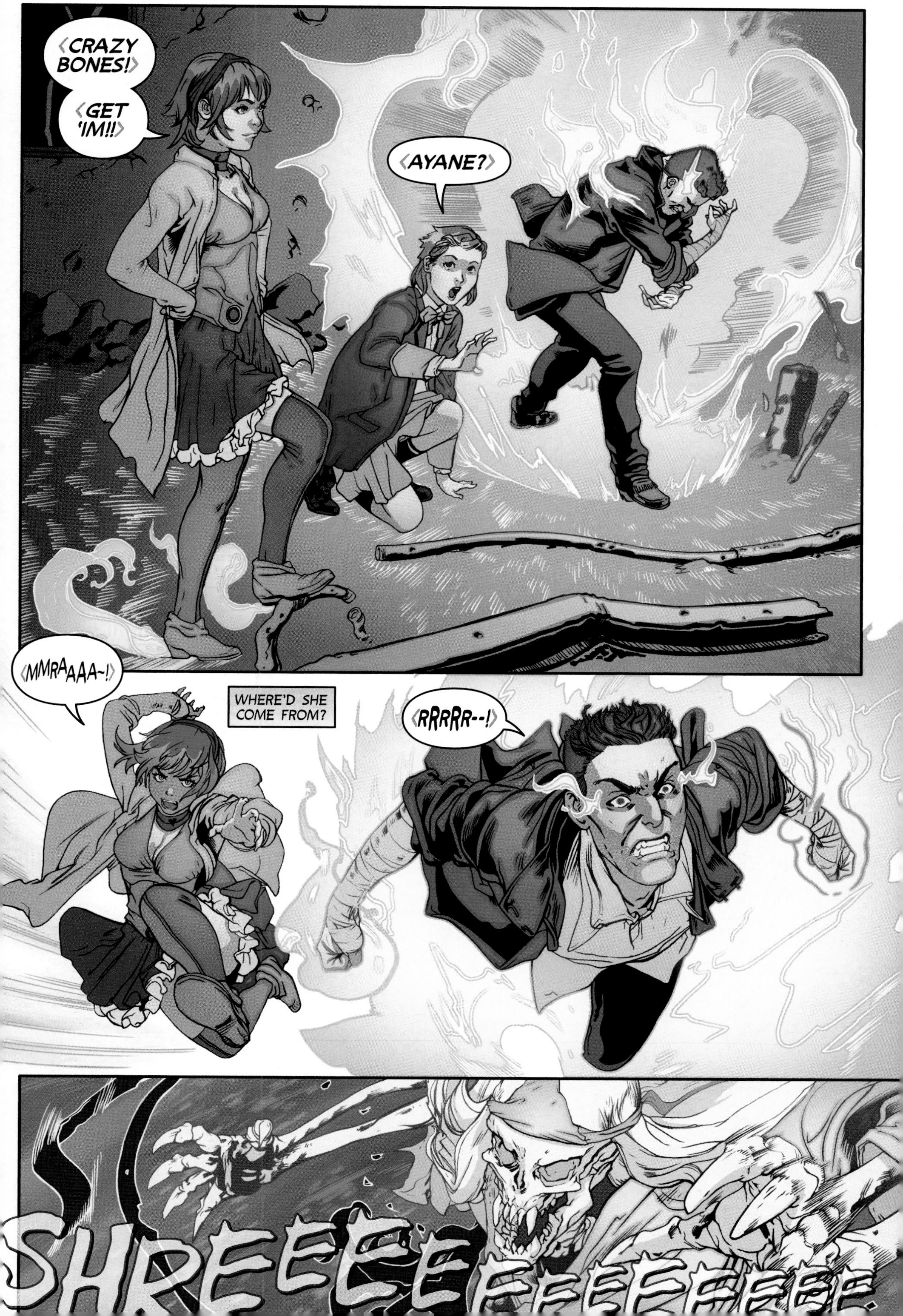

⟨CRAZY BONES!⟩
⟨GET 'IM!!⟩
⟨AYANE?⟩
⟨MMRAAAA~!⟩
WHERE'D SHE COME FROM?
⟨RRRRR--!⟩
SHREEEEEEEEEEEE.

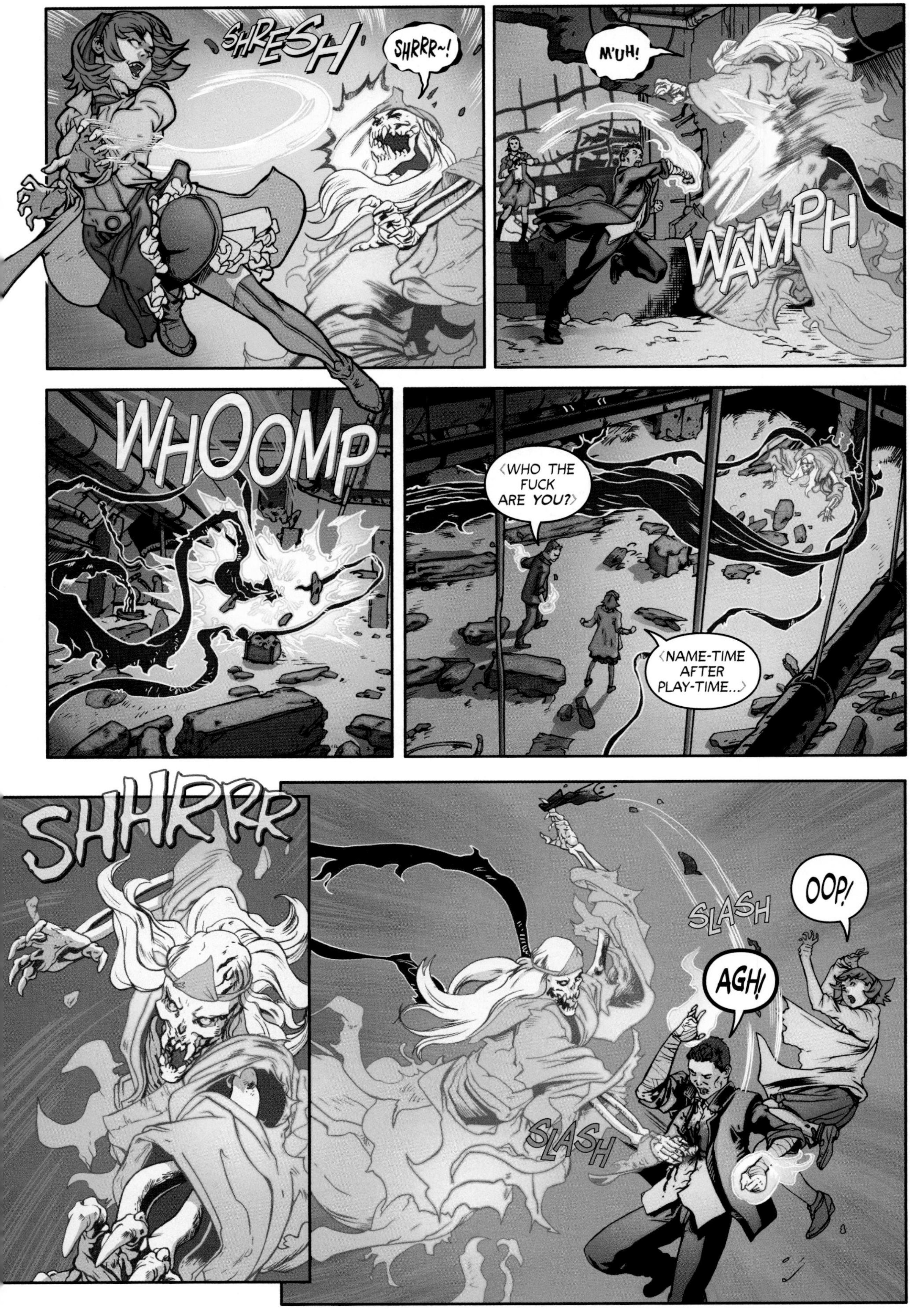
SHRESH
SHRRR~!
M'UH!
WAMPH
WHOOMP
⟨WHO THE FUCK ARE YOU?⟩
⟨NAME-TIME AFTER PLAY-TIME...⟩
SHHRRR
SLASH
OOP!
AGH!
SLASH

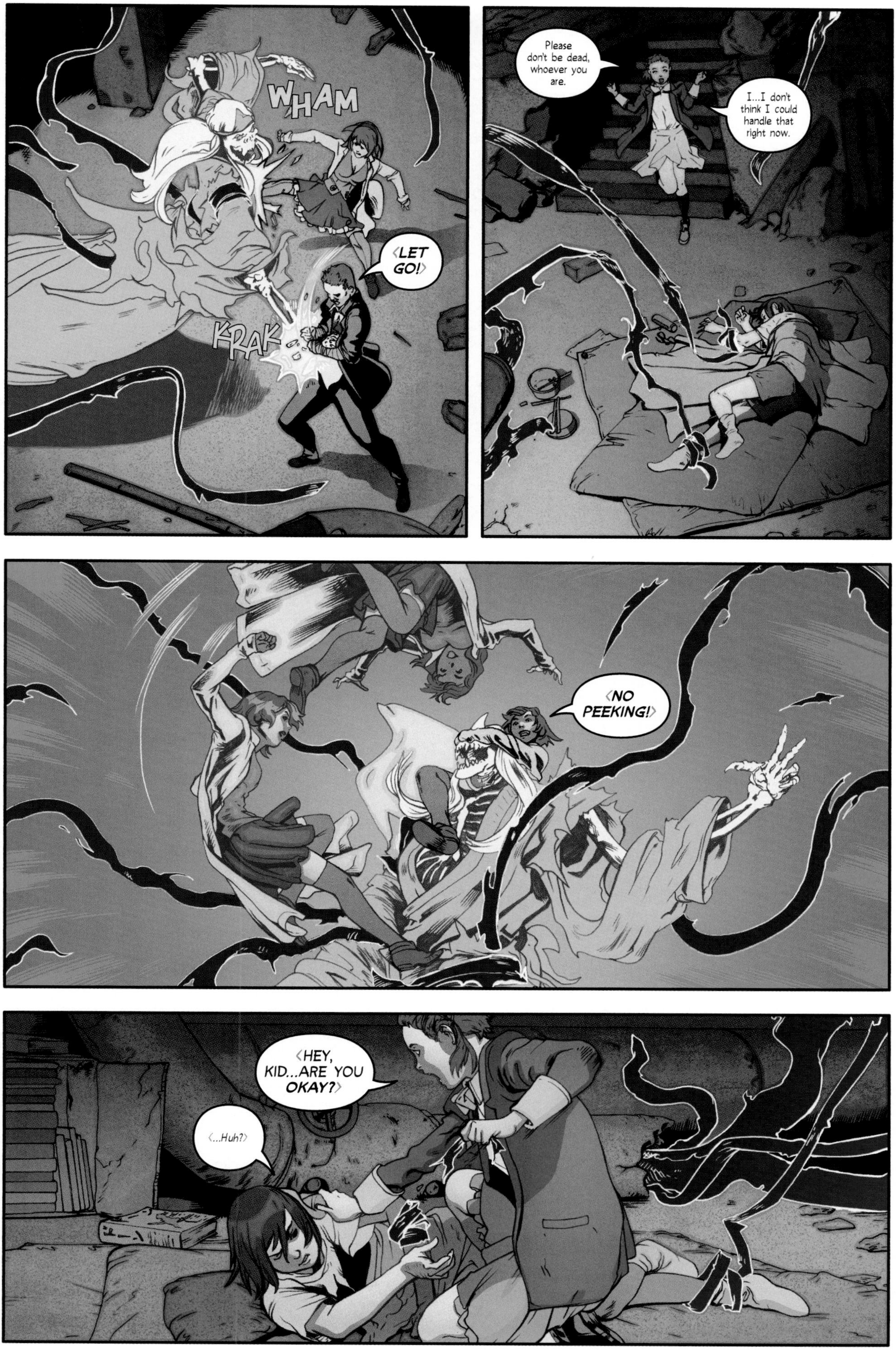
WHAM
‹LET GO!›
KRAK
Please don't be dead, whoever you are.
I...I don't think I could handle that right now.
‹NO PEEKING!›
‹HEY, KID...ARE YOU OKAY?›
‹...Huh?›

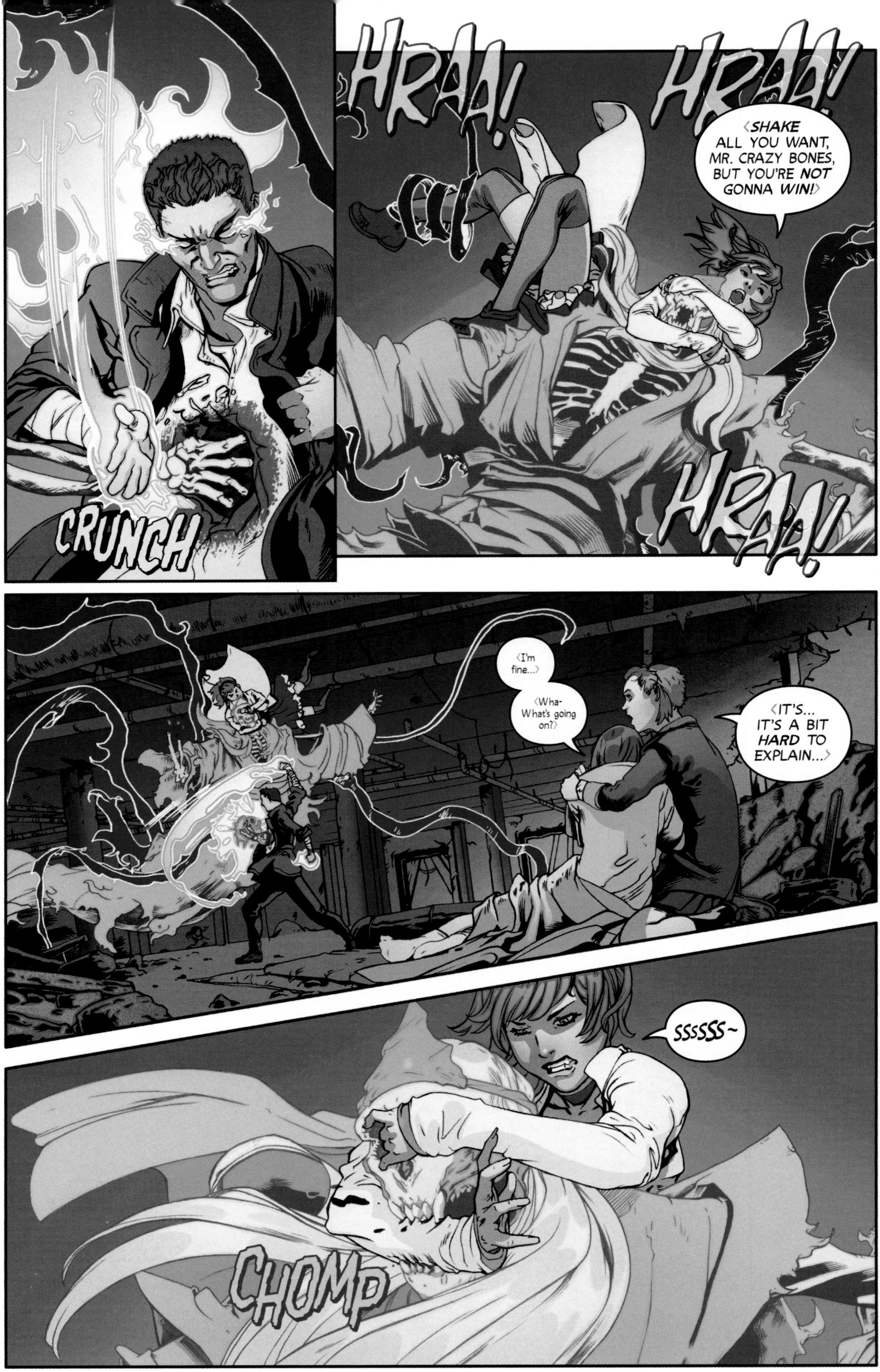
CRUNCH
HRAA!
HRAA!
‹SHAKE ALL YOU WANT, MR. CRAZY BONES, BUT YOU'RE NOT GONNA WIN!›
HRAA!
‹I'm fine...›
‹Wha- What's going on?›
‹IT'S... IT'S A BIT HARD TO EXPLAIN...›
SSSSSS~
CHOMP

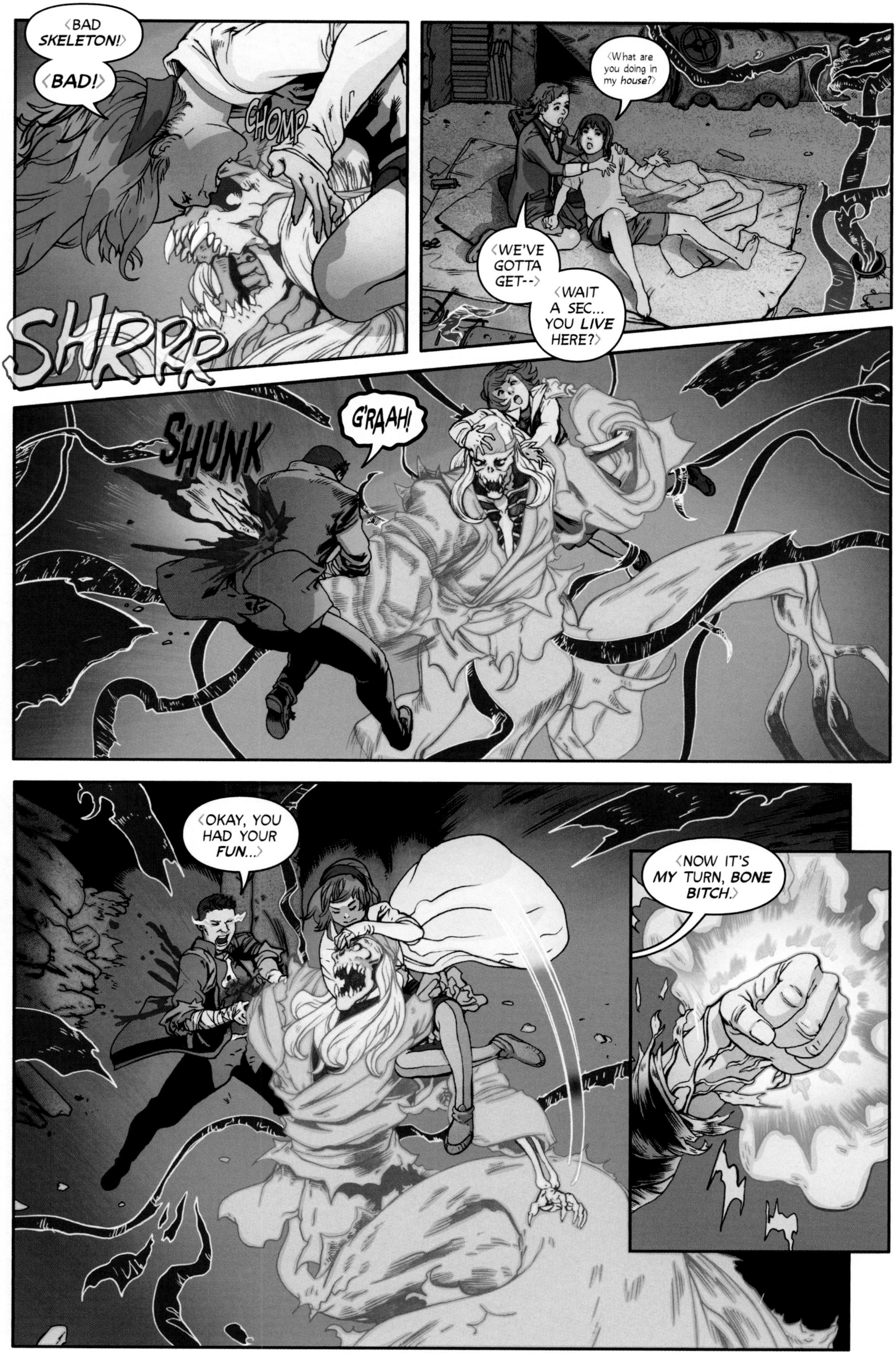
<BAD SKELETON!>
<BAD!>
CHOMP
SHRRR
<What are you doing in my house?>
<WE'VE GOTTA GET-->
<WAIT A SEC... YOU LIVE HERE?>
SHUNK
G'RAAH!
<OKAY, YOU HAD YOUR FUN...>
<NOW IT'S MY TURN, BONE BITCH.>

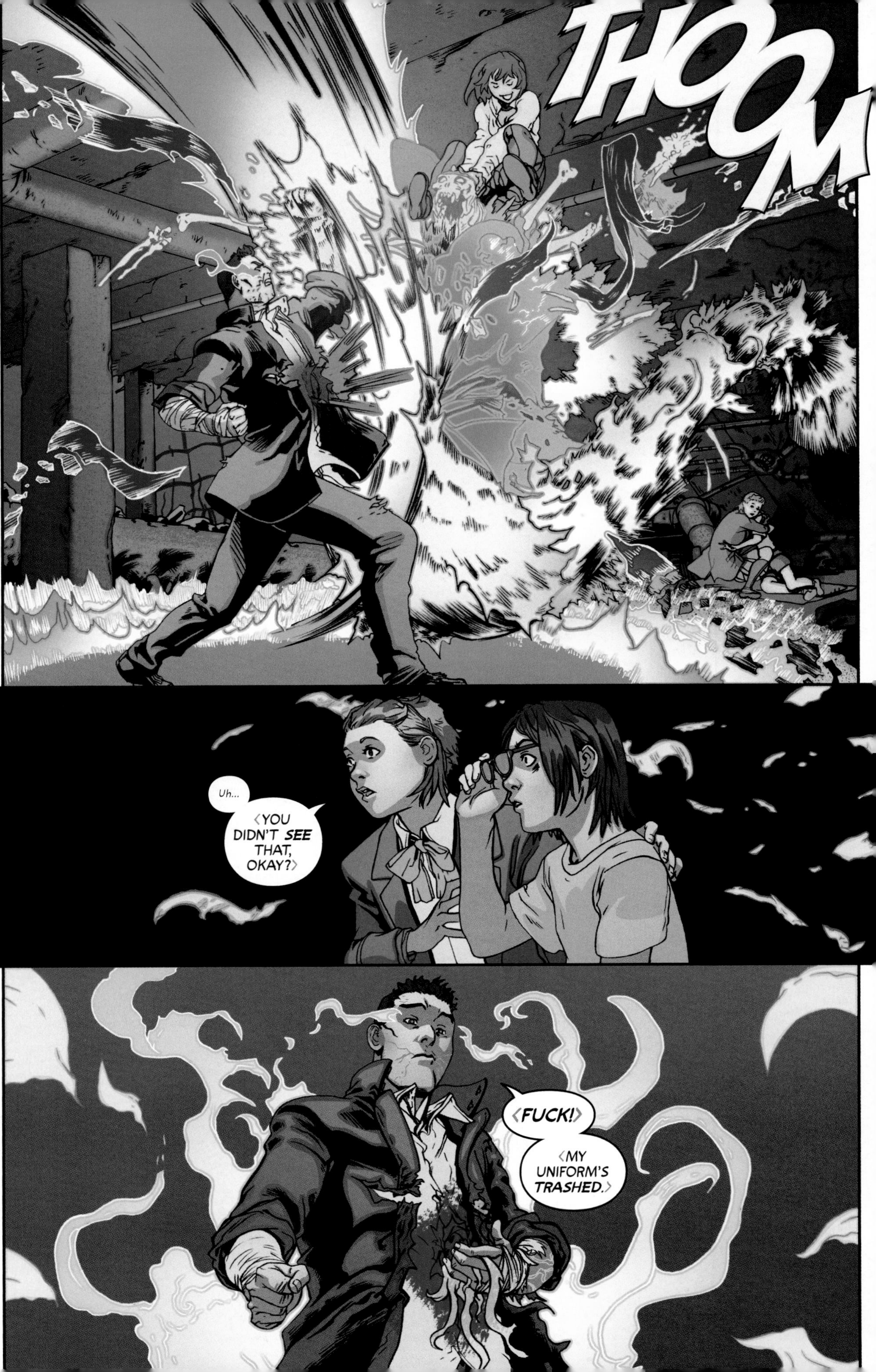
THOOM
Uh...
‹YOU DIDN'T SEE THAT, OKAY?›
‹FUCK!›
‹MY UNIFORM'S TRASHED.›

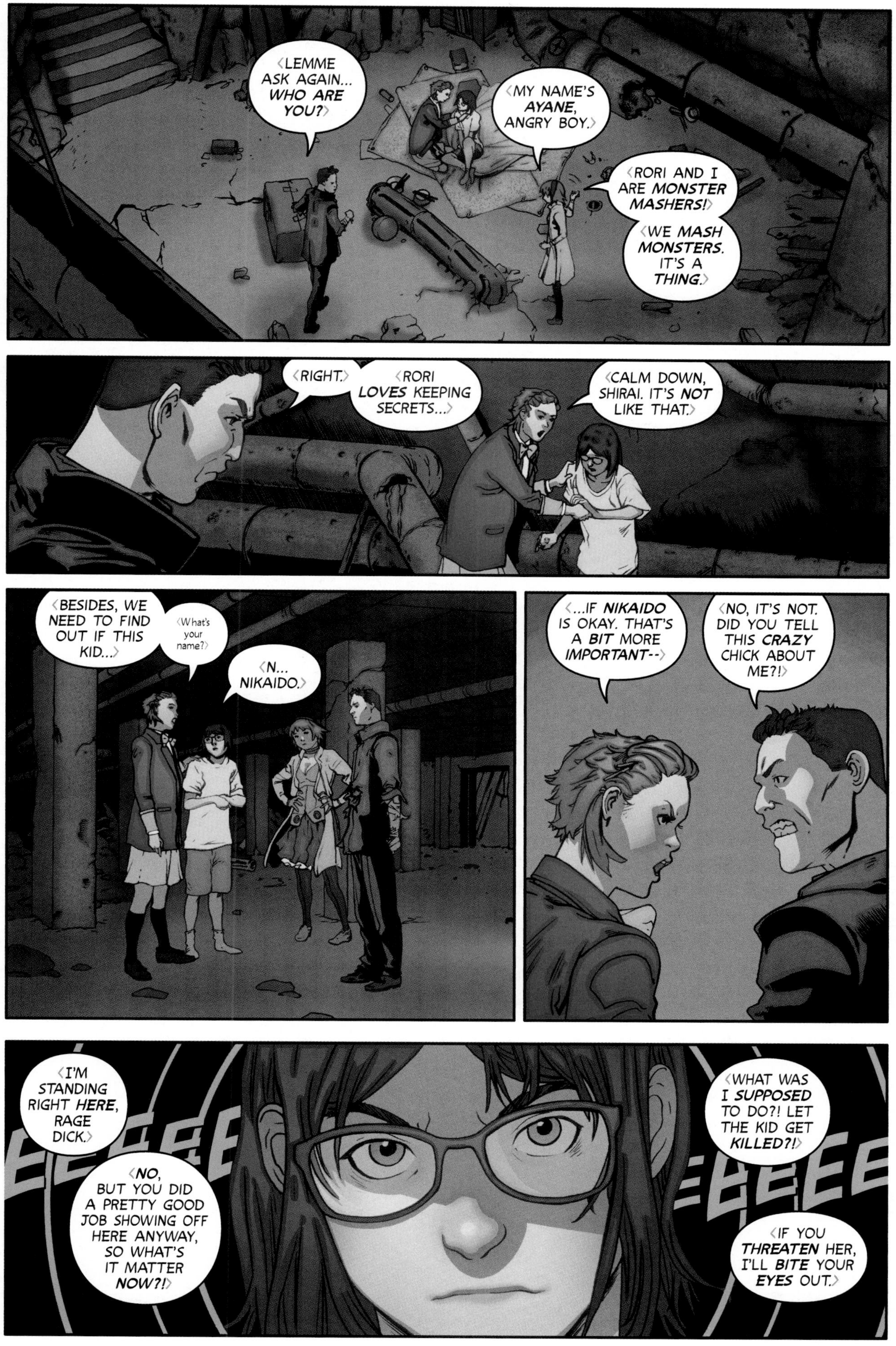
〈LEMME ASK AGAIN... WHO ARE YOU?〉
〈MY NAME'S AYANE, ANGRY BOY.〉
〈RORI AND I ARE MONSTER MASHERS!〉
〈WE MASH MONSTERS. IT'S A THING.〉
〈RIGHT.〉
〈RORI LOVES KEEPING SECRETS...〉
〈CALM DOWN, SHIRAI. IT'S NOT LIKE THAT.〉
〈BESIDES, WE NEED TO FIND OUT IF THIS KID...〉
〈What's your name?〉
〈N... NIKAIDO.〉
〈...IF NIKAIDO IS OKAY. THAT'S A BIT MORE IMPORTANT--〉
〈NO, IT'S NOT. DID YOU TELL THIS CRAZY CHICK ABOUT ME?!〉
〈I'M STANDING RIGHT HERE, RAGE DICK.〉
〈NO, BUT YOU DID A PRETTY GOOD JOB SHOWING OFF HERE ANYWAY, SO WHAT'S IT MATTER NOW?!〉
〈WHAT WAS I SUPPOSED TO DO?! LET THE KID GET KILLED?!〉
〈IF YOU THREATEN HER, I'LL BITE YOUR EYES OUT.〉

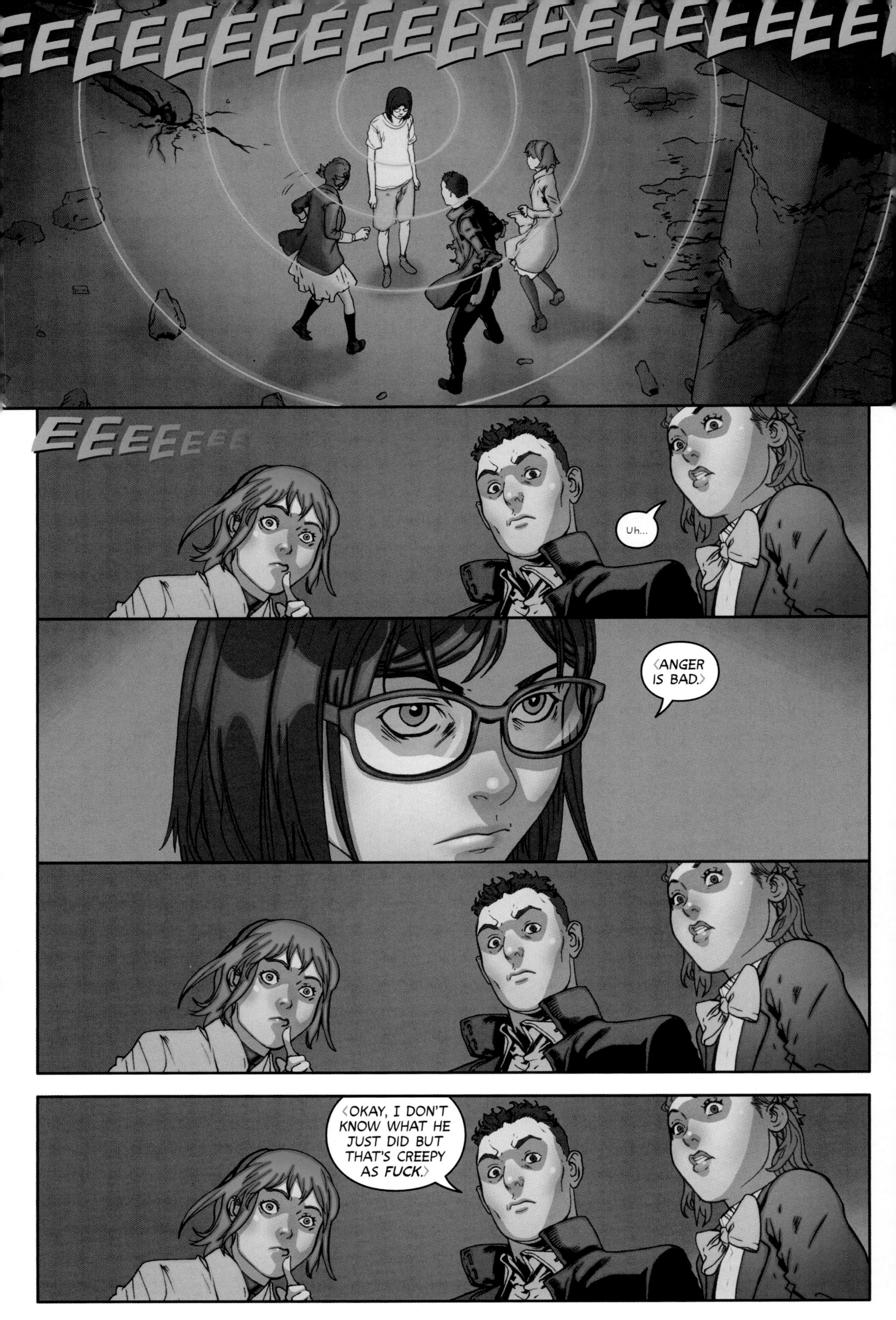
EEEEEEEEEEEEEEEEEE
EEEEEEE
Uh...
‹ANGER IS BAD.›
‹OKAY, I DON'T KNOW WHAT HE JUST DID BUT THAT'S CREEPY AS *FUCK*.›

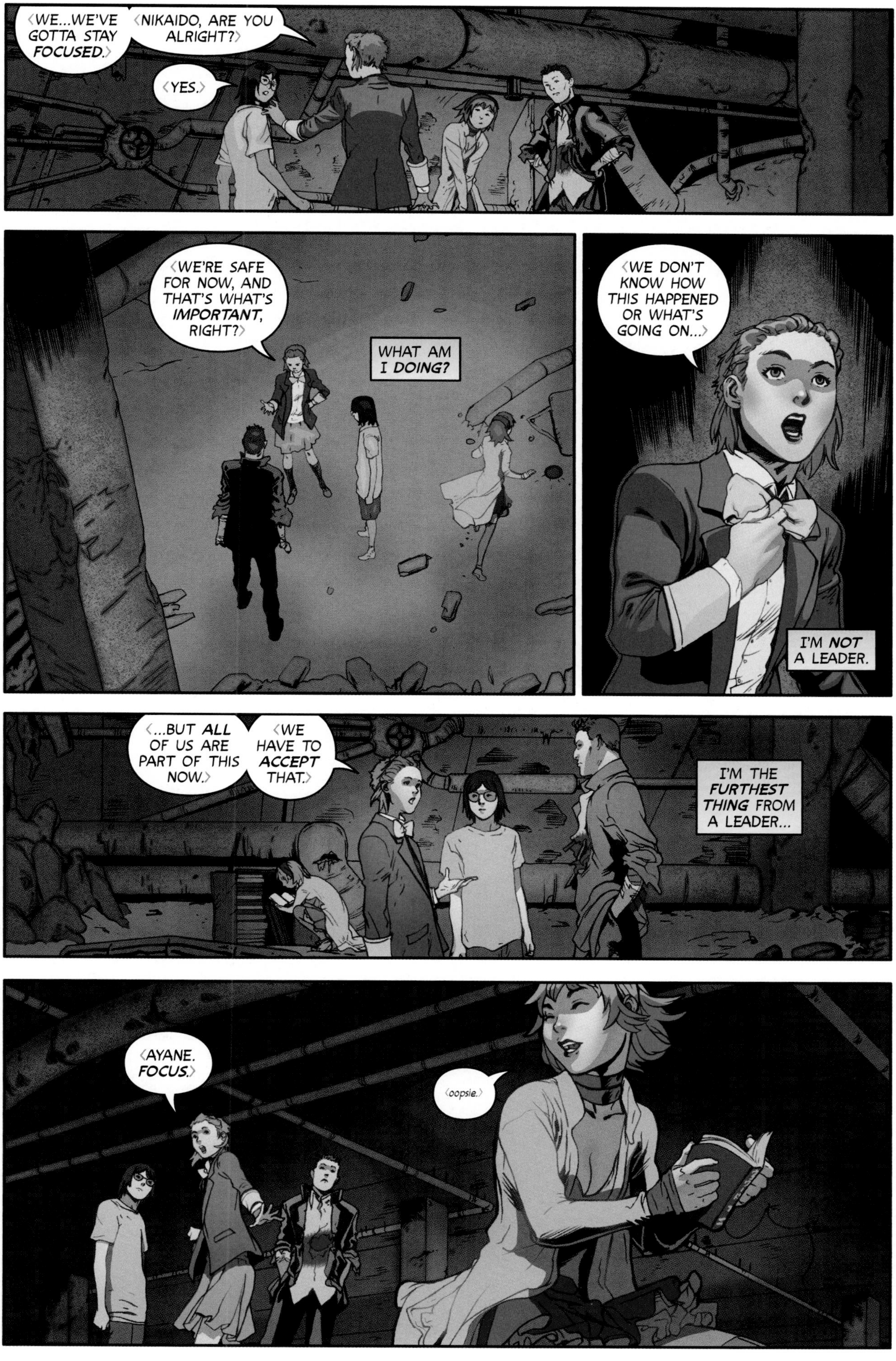
⟨WE...WE'VE GOTTA STAY FOCUSED.⟩
⟨NIKAIDO, ARE YOU ALRIGHT?⟩
⟨YES.⟩
⟨WE'RE SAFE FOR NOW, AND THAT'S WHAT'S IMPORTANT, RIGHT?⟩
WHAT AM I DOING?
⟨WE DON'T KNOW HOW THIS HAPPENED OR WHAT'S GOING ON...⟩
I'M NOT A LEADER.
⟨...BUT ALL OF US ARE PART OF THIS NOW.⟩
⟨WE HAVE TO ACCEPT THAT.⟩
I'M THE FURTHEST THING FROM A LEADER...
⟨AYANE. FOCUS.⟩
⟨oopsie.⟩

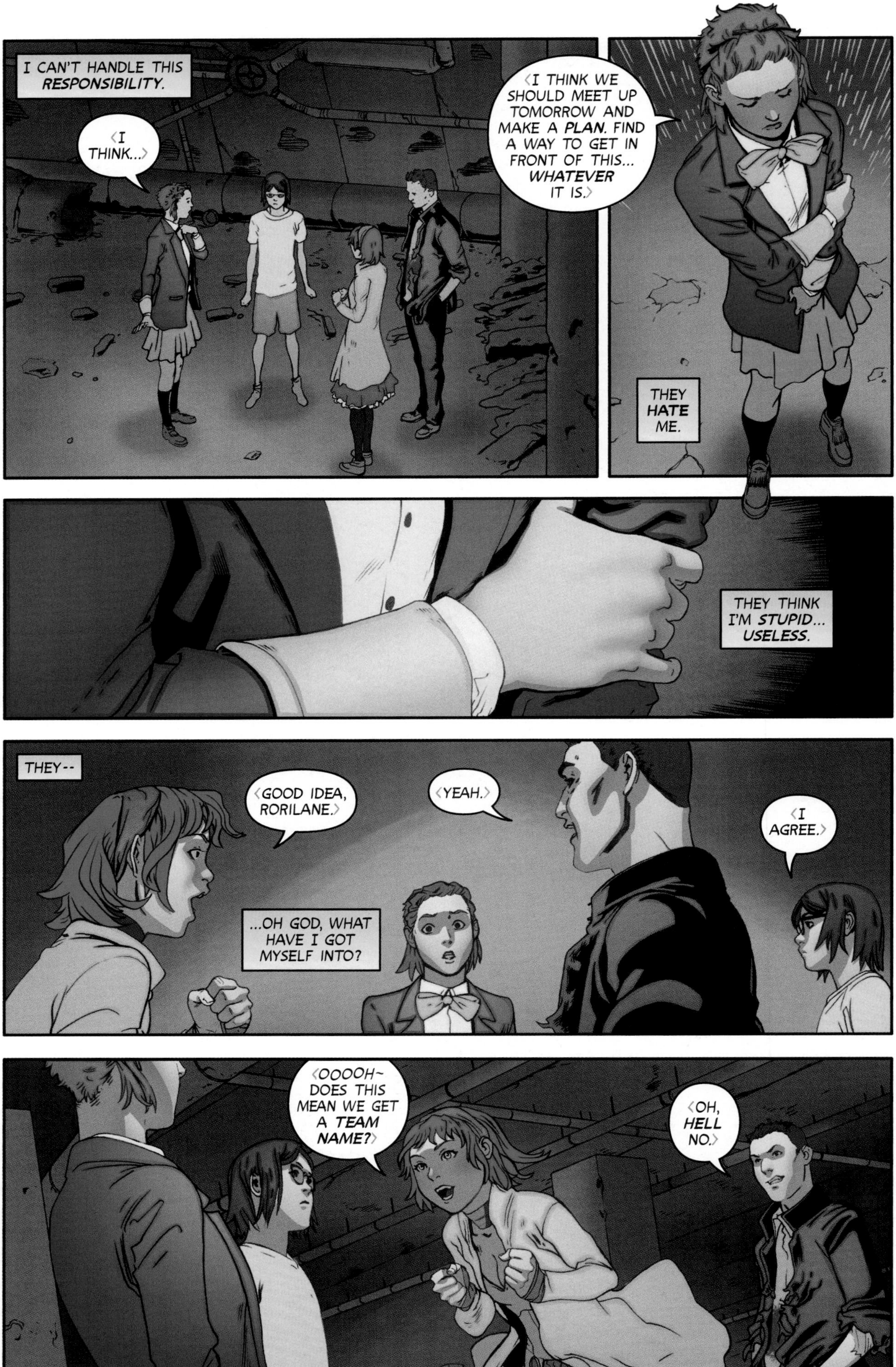
I CAN'T HANDLE THIS *RESPONSIBILITY.*
‹I THINK...›
‹I THINK WE SHOULD MEET UP TOMORROW AND MAKE A *PLAN*. FIND A WAY TO GET IN FRONT OF THIS... *WHATEVER* IT IS.›
THEY **HATE** ME.
THEY THINK I'M *STUPID*... *USELESS*.
THEY--
‹GOOD IDEA, RORILANE.›
‹YEAH.›
‹I AGREE.›
...OH GOD, WHAT HAVE I GOT MYSELF INTO?
‹OOOOH~ DOES THIS MEAN WE GET A *TEAM NAME?*›
‹OH, *HELL* NO.›

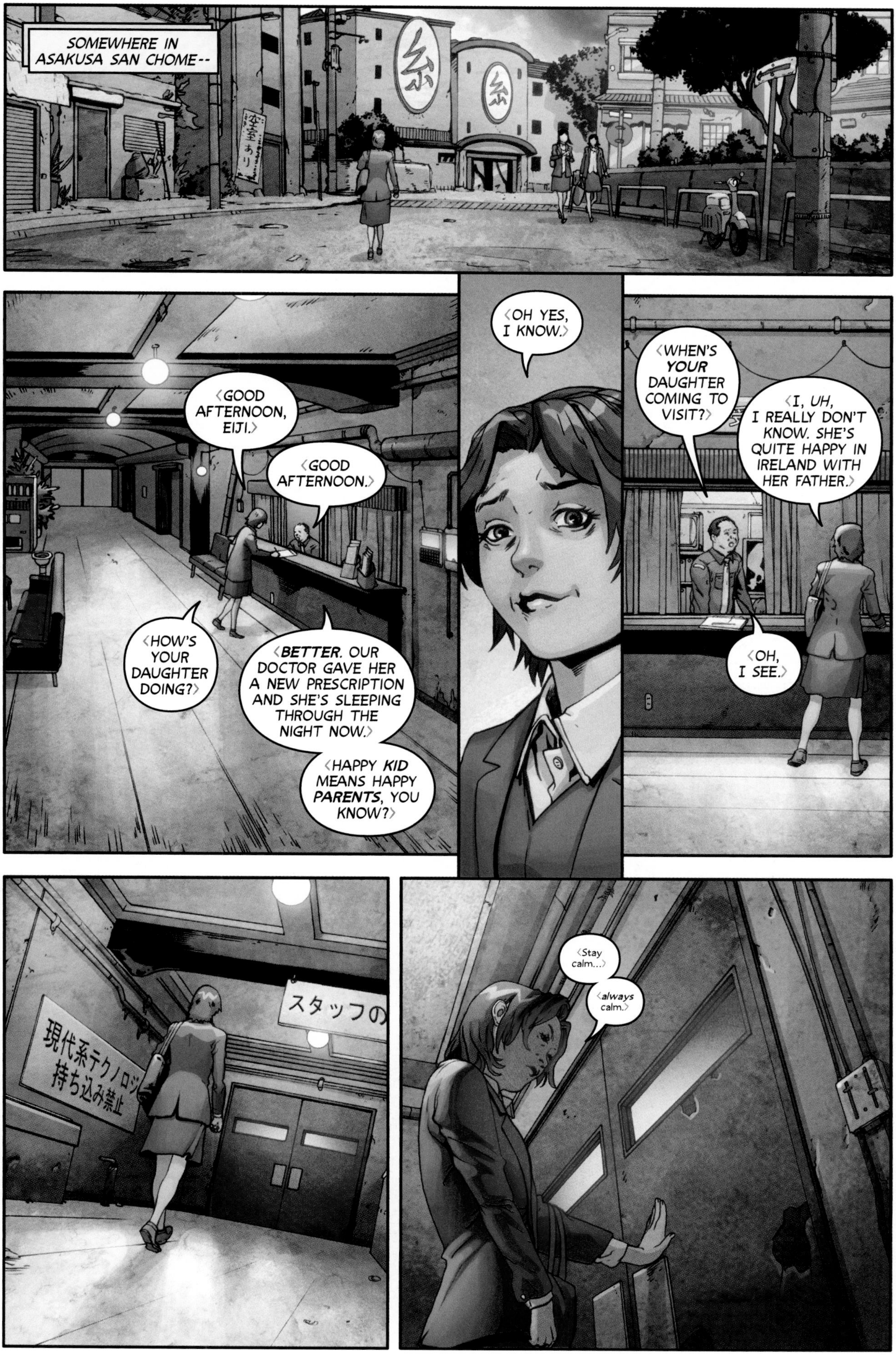
SOMEWHERE IN ASAKUSA SAN CHOME--
空室あり
‹GOOD AFTERNOON, EIJI.›
‹GOOD AFTERNOON.›
‹HOW'S YOUR DAUGHTER DOING?›
‹*BETTER*. OUR DOCTOR GAVE HER A NEW PRESCRIPTION AND SHE'S SLEEPING THROUGH THE NIGHT NOW.›
‹HAPPY *KID* MEANS HAPPY *PARENTS*, YOU KNOW?›
‹OH YES, I KNOW.›
‹WHEN'S *YOUR* DAUGHTER COMING TO VISIT?›
‹I, *UH*, I REALLY DON'T KNOW. SHE'S QUITE HAPPY IN IRELAND WITH HER FATHER.›
‹OH, I SEE.›
スタッフの
現代系テクノロジ
持ち込み禁止
‹Stay calm...›
‹*always* calm.›

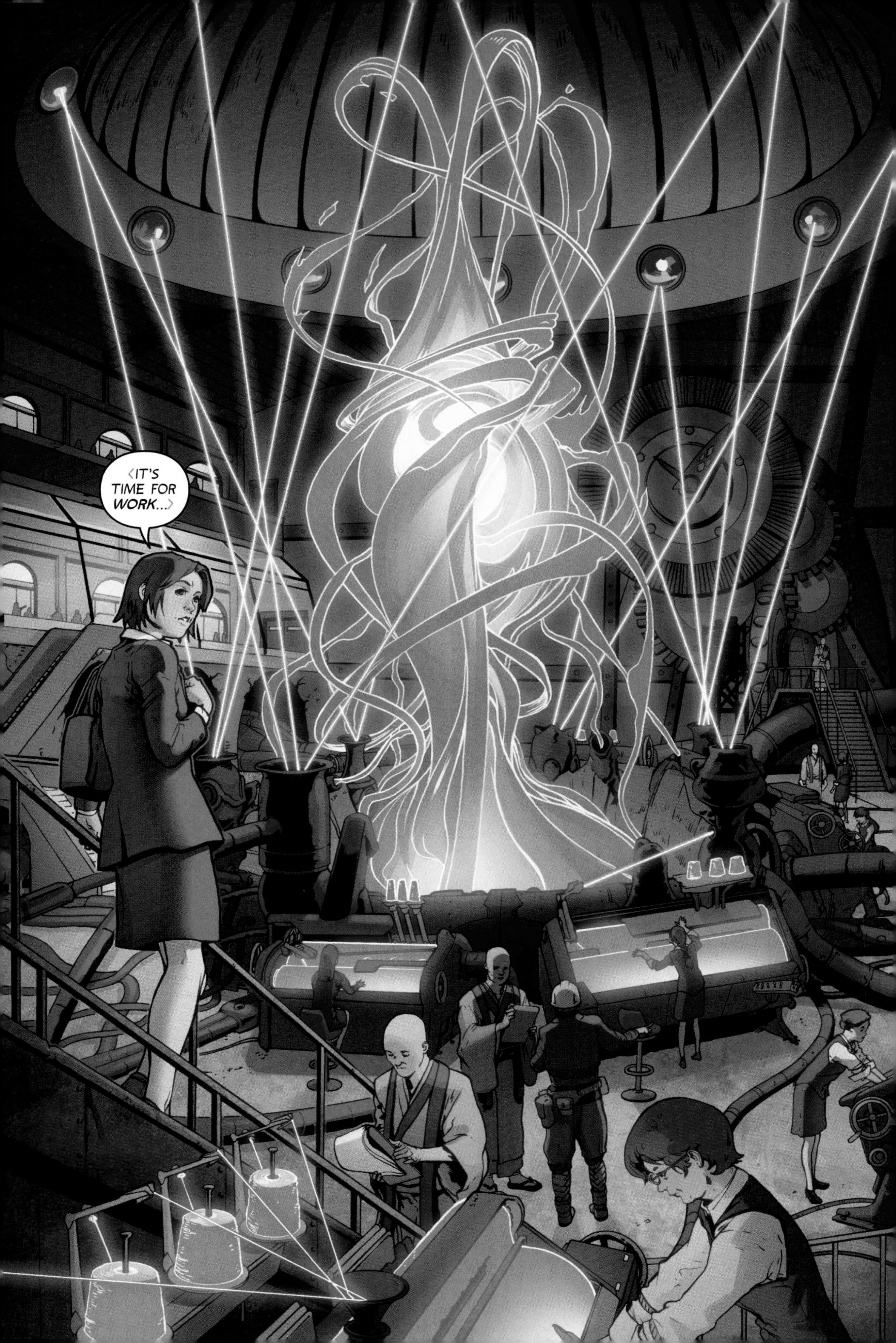
‹IT'S TIME FOR *WORK*...›

Chapter Four

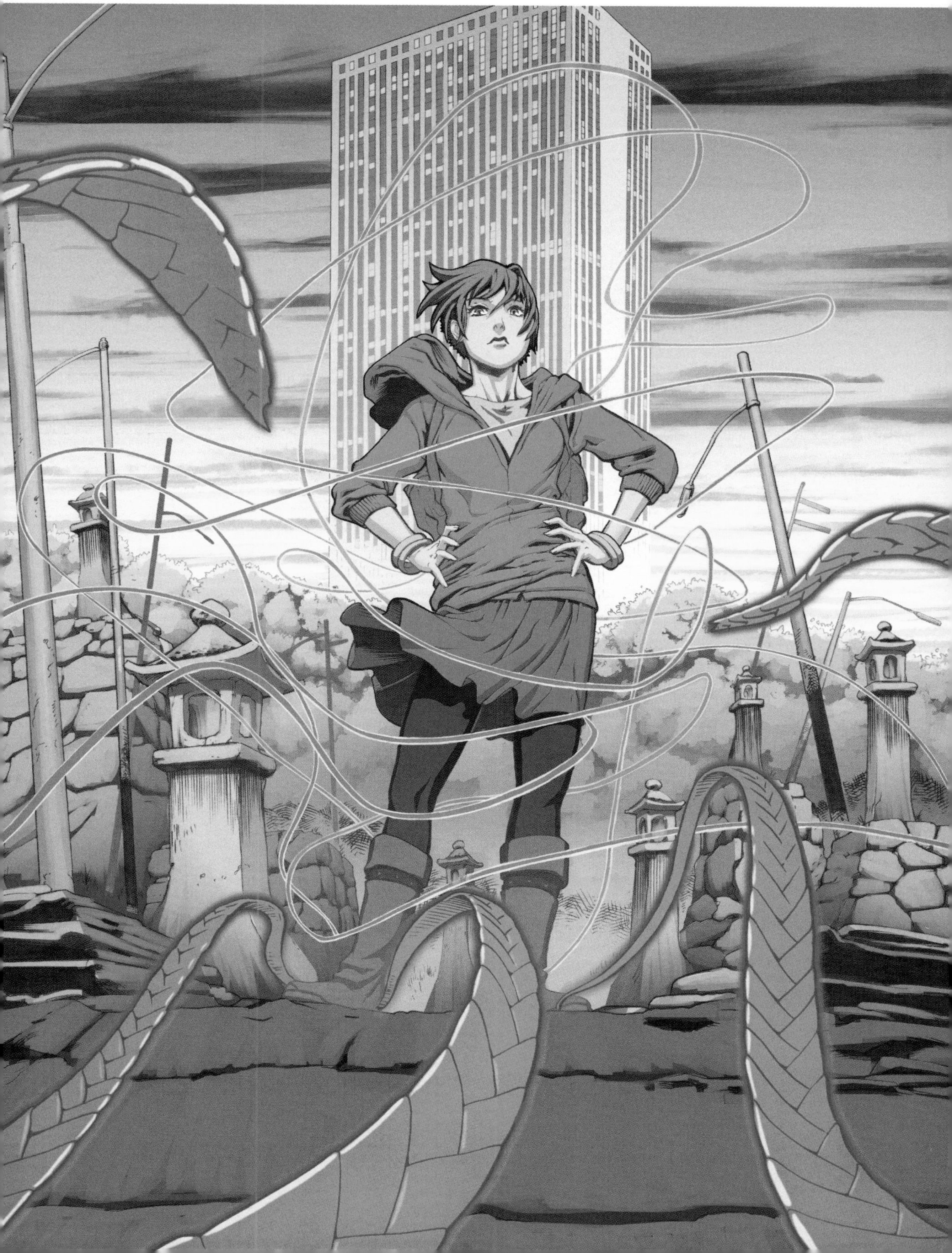

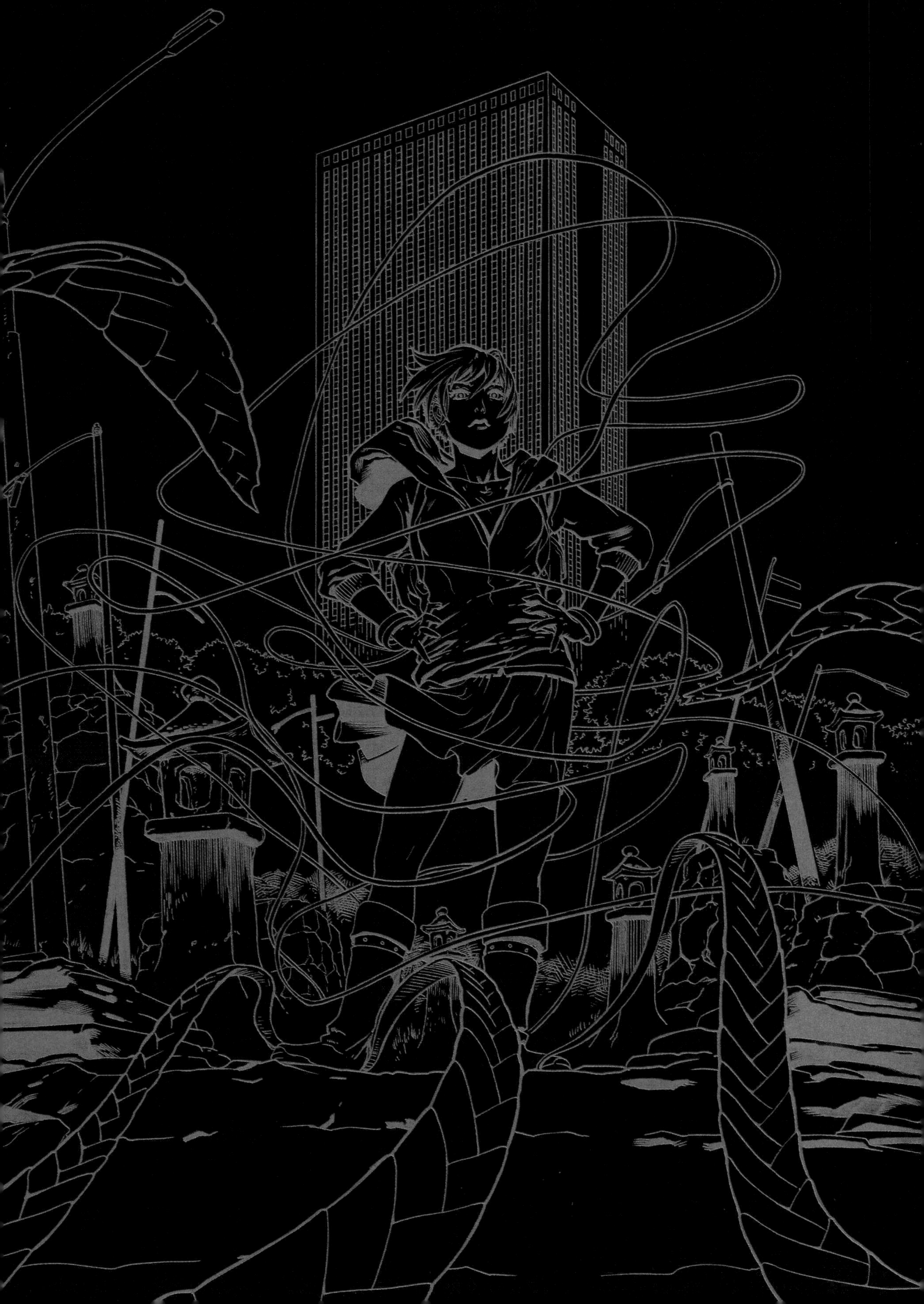

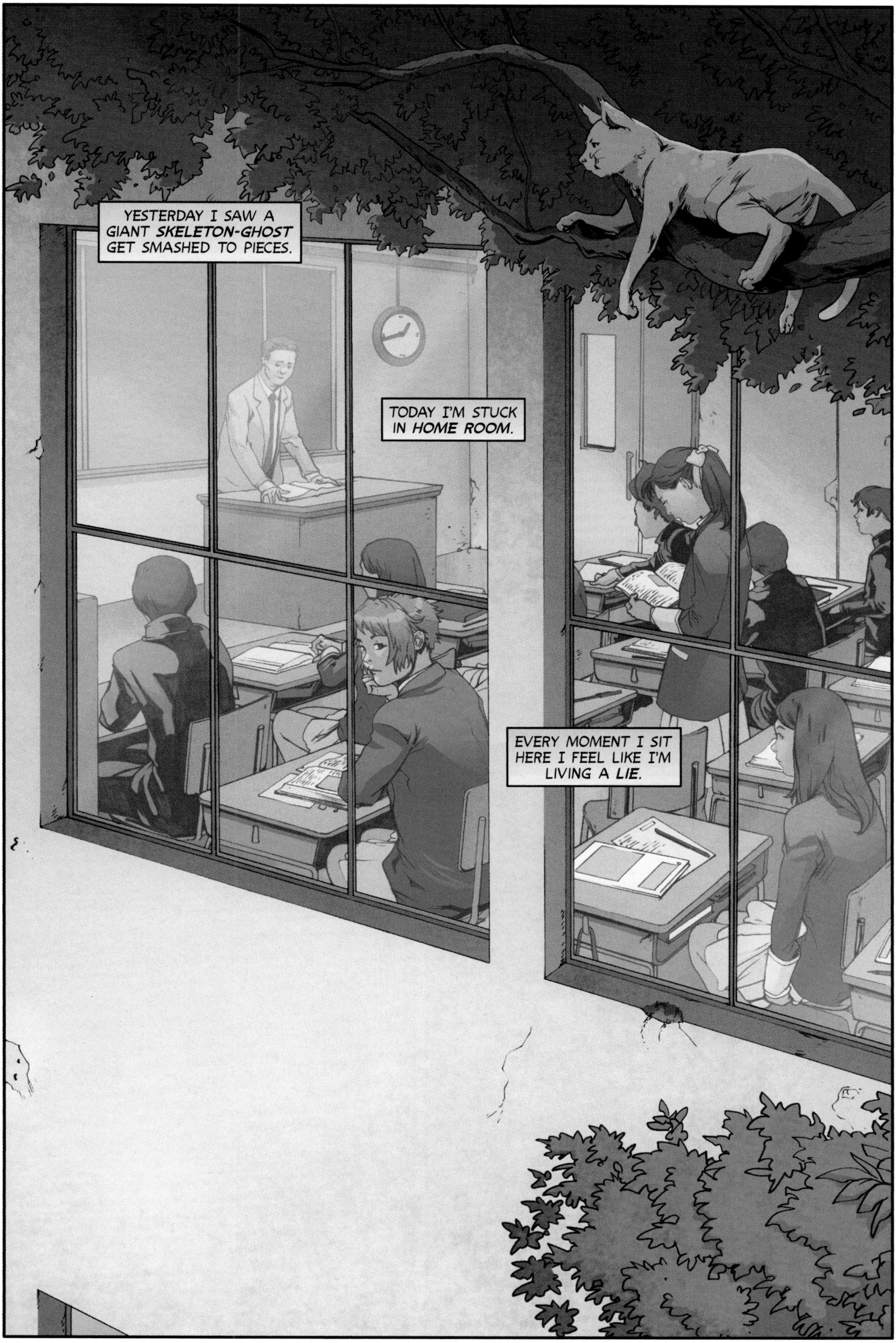
YESTERDAY I SAW A GIANT SKELETON-GHOST GET SMASHED TO PIECES.
TODAY I'M STUCK IN HOME ROOM.
EVERY MOMENT I SIT HERE I FEEL LIKE I'M LIVING A LIE.

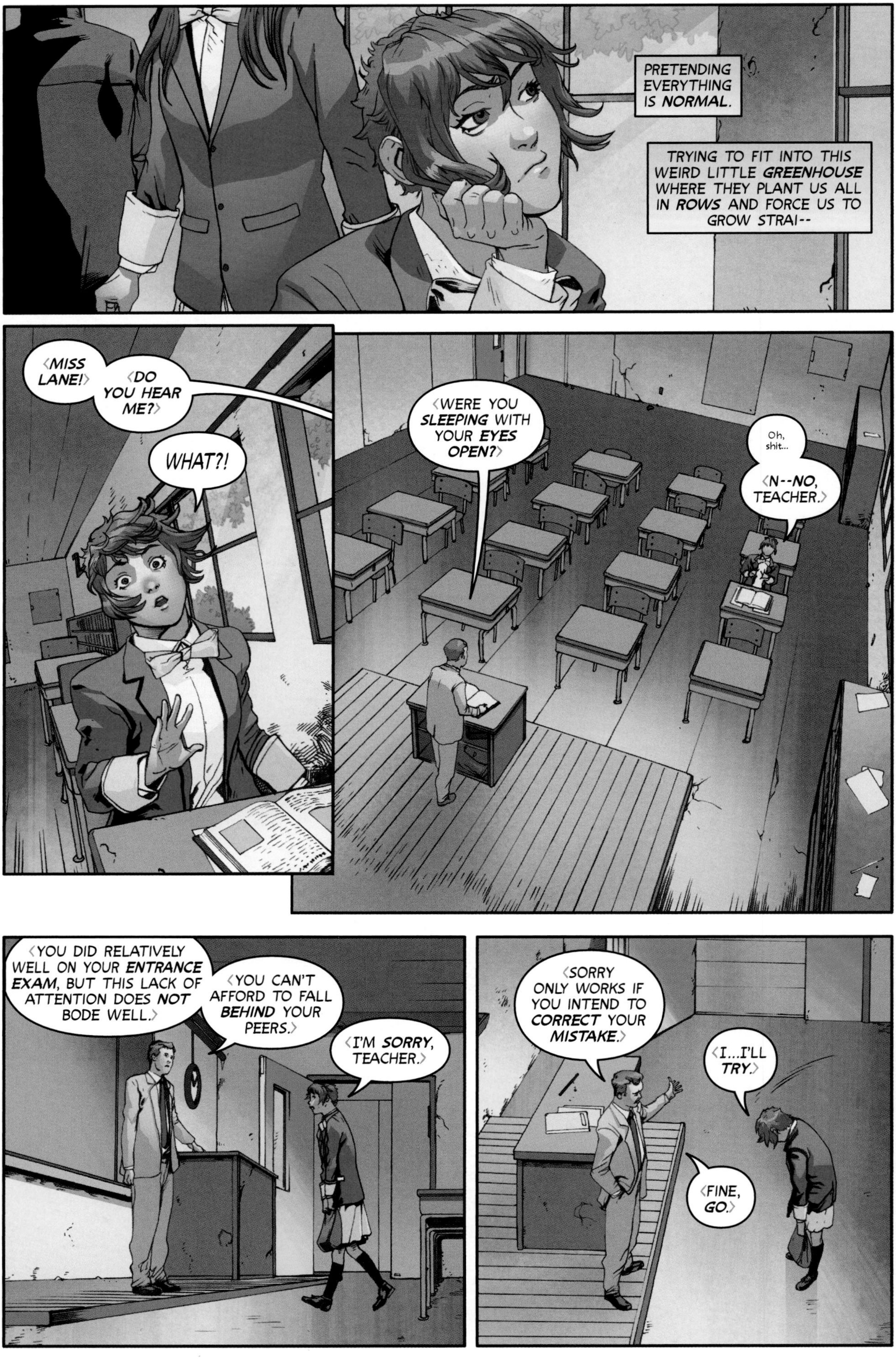

PRETENDING EVERYTHING IS NORMAL.
TRYING TO FIT INTO THIS WEIRD LITTLE GREENHOUSE WHERE THEY PLANT US ALL IN ROWS AND FORCE US TO GROW STRAI--
‹MISS LANE!›
‹DO YOU HEAR ME?›
WHAT?!
‹WERE YOU SLEEPING WITH YOUR EYES OPEN?›
Oh, shit...
‹N--NO, TEACHER.›
‹YOU DID RELATIVELY WELL ON YOUR ENTRANCE EXAM, BUT THIS LACK OF ATTENTION DOES NOT BODE WELL.›
‹YOU CAN'T AFFORD TO FALL BEHIND YOUR PEERS.›
‹I'M SORRY, TEACHER.›
‹SORRY ONLY WORKS IF YOU INTEND TO CORRECT YOUR MISTAKE.›
‹I...I'LL TRY.›
‹FINE, GO.›

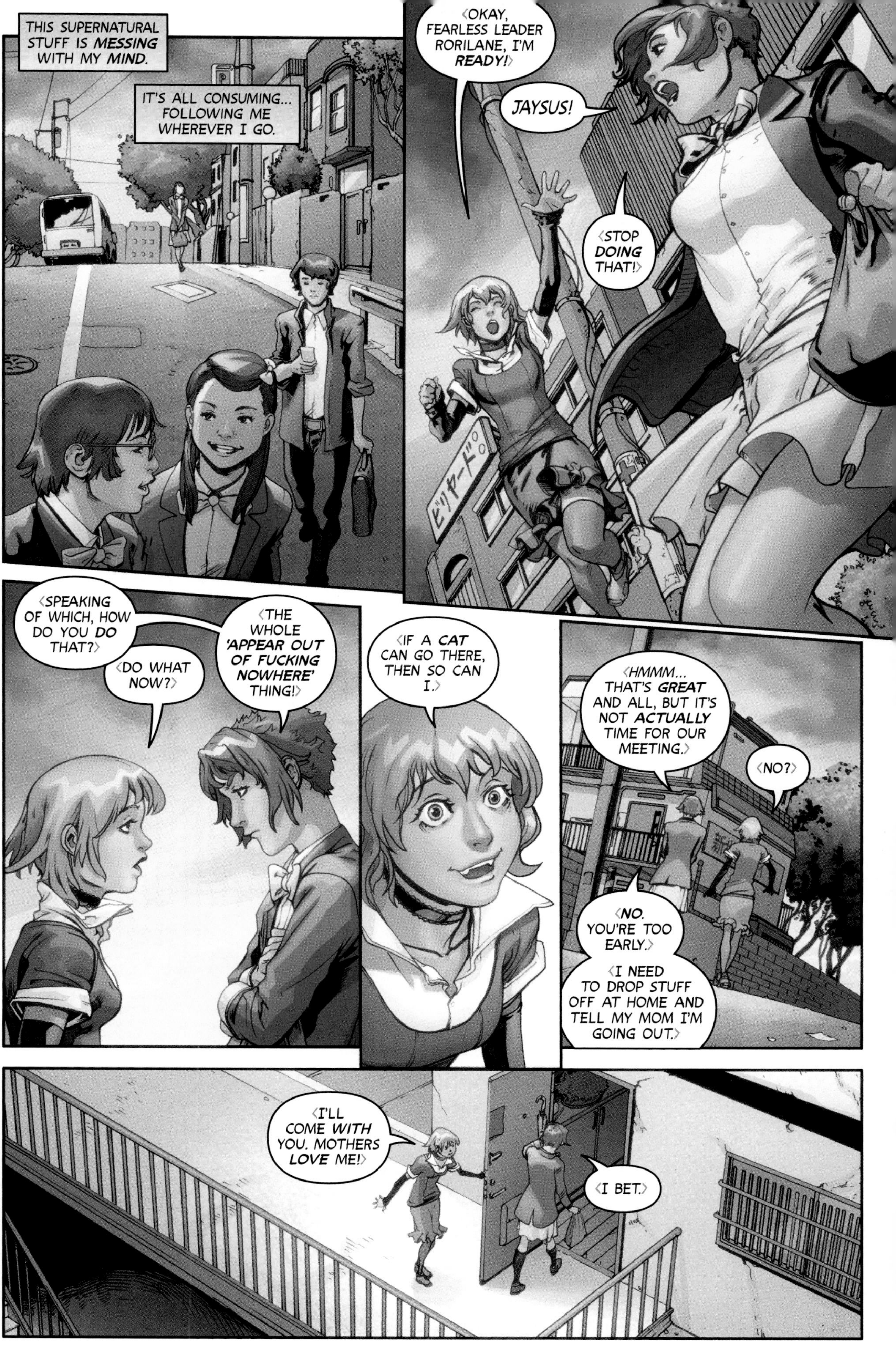
THIS SUPERNATURAL STUFF IS *MESSING* WITH MY *MIND.*
IT'S ALL CONSUMING... FOLLOWING ME WHEREVER I GO.
‹OKAY, FEARLESS LEADER RORILANE, I'M *READY!*›
JAYSUS!
‹STOP *DOING* THAT!›
ビリヤード
‹SPEAKING OF WHICH, HOW DO YOU *DO* THAT?›
‹DO WHAT NOW?›
‹THE WHOLE *'APPEAR OUT OF FUCKING NOWHERE'* THING!›
‹IF A *CAT* CAN GO THERE, THEN SO CAN I.›
‹HMMM... THAT'S *GREAT* AND ALL, BUT IT'S NOT *ACTUALLY* TIME FOR OUR MEETING.›
‹NO?›
‹*NO.* YOU'RE TOO EARLY.›
‹I NEED TO DROP STUFF OFF AT HOME AND TELL MY MOM I'M GOING OUT.›
‹I'LL COME *WITH* YOU. MOTHERS *LOVE* ME!›
‹I BET.›

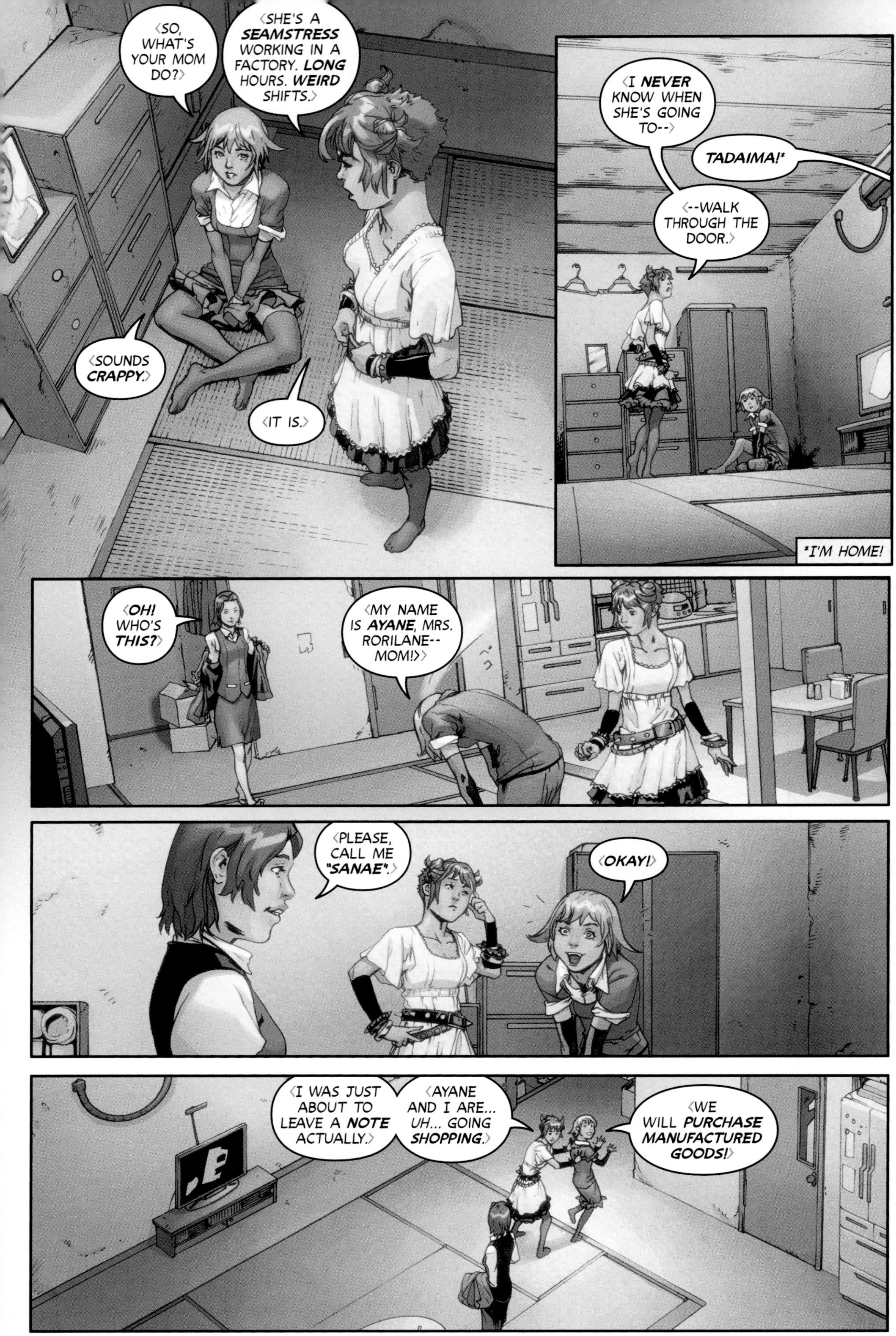
⟨SO, WHAT'S YOUR MOM DO?⟩
⟨SHE'S A ***SEAMSTRESS*** WORKING IN A FACTORY. ***LONG*** HOURS. ***WEIRD*** SHIFTS.⟩
⟨SOUNDS ***CRAPPY.***⟩
⟨IT IS.⟩
⟨I ***NEVER*** KNOW WHEN SHE'S GOING TO--⟩
TADAIMA!*
⟨--WALK THROUGH THE DOOR.⟩
*I'M HOME!
⟨***OH!*** WHO'S ***THIS?***⟩
⟨MY NAME IS ***AYANE***, MRS. RORILANE-- MOM!⟩⟩
⟨PLEASE, CALL ME ***"SANAE".***⟩
⟨***OKAY!***⟩
⟨I WAS JUST ABOUT TO LEAVE A ***NOTE*** ACTUALLY.⟩
⟨AYANE AND I ARE... UH... GOING ***SHOPPING***.⟩
⟨WE WILL ***PURCHASE MANUFACTURED GOODS!***⟩

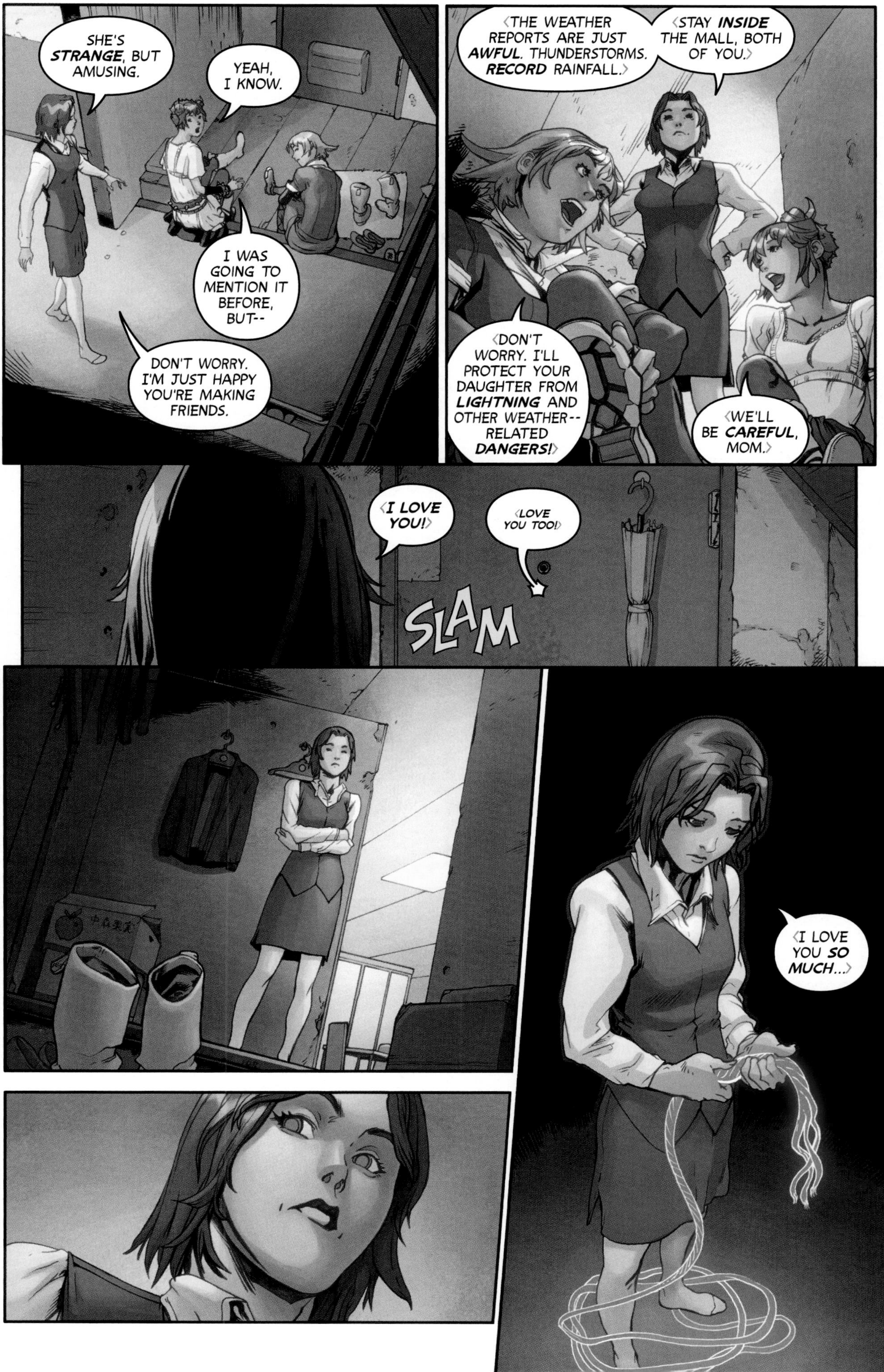
SHE'S STRANGE, BUT AMUSING.
YEAH, I KNOW.
I WAS GOING TO MENTION IT BEFORE, BUT--
DON'T WORRY. I'M JUST HAPPY YOU'RE MAKING FRIENDS.
‹THE WEATHER REPORTS ARE JUST AWFUL. THUNDERSTORMS. RECORD RAINFALL.›
‹STAY INSIDE THE MALL, BOTH OF YOU.›
‹DON'T WORRY. I'LL PROTECT YOUR DAUGHTER FROM LIGHTNING AND OTHER WEATHER--RELATED DANGERS!›
‹WE'LL BE CAREFUL, MOM.›
‹I LOVE YOU!›
‹LOVE YOU TOO!›
SLAM
‹I LOVE YOU SO MUCH...›

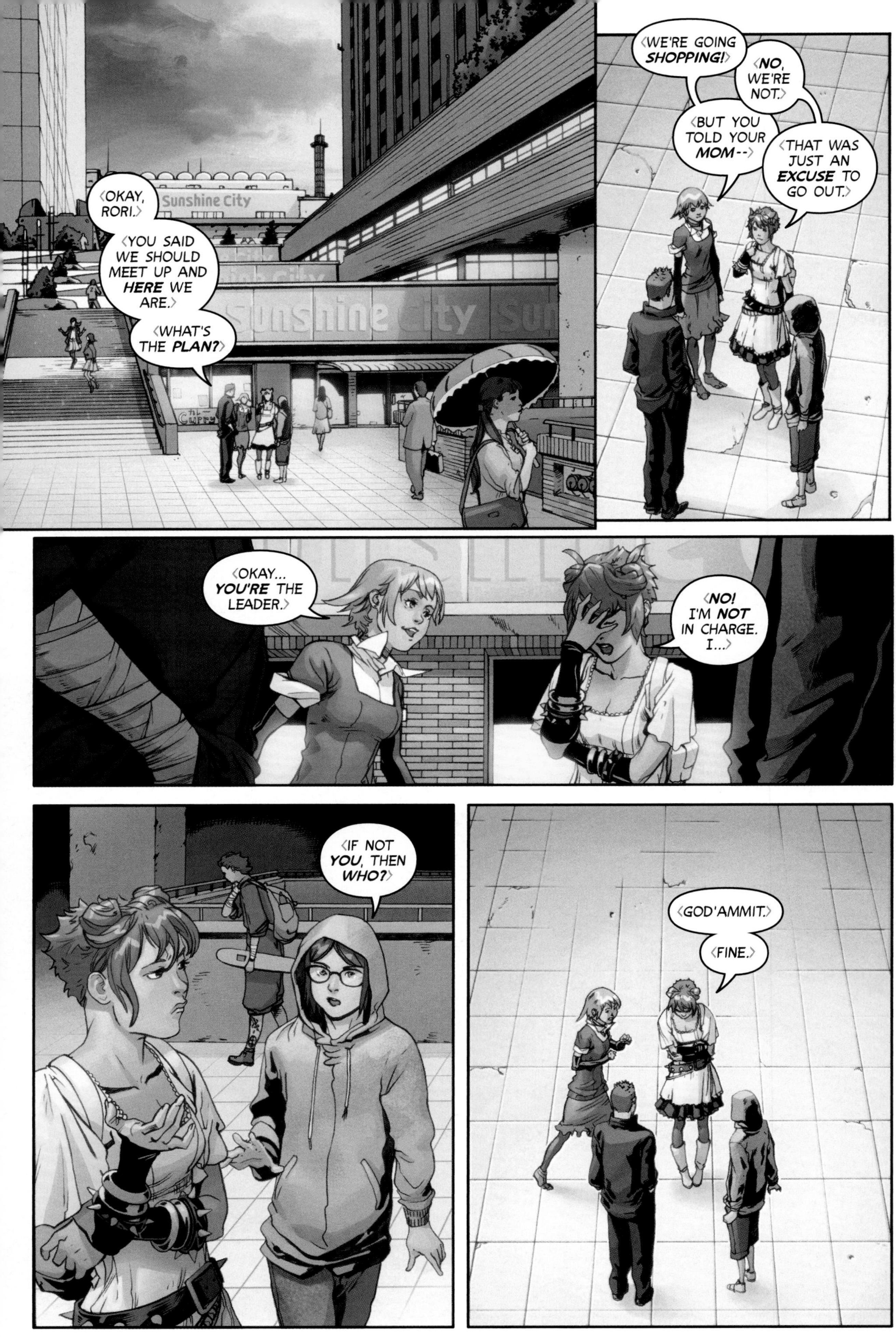
Sunshine City
〈OKAY, RORI.〉
〈YOU SAID WE SHOULD MEET UP AND HERE WE ARE.〉
〈WHAT'S THE PLAN?〉
Sunshine City
〈WE'RE GOING SHOPPING!〉
〈NO, WE'RE NOT.〉
〈BUT YOU TOLD YOUR MOM--〉
〈THAT WAS JUST AN EXCUSE TO GO OUT.〉
〈OKAY... YOU'RE THE LEADER.〉
〈NO! I'M NOT IN CHARGE. I...〉
〈IF NOT YOU, THEN WHO?〉
〈GOD'AMMIT.〉
〈FINE.〉

‹LOOK, EVERYONE NEEDS TO DISH ON WHAT THEY KNOW ABOUT THE SUPERNATURAL SO WE'RE ALL ON THE SAME PAGE.›

‹AYANE, YOU GO FIRST.›

‹ISN'T IT OBVIOUS? CAN'T YOU SMELL IT?›

‹SOMETHING IS RILING ALL THESE CREATURES UP.›

‹THEY'RE HUNTING.›

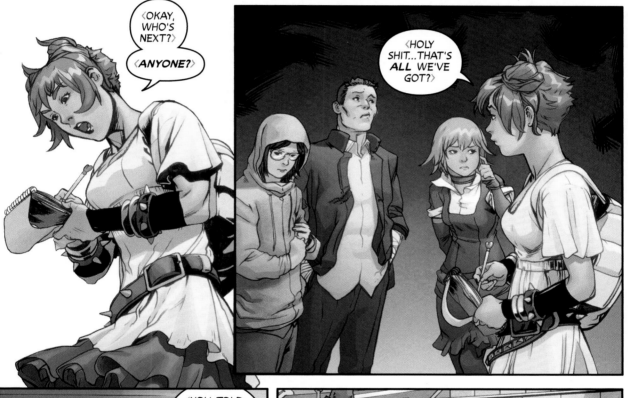

‹OKAY, WHO'S NEXT?›

‹ANYONE?›

‹HOLY SHIT...THAT'S ALL WE'VE GOT?›

‹YOU TOLD ME YOU SAW PATTERNS, THAT ALL THIS WAS CONNECTED SOMEHOW.›

‹SO, WHAT DO YOU SEE NOW? WHERE SHOULD WE GO?›

‹GIVE ME A SEC HERE...›

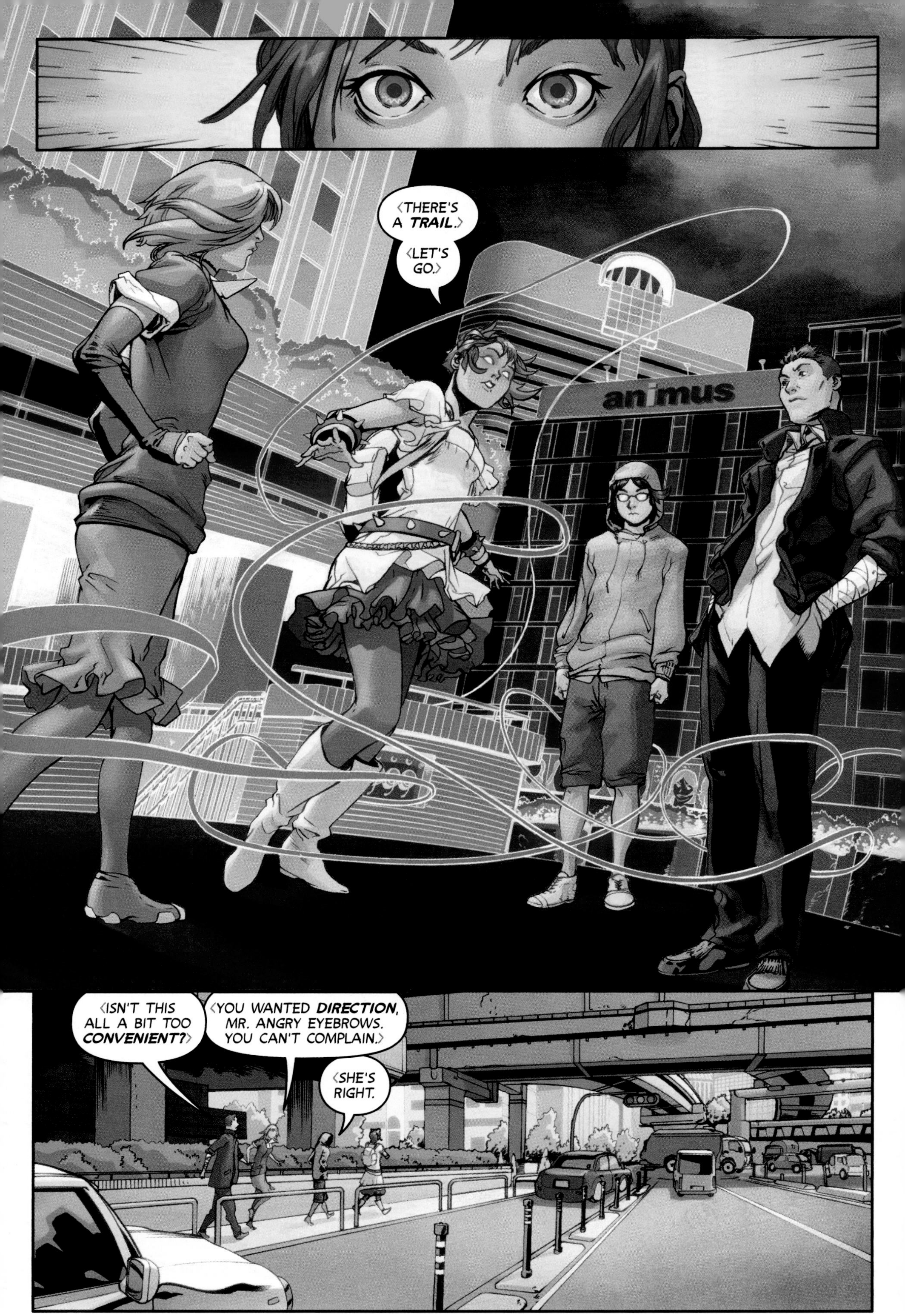
‹THERE'S A *TRAIL*.›
‹LET'S GO.›
animus
‹ISN'T THIS ALL A BIT TOO *CONVENIENT?*›
‹YOU WANTED *DIRECTION*, MR. ANGRY EYEBROWS. YOU CAN'T COMPLAIN.›
‹SHE'S RIGHT.›

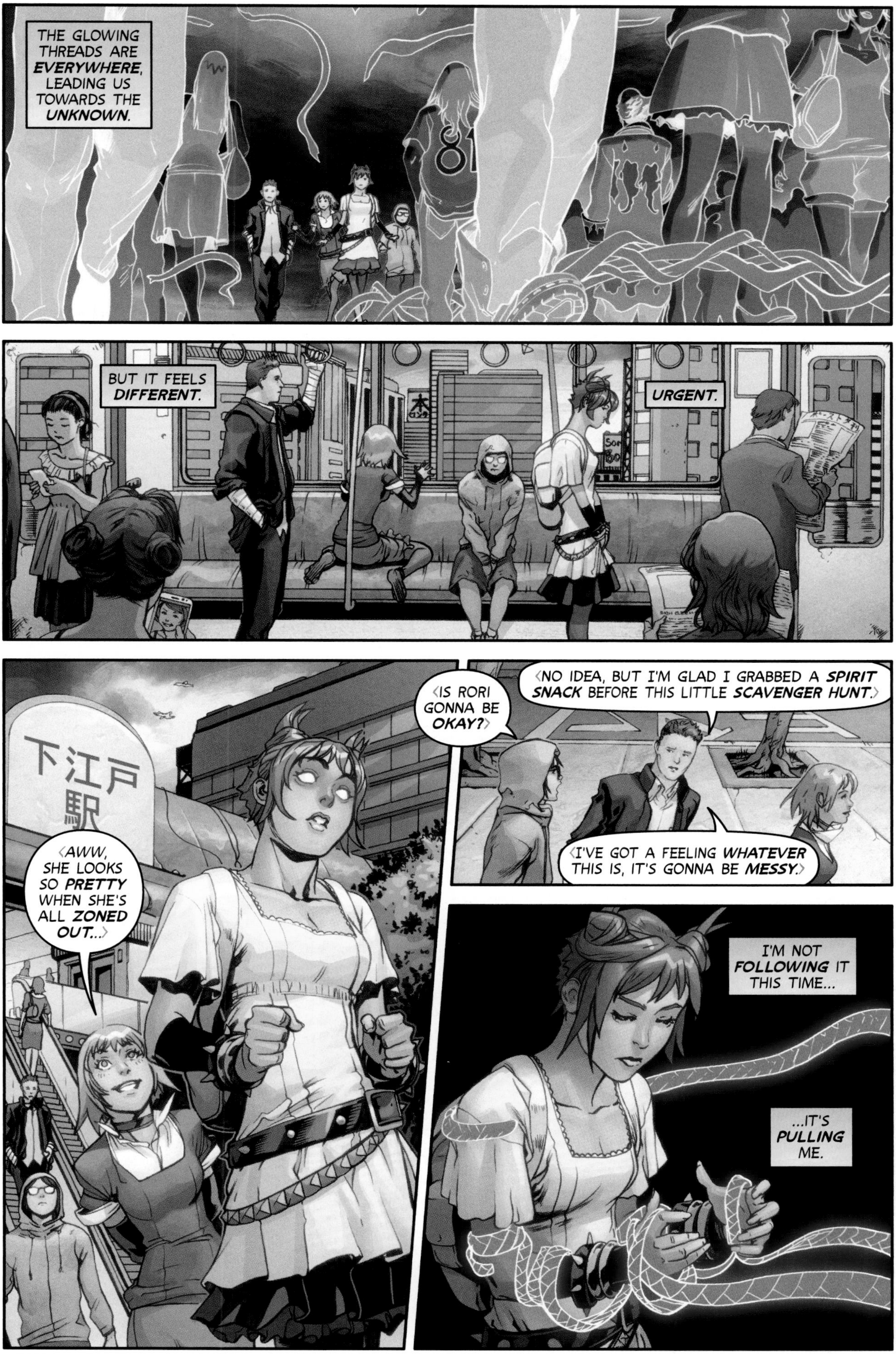
THE GLOWING THREADS ARE EVERYWHERE, LEADING US TOWARDS THE UNKNOWN.
BUT IT FEELS DIFFERENT.
URGENT.
下江戸駅
‹AWW, SHE LOOKS SO PRETTY WHEN SHE'S ALL ZONED OUT...›
‹IS RORI GONNA BE OKAY?›
‹NO IDEA, BUT I'M GLAD I GRABBED A SPIRIT SNACK BEFORE THIS LITTLE SCAVENGER HUNT.›
‹I'VE GOT A FEELING WHATEVER THIS IS, IT'S GONNA BE MESSY.›
I'M NOT FOLLOWING IT THIS TIME...
...IT'S PULLING ME.

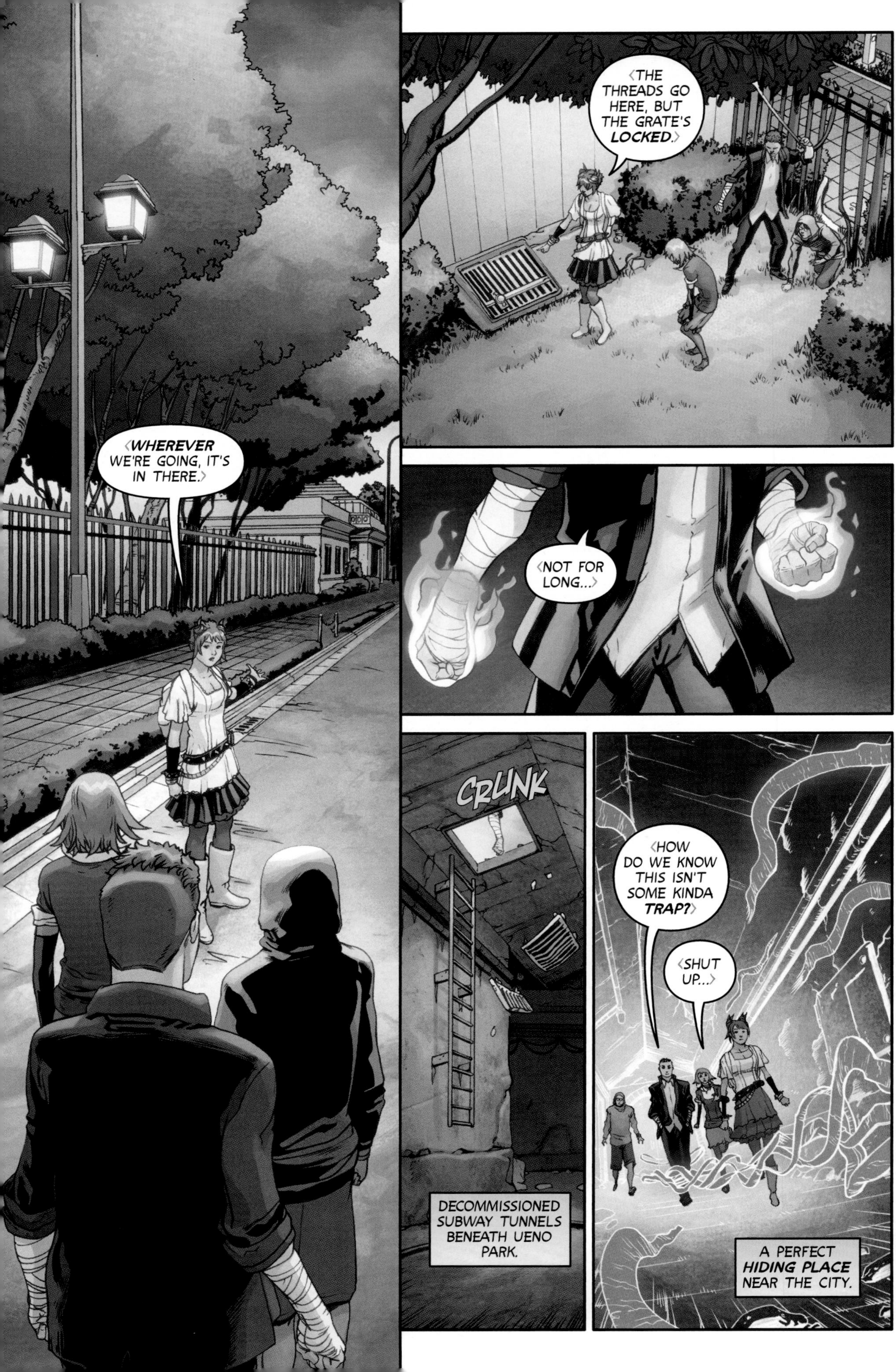
‹WHEREVER WE'RE GOING, IT'S IN THERE.›
‹THE THREADS GO HERE, BUT THE GRATE'S LOCKED.›
‹NOT FOR LONG...›
CRUNK
DECOMMISSIONED SUBWAY TUNNELS BENEATH UENO PARK.
‹HOW DO WE KNOW THIS ISN'T SOME KINDA TRAP?›
‹SHUT UP...›
A PERFECT HIDING PLACE NEAR THE CITY.

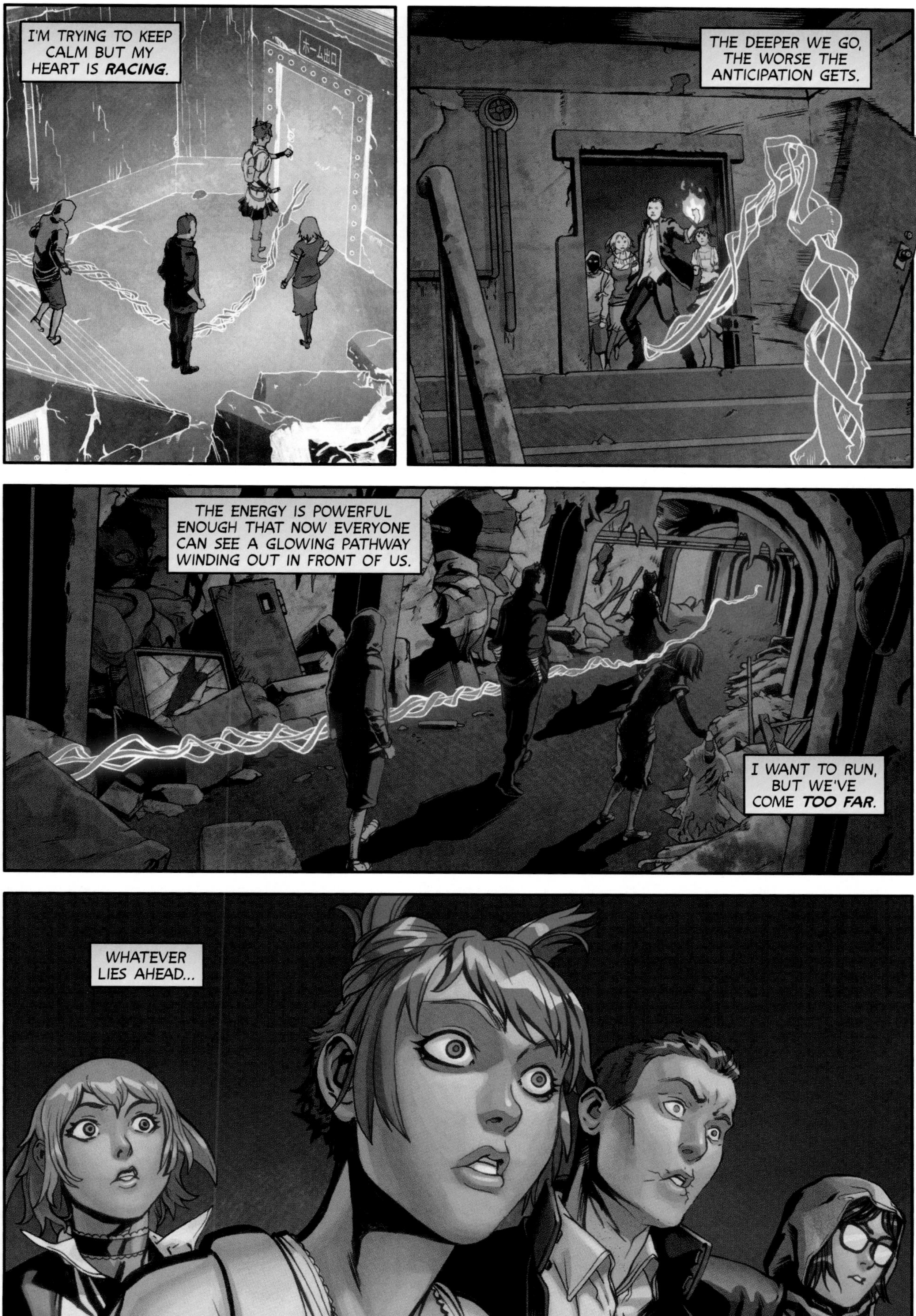
I'M TRYING TO KEEP CALM BUT MY HEART IS **RACING**.
ホーム出口
THE DEEPER WE GO, THE WORSE THE ANTICIPATION GETS.
THE ENERGY IS POWERFUL ENOUGH THAT NOW EVERYONE CAN SEE A GLOWING PATHWAY WINDING OUT IN FRONT OF US.
I WANT TO RUN, BUT WE'VE COME **TOO FAR**.
WHATEVER LIES AHEAD...

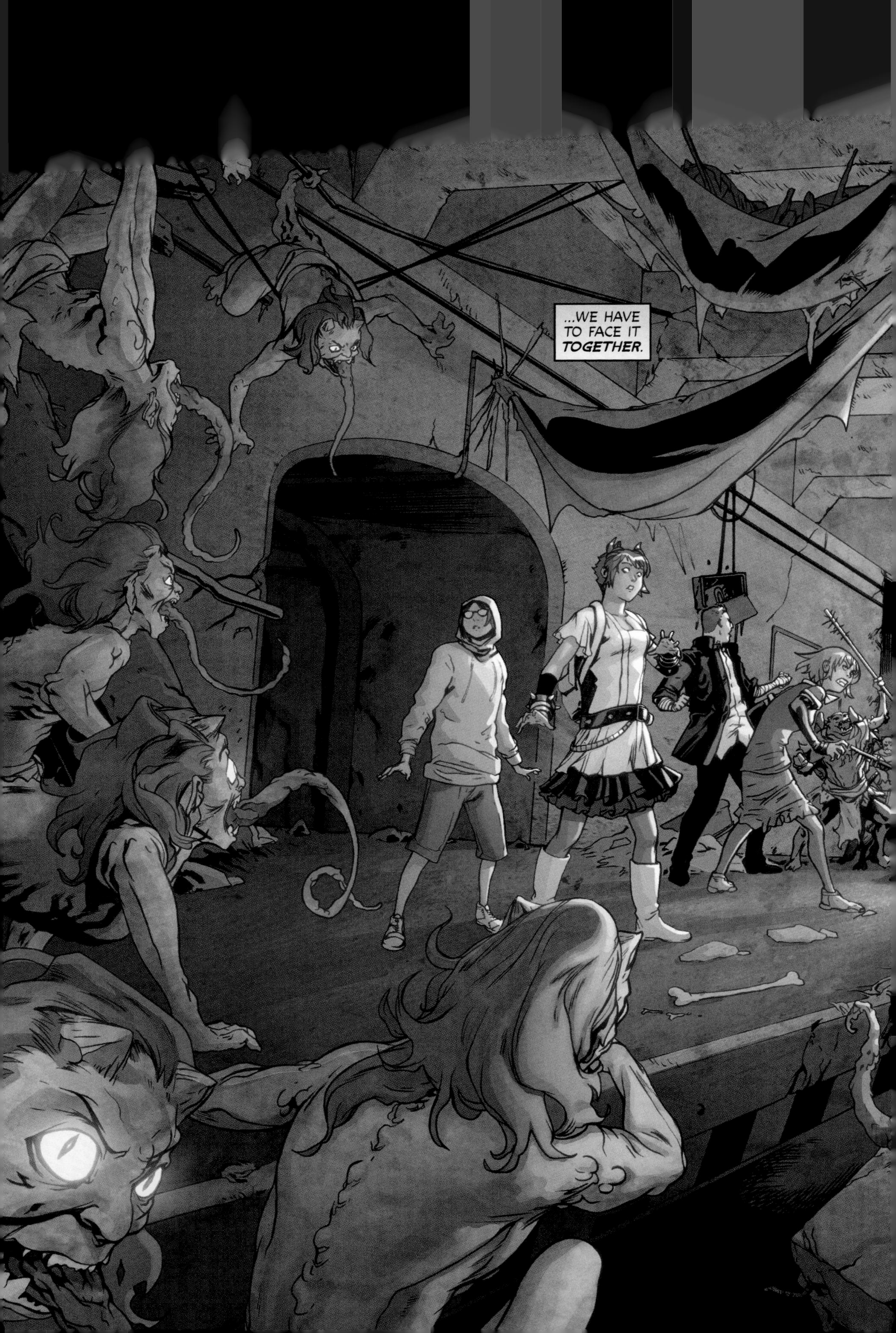
...WE HAVE TO FACE IT ***TOGETHER***.

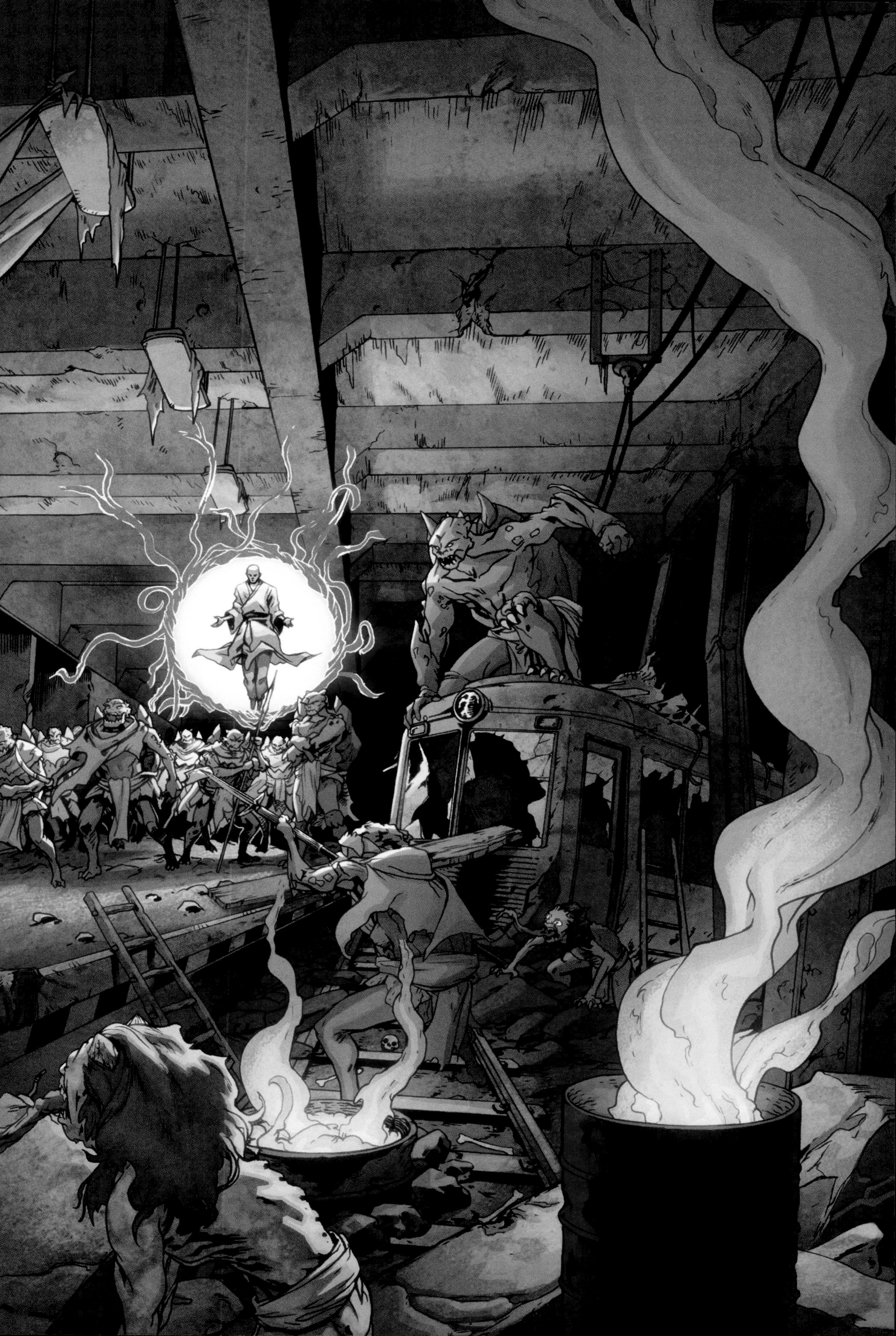

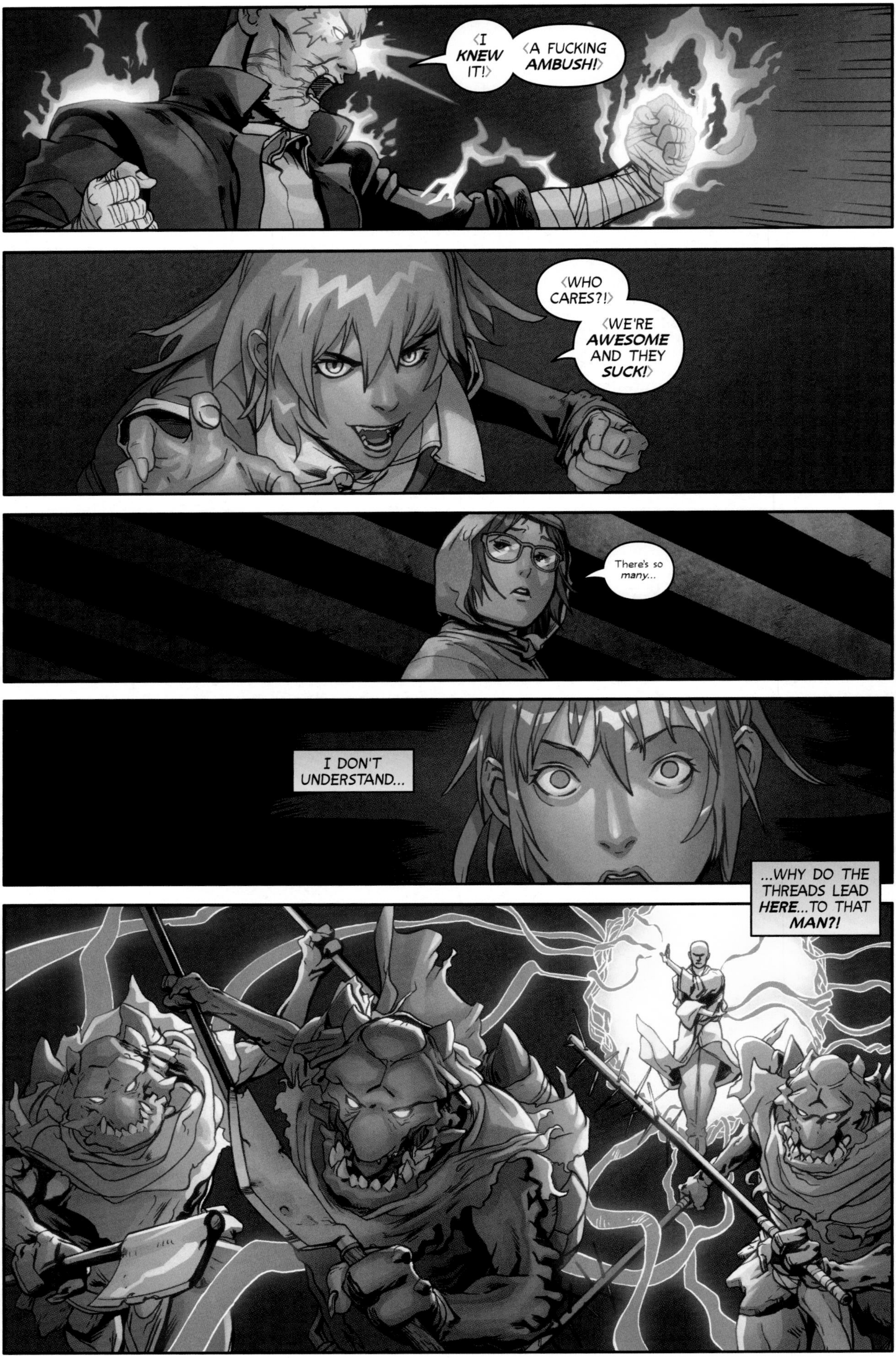
⟨I KNEW IT!⟩
⟨A FUCKING AMBUSH!⟩
⟨WHO CARES?!⟩
⟨WE'RE AWESOME AND THEY SUCK!⟩
There's so many...
I DON'T UNDERSTAND...
...WHY DO THE THREADS LEAD HERE...TO THAT MAN?!

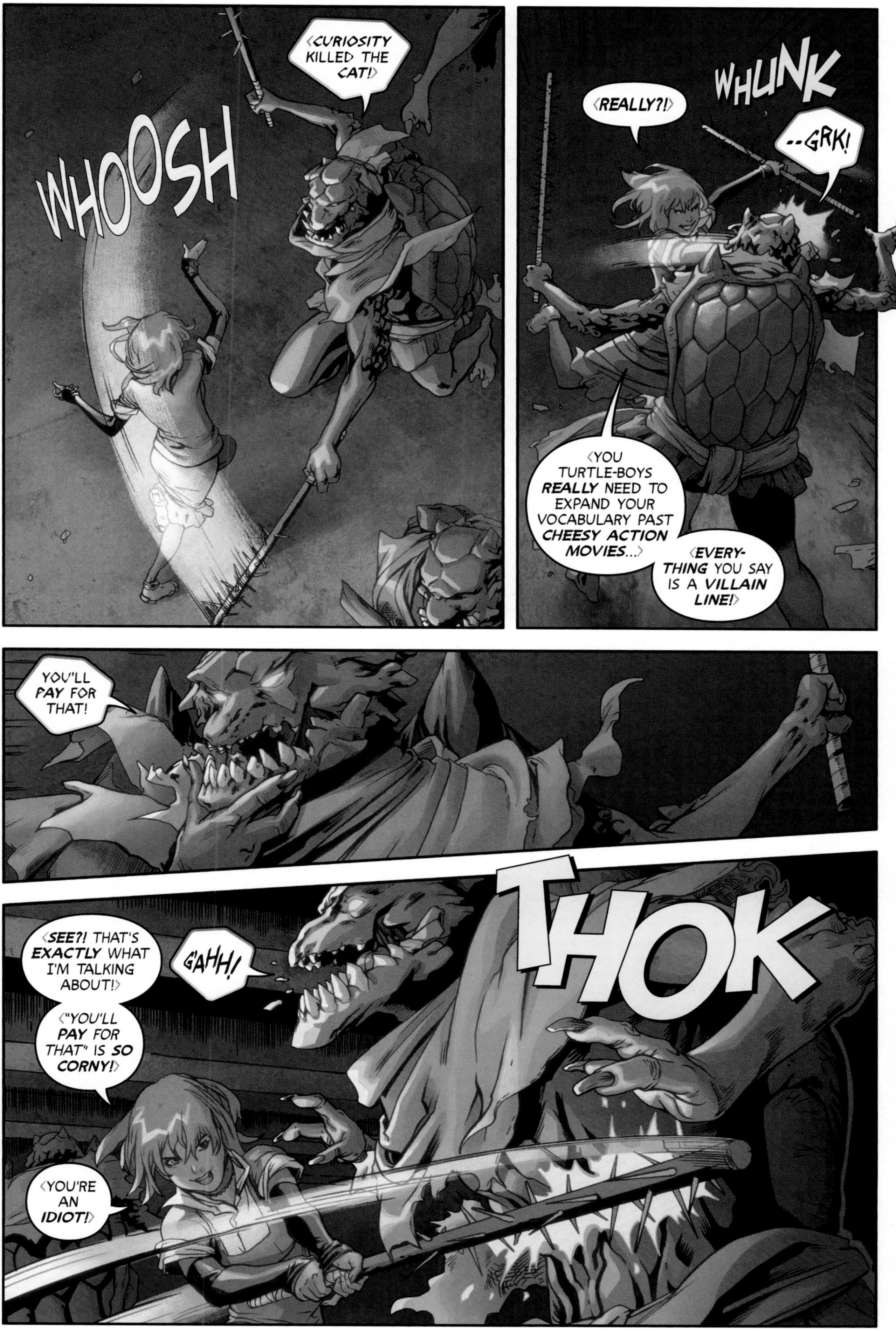
‹CURIOSITY KILLED THE CAT!›
WHOOSH
‹REALLY?!›
WHUNK
..GRK!
‹YOU TURTLE-BOYS REALLY NEED TO EXPAND YOUR VOCABULARY PAST CHEESY ACTION MOVIES...›
‹EVERY-THING YOU SAY IS A VILLAIN LINE!›
YOU'LL PAY FOR THAT!
‹SEE?! THAT'S EXACTLY WHAT I'M TALKING ABOUT!›
‹"YOU'LL PAY FOR THAT" IS SO CORNY!›
G'AHH!
THOK
‹YOU'RE AN IDIOT!›

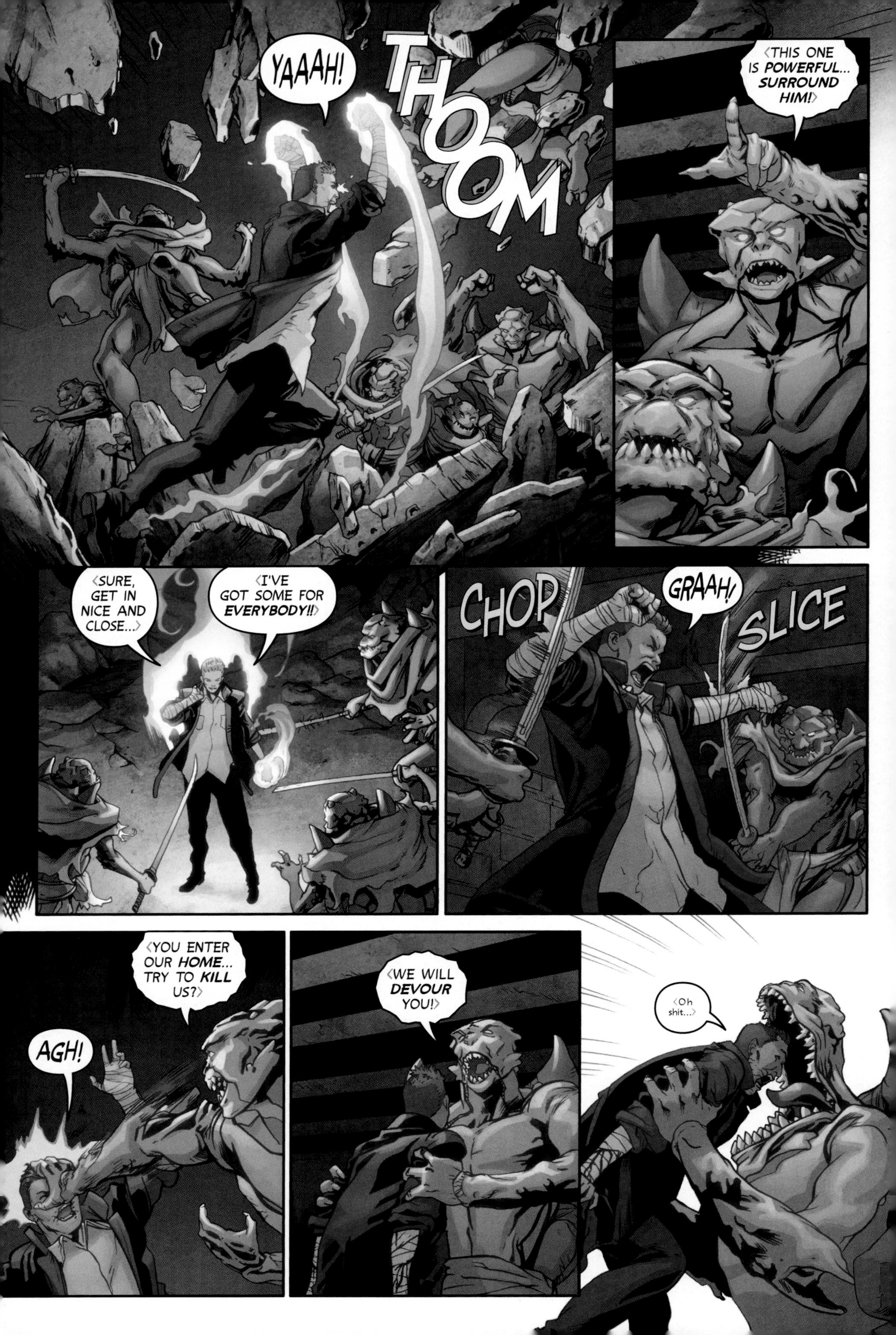
YAAAH!
THOOM
<THIS ONE IS POWERFUL... SURROUND HIM!>
<SURE, GET IN NICE AND CLOSE...>
<I'VE GOT SOME FOR EVERYBODY!!>
CHOP
GRAAH!
SLICE
<YOU ENTER OUR HOME... TRY TO KILL US?>
AGH!
<WE WILL DEVOUR YOU!>
<Oh shit...>

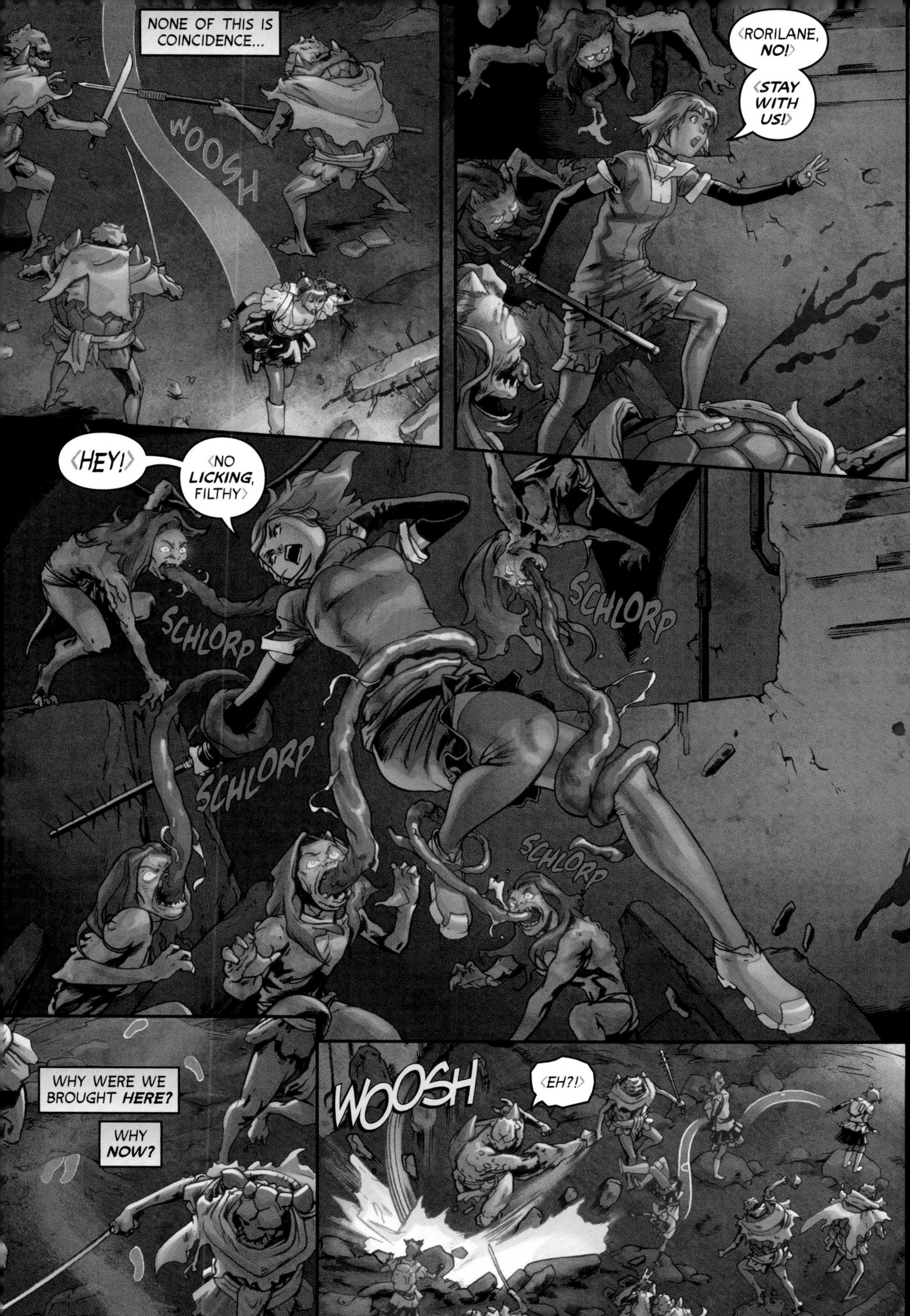
NONE OF THIS IS COINCIDENCE...
WOOSH
‹RORILANE, NO!›
‹STAY WITH US!›
‹HEY!›
‹NO LICKING, FILTHY›
SCHLORP
SCHLORP
SCHLORP
SCHLORP
WHY WERE WE BROUGHT HERE?
WHY NOW?
WOOSH
‹EH?!›
HOW DOES IT FIT THE PATTERN?

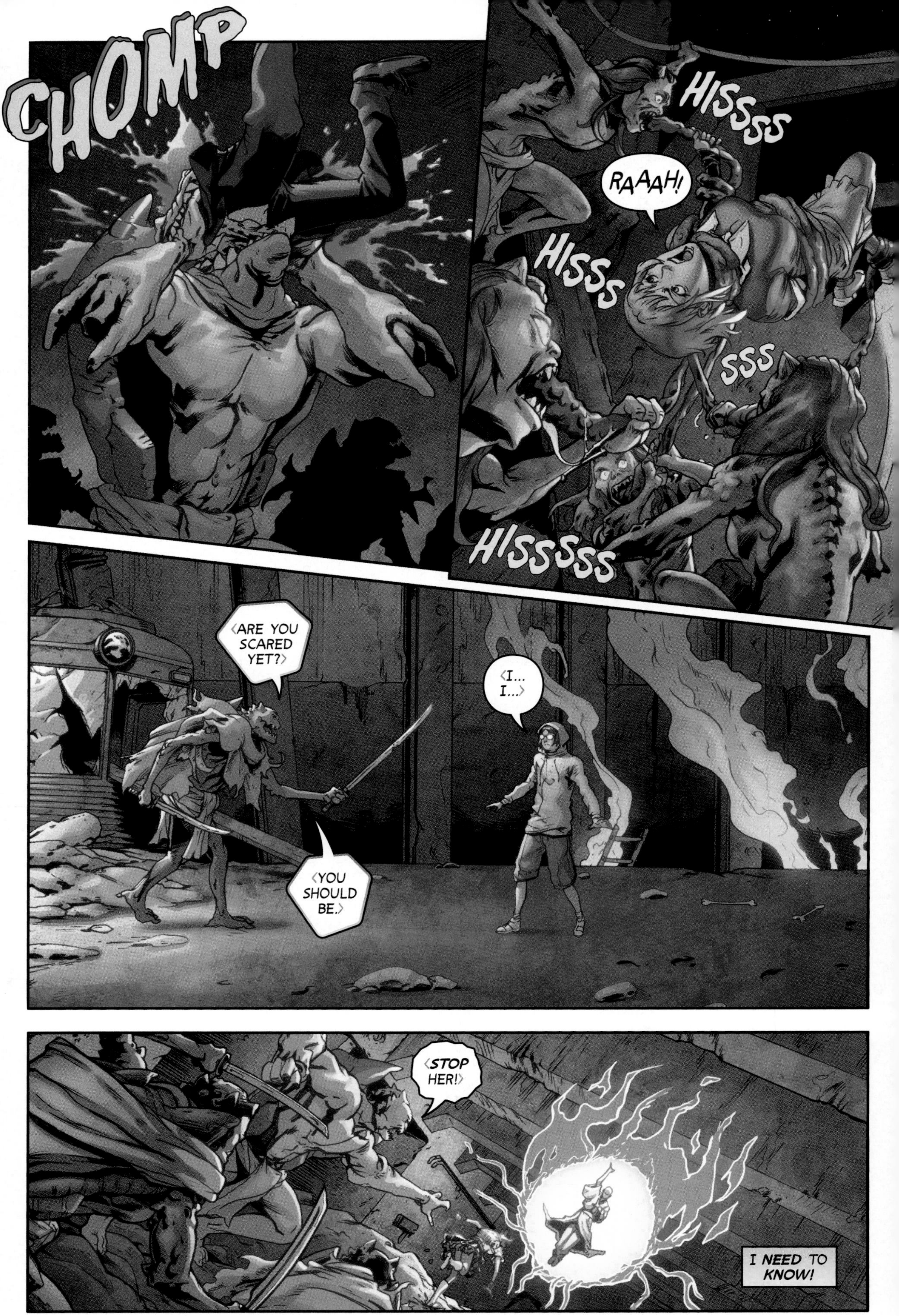
CHOMP
HISSSS
RAAAH!
HISSS
SSS
HISSSSS
‹ARE YOU SCARED YET?›
‹YOU SHOULD BE.›
‹I... I...›
‹STOP HER!›
I NEED TO KNOW!

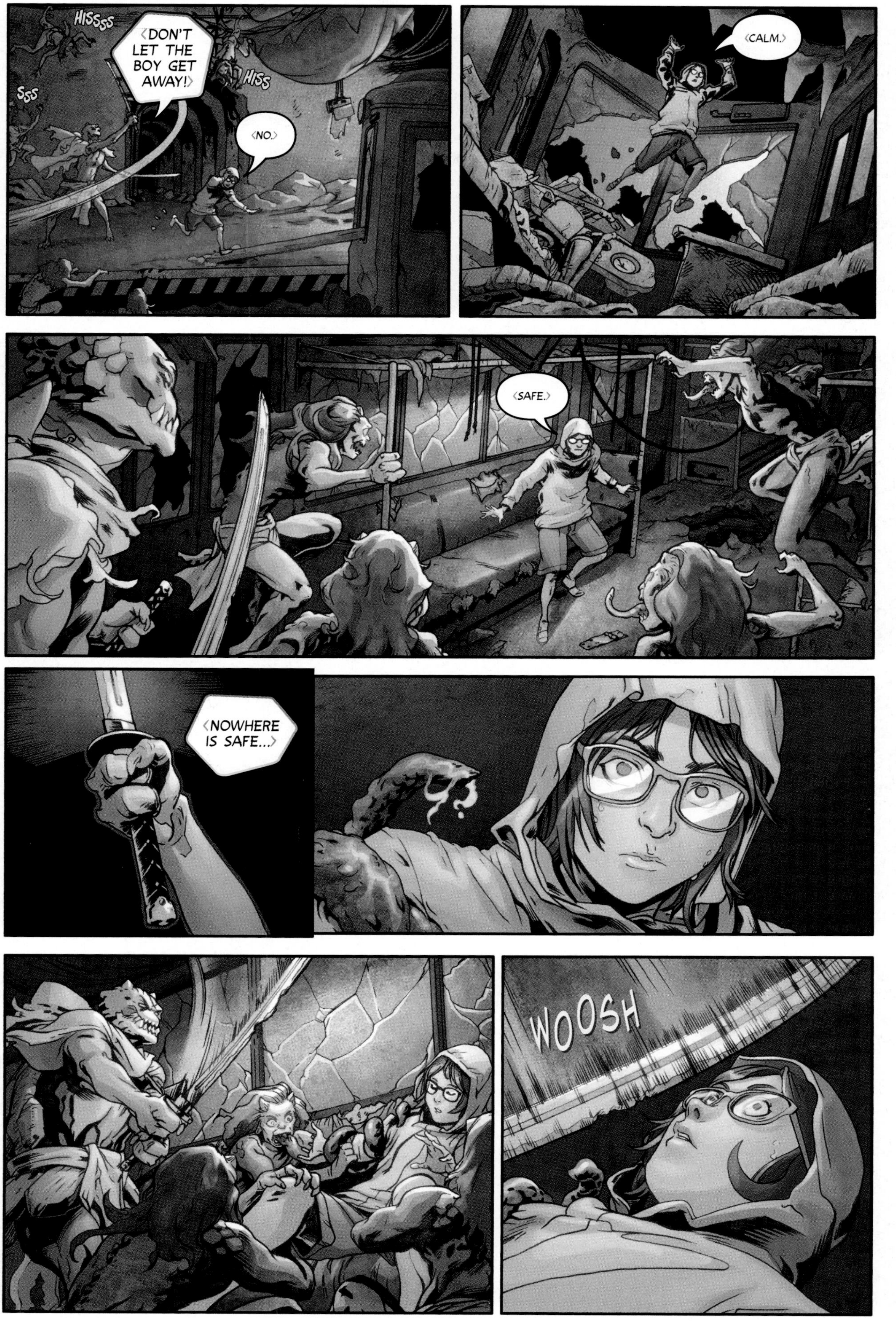
HISSSSS
SSS
⟨DON'T LET THE BOY GET AWAY!⟩
HISS
⟨NO.⟩
⟨CALM.⟩
⟨SAFE.⟩
⟨NOWHERE IS SAFE...⟩
WOOSH

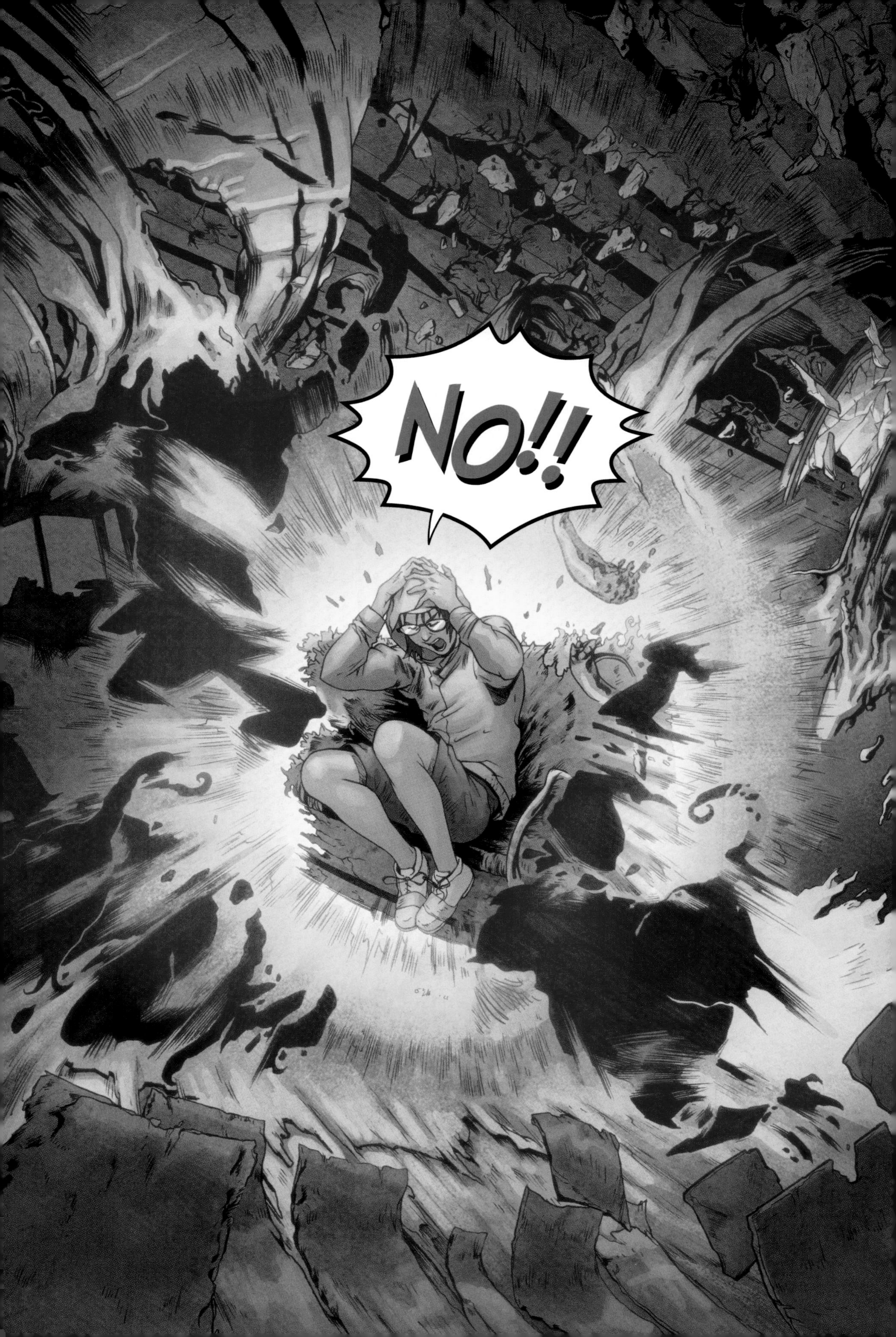
NO!!

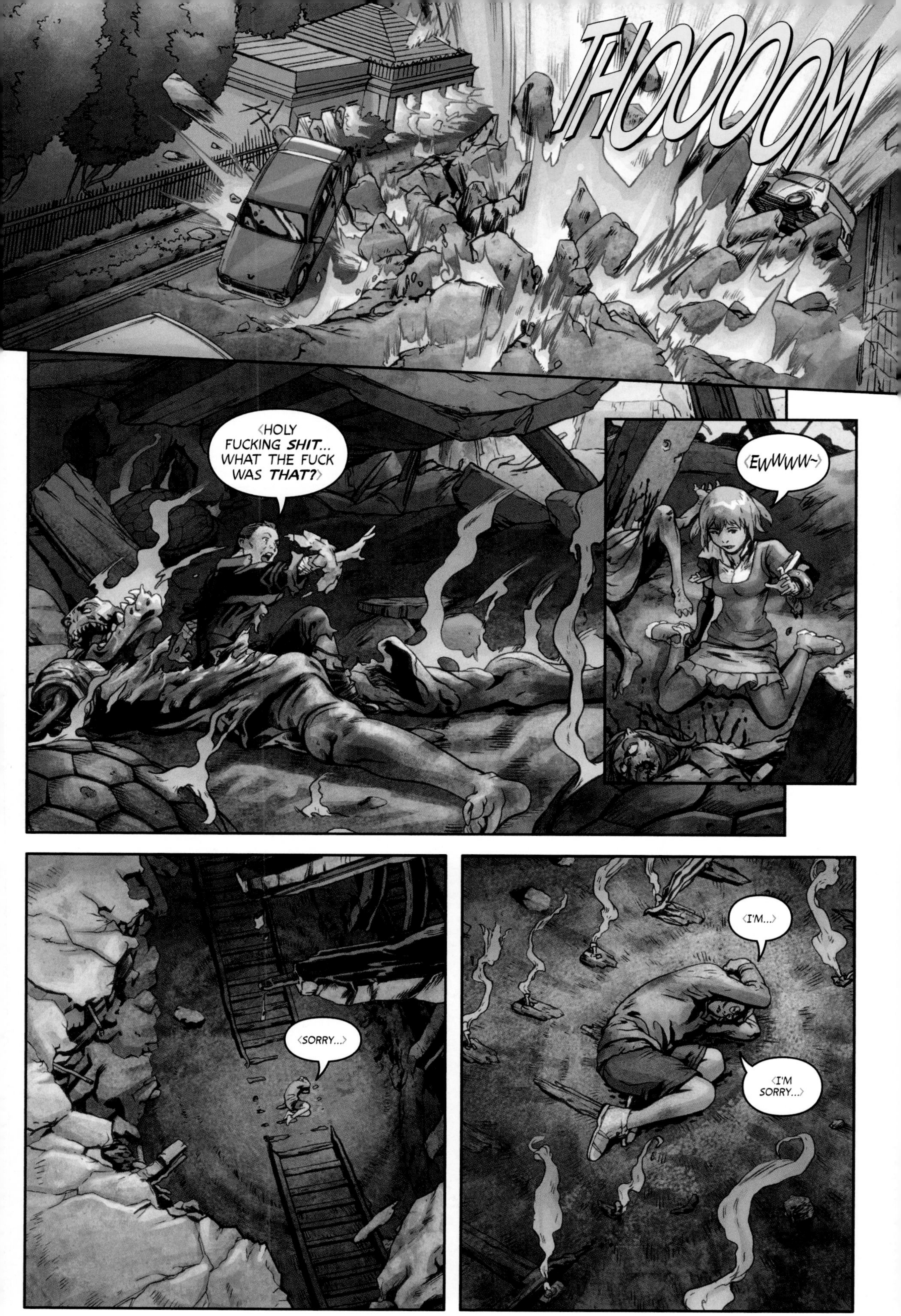
THOOOOM
⟨HOLY FUCKING **SHIT**... WHAT THE FUCK WAS **THAT?**⟩
⟨EWWWW~⟩
⟨SORRY...⟩
⟨I'M...⟩
⟨I'M SORRY...⟩

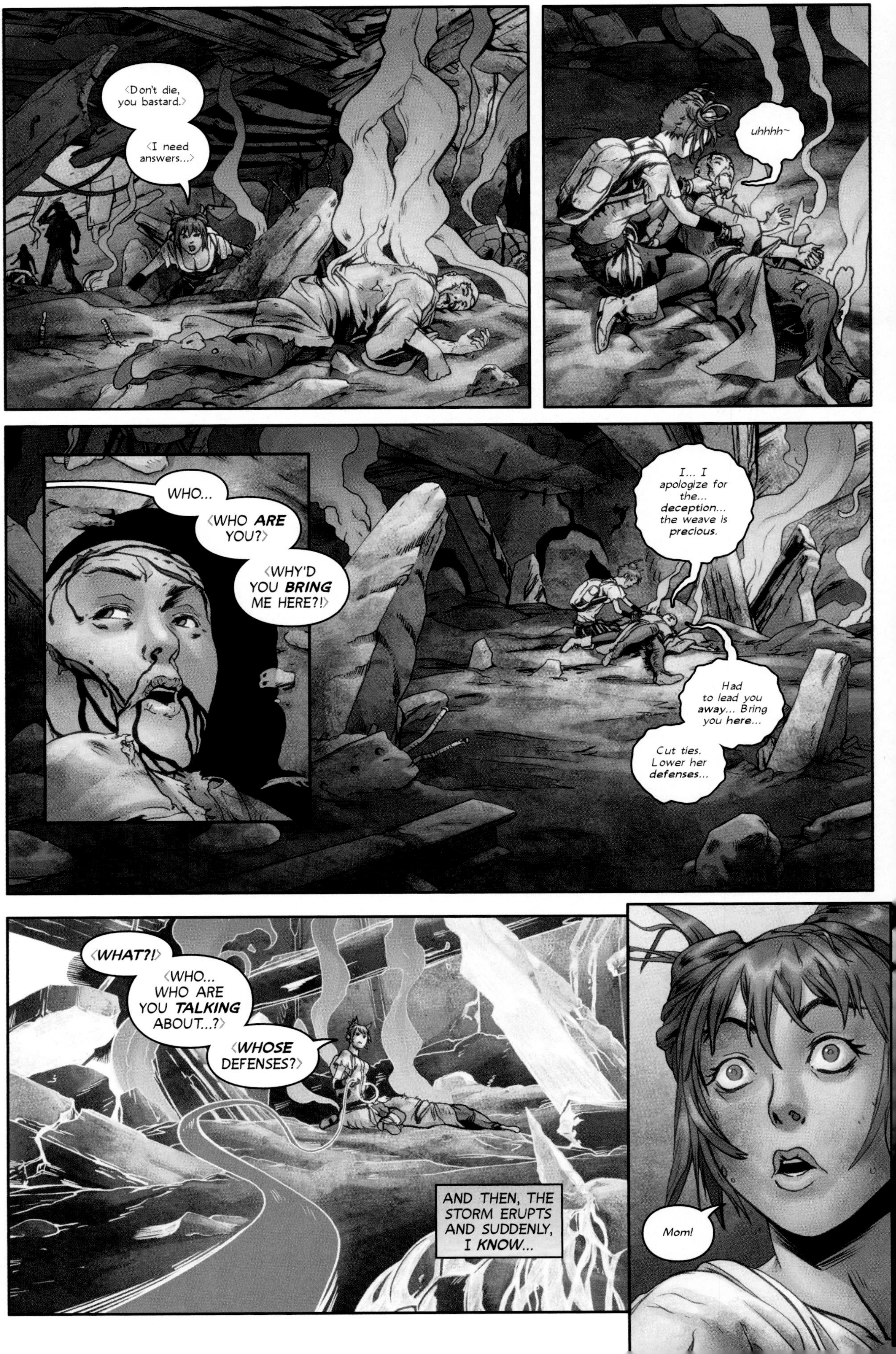

<Don't die, you bastard.>
<I need answers...>
uhhhh~
WHO...
<WHO ARE YOU?>
<WHY'D YOU BRING ME HERE?!>
I... I apologize for the... deception... the weave is precious.
Had to lead you away... Bring you here...
Cut ties. Lower her defenses...
<WHAT?!>
<WHO... WHO ARE YOU TALKING ABOUT...?>
<WHOSE DEFENSES?>
AND THEN, THE STORM ERUPTS AND SUDDENLY, I KNOW...
Mom!

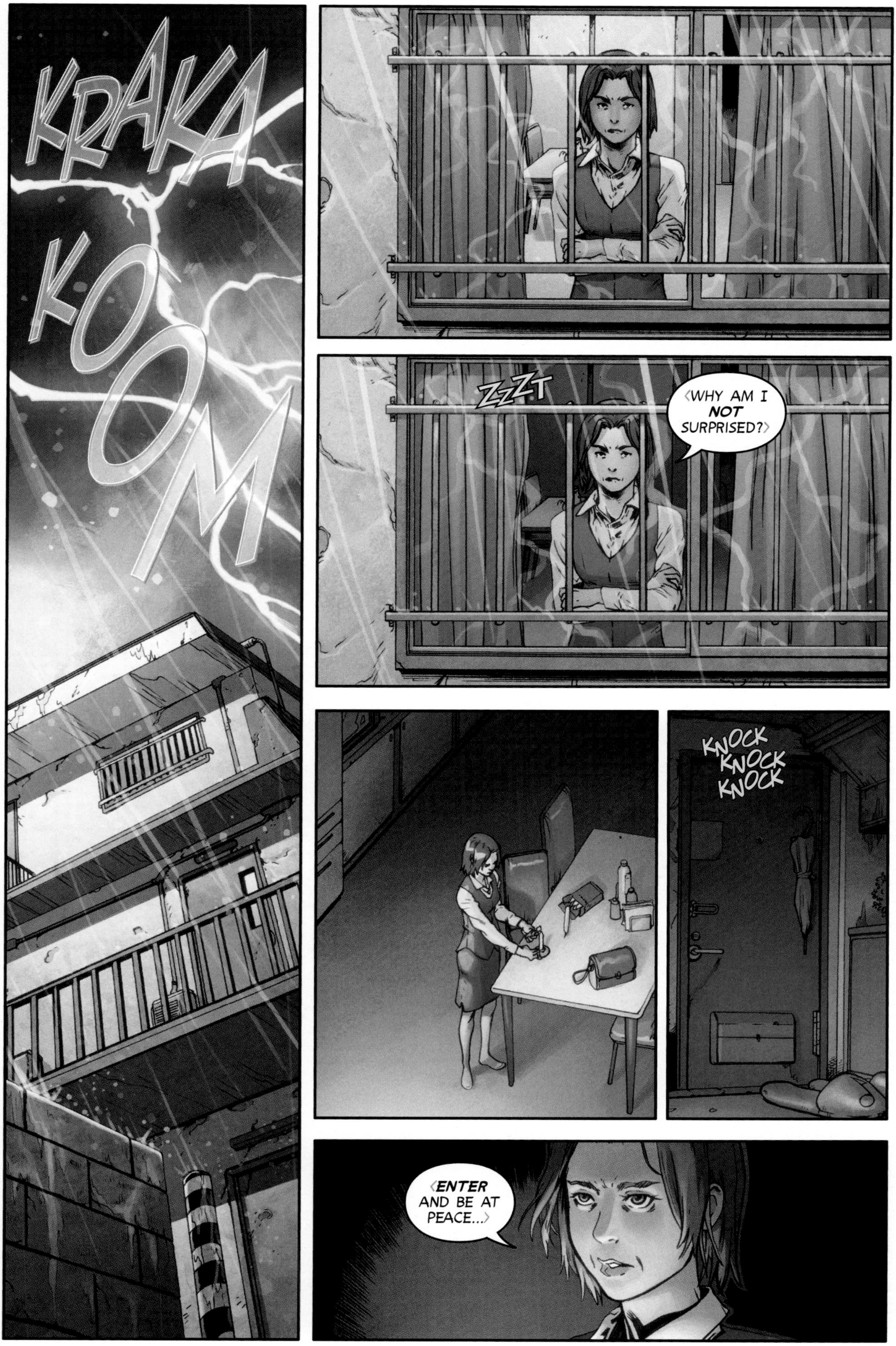
KRAKA
KOOM
ZZZT
⟨WHY AM I **NOT** SURPRISED?⟩
KNOCK
KNOCK
KNOCK
⟨**ENTER** AND BE AT PEACE...⟩

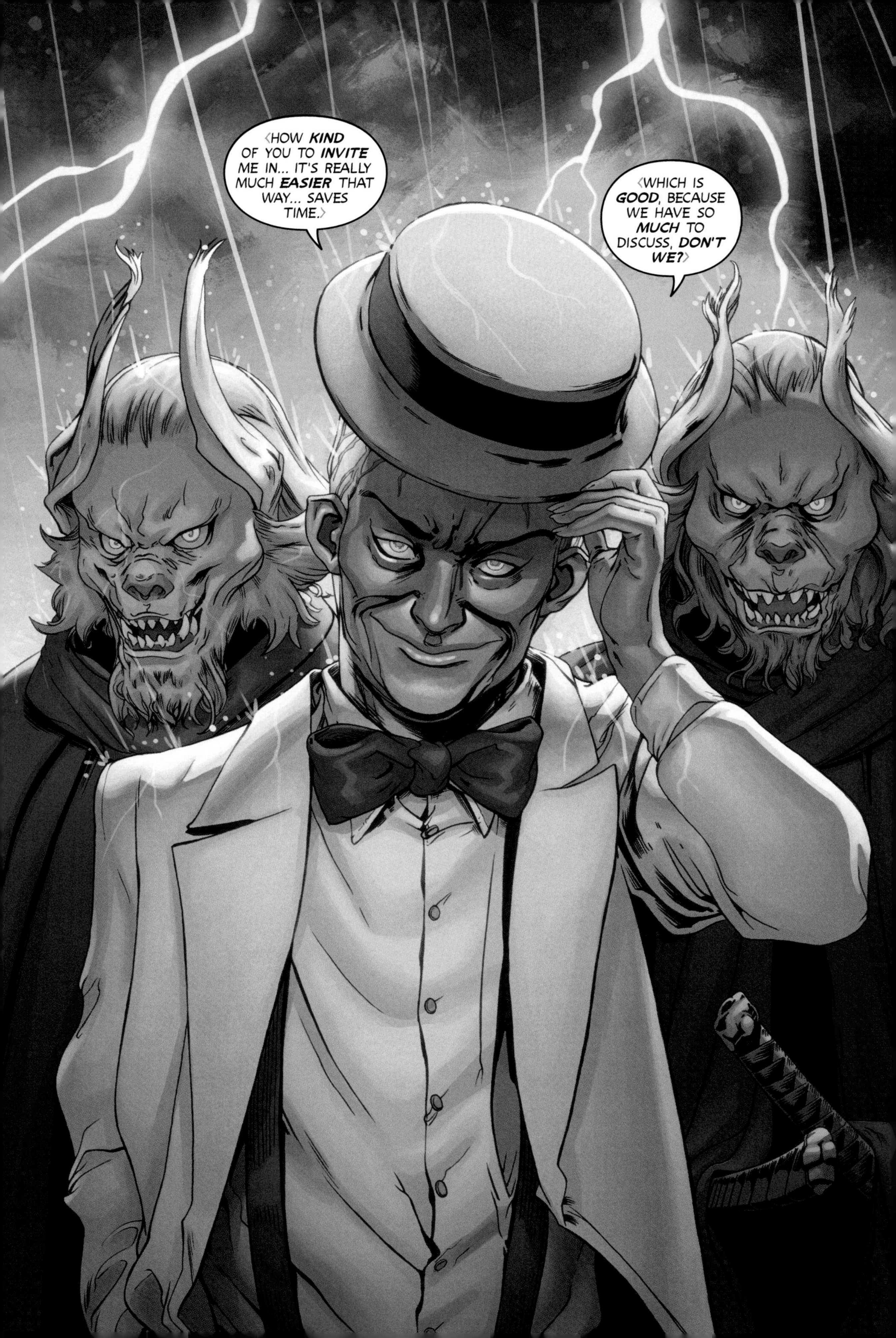
<HOW **KIND** OF YOU TO **INVITE** ME IN... IT'S REALLY MUCH **EASIER** THAT WAY... SAVES TIME.>
<WHICH IS **GOOD**, BECAUSE WE HAVE SO **MUCH** TO DISCUSS, **DON'T WE?**>

Chapter Five

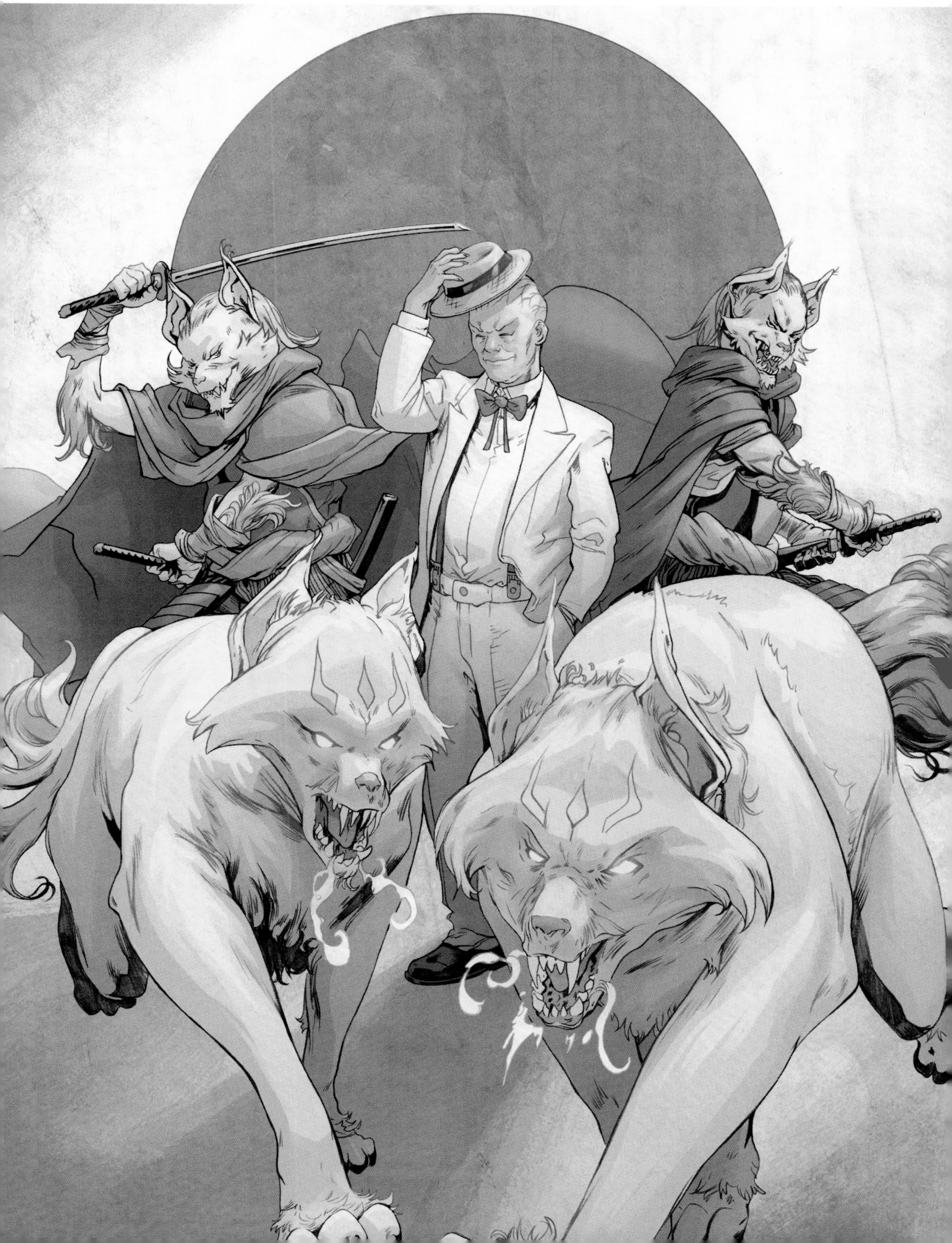

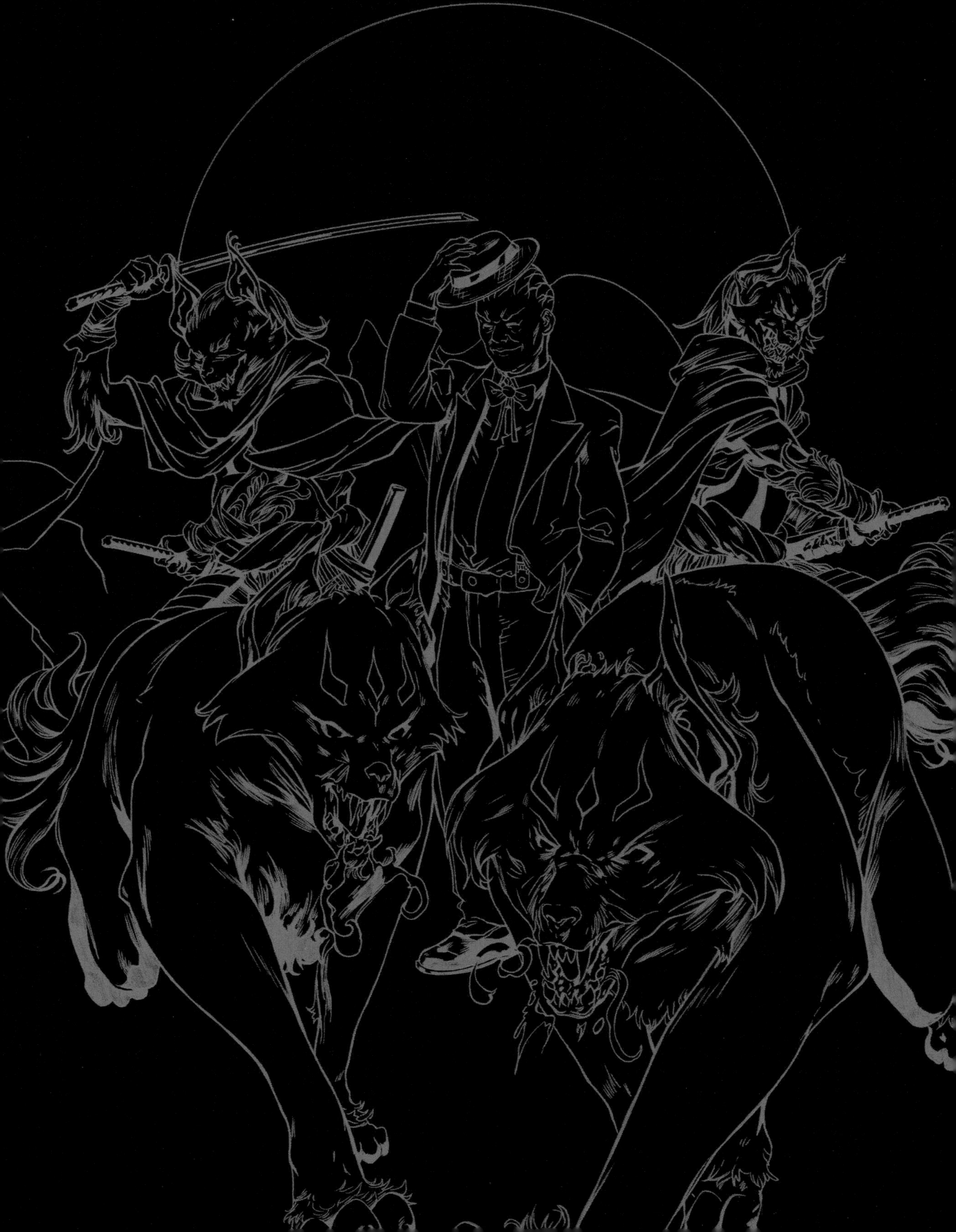

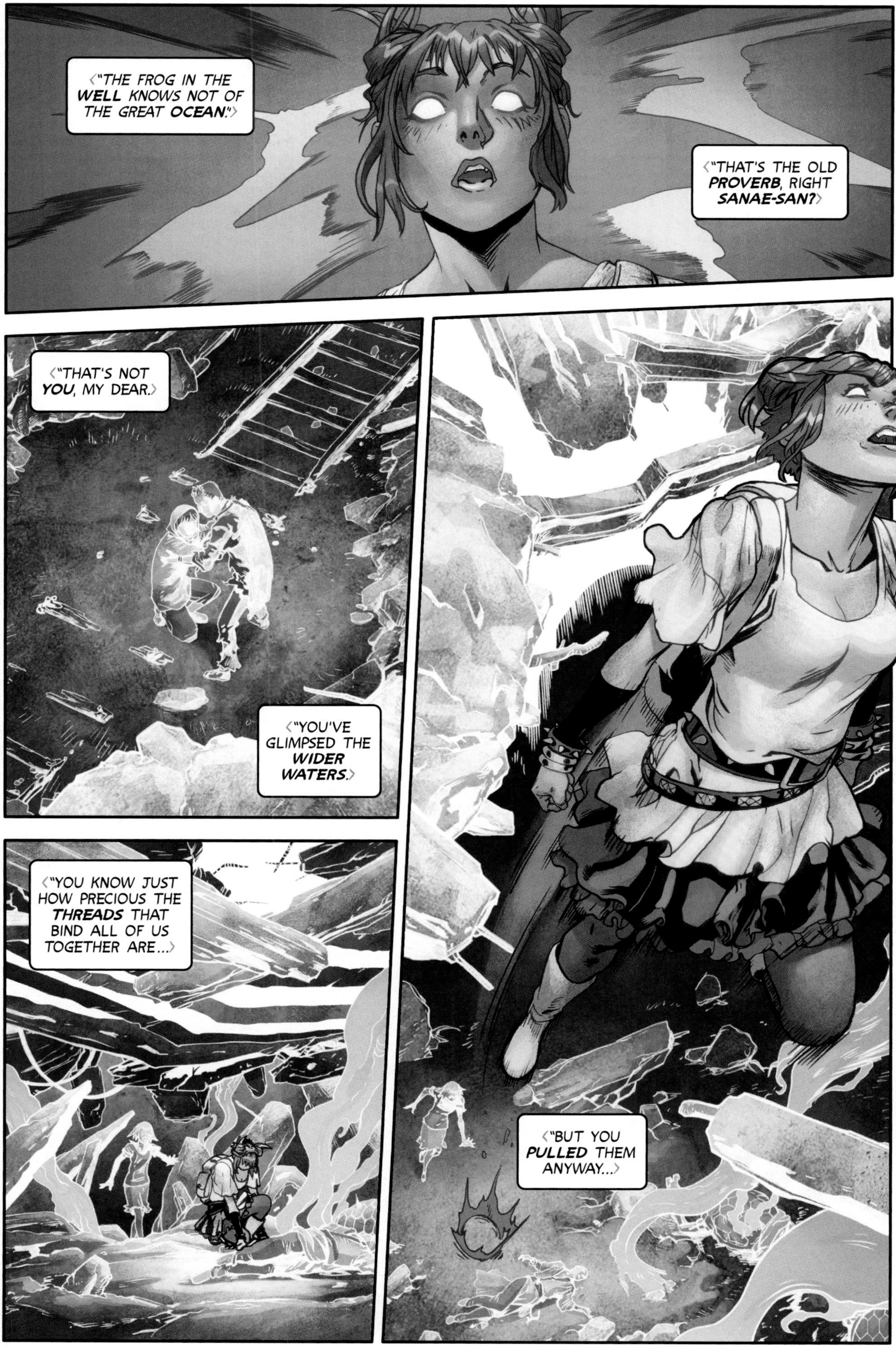
<"THE FROG IN THE **WELL** KNOWS NOT OF THE GREAT **OCEAN**.">
<"THAT'S THE OLD **PROVERB**, RIGHT **SANAE-SAN?**>
<"THAT'S NOT **YOU**, MY DEAR.>
<"YOU'VE GLIMPSED THE **WIDER WATERS**.>
<"YOU KNOW JUST HOW PRECIOUS THE **THREADS** THAT BIND ALL OF US TOGETHER ARE...>
<"BUT YOU **PULLED** THEM ANYWAY...>

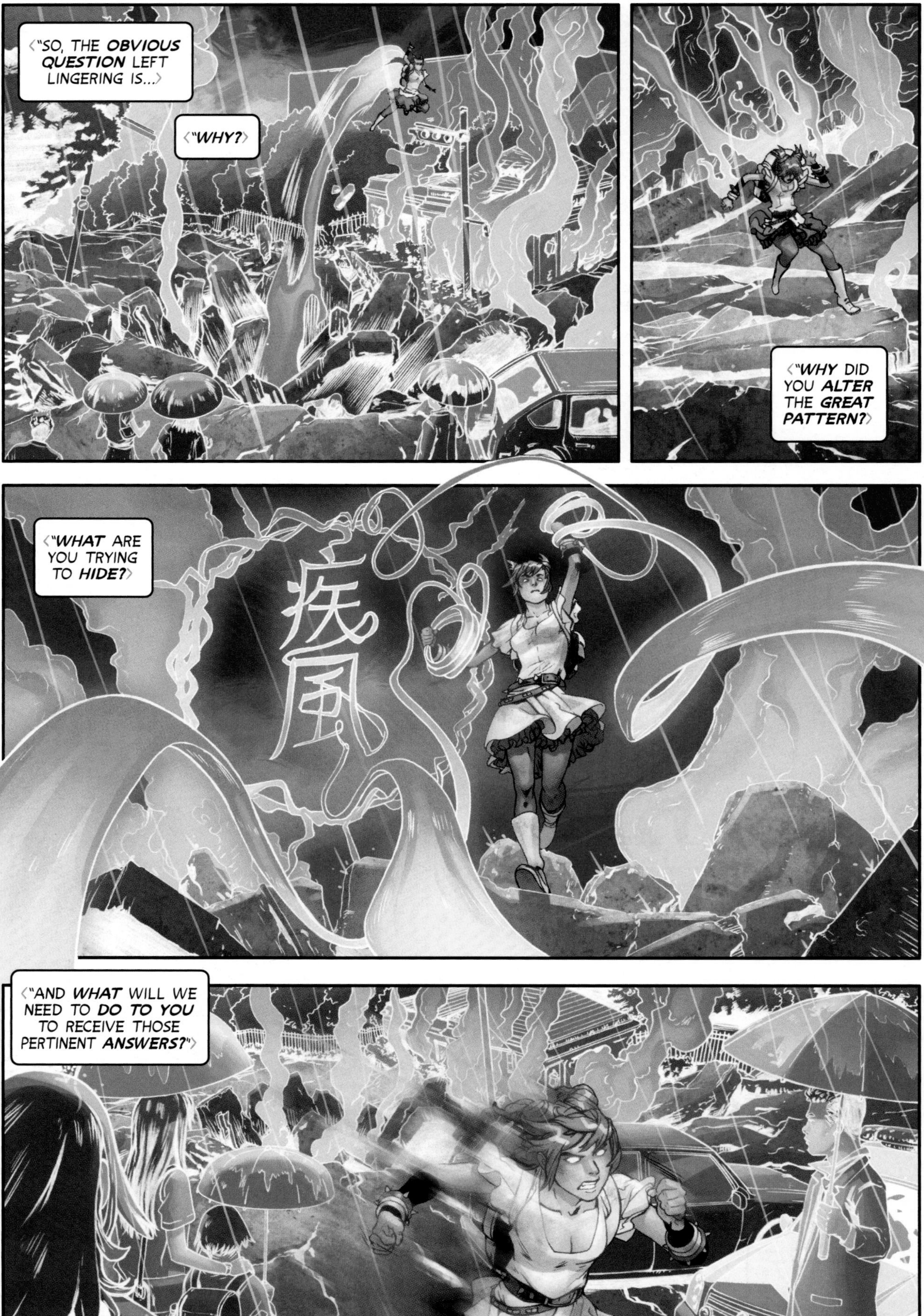
<"SO, THE OBVIOUS QUESTION LEFT LINGERING IS...>
<"WHY?>
<"WHY DID YOU ALTER THE GREAT PATTERN?>
<"WHAT ARE YOU TRYING TO HIDE?>
疾風
<"AND WHAT WILL WE NEED TO DO TO YOU TO RECEIVE THOSE PERTINENT ANSWERS?">

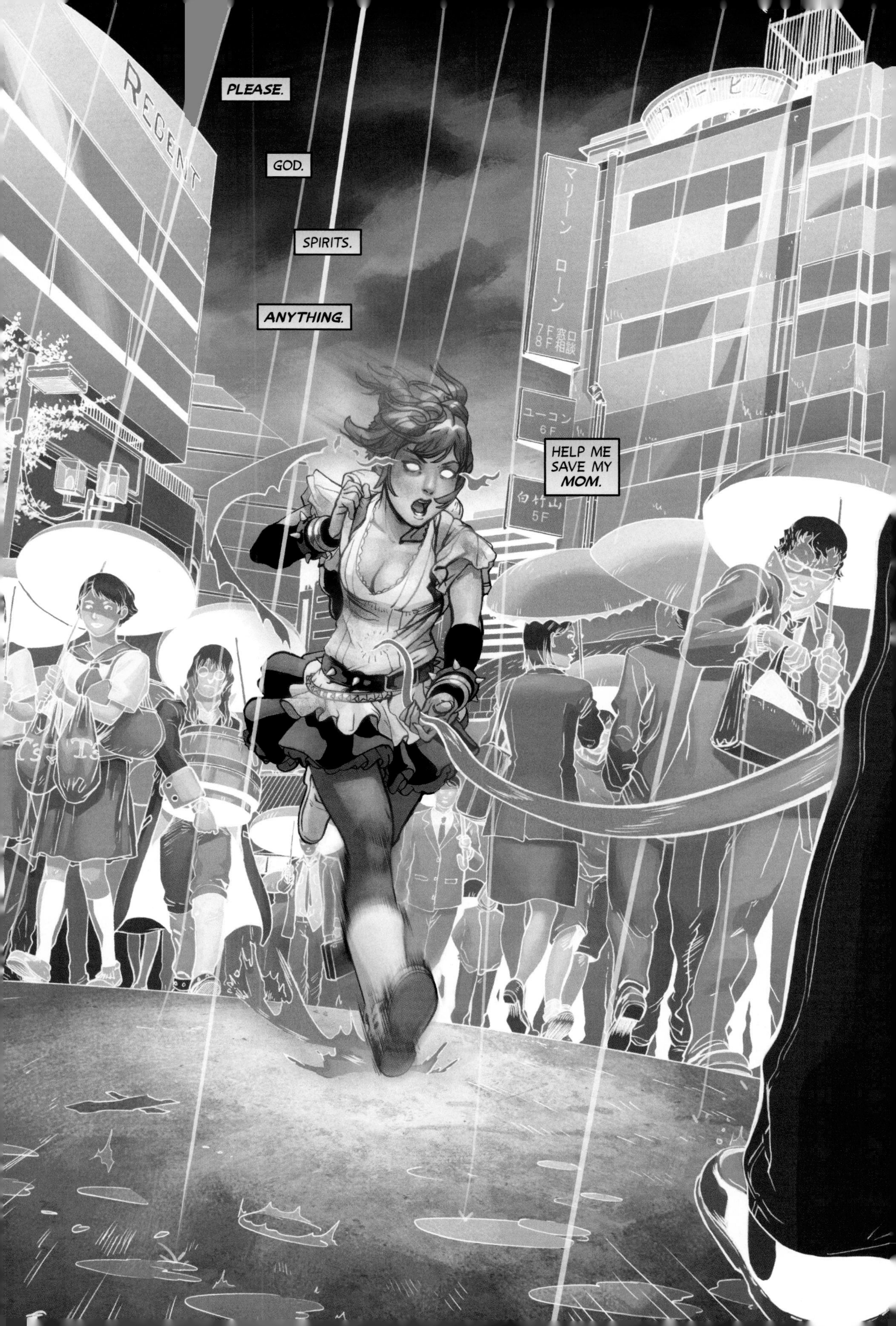
REGENT
PLEASE.
GOD.
SPIRITS.
ANYTHING.
マリーン ローン
7F窓口
8F相談
ユーコン
6F
HELP ME SAVE MY MOM.
白竹山
5F

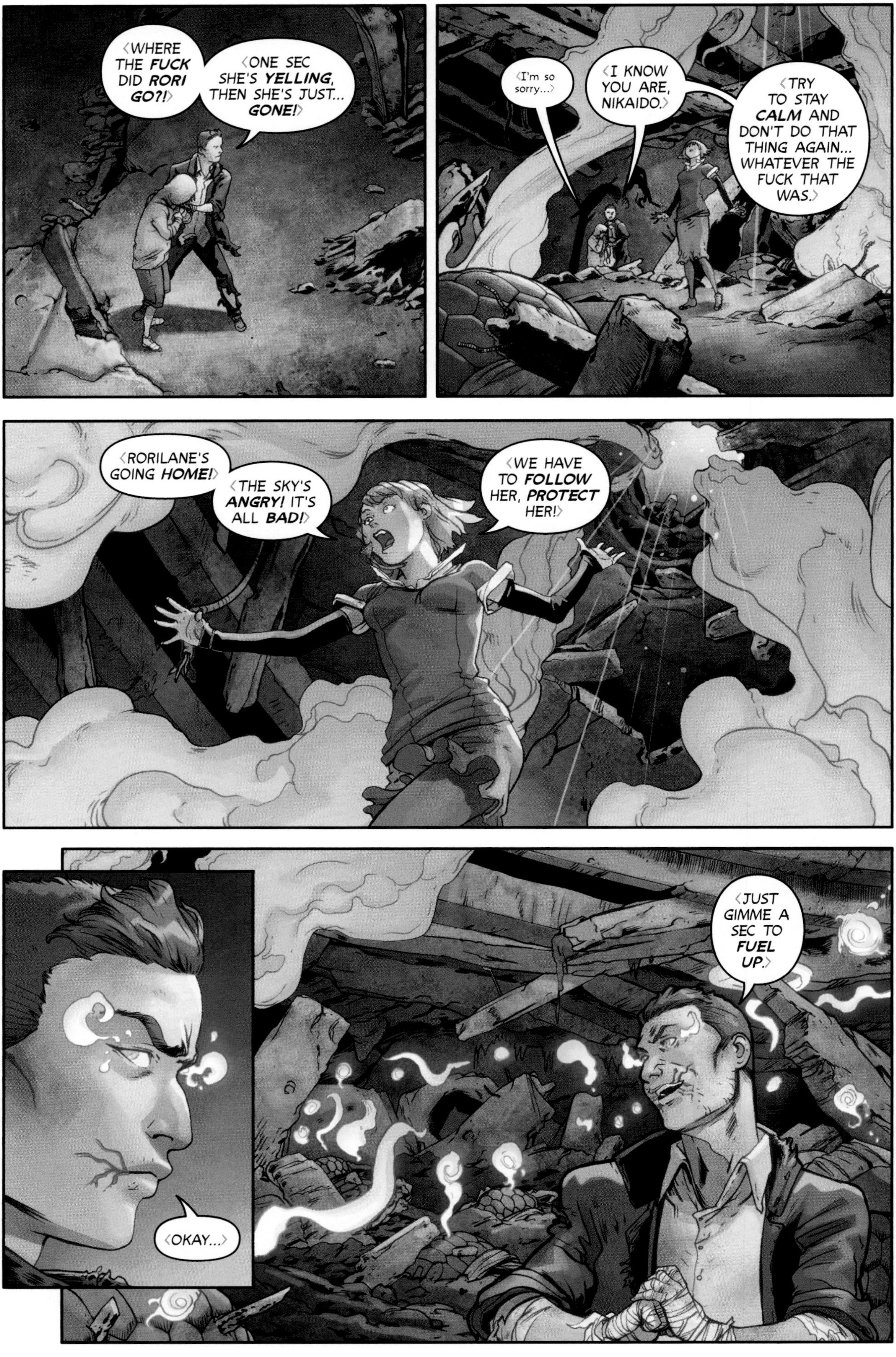

<WHERE THE **FUCK** DID **RORI** GO?!>
<ONE SEC SHE'S **YELLING**, THEN SHE'S JUST... **GONE!**>
<I'm so sorry...>
<I KNOW YOU ARE, NIKAIDO.>
<TRY TO STAY **CALM** AND DON'T DO THAT THING AGAIN... WHATEVER THE FUCK THAT WAS.>
<RORILANE'S GOING **HOME!**>
<THE SKY'S **ANGRY!** IT'S ALL **BAD!**>
<WE HAVE TO **FOLLOW** HER, **PROTECT** HER!>
<OKAY...>
<JUST GIMME A SEC TO **FUEL UP**.>

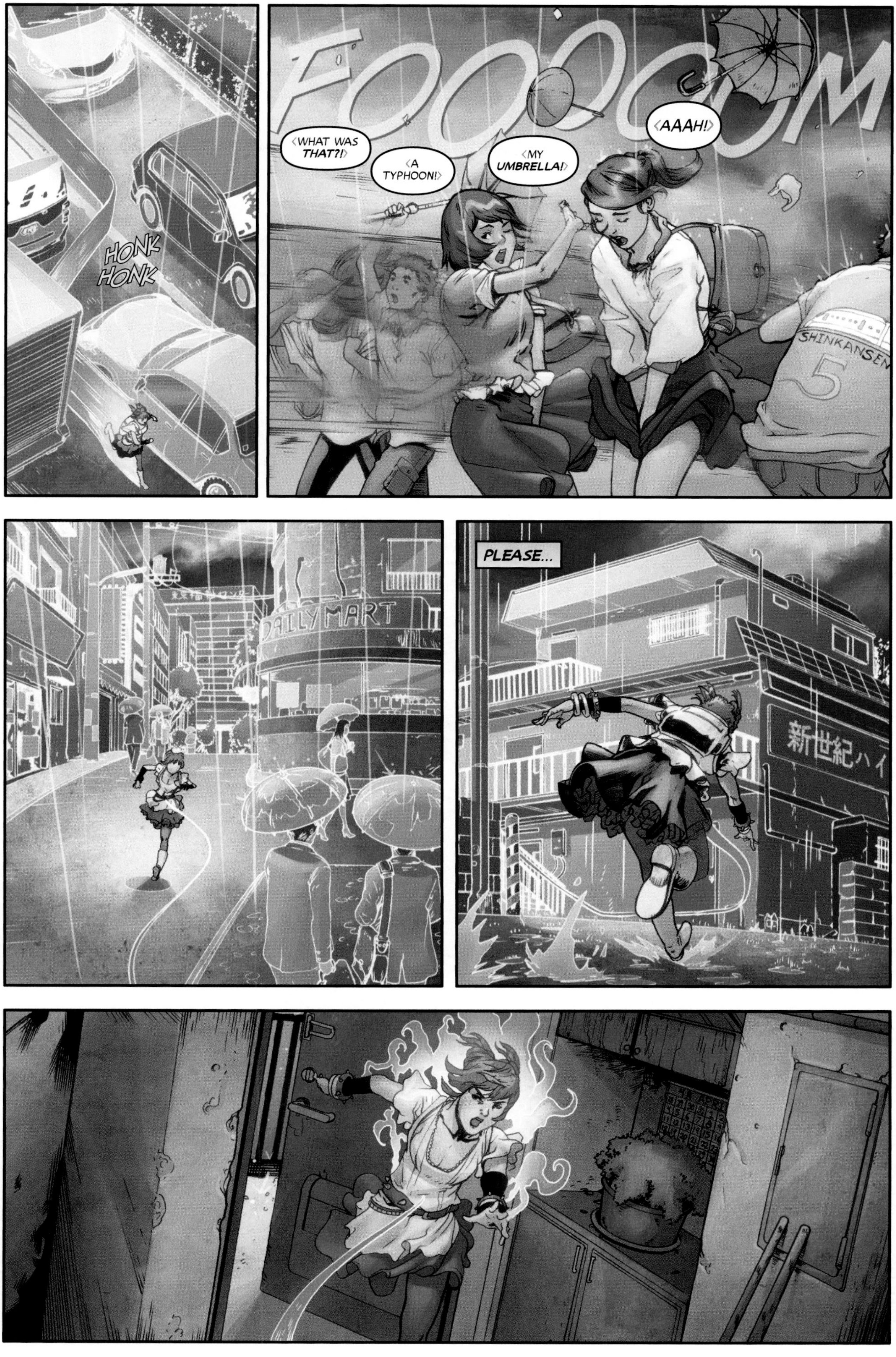
HONK
HONK
FOOOOM
<WHAT WAS THAT?!>
<A TYPHOON!>
<MY UMBRELLA!>
<AAAH!>
SHINKANSEN 5
DAILY MART
PLEASE...
新世紀ハイ

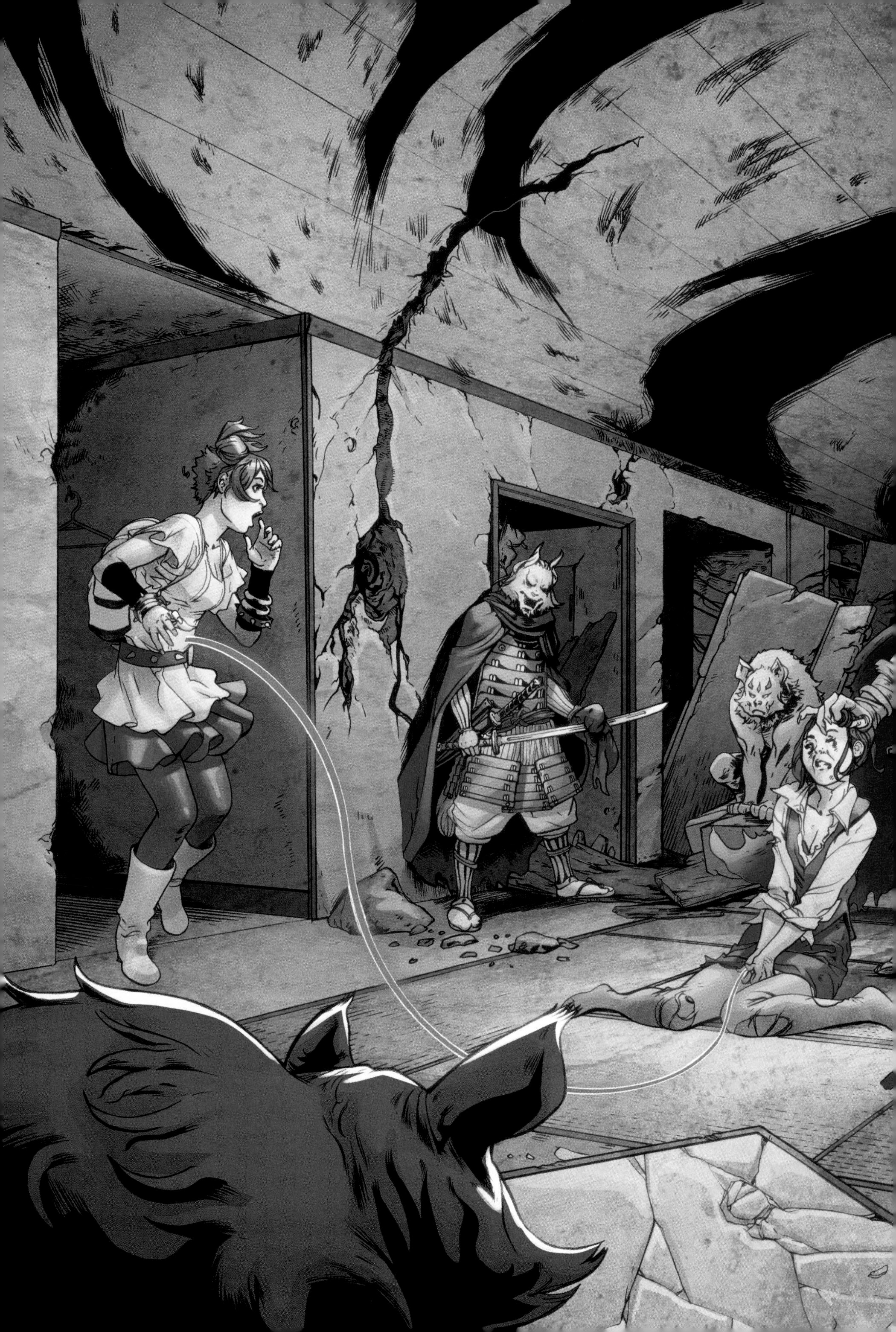

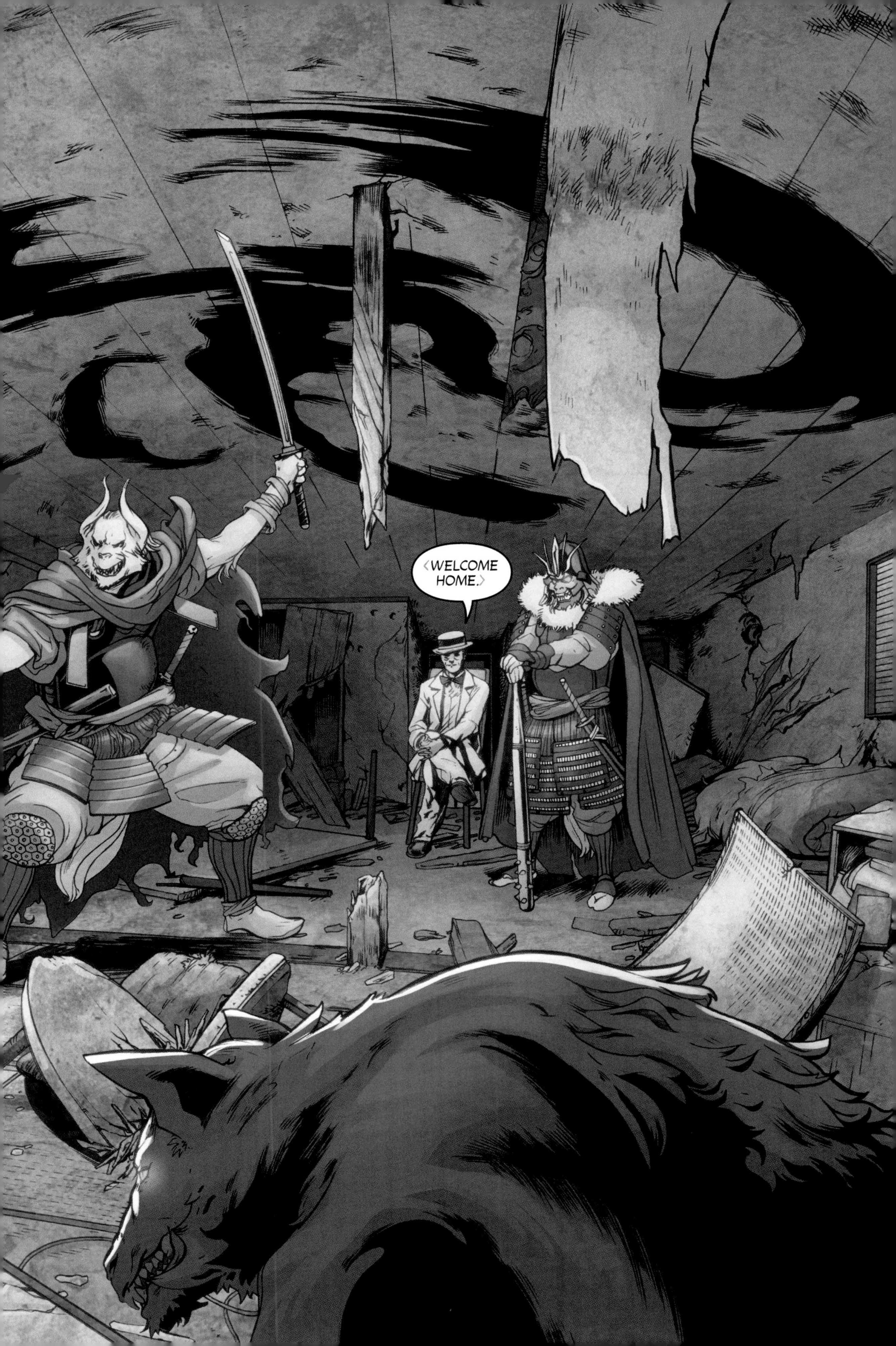
〈WELCOME HOME.〉

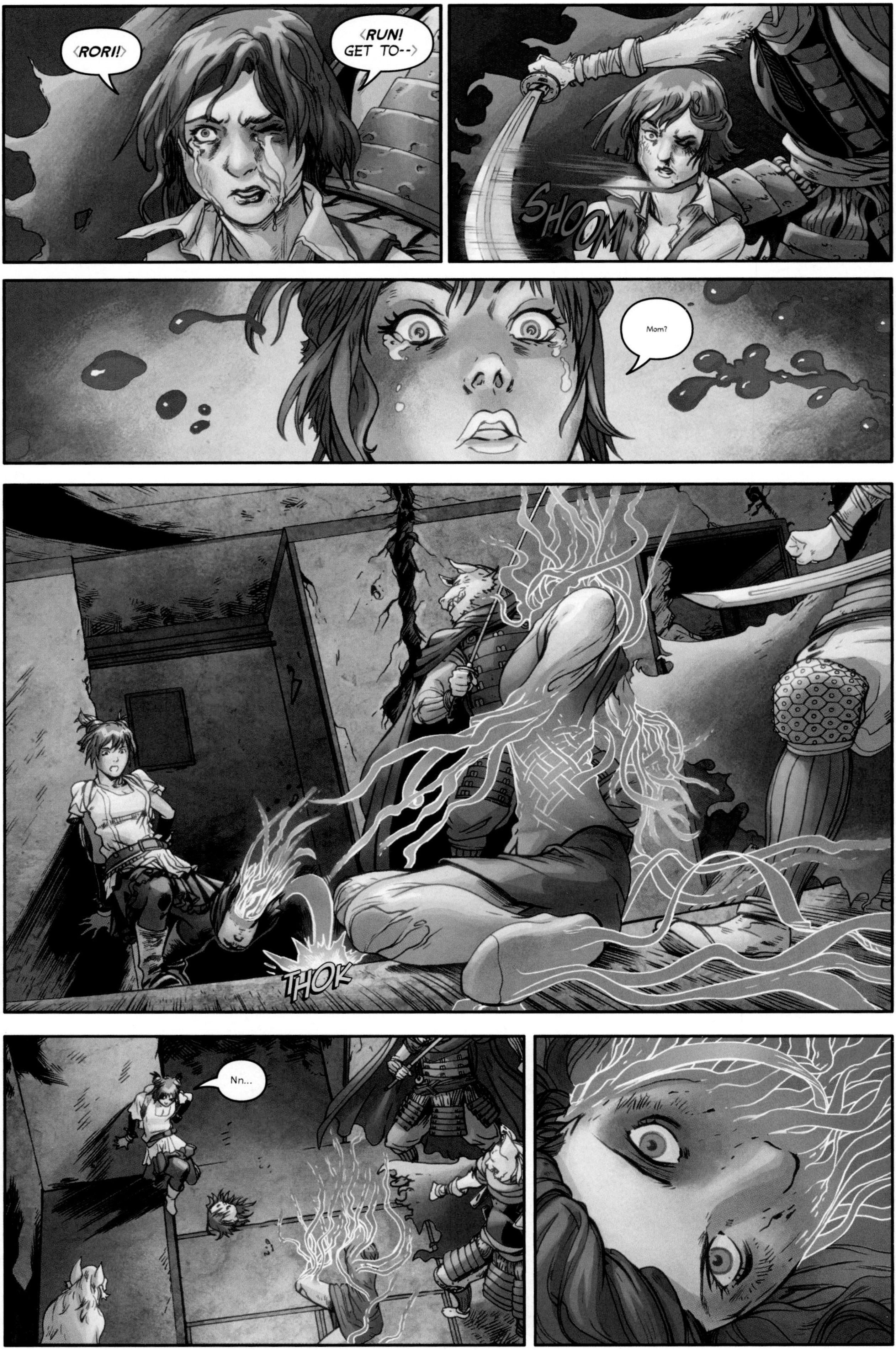
‹RORI!›
‹RUN! GET TO--›
SHOOM
Mom?
THOK
Nn...

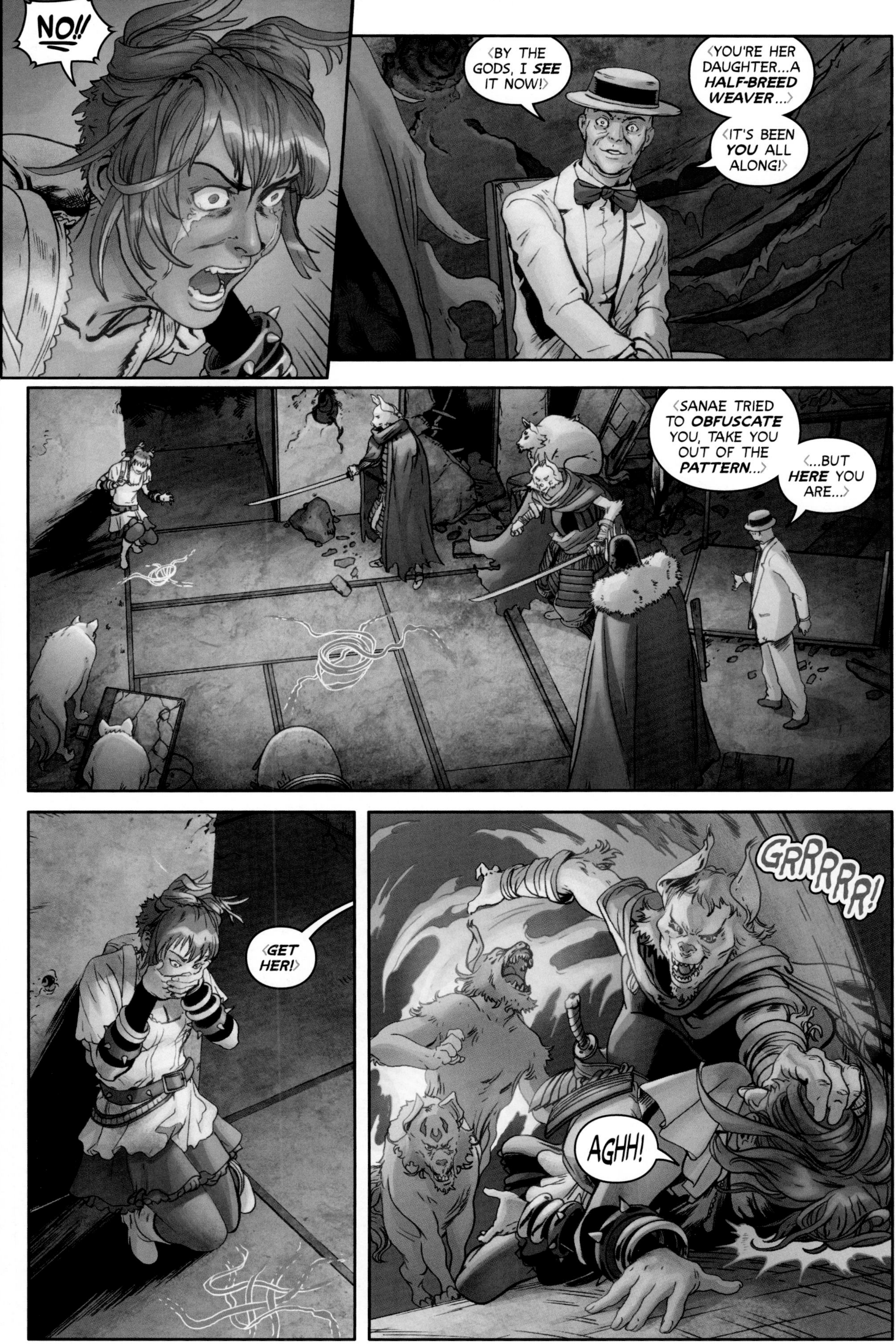
NO!!
⟨BY THE GODS, I SEE IT NOW!⟩
⟨YOU'RE HER DAUGHTER...A HALF-BREED WEAVER...⟩
⟨IT'S BEEN YOU ALL ALONG!⟩
⟨SANAE TRIED TO OBFUSCATE YOU, TAKE YOU OUT OF THE PATTERN...⟩
⟨...BUT HERE YOU ARE...⟩
⟨GET HER!⟩
GRRRRRR!
AGHH!

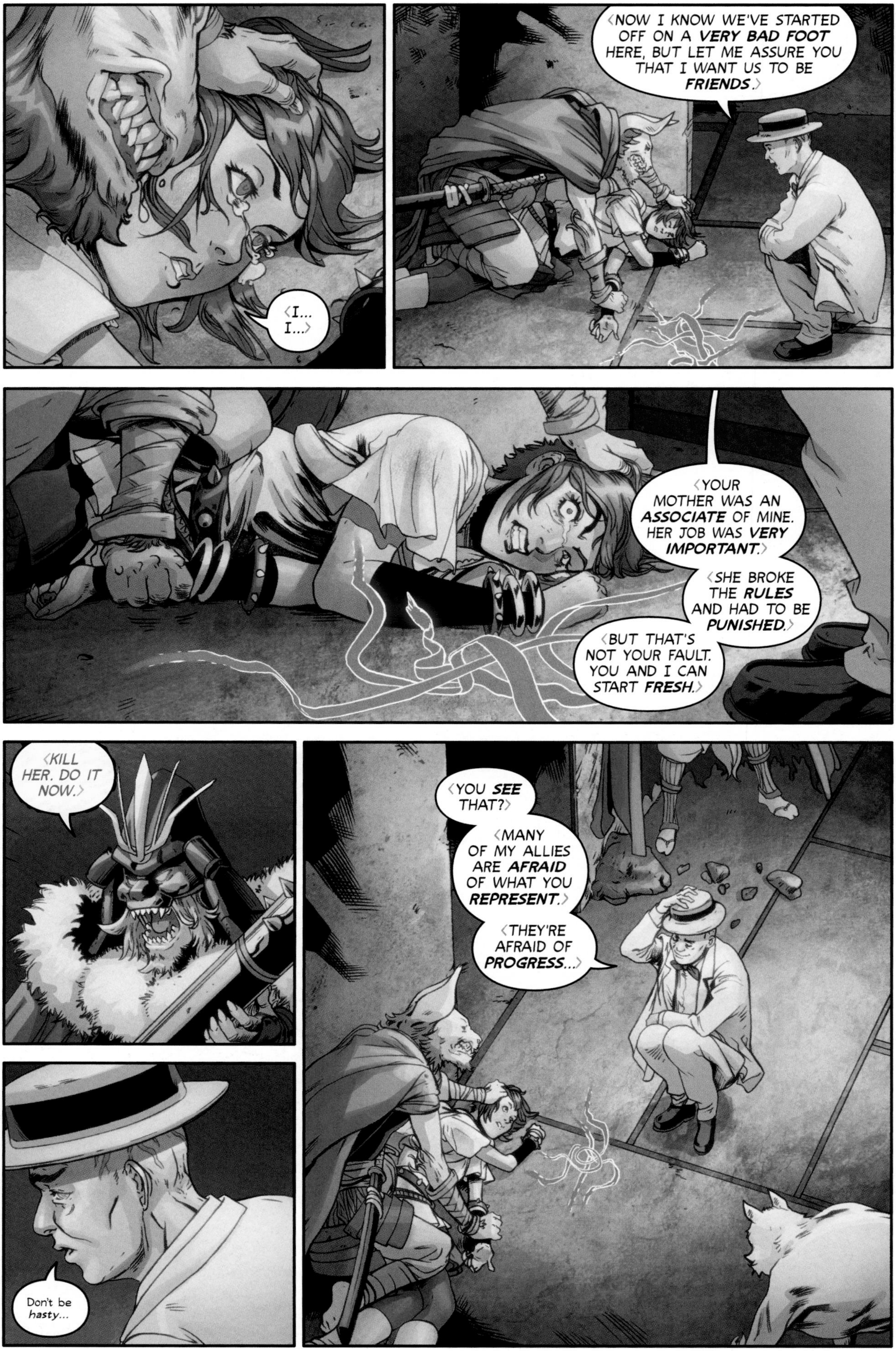

<I... I...>
<NOW I KNOW WE'VE STARTED OFF ON A **VERY BAD FOOT** HERE, BUT LET ME ASSURE YOU THAT I WANT US TO BE **FRIENDS**.>
<YOUR MOTHER WAS AN **ASSOCIATE** OF MINE. HER JOB WAS **VERY IMPORTANT**.>
<SHE BROKE THE **RULES** AND HAD TO BE **PUNISHED**.>
<BUT THAT'S NOT YOUR FAULT. YOU AND I CAN START **FRESH**.>
<KILL HER. DO IT NOW.>
Don't be *hasty*...
<YOU **SEE** THAT?>
<MANY OF MY ALLIES ARE **AFRAID** OF WHAT YOU **REPRESENT**.>
<THEY'RE AFRAID OF **PROGRESS**...>

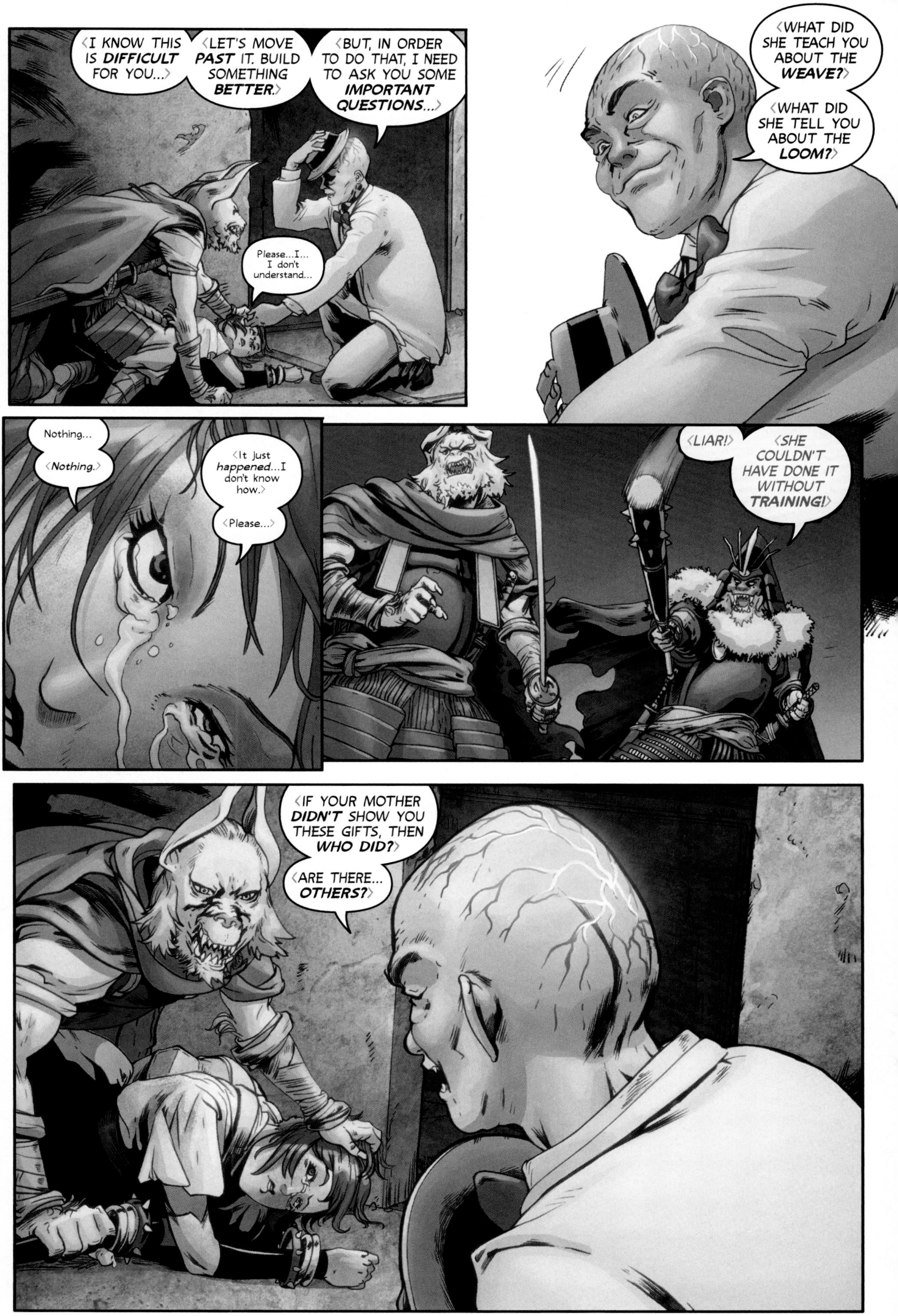
‹I KNOW THIS IS *DIFFICULT* FOR YOU...›
‹LET'S MOVE *PAST* IT. BUILD SOMETHING *BETTER.*›
‹BUT, IN ORDER TO DO THAT, I NEED TO ASK YOU SOME *IMPORTANT QUESTIONS...*›
Please...I... I don't understand...
‹WHAT DID SHE TEACH YOU ABOUT THE *WEAVE?*›
‹WHAT DID SHE TELL YOU ABOUT THE *LOOM?*›
Nothing...
‹*Nothing.*›
‹It just *happened*...I don't know how.›
‹Please...›
‹*LIAR!*›
‹*SHE COULDN'T HAVE DONE IT WITHOUT TRAINING!*›
‹IF YOUR MOTHER *DIDN'T* SHOW YOU THESE GIFTS, THEN *WHO DID?*›
‹ARE THERE... *OTHERS?*›

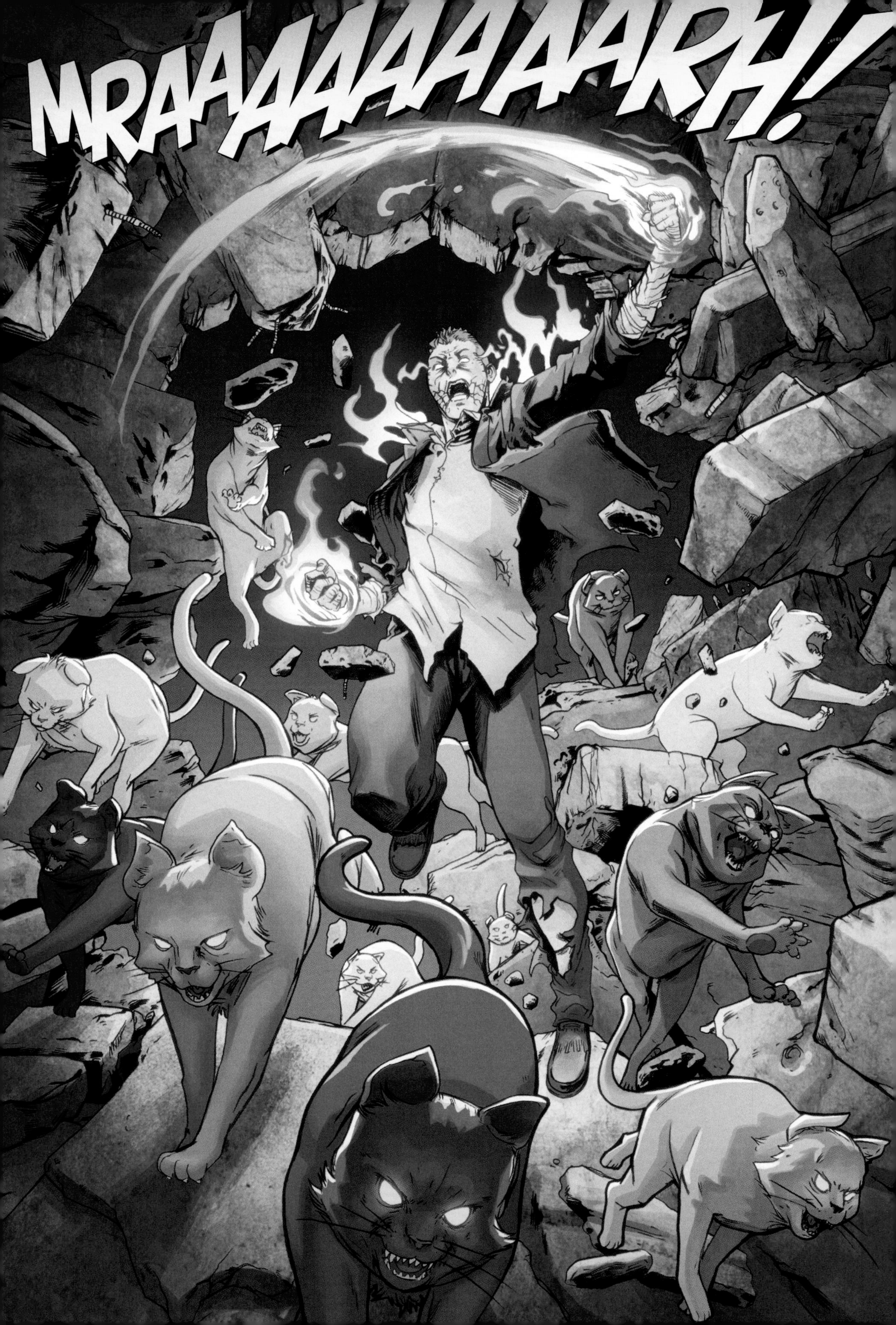
MRAAAAAAAAARH!

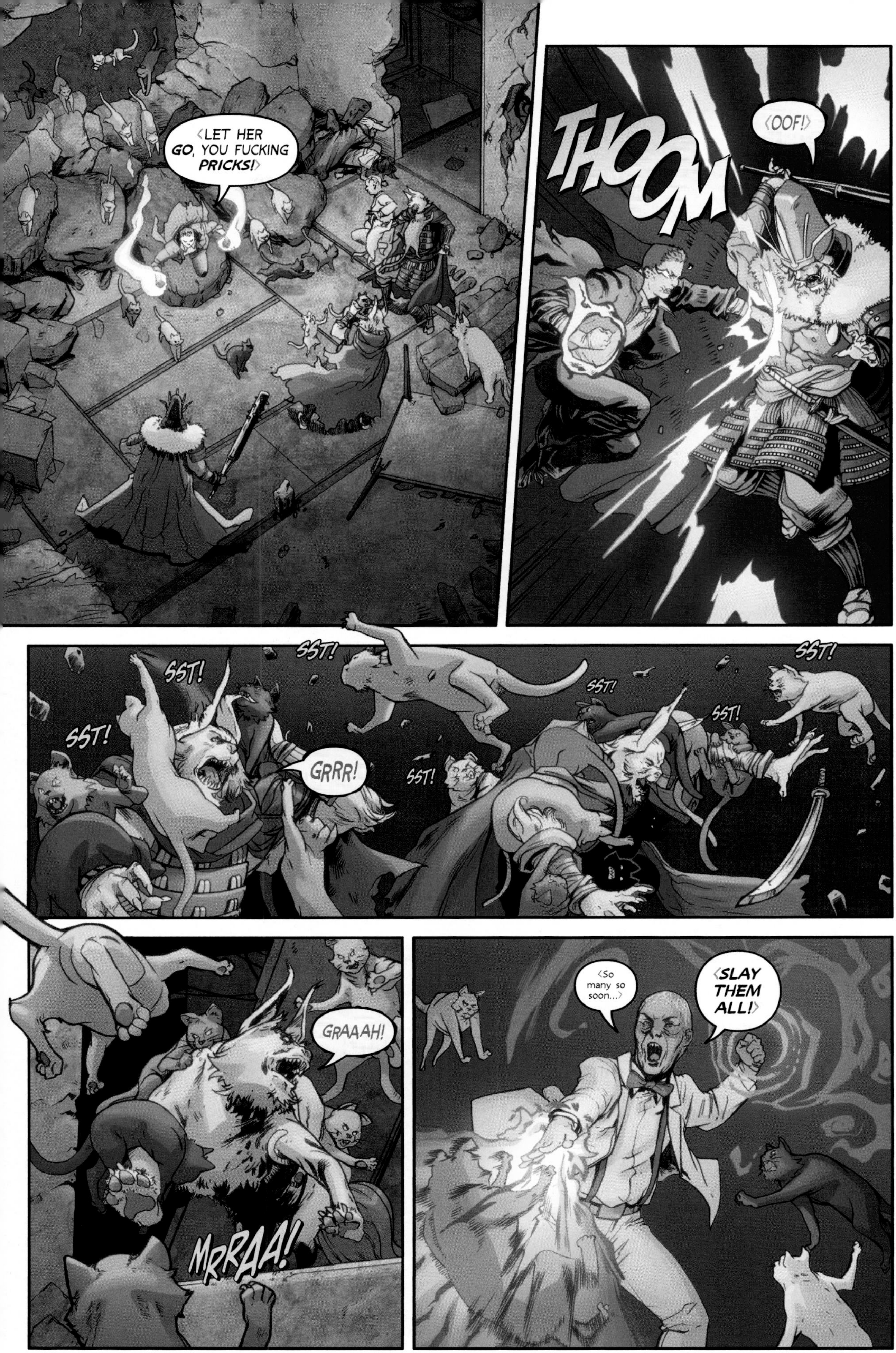

⟨LET HER GO, YOU FUCKING PRICKS!⟩
THOOM
⟨OOF!⟩
SST!
SST!
SST!
GRRR!
SST!
SST!
SST!
SST!
GRAAAH!
MRRAA!
⟨So many so soon...⟩
⟨SLAY THEM ALL!⟩

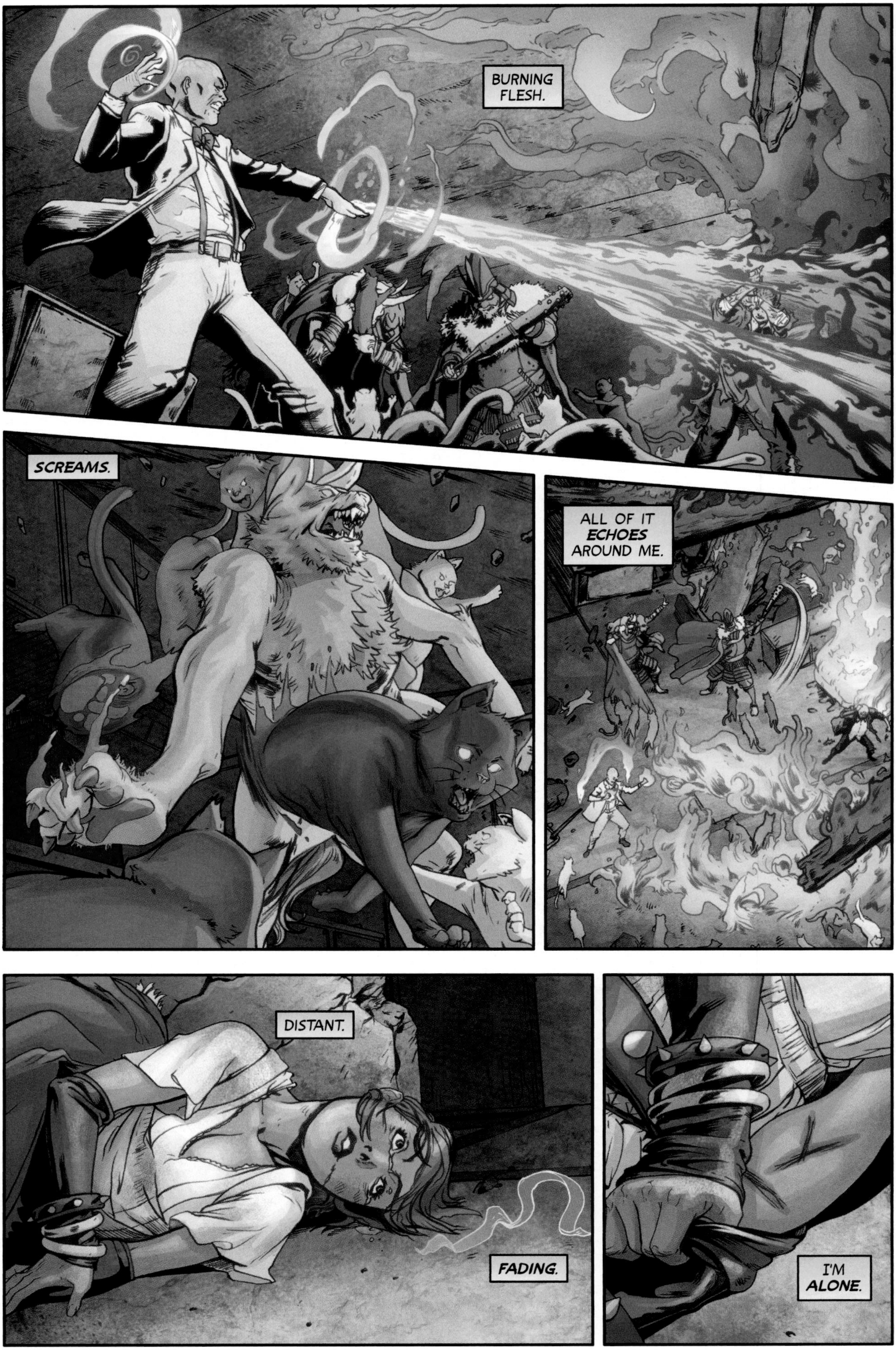
BURNING FLESH.
SCREAMS.
ALL OF IT ECHOES AROUND ME.
DISTANT.
FADING.
I'M ALONE.

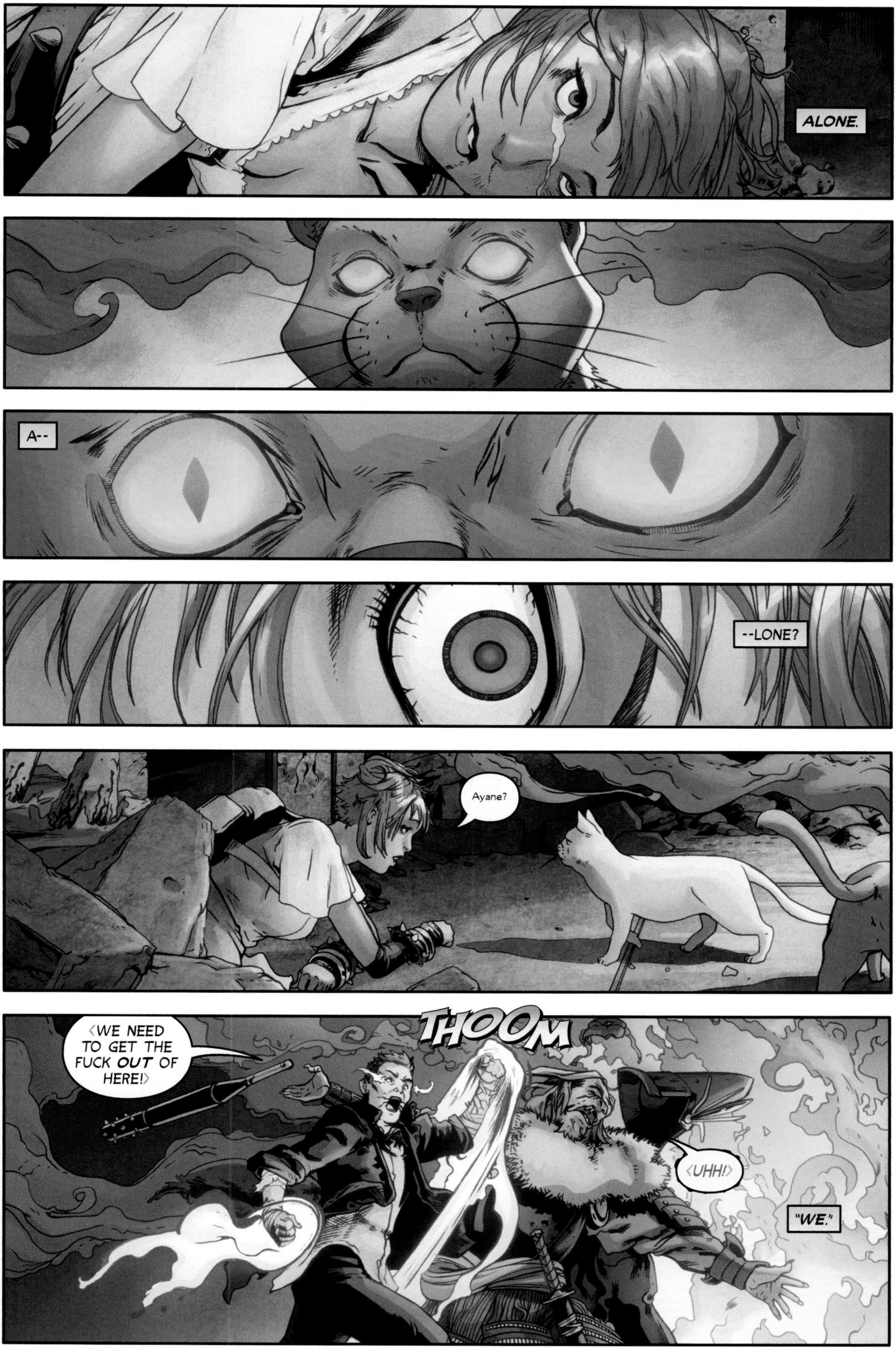
ALONE.
A--
--LONE?
Ayane?
THOOM
‹WE NEED TO GET THE FUCK OUT OF HERE!›
‹UHH!›
"WE."

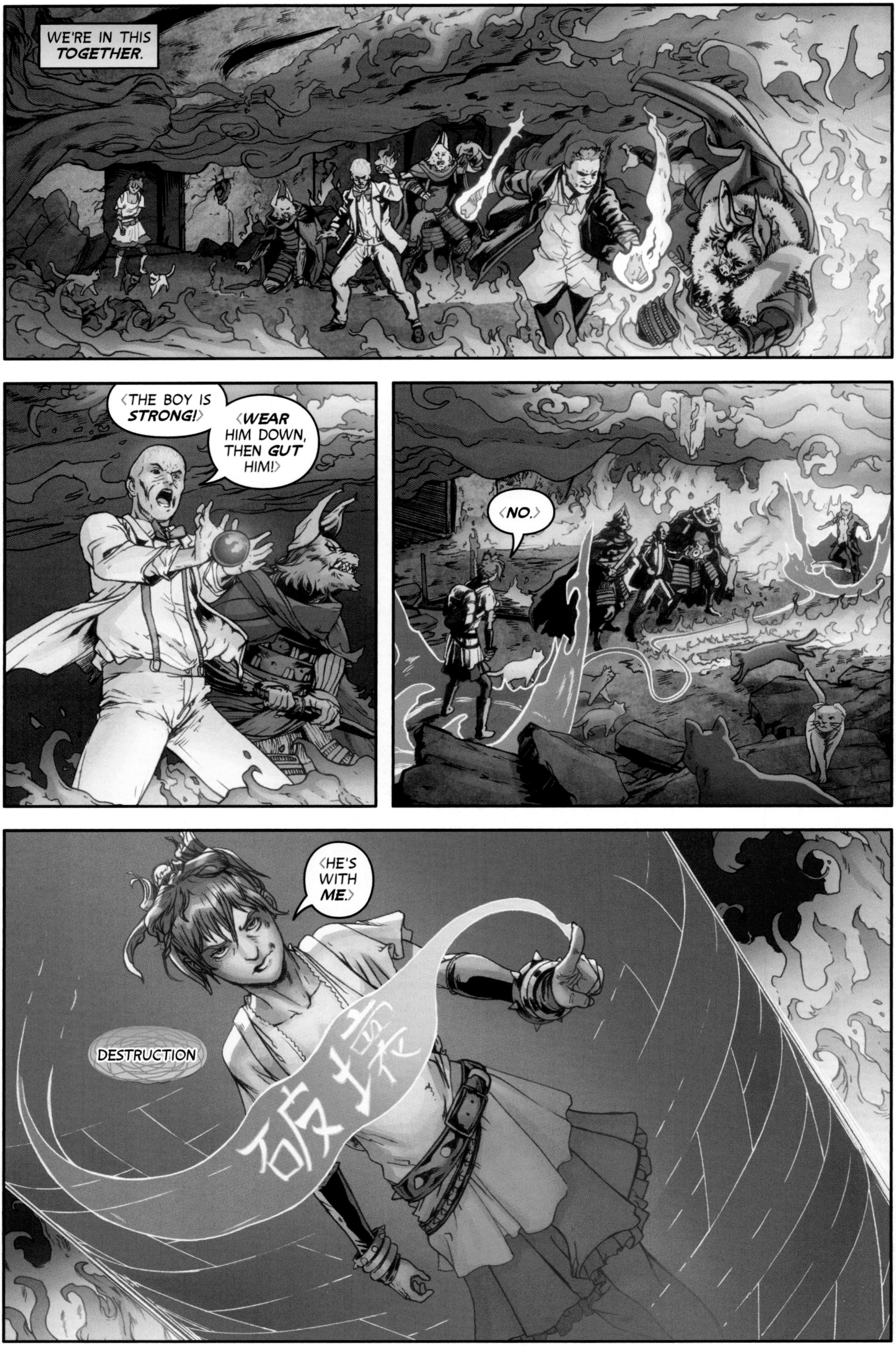

WE'RE IN THIS **TOGETHER**.
‹THE BOY IS **STRONG!**›
‹**WEAR** HIM DOWN, THEN **GUT** HIM!›
‹**NO.**›
‹HE'S WITH **ME.**›
DESTRUCTION
破壊

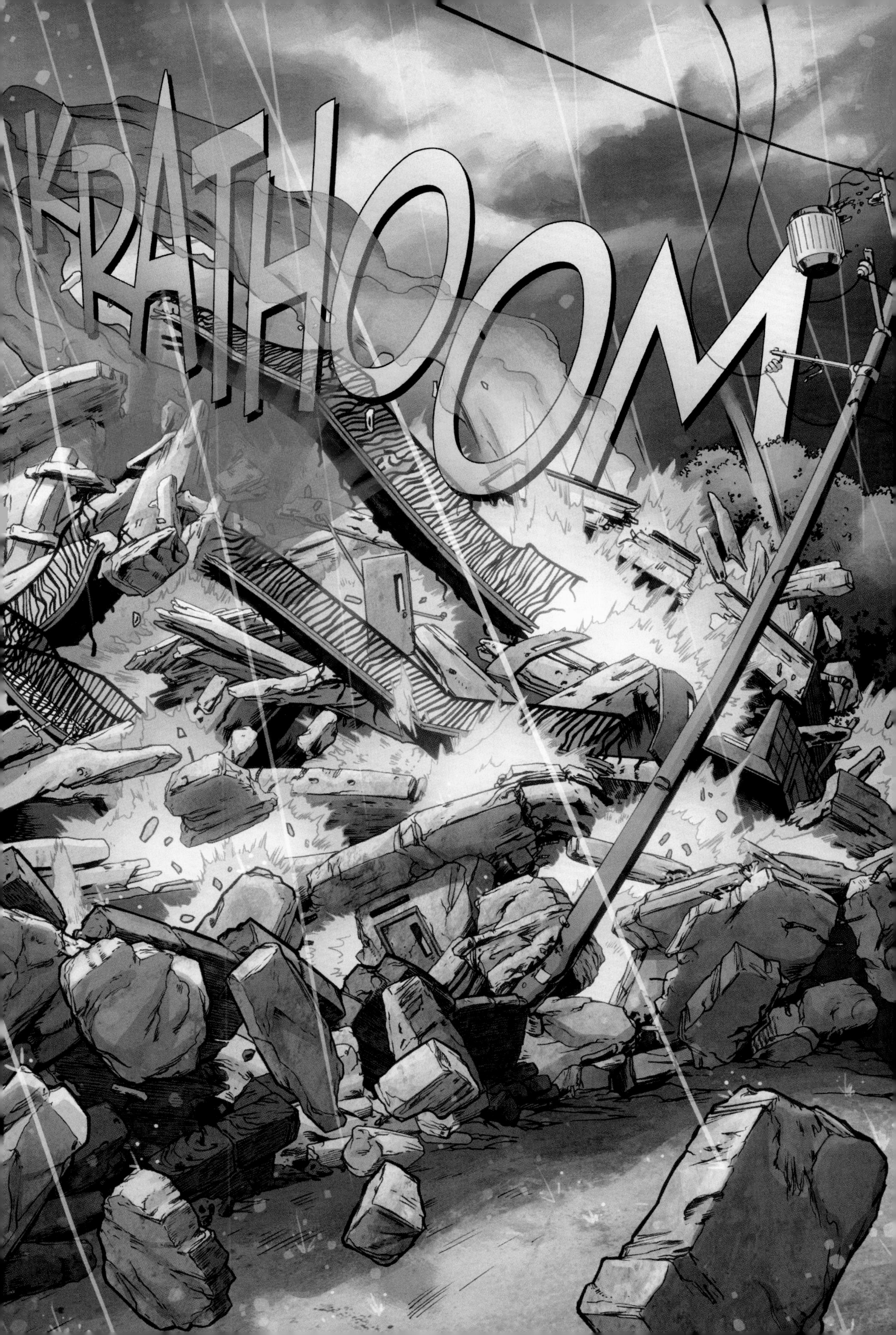
KRATHOOM

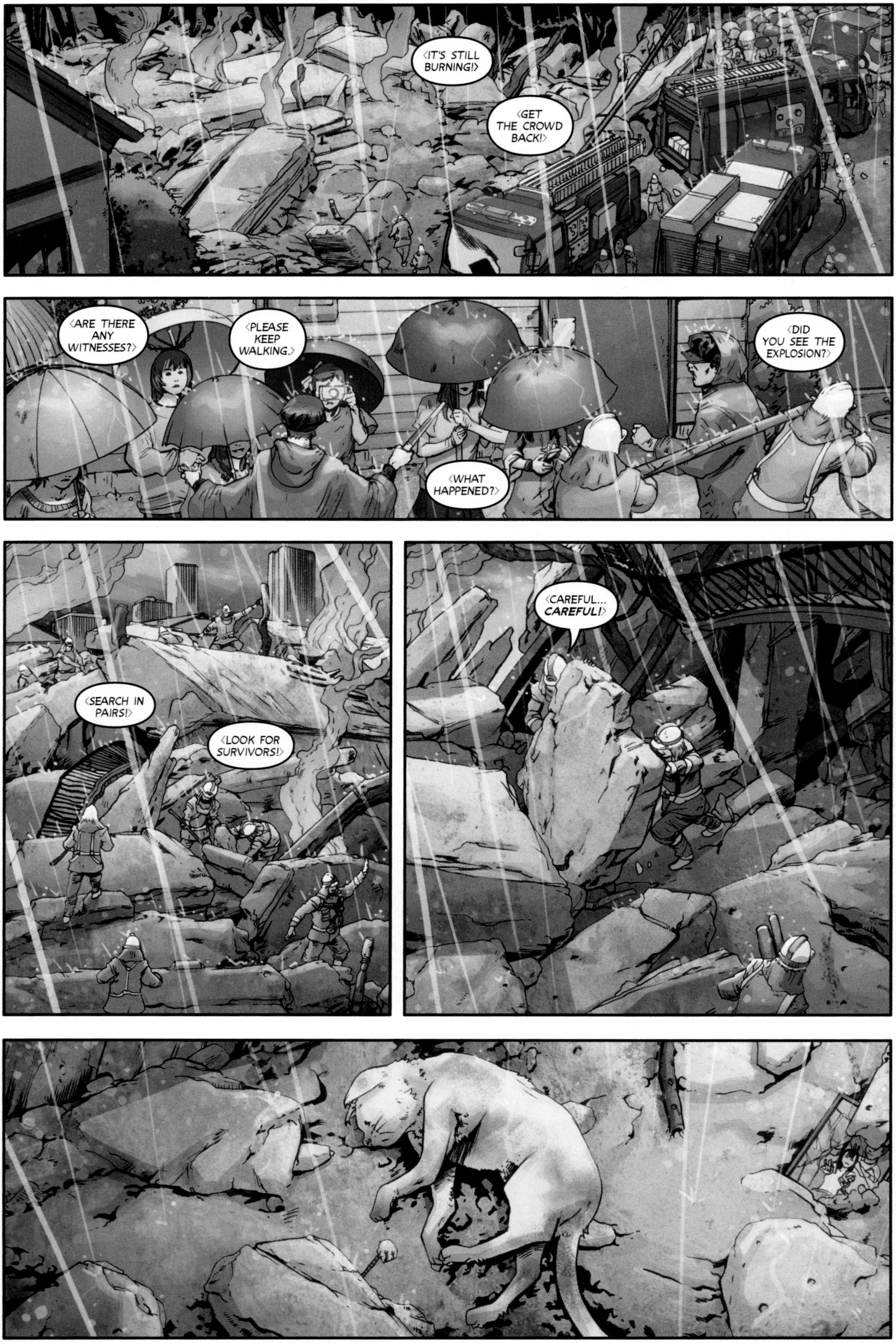

‹IT'S STILL BURNING!›
‹GET THE CROWD BACK!›
‹ARE THERE ANY WITNESSES?›
‹PLEASE KEEP WALKING.›
‹WHAT HAPPENED?›
‹DID YOU SEE THE EXPLOSION?›
‹SEARCH IN PAIRS!›
‹LOOK FOR SURVIVORS!›
‹CAREFUL... *CAREFUL!*›

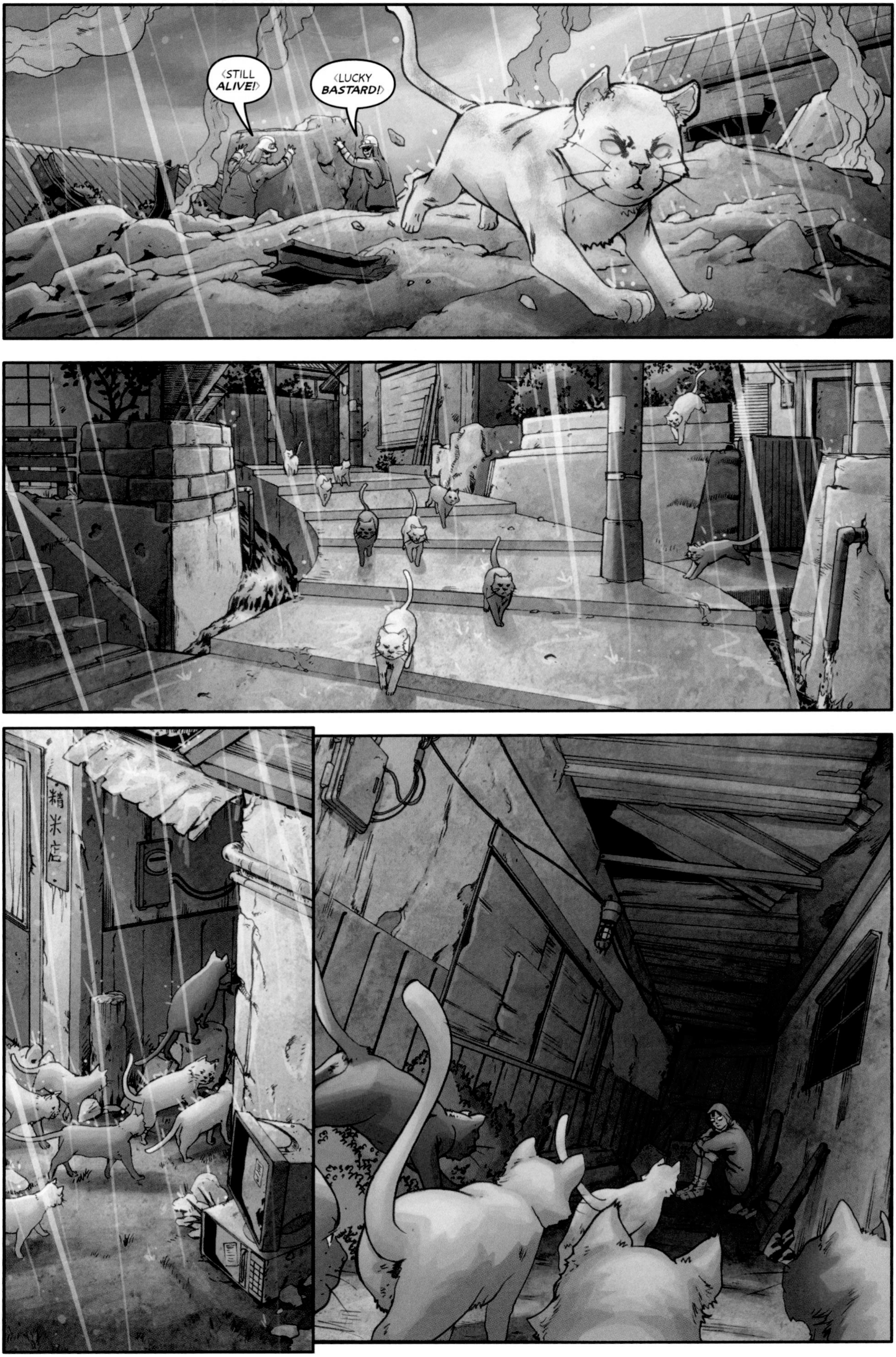
‹STILL ALIVE!›
‹LUCKY BASTARD!›
精米店

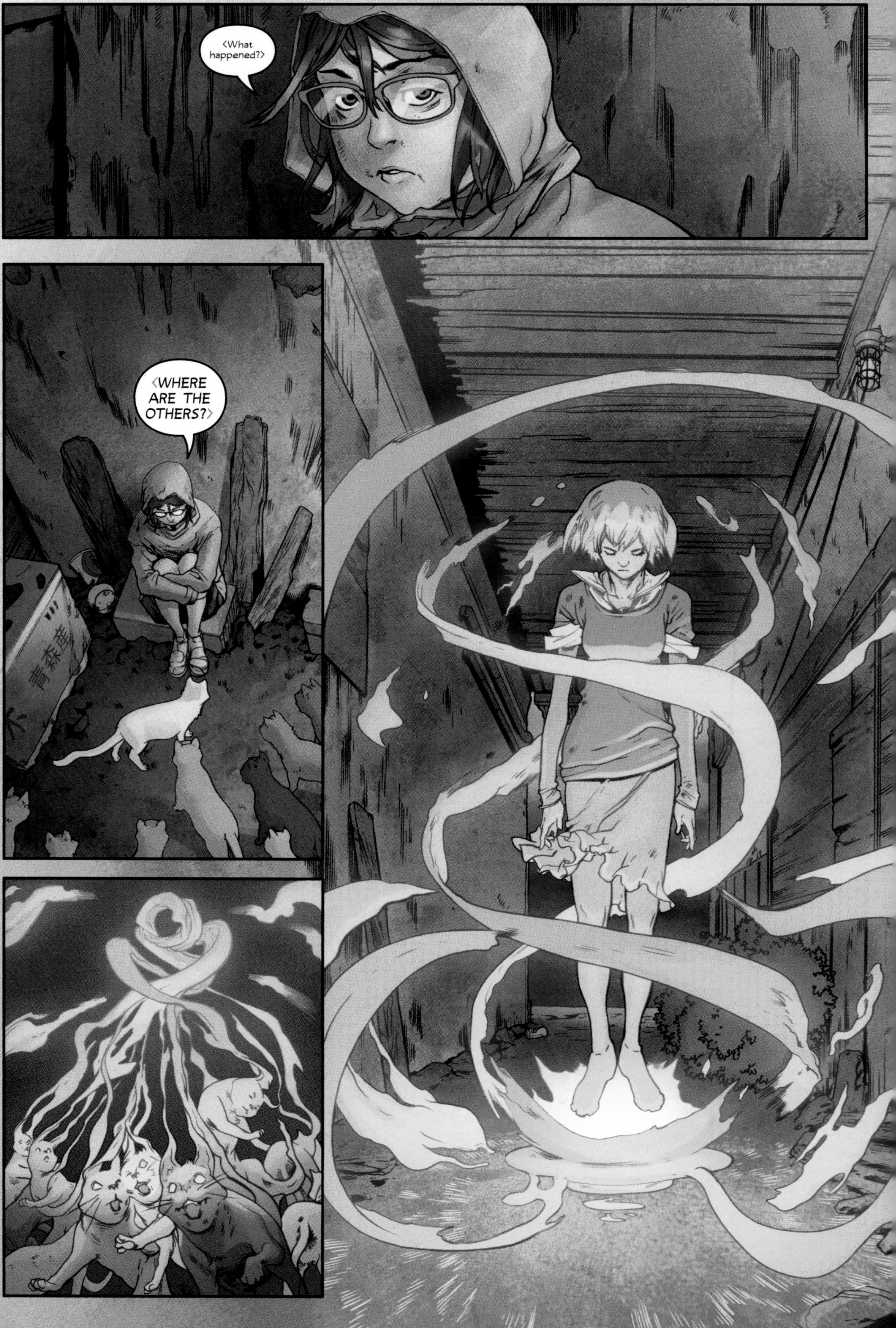
⟨What happened?⟩
⟨WHERE ARE THE OTHERS?⟩
青森産

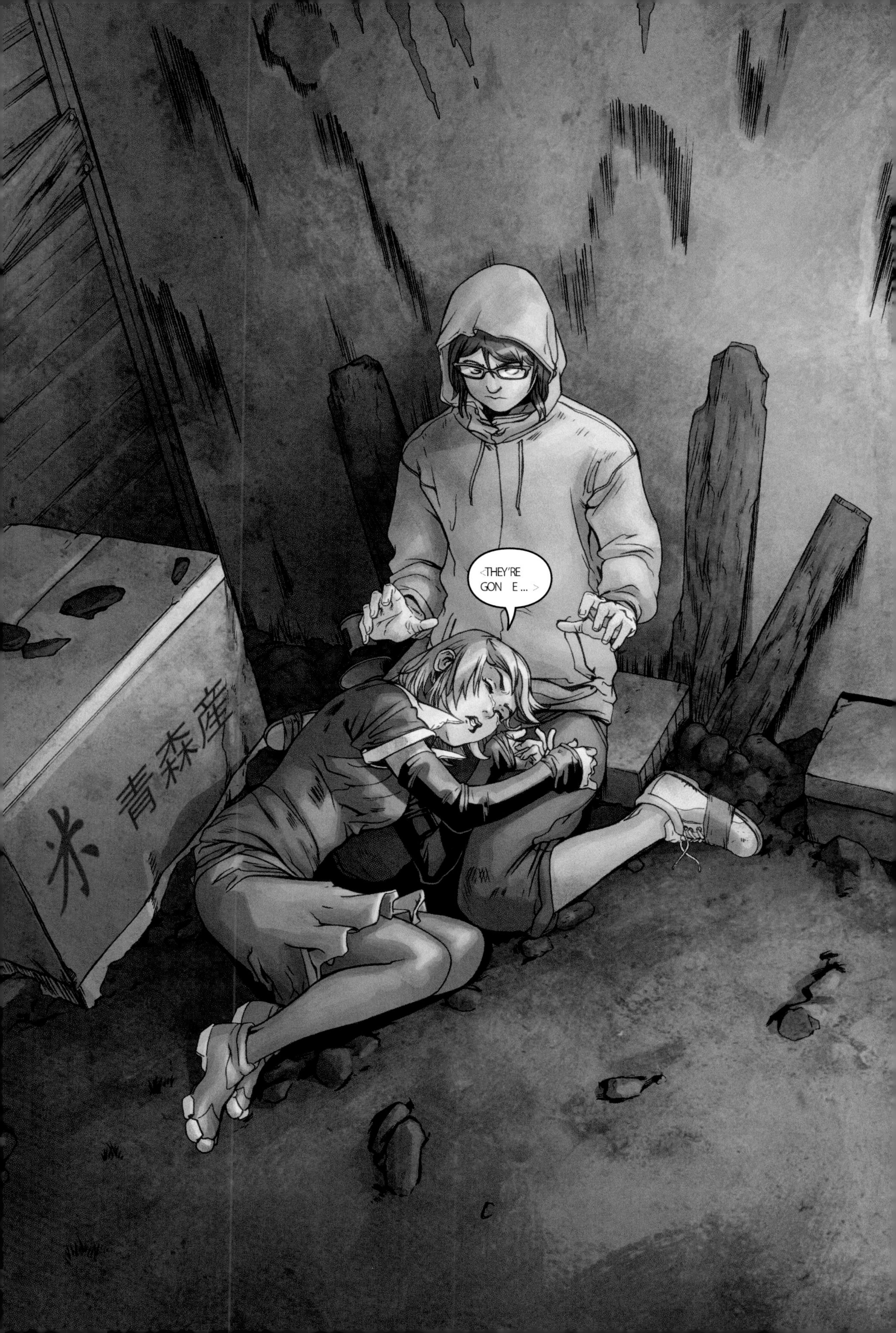

青森産
米
<THEY'RE GONE ...>

Chapter Six

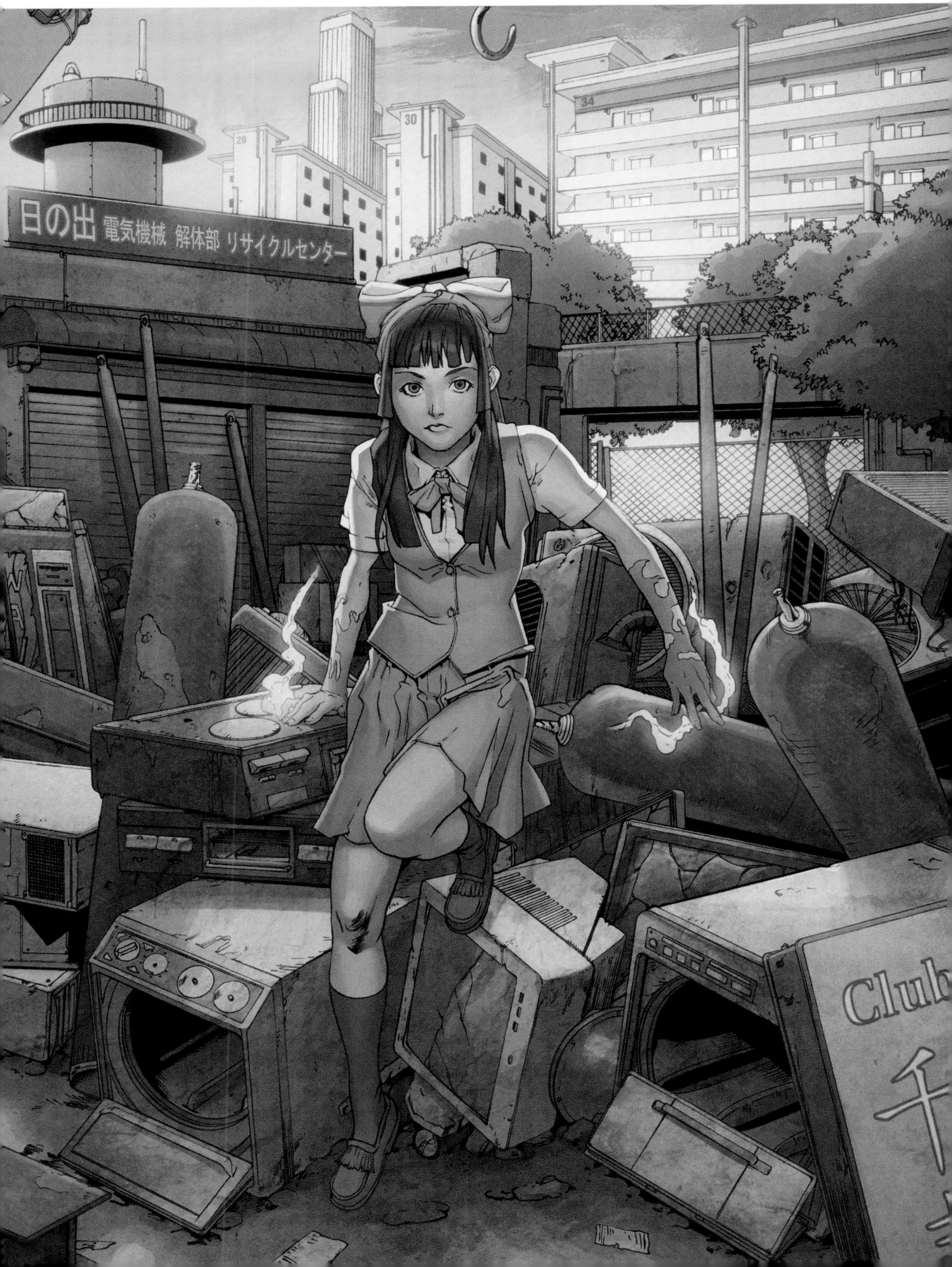
日の出 電気機械 解体部 リサイクルセンター
Club

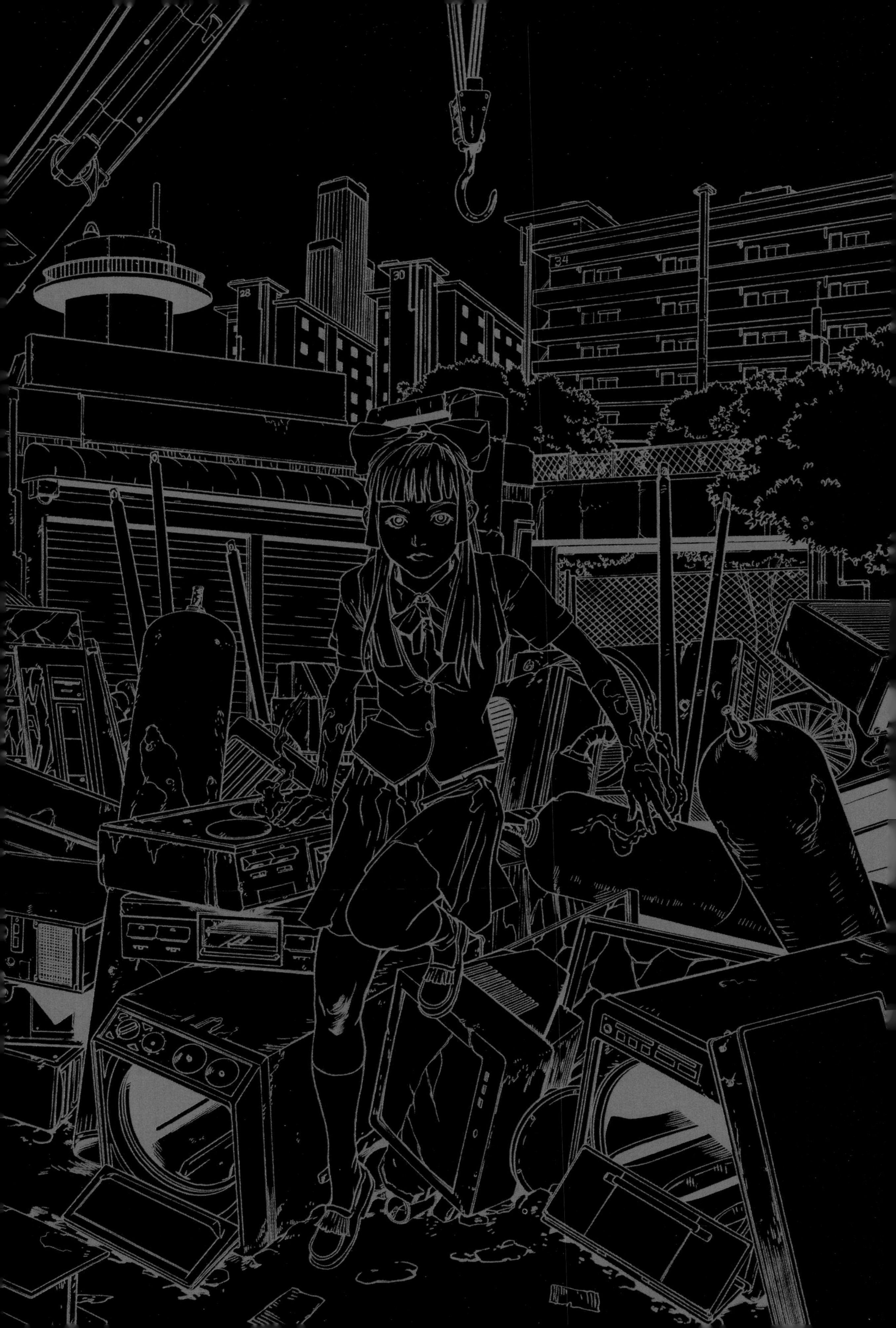
28
30
34

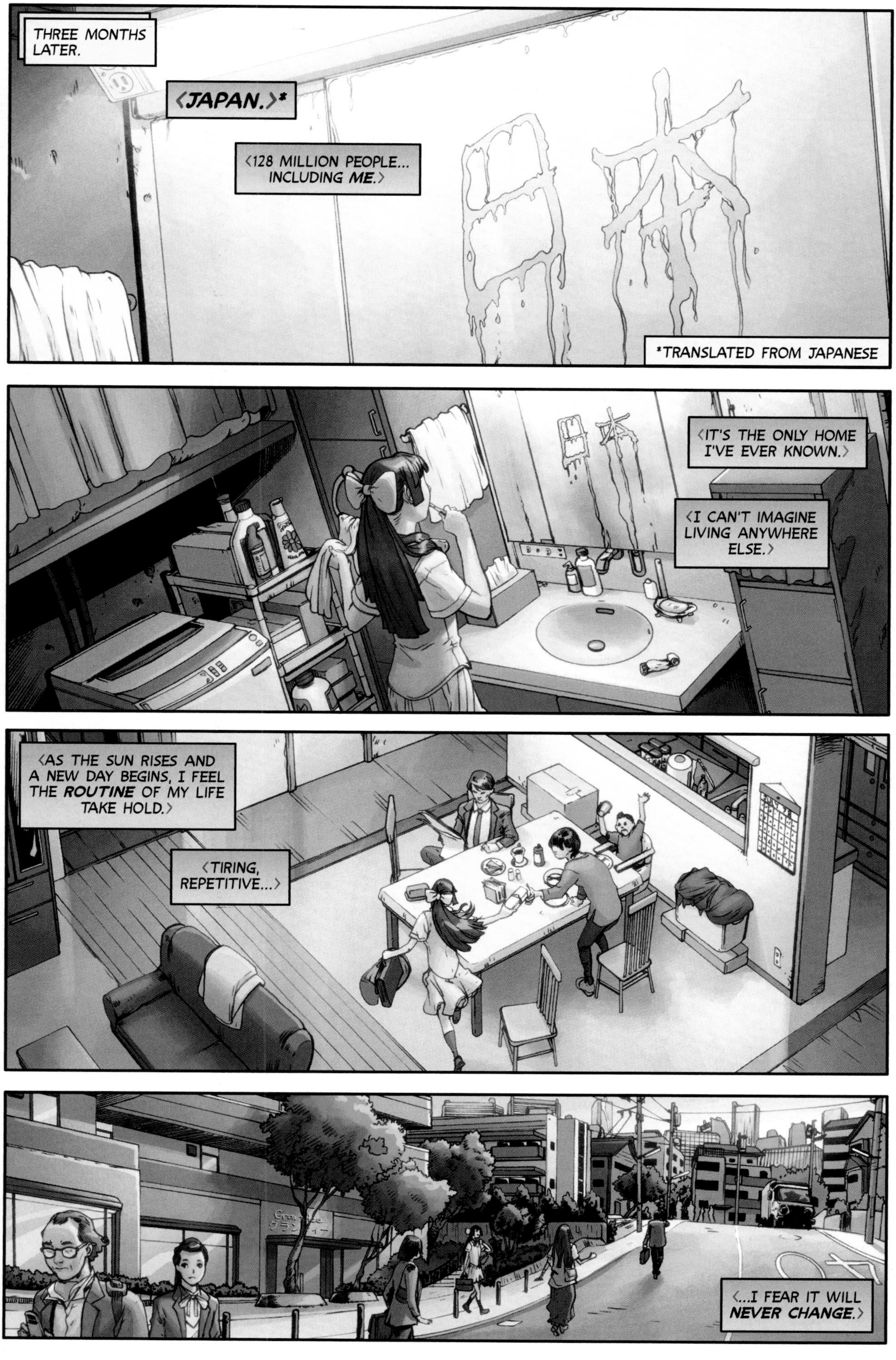
THREE MONTHS LATER.
⟨JAPAN.⟩*
⟨128 MILLION PEOPLE... INCLUDING ME.⟩
日本
*TRANSLATED FROM JAPANESE
⟨IT'S THE ONLY HOME I'VE EVER KNOWN.⟩
⟨I CAN'T IMAGINE LIVING ANYWHERE ELSE.⟩
⟨AS THE SUN RISES AND A NEW DAY BEGINS, I FEEL THE ROUTINE OF MY LIFE TAKE HOLD.⟩
⟨TIRING, REPETITIVE...⟩
⟨...I FEAR IT WILL NEVER CHANGE.⟩

⟨FATHER WORKS IN A CONSTRUCTION OFFICE.⟩

⟨MOTHER STAYS HOME TO TAKE CARE OF MY BABY BROTHER.⟩

⟨I'M THEIR DUTIFUL TEENAGE DAUGHTER.⟩

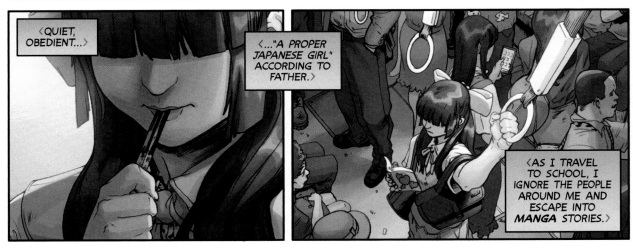

⟨QUIET, OBEDIENT...⟩

⟨..."A PROPER JAPANESE GIRL" ACCORDING TO FATHER.⟩

⟨AS I TRAVEL TO SCHOOL, I IGNORE THE PEOPLE AROUND ME AND ESCAPE INTO MANGA STORIES.⟩

⟨THE GIRLS ARE SO BEAUTIFUL. THEIR LIVES ARE EXCITING.⟩

⟨I SECRETLY WANT TO BE LIKE THEM.⟩

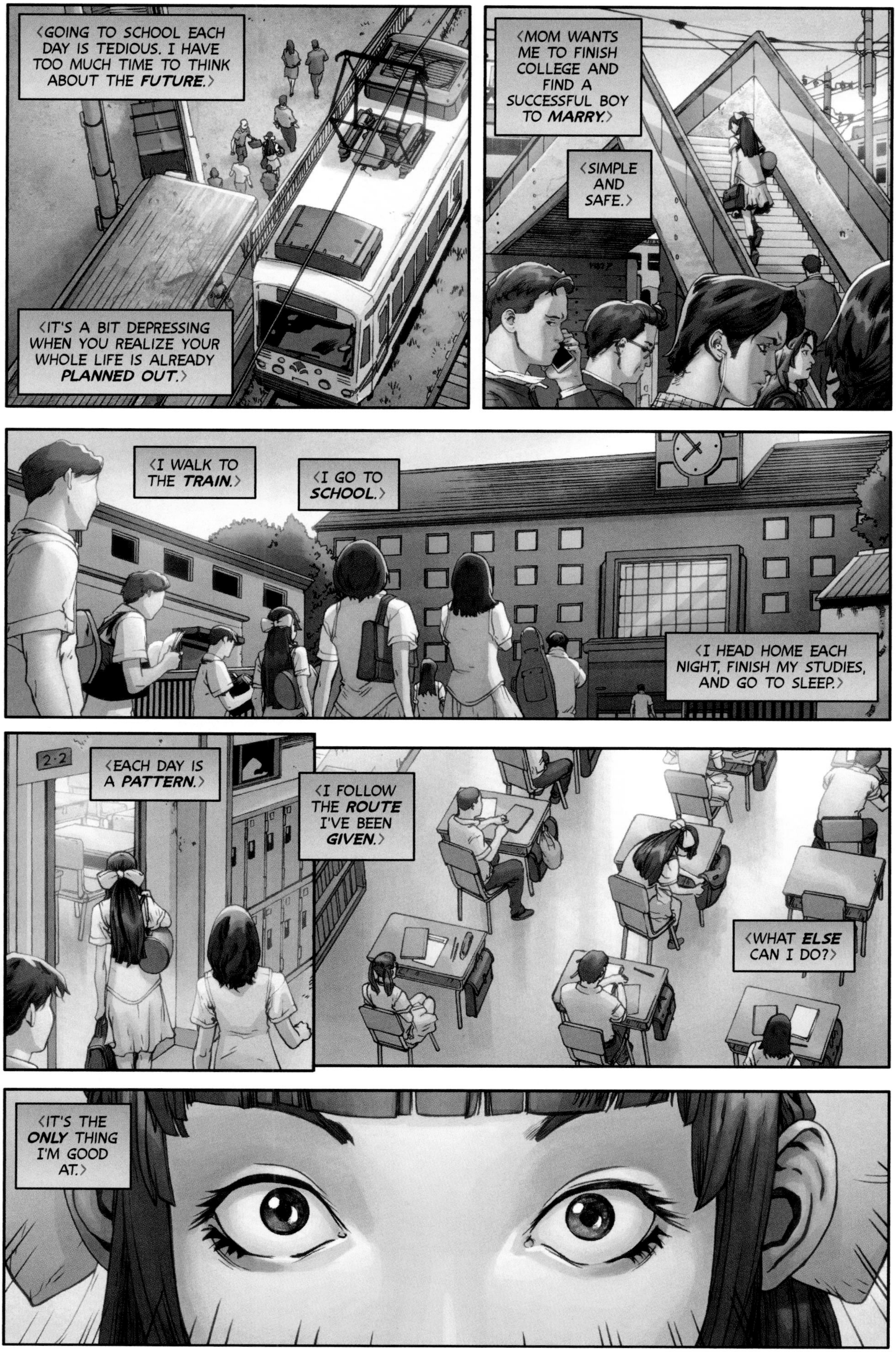
‹GOING TO SCHOOL EACH DAY IS TEDIOUS. I HAVE TOO MUCH TIME TO THINK ABOUT THE ***FUTURE.***›
‹IT'S A BIT DEPRESSING WHEN YOU REALIZE YOUR WHOLE LIFE IS ALREADY ***PLANNED OUT.***›
‹MOM WANTS ME TO FINISH COLLEGE AND FIND A SUCCESSFUL BOY TO ***MARRY.***›
‹SIMPLE AND SAFE.›
‹I WALK TO THE ***TRAIN.***›
‹I GO TO ***SCHOOL.***›
‹I HEAD HOME EACH NIGHT, FINISH MY STUDIES, AND GO TO SLEEP.›
2-2
‹EACH DAY IS A ***PATTERN.***›
‹I FOLLOW THE ***ROUTE*** I'VE BEEN ***GIVEN.***›
‹WHAT ***ELSE*** CAN I DO?›
‹IT'S THE ***ONLY*** THING I'M GOOD AT.›

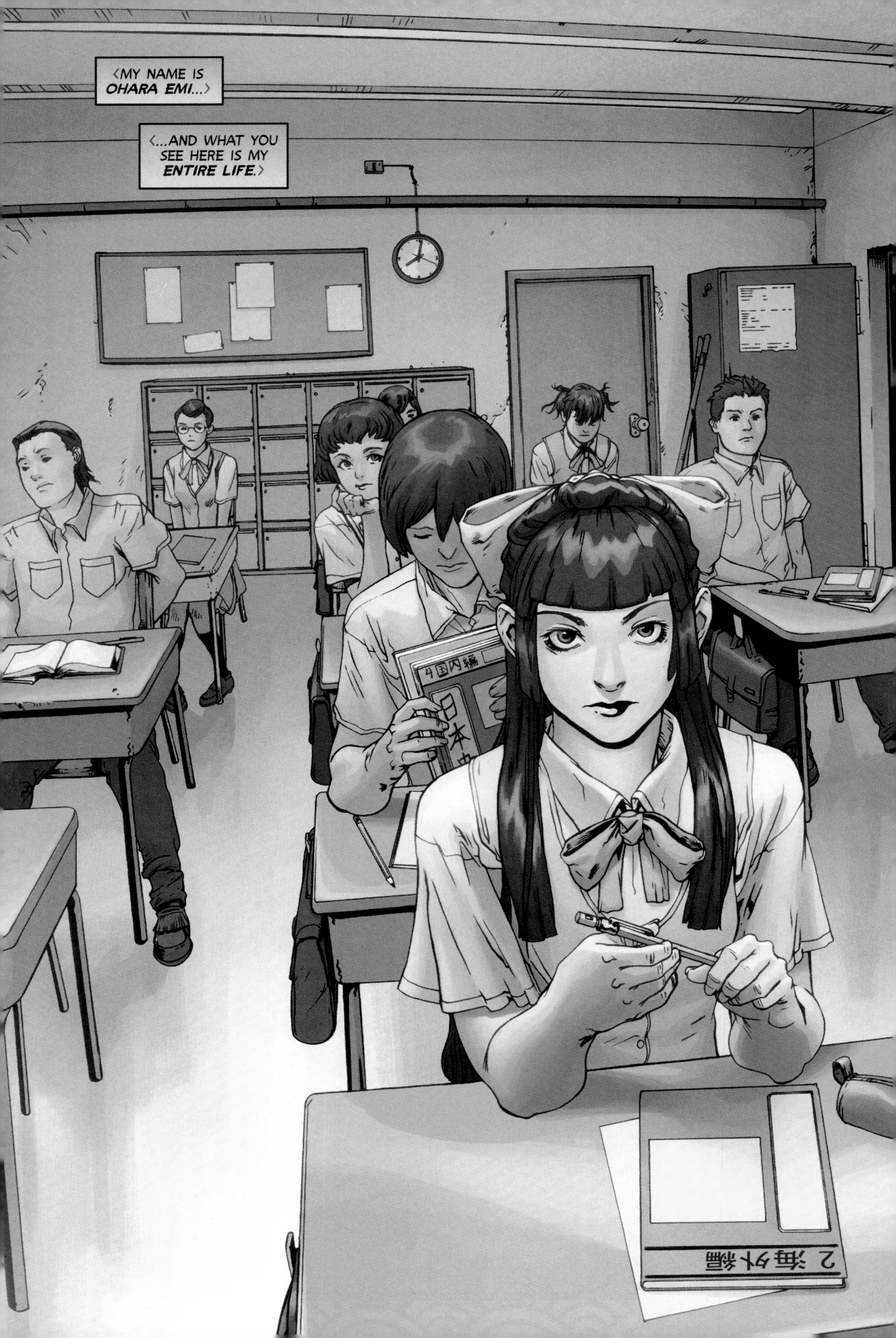
<MY NAME IS OHARA EMI...>
<...AND WHAT YOU SEE HERE IS MY ENTIRE LIFE.>
4国内編

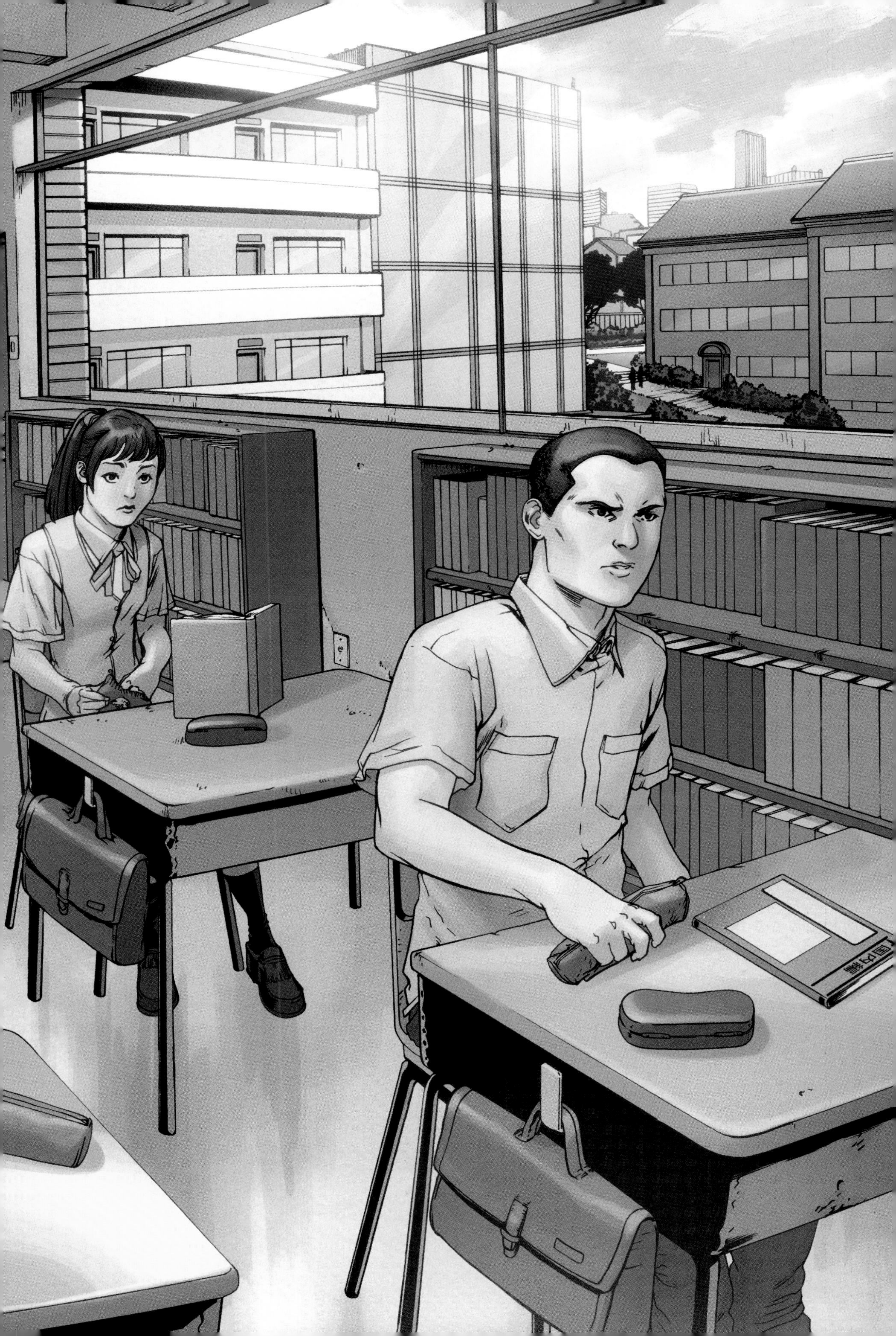

〈AT LUNCHTIME, MY FRIENDS SHARE GOSSIP OR PINE OVER BOYS.〉

〈DID YOU KNOW THEY'RE STILL SEARCHING FOR THOSE TWO *MISSING STUDENTS?*〉

〈WHO?〉

〈I THINK THE FOREIGN GIRL'S NAME WAS *"LORI."* THE ONE IN *7-B.*〉

〈YEAH. I HEARD SHE AND THAT UGLY BOY FELL IN *LOVE* AND WENT ON A *MURDER CRIME SPREE.*〉

〈THEY BLEW UP HER APARTMENT BUILDING WITH *EXPLOSIVES* AND RAN AWAY TOGETHER TO THE AOKIGAHARA *SUICIDE FOREST.*〉

〈*NO WAY!*〉

〈I HEARD THAT *TOO!*〉

〈SO *SCARY!*〉

〈UH... PARDON ME.〉

〈EH?〉

〈OHARA, YOU *OKAY?*〉

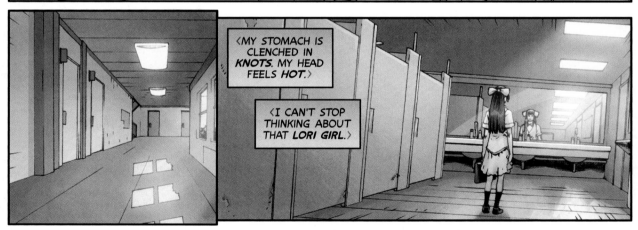

〈MY STOMACH IS CLENCHED IN *KNOTS.* MY HEAD FEELS *HOT.*〉

〈I CAN'T STOP THINKING ABOUT THAT *LORI GIRL.*〉

〈I MET HER ONCE, JUST IN PASSING.〉

〈EX- EXCUSE ME...〉

〈OH!〉

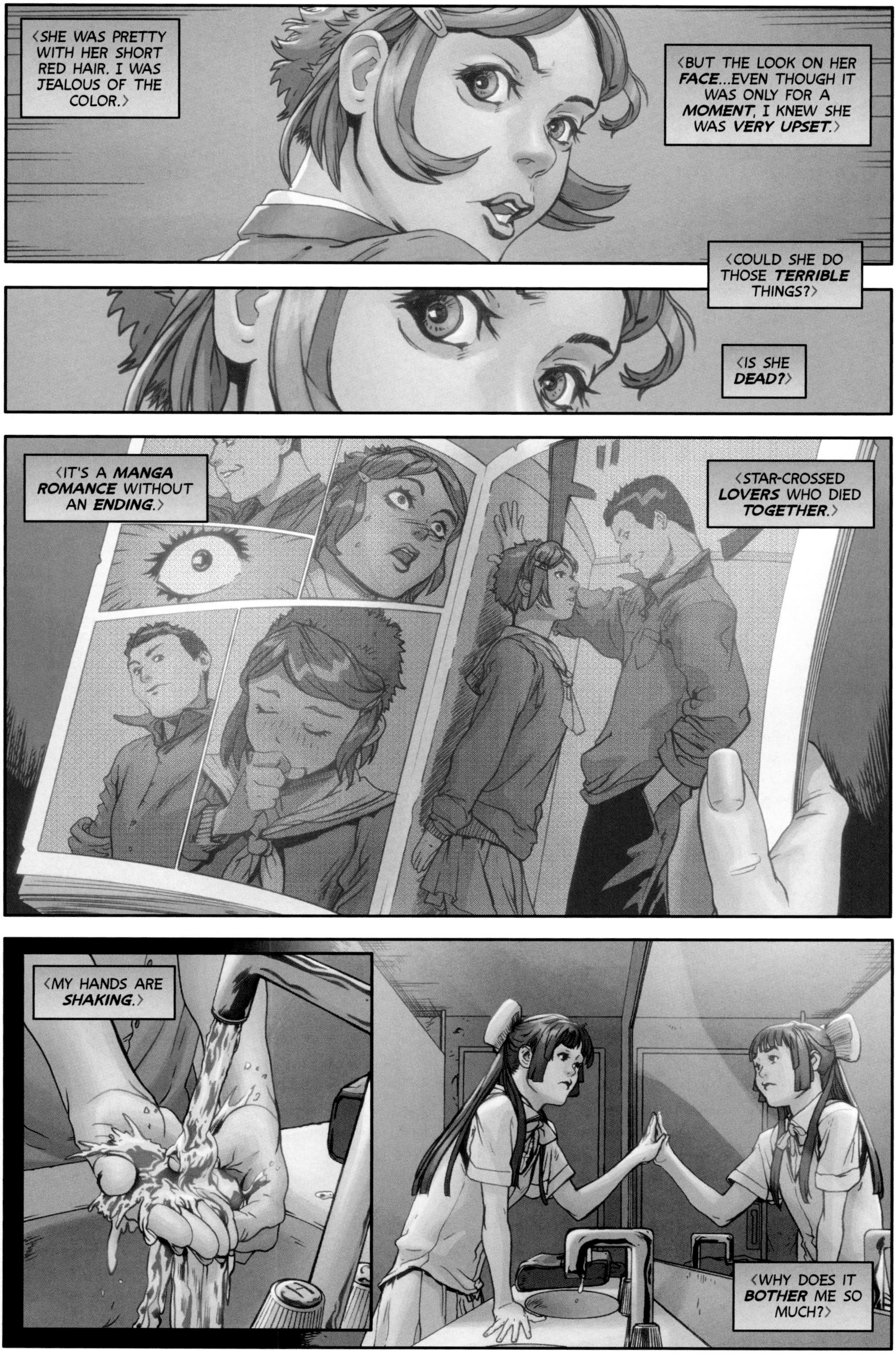
‹SHE WAS PRETTY WITH HER SHORT RED HAIR. I WAS JEALOUS OF THE COLOR.›
‹BUT THE LOOK ON HER FACE...EVEN THOUGH IT WAS ONLY FOR A MOMENT, I KNEW SHE WAS VERY UPSET.›
‹COULD SHE DO THOSE TERRIBLE THINGS?›
‹IS SHE DEAD?›
‹IT'S A MANGA ROMANCE WITHOUT AN ENDING.›
‹STAR-CROSSED LOVERS WHO DIED TOGETHER.›
‹MY HANDS ARE SHAKING.›
‹WHY DOES IT BOTHER ME SO MUCH?›

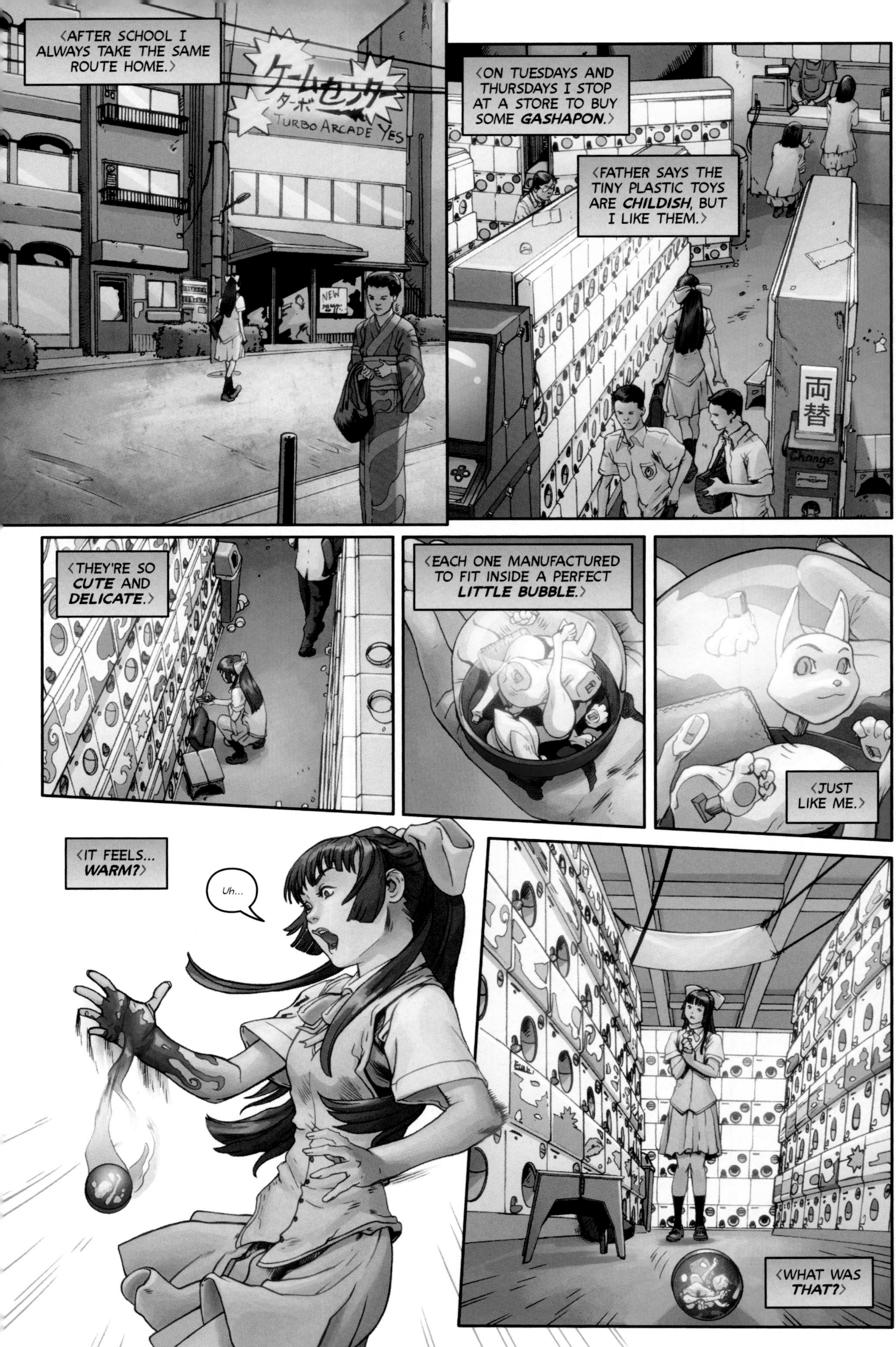
‹AFTER SCHOOL I ALWAYS TAKE THE SAME ROUTE HOME.›
ゲームセンター
ターボ
TURBO ARCADE
YES
NEW
‹ON TUESDAYS AND THURSDAYS I STOP AT A STORE TO BUY SOME **GASHAPON**.›
‹FATHER SAYS THE TINY PLASTIC TOYS ARE **CHILDISH**, BUT I LIKE THEM.›
両替
Change
‹THEY'RE SO **CUTE** AND **DELICATE**.›
‹EACH ONE MANUFACTURED TO FIT INSIDE A PERFECT **LITTLE BUBBLE**.›
‹JUST LIKE ME.›
‹IT FEELS... **WARM?**›
Uh...
‹WHAT WAS **THAT?**›

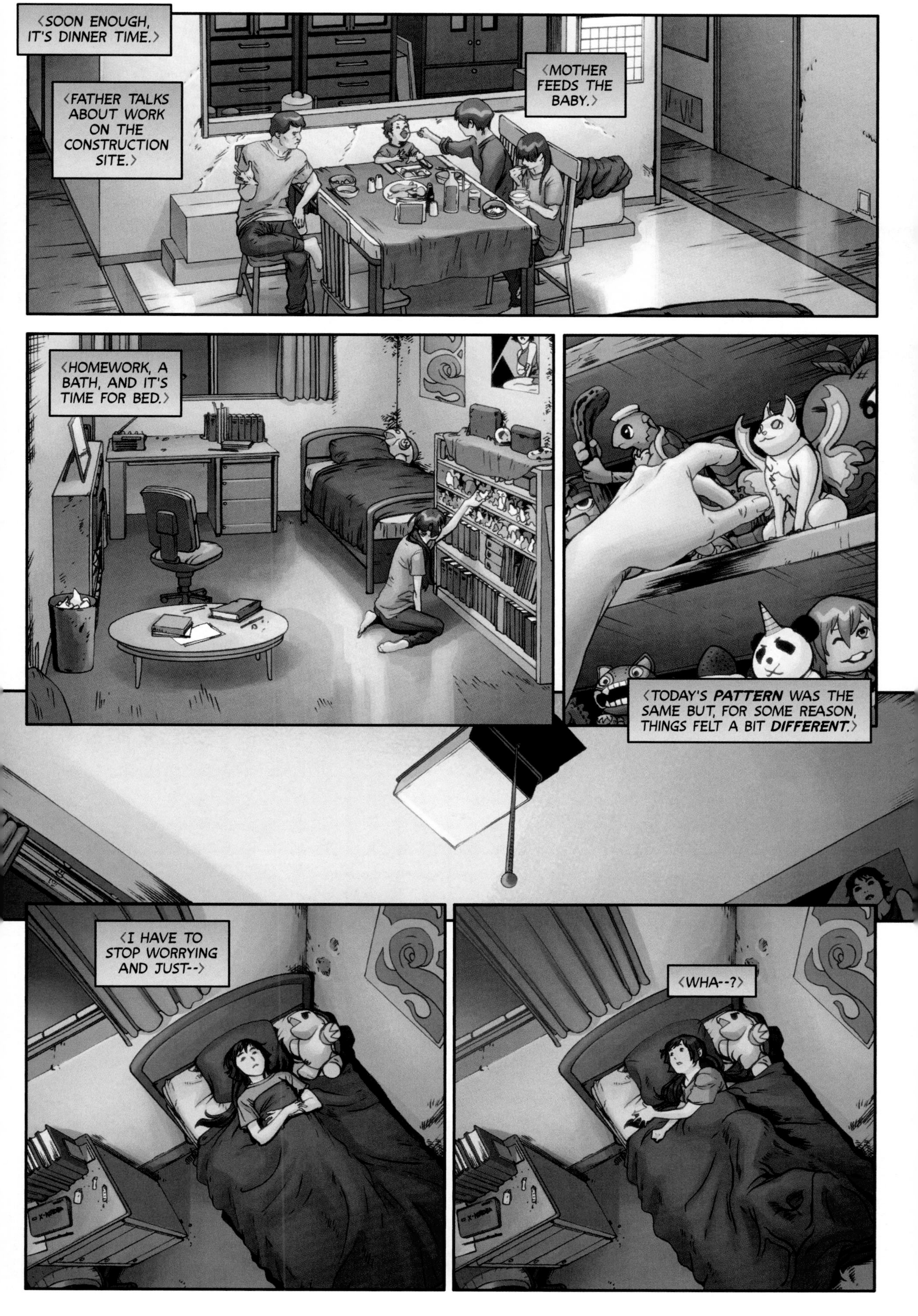
‹SOON ENOUGH, IT'S DINNER TIME.›
‹FATHER TALKS ABOUT WORK ON THE CONSTRUCTION SITE.›
‹MOTHER FEEDS THE BABY.›
‹HOMEWORK, A BATH, AND IT'S TIME FOR BED.›
‹TODAY'S PATTERN WAS THE SAME BUT, FOR SOME REASON, THINGS FELT A BIT DIFFERENT.›
‹I HAVE TO STOP WORRYING AND JUST--›
‹WHA--?›

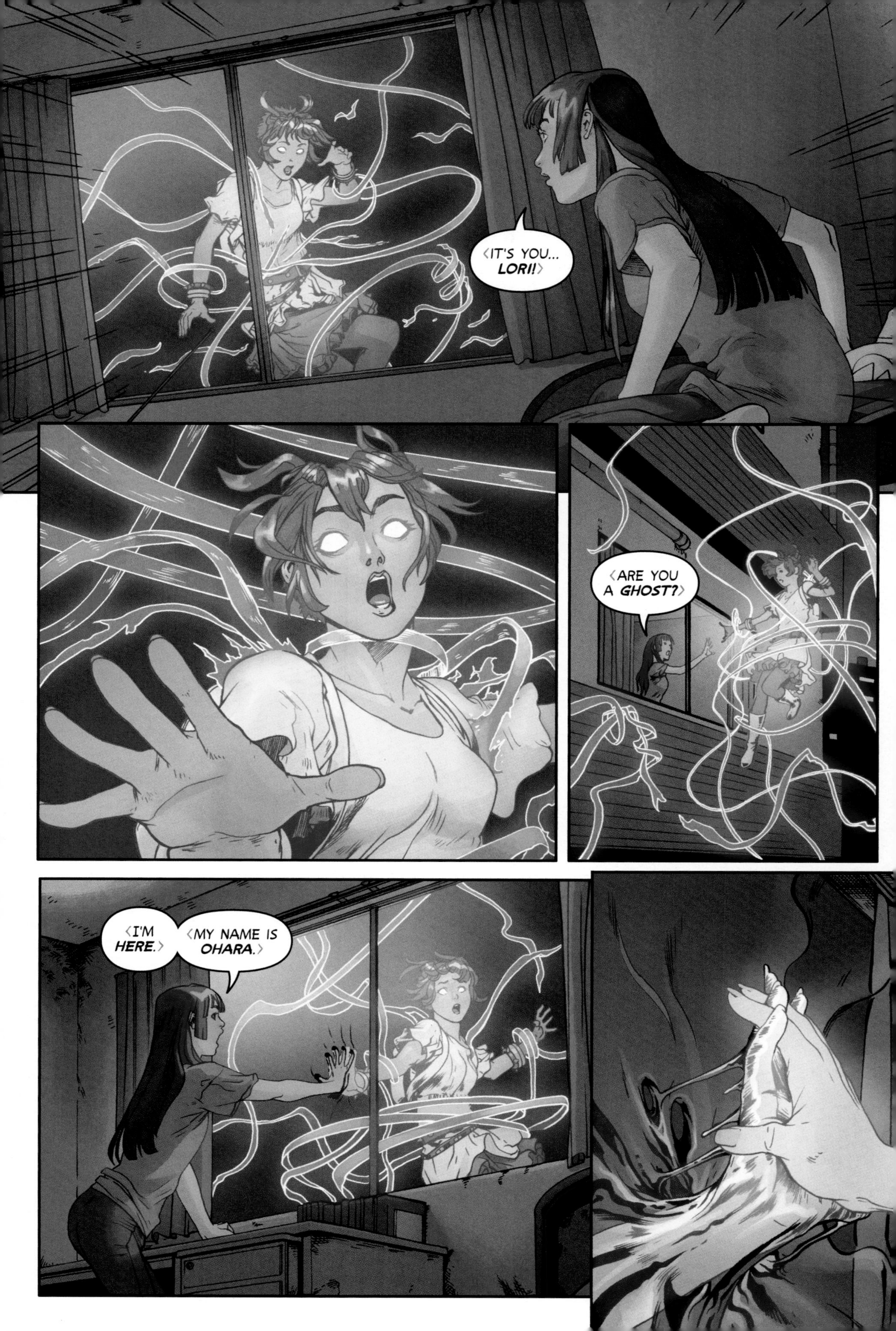
<IT'S YOU... LORI!>
<ARE YOU A GHOST?>
<I'M HERE.>
<MY NAME IS OHARA.>

⟨Huh?⟩

⟨IT'S **MORNING.**⟩

⟨Wha...⟩

⟨What happened?⟩

⟨**EMI-DEAR,** IT'S TIME TO **GET UP!**⟩

⟨YES, MOTHER, I **KNOW!**⟩

⟨WAS... WAS THAT A **DREAM?**⟩

⟨LORI'S GHOST...IT FELT SO **REAL.**⟩

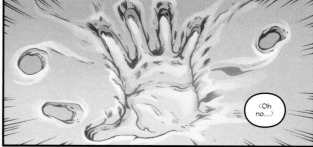

⟨Oh no...⟩

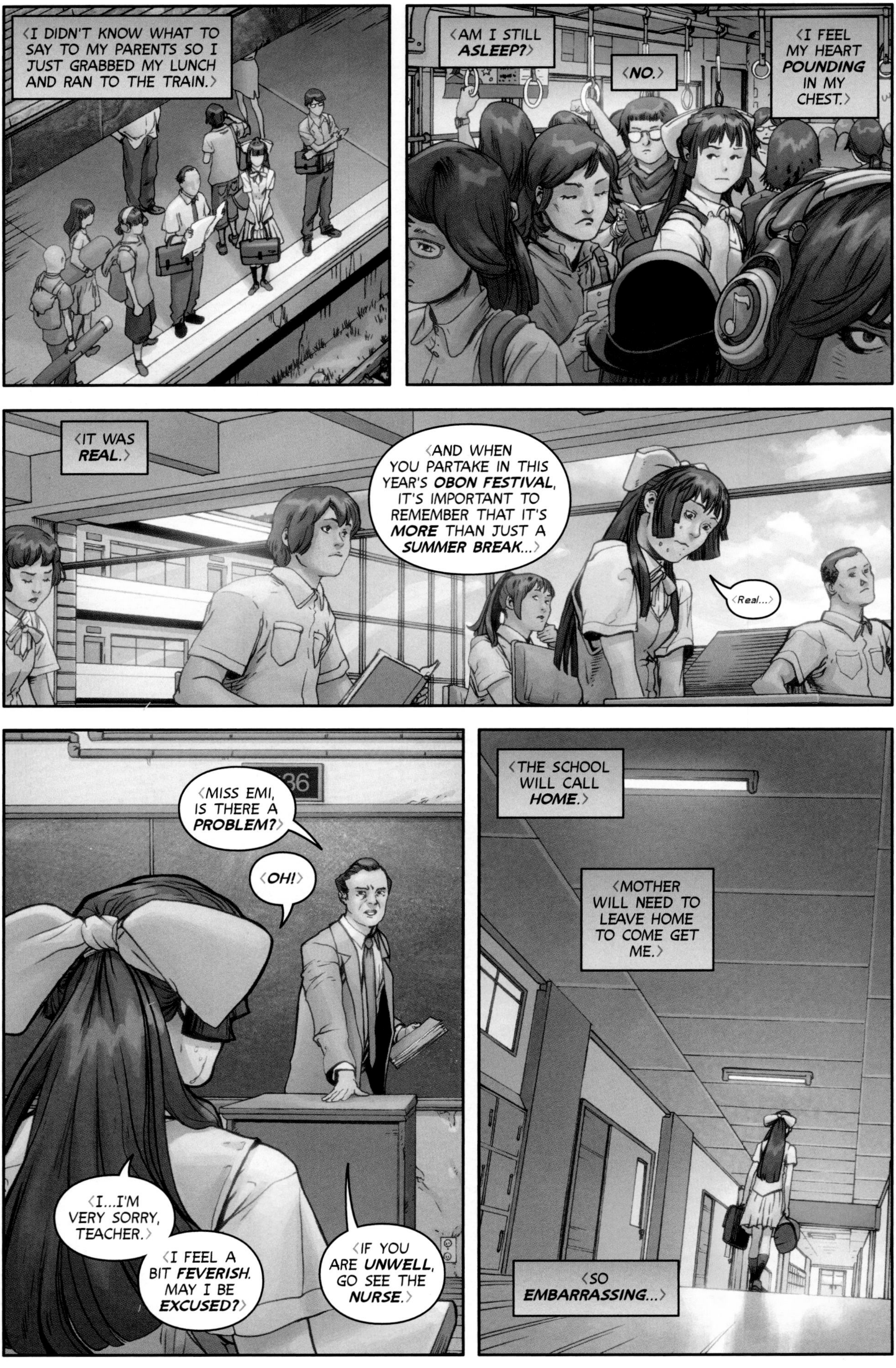
⟨I DIDN'T KNOW WHAT TO SAY TO MY PARENTS SO I JUST GRABBED MY LUNCH AND RAN TO THE TRAIN.⟩
⟨AM I STILL ASLEEP?⟩
⟨NO.⟩
⟨I FEEL MY HEART POUNDING IN MY CHEST.⟩
⟨IT WAS REAL.⟩
⟨AND WHEN YOU PARTAKE IN THIS YEAR'S OBON FESTIVAL, IT'S IMPORTANT TO REMEMBER THAT IT'S MORE THAN JUST A SUMMER BREAK...⟩
⟨Real...⟩
36
⟨MISS EMI, IS THERE A PROBLEM?⟩
⟨OH!⟩
⟨I...I'M VERY SORRY, TEACHER.⟩
⟨I FEEL A BIT FEVERISH. MAY I BE EXCUSED?⟩
⟨IF YOU ARE UNWELL, GO SEE THE NURSE.⟩
⟨THE SCHOOL WILL CALL HOME.⟩
⟨MOTHER WILL NEED TO LEAVE HOME TO COME GET ME.⟩
⟨SO EMBARRASSING...⟩

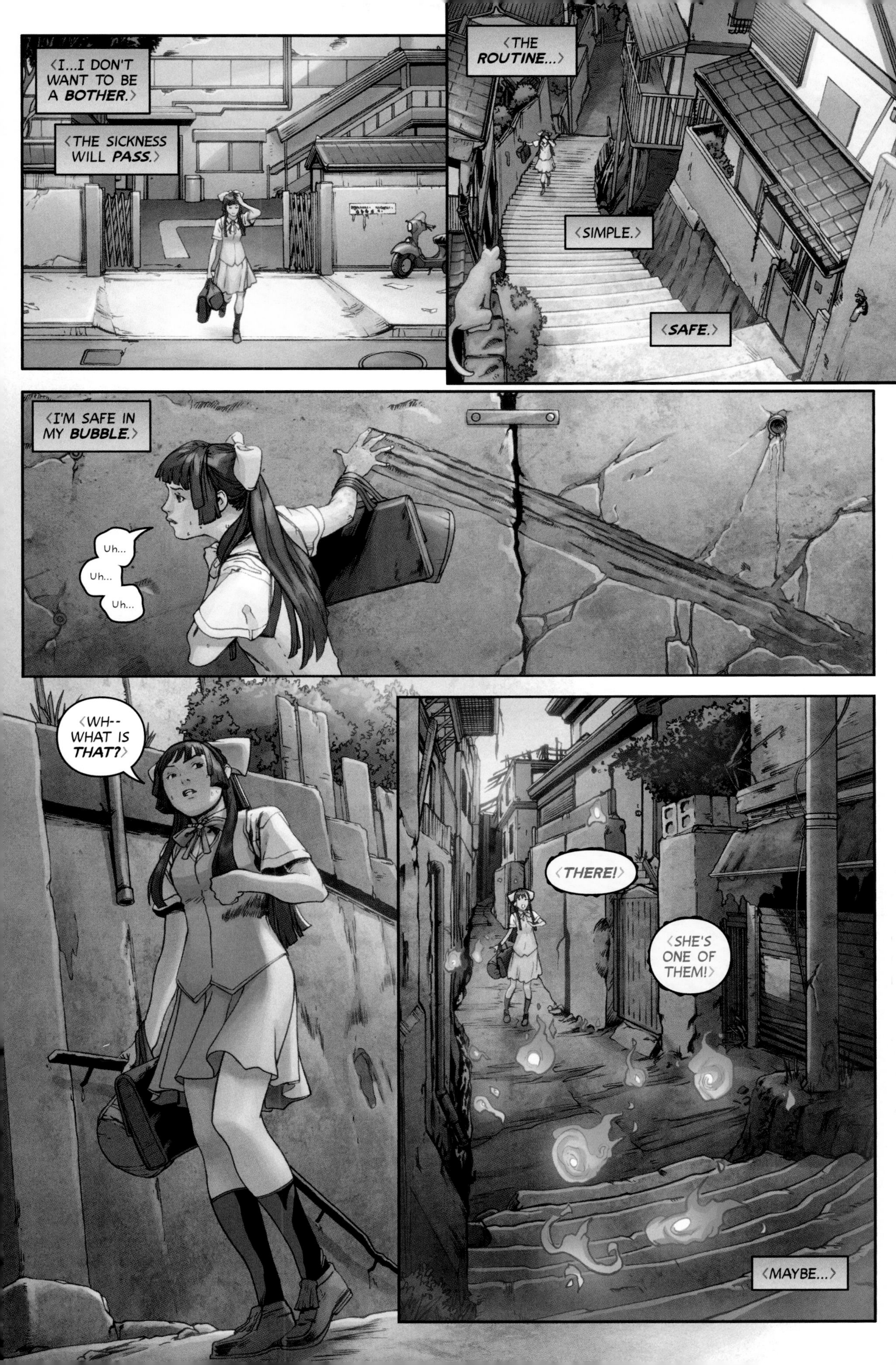
‹I...I DON'T WANT TO BE A *BOTHER*.›
‹THE SICKNESS WILL *PASS*.›
‹THE *ROUTINE*...›
‹SIMPLE.›
‹*SAFE*.›
‹I'M SAFE IN MY *BUBBLE*.›
Uh...
Uh...
Uh...
‹WH-- WHAT IS *THAT?*›
‹*THERE!*›
‹SHE'S ONE OF THEM!›
‹MAYBE...›

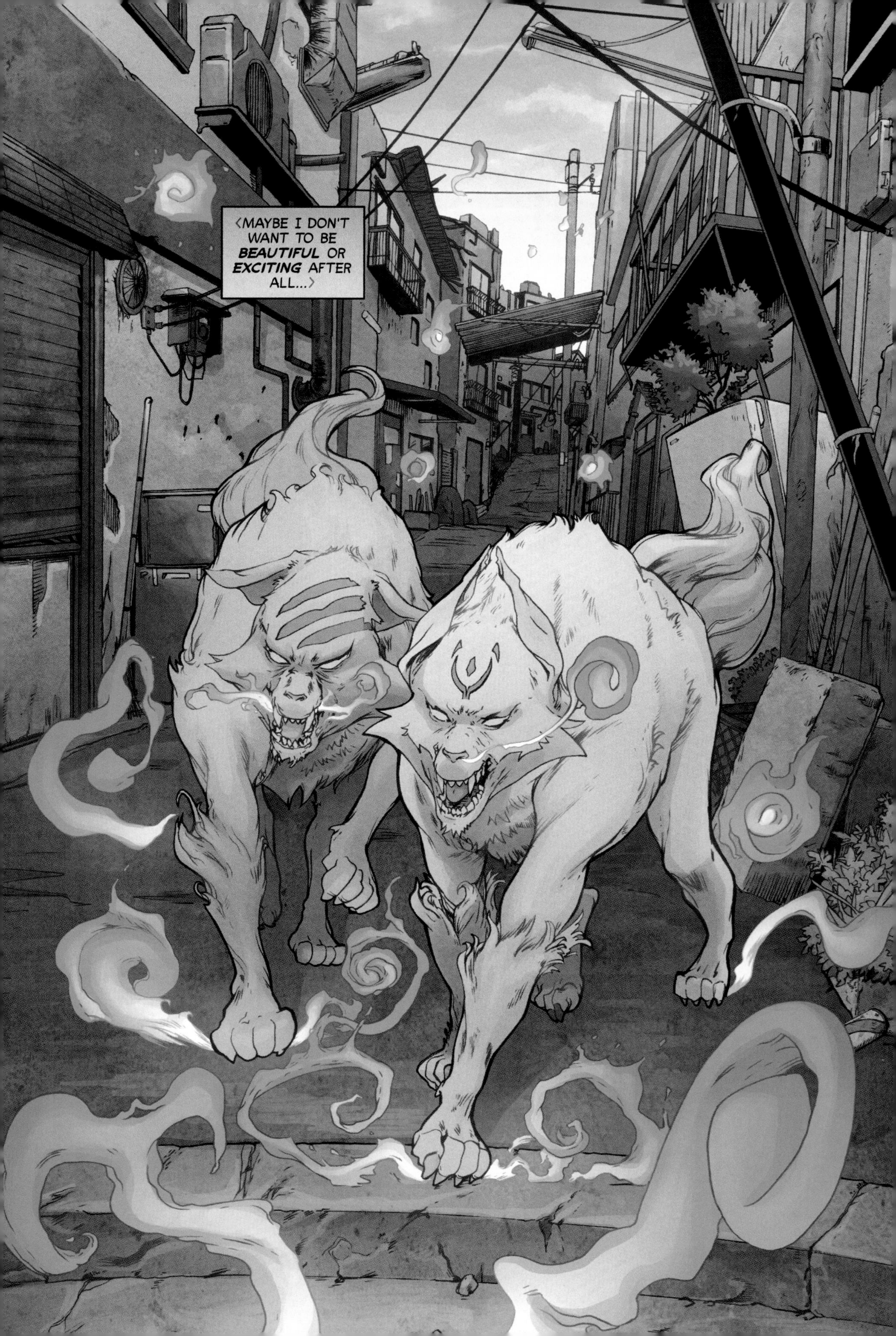
<MAYBE I DON'T WANT TO BE **BEAUTIFUL** OR **EXCITING** AFTER ALL...>

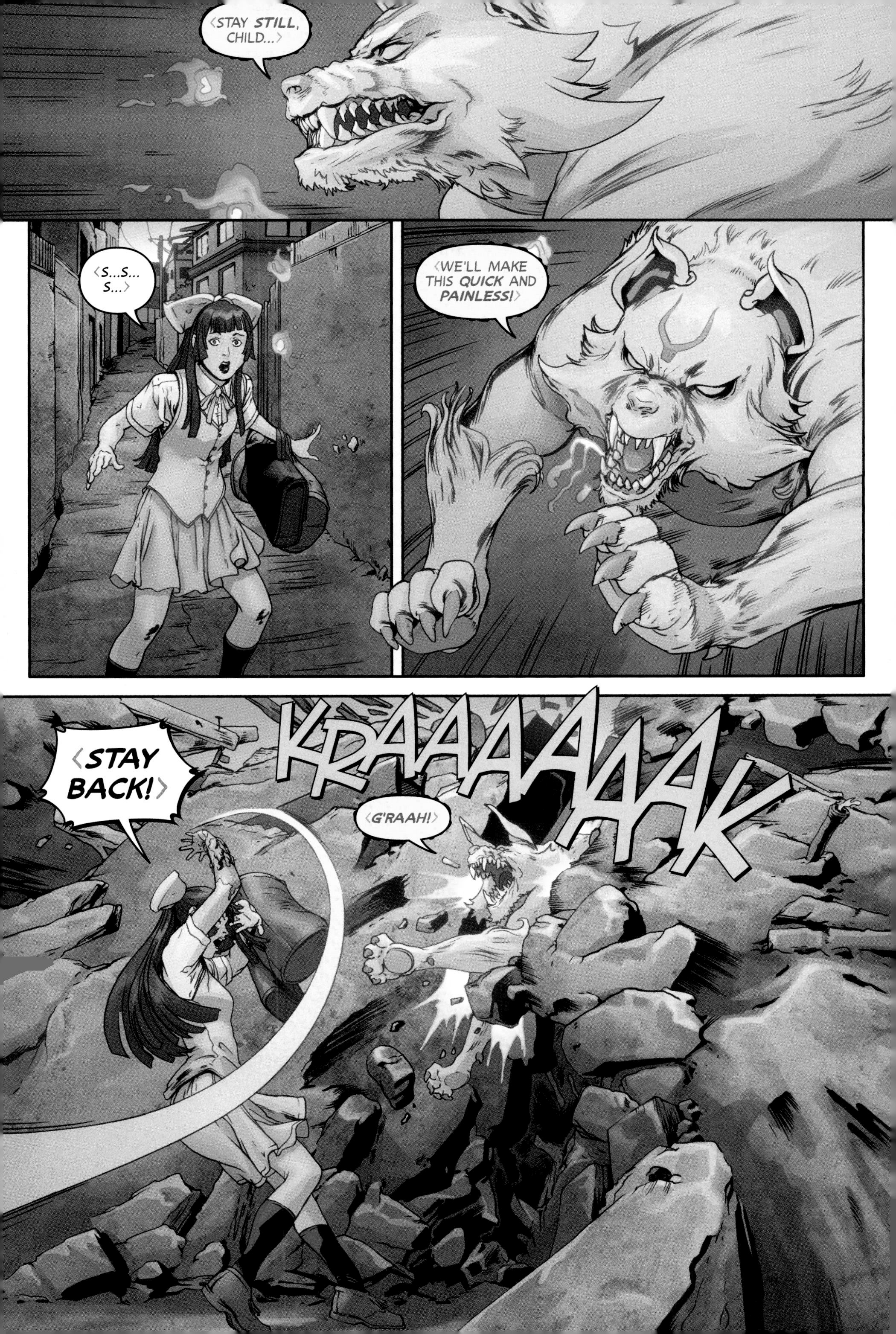
⟨STAY STILL, CHILD...⟩
⟨S...S... S...⟩
⟨WE'LL MAKE THIS QUICK AND PAINLESS!⟩
⟨STAY BACK!⟩
KRAAAAAAAK
⟨G'RAAH!⟩

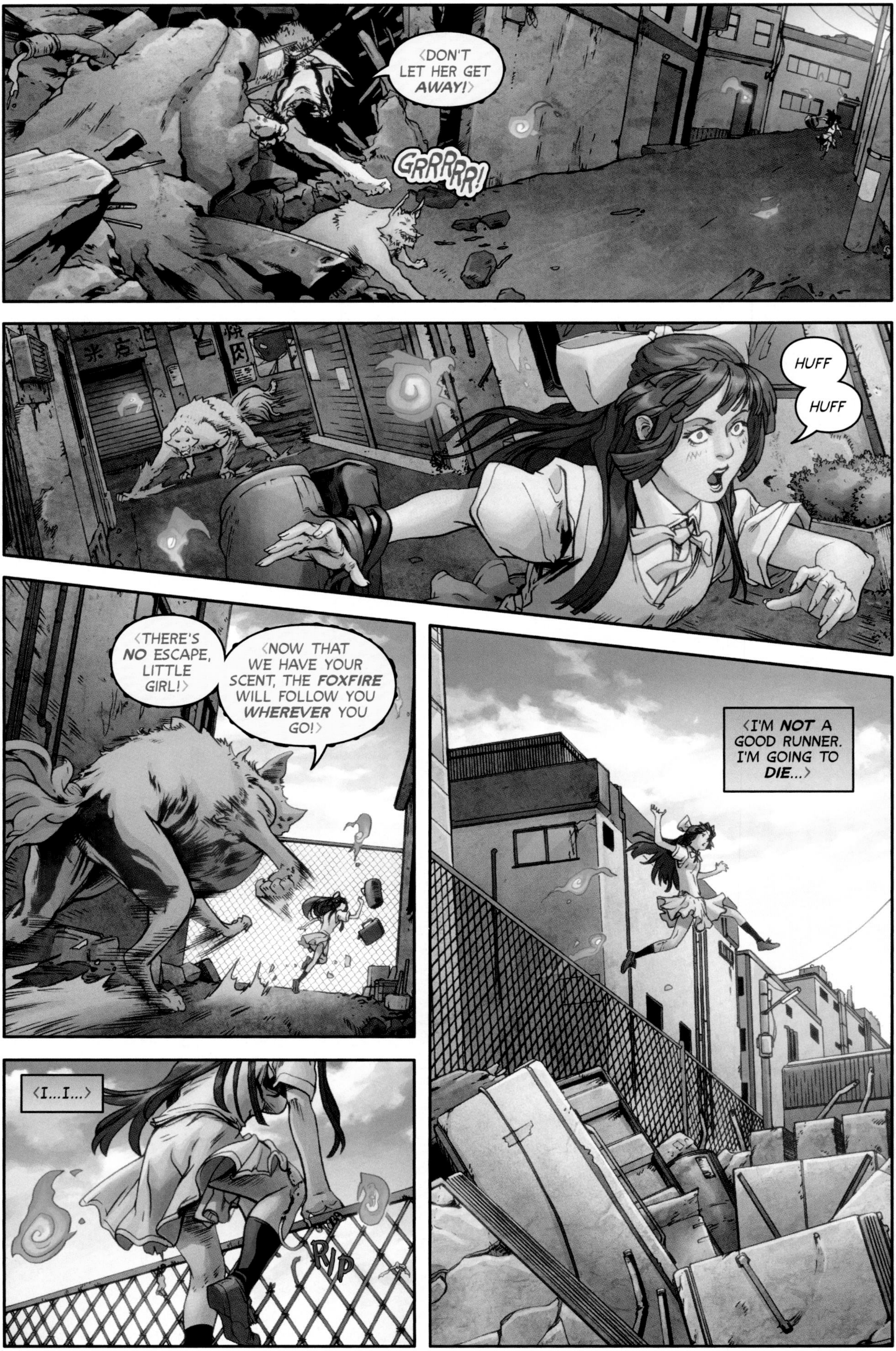
‹DON'T LET HER GET AWAY!›
GRRRRR!
HUFF
HUFF
‹THERE'S NO ESCAPE, LITTLE GIRL!›
‹NOW THAT WE HAVE YOUR SCENT, THE FOXFIRE WILL FOLLOW YOU WHEREVER YOU GO!›
‹I...I...›
RIP
‹I'M NOT A GOOD RUNNER. I'M GOING TO DIE...›

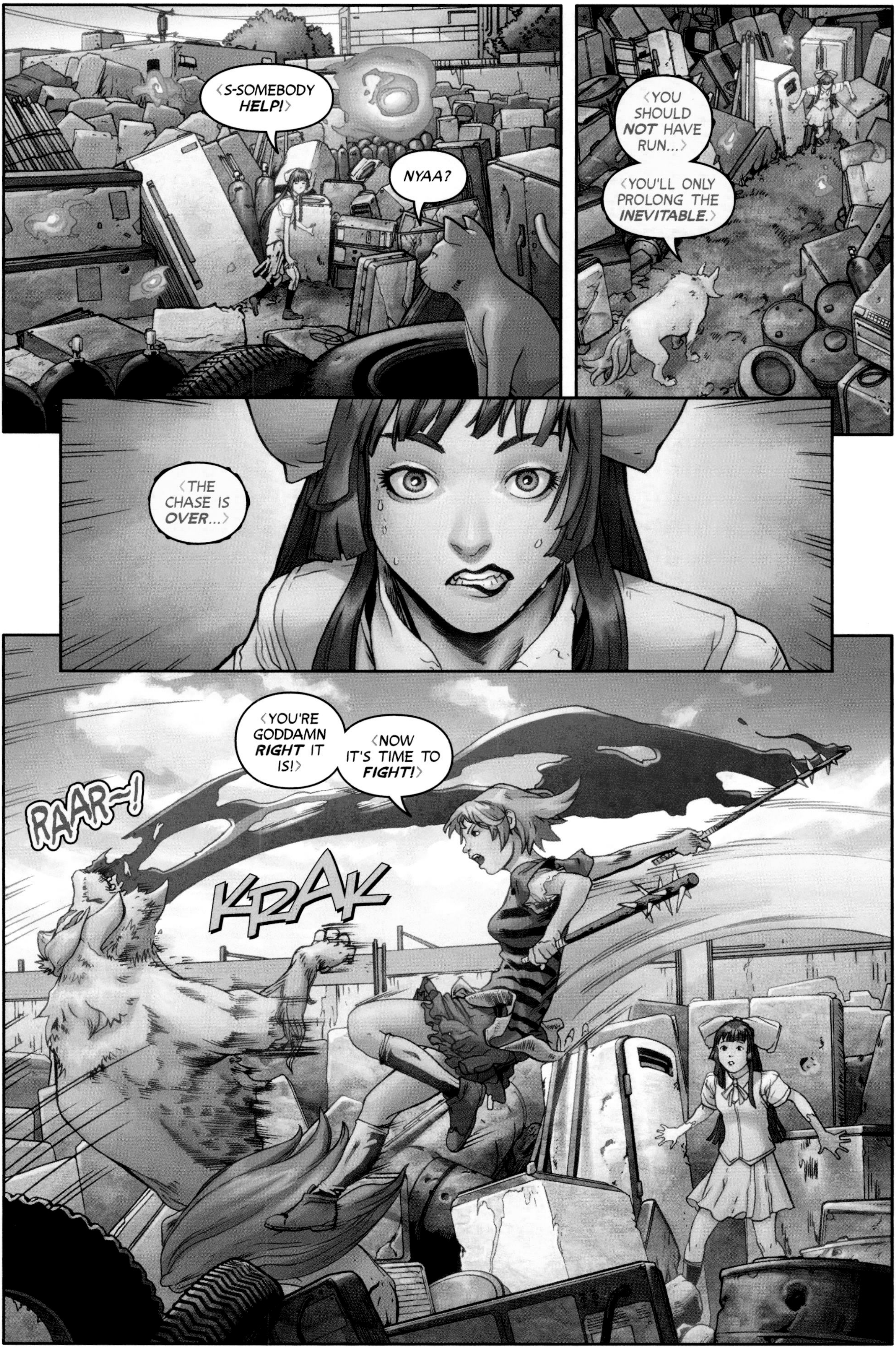

<S-SOMEBODY HELP!>
NYAA?
<YOU SHOULD NOT HAVE RUN...>
<YOU'LL ONLY PROLONG THE INEVITABLE.>
<THE CHASE IS OVER...>
RAAR~!
<YOU'RE GODDAMN RIGHT IT IS!>
<NOW IT'S TIME TO FIGHT!>
KRAK

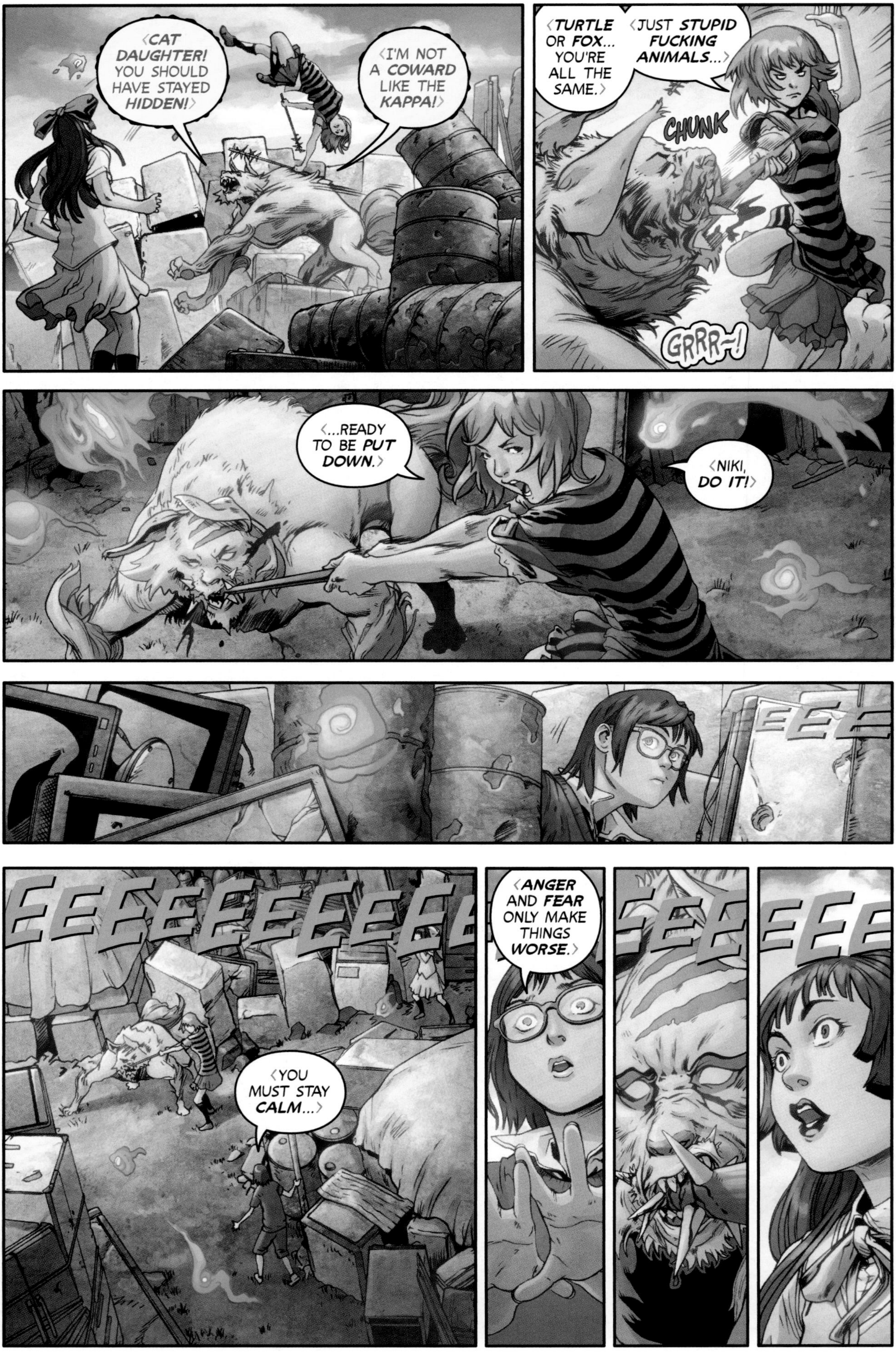

‹CAT DAUGHTER! YOU SHOULD HAVE STAYED HIDDEN!›
‹I'M NOT A COWARD LIKE THE KAPPA!›
‹TURTLE OR FOX... YOU'RE ALL THE SAME.›
‹JUST STUPID FUCKING ANIMALS...›
CHUNK
GRRR~!
‹...READY TO BE PUT DOWN.›
‹NIKI, DO IT!›
EEE
EEEEEEEEE
‹YOU MUST STAY CALM...›
‹ANGER AND FEAR ONLY MAKE THINGS WORSE.›
EEE
EEEE

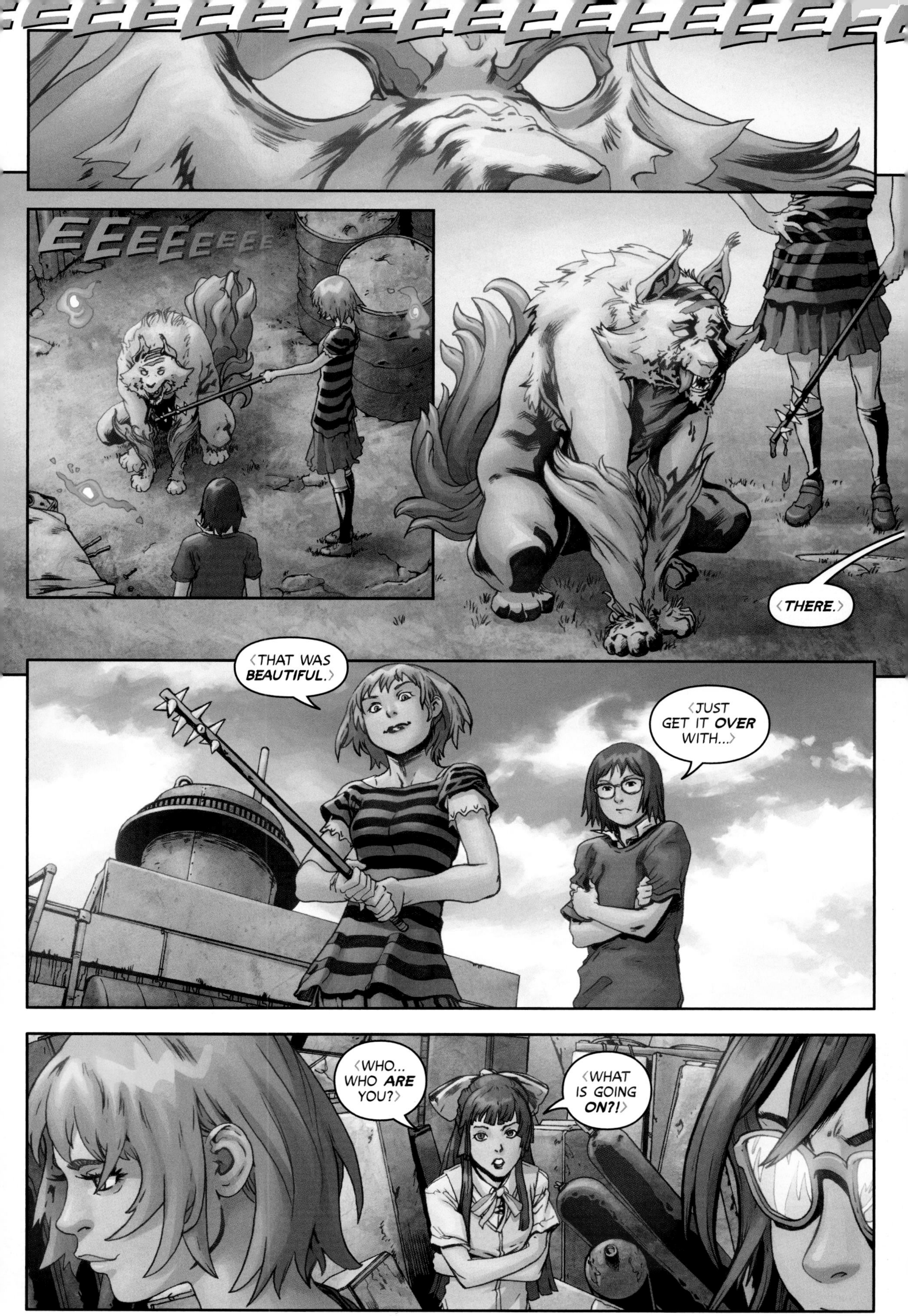
EEEEEEEEEEEEEEEEEEEEE
EEEEEEEEE
〈THERE.〉
〈THAT WAS BEAUTIFUL.〉
〈JUST GET IT OVER WITH...〉
〈WHO... WHO ARE YOU?〉
〈WHAT IS GOING ON?!〉

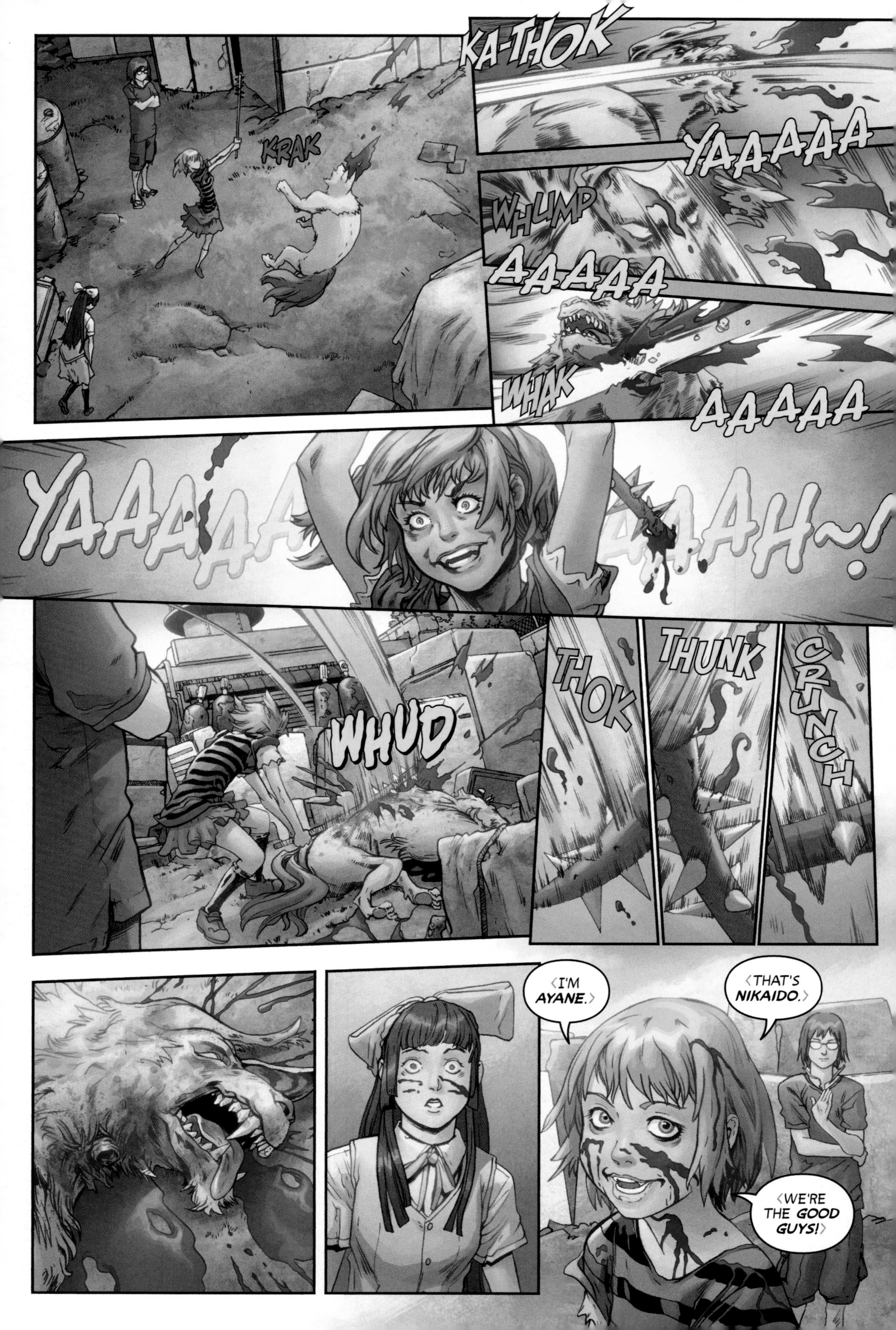
KRAK
KA-THOK
YAAAAAA
WHUMP
AAAAAA
WHAK
AAAAAA
YAAAAAAAAAAH~!
WHUD
THOK
THUNK
CRUNCH
‹I'M AYANE.›
‹THAT'S NIKAIDO.›
‹WE'RE THE GOOD GUYS!›

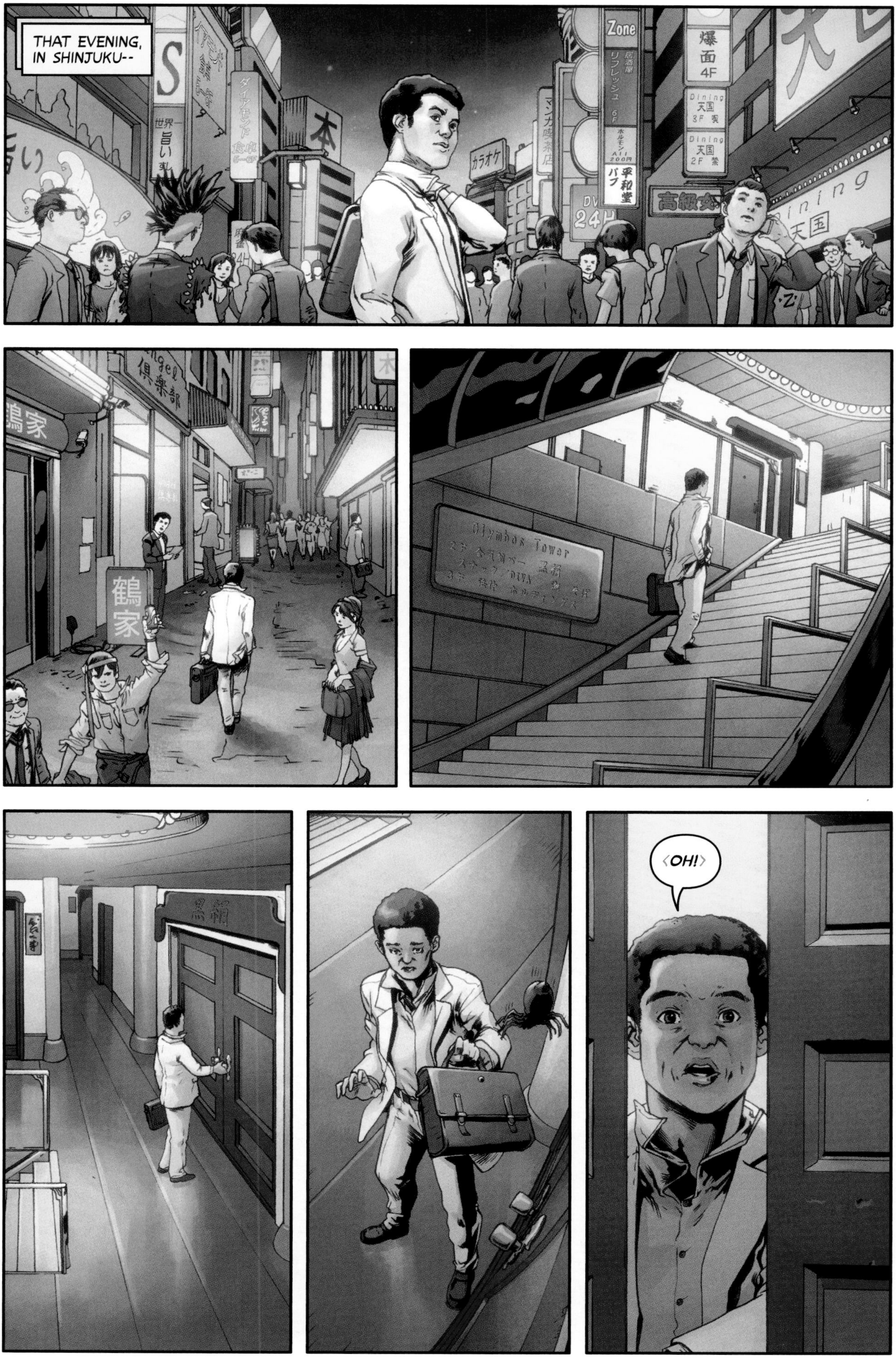
THAT EVENING, IN SHINJUKU--
‹OH!›

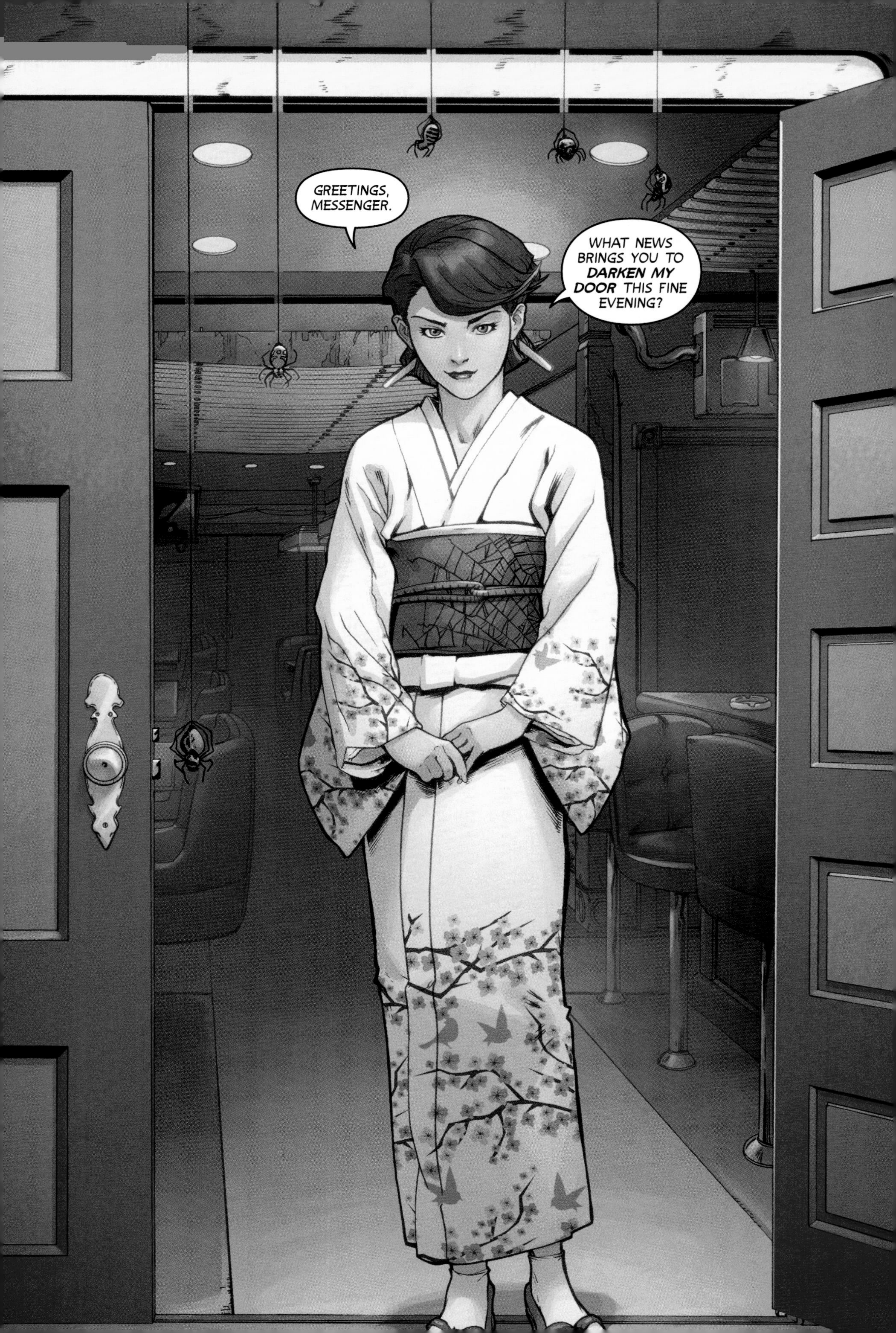
GREETINGS, MESSENGER.
WHAT NEWS BRINGS YOU TO DARKEN MY DOOR THIS FINE EVENING?

Chapter Seven

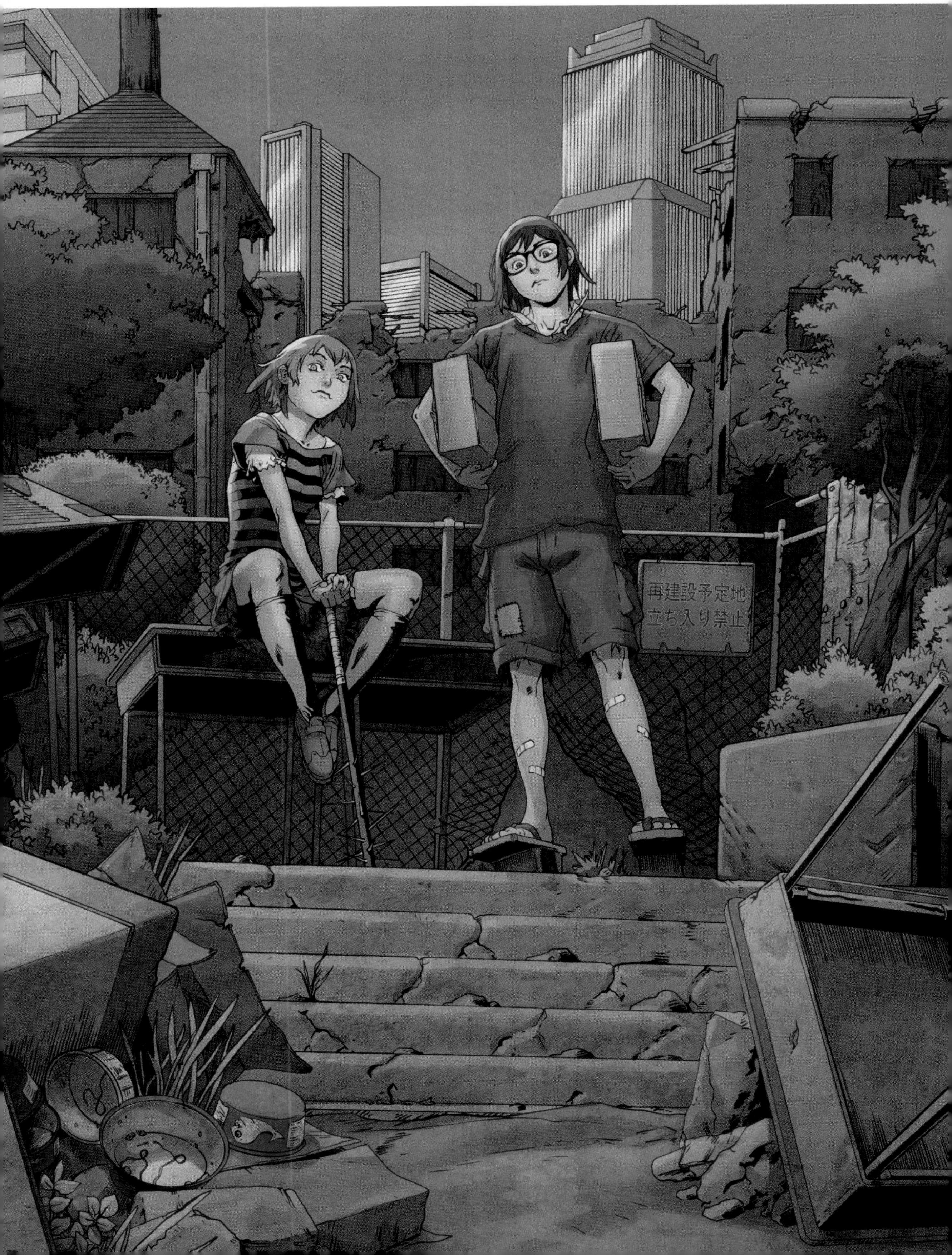

再建設予定地
立ち入り禁止

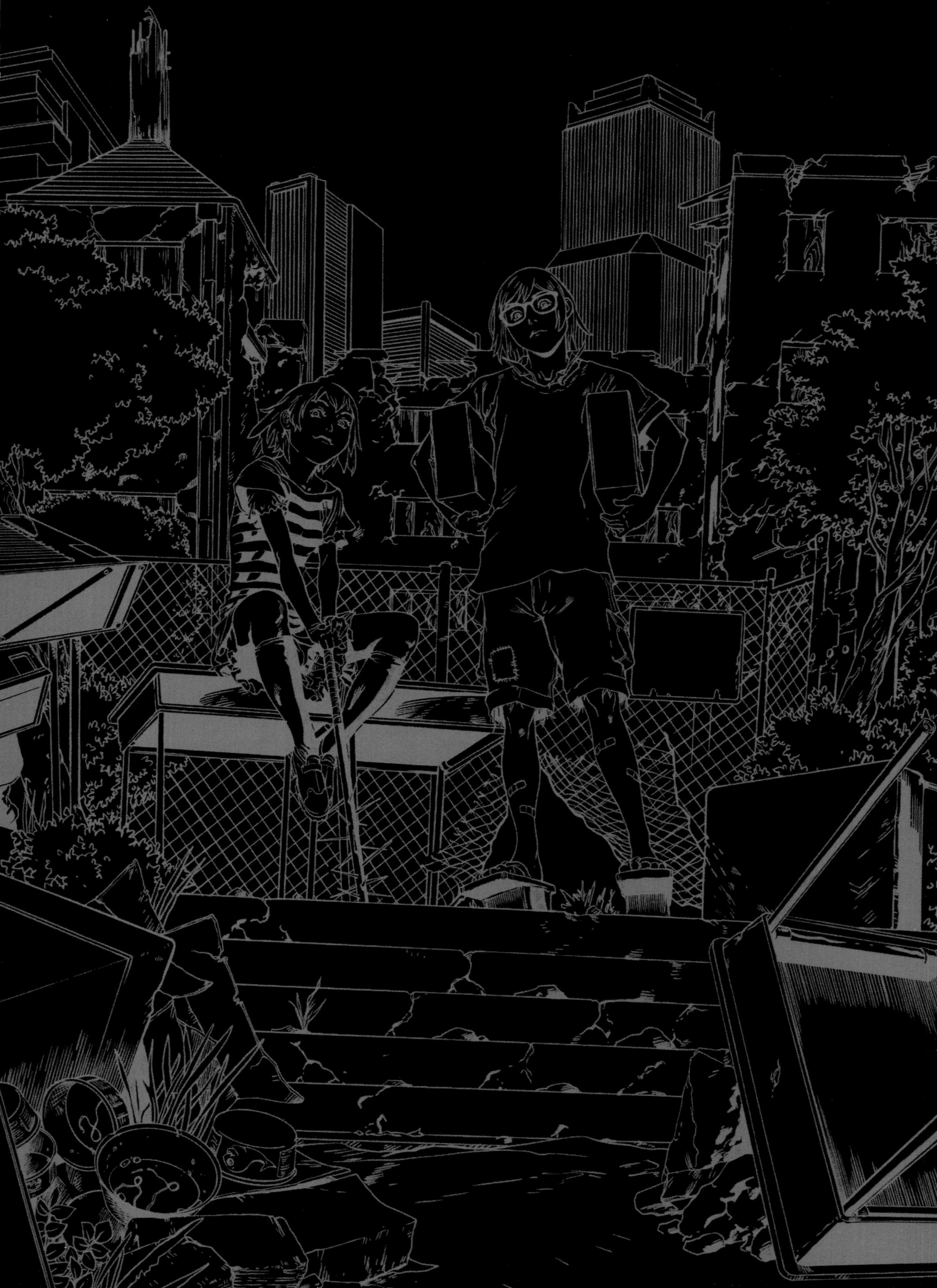

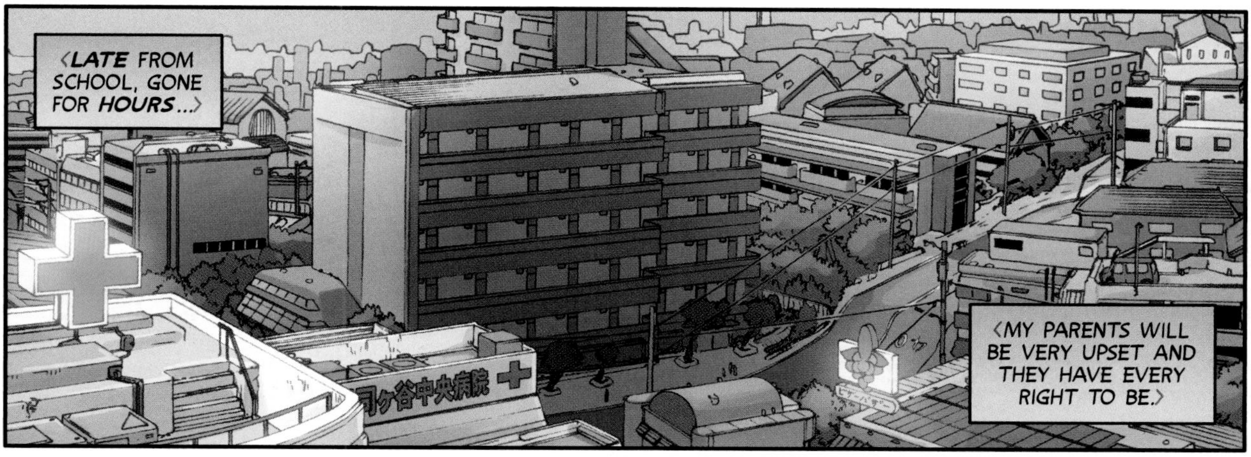
<**LATE** FROM SCHOOL, GONE FOR **HOURS**...>
ヶ谷中央病院
<MY PARENTS WILL BE VERY UPSET AND THEY HAVE EVERY RIGHT TO BE.>

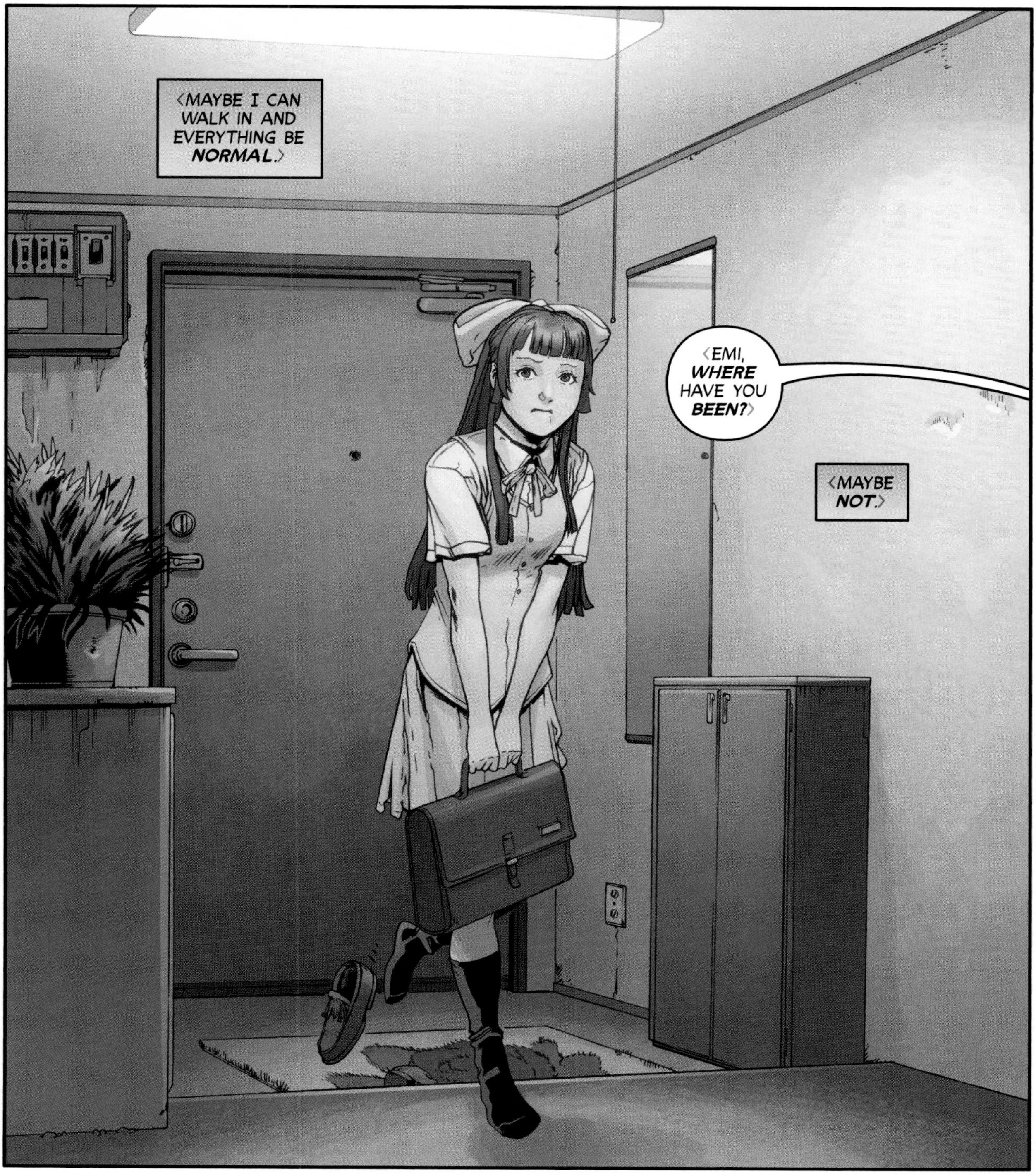
<MAYBE I CAN WALK IN AND EVERYTHING BE **NORMAL**.>
<EMI, **WHERE** HAVE YOU **BEEN?**>
<MAYBE **NOT**.>

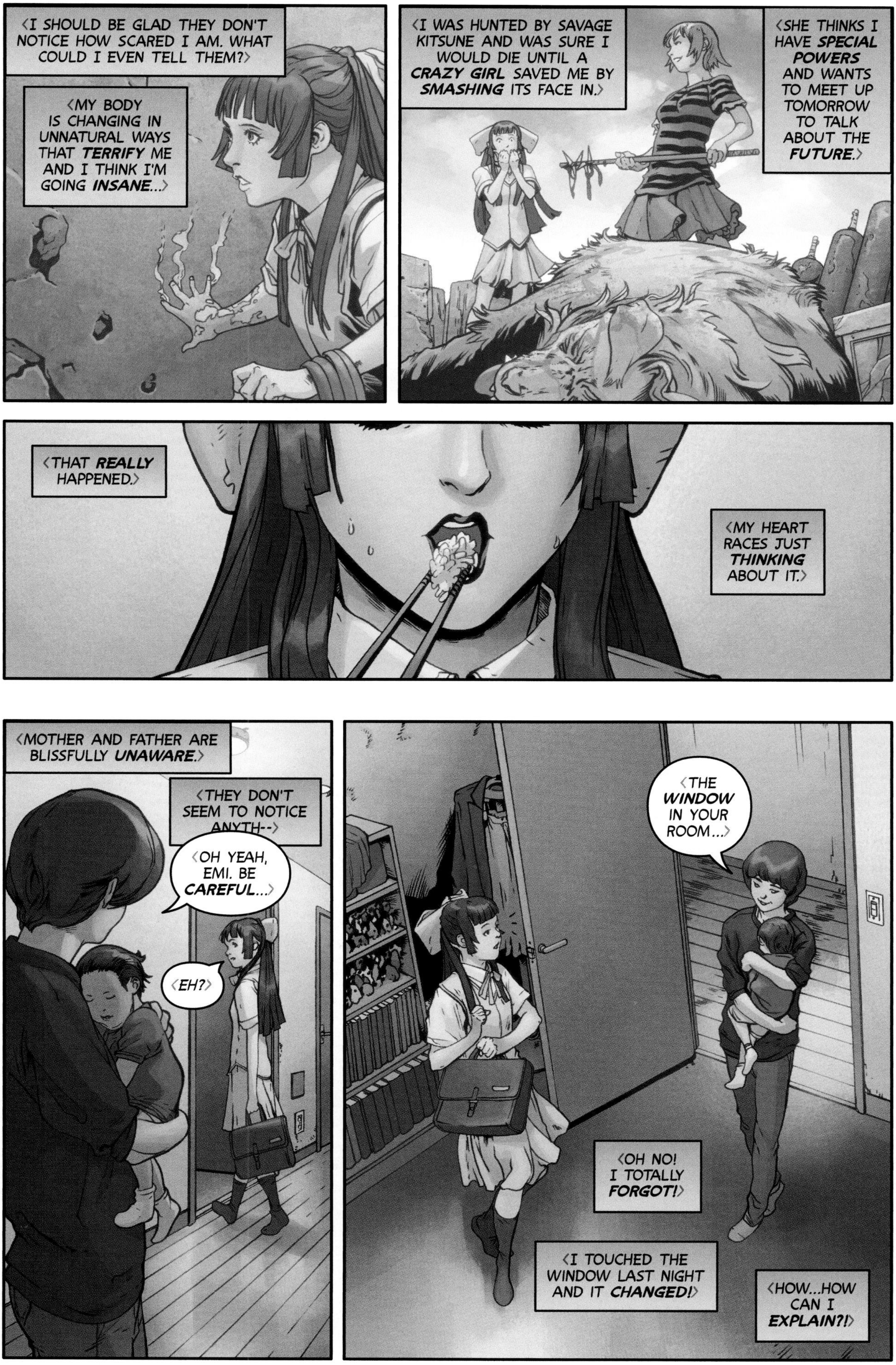

<I SHOULD BE GLAD THEY DON'T NOTICE HOW SCARED I AM. WHAT COULD I EVEN TELL THEM?>
<MY BODY IS CHANGING IN UNNATURAL WAYS THAT TERRIFY ME AND I THINK I'M GOING INSANE...>
<I WAS HUNTED BY SAVAGE KITSUNE AND WAS SURE I WOULD DIE UNTIL A CRAZY GIRL SAVED ME BY SMASHING ITS FACE IN.>
<SHE THINKS I HAVE SPECIAL POWERS AND WANTS TO MEET UP TOMORROW TO TALK ABOUT THE FUTURE.>
<THAT REALLY HAPPENED.>
<MY HEART RACES JUST THINKING ABOUT IT.>
<MOTHER AND FATHER ARE BLISSFULLY UNAWARE.>
<THEY DON'T SEEM TO NOTICE ANYTH-->
<OH YEAH, EMI. BE CAREFUL...>
<EH?>
<THE WINDOW IN YOUR ROOM...>
<OH NO! I TOTALLY FORGOT!>
<I TOUCHED THE WINDOW LAST NIGHT AND IT CHANGED!>
<HOW...HOW CAN I EXPLAIN?!>

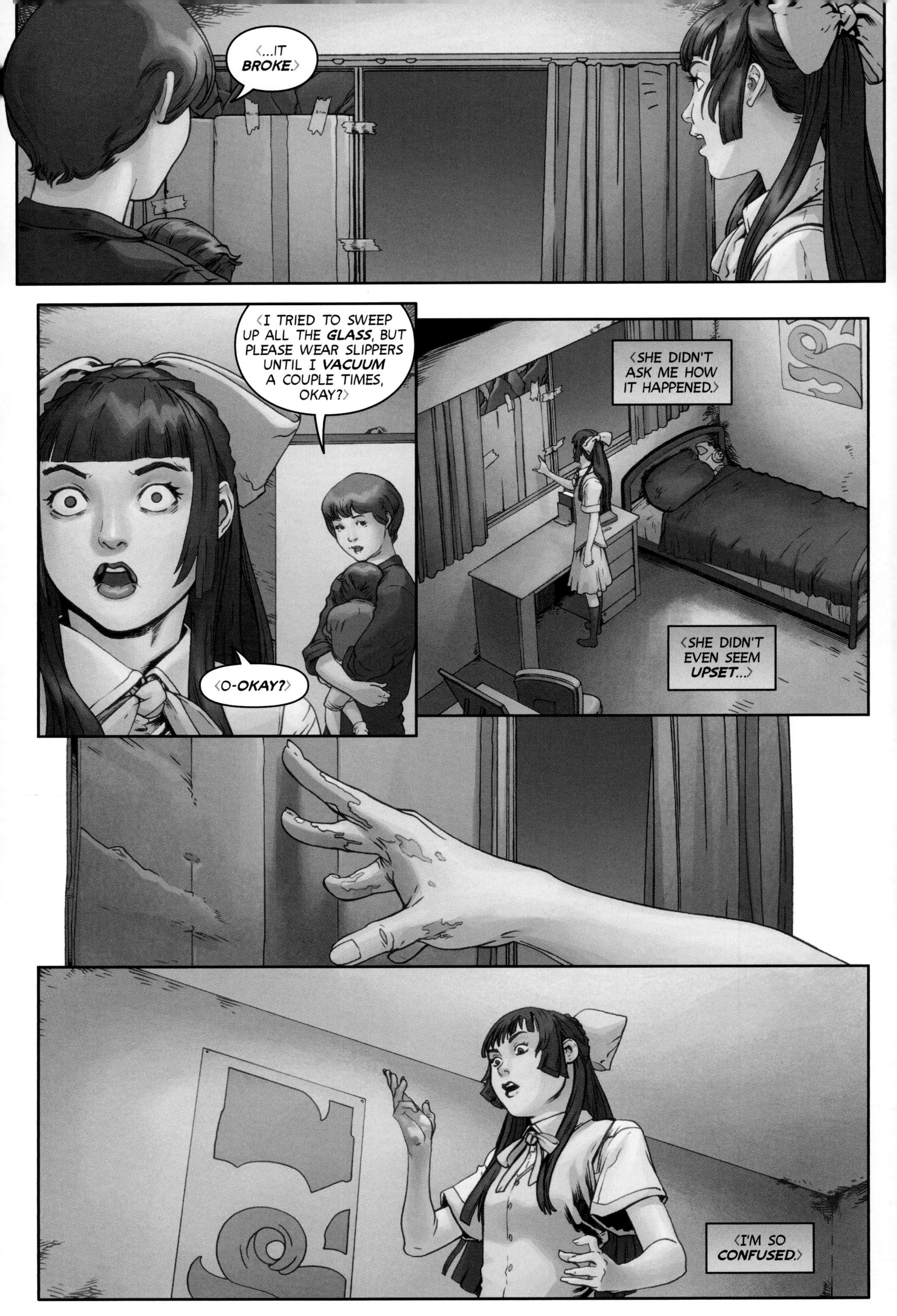
〈...IT BROKE.〉
〈I TRIED TO SWEEP UP ALL THE GLASS, BUT PLEASE WEAR SLIPPERS UNTIL I VACUUM A COUPLE TIMES, OKAY?〉
〈O-OKAY?〉
〈SHE DIDN'T ASK ME HOW IT HAPPENED.〉
〈SHE DIDN'T EVEN SEEM UPSET...〉
〈I'M SO CONFUSED.〉

ELSEWHERE.

‹WE HEARD RUMORS OF YOUR *DEMISE*, NURARIHYON.›

‹WELL, GENTLEMEN, *THAT'S* WHY WE'VE GATHERED HERE. I WANT TO DISPEL ALL THESE *"RUMORS".*›

‹ACCURATE INFORMATION IS CRUCIAL.›

‹SO THERE'S NO TRUTH TO THE SPIRIT CHATTER WE'VE BEEN HEARING ABOUT *CORRUPT CHILDREN* RUNNING *AMUCK?*›

‹IT'S...›

‹...COMPLICATED...›

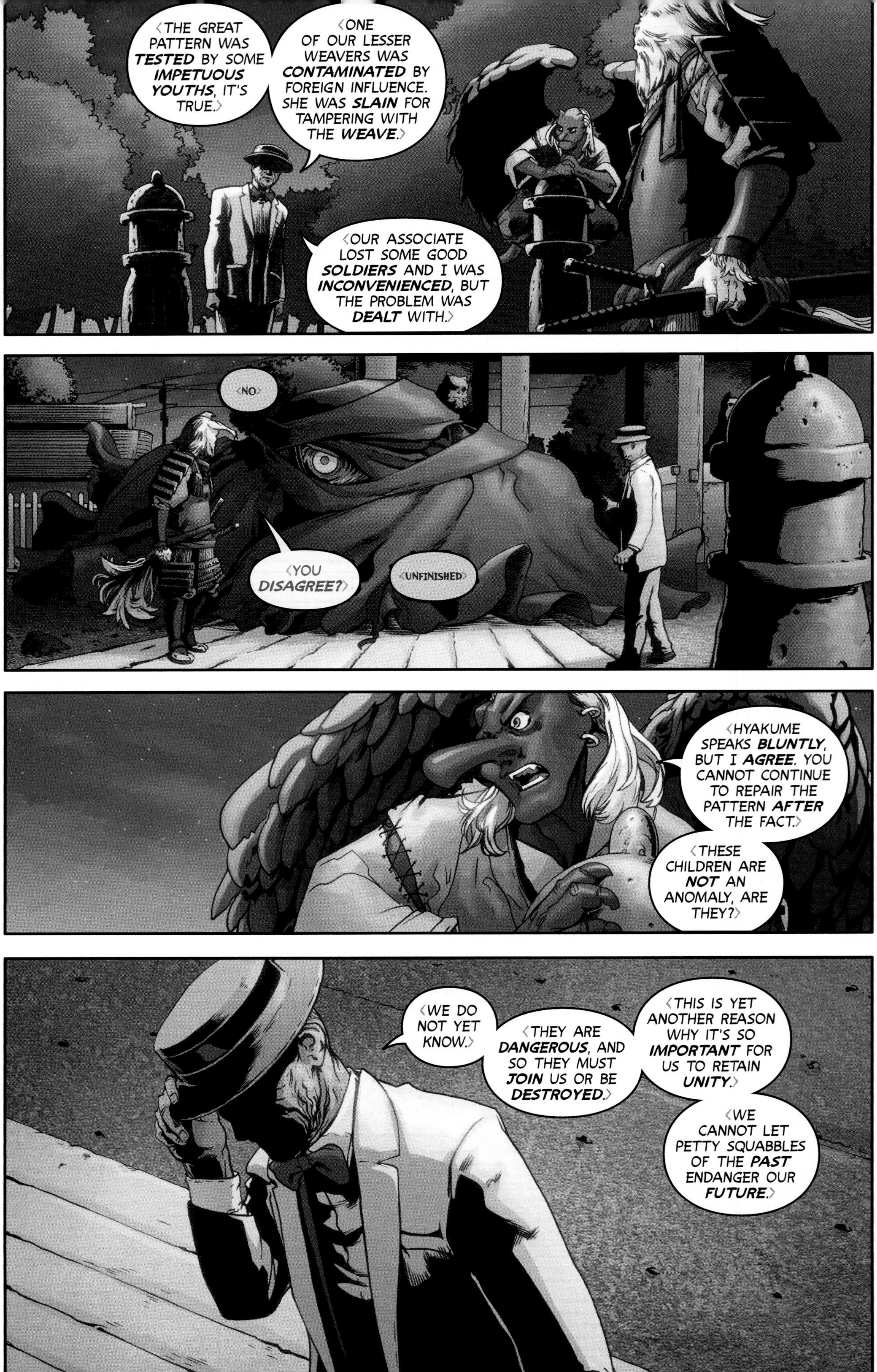
‹THE GREAT PATTERN WAS TESTED BY SOME IMPETUOUS YOUTHS, IT'S TRUE.›
‹ONE OF OUR LESSER WEAVERS WAS CONTAMINATED BY FOREIGN INFLUENCE. SHE WAS SLAIN FOR TAMPERING WITH THE WEAVE.›
‹OUR ASSOCIATE LOST SOME GOOD SOLDIERS AND I WAS INCONVENIENCED, BUT THE PROBLEM WAS DEALT WITH.›
‹NO›
‹YOU DISAGREE?›
‹UNFINISHED›
‹HYAKUME SPEAKS BLUNTLY, BUT I AGREE. YOU CANNOT CONTINUE TO REPAIR THE PATTERN AFTER THE FACT.›
‹THESE CHILDREN ARE NOT AN ANOMALY, ARE THEY?›
‹WE DO NOT YET KNOW.›
‹THEY ARE DANGEROUS, AND SO THEY MUST JOIN US OR BE DESTROYED.›
‹THIS IS YET ANOTHER REASON WHY IT'S SO IMPORTANT FOR US TO RETAIN UNITY.›
‹WE CANNOT LET PETTY SQUABBLES OF THE PAST ENDANGER OUR FUTURE.›

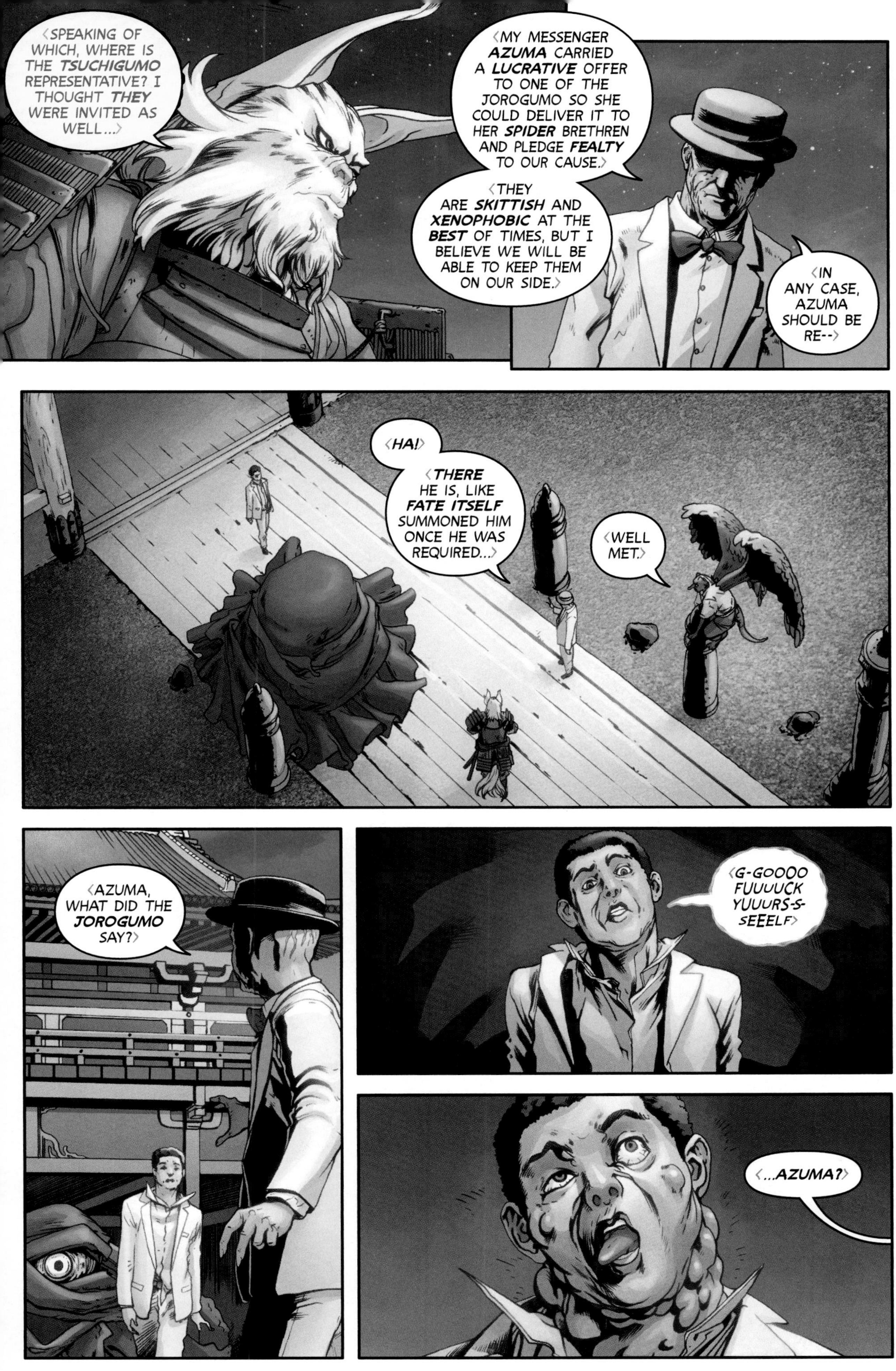
⟨SPEAKING OF WHICH, WHERE IS THE TSUCHIGUMO REPRESENTATIVE? I THOUGHT THEY WERE INVITED AS WELL...⟩
⟨MY MESSENGER AZUMA CARRIED A LUCRATIVE OFFER TO ONE OF THE JOROGUMO SO SHE COULD DELIVER IT TO HER SPIDER BRETHREN AND PLEDGE FEALTY TO OUR CAUSE.⟩
⟨THEY ARE SKITTISH AND XENOPHOBIC AT THE BEST OF TIMES, BUT I BELIEVE WE WILL BE ABLE TO KEEP THEM ON OUR SIDE.⟩
⟨IN ANY CASE, AZUMA SHOULD BE RE--⟩
⟨HA!⟩
⟨THERE HE IS, LIKE FATE ITSELF SUMMONED HIM ONCE HE WAS REQUIRED...⟩
⟨WELL MET.⟩
⟨AZUMA, WHAT DID THE JOROGUMO SAY?⟩
⟨G-GOOOO FUUUUCK YUUURS-S-SEEELF⟩
⟨...AZUMA?⟩

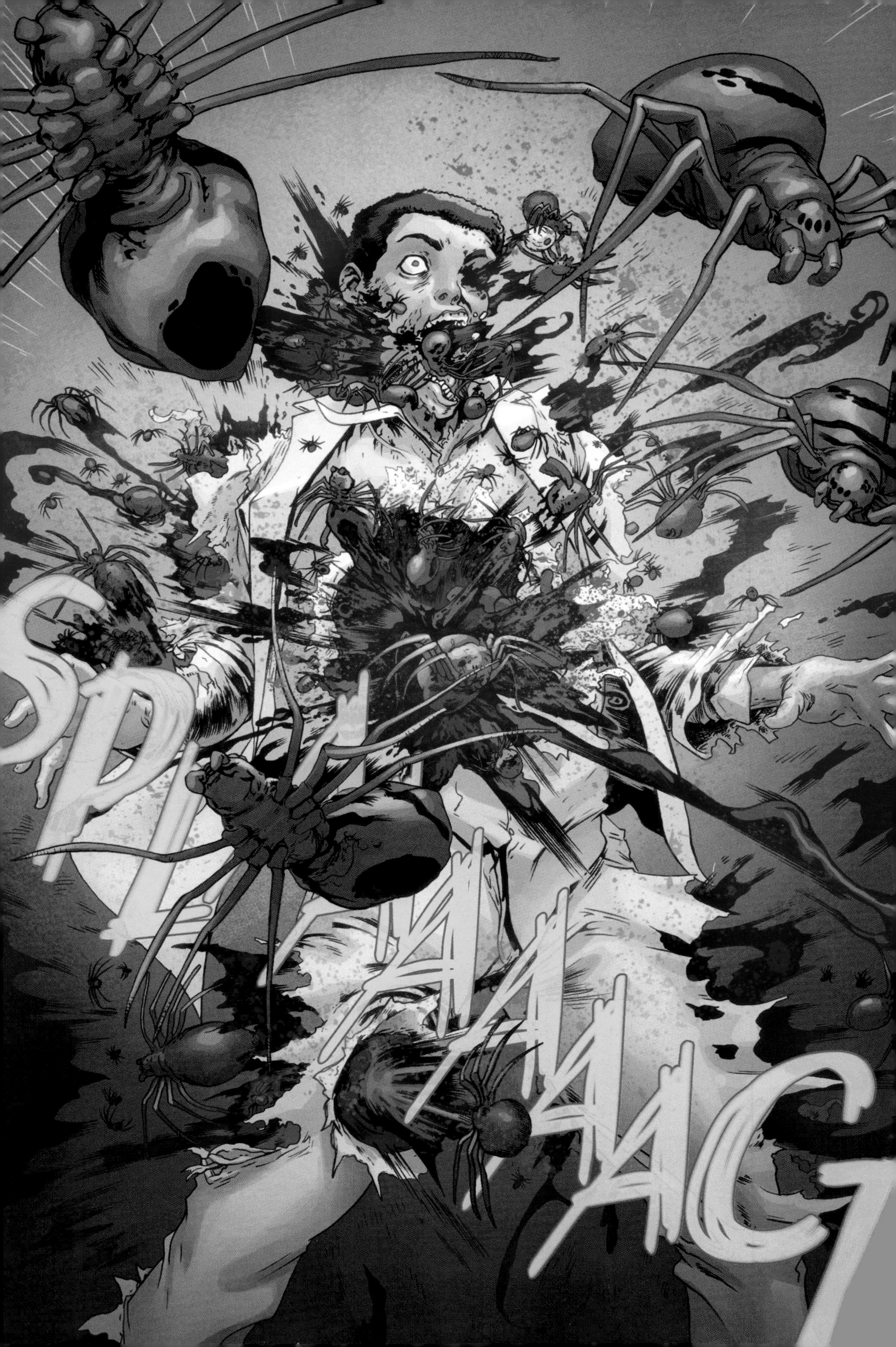
SPLAAAAG

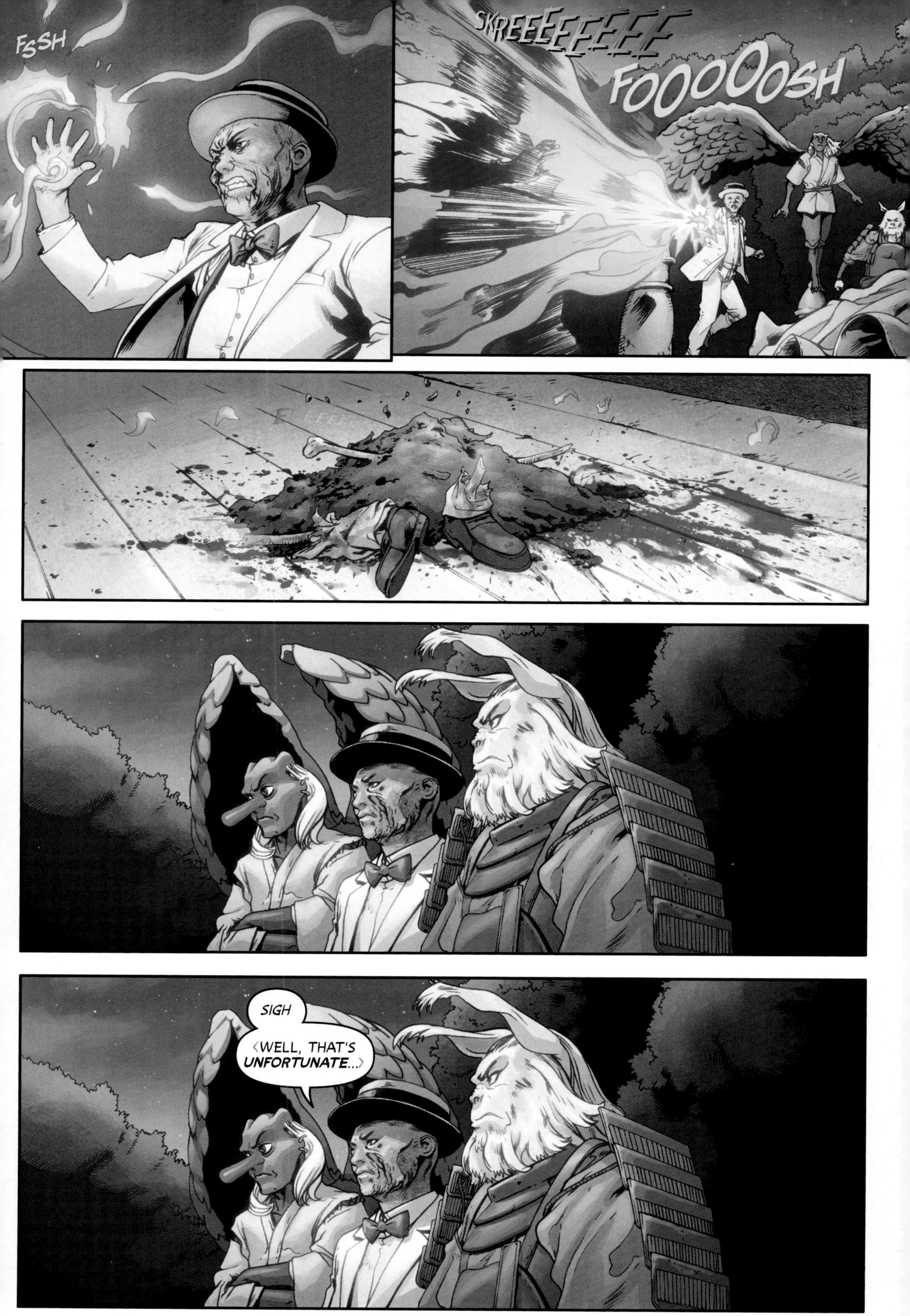
FSSH
SKREEEEEEEEE
FOOOOOSH
SIGH
‹WELL, THAT'S UNFORTUNATE...›

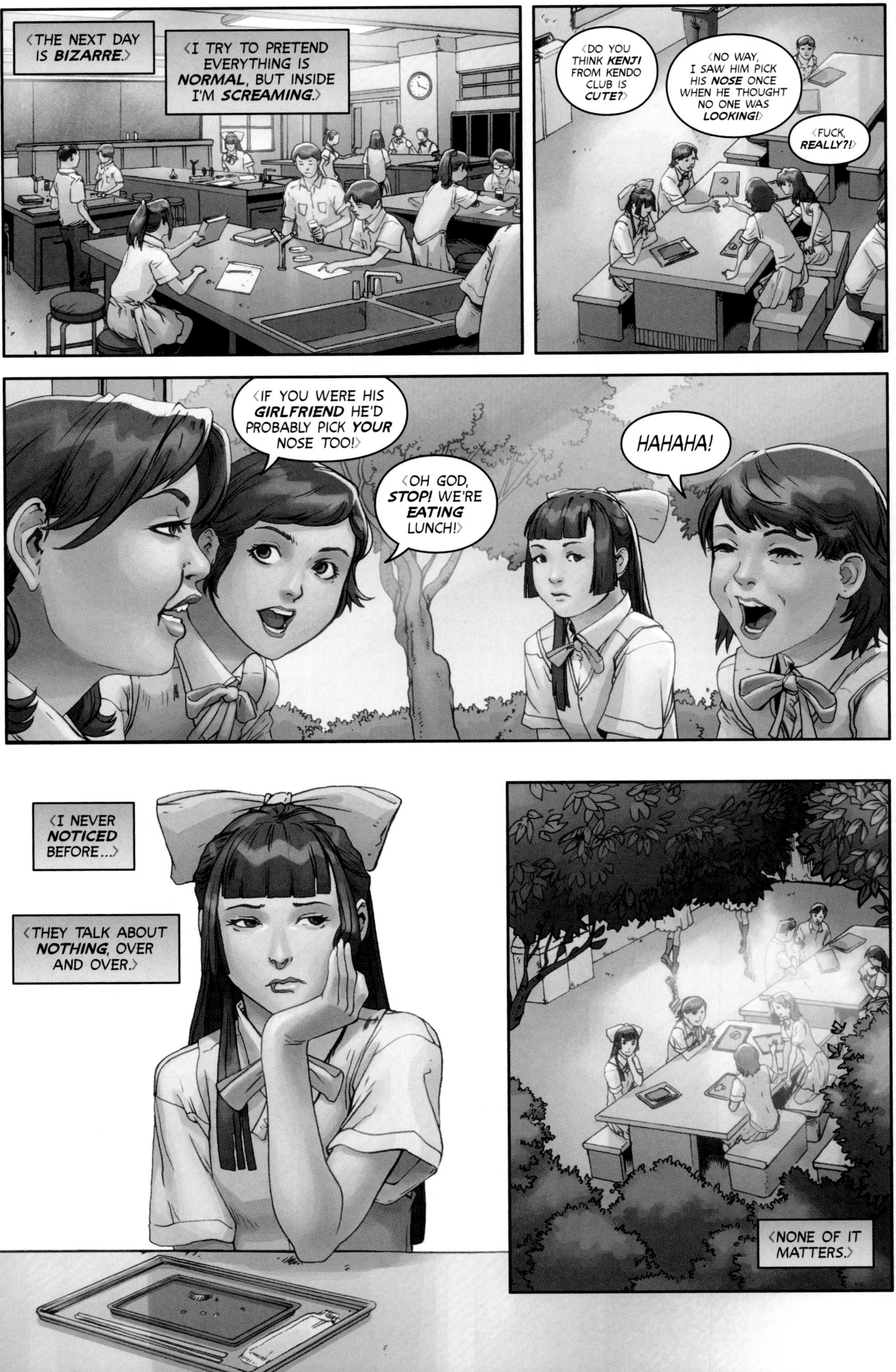

‹THE NEXT DAY IS ***BIZARRE***.›
‹I TRY TO PRETEND EVERYTHING IS ***NORMAL***, BUT INSIDE I'M ***SCREAMING***.›
‹DO YOU THINK ***KENJI*** FROM KENDO CLUB IS ***CUTE?***›
‹NO WAY, I SAW HIM PICK HIS ***NOSE*** ONCE WHEN HE THOUGHT NO ONE WAS ***LOOKING!***›
‹FUCK, ***REALLY?!***›
‹IF YOU WERE HIS ***GIRLFRIEND*** HE'D PROBABLY PICK ***YOUR*** NOSE TOO!›
‹OH GOD, ***STOP!*** WE'RE ***EATING*** LUNCH!›
HAHAHA!
‹I NEVER ***NOTICED*** BEFORE...›
‹THEY TALK ABOUT ***NOTHING***, OVER AND OVER.›
‹NONE OF IT MATTERS.›

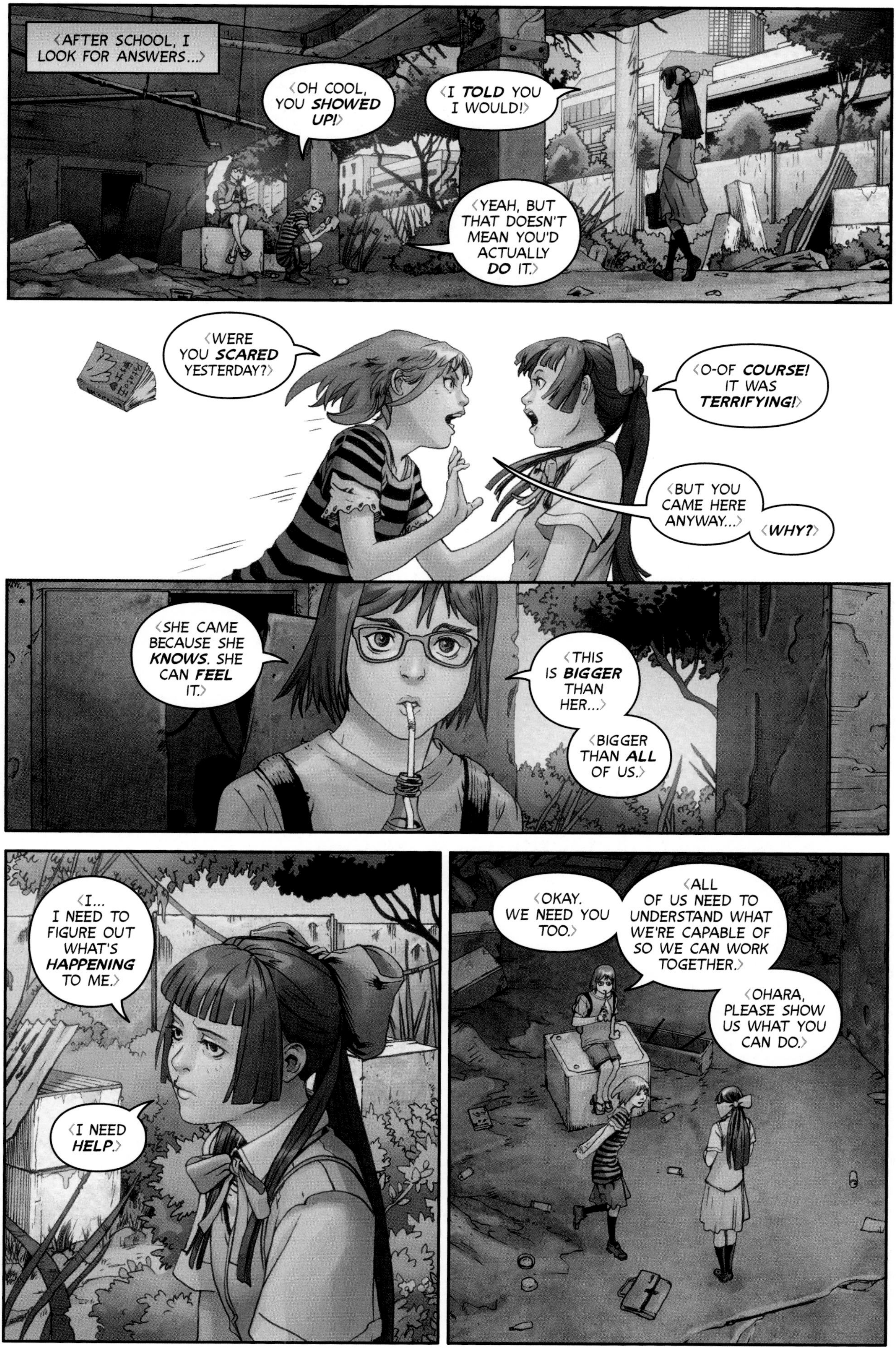

‹AFTER SCHOOL, I LOOK FOR ANSWERS...›
‹OH COOL, YOU SHOWED UP!›
‹I TOLD YOU I WOULD!›
‹YEAH, BUT THAT DOESN'T MEAN YOU'D ACTUALLY DO IT.›
‹WERE YOU SCARED YESTERDAY?›
‹O-OF COURSE! IT WAS TERRIFYING!›
‹BUT YOU CAME HERE ANYWAY...›
‹WHY?›
‹SHE CAME BECAUSE SHE KNOWS. SHE CAN FEEL IT.›
‹THIS IS BIGGER THAN HER...›
‹BIGGER THAN ALL OF US.›
‹I... I NEED TO FIGURE OUT WHAT'S HAPPENING TO ME.›
‹I NEED HELP.›
‹OKAY. WE NEED YOU TOO.›
‹ALL OF US NEED TO UNDERSTAND WHAT WE'RE CAPABLE OF SO WE CAN WORK TOGETHER.›
‹OHARA, PLEASE SHOW US WHAT YOU CAN DO.›

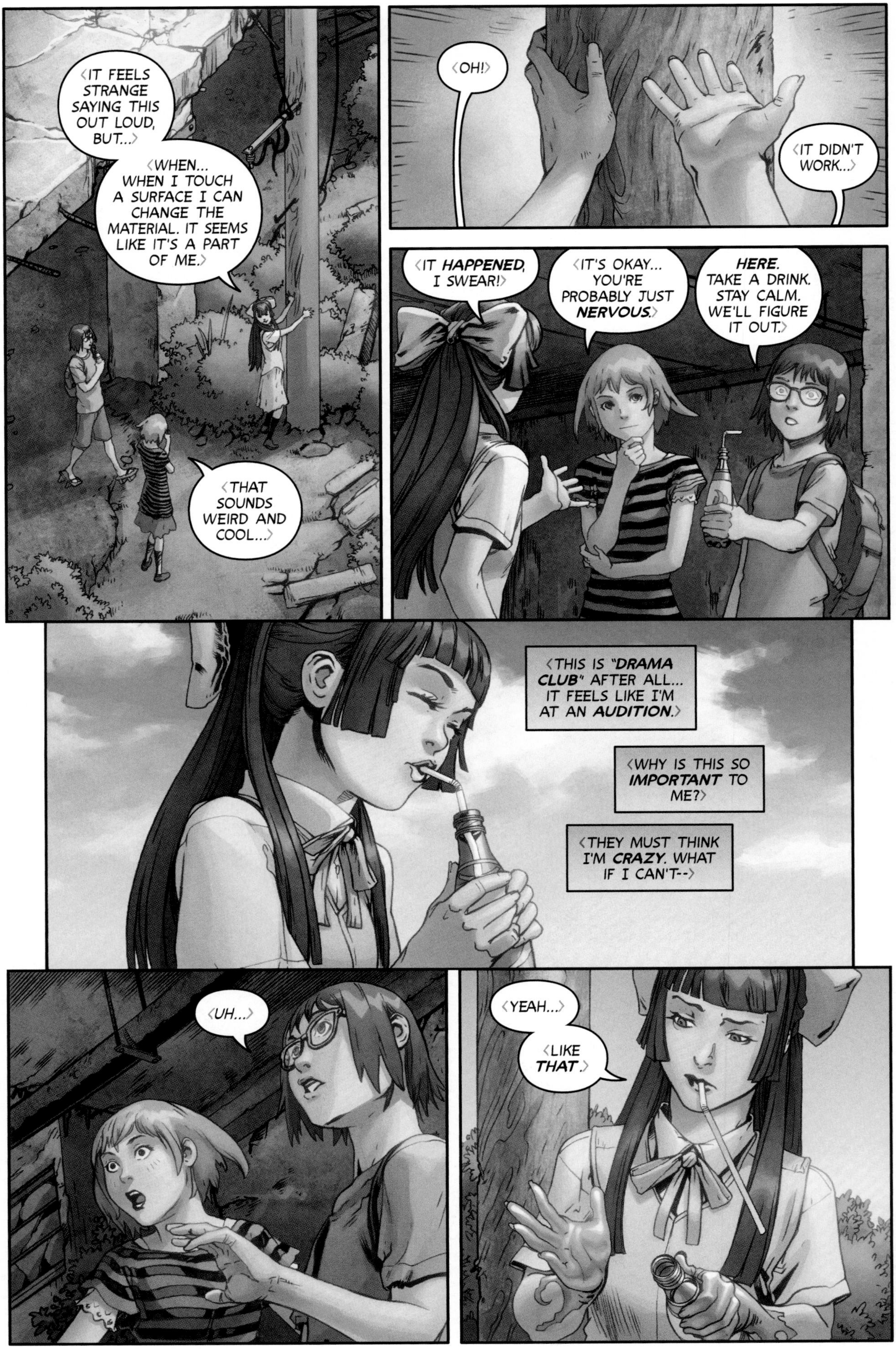
⟨IT FEELS STRANGE SAYING THIS OUT LOUD, BUT...⟩
⟨WHEN... WHEN I TOUCH A SURFACE I CAN CHANGE THE MATERIAL. IT SEEMS LIKE IT'S A PART OF ME.⟩
⟨THAT SOUNDS WEIRD AND COOL...⟩
⟨OH!⟩
⟨IT DIDN'T WORK...⟩
⟨IT *HAPPENED*, I SWEAR!⟩
⟨IT'S OKAY... YOU'RE PROBABLY JUST *NERVOUS*.⟩
⟨*HERE*. TAKE A DRINK. STAY CALM. WE'LL FIGURE IT OUT.⟩
⟨THIS IS "*DRAMA CLUB*" AFTER ALL... IT FEELS LIKE I'M AT AN *AUDITION*.⟩
⟨WHY IS THIS SO *IMPORTANT* TO ME?⟩
⟨THEY MUST THINK I'M *CRAZY*. WHAT IF I CAN'T--⟩
⟨UH...⟩
⟨YEAH...⟩
⟨LIKE *THAT*.⟩

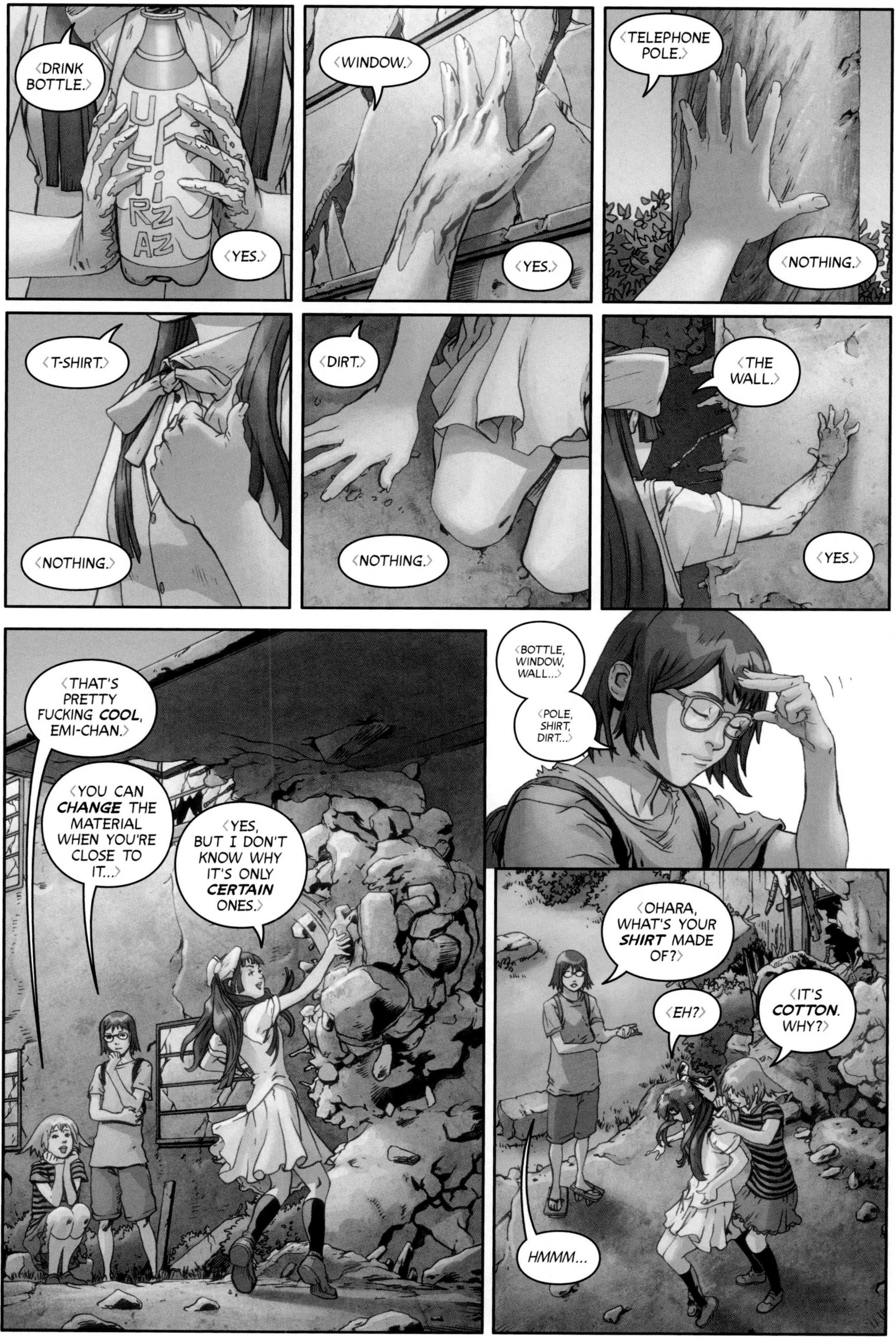
<DRINK BOTTLE.>
<YES.>
<WINDOW.>
<YES.>
<TELEPHONE POLE.>
<NOTHING.>
<T-SHIRT.>
<NOTHING.>
<DIRT.>
<NOTHING.>
<THE WALL.>
<YES.>
<THAT'S PRETTY FUCKING **COOL**, EMI-CHAN.>
<YOU CAN **CHANGE** THE MATERIAL WHEN YOU'RE CLOSE TO IT...>
<YES, BUT I DON'T KNOW WHY IT'S ONLY **CERTAIN** ONES.>
<BOTTLE, WINDOW, WALL...>
<POLE, SHIRT, DIRT...>
<OHARA, WHAT'S YOUR **SHIRT** MADE OF?>
<*EH?*>
<IT'S **COTTON**. WHY?>
HMMM...

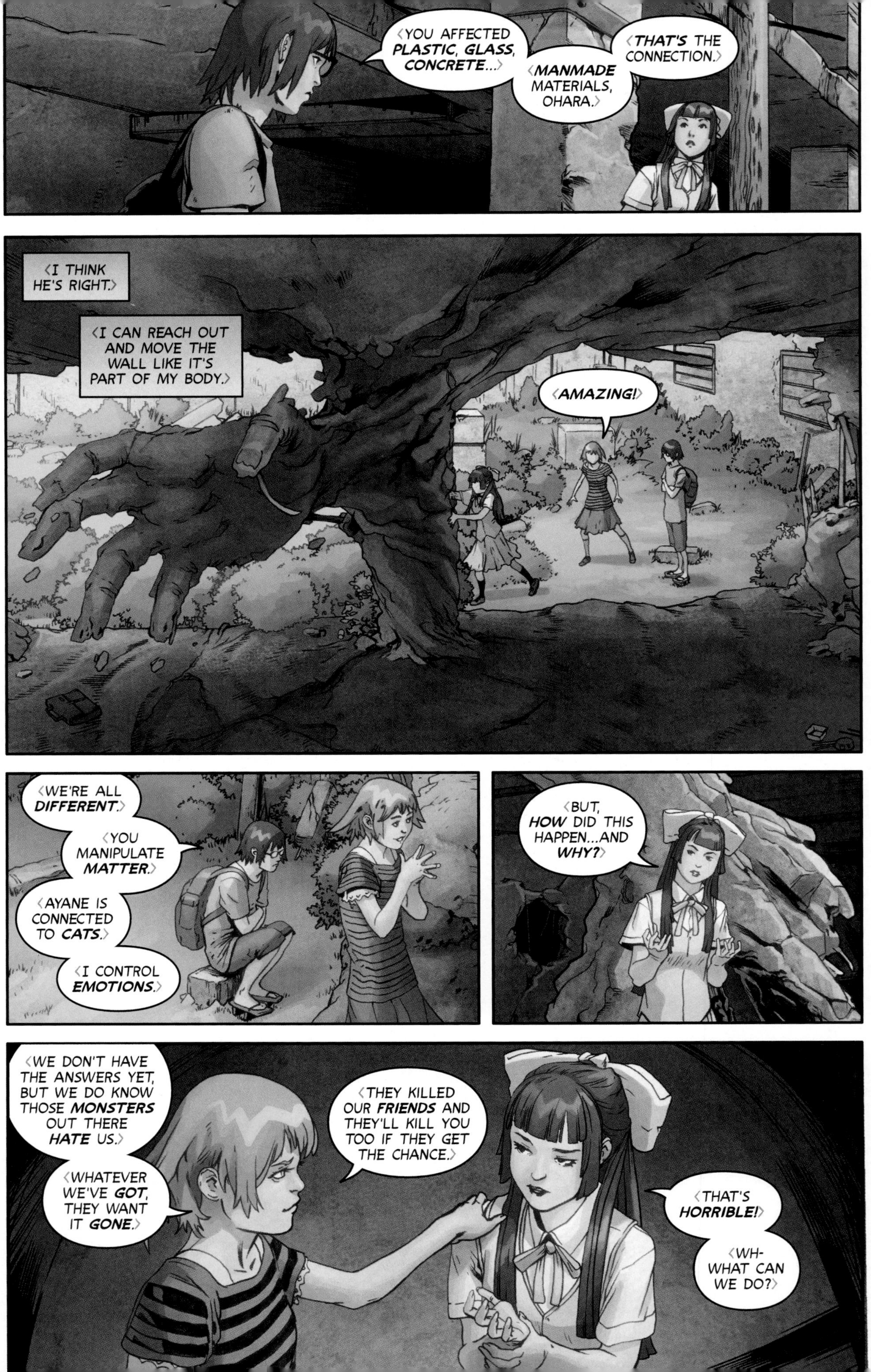

<YOU AFFECTED PLASTIC, GLASS, CONCRETE...>
<MANMADE MATERIALS, OHARA.>
<THAT'S THE CONNECTION.>
<I THINK HE'S RIGHT.>
<I CAN REACH OUT AND MOVE THE WALL LIKE IT'S PART OF MY BODY.>
<AMAZING!>
<WE'RE ALL DIFFERENT.>
<YOU MANIPULATE MATTER.>
<AYANE IS CONNECTED TO CATS.>
<I CONTROL EMOTIONS.>
<BUT, HOW DID THIS HAPPEN...AND WHY?>
<WE DON'T HAVE THE ANSWERS YET, BUT WE DO KNOW THOSE MONSTERS OUT THERE HATE US.>
<WHATEVER WE'VE GOT, THEY WANT IT GONE.>
<THEY KILLED OUR FRIENDS AND THEY'LL KILL YOU TOO IF THEY GET THE CHANCE.>
<THAT'S HORRIBLE!>
<WH- WHAT CAN WE DO?>

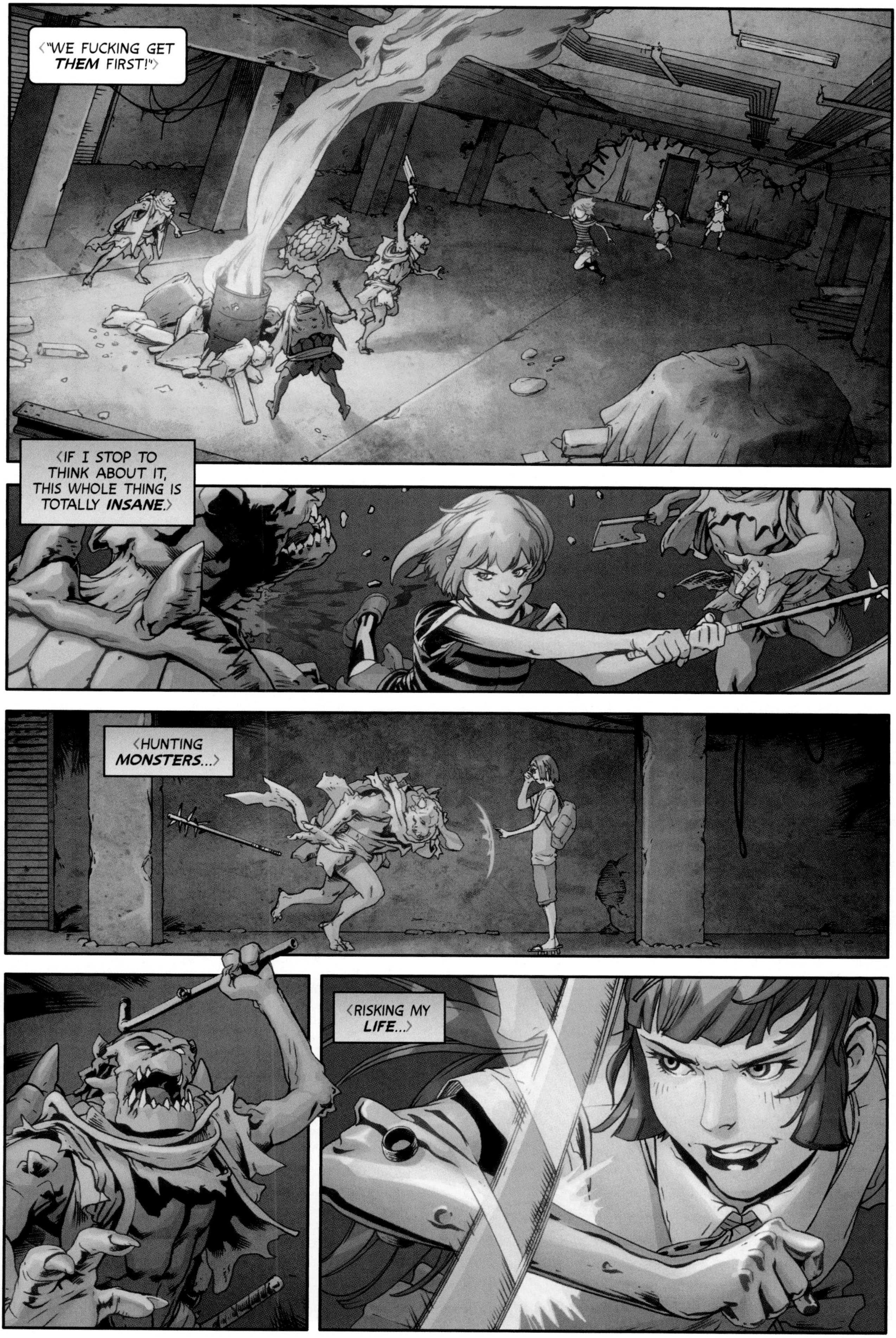
〈"WE FUCKING GET THEM FIRST!"〉
〈IF I STOP TO THINK ABOUT IT, THIS WHOLE THING IS TOTALLY INSANE.〉
〈HUNTING MONSTERS...〉
〈RISKING MY LIFE...〉

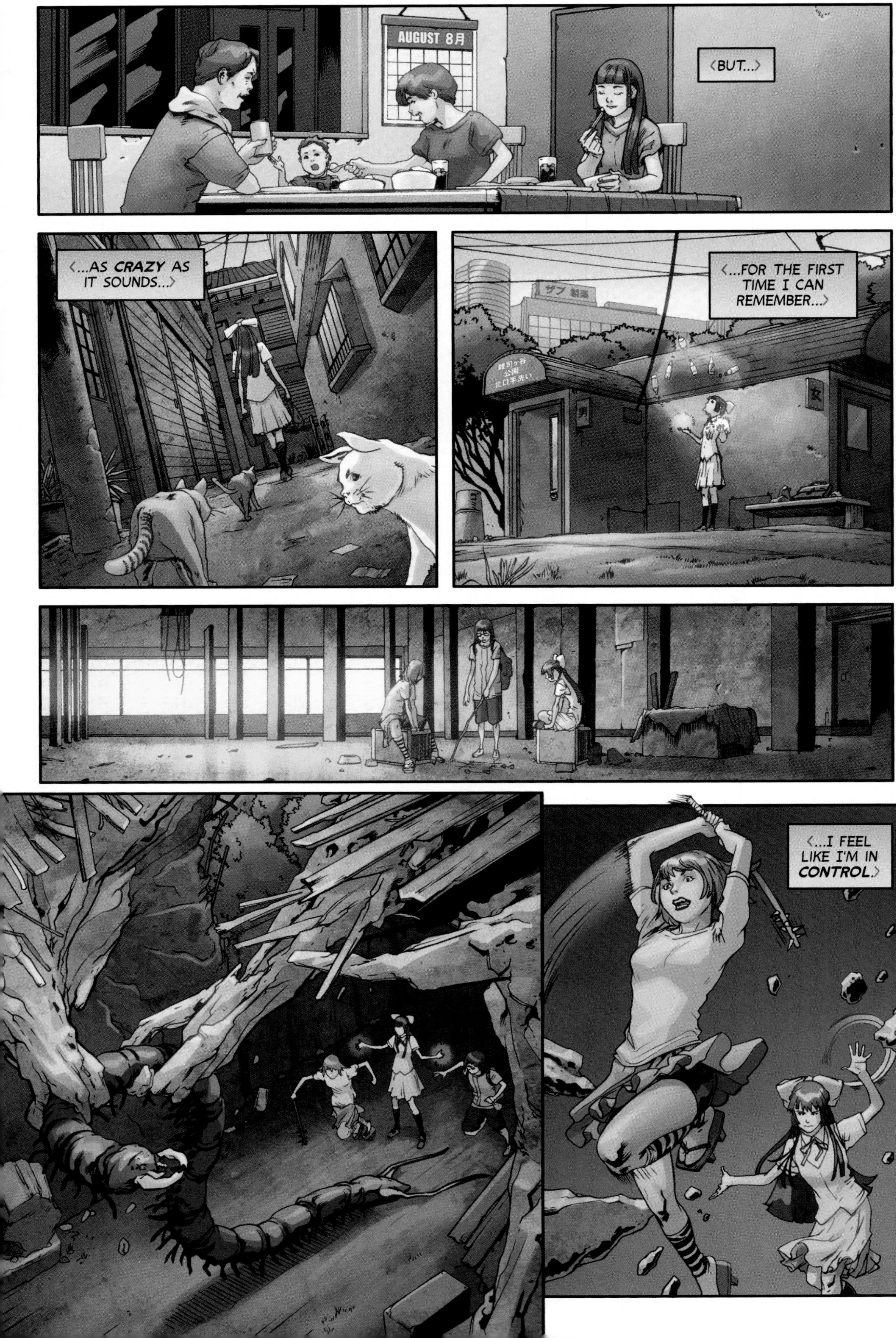
AUGUST 8月
‹BUT...›
‹...AS *CRAZY* AS IT SOUNDS...›
‹...FOR THE FIRST TIME I CAN REMEMBER...›
‹...I FEEL LIKE I'M IN *CONTROL*.›

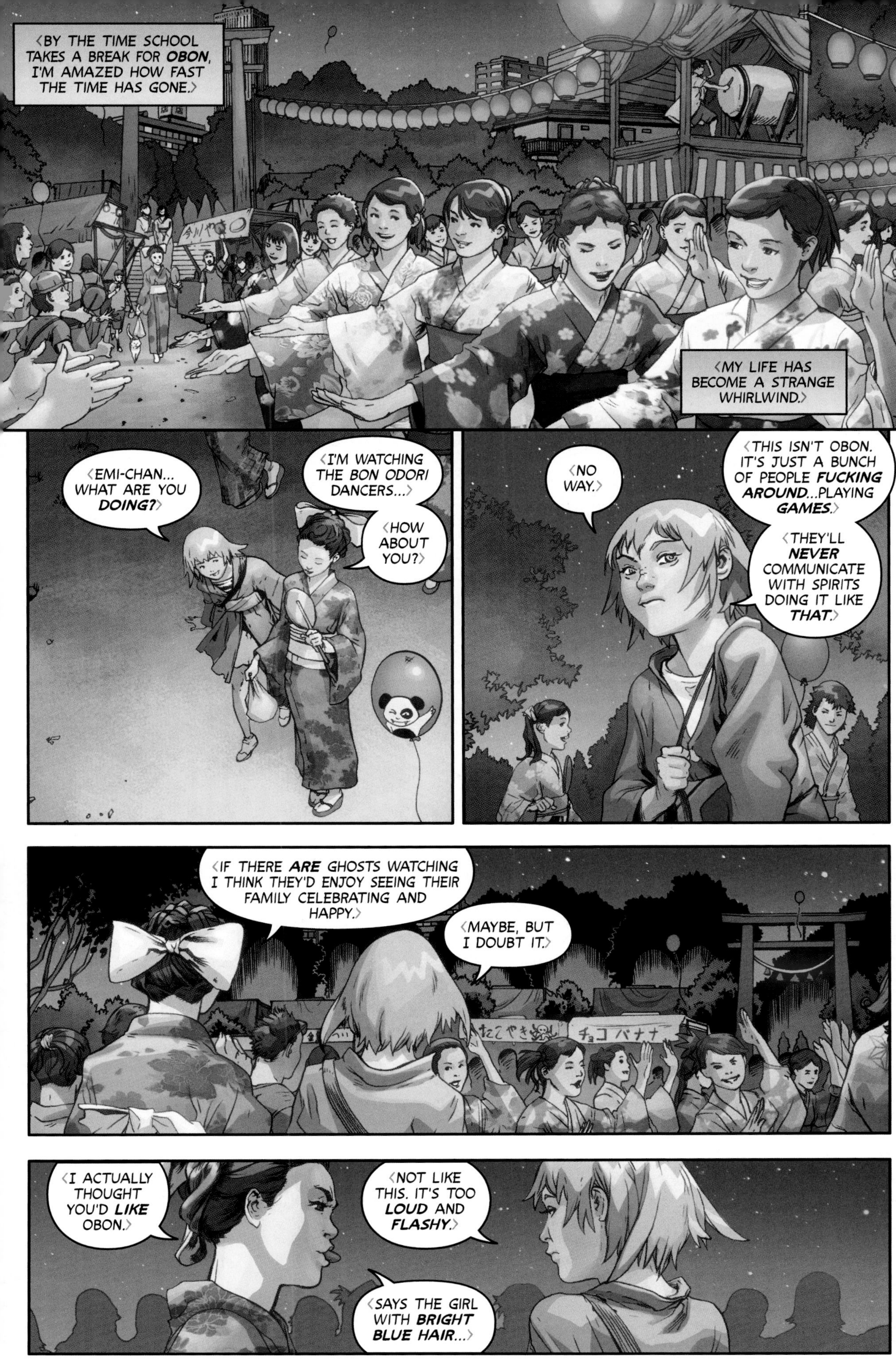
‹BY THE TIME SCHOOL TAKES A BREAK FOR **OBON**, I'M AMAZED HOW FAST THE TIME HAS GONE.›
‹MY LIFE HAS BECOME A STRANGE WHIRLWIND.›
‹EMI-CHAN... WHAT ARE YOU **DOING?**›
‹I'M WATCHING THE *BON ODORI* DANCERS...›
‹HOW ABOUT YOU?›
‹NO WAY.›
‹THIS ISN'T OBON. IT'S JUST A BUNCH OF PEOPLE **FUCKING AROUND**...PLAYING **GAMES**.›
‹THEY'LL **NEVER** COMMUNICATE WITH SPIRITS DOING IT LIKE **THAT**.›
‹IF THERE **ARE** GHOSTS WATCHING I THINK THEY'D ENJOY SEEING THEIR FAMILY CELEBRATING AND HAPPY.›
‹MAYBE, BUT I DOUBT IT.›
たこやき
チョコバナナ
‹I ACTUALLY THOUGHT YOU'D **LIKE** OBON.›
‹NOT LIKE THIS. IT'S TOO **LOUD** AND **FLASHY**.›
‹SAYS THE GIRL WITH **BRIGHT BLUE HAIR**...›

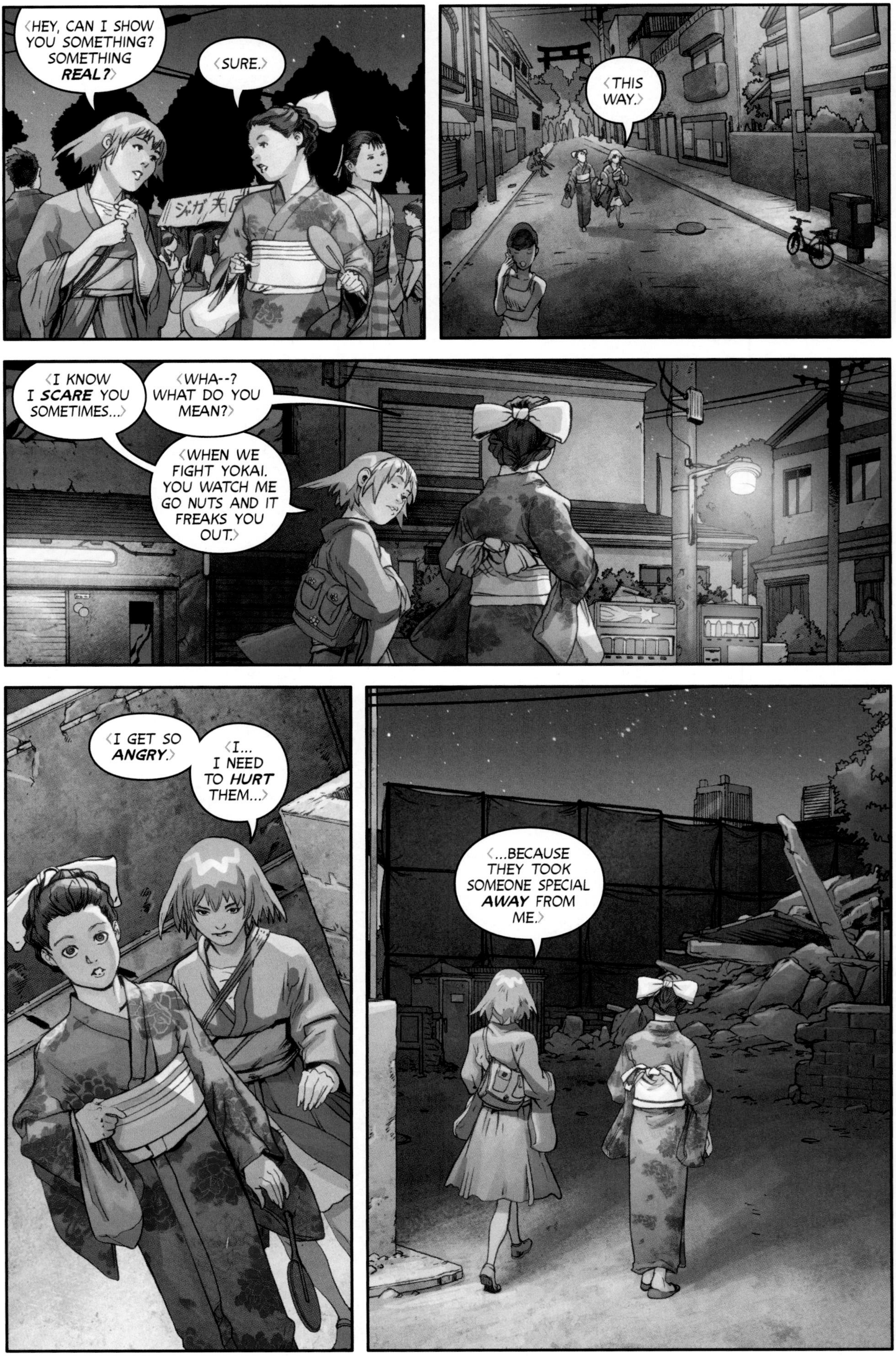

〈HEY, CAN I SHOW YOU SOMETHING? SOMETHING **REAL?**〉
〈SURE.〉
ジガ天
〈THIS WAY.〉
〈I KNOW I **SCARE** YOU SOMETIMES...〉
〈WHA--? WHAT DO YOU MEAN?〉
〈WHEN WE FIGHT YOKAI. YOU WATCH ME GO NUTS AND IT FREAKS YOU OUT.〉
〈I GET SO **ANGRY**.〉
〈I... I NEED TO **HURT** THEM...〉
〈...BECAUSE THEY TOOK SOMEONE SPECIAL **AWAY** FROM ME.〉

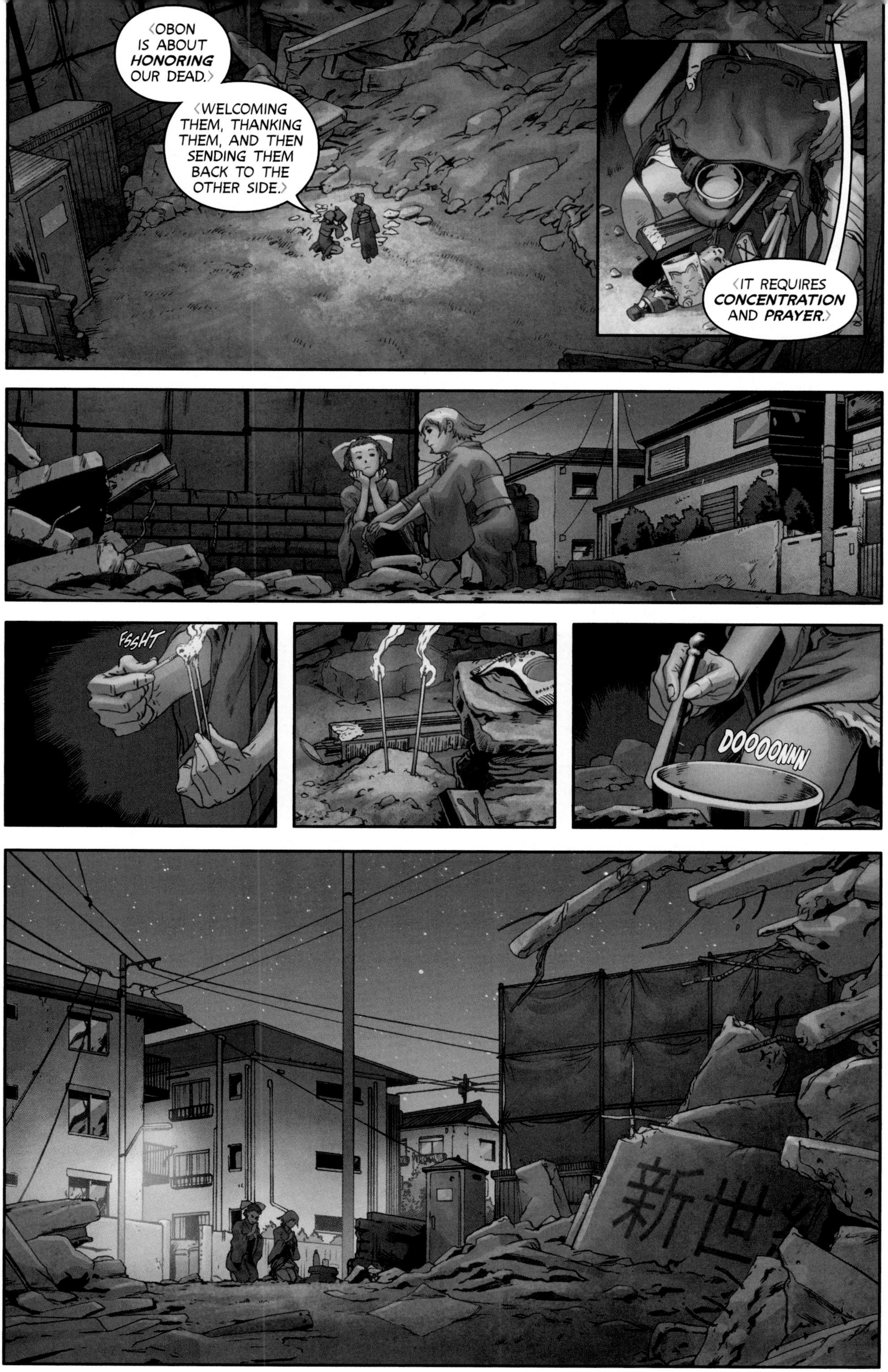
‹OBON IS ABOUT ***HONORING*** OUR DEAD.›
‹WELCOMING THEM, THANKING THEM, AND THEN SENDING THEM BACK TO THE OTHER SIDE.›
‹IT REQUIRES ***CONCENTRATION*** AND ***PRAYER.***›
FSSHT
DOOOONNN
新世

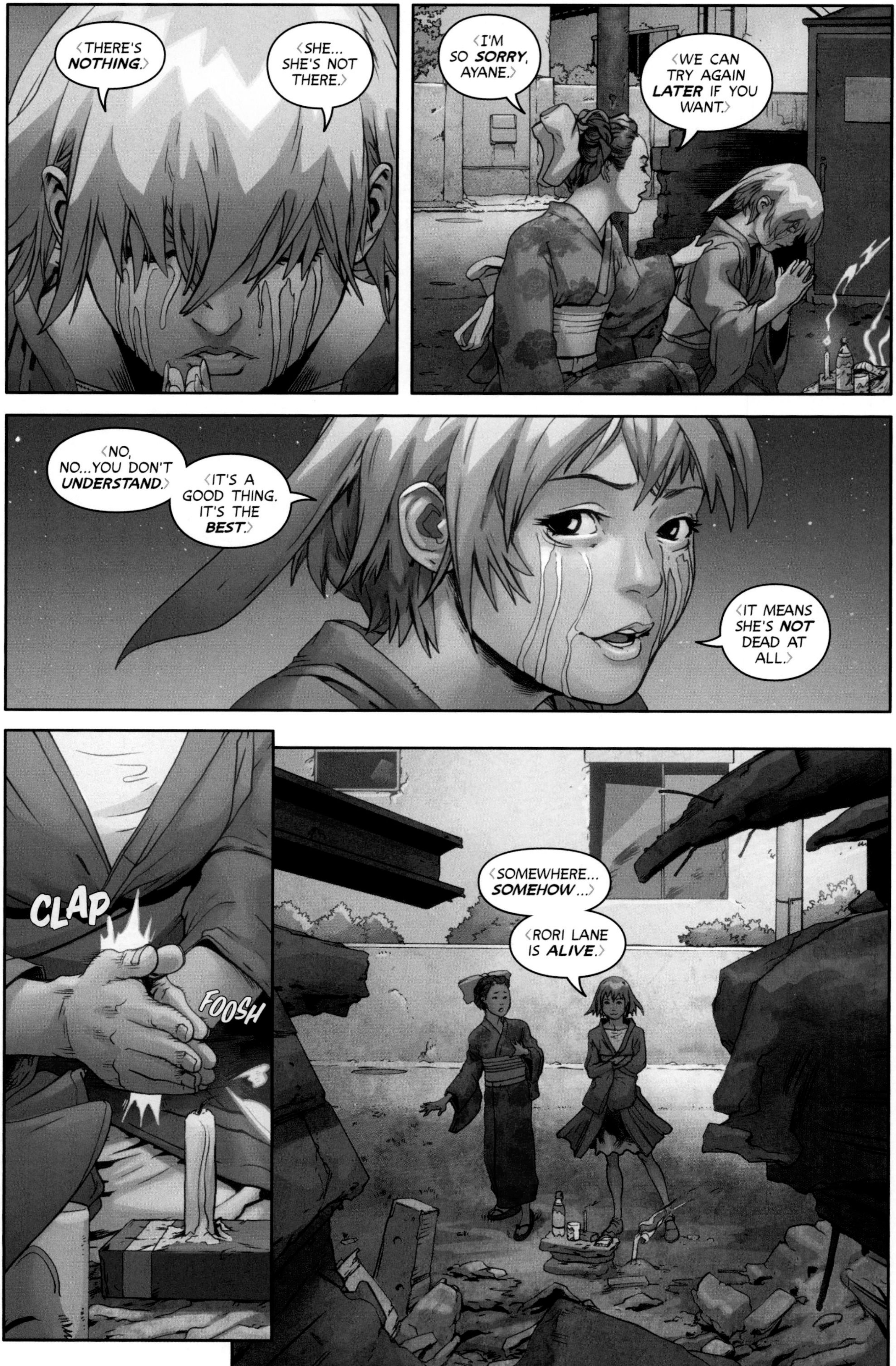
<THERE'S NOTHING.>
<SHE... SHE'S NOT THERE.>
<I'M SO SORRY, AYANE.>
<WE CAN TRY AGAIN LATER IF YOU WANT.>
<NO, NO...YOU DON'T UNDERSTAND.>
<IT'S A GOOD THING. IT'S THE BEST.>
<IT MEANS SHE'S NOT DEAD AT ALL.>
CLAP
FOOSH
<SOMEWHERE... SOMEHOW...>
<RORI LANE IS ALIVE.>

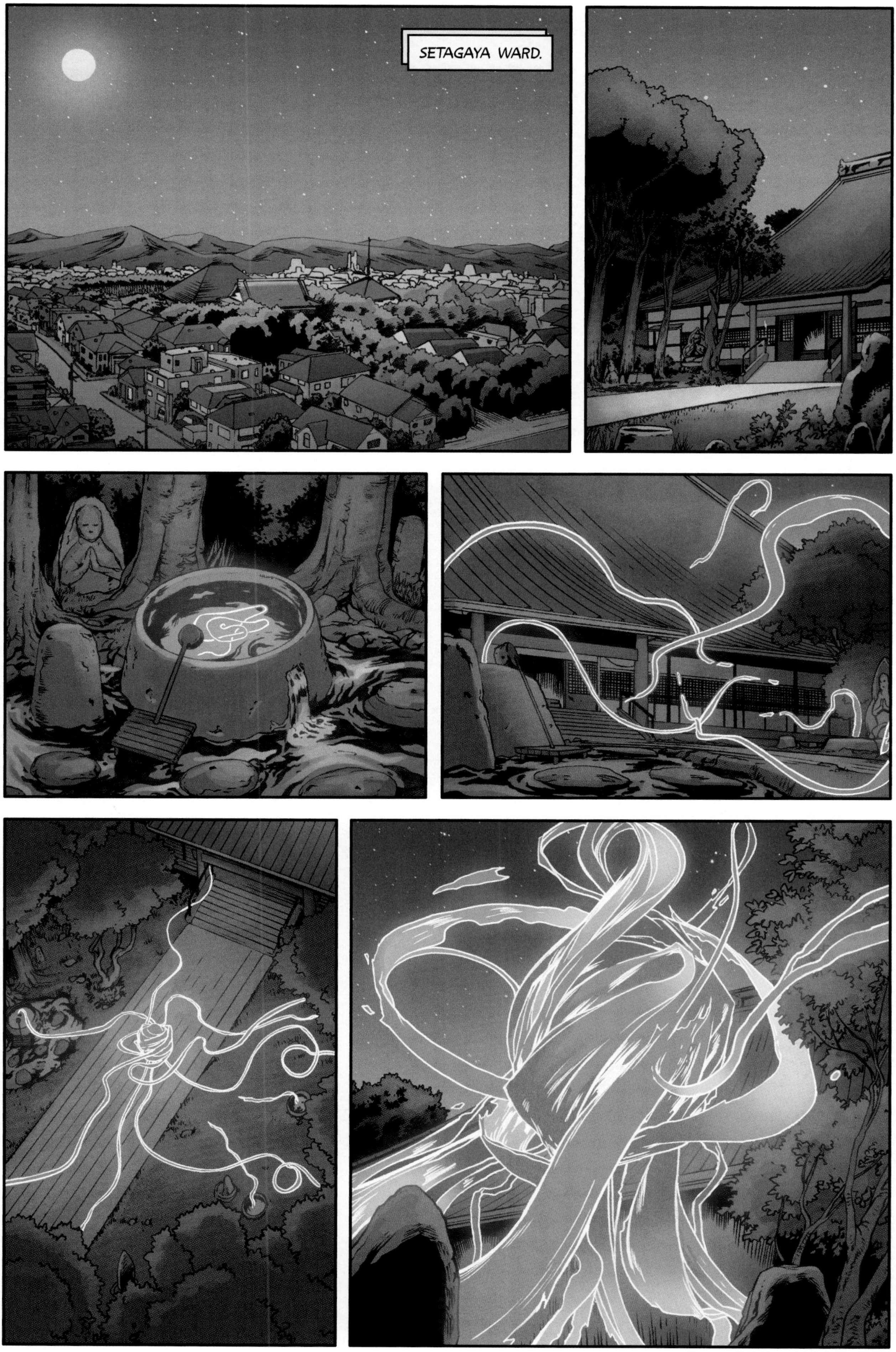
SETAGAYA WARD.

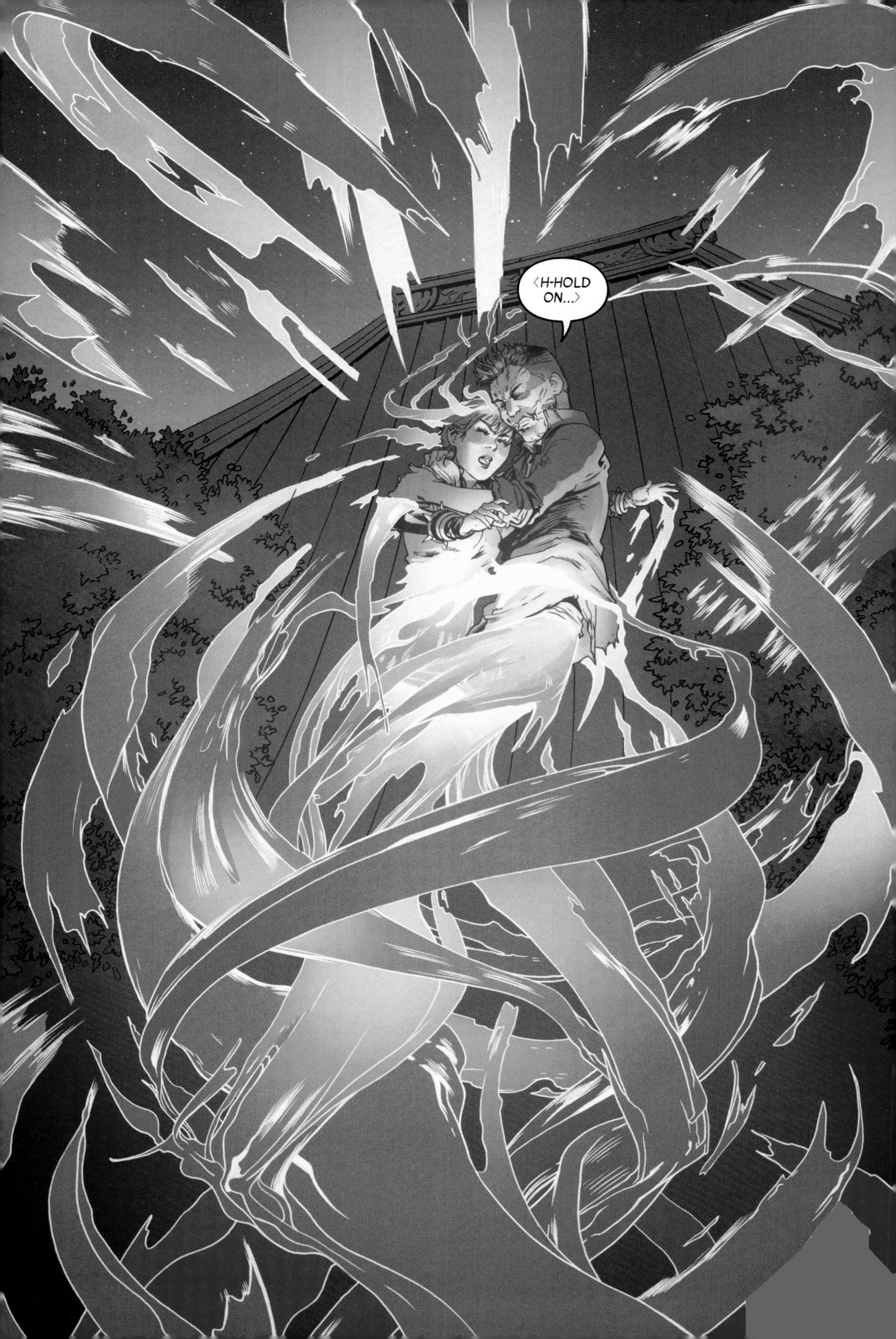
<H-HOLD ON...>

Chapter Eight

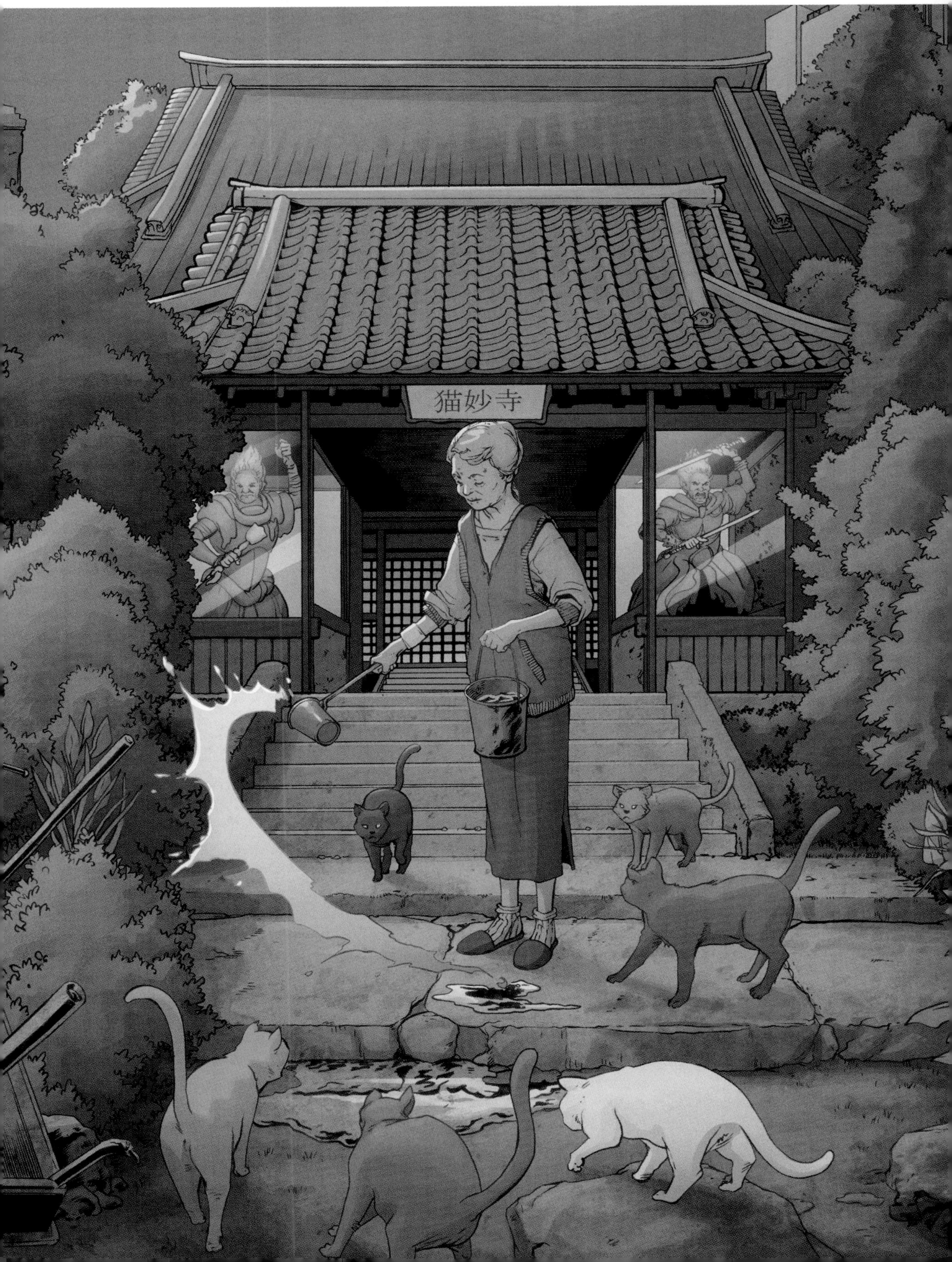
猫妙寺

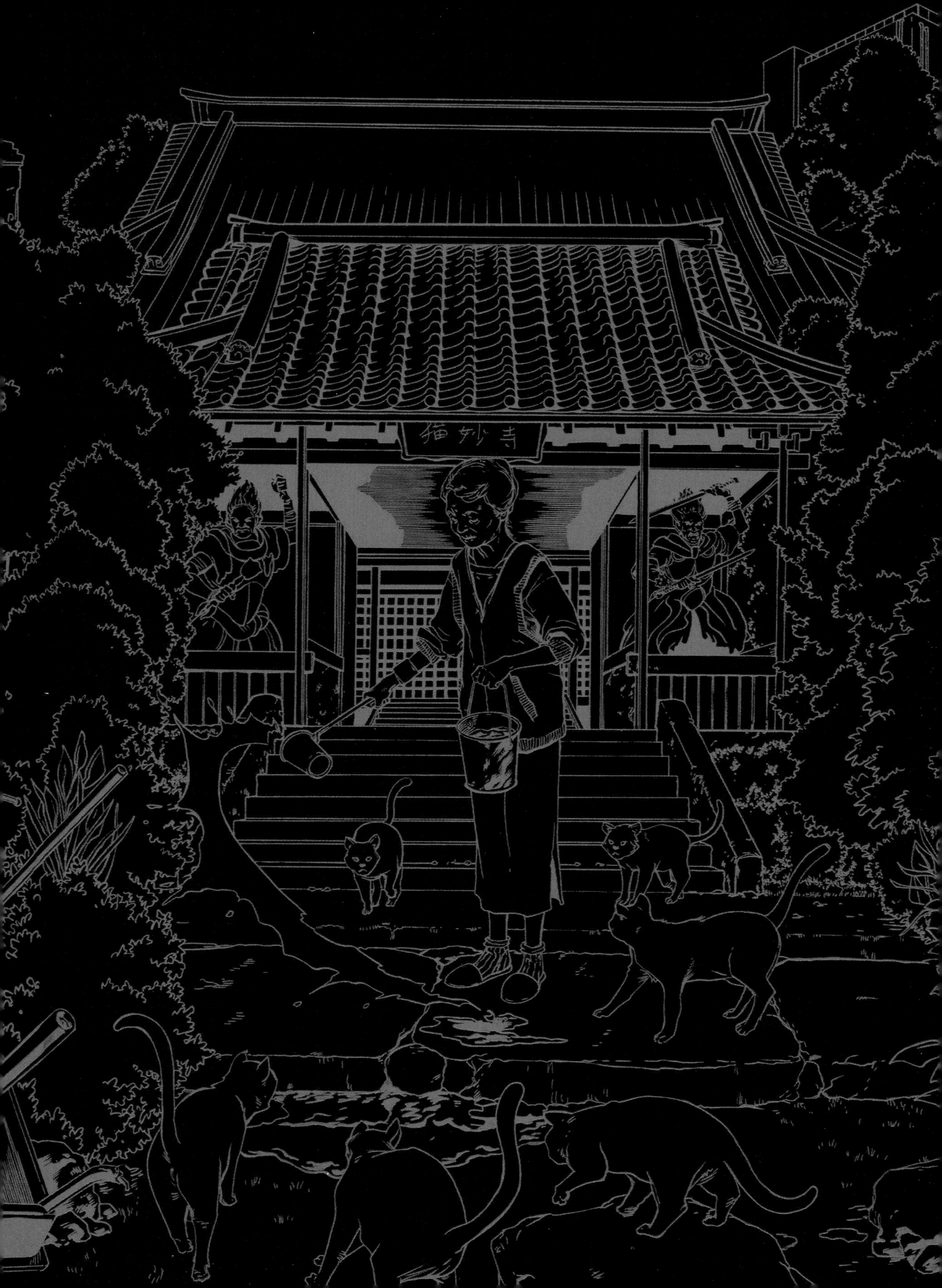
猫妙寺

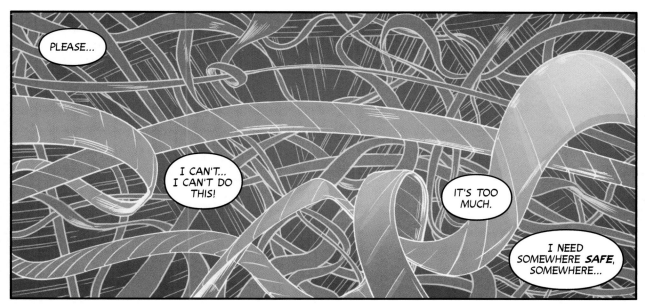

PLEASE...

I CAN'T... I CAN'T DO THIS!

IT'S TOO MUCH.

I NEED SOMEWHERE *SAFE*, SOMEWHERE...

WHA--?

OOF!

♪TERU-TERU-BOZU, TERU BOZU♪ ♪MAKE TOMORROW A SUNNY DAY♪ ♪LIKE THE SKY IN A DREAM SOMETIME♪ ♪IF IT'S SUNNY I'LL GIVE YOU A GOLDEN BELL♪

♪TERU-TERU-BOZU, TERU BOZU♪,

♪MAKE TOMORROW A SUNNY DAY♪

♪IF YOU MAKE MY WISH COME TRUE♪

♪WE'LL DRINK LOTS OF SWEET SAKE♪*

HUH?

♪TERU-TERU-BOZU, TERU BOZU♪

♪MAKE TOMORROW A SUNNY DAY♪

♪BUT IF IT'S CLOUDY AND I FIND YOU CRYING♪

♪THEN I SHALL SNIP YOUR HEAD OFF♪

SPLISH

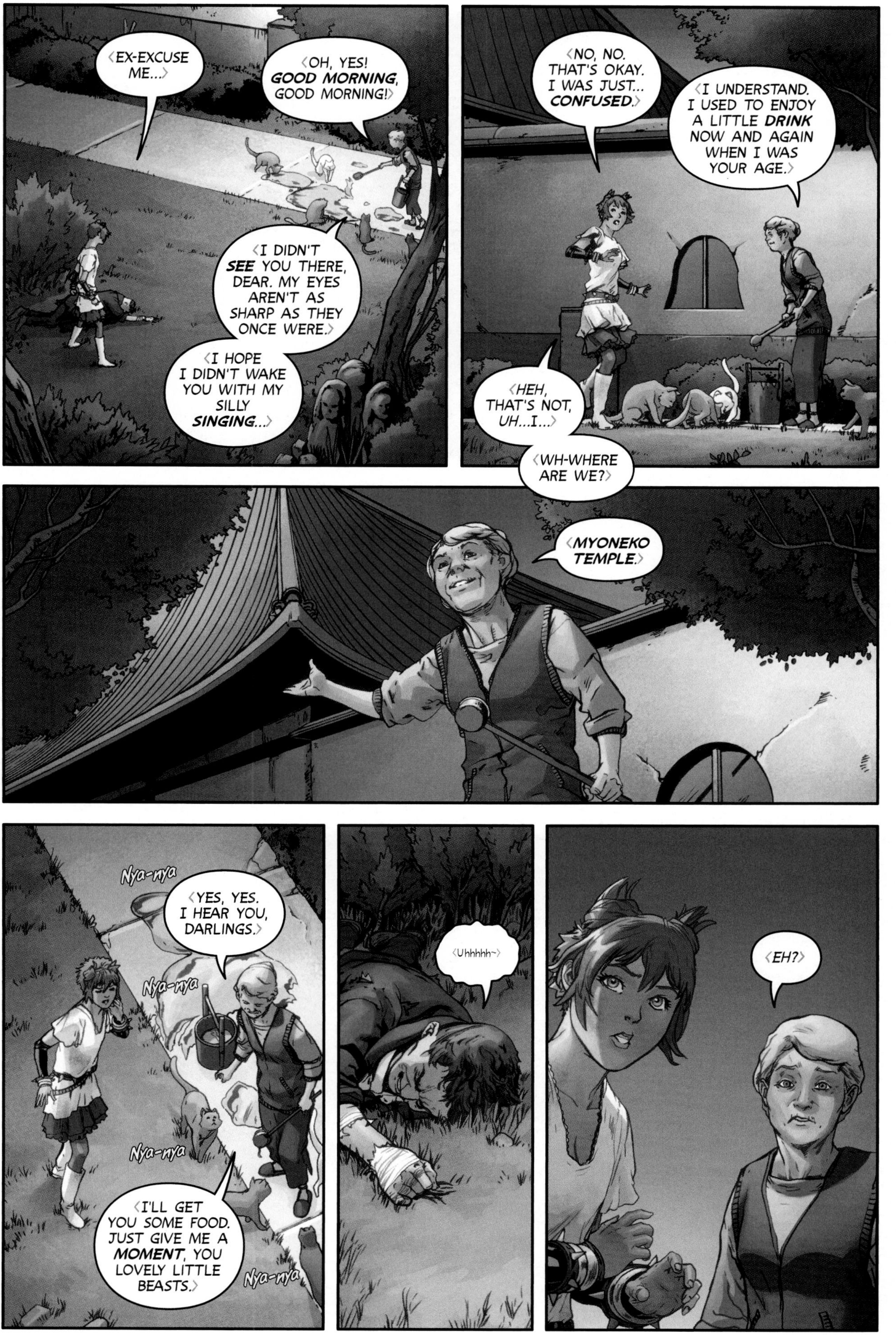
〈EX-EXCUSE ME...〉
〈OH, YES! **GOOD MORNING**, GOOD MORNING!〉
〈I DIDN'T **SEE** YOU THERE, DEAR. MY EYES AREN'T AS SHARP AS THEY ONCE WERE.〉
〈I HOPE I DIDN'T WAKE YOU WITH MY SILLY **SINGING**...〉
〈NO, NO. THAT'S OKAY. I WAS JUST... **CONFUSED**.〉
〈I UNDERSTAND. I USED TO ENJOY A LITTLE **DRINK** NOW AND AGAIN WHEN I WAS YOUR AGE.〉
〈HEH, THAT'S NOT, UH...I...〉
〈WH-WHERE ARE WE?〉
〈**MYONEKO TEMPLE**.〉
Nya-nya
〈YES, YES. I HEAR YOU, DARLINGS.〉
Nya-nya
Nya-nya
〈I'LL GET YOU SOME FOOD. JUST GIVE ME A **MOMENT**, YOU LOVELY LITTLE BEASTS.〉
Nya-nya
〈Uhhhhh~〉
〈EH?〉

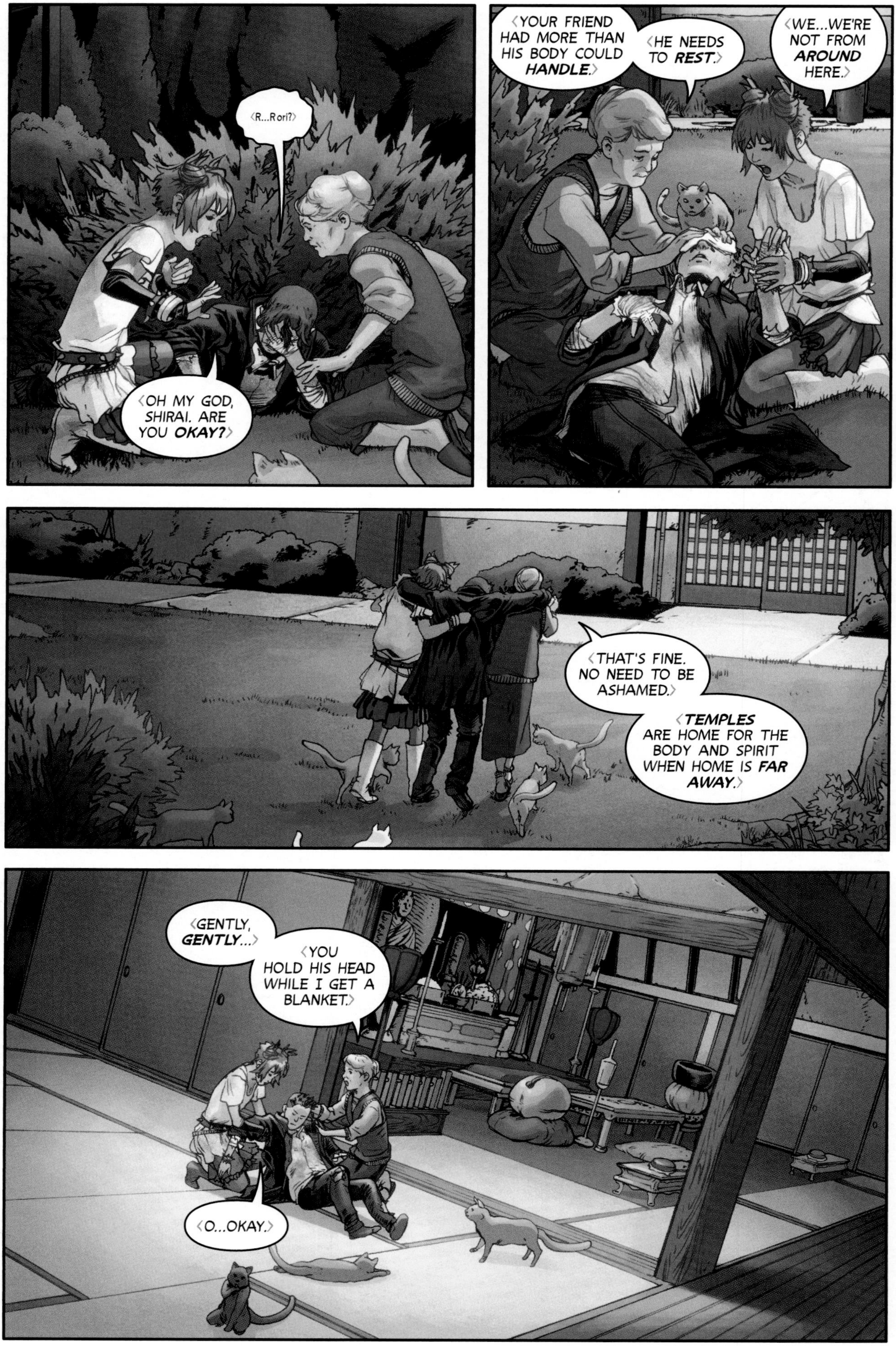
〈R...Rori?〉
〈OH MY GOD, SHIRAI. ARE YOU **OKAY?**〉
〈YOUR FRIEND HAD MORE THAN HIS BODY COULD **HANDLE.**〉
〈HE NEEDS TO **REST.**〉
〈WE...WE'RE NOT FROM **AROUND** HERE.〉
〈THAT'S FINE. NO NEED TO BE ASHAMED.〉
〈**TEMPLES** ARE HOME FOR THE BODY AND SPIRIT WHEN HOME IS **FAR AWAY.**〉
〈GENTLY, **GENTLY**...〉
〈YOU HOLD HIS HEAD WHILE I GET A BLANKET.〉
〈O...OKAY.〉

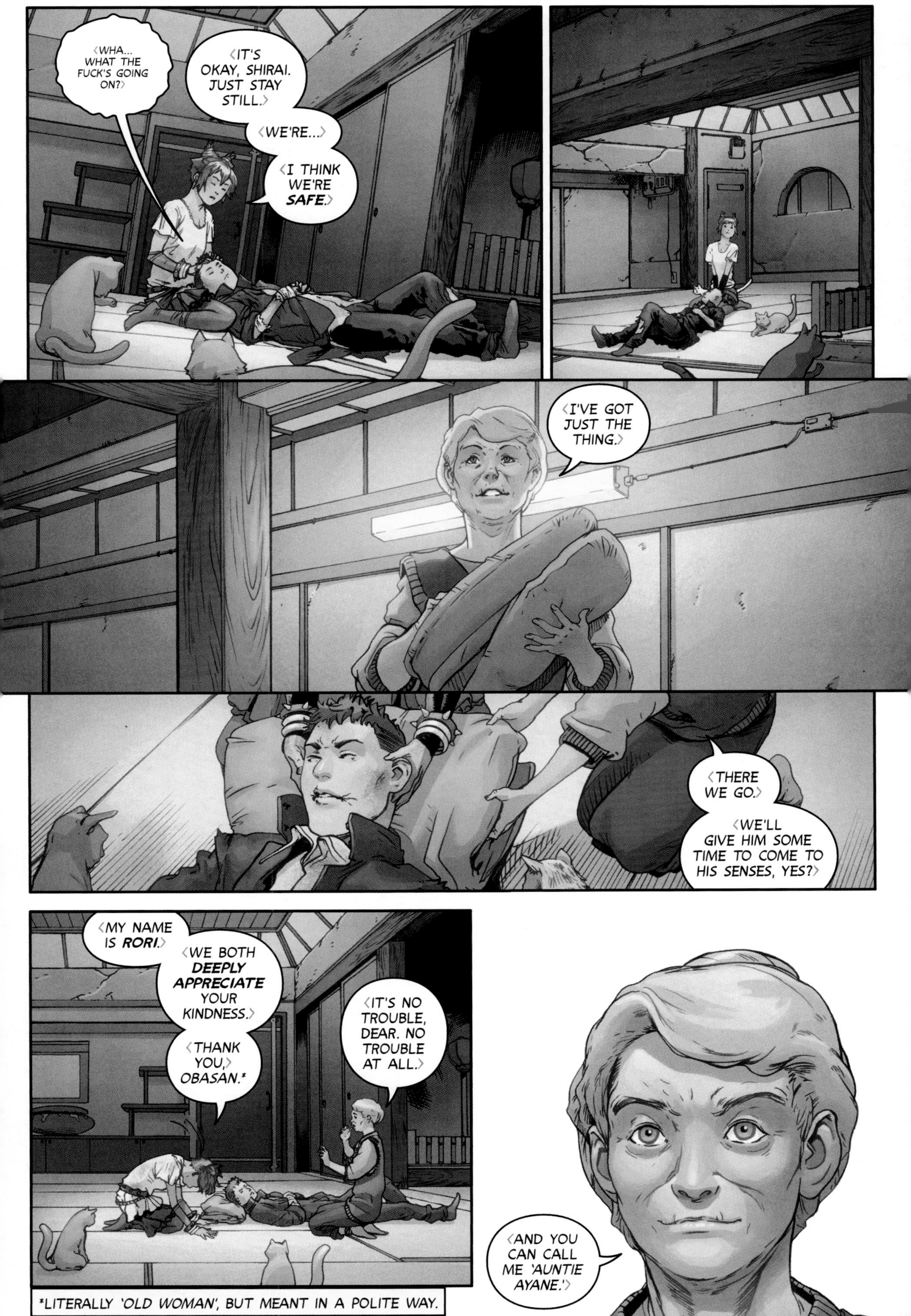

‹WHA... WHAT THE FUCK'S GOING ON?›
‹IT'S OKAY, SHIRAI. JUST STAY STILL.›
‹WE'RE...›
‹I THINK WE'RE **SAFE**.›
‹I'VE GOT JUST THE THING.›
‹THERE WE GO.›
‹WE'LL GIVE HIM SOME TIME TO COME TO HIS SENSES, YES?›
‹MY NAME IS **RORI**.›
‹WE BOTH **DEEPLY APPRECIATE** YOUR KINDNESS.›
‹THANK YOU,› OBASAN.*
‹IT'S NO TROUBLE, DEAR. NO TROUBLE AT ALL.›
*LITERALLY *'OLD WOMAN'*, BUT MEANT IN A POLITE WAY.
‹AND YOU CAN CALL ME *'AUNTIE AYANE.'*›

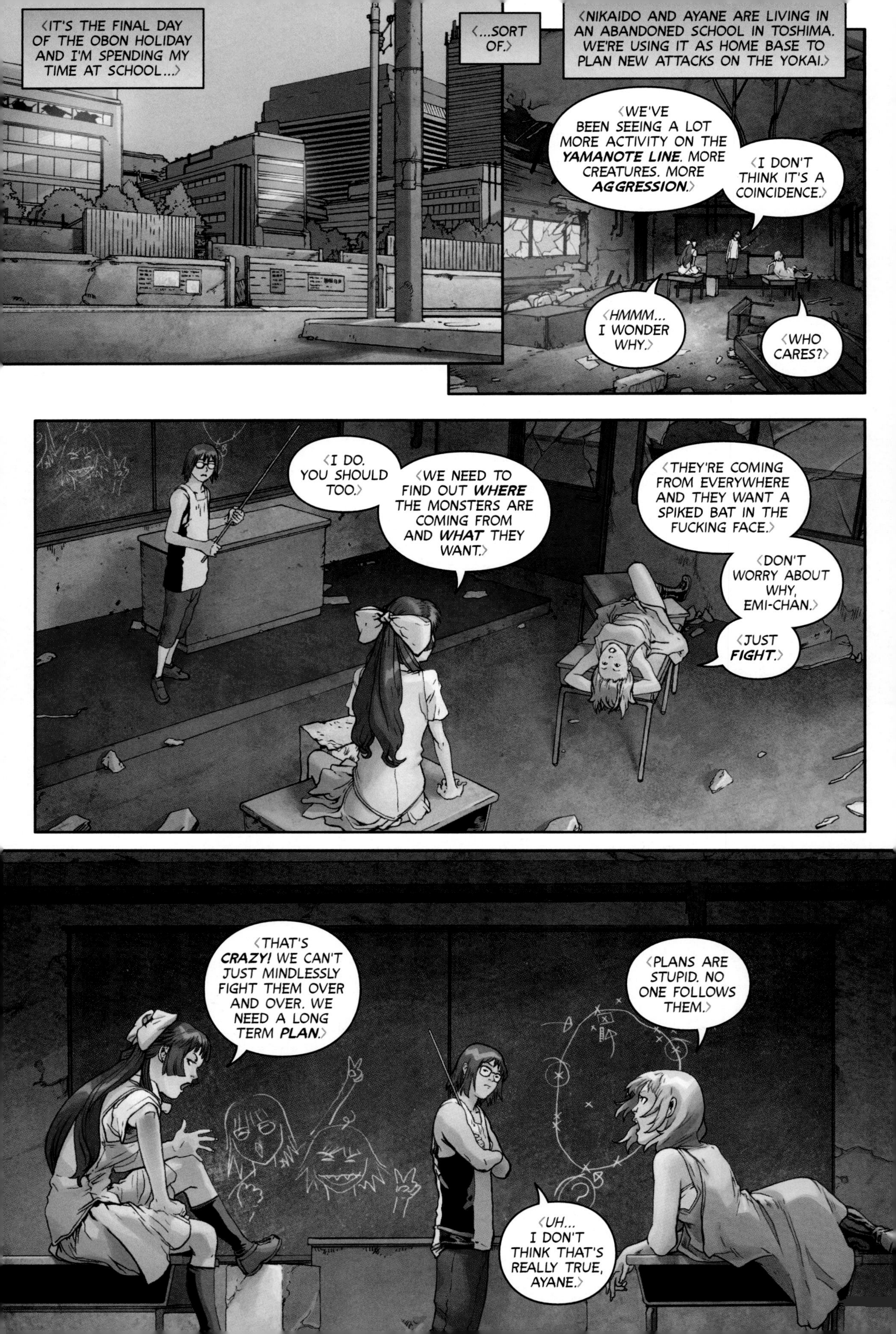
‹IT'S THE FINAL DAY OF THE OBON HOLIDAY AND I'M SPENDING MY TIME AT SCHOOL...›
‹...SORT OF.›
‹NIKAIDO AND AYANE ARE LIVING IN AN ABANDONED SCHOOL IN TOSHIMA. WE'RE USING IT AS HOME BASE TO PLAN NEW ATTACKS ON THE YOKAI.›
‹WE'VE BEEN SEEING A LOT MORE ACTIVITY ON THE ***YAMANOTE LINE***. MORE CREATURES. MORE ***AGGRESSION***.›
‹I DON'T THINK IT'S A COINCIDENCE.›
‹HMMM... I WONDER WHY.›
‹WHO CARES?›
‹I DO. YOU SHOULD TOO.›
‹WE NEED TO FIND OUT ***WHERE*** THE MONSTERS ARE COMING FROM AND ***WHAT*** THEY WANT.›
‹THEY'RE COMING FROM EVERYWHERE AND THEY WANT A SPIKED BAT IN THE FUCKING FACE.›
‹DON'T WORRY ABOUT WHY, EMI-CHAN.›
‹JUST ***FIGHT***.›
‹THAT'S ***CRAZY!*** WE CAN'T JUST MINDLESSLY FIGHT THEM OVER AND OVER. WE NEED A LONG TERM ***PLAN***.›
‹PLANS ARE STUPID. NO ONE FOLLOWS THEM.›
‹UH... I DON'T THINK THAT'S REALLY TRUE, AYANE.›

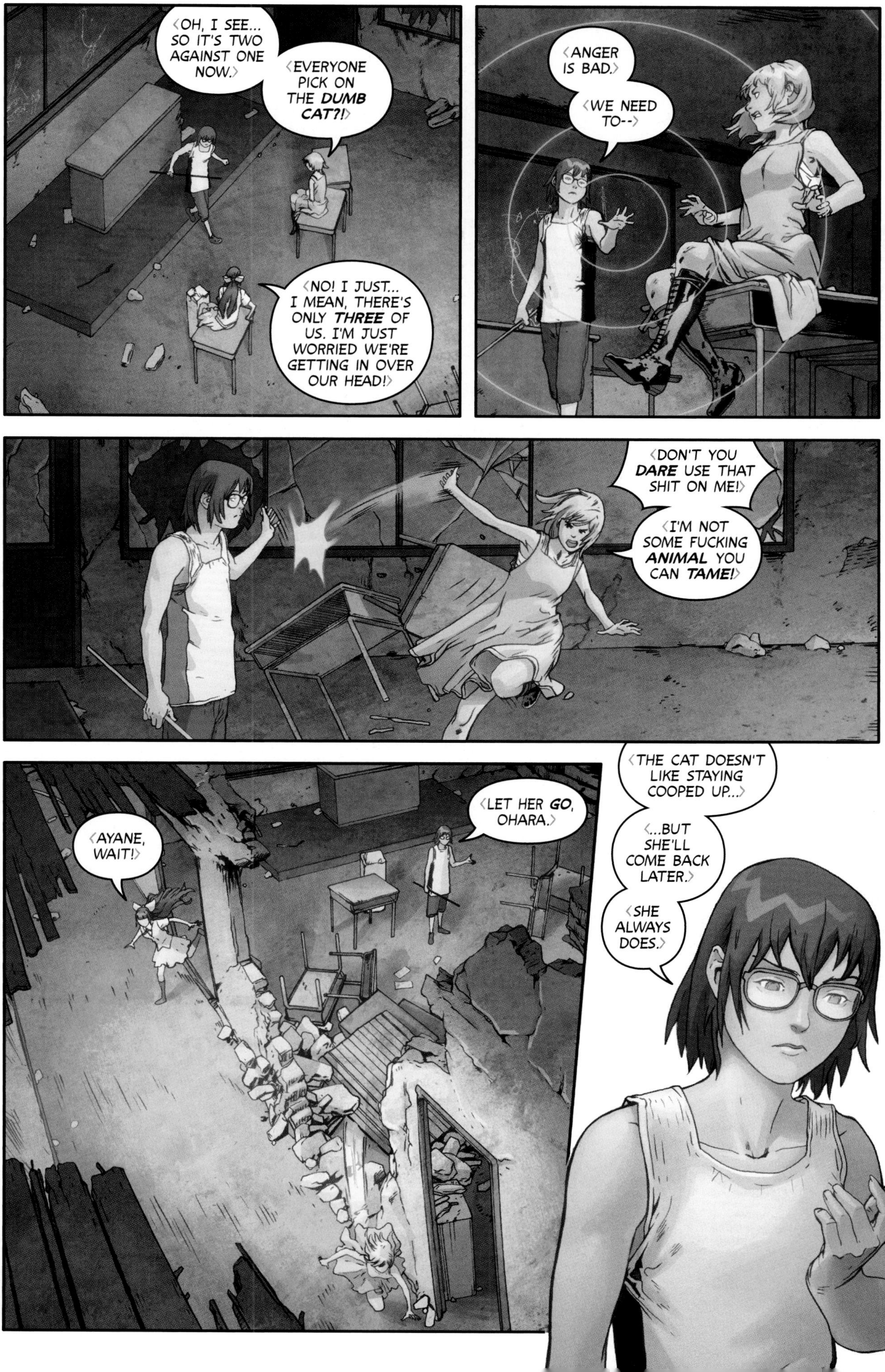
‹OH, I SEE... SO IT'S TWO AGAINST ONE NOW.›
‹EVERYONE PICK ON THE *DUMB CAT?!*›
‹NO! I JUST... I MEAN, THERE'S ONLY *THREE* OF US. I'M JUST WORRIED WE'RE GETTING IN OVER OUR HEAD!›
‹ANGER IS BAD.›
‹WE NEED TO--›
‹DON'T YOU *DARE* USE THAT SHIT ON ME!›
‹I'M NOT SOME FUCKING *ANIMAL* YOU CAN *TAME!*›
‹AYANE, WAIT!›
‹LET HER *GO*, OHARA.›
‹THE CAT DOESN'T LIKE STAYING COOPED UP...›
‹...BUT SHE'LL COME BACK LATER.›
‹SHE ALWAYS DOES.›

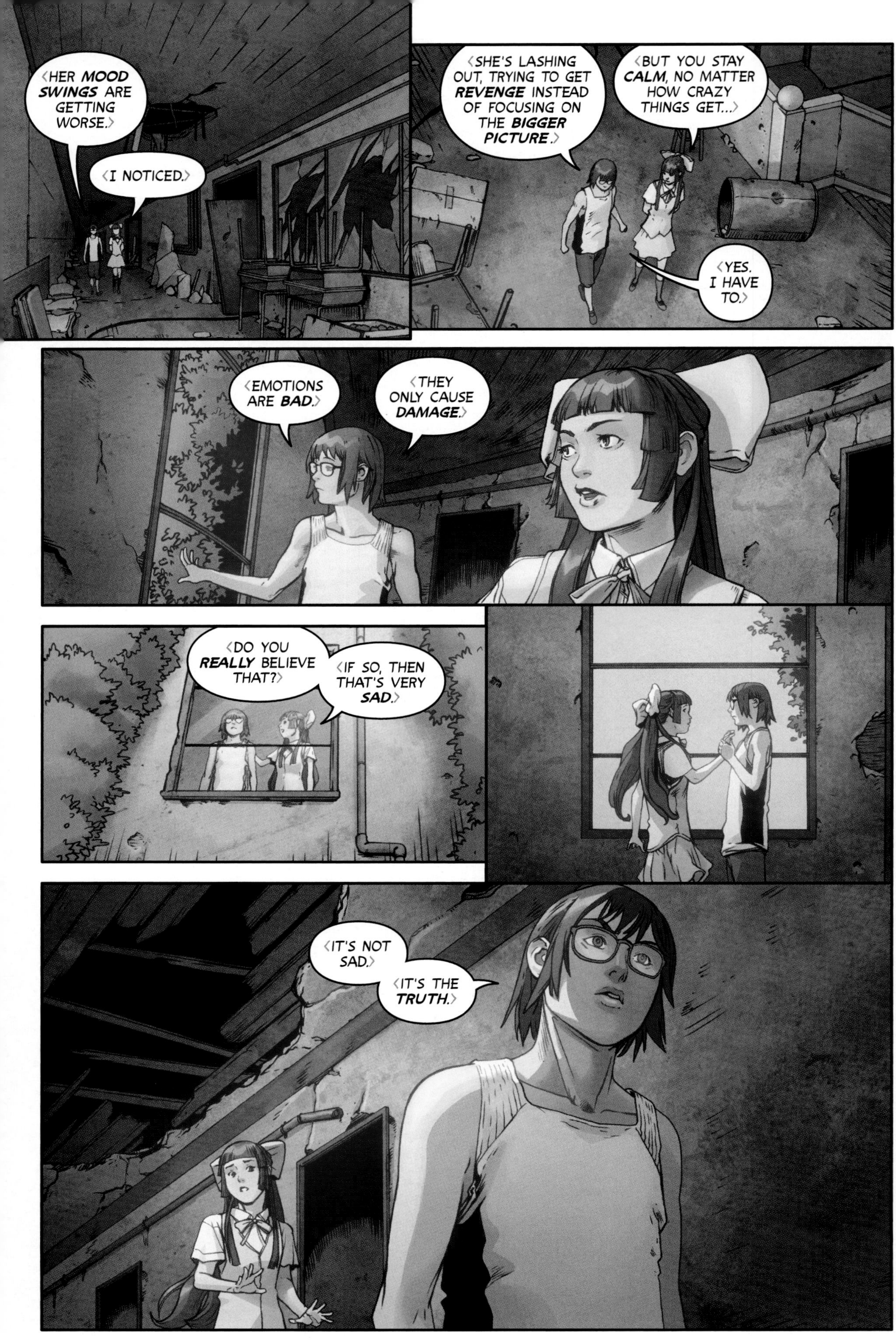
⟨HER **MOOD SWINGS** ARE GETTING WORSE.⟩
⟨I NOTICED.⟩
⟨SHE'S LASHING OUT, TRYING TO GET **REVENGE** INSTEAD OF FOCUSING ON THE **BIGGER PICTURE**.⟩
⟨BUT YOU STAY **CALM**, NO MATTER HOW CRAZY THINGS GET...⟩
⟨YES. I HAVE TO.⟩
⟨EMOTIONS ARE **BAD**.⟩
⟨THEY ONLY CAUSE **DAMAGE**.⟩
⟨DO YOU **REALLY** BELIEVE THAT?⟩
⟨IF SO, THEN THAT'S VERY **SAD**.⟩
⟨IT'S NOT SAD.⟩
⟨IT'S THE **TRUTH**.⟩

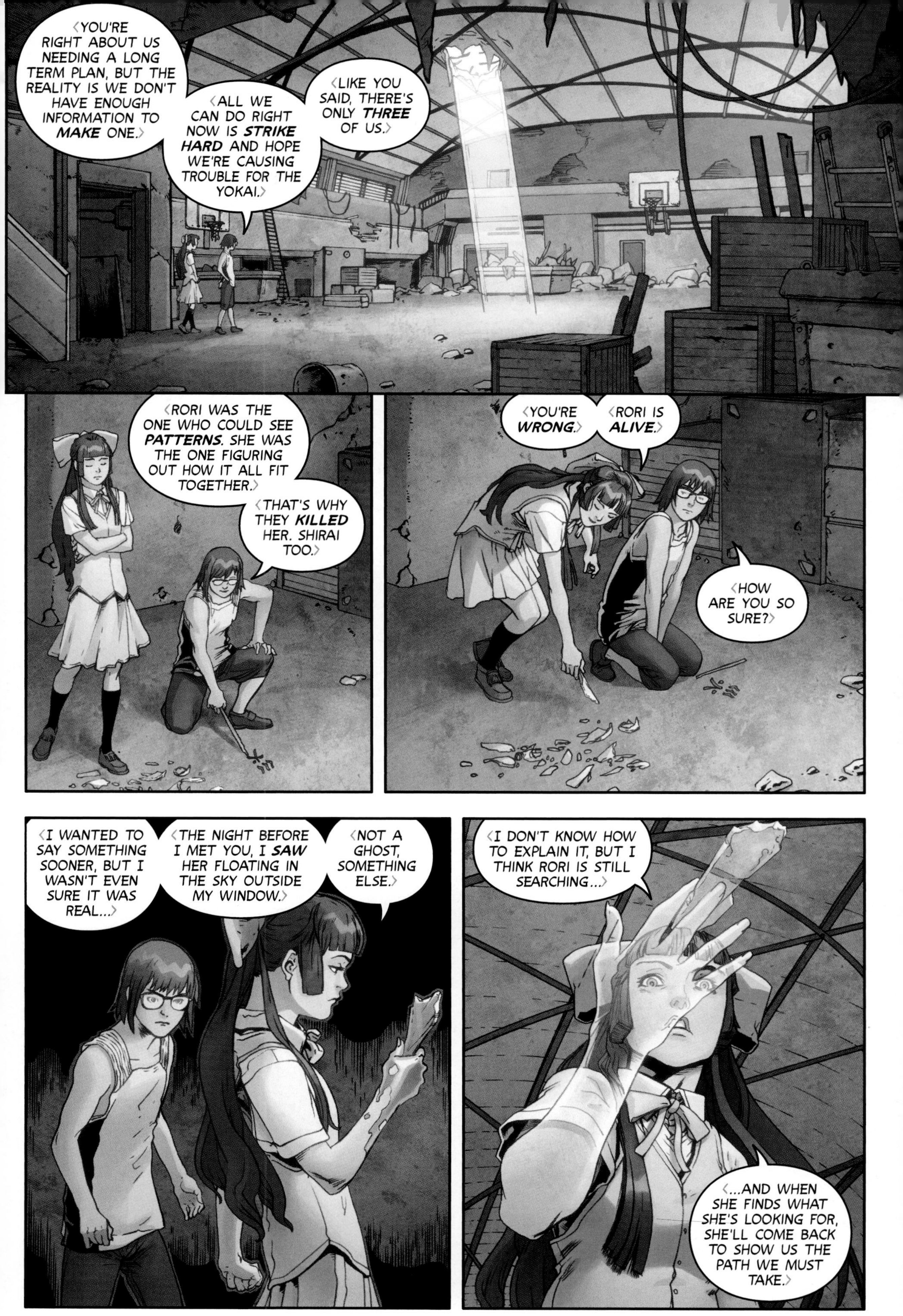

‹YOU'RE RIGHT ABOUT US NEEDING A LONG TERM PLAN, BUT THE REALITY IS WE DON'T HAVE ENOUGH INFORMATION TO MAKE ONE.›
‹ALL WE CAN DO RIGHT NOW IS STRIKE HARD AND HOPE WE'RE CAUSING TROUBLE FOR THE YOKAI.›
‹LIKE YOU SAID, THERE'S ONLY THREE OF US.›
‹RORI WAS THE ONE WHO COULD SEE PATTERNS. SHE WAS THE ONE FIGURING OUT HOW IT ALL FIT TOGETHER.›
‹THAT'S WHY THEY KILLED HER. SHIRAI TOO.›
‹YOU'RE WRONG.›
‹RORI IS ALIVE.›
‹HOW ARE YOU SO SURE?›
‹I WANTED TO SAY SOMETHING SOONER, BUT I WASN'T EVEN SURE IT WAS REAL...›
‹THE NIGHT BEFORE I MET YOU, I SAW HER FLOATING IN THE SKY OUTSIDE MY WINDOW.›
‹NOT A GHOST, SOMETHING ELSE.›
‹I DON'T KNOW HOW TO EXPLAIN IT, BUT I THINK RORI IS STILL SEARCHING...›
‹...AND WHEN SHE FINDS WHAT SHE'S LOOKING FOR, SHE'LL COME BACK TO SHOW US THE PATH WE MUST TAKE.›

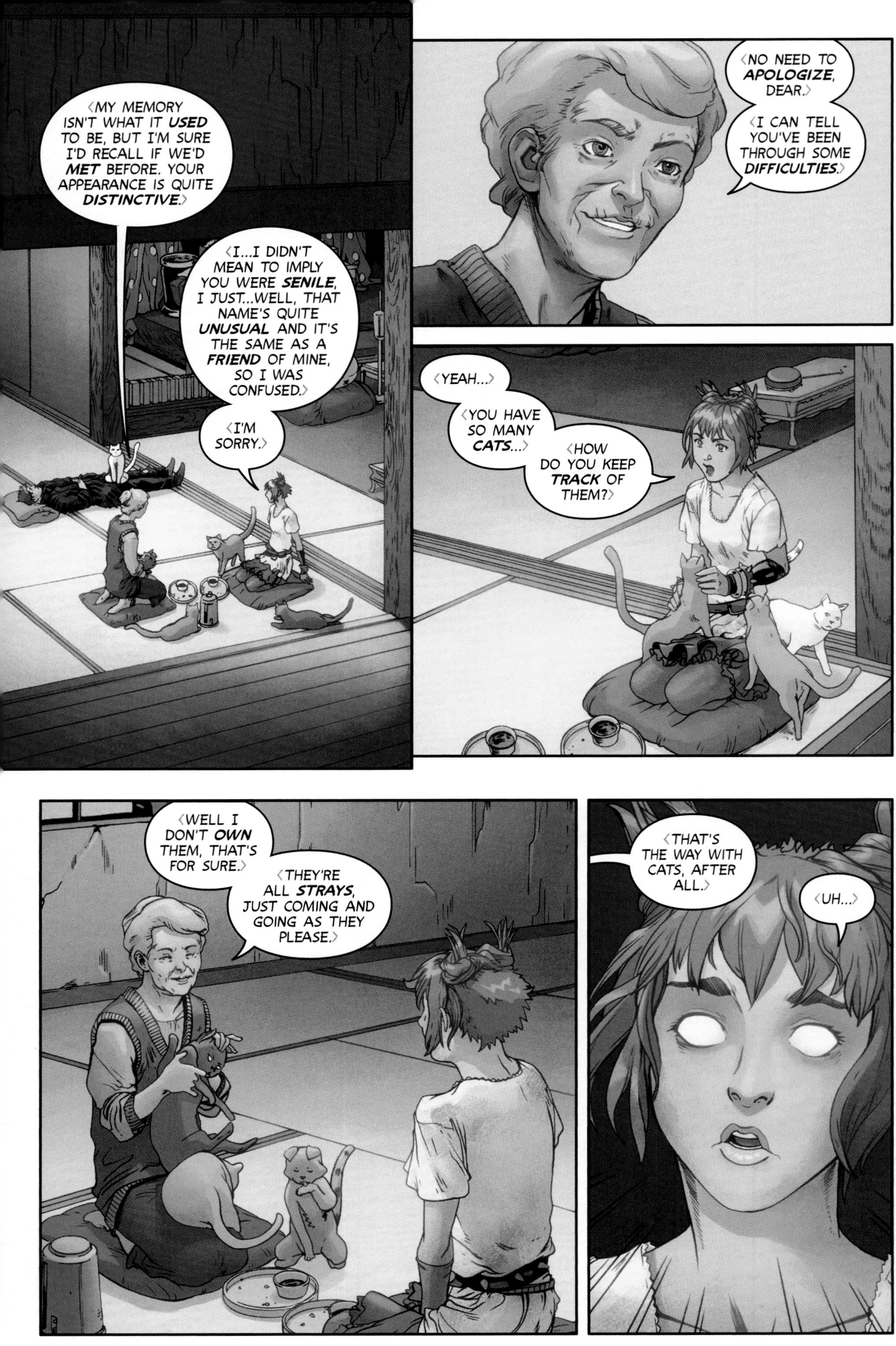
‹MY MEMORY ISN'T WHAT IT USED TO BE, BUT I'M SURE I'D RECALL IF WE'D MET BEFORE. YOUR APPEARANCE IS QUITE DISTINCTIVE.›
‹I...I DIDN'T MEAN TO IMPLY YOU WERE SENILE, I JUST...WELL, THAT NAME'S QUITE UNUSUAL AND IT'S THE SAME AS A FRIEND OF MINE, SO I WAS CONFUSED.›
‹I'M SORRY.›
‹NO NEED TO APOLOGIZE, DEAR.›
‹I CAN TELL YOU'VE BEEN THROUGH SOME DIFFICULTIES.›
‹YEAH...›
‹YOU HAVE SO MANY CATS...›
‹HOW DO YOU KEEP TRACK OF THEM?›
‹WELL I DON'T OWN THEM, THAT'S FOR SURE.›
‹THEY'RE ALL STRAYS, JUST COMING AND GOING AS THEY PLEASE.›
‹THAT'S THE WAY WITH CATS, AFTER ALL.›
‹UH...›

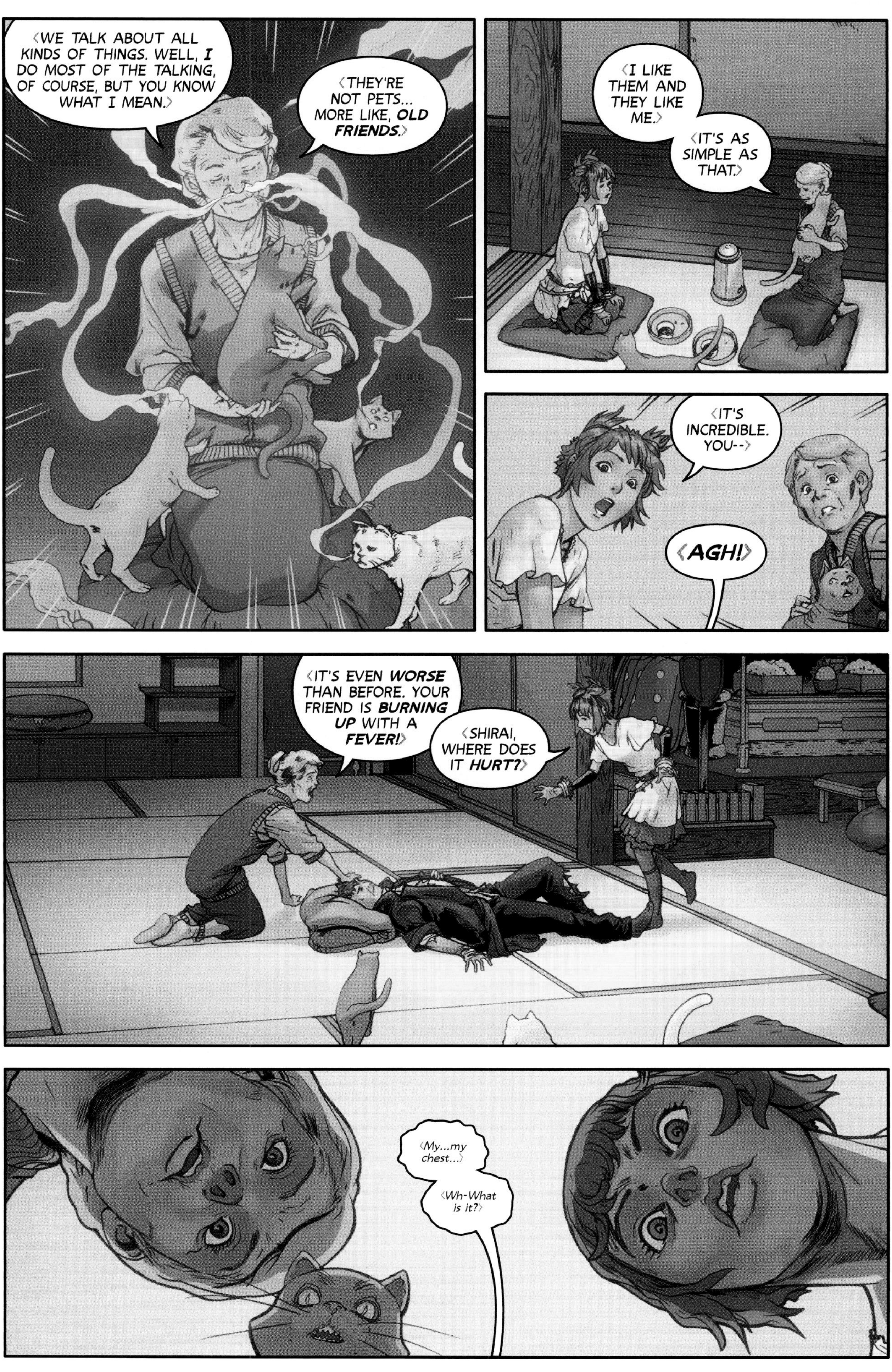
‹WE TALK ABOUT ALL KINDS OF THINGS. WELL, ***I*** DO MOST OF THE TALKING, OF COURSE, BUT YOU KNOW WHAT I MEAN.›
‹THEY'RE NOT PETS... MORE LIKE, ***OLD FRIENDS.***›
‹I LIKE THEM AND THEY LIKE ME.›
‹IT'S AS SIMPLE AS THAT.›
‹IT'S INCREDIBLE. YOU--›
‹***AGH!***›
‹IT'S EVEN ***WORSE*** THAN BEFORE. YOUR FRIEND IS ***BURNING UP*** WITH A ***FEVER!***›
‹SHIRAI, WHERE DOES IT ***HURT?***›
‹*My...my chest...*›
‹*Wh-What is it?*›

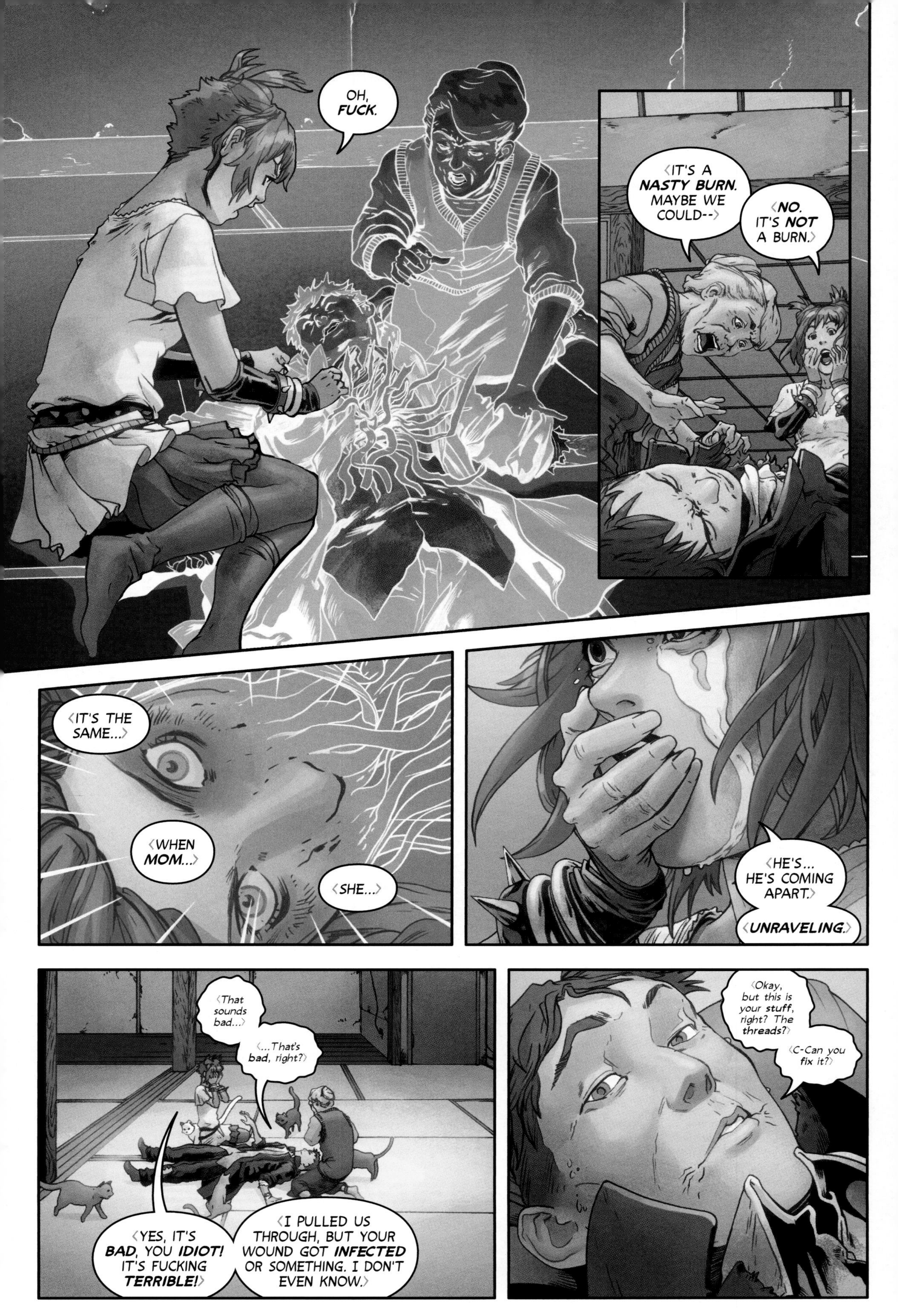
OH, **FUCK**.
‹IT'S A **NASTY BURN**. MAYBE WE COULD--›
‹**NO**. IT'S **NOT** A BURN.›
‹IT'S THE SAME...›
‹WHEN **MOM**...›
‹SHE...›
‹HE'S... HE'S COMING APART.›
‹**UNRAVELING**.›
‹*That sounds bad...*›
‹*...That's **bad**, right?*›
‹YES, IT'S **BAD**, YOU **IDIOT!** IT'S FUCKING **TERRIBLE!**›
‹I PULLED US THROUGH, BUT YOUR WOUND GOT **INFECTED** OR SOMETHING. I DON'T EVEN KNOW.›
‹*Okay, but this is your **stuff**, right? The **threads**?*›
‹*C-Can you **fix** it?*›

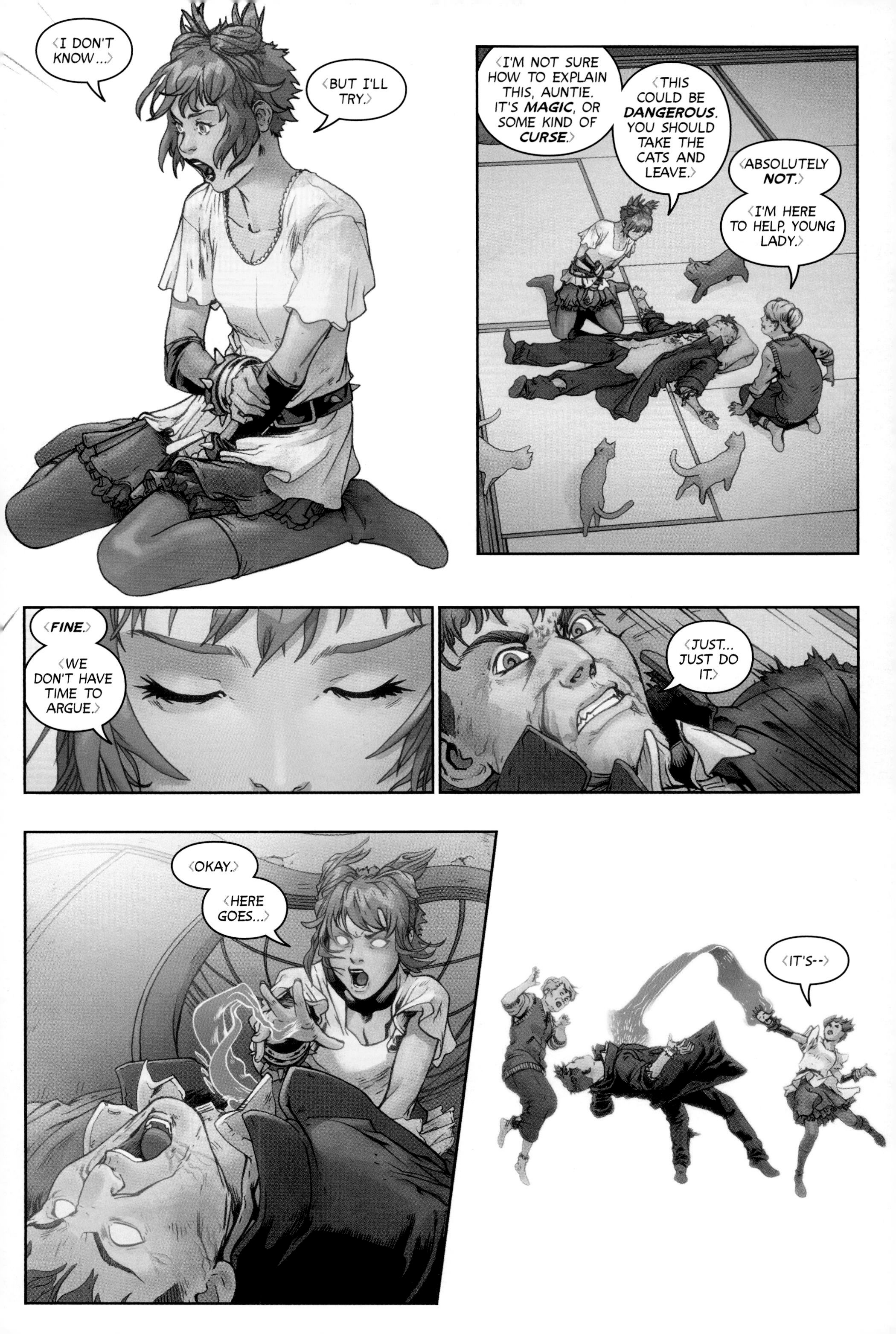

‹I DON'T KNOW...›
‹BUT I'LL TRY.›
‹I'M NOT SURE HOW TO EXPLAIN THIS, AUNTIE. IT'S **MAGIC**, OR SOME KIND OF **CURSE**.›
‹THIS COULD BE **DANGEROUS**. YOU SHOULD TAKE THE CATS AND LEAVE.›
‹ABSOLUTELY **NOT**.›
‹I'M HERE TO HELP, YOUNG LADY.›
‹**FINE**.›
‹WE DON'T HAVE TIME TO ARGUE.›
‹JUST... JUST DO IT.›
‹OKAY.›
‹HERE GOES...›
‹IT'S--›

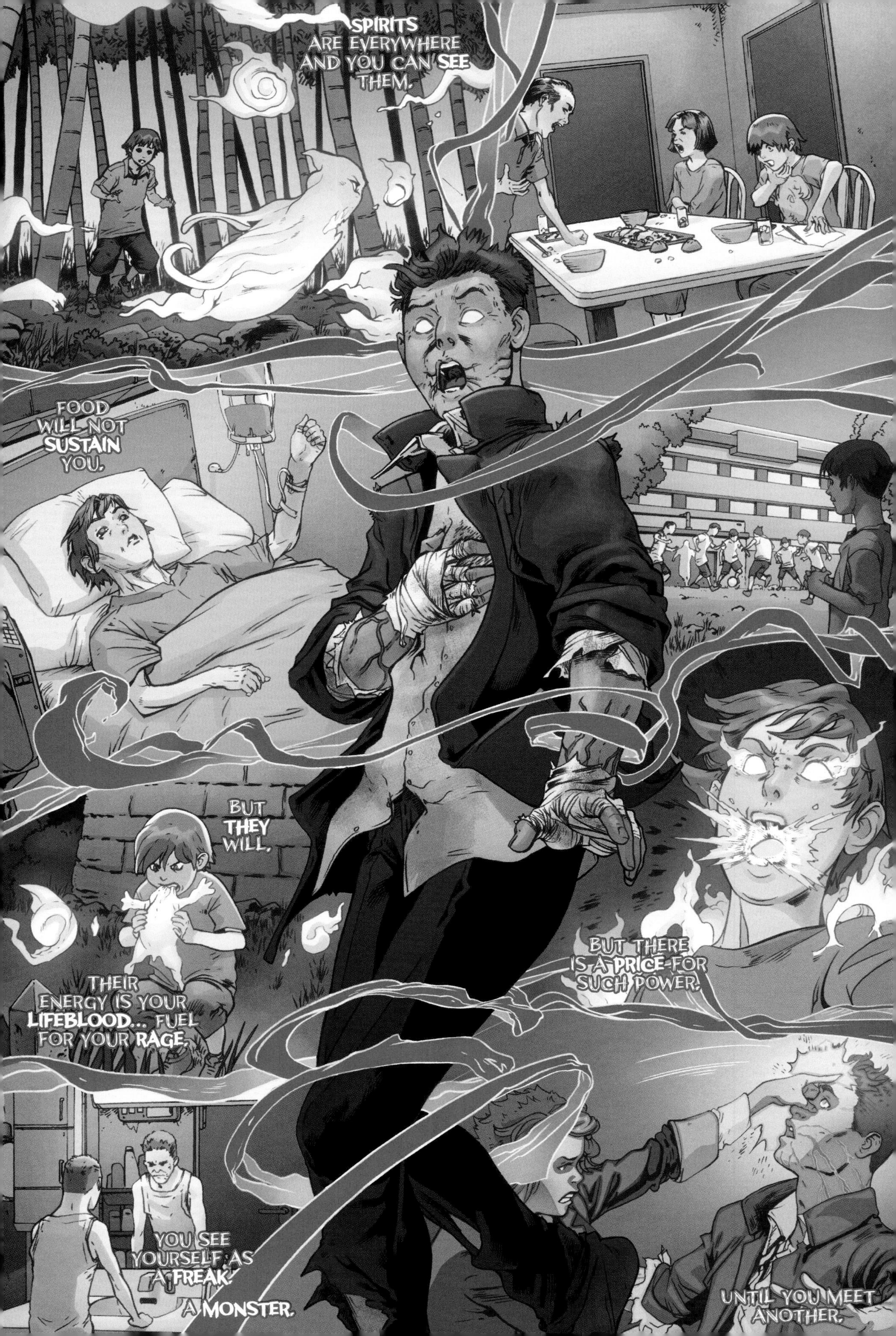
SPIRITS ARE EVERYWHERE AND YOU CAN SEE THEM.
FOOD WILL NOT SUSTAIN YOU.
BUT THEY WILL.
THEIR ENERGY IS YOUR LIFEBLOOD... FUEL FOR YOUR RAGE.
BUT THERE IS A PRICE FOR SUCH POWER.
YOU SEE YOURSELF AS A FREAK.
A MONSTER.
UNTIL YOU MEET ANOTHER.

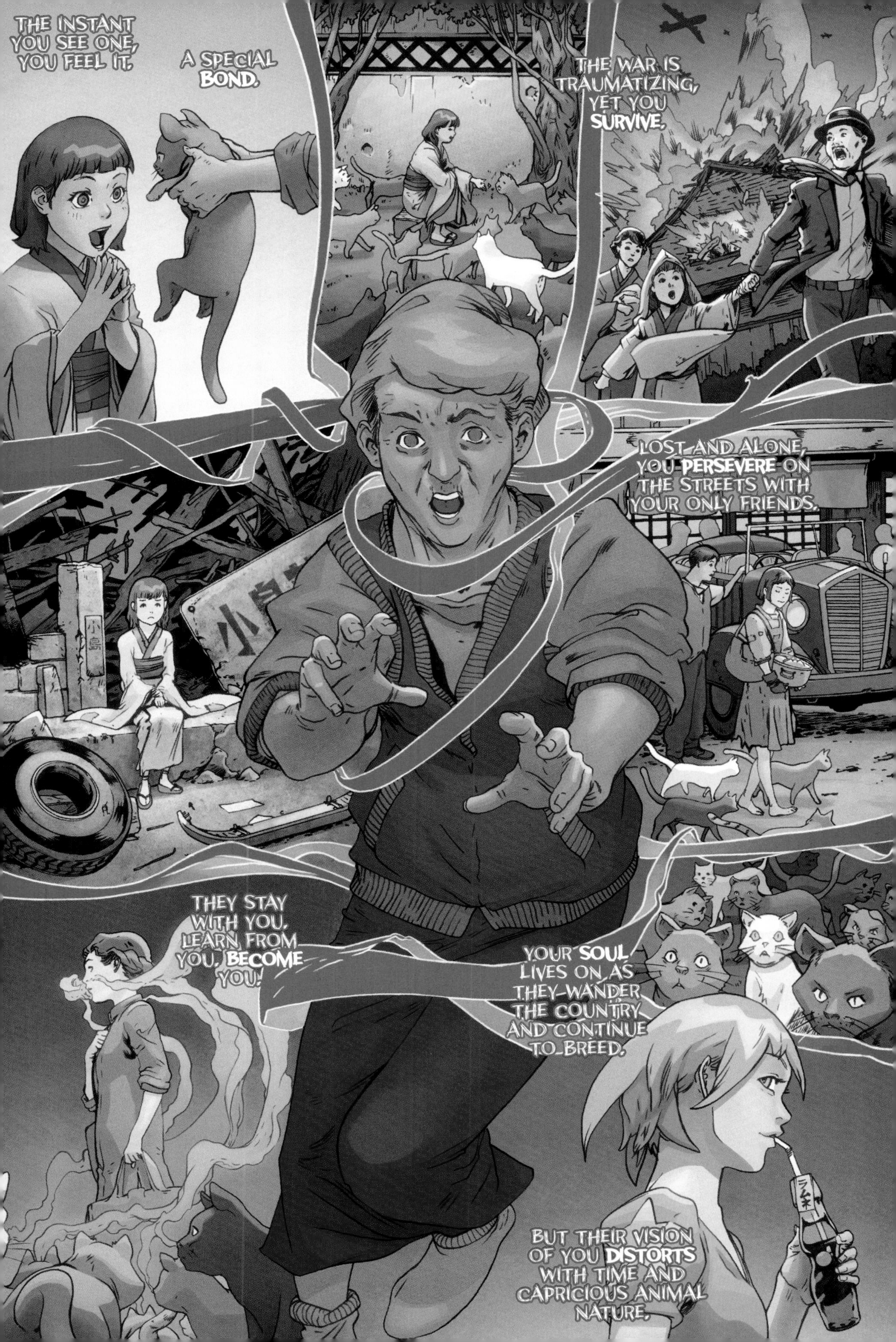
THE INSTANT YOU SEE ONE, YOU FEEL IT.
A SPECIAL BOND.
THE WAR IS TRAUMATIZING, YET YOU SURVIVE.
LOST AND ALONE, YOU PERSEVERE ON THE STREETS WITH YOUR ONLY FRIENDS.
小島
THEY STAY WITH YOU, LEARN FROM YOU, BECOME YOU!
YOUR SOUL LIVES ON AS THEY WANDER THE COUNTRY AND CONTINUE TO BREED.
ラムネ
BUT THEIR VISION OF YOU DISTORTS WITH TIME AND CAPRICIOUS ANIMAL NATURE.

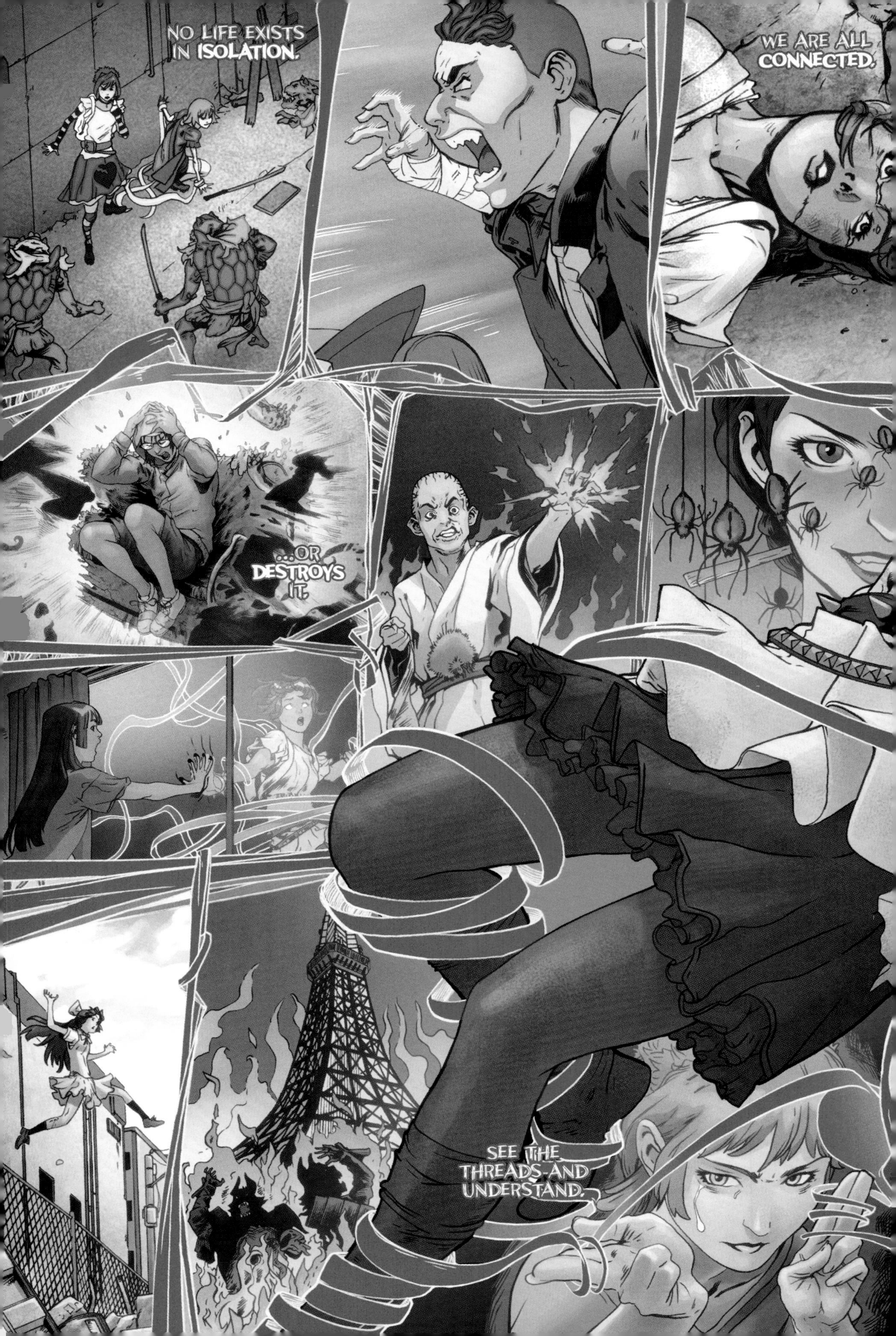
NO LIFE EXISTS IN ISOLATION.
WE ARE ALL CONNECTED.
...OR DESTROYS IT.
SEE THE THREADS AND UNDERSTAND.

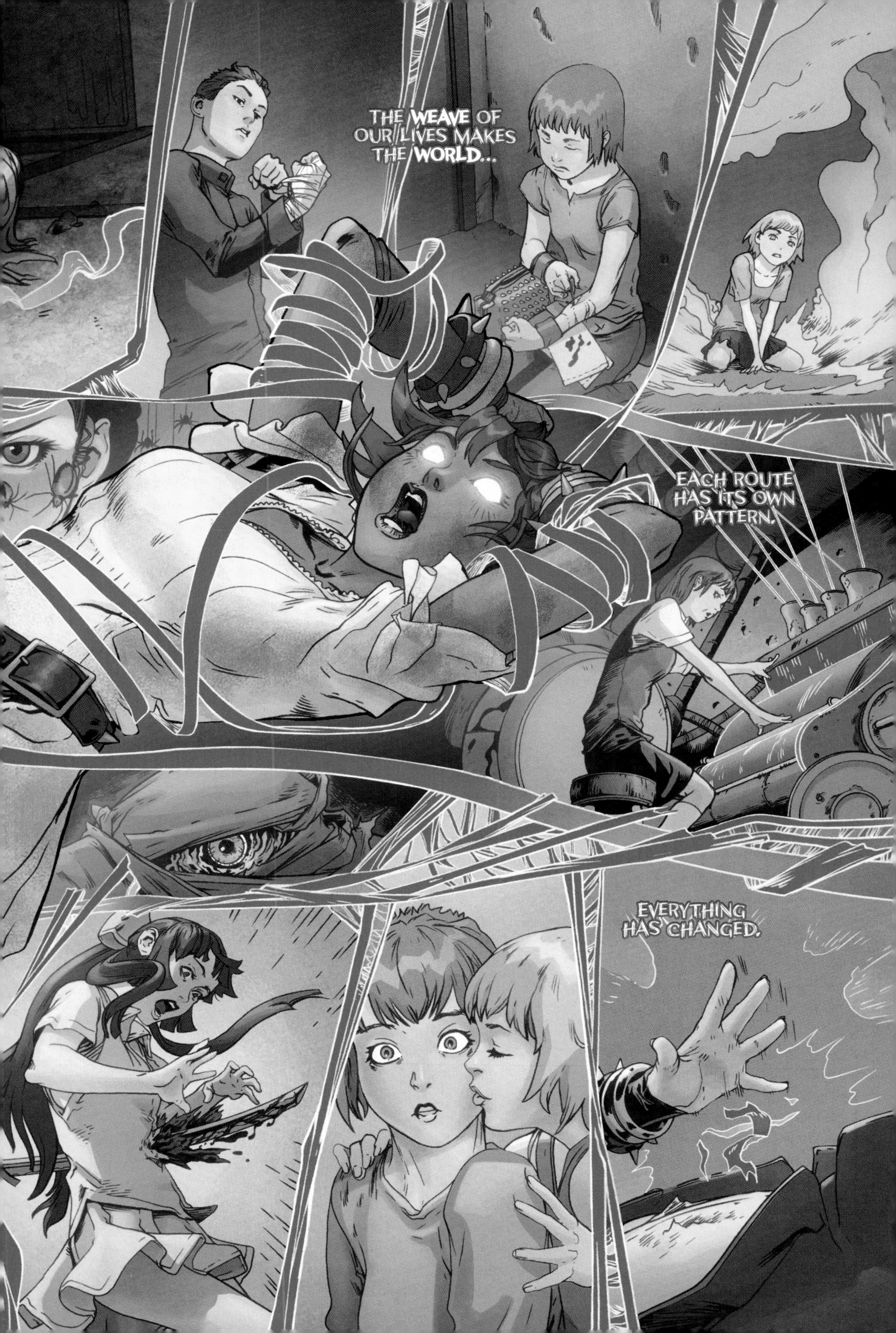
THE WEAVE OF OUR LIVES MAKES THE WORLD...
EACH ROUTE HAS ITS OWN PATTERN.
EVERYTHING HAS CHANGED.

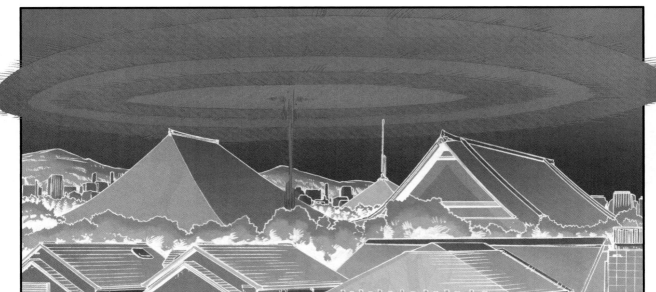

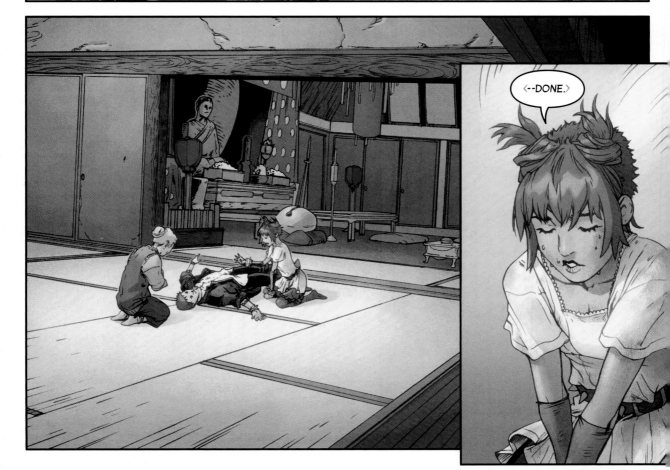

‹--DONE.›

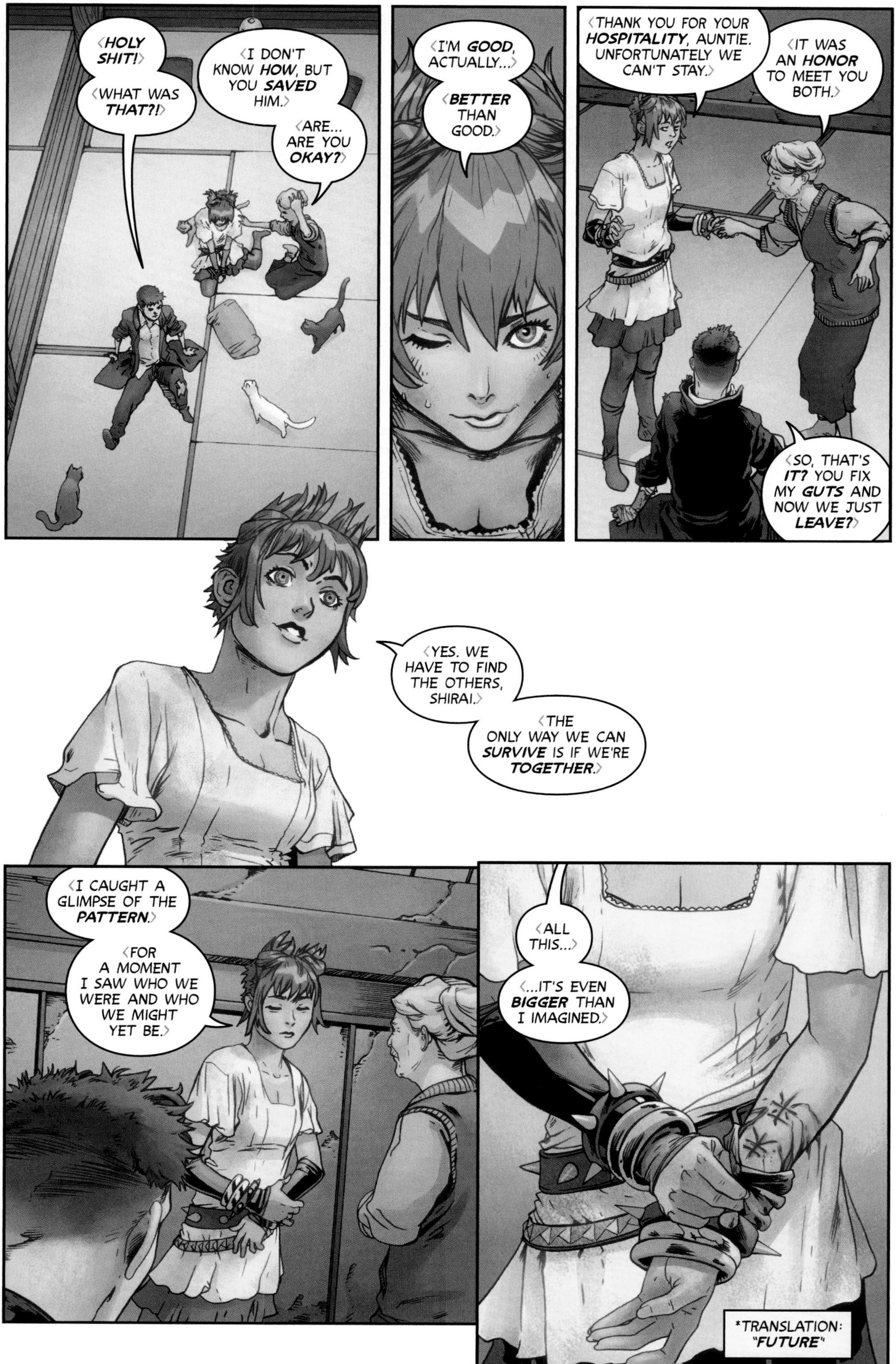

⟨HOLY SHIT!⟩
⟨WHAT WAS THAT?!⟩
⟨I DON'T KNOW HOW, BUT YOU SAVED HIM.⟩
⟨ARE... ARE YOU OKAY?⟩
⟨I'M GOOD, ACTUALLY...⟩
⟨BETTER THAN GOOD.⟩
⟨THANK YOU FOR YOUR HOSPITALITY, AUNTIE. UNFORTUNATELY WE CAN'T STAY.⟩
⟨IT WAS AN HONOR TO MEET YOU BOTH.⟩
⟨SO, THAT'S IT? YOU FIX MY GUTS AND NOW WE JUST LEAVE?⟩
⟨YES. WE HAVE TO FIND THE OTHERS, SHIRAI.⟩
⟨THE ONLY WAY WE CAN SURVIVE IS IF WE'RE TOGETHER.⟩
⟨I CAUGHT A GLIMPSE OF THE PATTERN.⟩
⟨FOR A MOMENT I SAW WHO WE WERE AND WHO WE MIGHT YET BE.⟩
⟨ALL THIS...⟩
⟨...IT'S EVEN BIGGER THAN I IMAGINED.⟩
*TRANSLATION: "FUTURE"

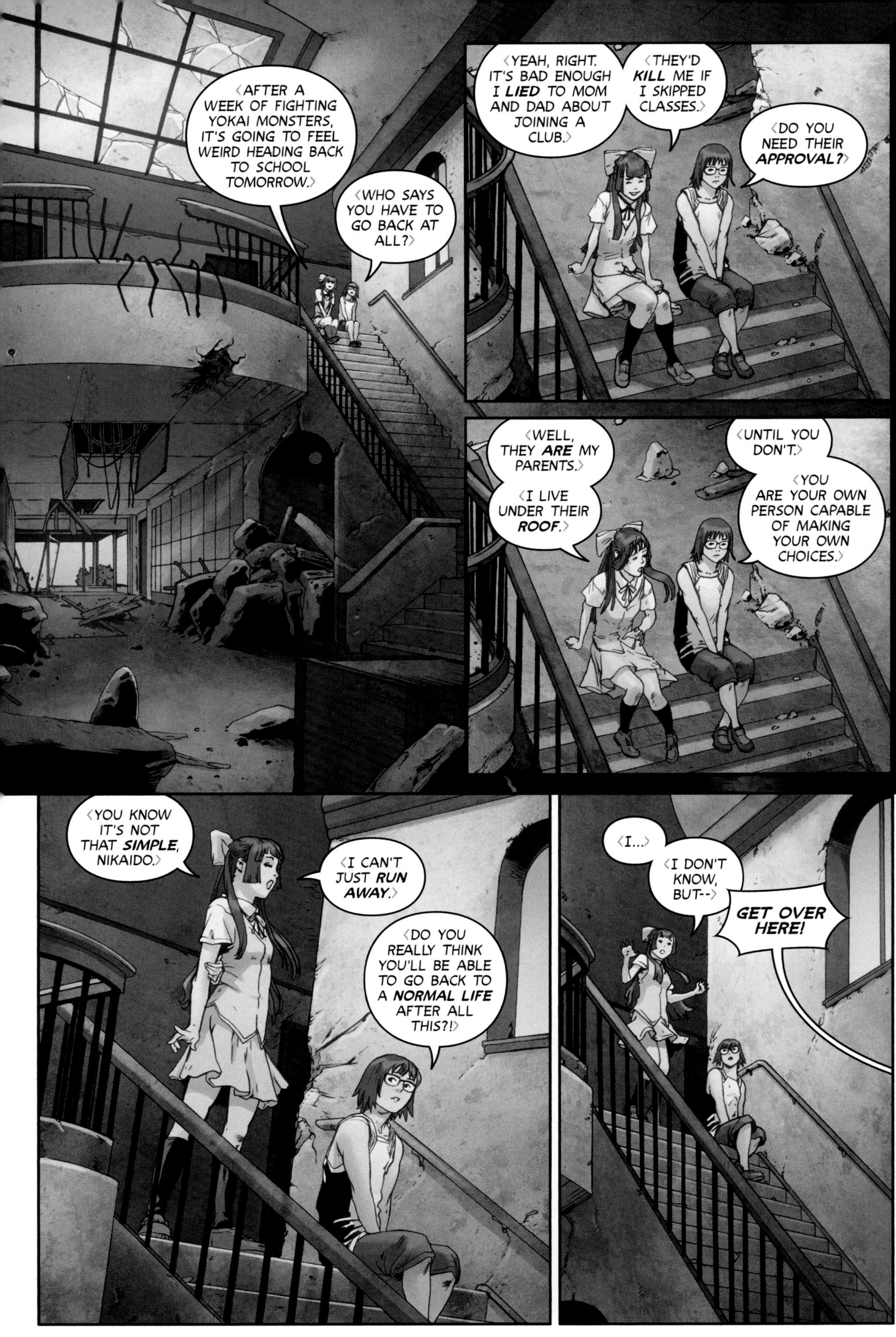
‹AFTER A WEEK OF FIGHTING YOKAI MONSTERS, IT'S GOING TO FEEL WEIRD HEADING BACK TO SCHOOL TOMORROW.›
‹WHO SAYS YOU HAVE TO GO BACK AT ALL?›
‹YEAH, RIGHT. IT'S BAD ENOUGH I LIED TO MOM AND DAD ABOUT JOINING A CLUB.›
‹THEY'D KILL ME IF I SKIPPED CLASSES.›
‹DO YOU NEED THEIR APPROVAL?›
‹WELL, THEY ARE MY PARENTS.›
‹I LIVE UNDER THEIR ROOF.›
‹UNTIL YOU DON'T.›
‹YOU ARE YOUR OWN PERSON CAPABLE OF MAKING YOUR OWN CHOICES.›
‹YOU KNOW IT'S NOT THAT SIMPLE, NIKAIDO.›
‹I CAN'T JUST RUN AWAY.›
‹DO YOU REALLY THINK YOU'LL BE ABLE TO GO BACK TO A NORMAL LIFE AFTER ALL THIS?!›
‹I...›
‹I DON'T KNOW, BUT--›
GET OVER HERE!

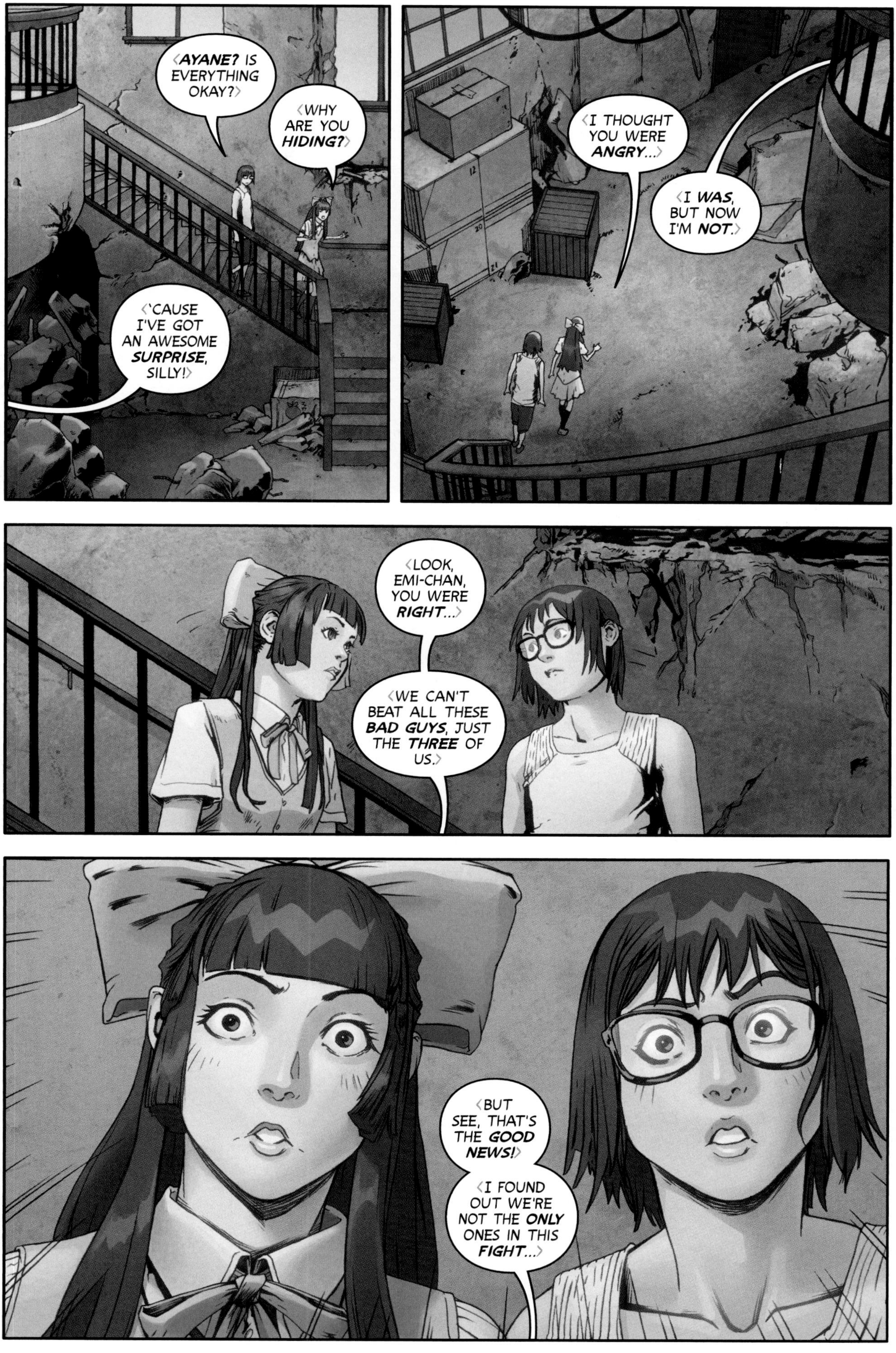

⟨AYANE? IS EVERYTHING OKAY?⟩
⟨WHY ARE YOU HIDING?⟩
⟨'CAUSE I'VE GOT AN AWESOME SURPRISE, SILLY!⟩
⟨I THOUGHT YOU WERE ANGRY...⟩
⟨I WAS, BUT NOW I'M NOT.⟩
⟨LOOK, EMI-CHAN, YOU WERE RIGHT...⟩
⟨WE CAN'T BEAT ALL THESE BAD GUYS, JUST THE THREE OF US.⟩
⟨BUT SEE, THAT'S THE GOOD NEWS!⟩
⟨I FOUND OUT WE'RE NOT THE ONLY ONES IN THIS FIGHT...⟩

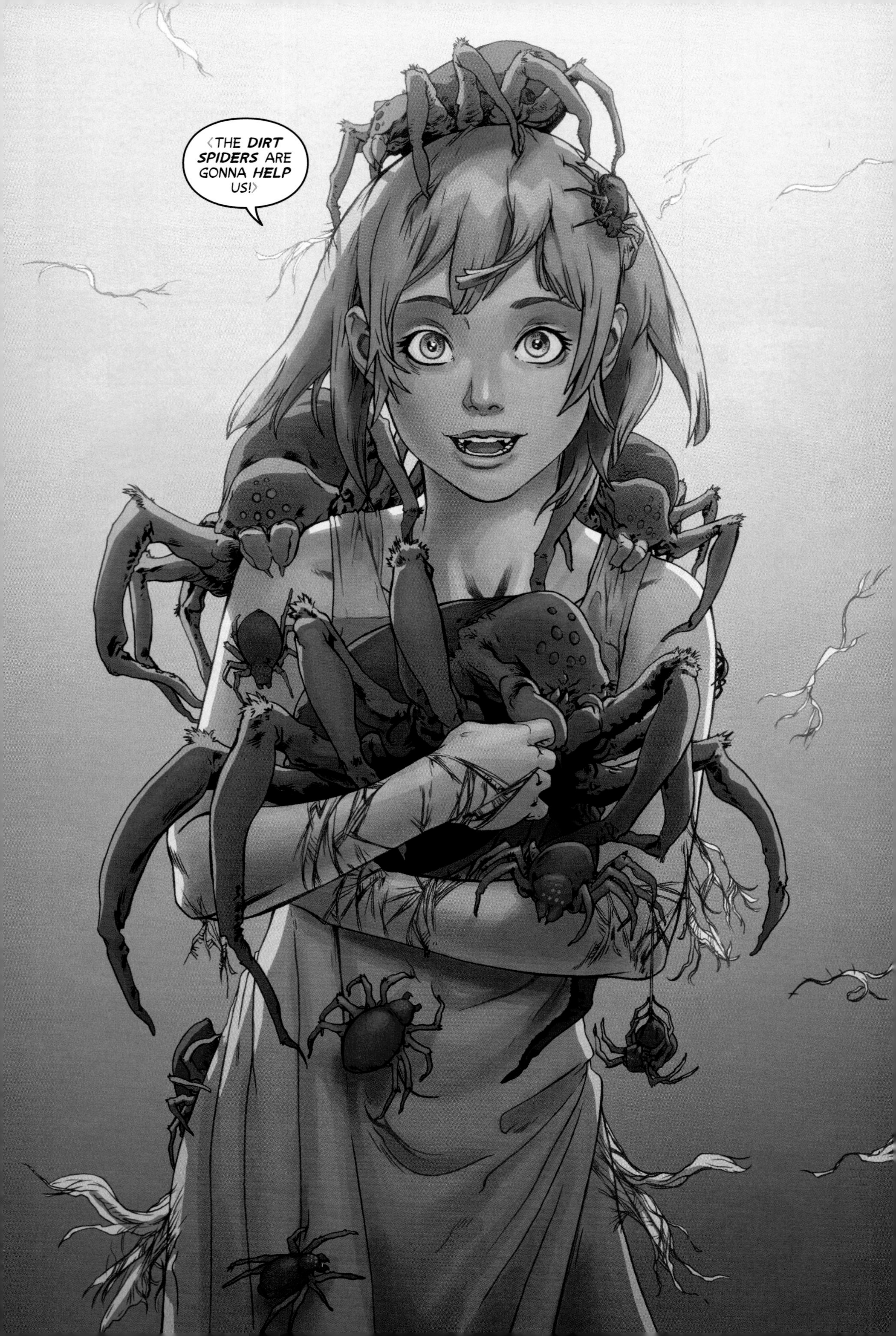
<THE DIRT SPIDERS ARE GONNA HELP US!>

Chapter Nine

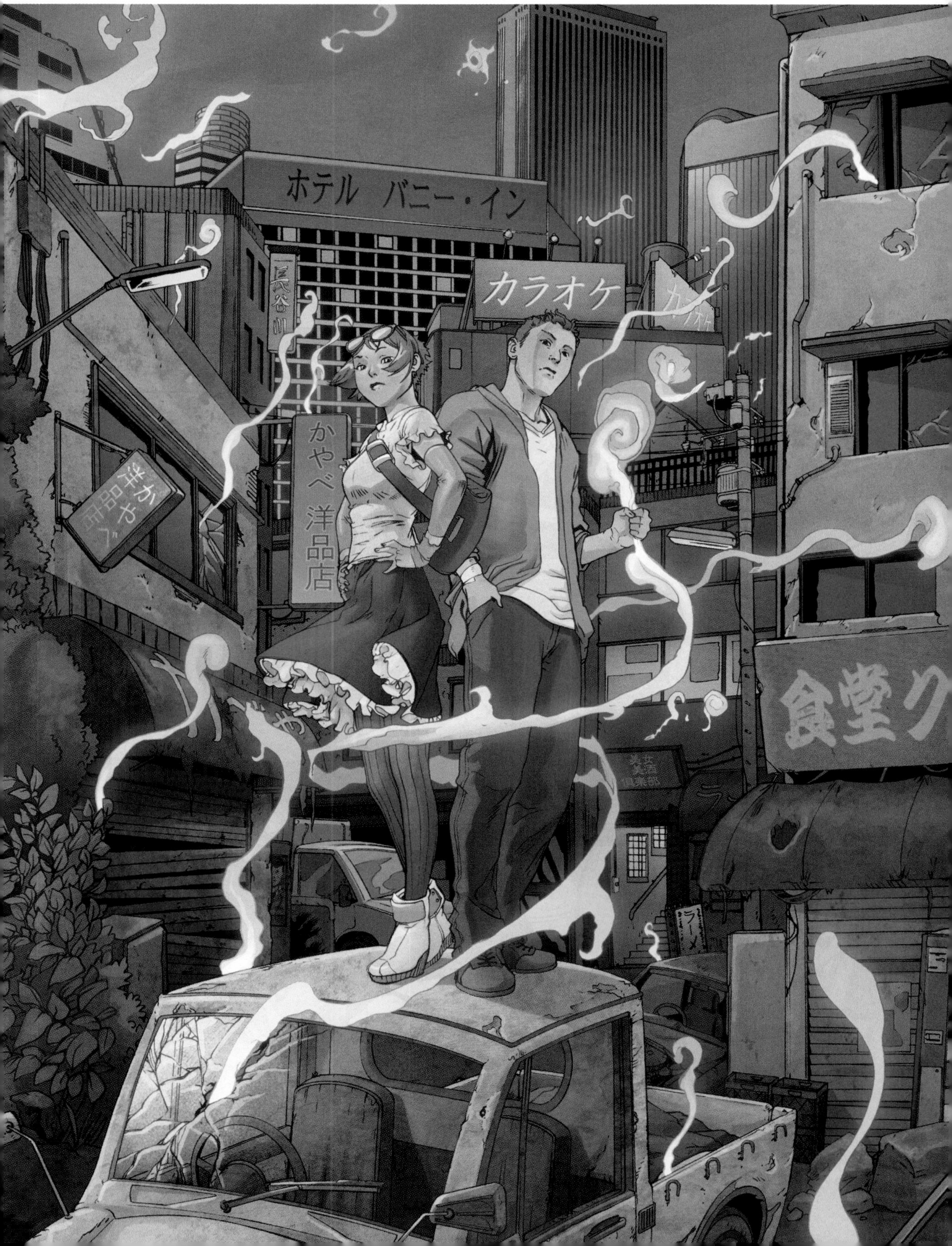
ホテル　バニー・イン
カラオケ
かやべ洋品店
食堂ク

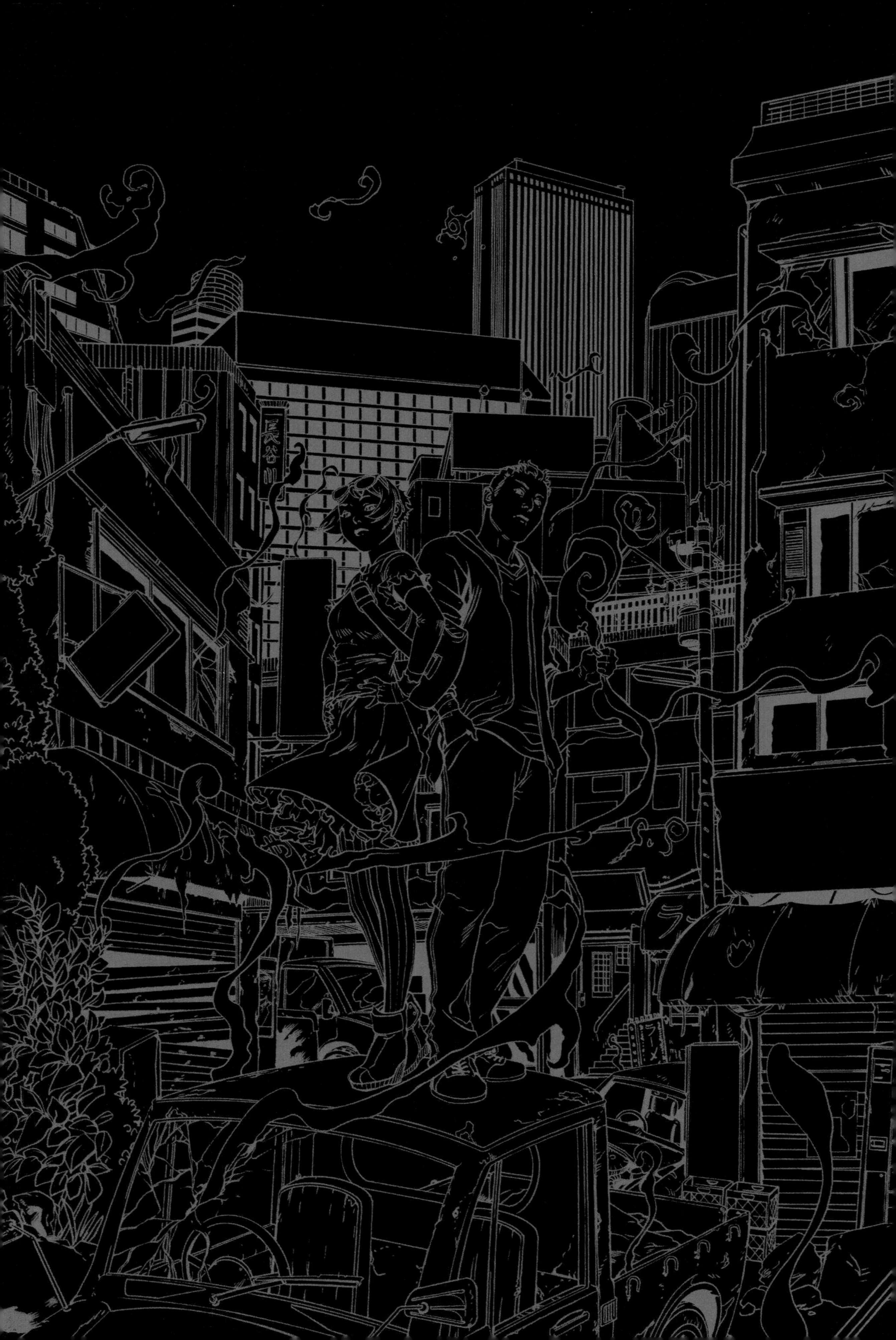
長谷川

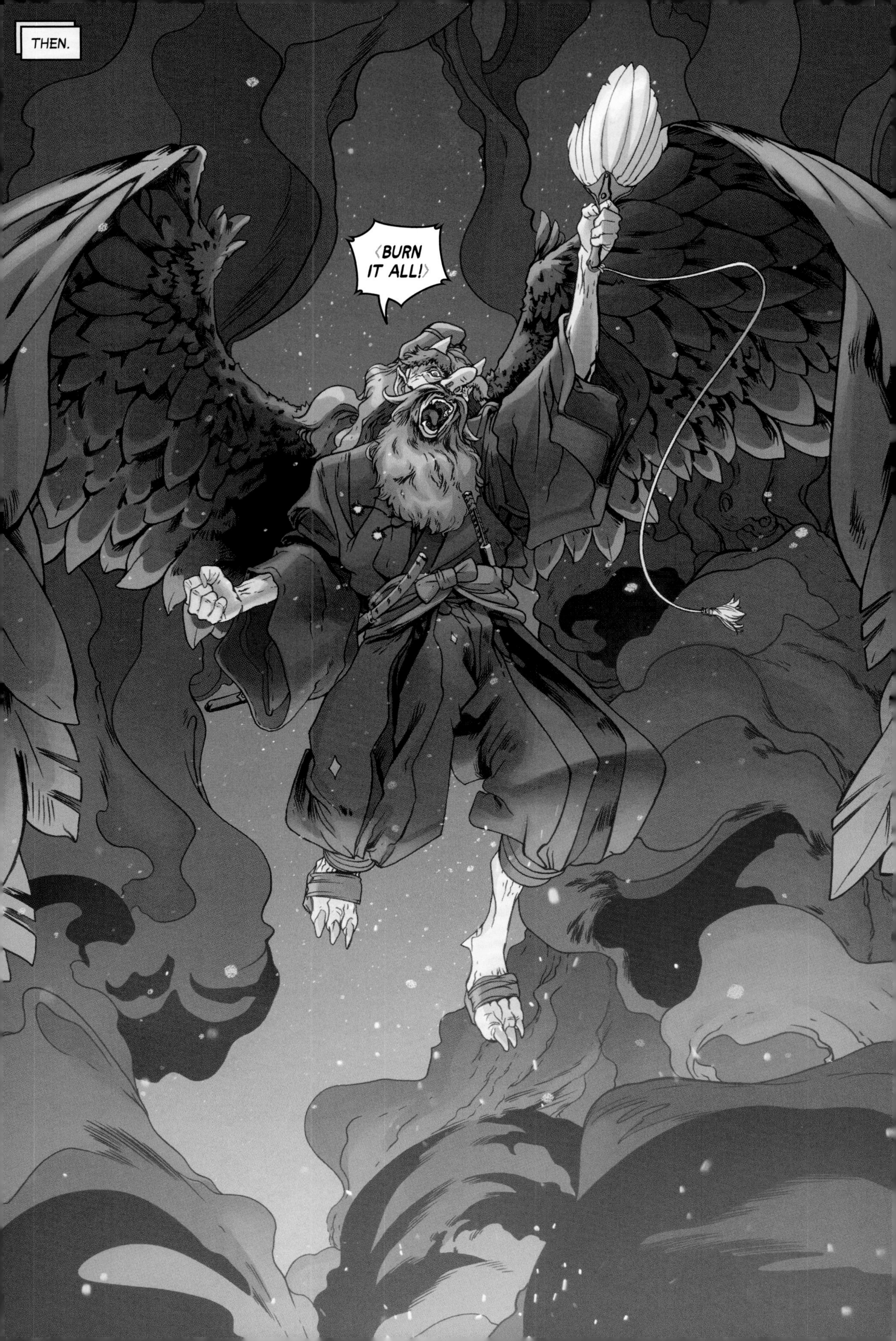
THEN.
⟨BURN IT ALL!⟩

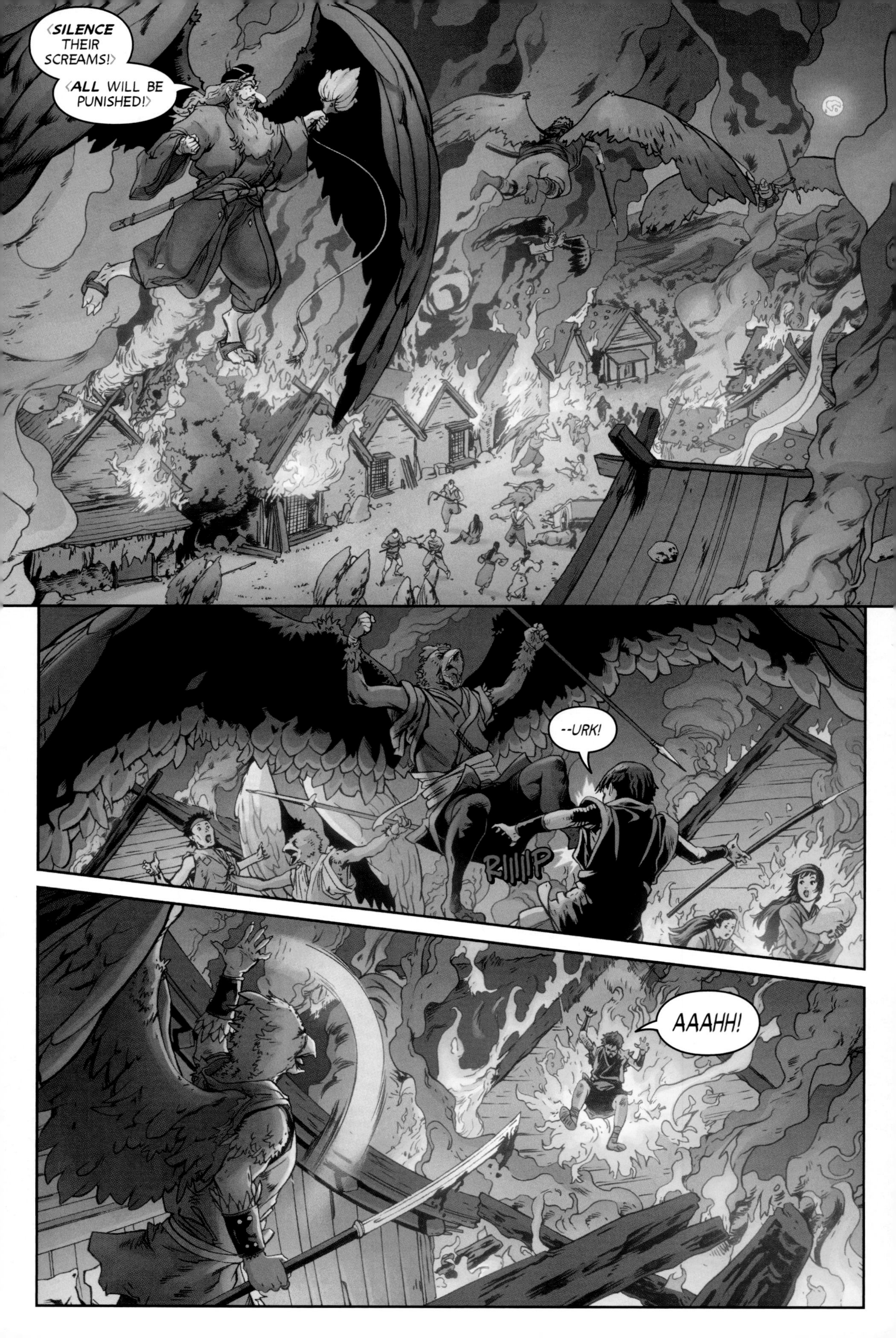

‹SILENCE THEIR SCREAMS!›
‹ALL WILL BE PUNISHED!›
--URK!
RIIIIP
AAAHH!

‹DARANIBŌ OF THE MOUNTAINS, I *IMPLORE* YOU--›

‹*STOP* THIS *CARNAGE!*›

‹I WILL NOT.›

‹NOT UNLESS YOU GIVE US THE *GIRL.*›

‹*SHE* IS THE KEY TO *SURVIVAL.*›

‹SHE...›

‹SHE'S *NOT* HERE.›

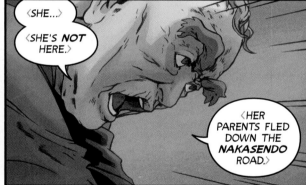

‹HER PARENTS FLED DOWN THE *NAKASENDO* ROAD.›

HALT! ‹STOP THE ATTACK.›

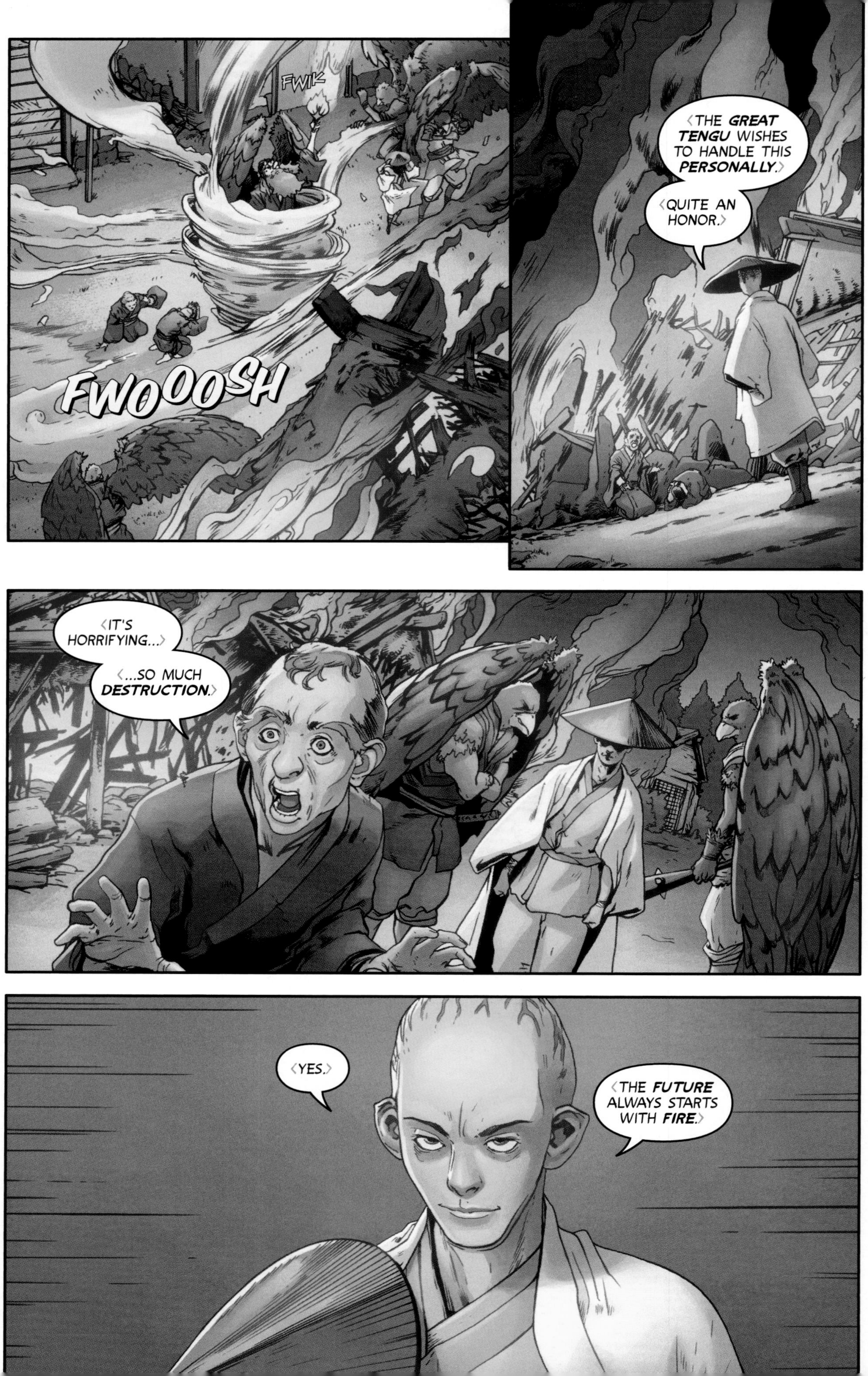
FWIK
FWOOOSH
‹THE GREAT TENGU WISHES TO HANDLE THIS PERSONALLY.›
‹QUITE AN HONOR.›
‹IT'S HORRIFYING...›
‹...SO MUCH DESTRUCTION.›
‹YES.›
‹THE FUTURE ALWAYS STARTS WITH FIRE.›

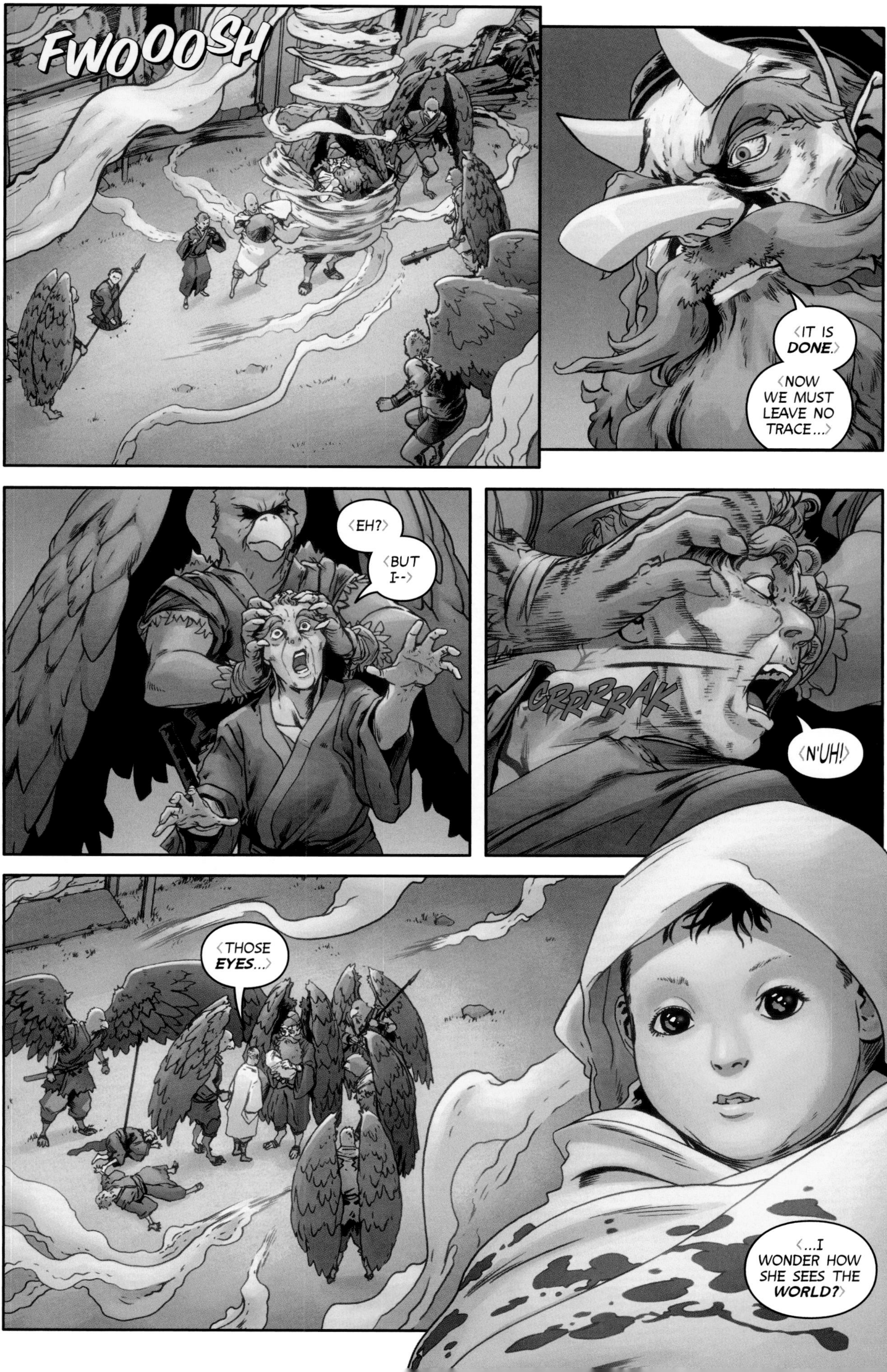
FWOOOSH
‹IT IS DONE.›
‹NOW WE MUST LEAVE NO TRACE...›
‹EH?›
‹BUT I--›
CRRRRAK
‹N'UH!›
‹THOSE EYES...›
‹...I WONDER HOW SHE SEES THE WORLD?›

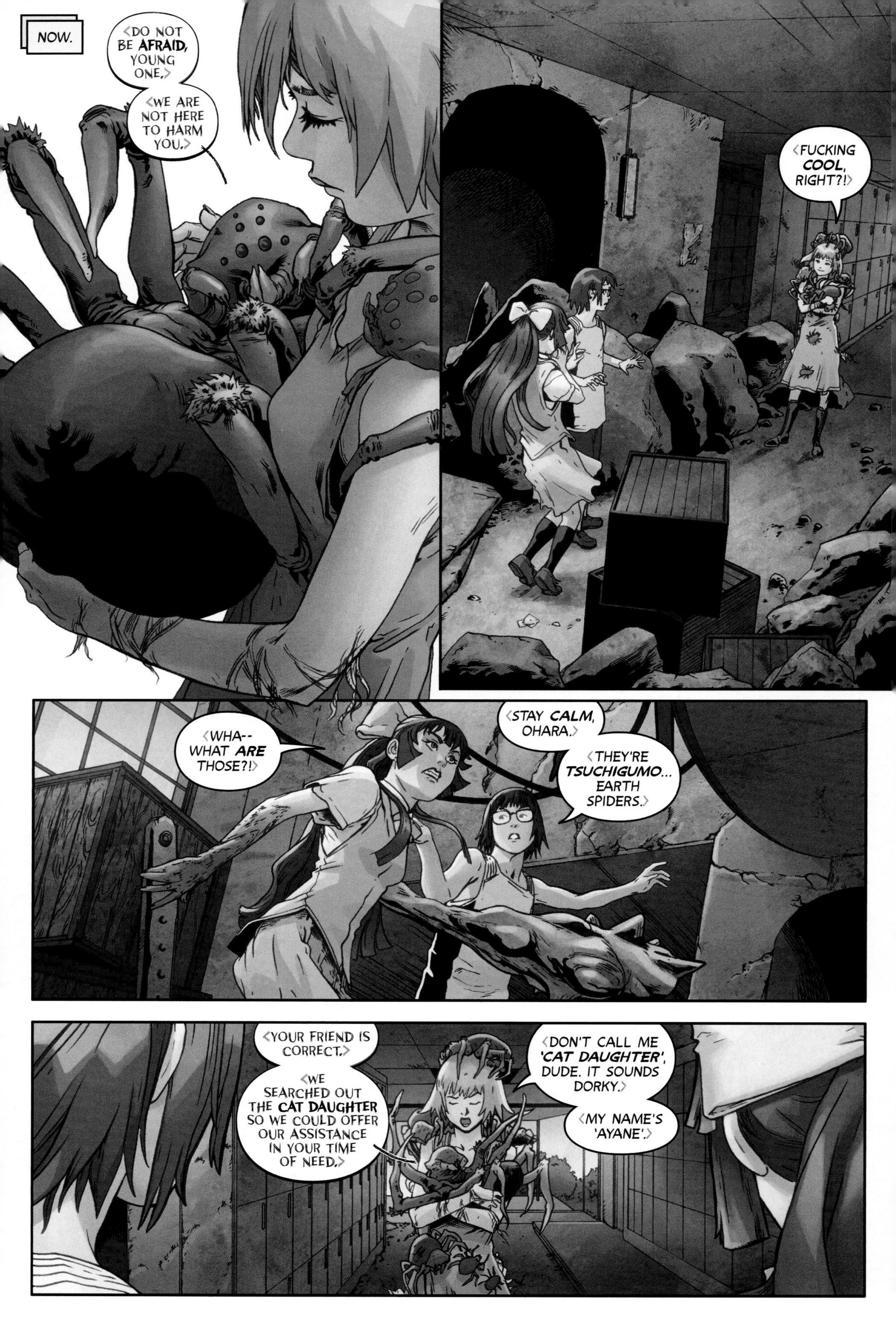
NOW.
<DO NOT BE AFRAID, YOUNG ONE.>
<WE ARE NOT HERE TO HARM YOU.>
<FUCKING COOL, RIGHT?!>
<WHA-- WHAT ARE THOSE?!>
<STAY CALM, OHARA.>
<THEY'RE TSUCHIGUMO... EARTH SPIDERS.>
<YOUR FRIEND IS CORRECT.>
<WE SEARCHED OUT THE CAT DAUGHTER SO WE COULD OFFER OUR ASSISTANCE IN YOUR TIME OF NEED.>
<DON'T CALL ME 'CAT DAUGHTER', DUDE. IT SOUNDS DORKY.>
<MY NAME'S 'AYANE'.>

"ASSISTANCE?"

WHY PUT YOURSELVES AT RISK?

YOU ARE BEING HUNTED BY NURARIHYON AND HIS ILK BECAUSE THEY DESTROY THAT WHICH THEY CANNOT CONTROL.

WE HAVE ALSO BEEN TARGETS OF THEIR IRE IN THE PAST.

THE TSUCHIGUMO ARE ALWAYS DISMISSED UNLESS WE'RE NEEDED BY THE POWERS THAT BE...

...UNTIL NOW.

SEE?! THEY HATE THOSE ASSHOLES JUST AS MUCH AS WE DO!

WE CAN TOTALLY PULL TOGETHER A SPIDER-CAT ARMY AND FUCK THEM ALL UP.

HOW... HOW DO WE KNOW WE CAN TRUST YOU?

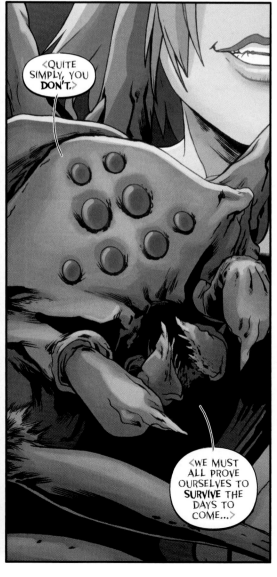

QUITE SIMPLY, YOU DON'T.

WE MUST ALL PROVE OURSELVES TO SURVIVE THE DAYS TO COME...

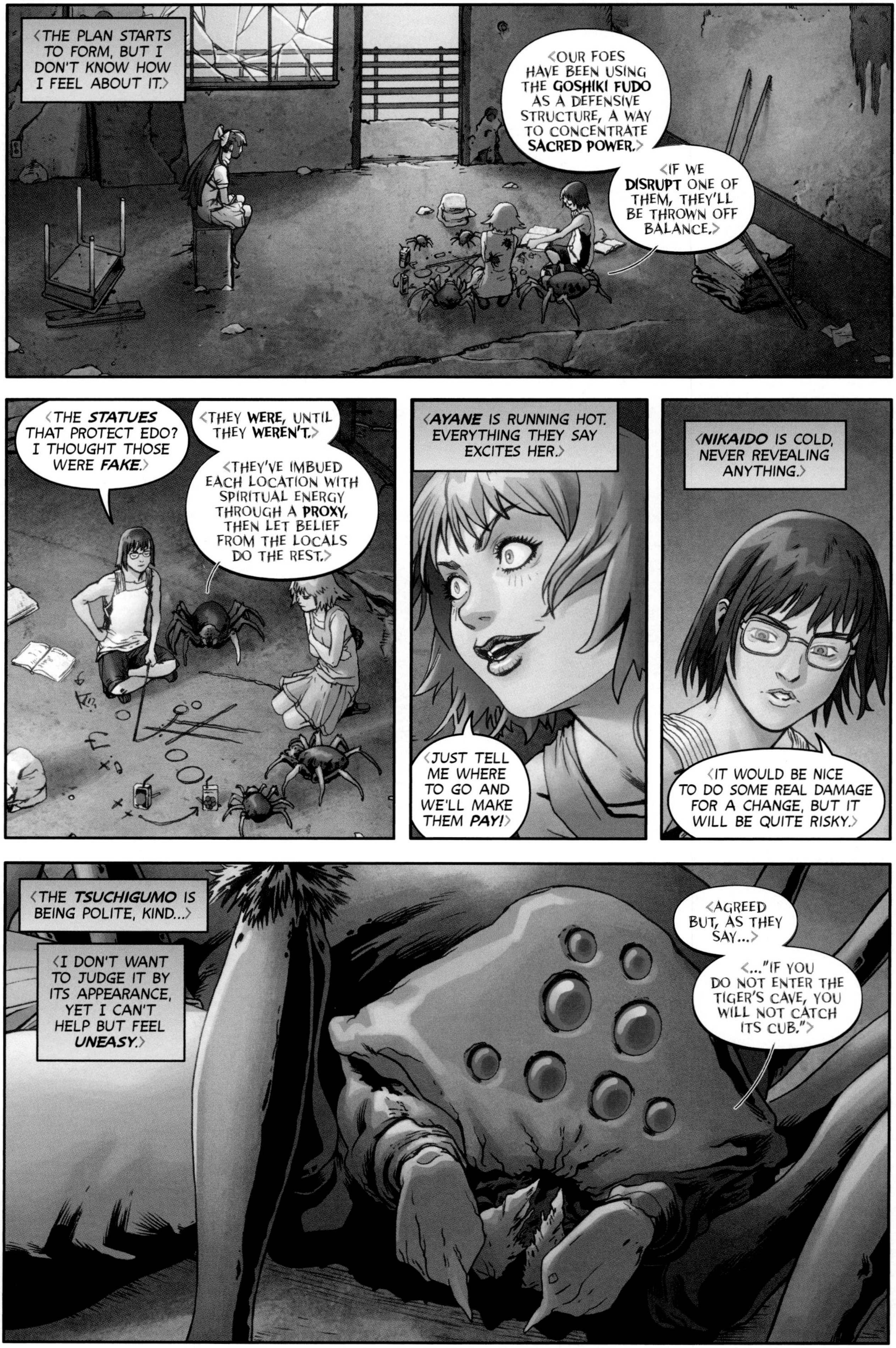
<THE PLAN STARTS TO FORM, BUT I DON'T KNOW HOW I FEEL ABOUT IT.>
<OUR FOES HAVE BEEN USING THE **GOSHIKI FUDO** AS A DEFENSIVE STRUCTURE, A WAY TO CONCENTRATE **SACRED POWER.**>
<IF WE **DISRUPT** ONE OF THEM, THEY'LL BE THROWN OFF BALANCE.>
<THE ***STATUES*** THAT PROTECT EDO? I THOUGHT THOSE WERE ***FAKE***.>
<THEY **WERE**, UNTIL THEY **WEREN'T.**>
<THEY'VE IMBUED EACH LOCATION WITH SPIRITUAL ENERGY THROUGH A **PROXY**, THEN LET BELIEF FROM THE LOCALS DO THE REST.>
<***AYANE*** IS RUNNING HOT. EVERYTHING THEY SAY EXCITES HER.>
<JUST TELL ME WHERE TO GO AND WE'LL MAKE THEM ***PAY!***>
<***NIKAIDO*** IS COLD, NEVER REVEALING ANYTHING.>
<IT WOULD BE NICE TO DO SOME REAL DAMAGE FOR A CHANGE, BUT IT WILL BE QUITE RISKY.>
<THE ***TSUCHIGUMO*** IS BEING POLITE, KIND...>
<I DON'T WANT TO JUDGE IT BY ITS APPEARANCE, YET I CAN'T HELP BUT FEEL ***UNEASY***.>
<AGREED BUT, AS THEY SAY...>
<..."IF YOU DO NOT ENTER THE TIGER'S CAVE, YOU WILL NOT CATCH ITS CUB.">

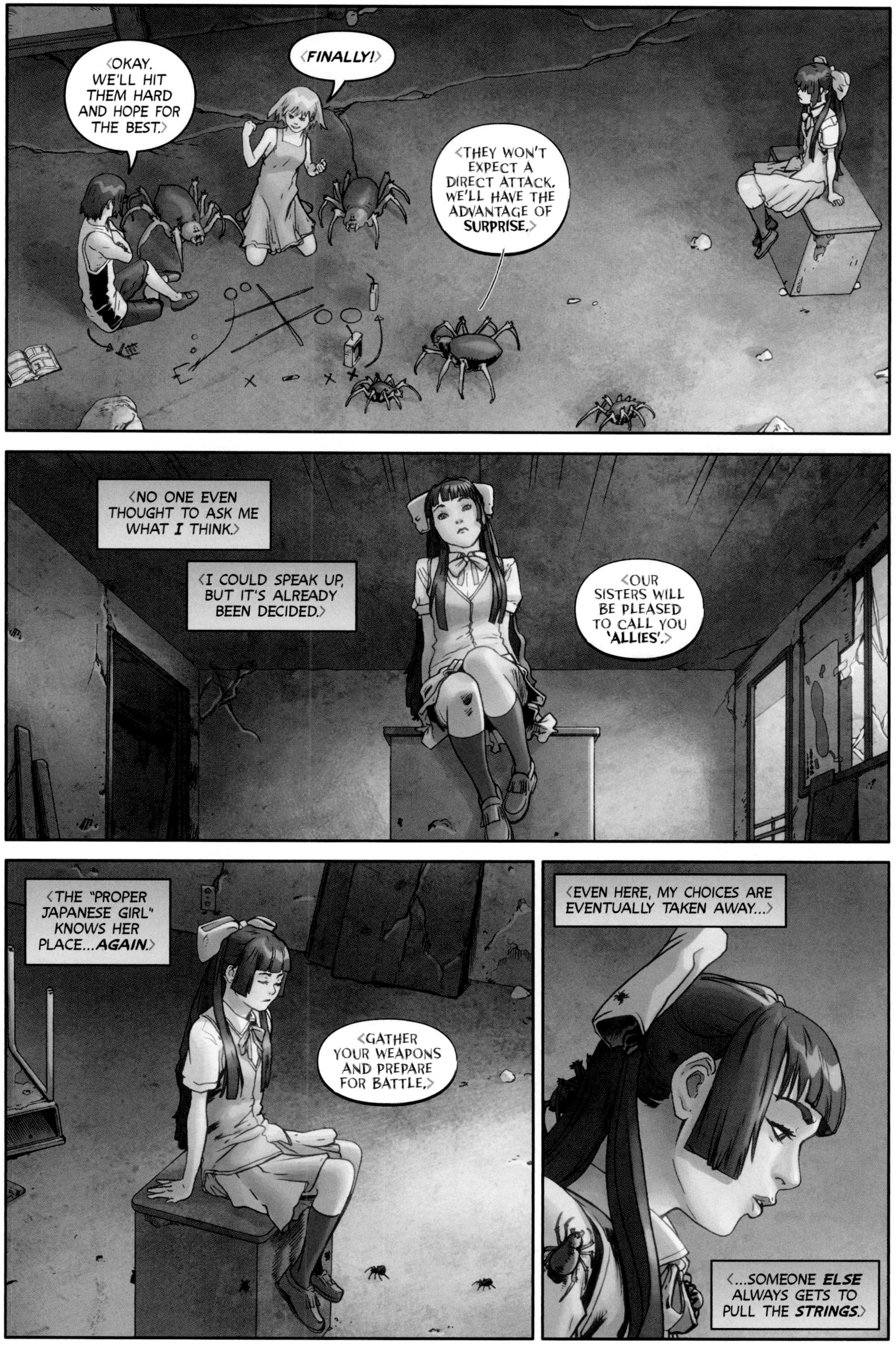

<OKAY. WE'LL HIT THEM HARD AND HOPE FOR THE BEST.>
<FINALLY!>
<THEY WON'T EXPECT A DIRECT ATTACK. WE'LL HAVE THE ADVANTAGE OF SURPRISE.>
<NO ONE EVEN THOUGHT TO ASK ME WHAT I THINK.>
<I COULD SPEAK UP, BUT IT'S ALREADY BEEN DECIDED.>
<OUR SISTERS WILL BE PLEASED TO CALL YOU 'ALLIES'.>
<THE "PROPER JAPANESE GIRL" KNOWS HER PLACE...AGAIN.>
<GATHER YOUR WEAPONS AND PREPARE FOR BATTLE.>
<EVEN HERE, MY CHOICES ARE EVENTUALLY TAKEN AWAY...>
<...SOMEONE ELSE ALWAYS GETS TO PULL THE STRINGS.>

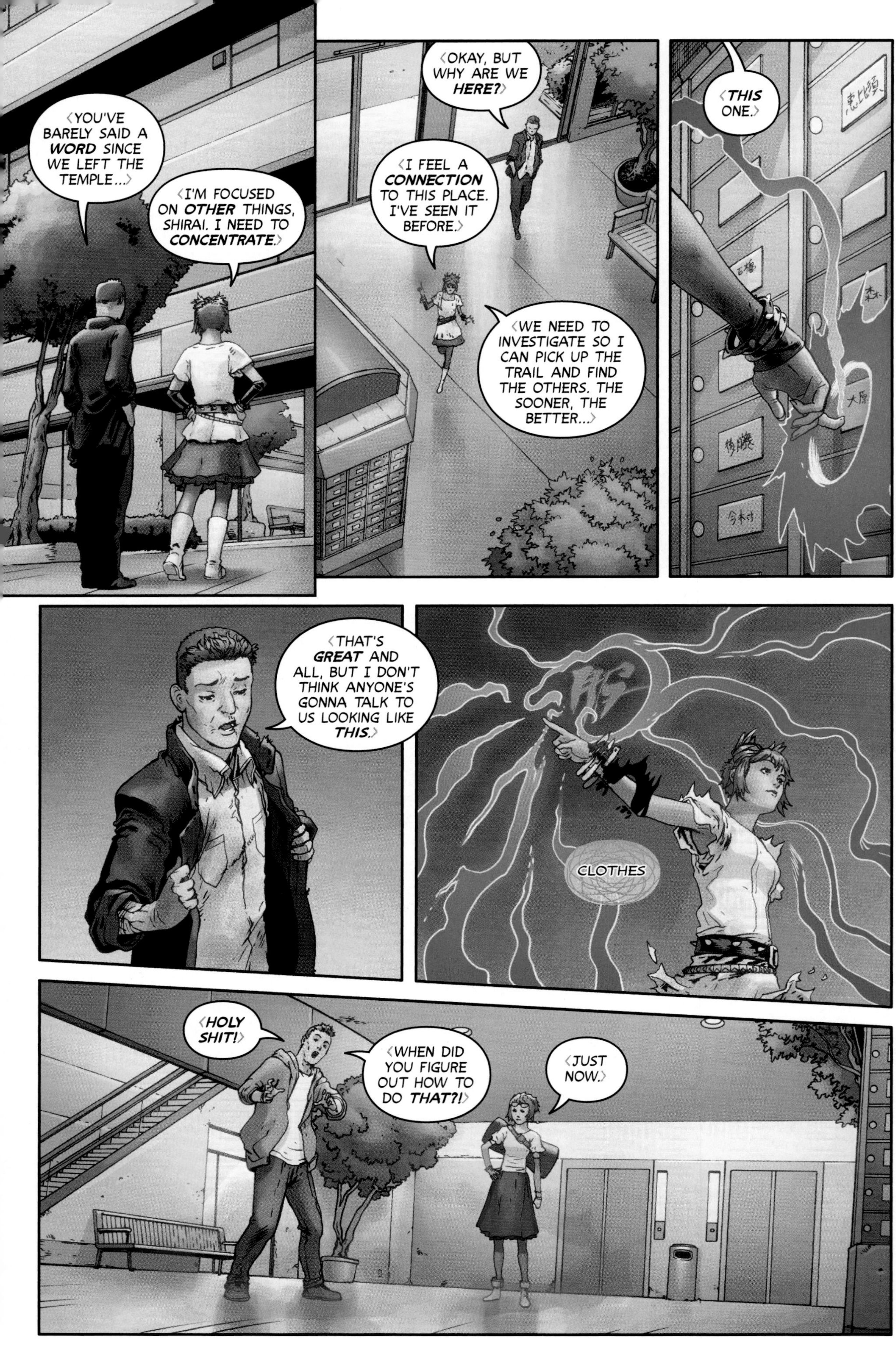
⟨YOU'VE BARELY SAID A **WORD** SINCE WE LEFT THE TEMPLE...⟩
⟨I'M FOCUSED ON **OTHER** THINGS, SHIRAI. I NEED TO **CONCENTRATE.**⟩
⟨OKAY, BUT WHY ARE WE **HERE?**⟩
⟨I FEEL A **CONNECTION** TO THIS PLACE. I'VE SEEN IT BEFORE.⟩
⟨WE NEED TO INVESTIGATE SO I CAN PICK UP THE TRAIL AND FIND THE OTHERS. THE SOONER, THE BETTER...⟩
⟨**THIS** ONE.⟩
⟨THAT'S **GREAT** AND ALL, BUT I DON'T THINK ANYONE'S GONNA TALK TO US LOOKING LIKE **THIS.**⟩
CLOTHES
⟨**HOLY SHIT!**⟩
⟨WHEN DID YOU FIGURE OUT HOW TO DO **THAT?!**⟩
⟨JUST NOW.⟩

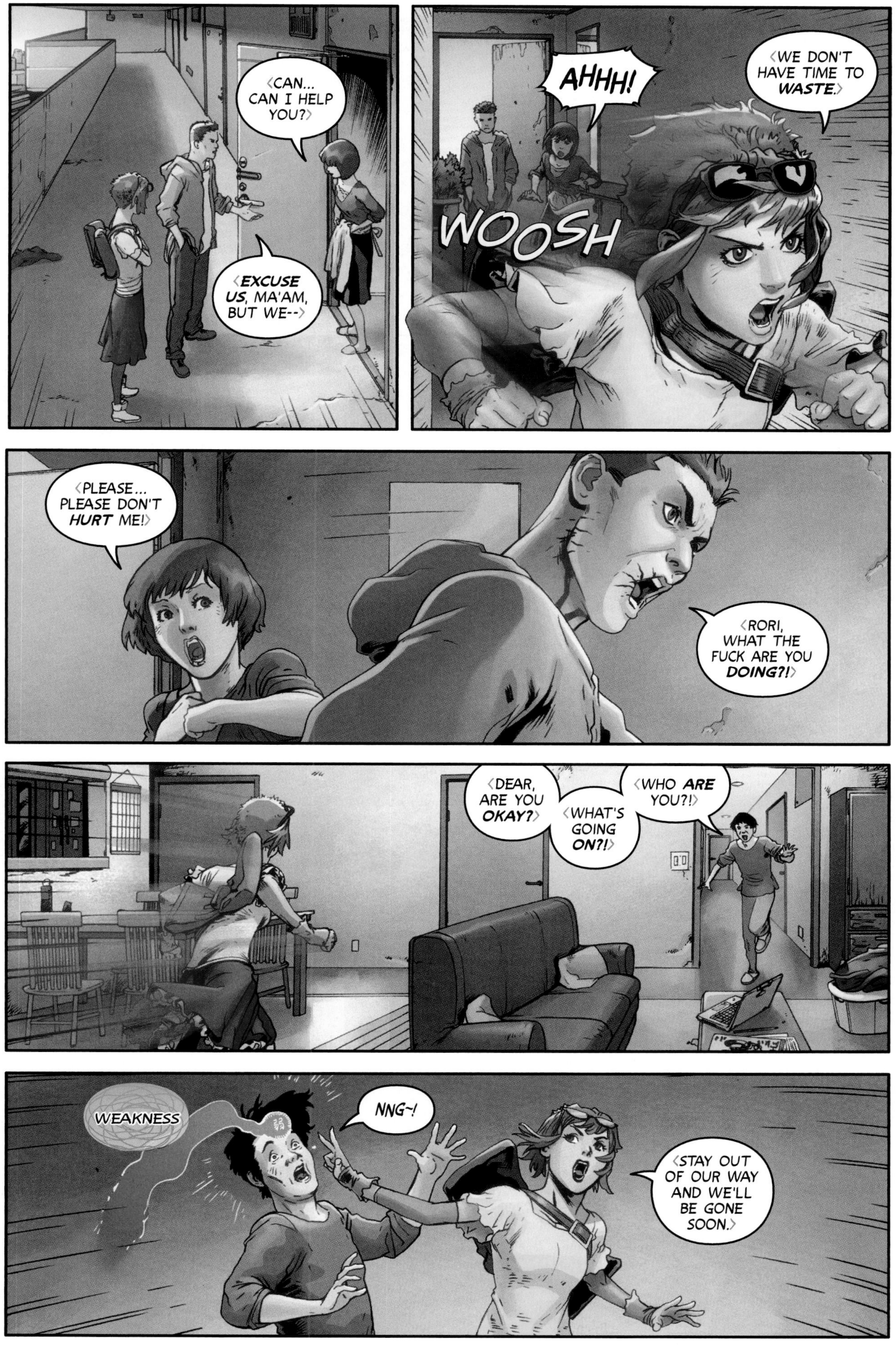

<CAN... CAN I HELP YOU?>
<EXCUSE US, MA'AM, BUT WE-->
AHHH!
<WE DON'T HAVE TIME TO WASTE.>
WOOSH
<PLEASE... PLEASE DON'T HURT ME!>
<RORI, WHAT THE FUCK ARE YOU DOING?!>
<DEAR, ARE YOU OKAY?>
<WHAT'S GOING ON?!>
<WHO ARE YOU?!>
WEAKNESS
NNG~!
<STAY OUT OF OUR WAY AND WE'LL BE GONE SOON.>

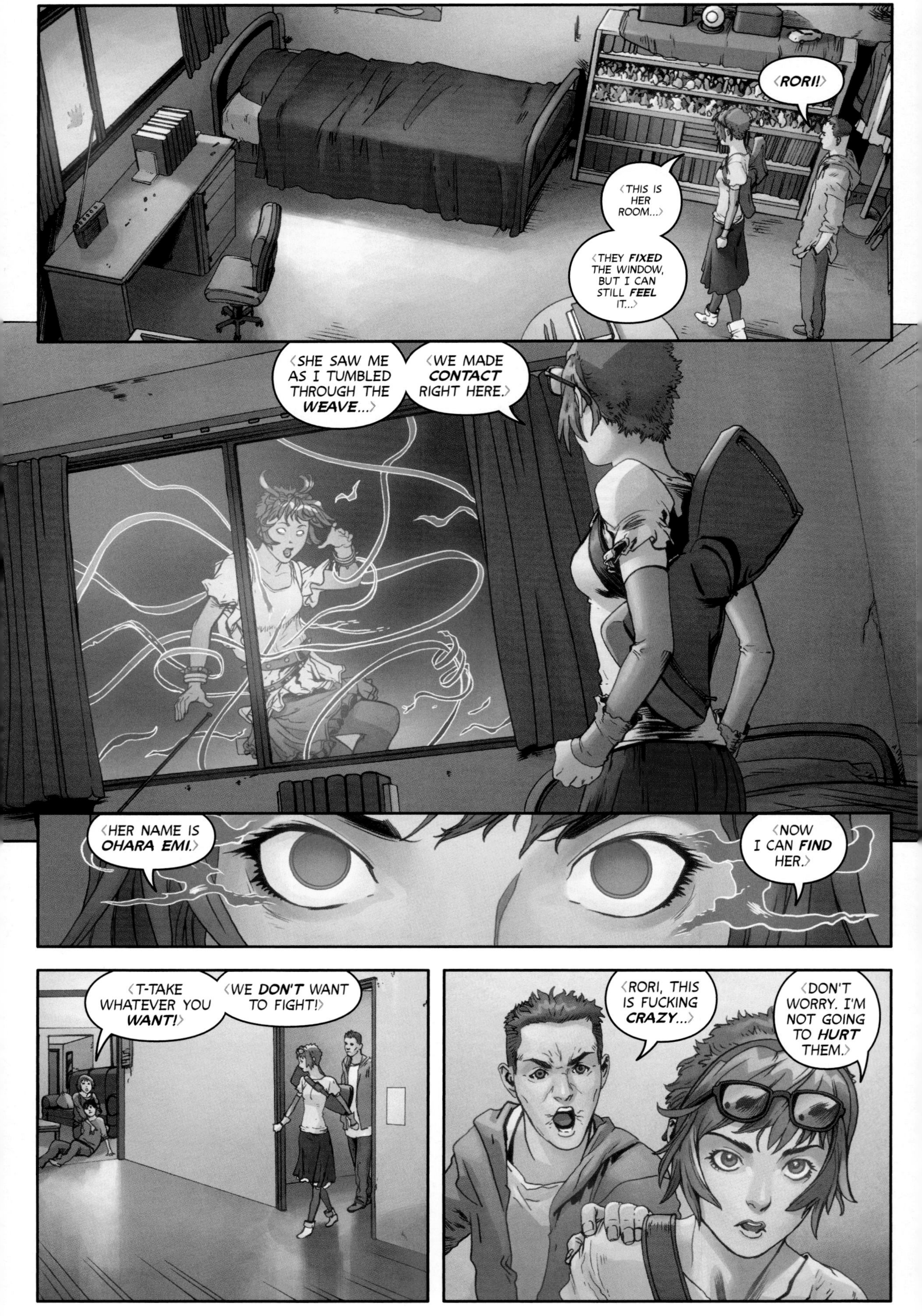

〈RORI!〉
〈THIS IS HER ROOM...〉
〈THEY FIXED THE WINDOW, BUT I CAN STILL FEEL IT...〉
〈SHE SAW ME AS I TUMBLED THROUGH THE WEAVE...〉
〈WE MADE CONTACT RIGHT HERE.〉
〈HER NAME IS OHARA EMI.〉
〈NOW I CAN FIND HER.〉
〈T-TAKE WHATEVER YOU WANT!〉
〈WE DON'T WANT TO FIGHT!〉
〈RORI, THIS IS FUCKING CRAZY...〉
〈DON'T WORRY. I'M NOT GOING TO HURT THEM.〉

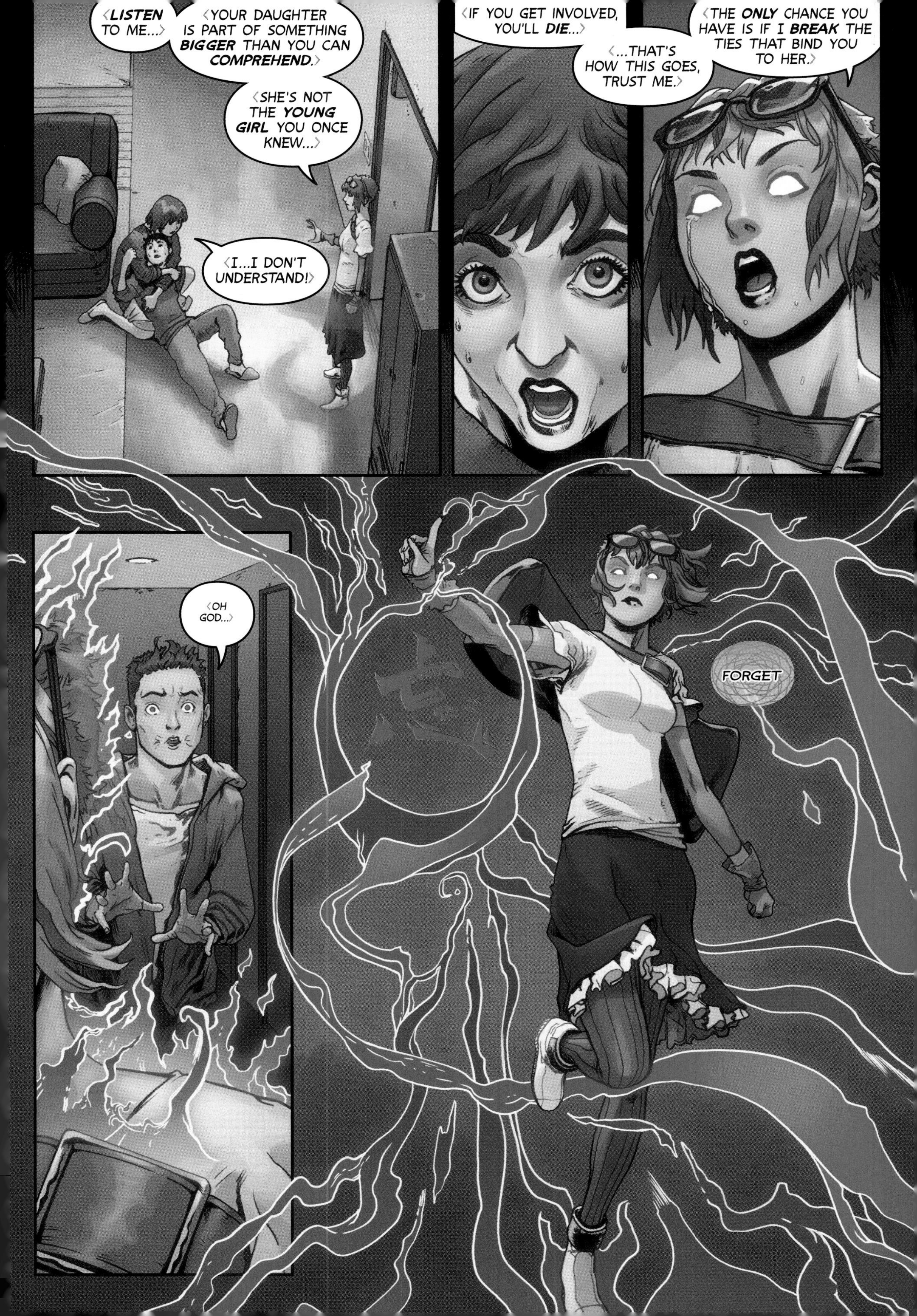

<LISTEN TO ME...>
<YOUR DAUGHTER IS PART OF SOMETHING BIGGER THAN YOU CAN COMPREHEND.>
<SHE'S NOT THE YOUNG GIRL YOU ONCE KNEW...>
<I...I DON'T UNDERSTAND!>
<IF YOU GET INVOLVED, YOU'LL DIE...>
<...THAT'S HOW THIS GOES, TRUST ME.>
<THE ONLY CHANCE YOU HAVE IS IF I BREAK THE TIES THAT BIND YOU TO HER.>
<OH GOD...>
FORGET

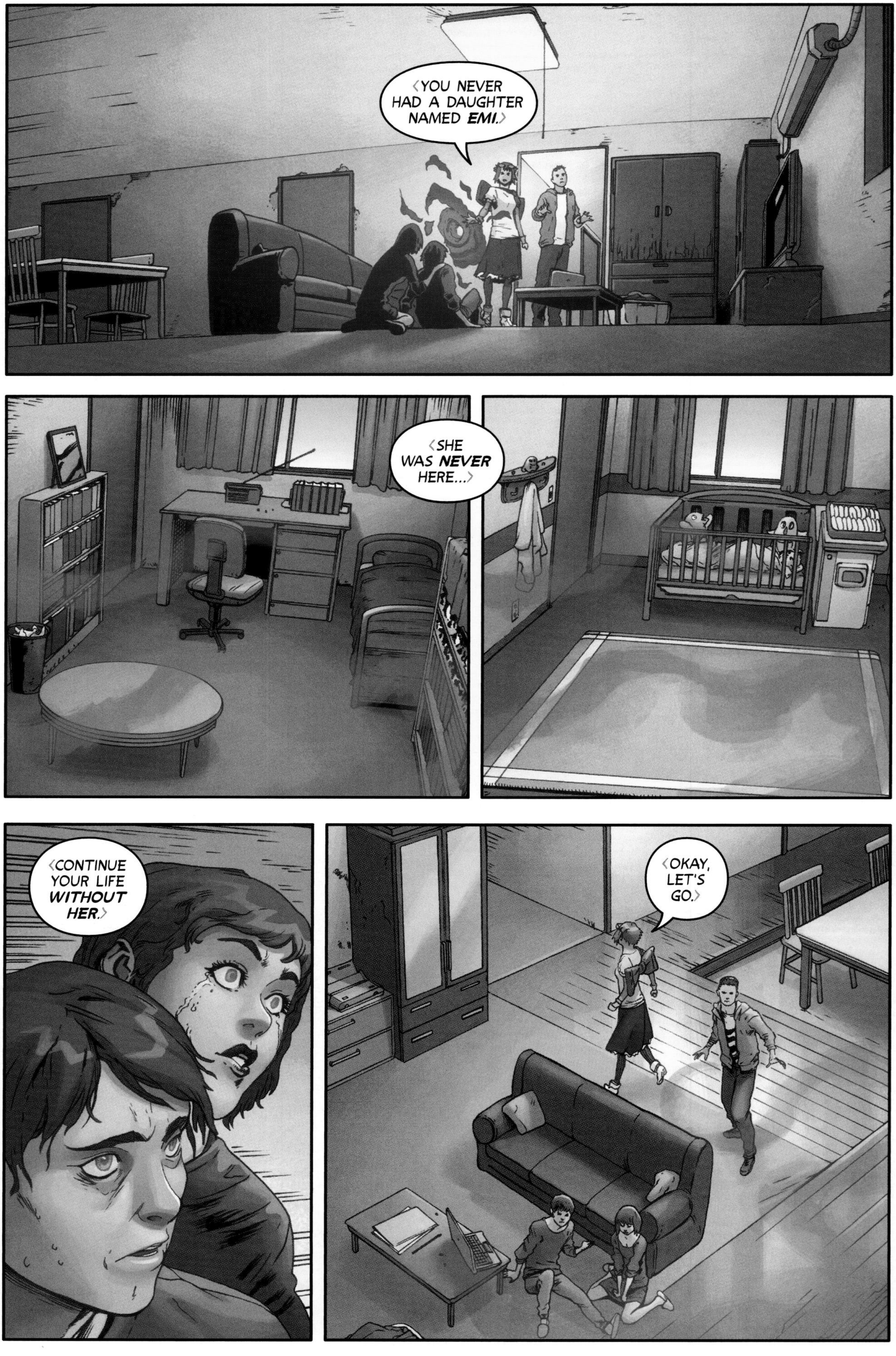
‹YOU NEVER HAD A DAUGHTER NAMED **EMI**.›
‹SHE WAS **NEVER** HERE...›
‹CONTINUE YOUR LIFE **WITHOUT HER**.›
‹OKAY, LET'S GO.›

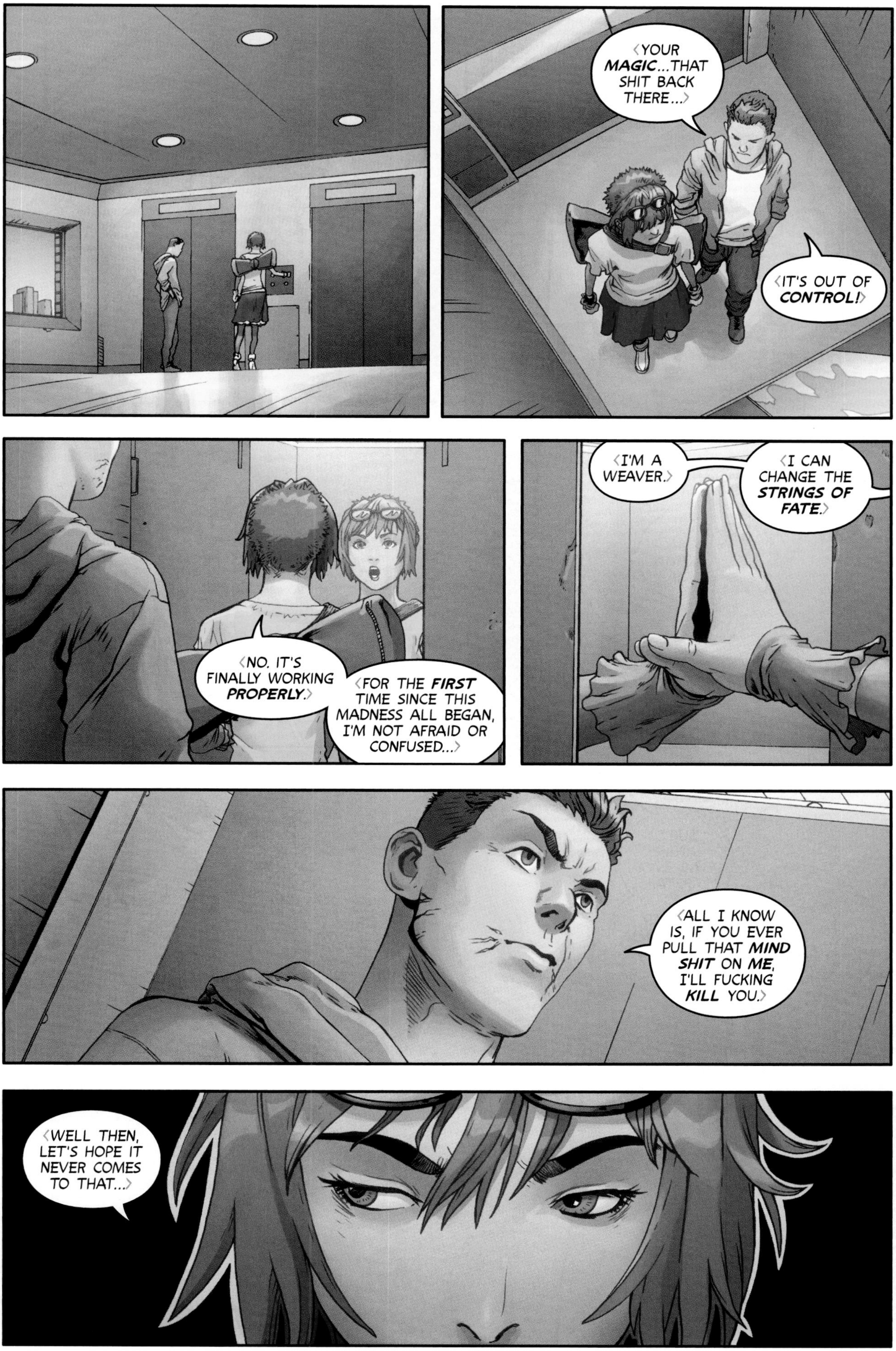
<YOUR MAGIC...THAT SHIT BACK THERE...>
<IT'S OUT OF CONTROL!>
<NO. IT'S FINALLY WORKING PROPERLY.>
<FOR THE FIRST TIME SINCE THIS MADNESS ALL BEGAN, I'M NOT AFRAID OR CONFUSED...>
<I'M A WEAVER.>
<I CAN CHANGE THE STRINGS OF FATE.>
<ALL I KNOW IS, IF YOU EVER PULL THAT MIND SHIT ON ME, I'LL FUCKING KILL YOU.>
<WELL THEN, LET'S HOPE IT NEVER COMES TO THAT...>

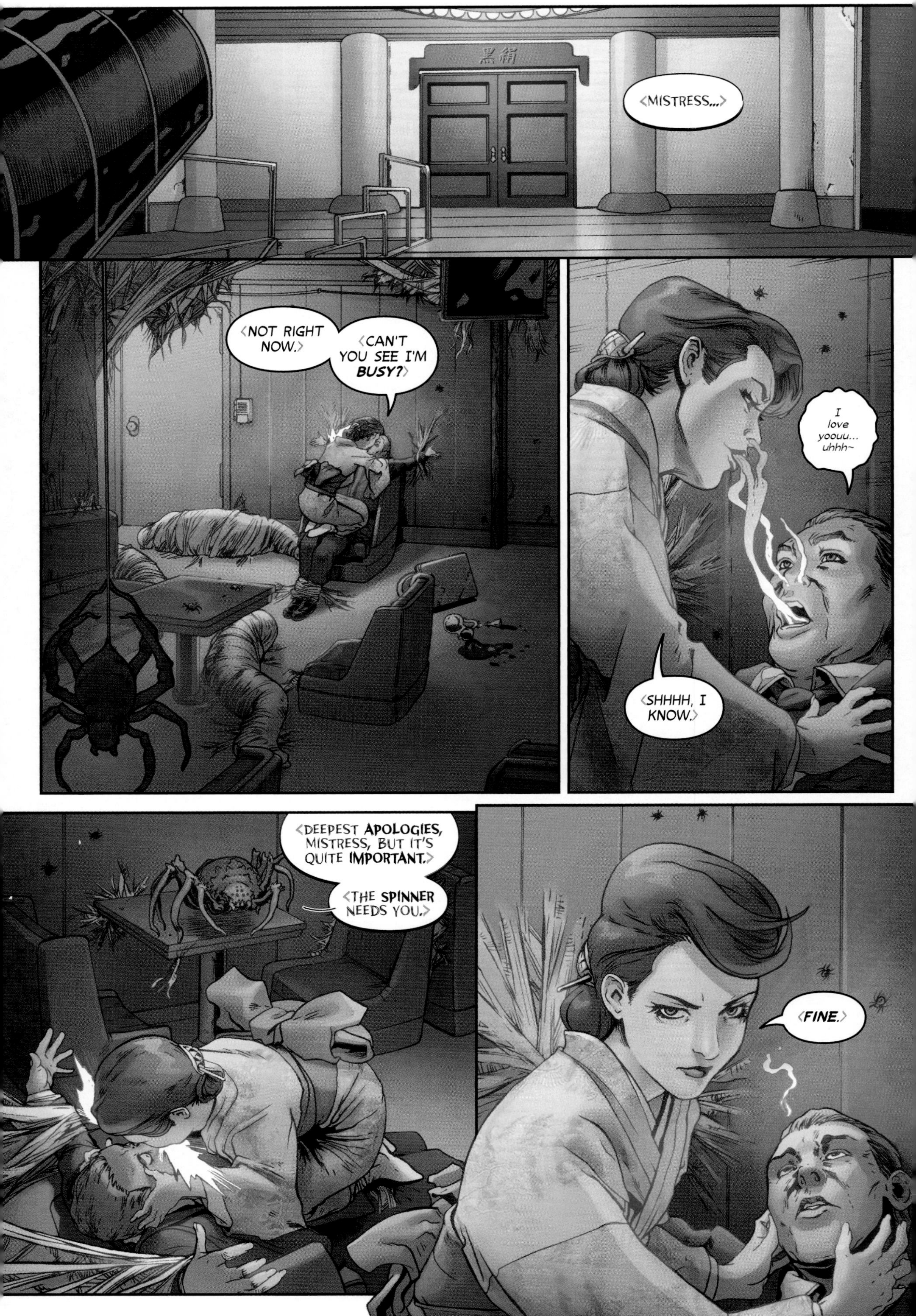

<MISTRESS...>
<NOT RIGHT NOW.>
<CAN'T YOU SEE I'M BUSY?>
I love yoouu... uhhh~
<SHHHH, I KNOW.>
<DEEPEST APOLOGIES, MISTRESS, BUT IT'S QUITE IMPORTANT.>
<THE SPINNER NEEDS YOU.>
<FINE.>

‹I SENSE **NEW** ENERGY ALONG THE WEAVE.›

‹**GREAT POWER** BRINGING **GREAT CHANGE.**›

‹THE **CHILDREN?**›

‹YES.›

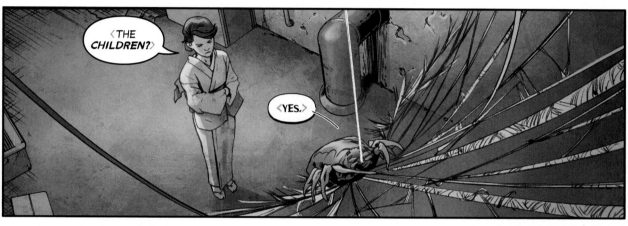

‹THE **WEAVE** IS **BEING TORN.**›

‹THE **PATTERN** WOVEN WITHOUT **CARE**, SUCH AS I HAVE **NEVER** FELT BEFORE.›

‹MISTRESS, I'M **AFRAID.**›

‹**DON'T** BE. WE'VE PICKED THE **WINNING** SIDE.›

‹ONCE WE BRING THEM INTO THE **WEB**, OUR **FUTURE** WILL BE **SECURE.**›

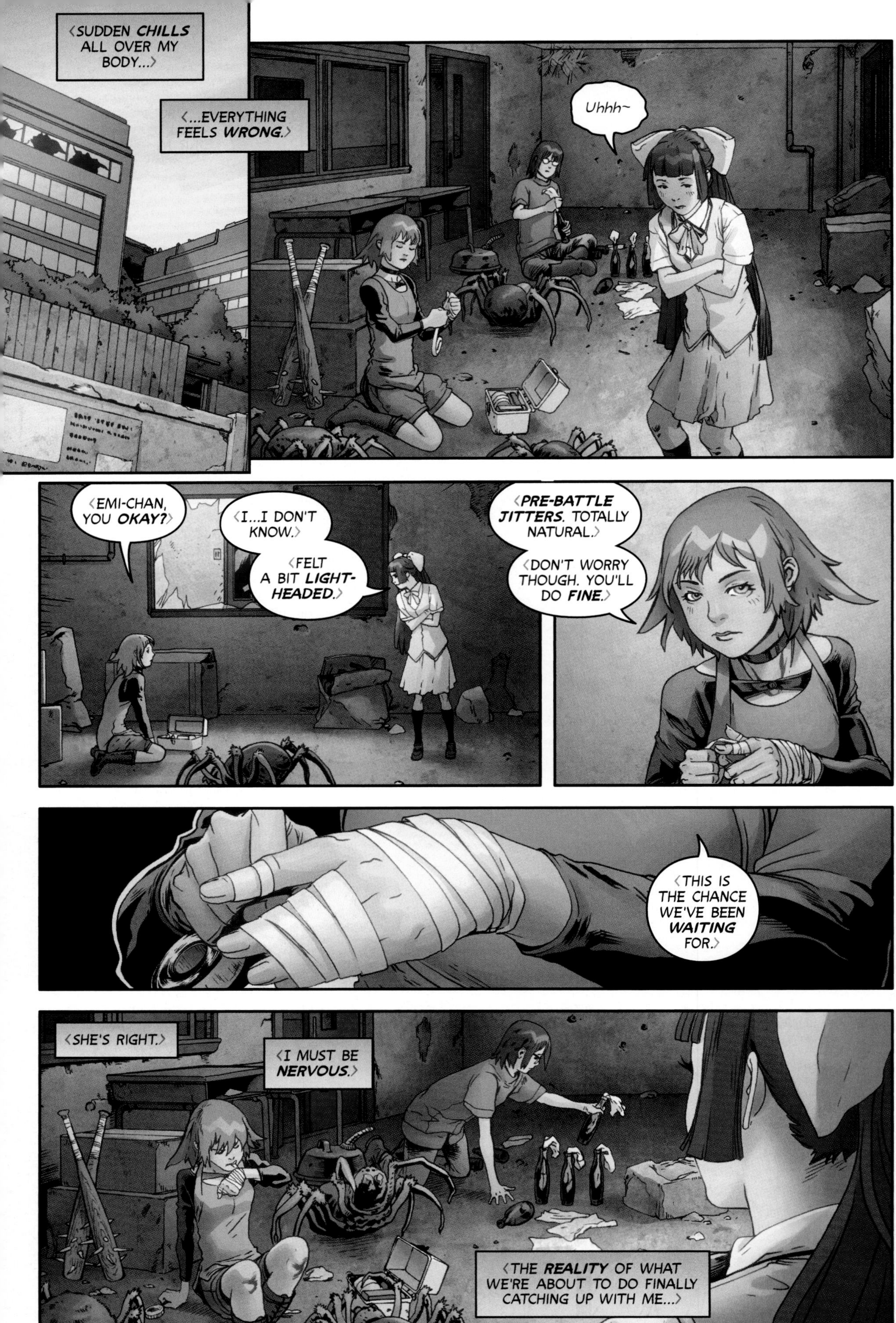
‹SUDDEN CHILLS ALL OVER MY BODY...›
‹...EVERYTHING FEELS WRONG.›
Uhhh~
‹EMI-CHAN, YOU OKAY?›
‹I...I DON'T KNOW.›
‹FELT A BIT LIGHT-HEADED.›
‹PRE-BATTLE JITTERS. TOTALLY NATURAL.›
‹DON'T WORRY THOUGH. YOU'LL DO FINE.›
‹THIS IS THE CHANCE WE'VE BEEN WAITING FOR.›
‹SHE'S RIGHT.›
‹I MUST BE NERVOUS.›
‹THE REALITY OF WHAT WE'RE ABOUT TO DO FINALLY CATCHING UP WITH ME...›

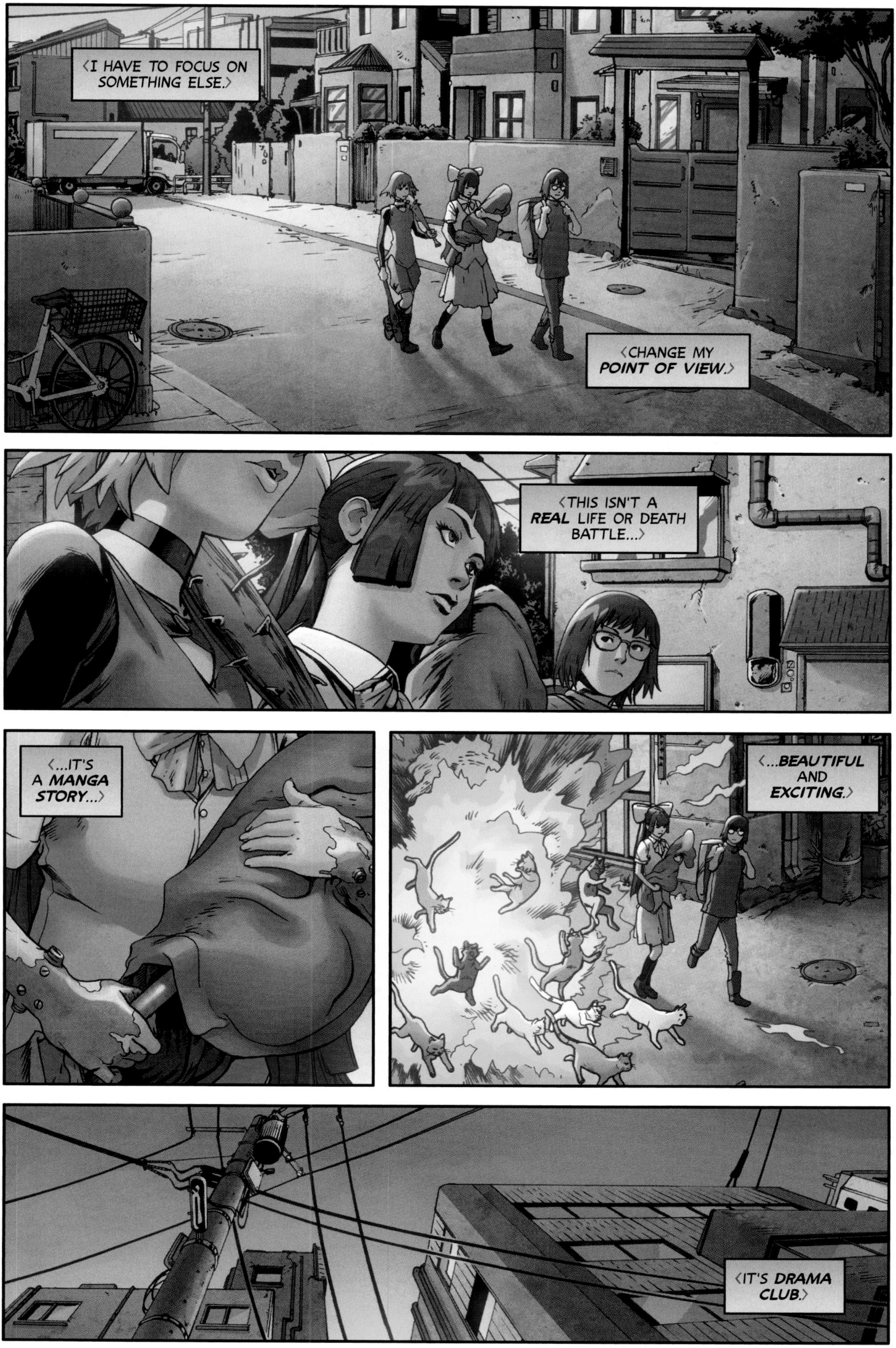
⟨I HAVE TO FOCUS ON SOMETHING ELSE.⟩
⟨CHANGE MY *POINT OF VIEW.*⟩
⟨THIS ISN'T A ***REAL*** LIFE OR DEATH BATTLE...⟩
⟨...IT'S A *MANGA STORY*...⟩
⟨...*BEAUTIFUL* AND *EXCITING.*⟩
⟨IT'S *DRAMA CLUB.*⟩

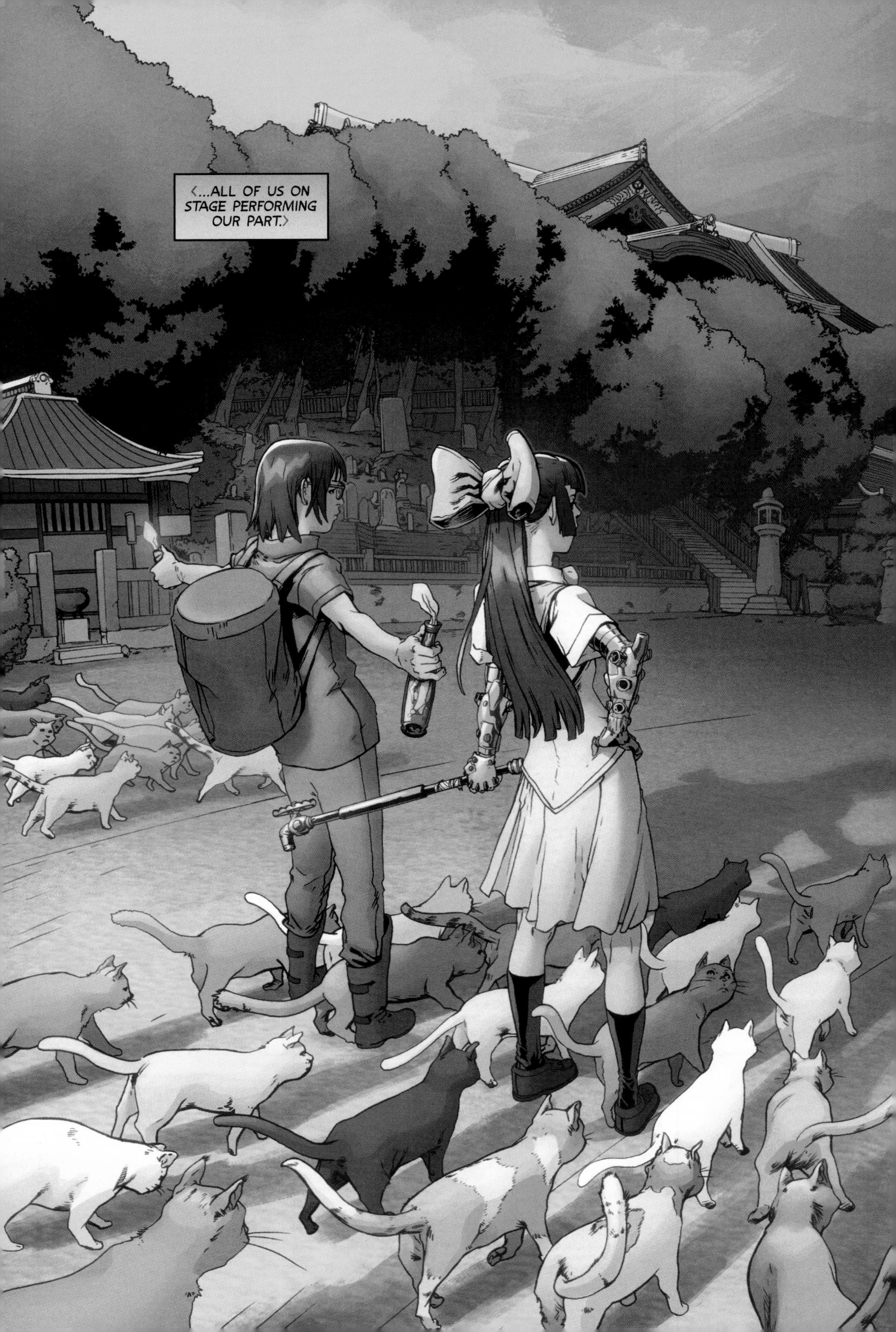
<...ALL OF US ON STAGE PERFORMING OUR PART.>

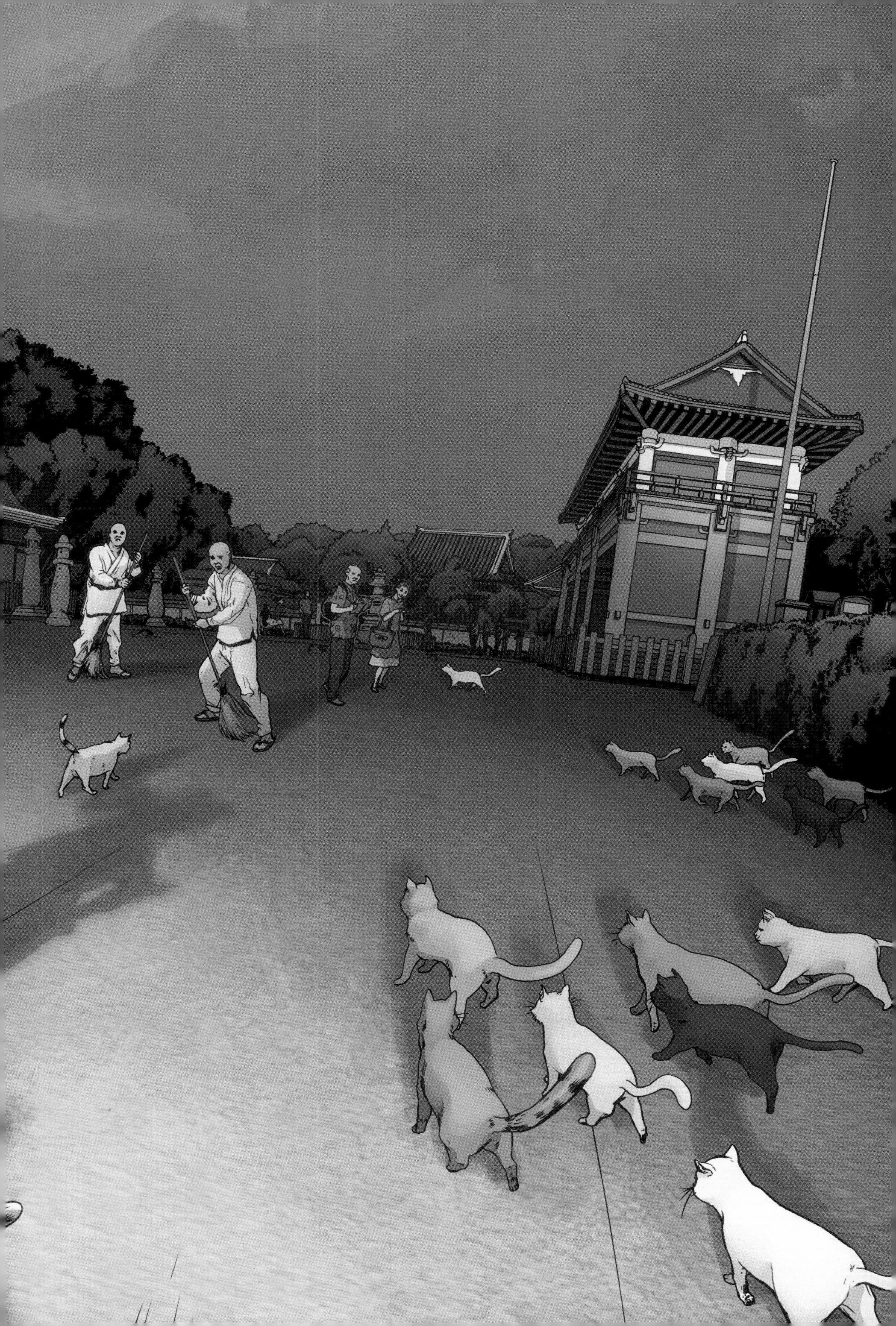

Chapter Ten

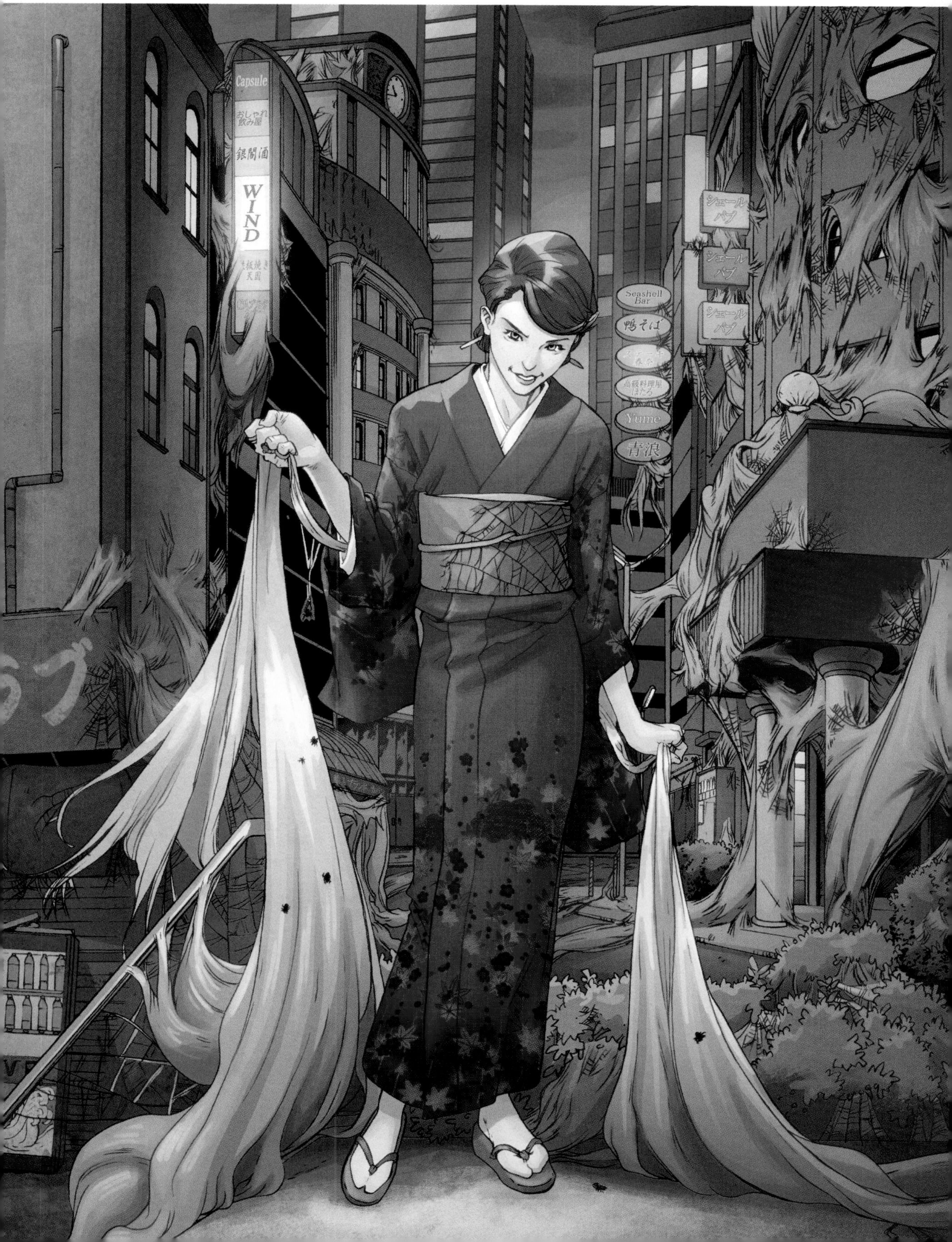
Capsule
おしゃれ飲み屋
銀閣酒
WIND
Seashell Bar
鴨そば
Yume
青浪
シェールパブ
シェールパブ
シェールパブ

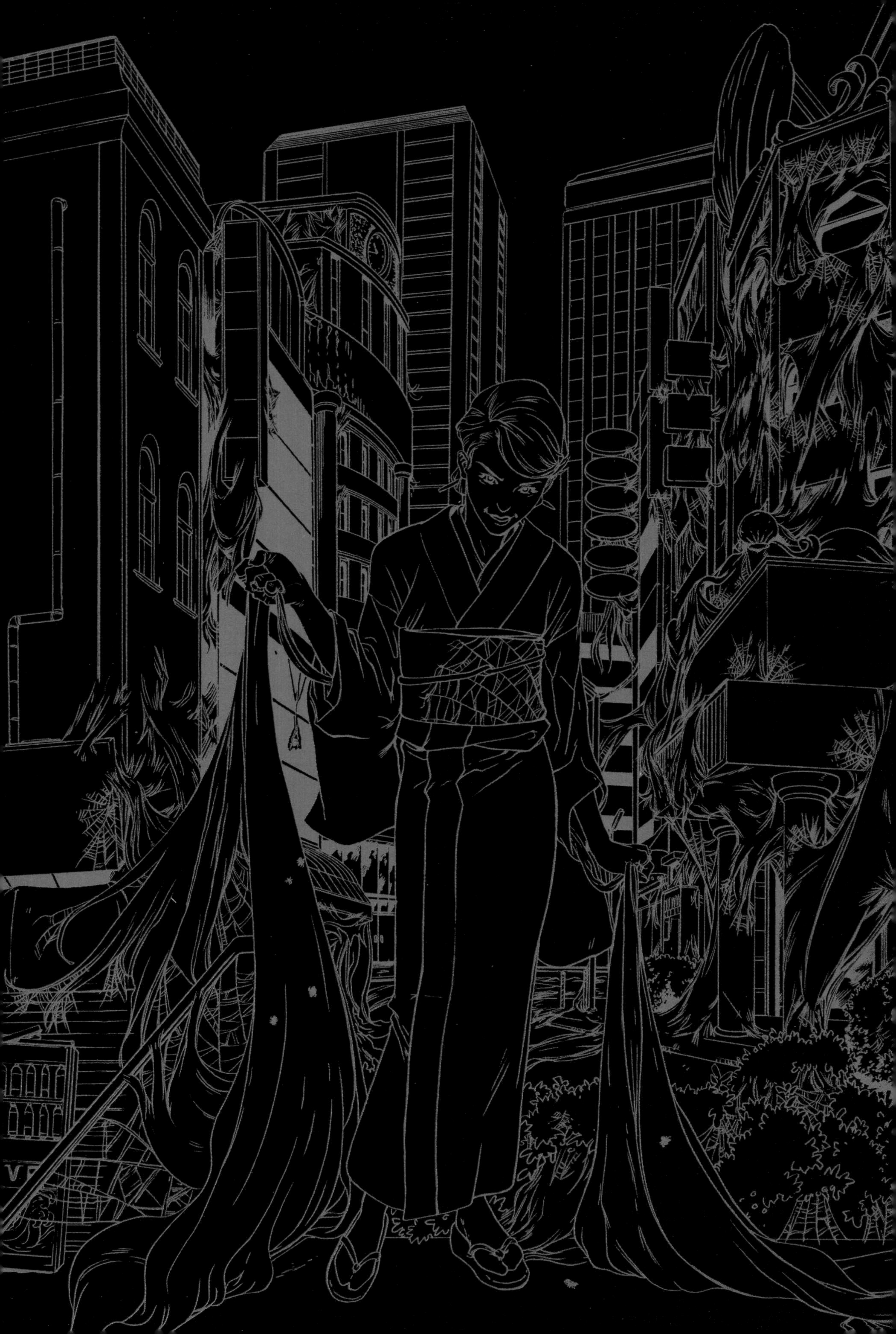

THEN.

<MASTER, CAN YOU *HEAR* ME?>

<DO NOT *SPEAK* TO HIM, BROTHER.>

<*DEEP MEDITATION* CLOSES HIM OFF FROM THE *PHYSICAL REALM* NOW AND FOREVER MORE.>

<HE IS ONE WITH THE *WEAVE*.>

<HIS STRENGTH *PROTECTS* US FROM THE *UNKNOWN*.>

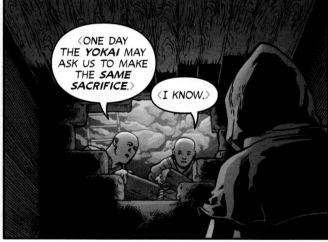

<ONE DAY THE *YOKAI* MAY ASK US TO MAKE THE *SAME SACRIFICE*.>

<I KNOW.>

<ARE... ARE YOU AFRAID OF *SOKUSHIN-BUTSU?**>

*SELF MUMMIFICATION.

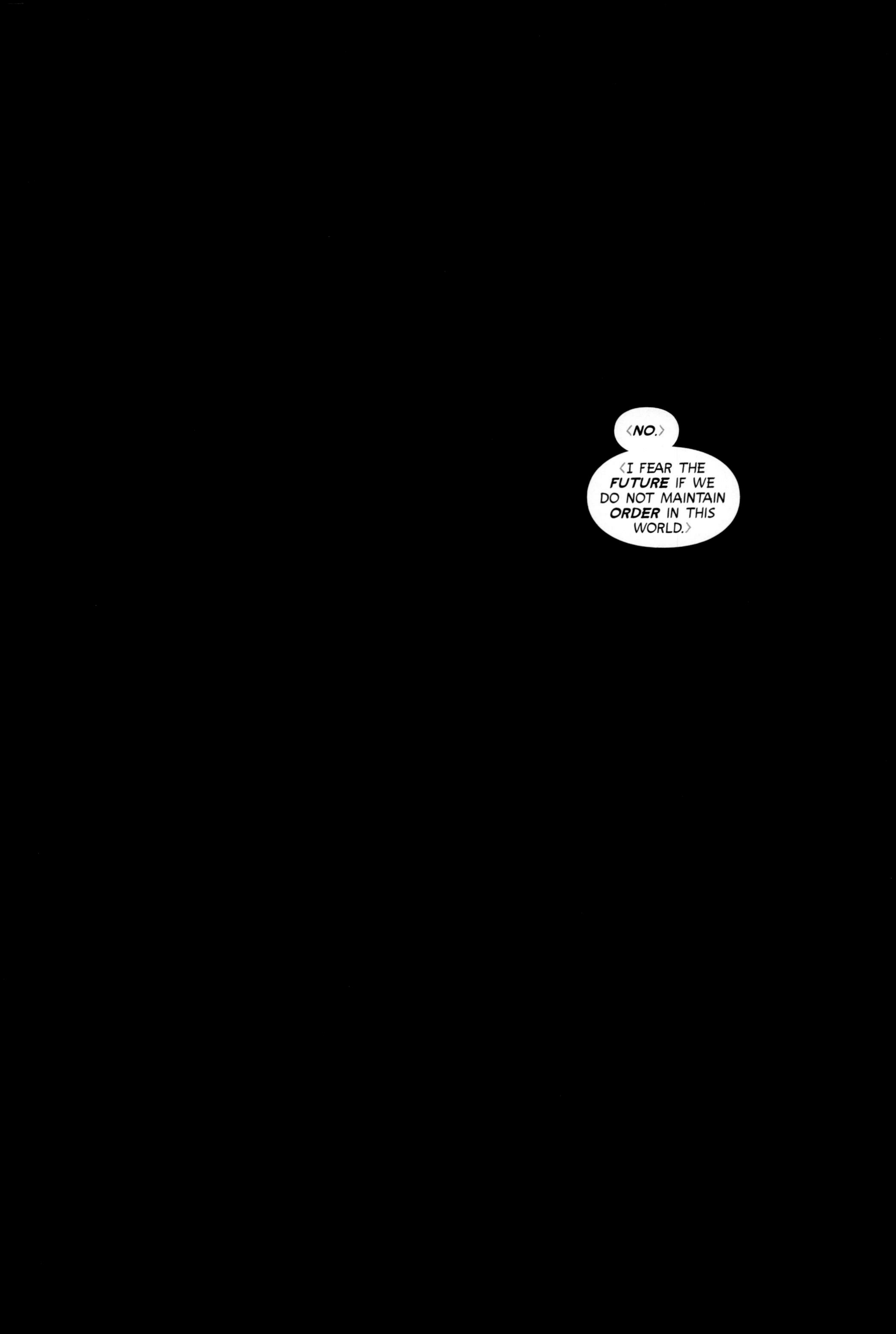
<NO.>
<I FEAR THE FUTURE IF WE DO NOT MAINTAIN ORDER IN THIS WORLD.>

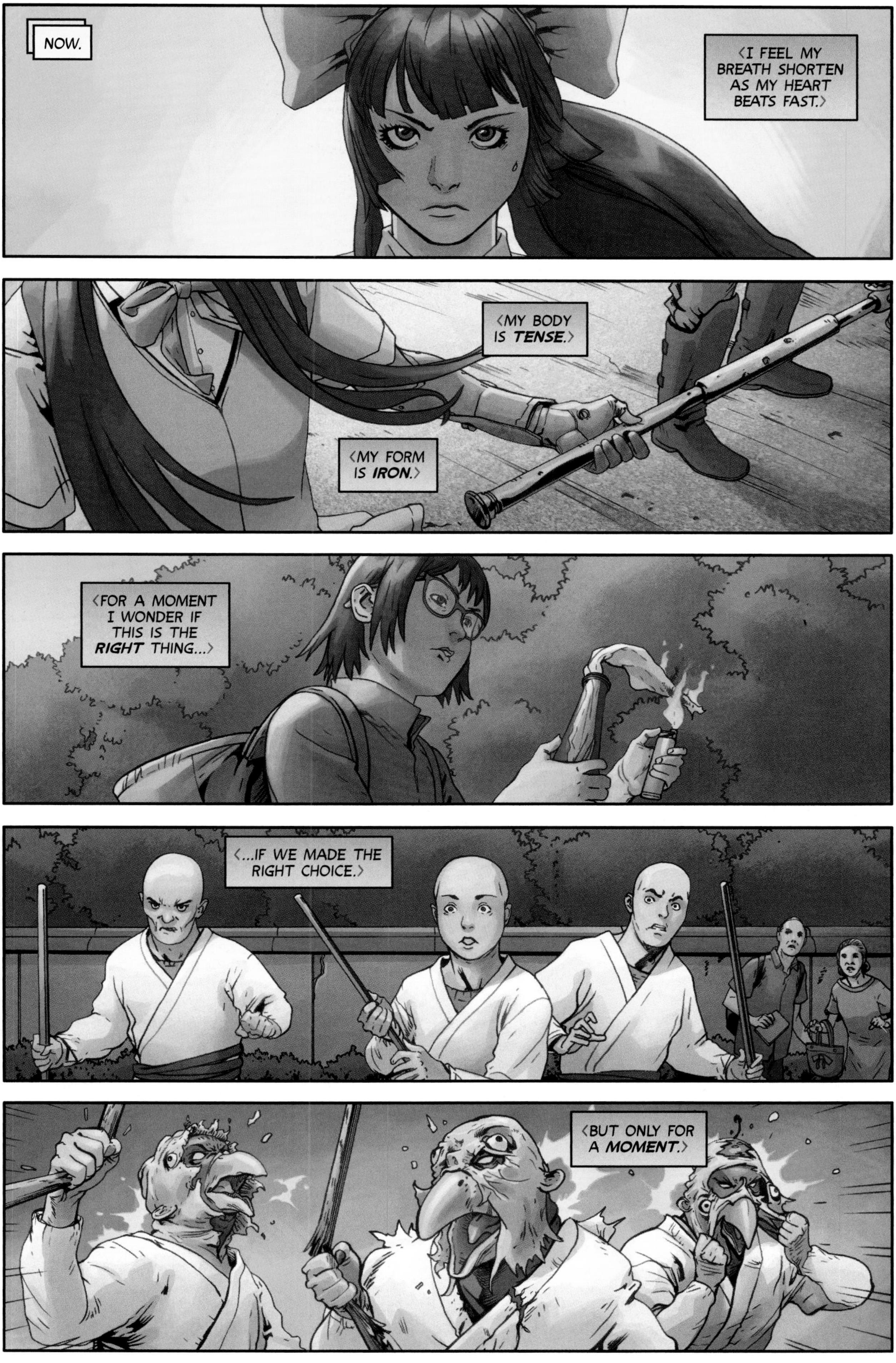
NOW.
<I FEEL MY BREATH SHORTEN AS MY HEART BEATS FAST.>
<MY BODY IS TENSE.>
<MY FORM IS IRON.>
<FOR A MOMENT I WONDER IF THIS IS THE RIGHT THING...>
<...IF WE MADE THE RIGHT CHOICE.>
<BUT ONLY FOR A MOMENT.>

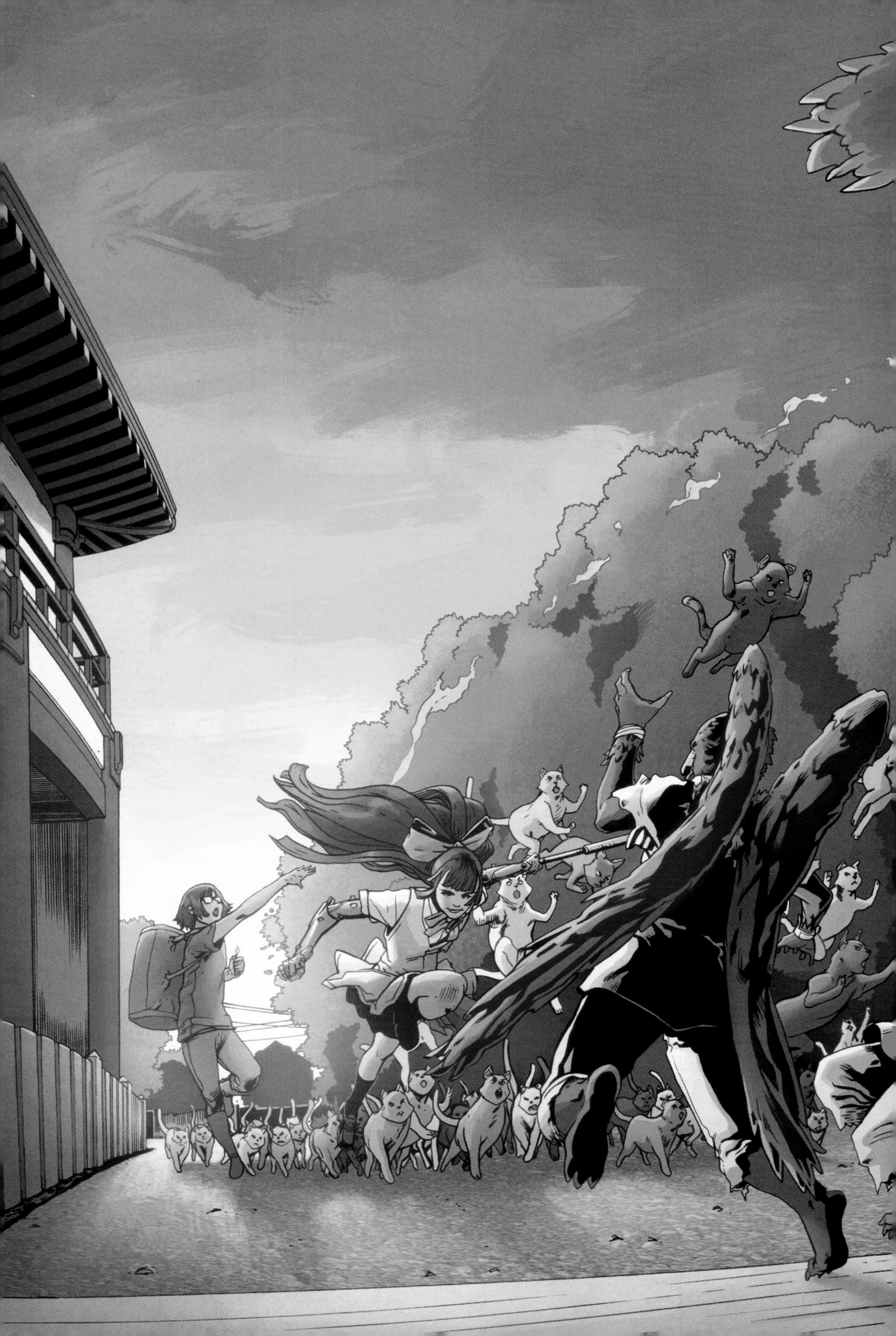

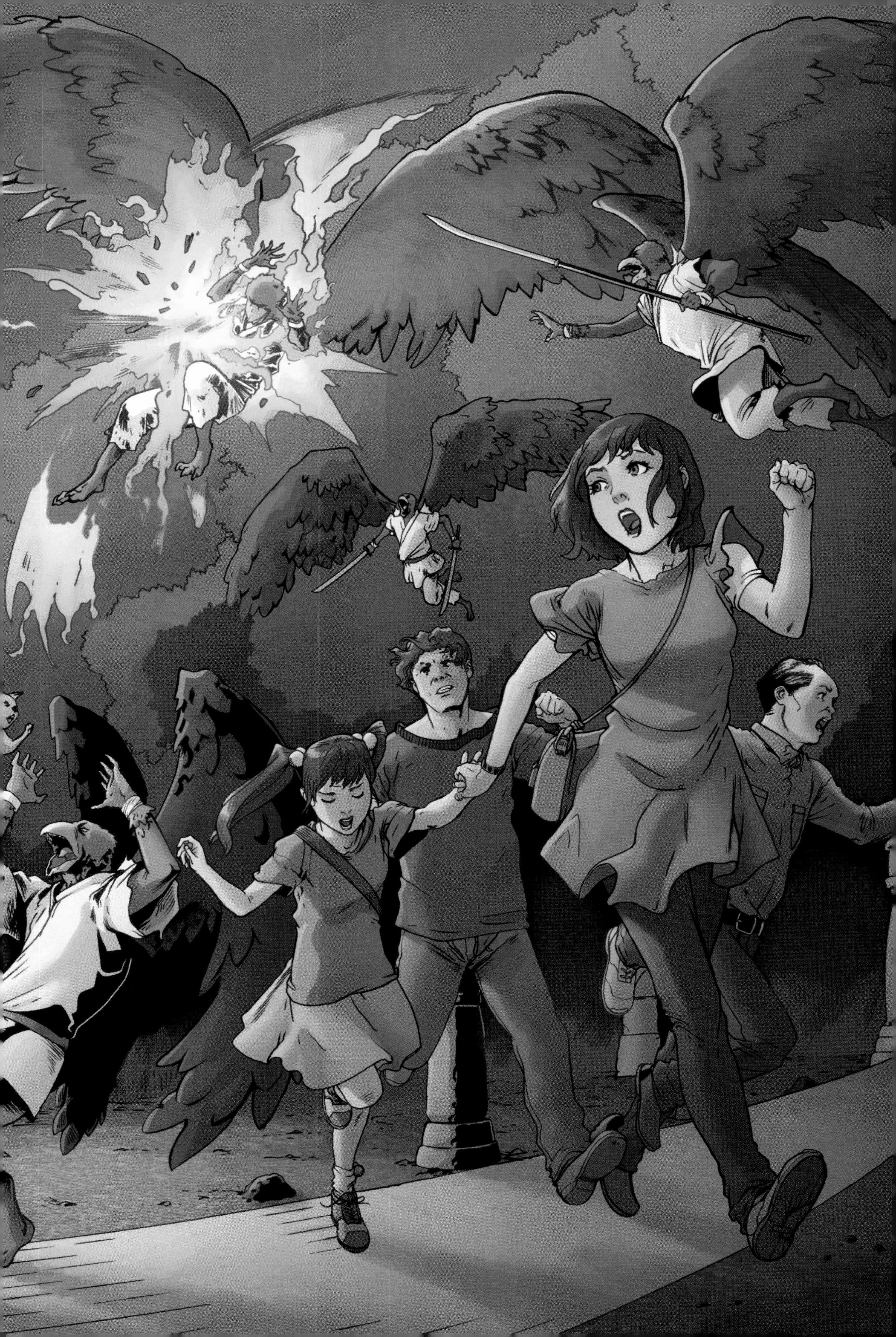

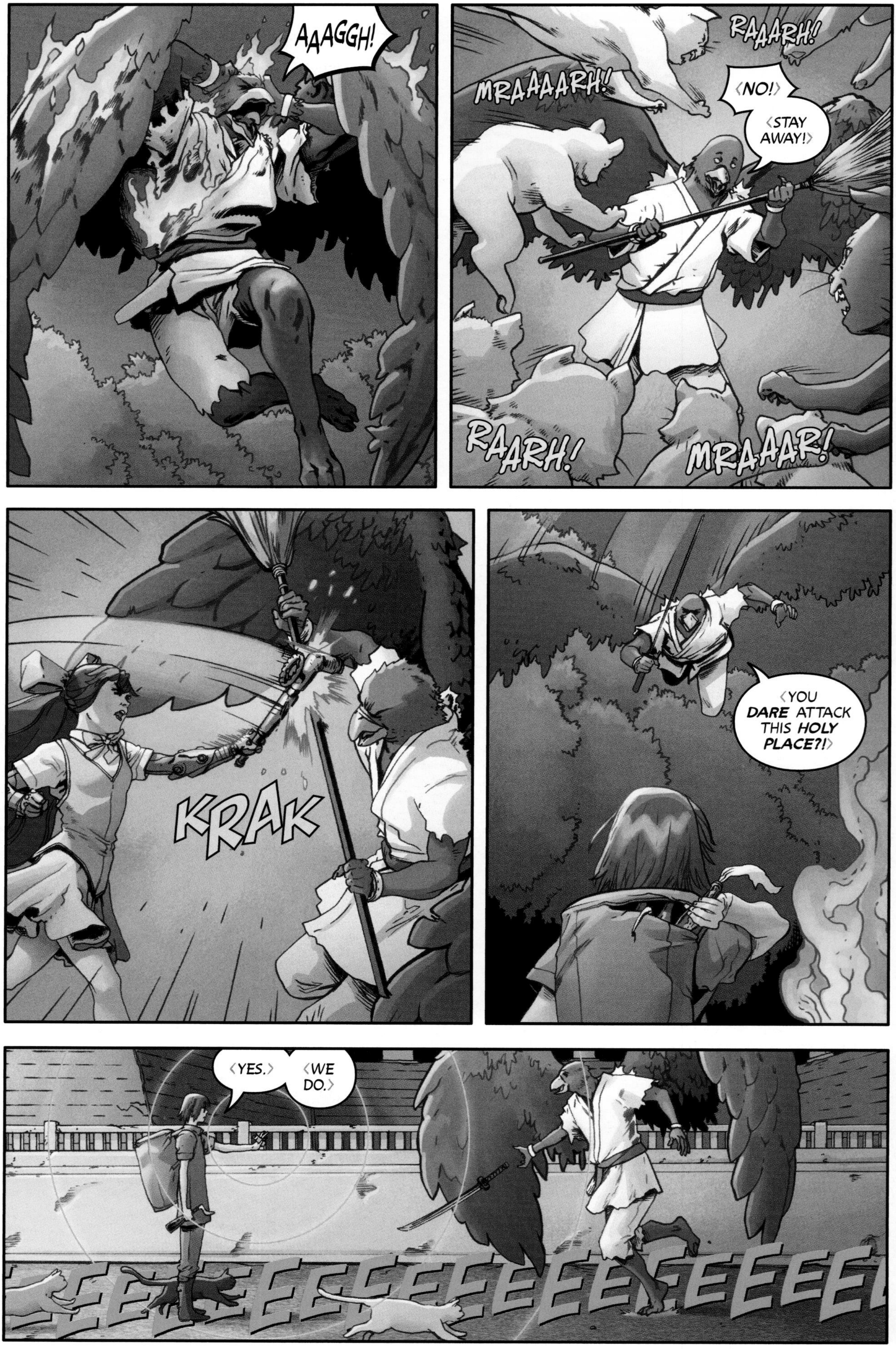
AAAGGH!
RAAARH!
MRAAAARH!
‹NO!›
‹STAY AWAY!›
RAARH!
MRAAAR!
KRAK
‹YOU DARE ATTACK THIS HOLY PLACE?!›
‹YES.›
‹WE DO.›
EEEEEEEEEEEEEEEEEE

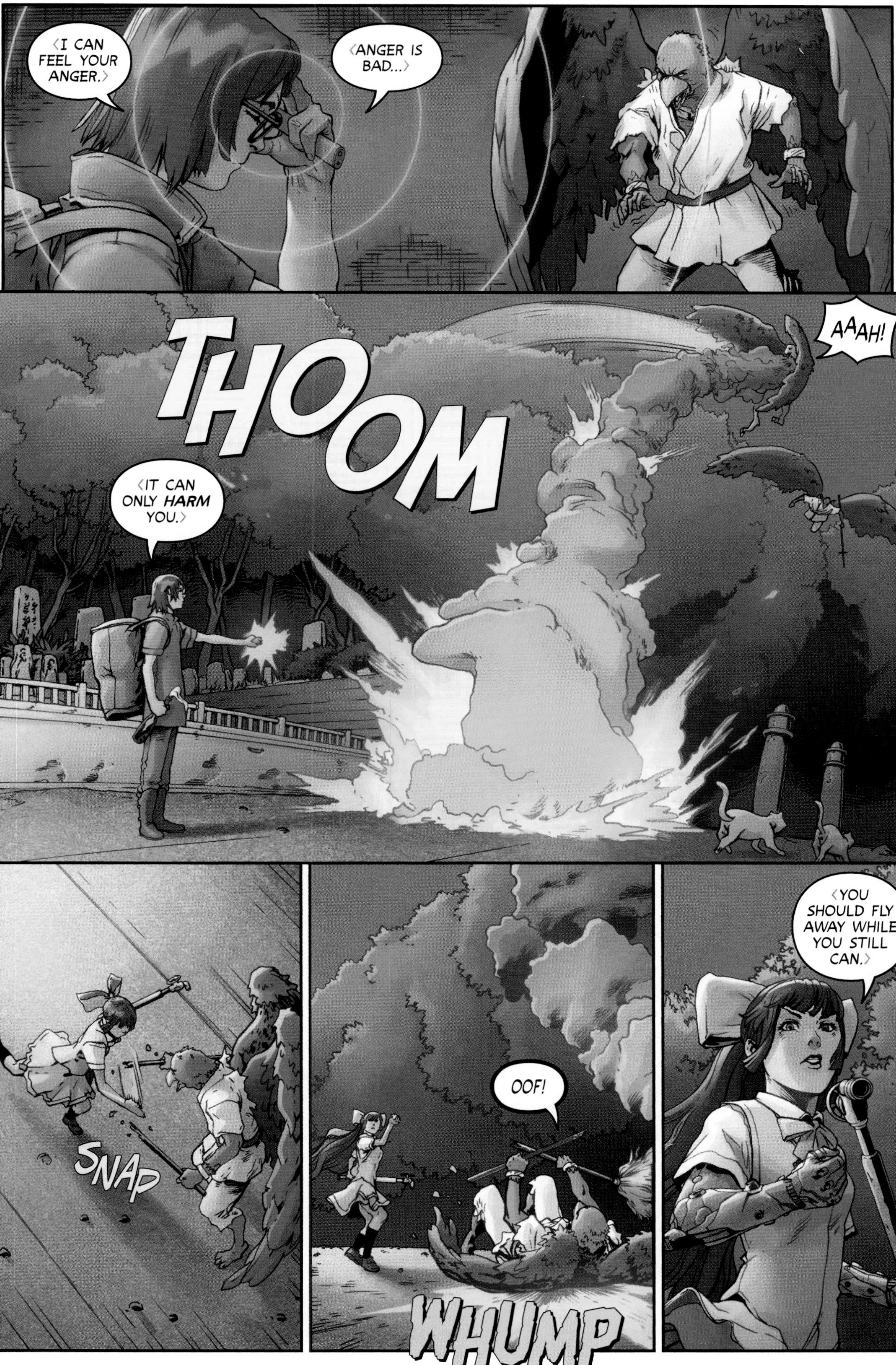

〈I CAN FEEL YOUR ANGER.〉
〈ANGER IS BAD...〉
THOOM
AAAH!
〈IT CAN ONLY *HARM* YOU.〉
SNAP
OOF!
WHUMP
〈YOU SHOULD FLY AWAY WHILE YOU STILL CAN.〉

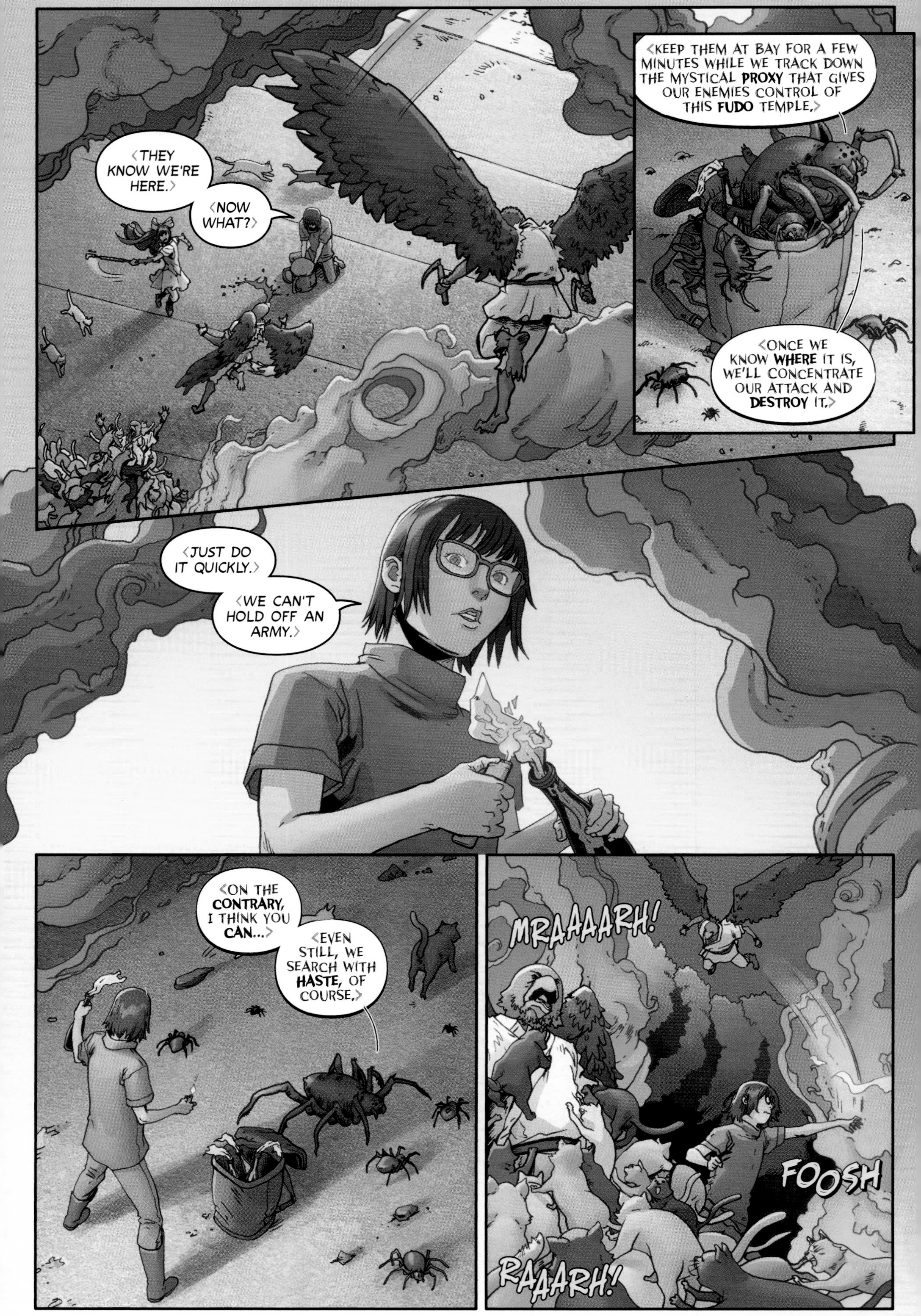
<THEY KNOW WE'RE HERE.>
<NOW WHAT?>
<KEEP THEM AT BAY FOR A FEW MINUTES WHILE WE TRACK DOWN THE MYSTICAL **PROXY** THAT GIVES OUR ENEMIES CONTROL OF THIS **FUDO** TEMPLE.>
<ONCE WE KNOW **WHERE** IT IS, WE'LL CONCENTRATE OUR ATTACK AND **DESTROY** IT.>
<JUST DO IT QUICKLY.>
<WE CAN'T HOLD OFF AN ARMY.>
<ON THE **CONTRARY**, I THINK YOU **CAN**...>
<EVEN STILL, WE SEARCH WITH **HASTE**, OF COURSE.>
MRAAAAARH!
FOOSH
RAAARH!

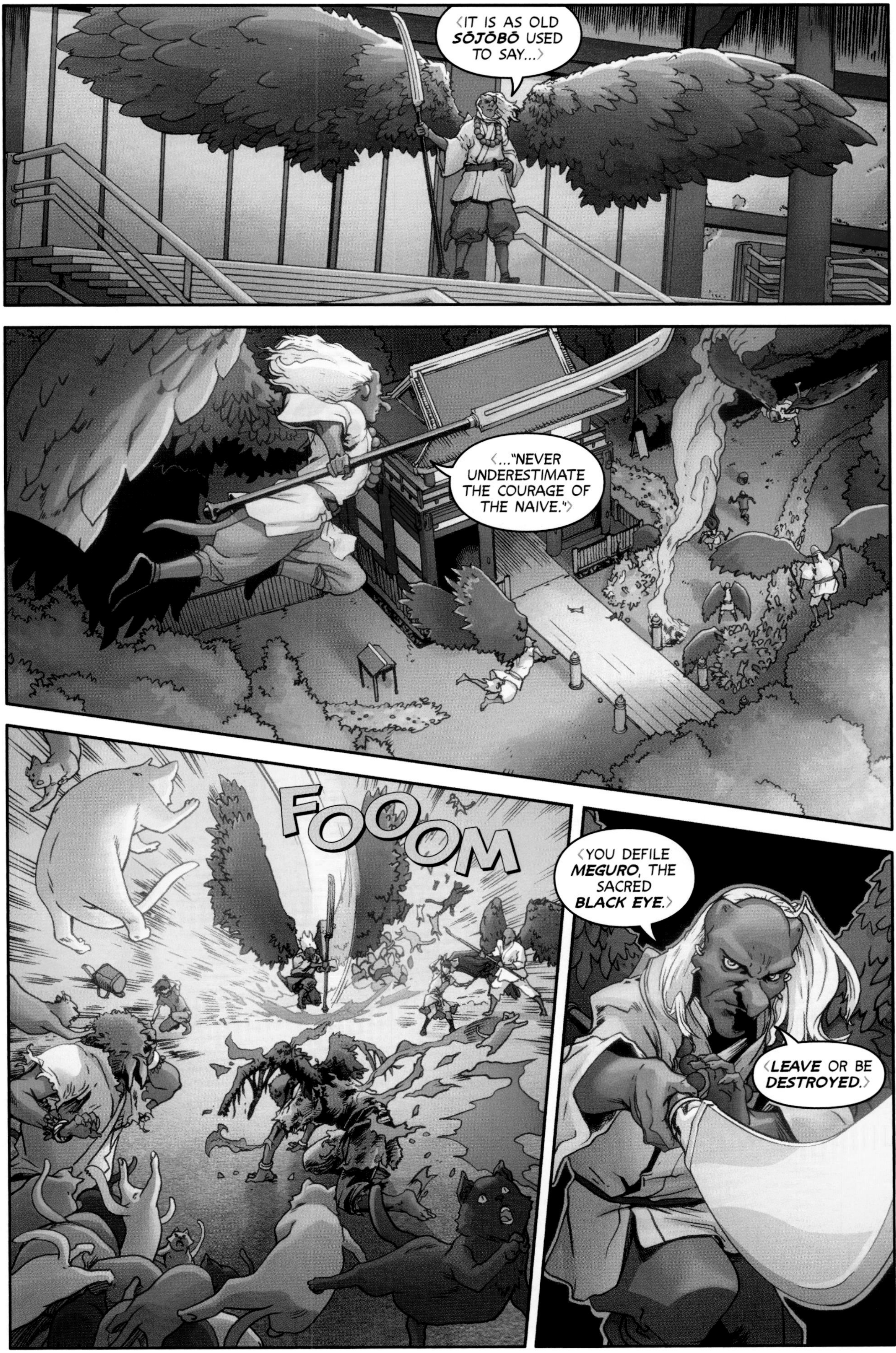
‹IT IS AS OLD SŌJŌBŌ USED TO SAY...›
‹..."NEVER UNDERESTIMATE THE COURAGE OF THE NAIVE."›
FOOOM
‹YOU DEFILE MEGURO, THE SACRED BLACK EYE.›
‹LEAVE OR BE DESTROYED.›

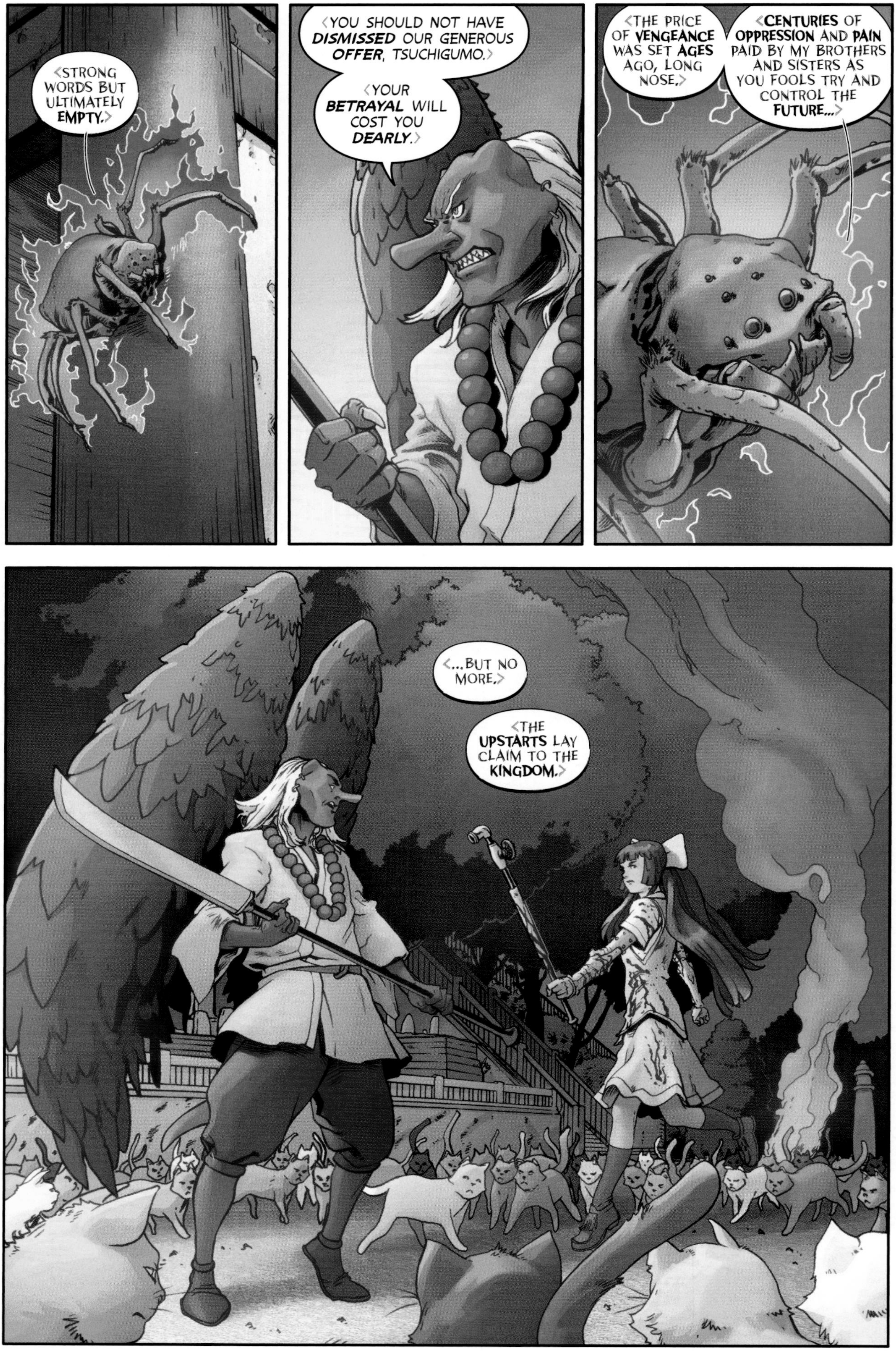
<STRONG WORDS BUT ULTIMATELY EMPTY.>
<YOU SHOULD NOT HAVE DISMISSED OUR GENEROUS OFFER, TSUCHIGUMO.>
<YOUR BETRAYAL WILL COST YOU DEARLY.>
<THE PRICE OF VENGEANCE WAS SET AGES AGO, LONG NOSE.>
<CENTURIES OF OPPRESSION AND PAIN PAID BY MY BROTHERS AND SISTERS AS YOU FOOLS TRY AND CONTROL THE FUTURE...>
<...BUT NO MORE.>
<THE UPSTARTS LAY CLAIM TO THE KINGDOM.>

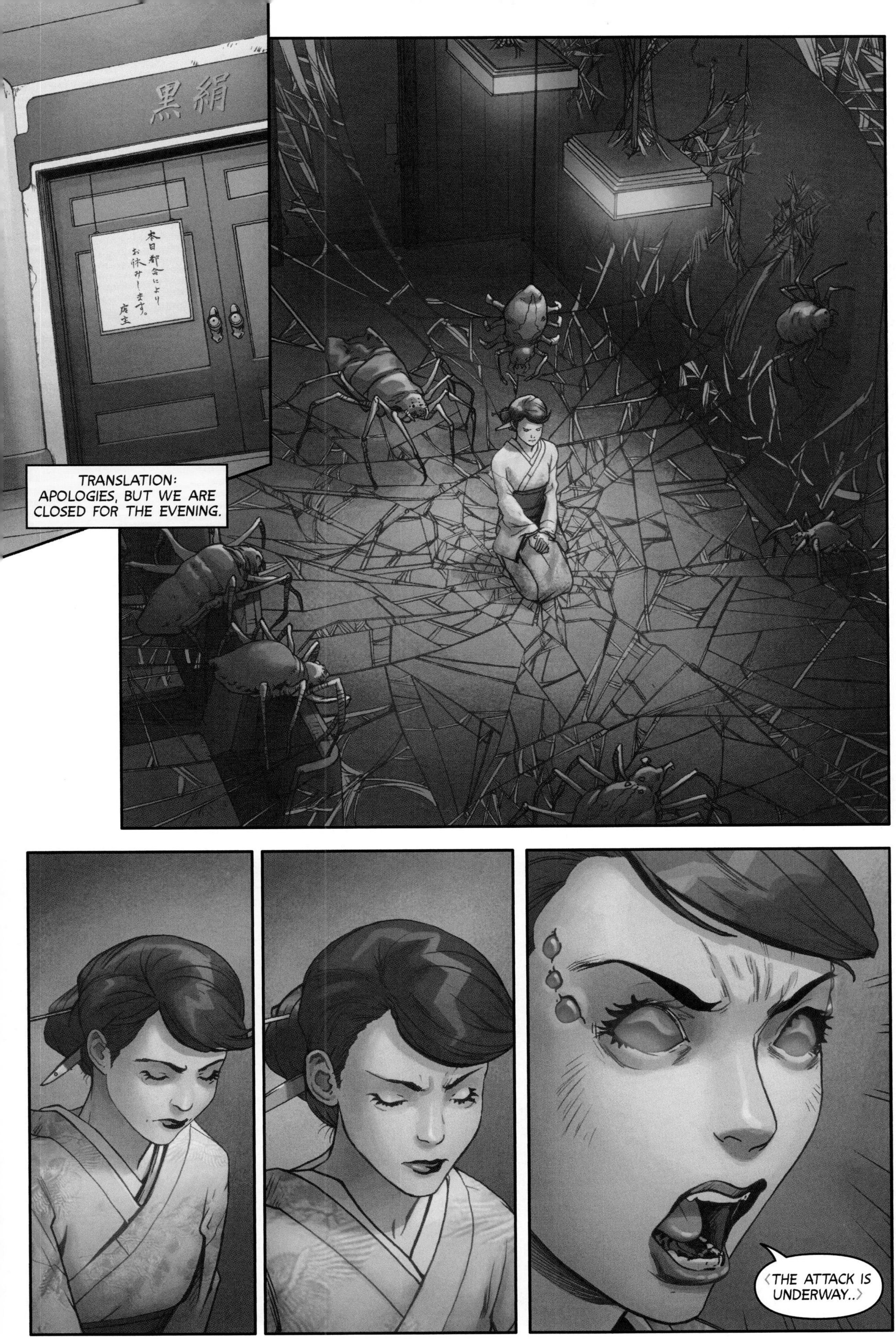
黒絹
本日都合により お休みします。 店主
TRANSLATION: APOLOGIES, BUT WE ARE CLOSED FOR THE EVENING.
〈THE ATTACK IS UNDERWAY..〉

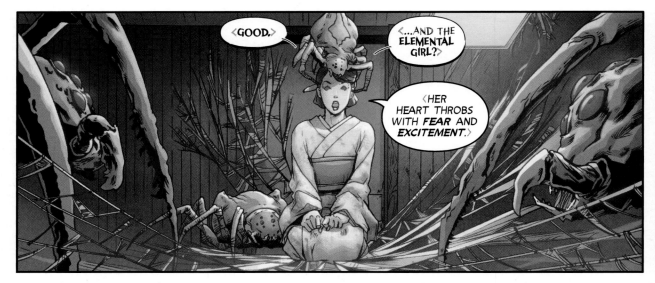

‹GOOD.›

‹...AND THE ELEMENTAL GIRL?›

‹HER HEART THROBS WITH *FEAR* AND *EXCITEMENT*.›

‹REACH OUT TO HER.›

‹YES.›

‹DIRECT HER.›

‹GIVE HER STRENGTH.›

‹ATTACK!›

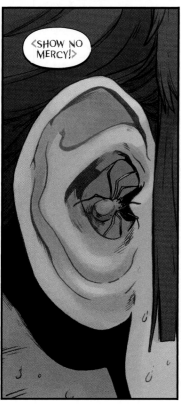

‹SHOW NO MERCY!›

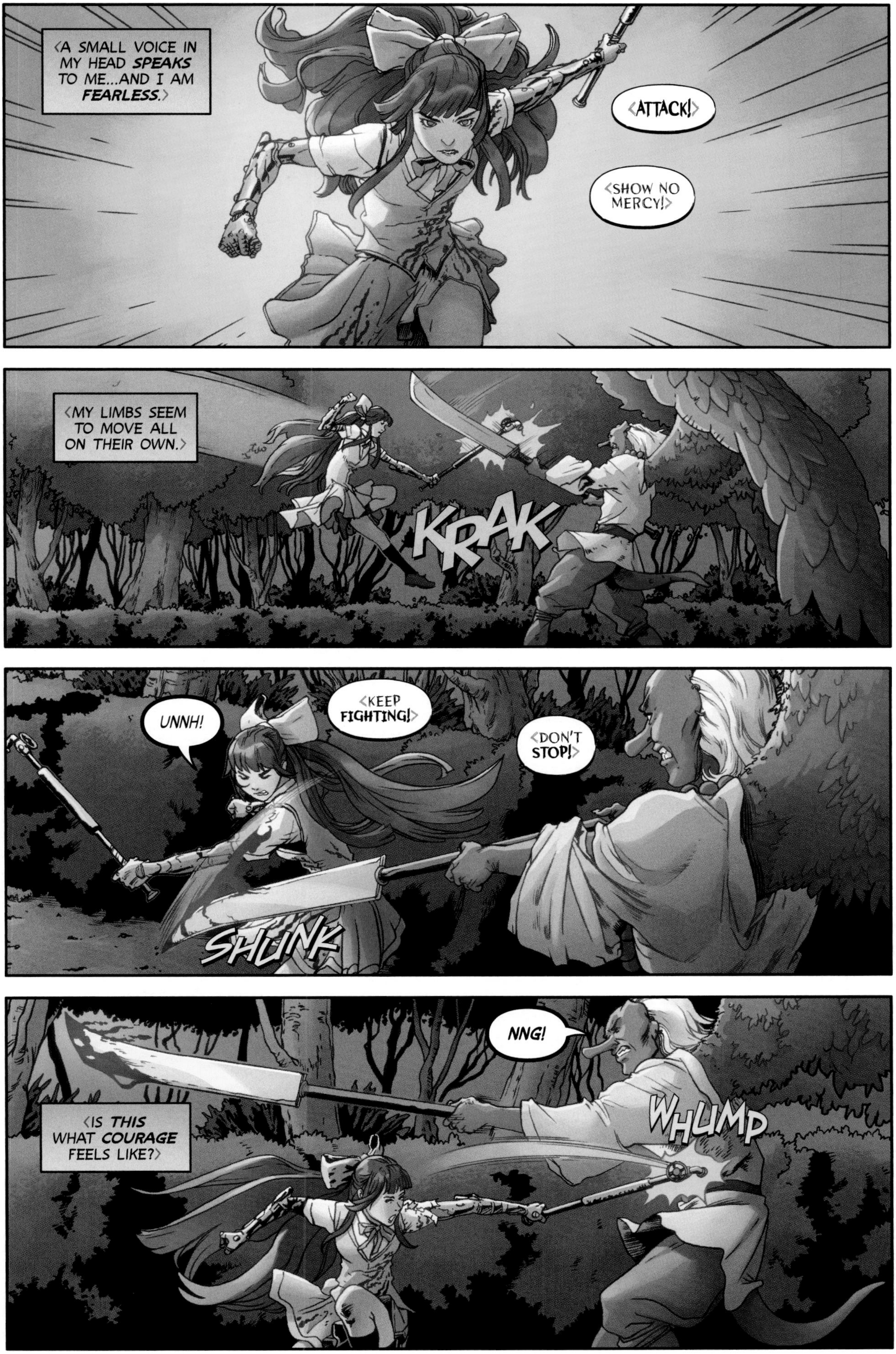
‹A SMALL VOICE IN MY HEAD SPEAKS TO ME...AND I AM FEARLESS.›
‹ATTACK!›
‹SHOW NO MERCY!›
‹MY LIMBS SEEM TO MOVE ALL ON THEIR OWN.›
KRAK
UNNH!
‹KEEP FIGHTING!›
‹DON'T STOP!›
SHUNK
NNG!
‹IS THIS WHAT COURAGE FEELS LIKE?›
WHUMP

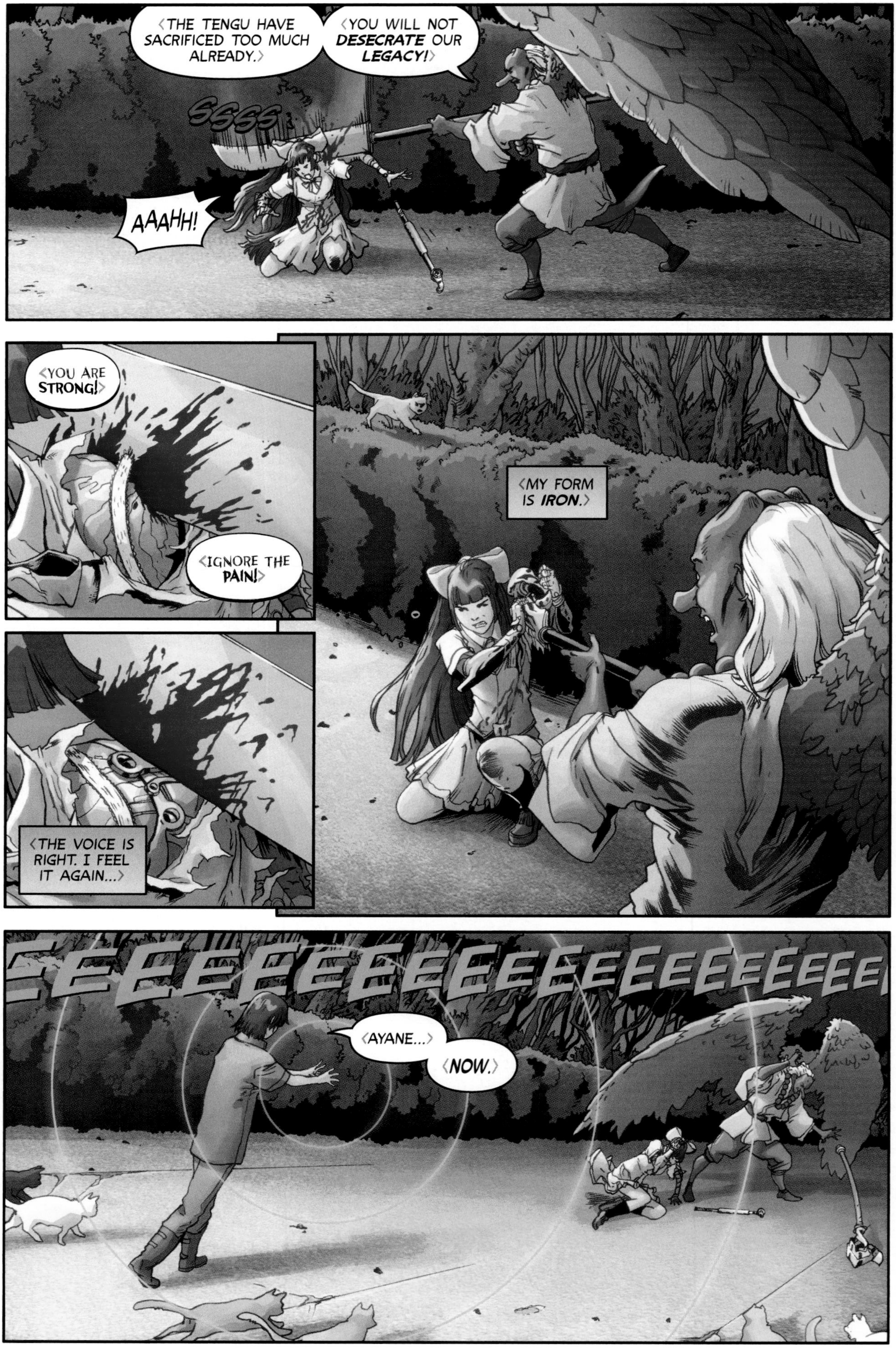

〈THE TENGU HAVE SACRIFICED TOO MUCH ALREADY.〉
〈YOU WILL NOT DESECRATE OUR LEGACY!〉
SSSS
AAAHH!
〈YOU ARE STRONG!〉
〈IGNORE THE PAIN!〉
〈THE VOICE IS RIGHT. I FEEL IT AGAIN...〉
〈MY FORM IS IRON.〉
EEEEEEEEEEEEEEEEEEEE
〈AYANE...〉
〈NOW.〉

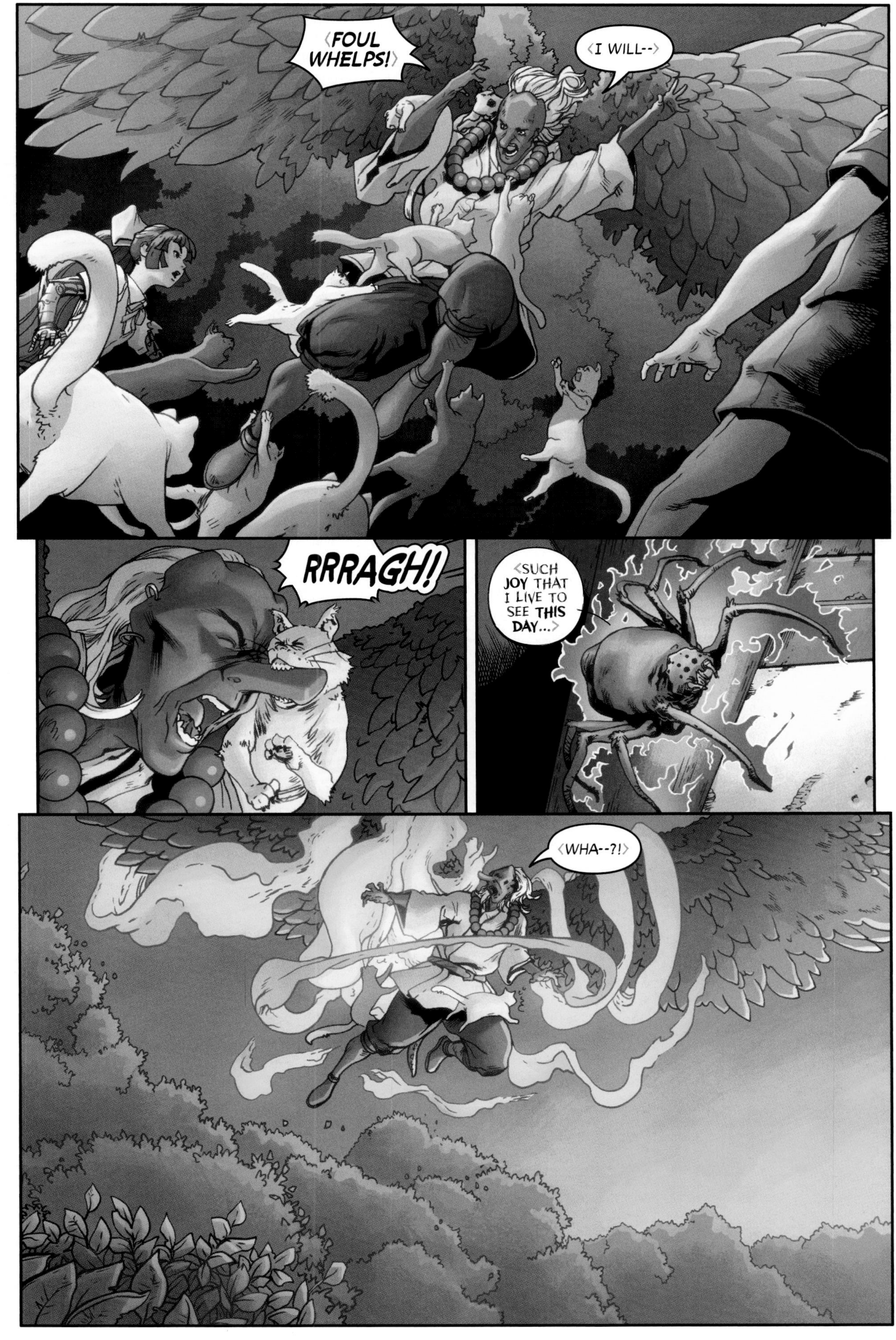
⟨FOUL WHELPS!⟩
⟨I WILL--⟩
RRRAGH!
⟨SUCH JOY THAT I LIVE TO SEE THIS DAY...⟩
⟨WHA--?!⟩

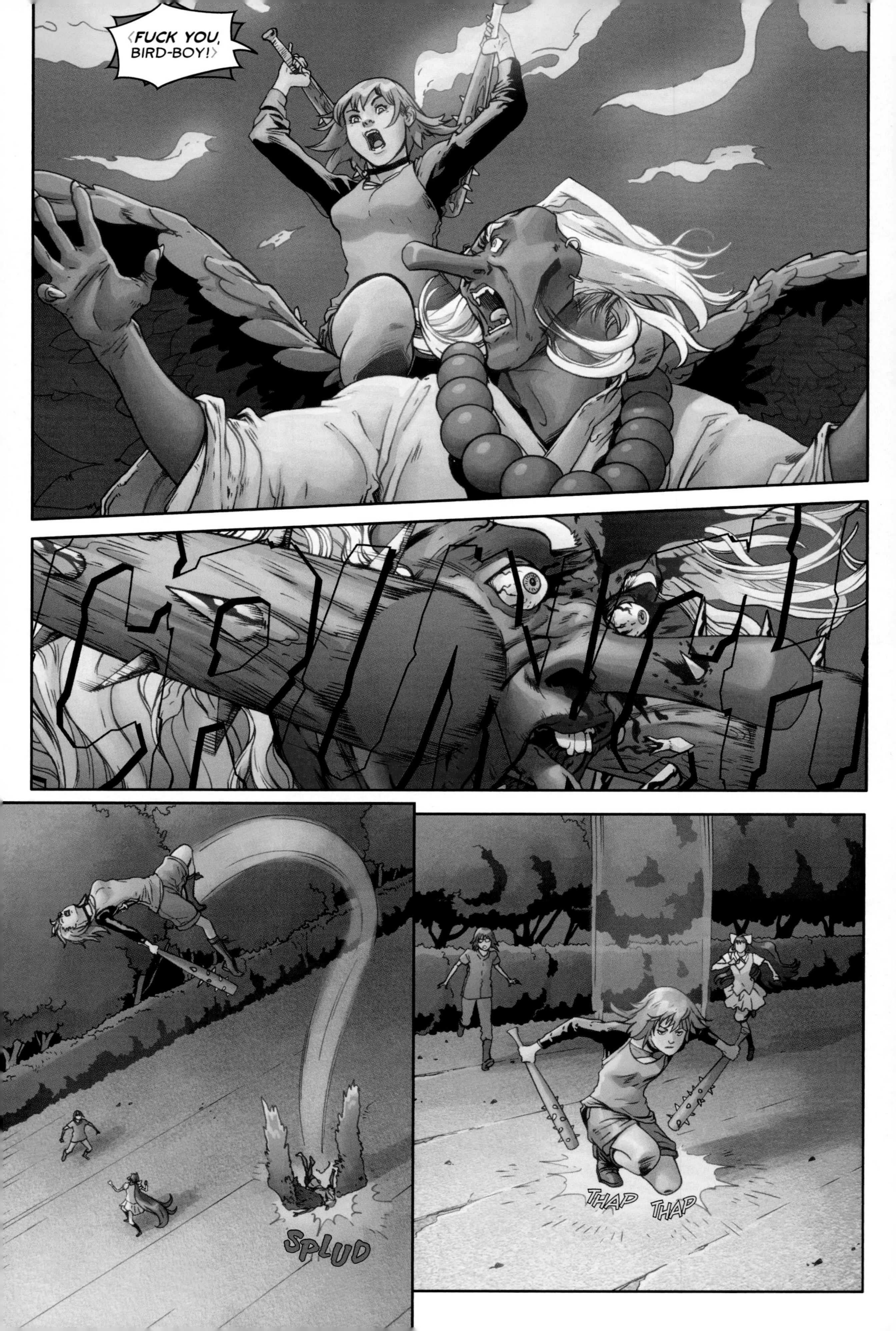
⟨FUCK YOU, BIRD-BOY!⟩
SPLUD
THAP THAP

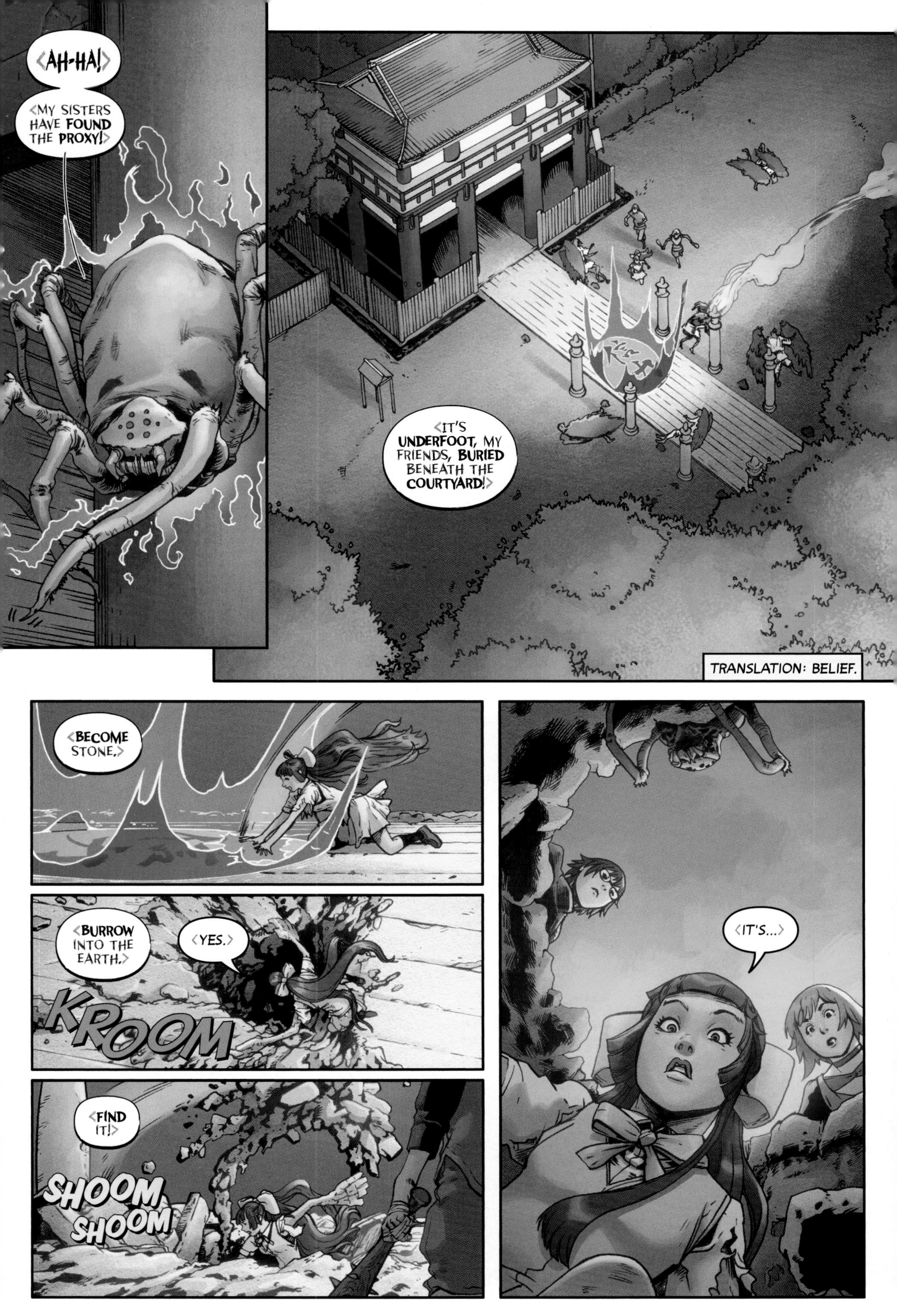
<AH-HA!>
<MY SISTERS HAVE FOUND THE PROXY!>
<IT'S UNDERFOOT, MY FRIENDS, BURIED BENEATH THE COURTYARD!>
TRANSLATION: BELIEF.
<BECOME STONE.>
<BURROW INTO THE EARTH.>
<YES.>
KROOM
<FIND IT!>
SHOOM
SHOOM
<IT'S...>

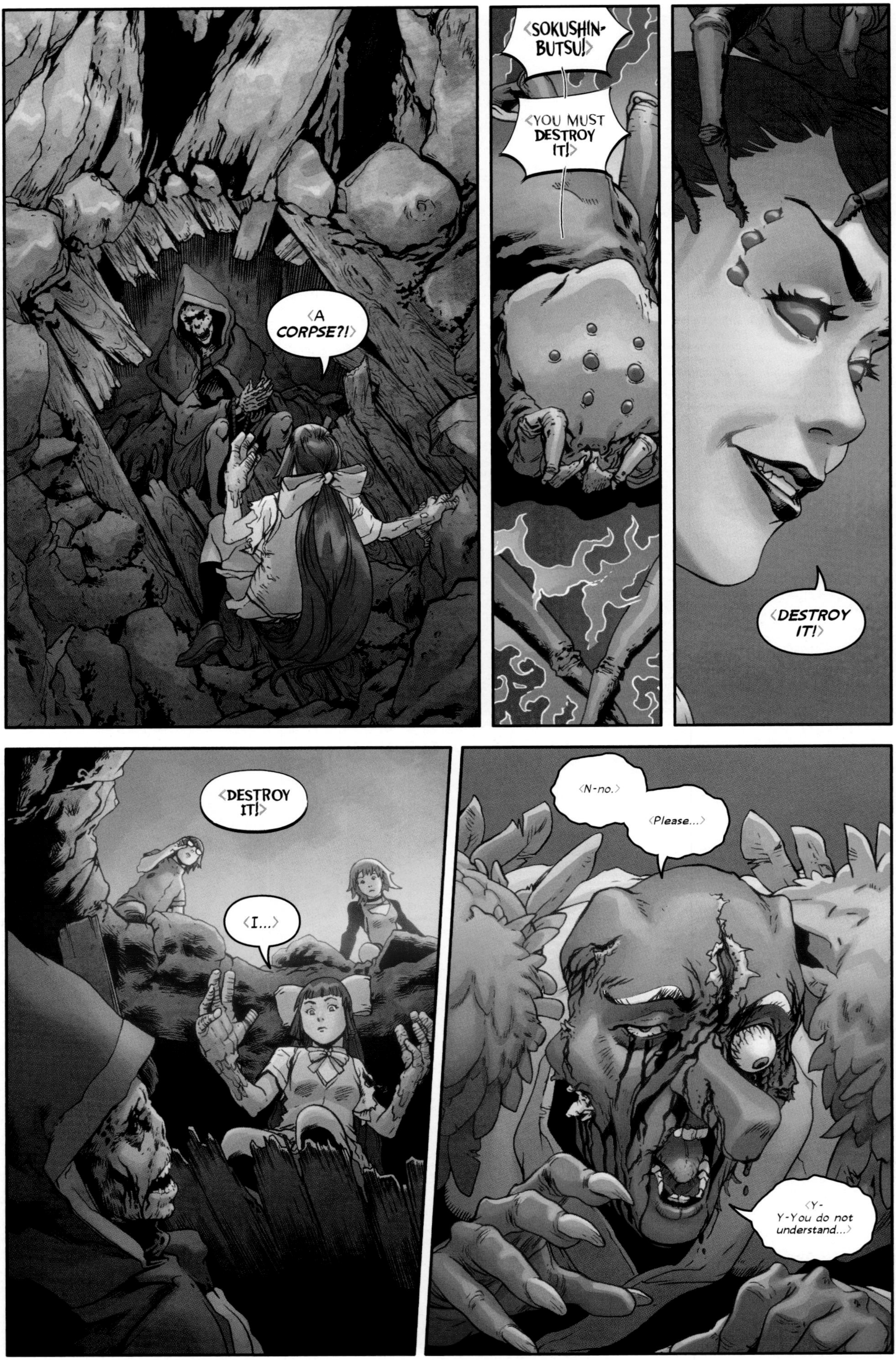

<A CORPSE?!>
<SOKUSHIN-BUTSU!>
<YOU MUST DESTROY IT!>
<DESTROY IT!>
<DESTROY IT!>
<I...>
<N-no.>
<Please...>
<Y- Y-You do not understand...>

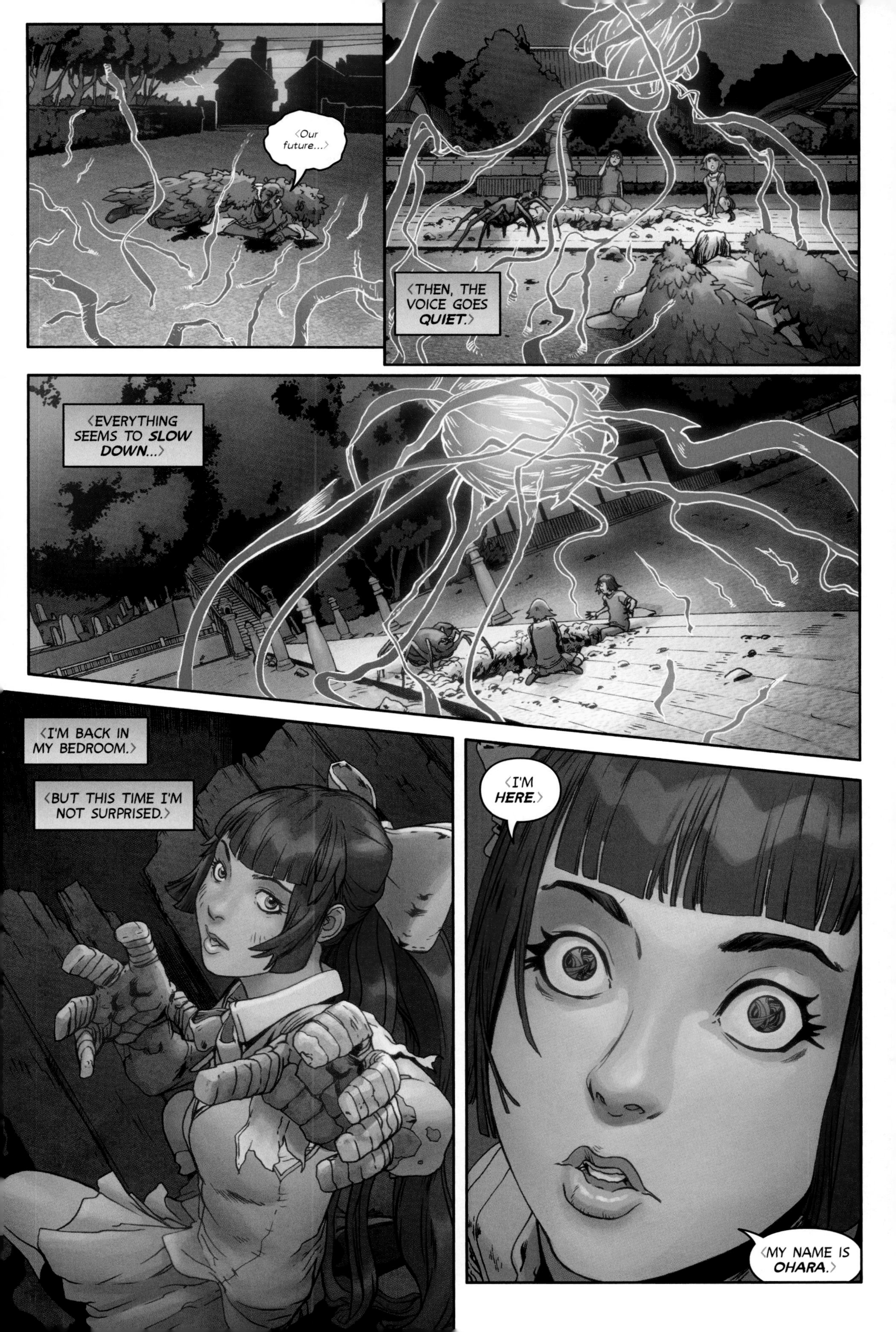
〈Our future...〉
〈THEN, THE VOICE GOES QUIET.〉
〈EVERYTHING SEEMS TO SLOW DOWN...〉
〈I'M BACK IN MY BEDROOM.〉
〈BUT THIS TIME I'M NOT SURPRISED.〉
〈I'M HERE.〉
〈MY NAME IS OHARA.〉

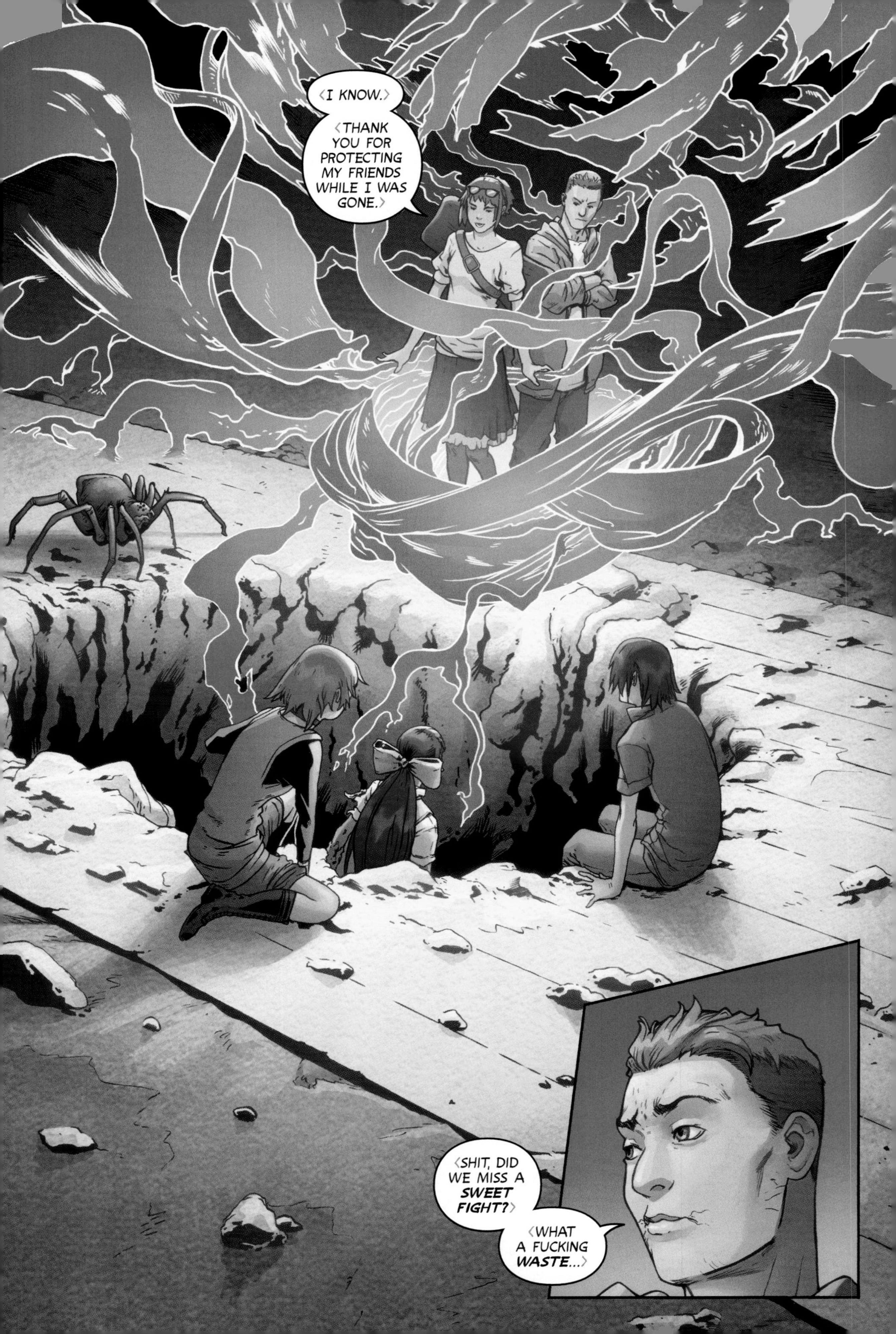

<I KNOW.>
<THANK YOU FOR PROTECTING MY FRIENDS WHILE I WAS GONE.>
<SHIT, DID WE MISS A **SWEET FIGHT?**>
<WHAT A FUCKING ***WASTE...***>

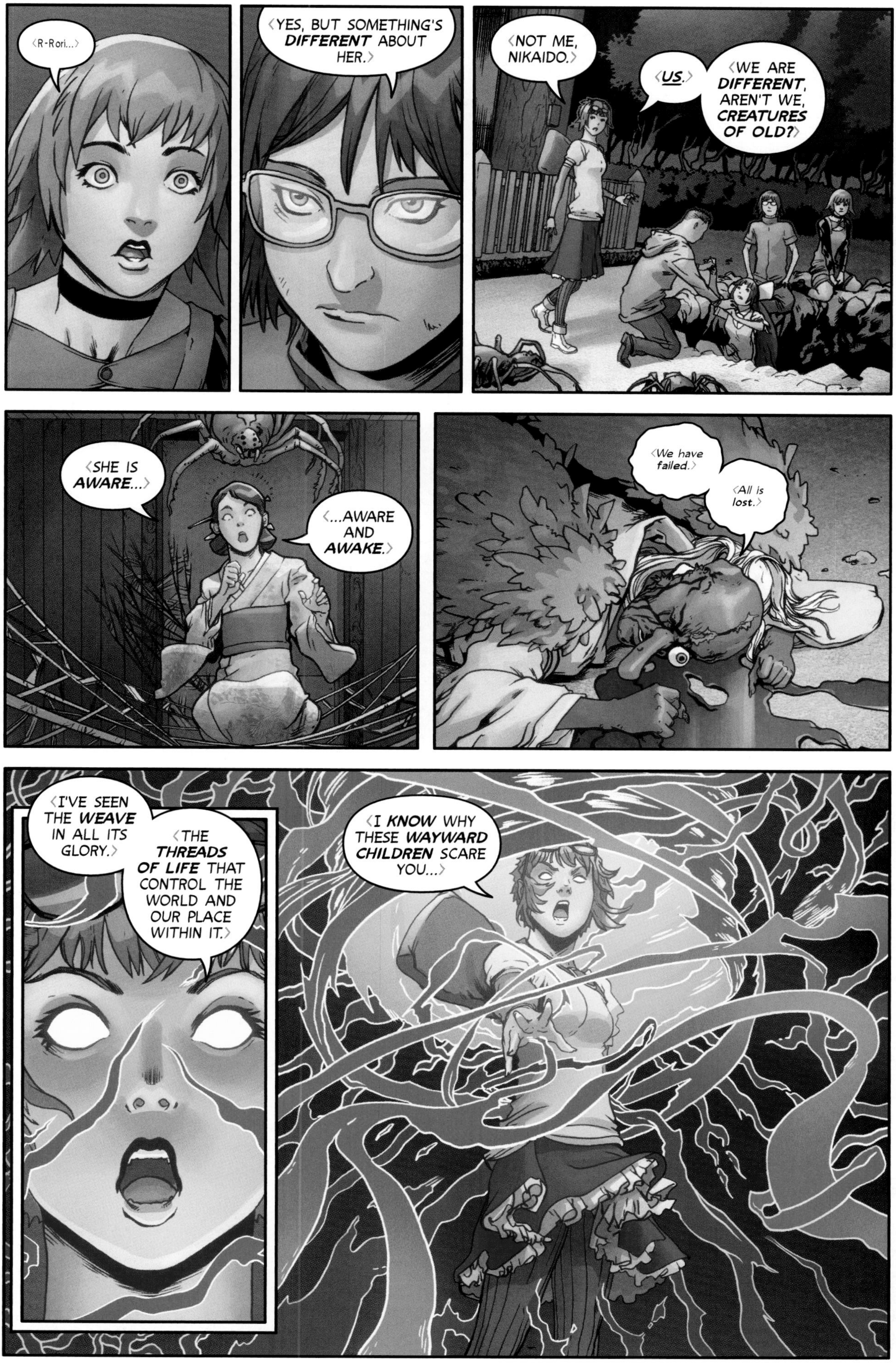

〈R-Rori...〉
〈YES, BUT SOMETHING'S ***DIFFERENT*** ABOUT HER.〉
〈NOT ME, NIKAIDO.〉
〈***US***.〉
〈WE ARE ***DIFFERENT***, AREN'T WE, ***CREATURES OF OLD?***〉
〈SHE IS ***AWARE...***〉
〈...AWARE AND ***AWAKE***.〉
〈We have failed.〉
〈All is lost.〉
〈I'VE SEEN THE ***WEAVE*** IN ALL ITS GLORY.〉
〈THE ***THREADS OF LIFE*** THAT CONTROL THE WORLD AND OUR PLACE WITHIN IT.〉
〈I ***KNOW*** WHY THESE ***WAYWARD CHILDREN*** SCARE YOU...〉

MEKI, THE YELLOW EYE FUDO TEMPLE

‹WHY YOU TRIED TO *SEPARATE* US...›

MEAO, THE BLUE EYE FUDO TEMPLE

‹...CONTROL US...›

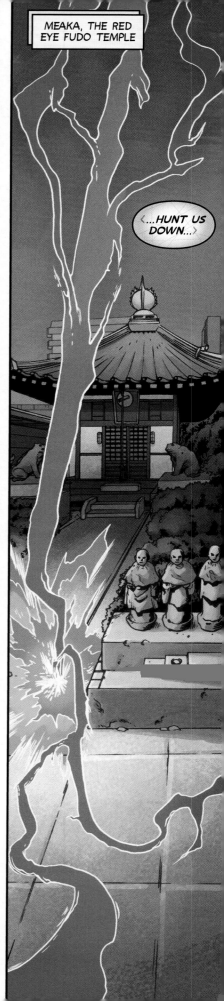

MEAKA, THE RED EYE FUDO TEMPLE

‹...HUNT US DOWN...›

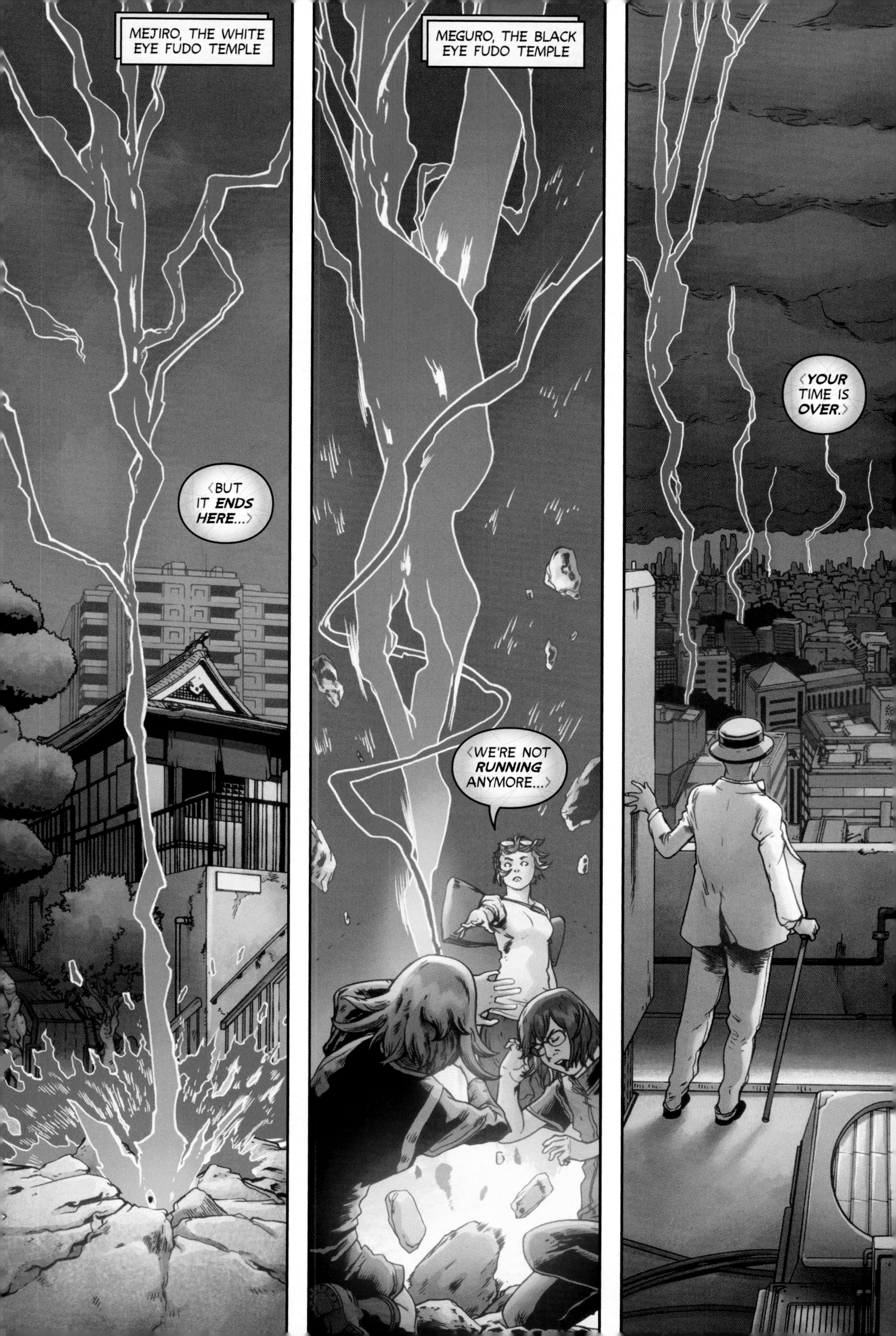
MEJIRO, THE WHITE EYE FUDO TEMPLE
‹BUT IT ENDS HERE...›
MEGURO, THE BLACK EYE FUDO TEMPLE
‹WE'RE NOT RUNNING ANYMORE...›
‹YOUR TIME IS OVER.›

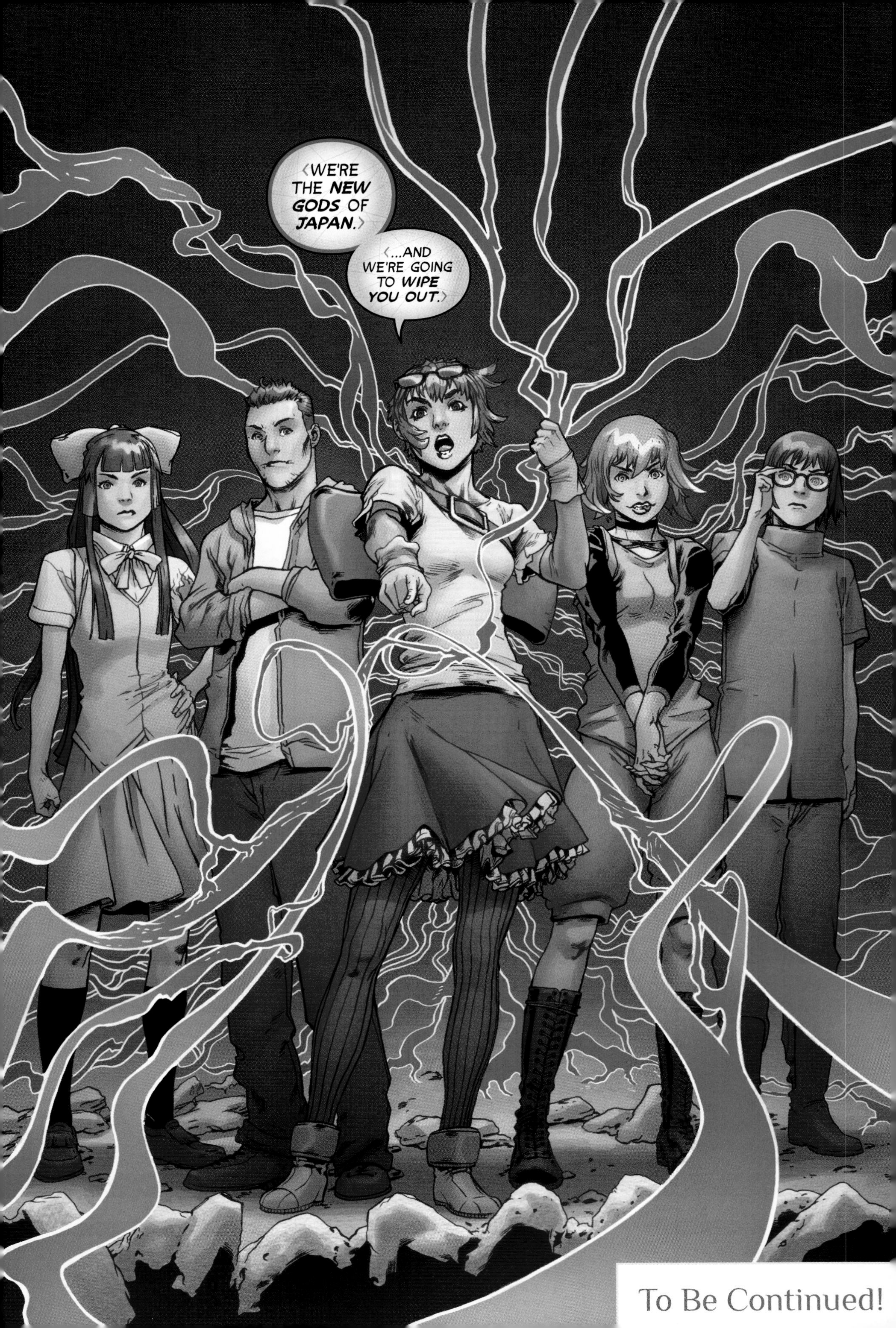
‹WE'RE THE **NEW GODS** OF **JAPAN.**›
‹...AND WE'RE GOING TO **WIPE YOU OUT.**›
To Be Continued!

Wayward
COVER GALLERY

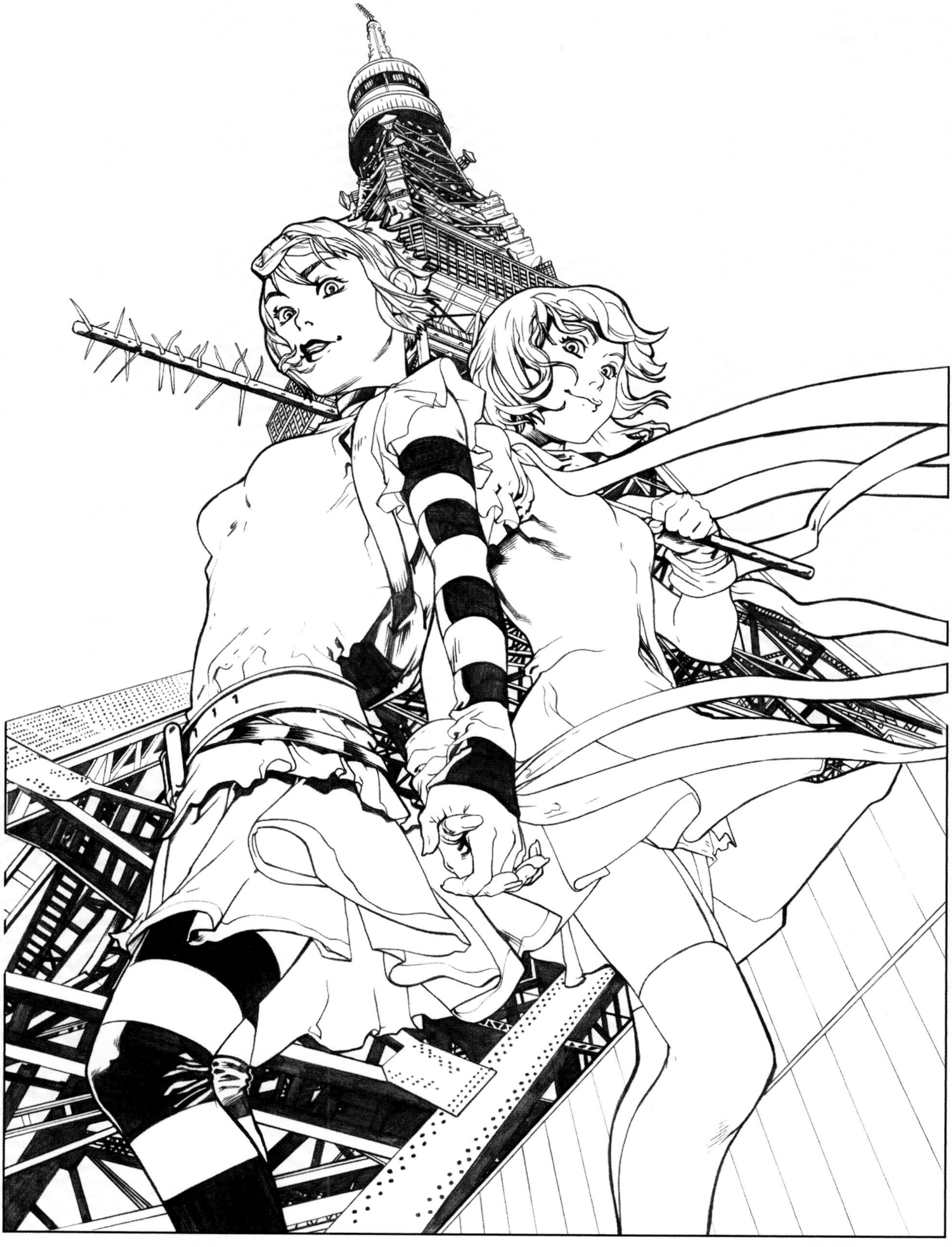

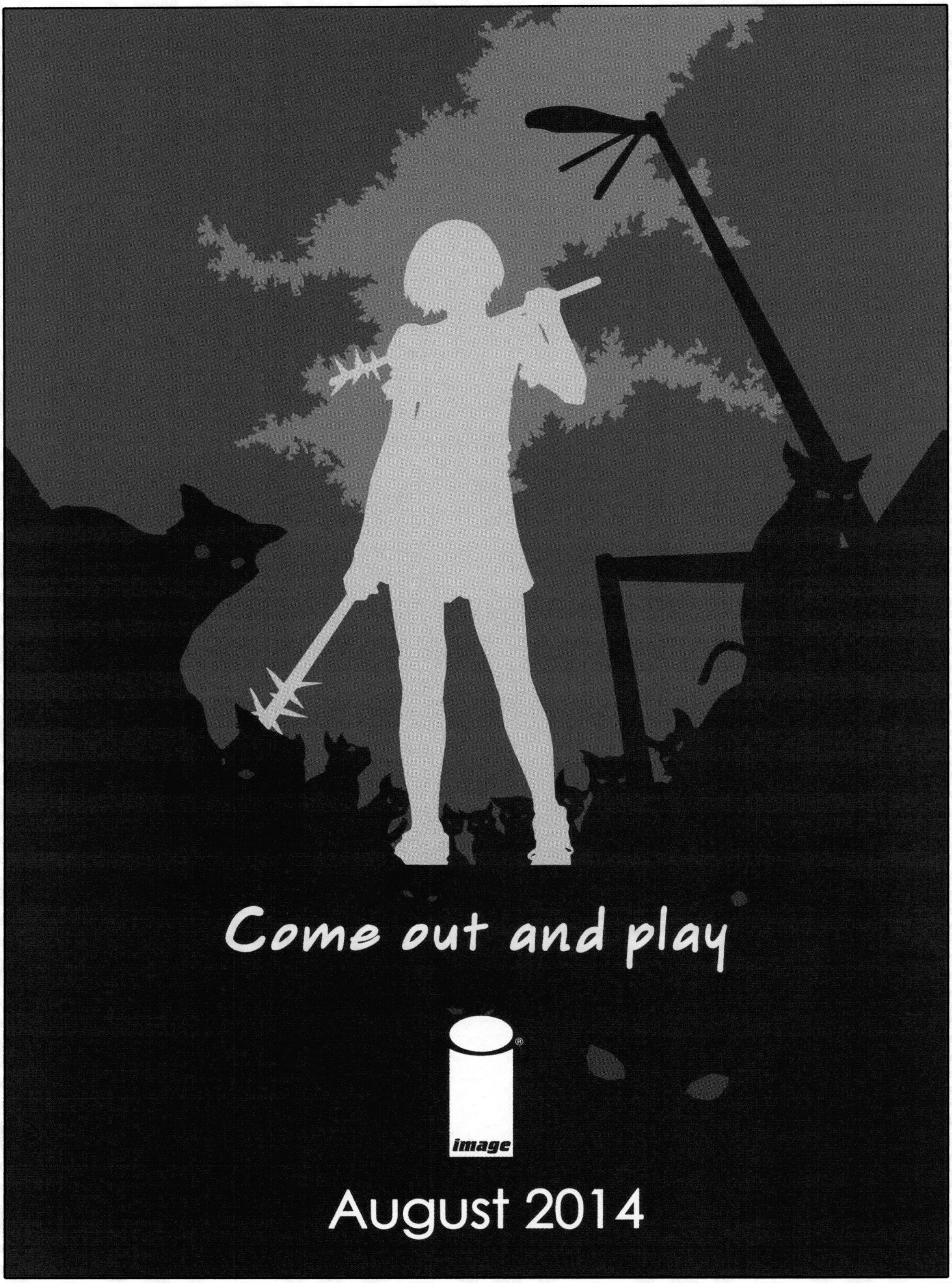
Come out and play
image
August 2014

WAYWARD Teaser
Artwork by Steve Cummings and Layout by Jim Zub

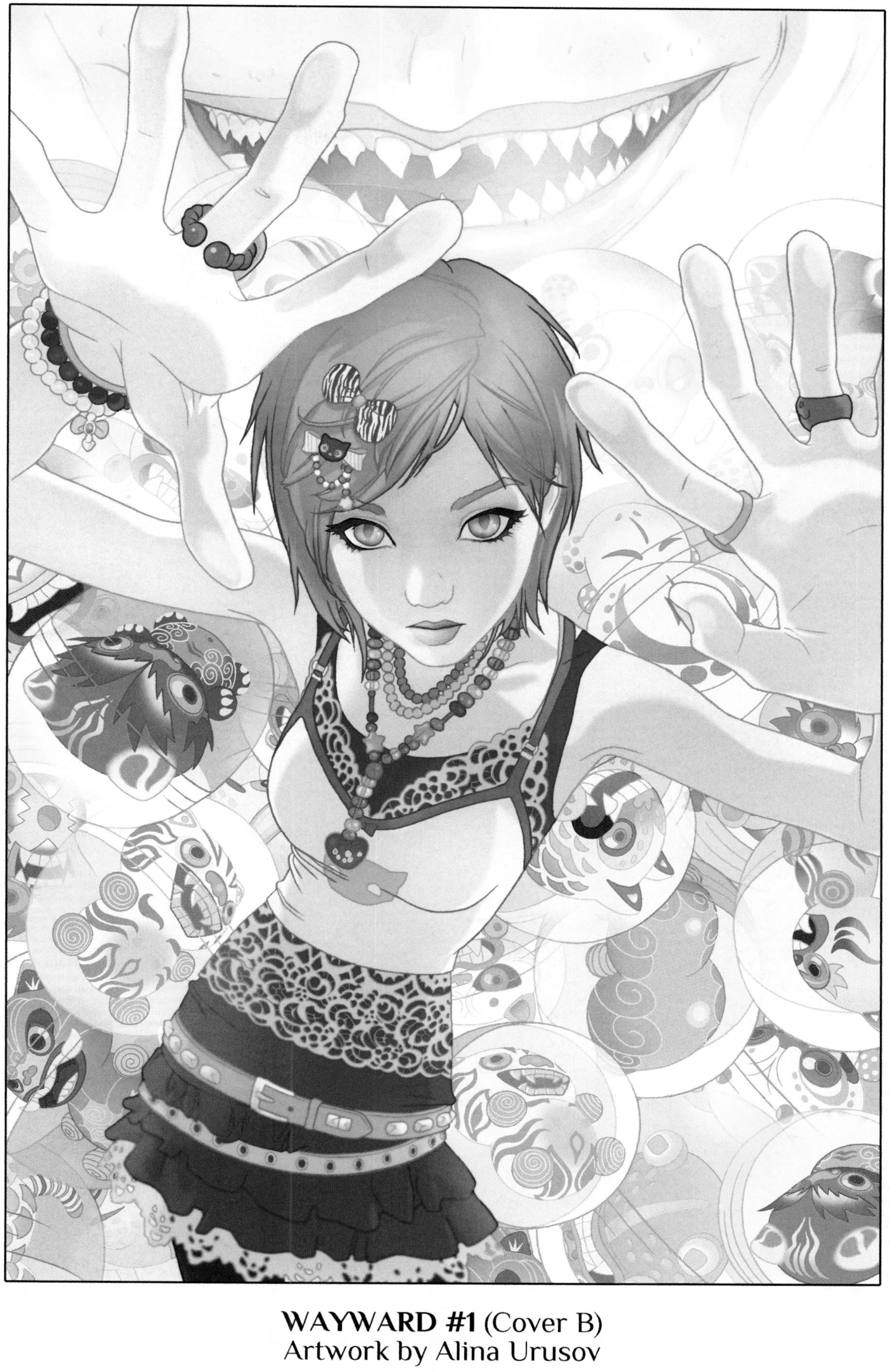

WAYWARD #1 (Cover B)
Artwork by Alina Urusov

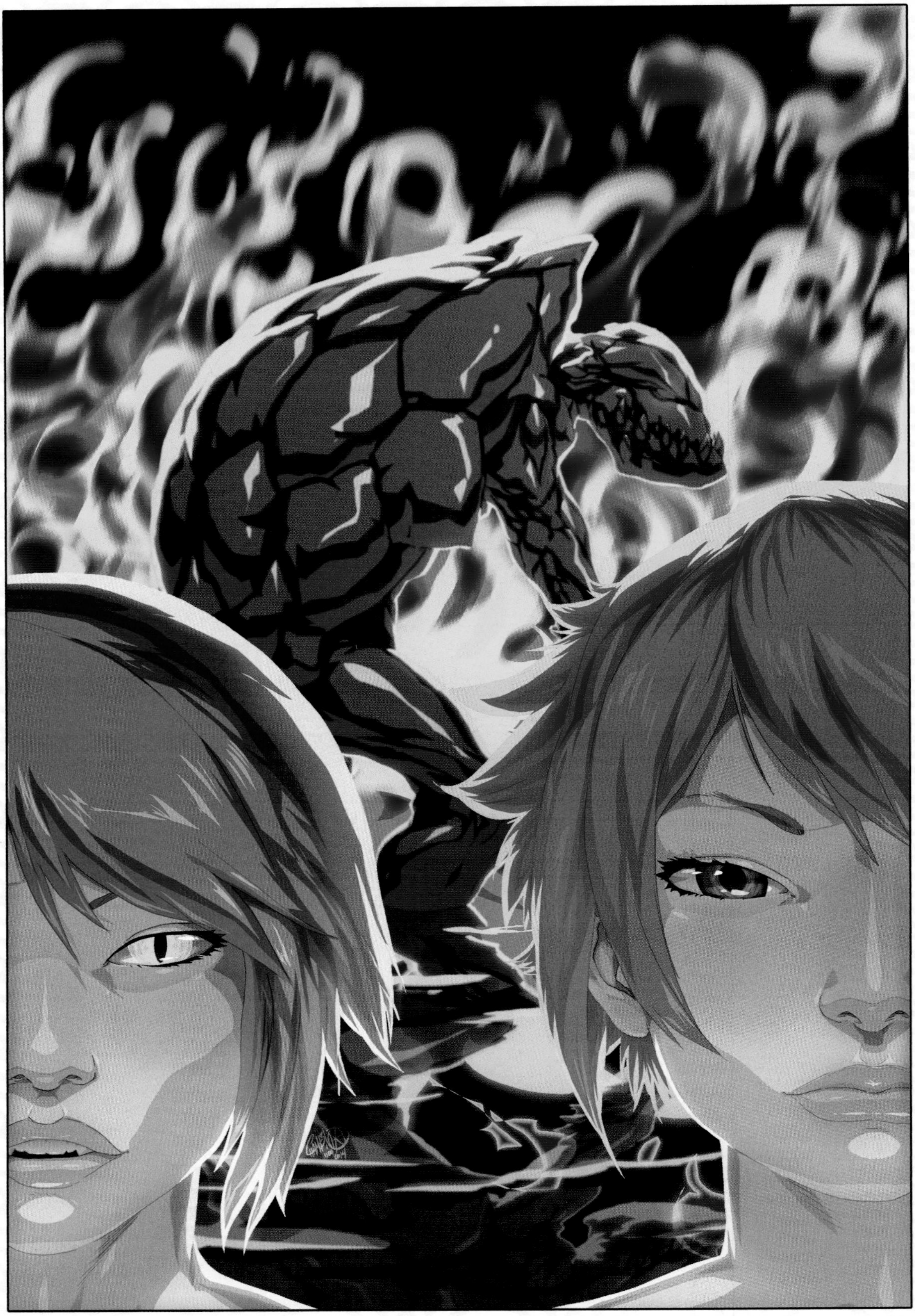

WAYWARD #1 (Cover C)
Artwork by Jeff "Chamba" Cruz

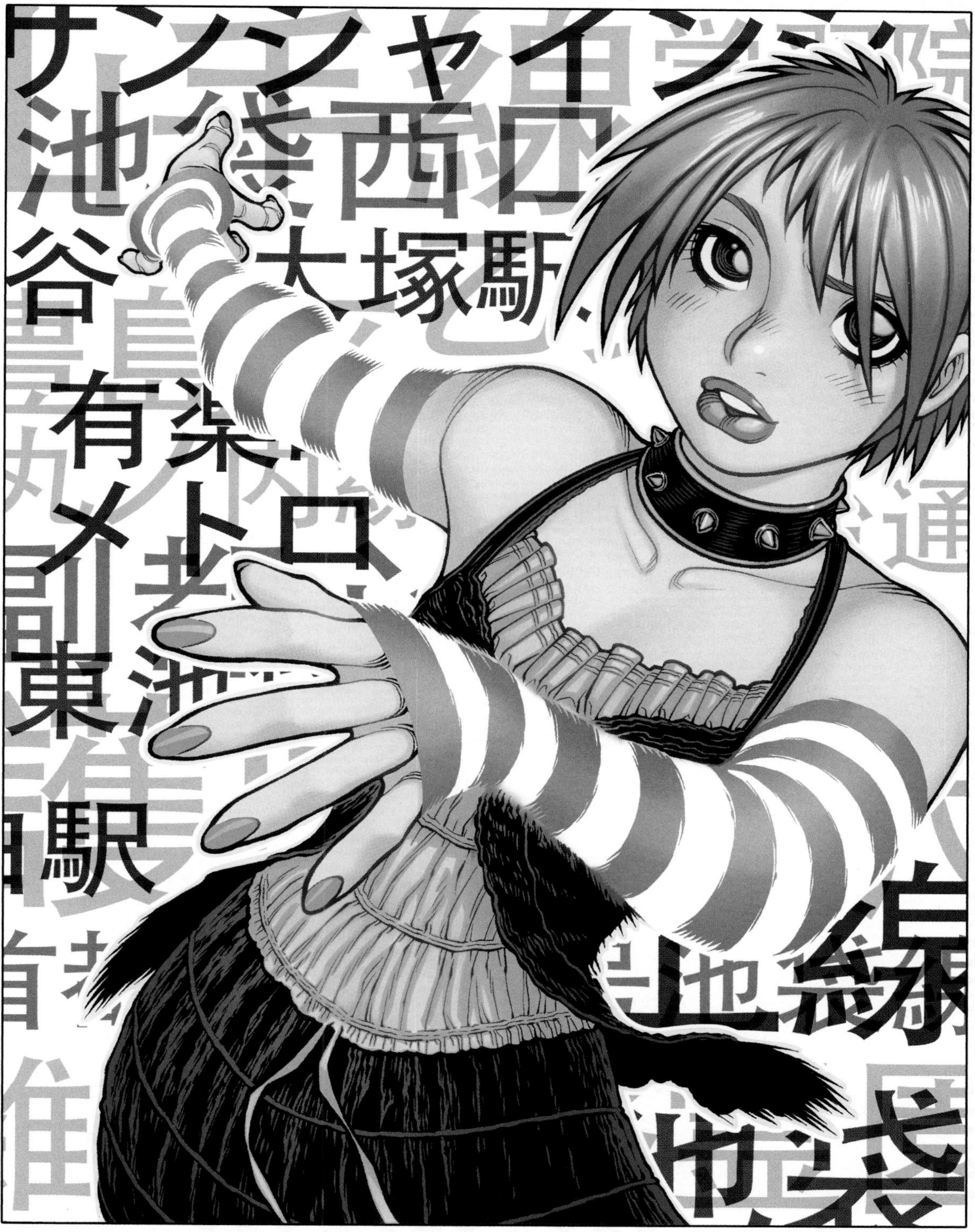
サンシャイン
池袋西口
大塚駅
有楽
メトロ

WAYWARD #1 (Cover D)
Artwork by Adam Warren and John Rauch

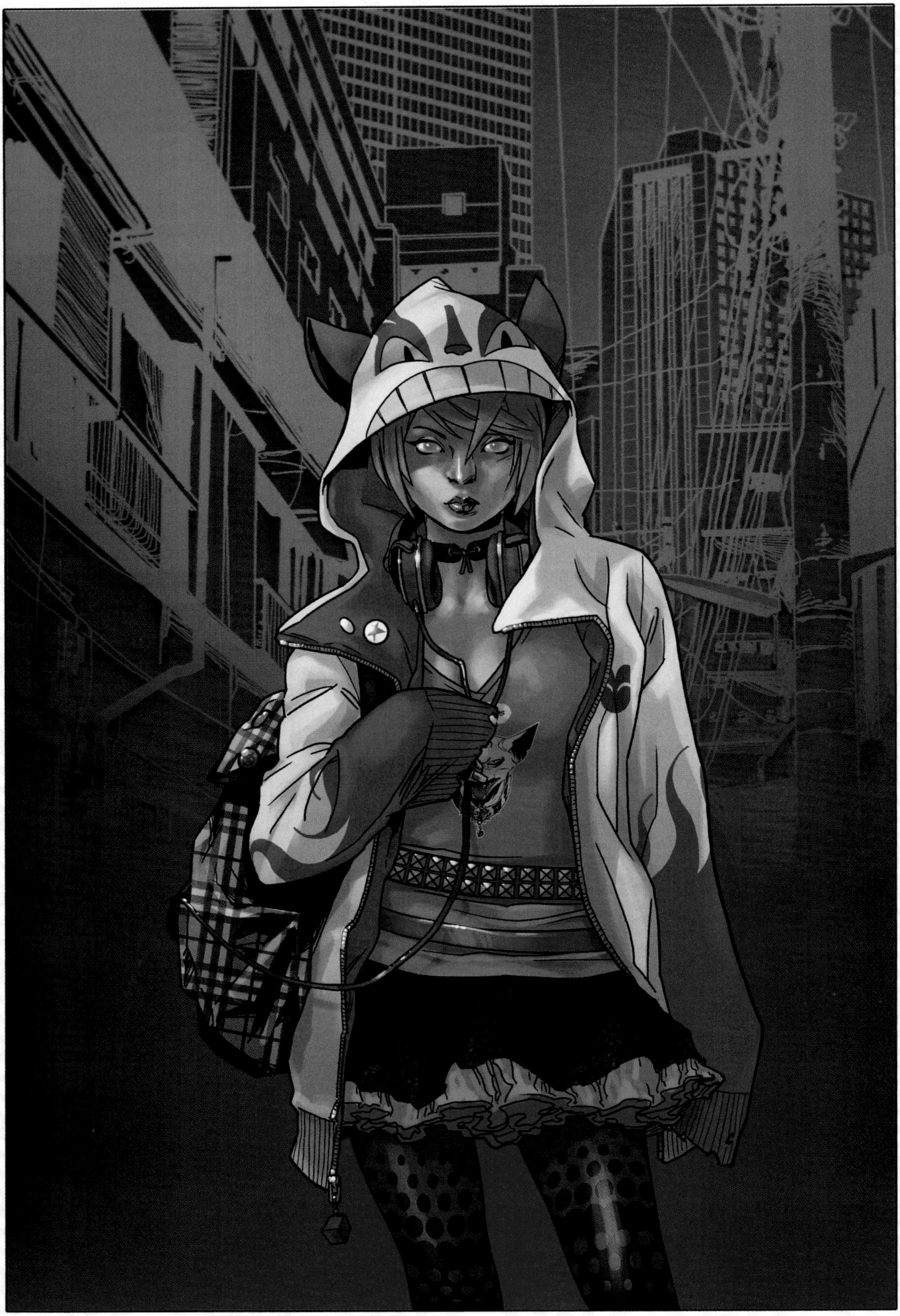

WAYWARD #1 (Fan Expo Canada Cover)
Artwork by Kalman Andrasofszky

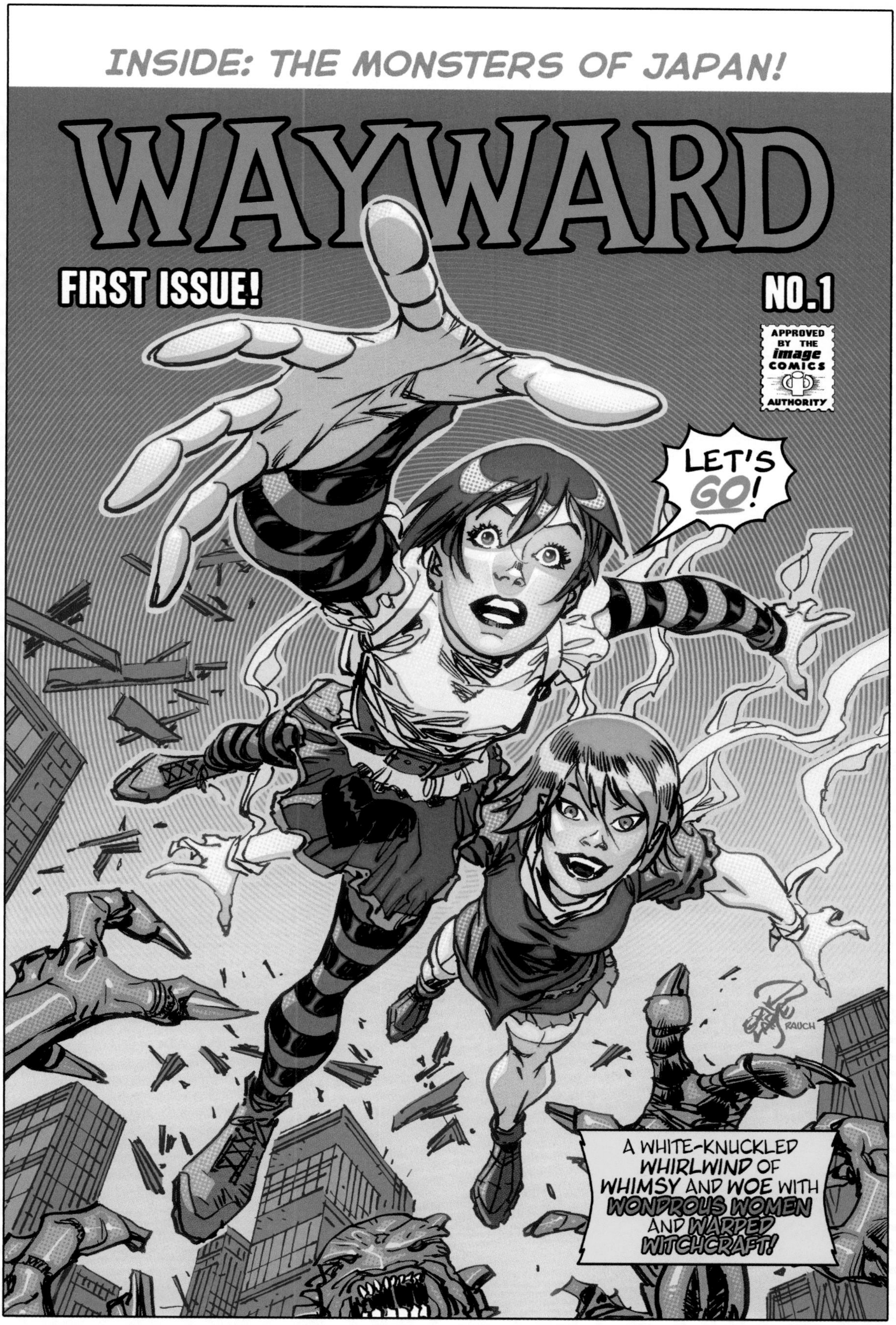
INSIDE: THE MONSTERS OF JAPAN!
WAYWARD
FIRST ISSUE!
NO.1
APPROVED BY THE image COMICS AUTHORITY
LET'S GO!
A WHITE-KNUCKLED WHIRLWIND OF WHIMSY AND WOE WITH WONDROUS WOMEN AND WARPED WITCHCRAFT!
RAUCH

WAYWARD #1 (Rose City Comic Con Cover)
Artwork by Erik Larsen and John Rauch

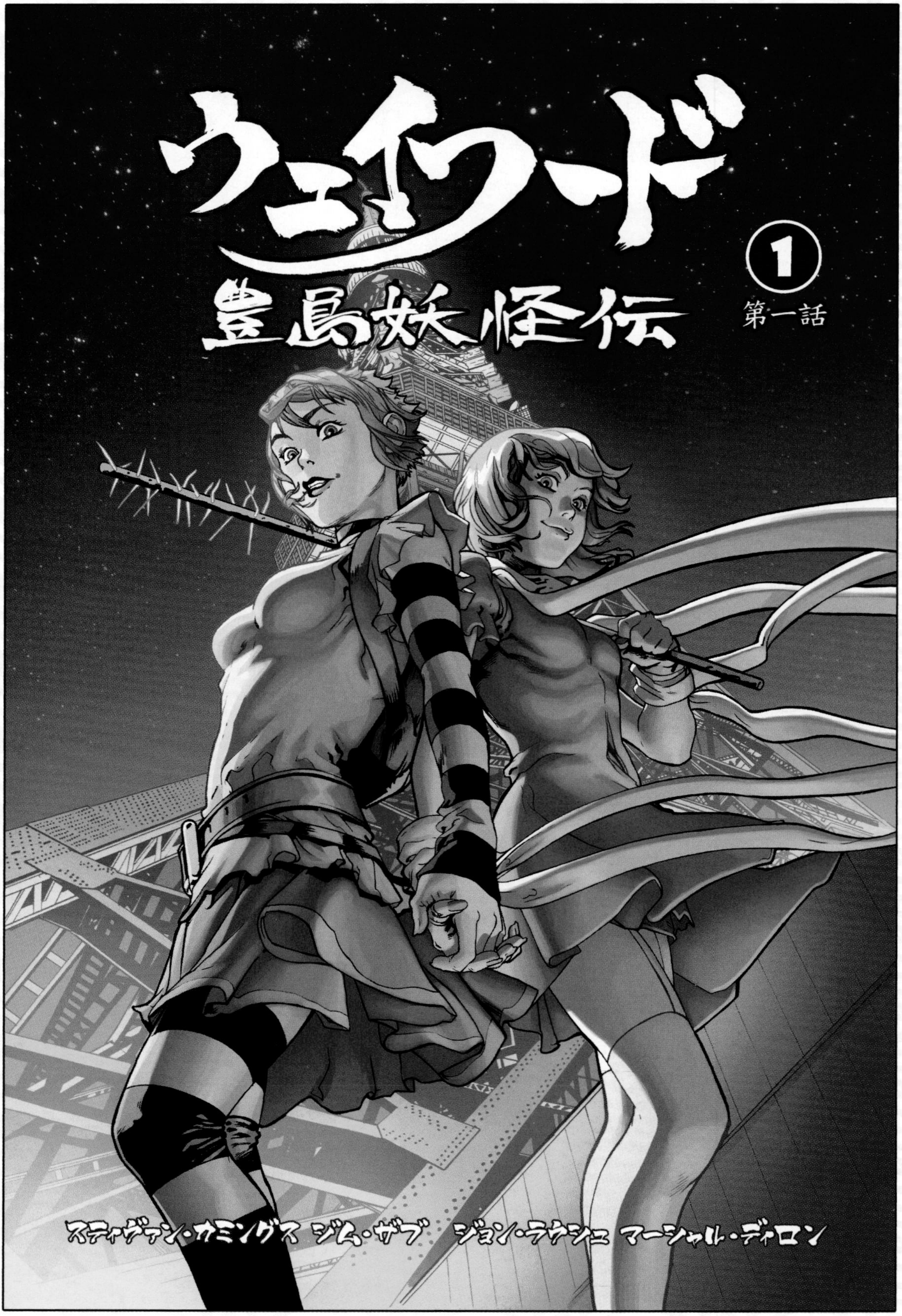
ウェイワード
豊島妖怪伝
1
第一話
スティヴァン・カミングス ジム・ザブ ジョン・ラウシュ マーシャル・ディロン

WAYWARD #1 (Happy Harbor Retailer Cover)
Artwork by Steve Cummings and Tamra Bonvillain

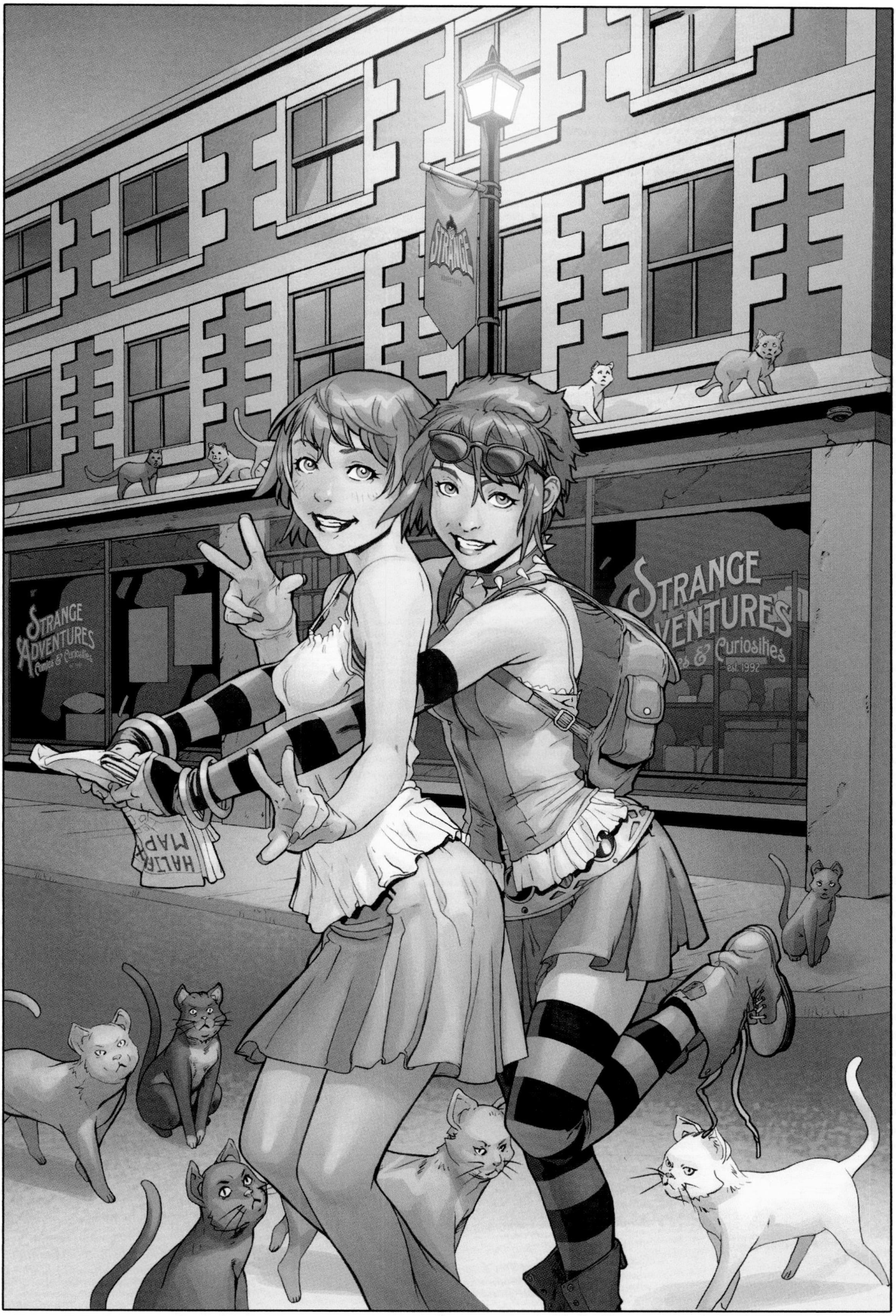
STRANGE ADVENTURES
Comics & Curiosities
STRANGE ADVENTURES
& Curiosities
est. 1992

WAYWARD #1 (Strange Adventures Retailer Cover)
Artwork by Steve Cummings and Tamra Bonvillain

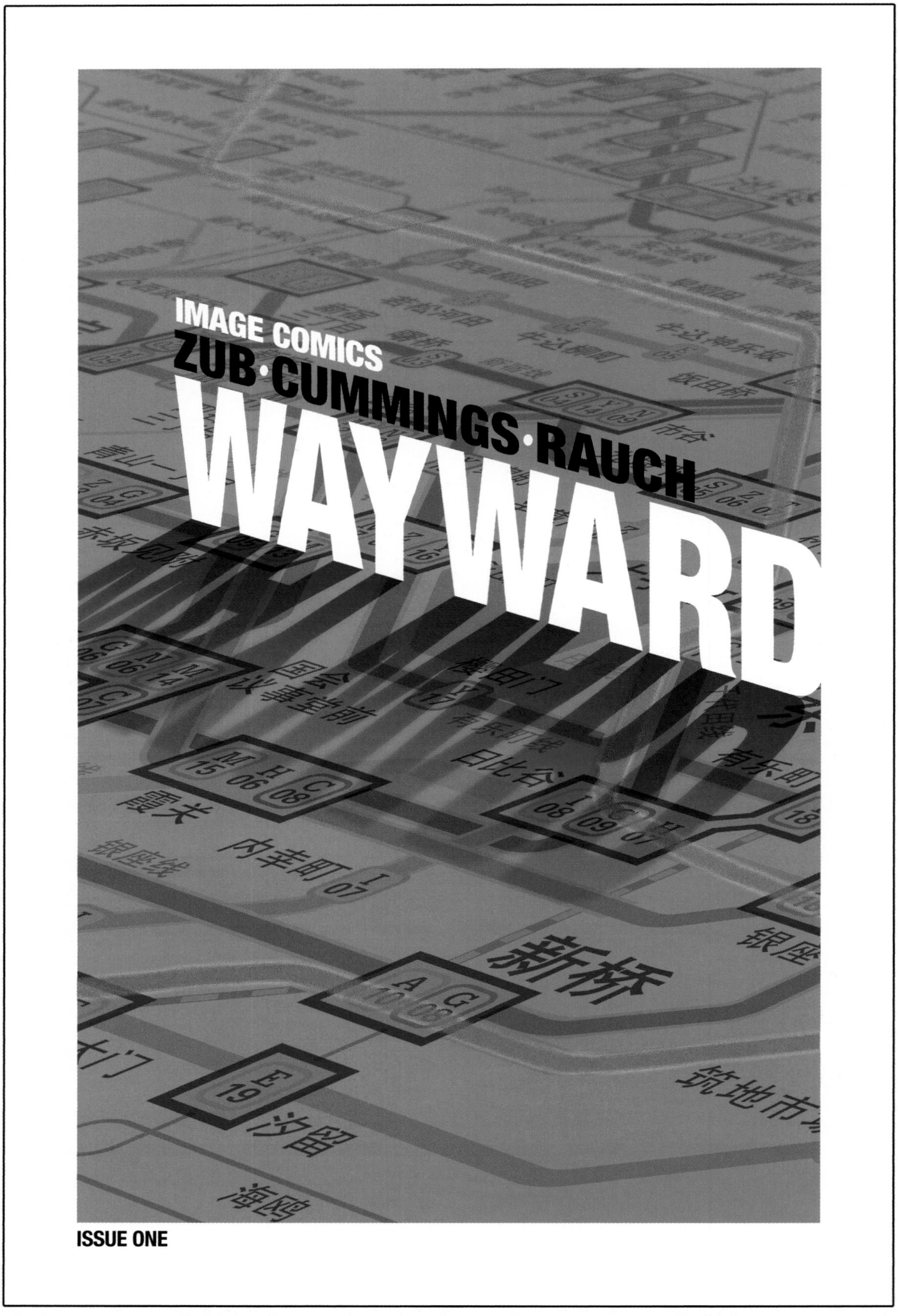
IMAGE COMICS
ZUB·CUMMINGS·RAUCH
WAYWARD
ISSUE ONE

WAYWARD #1 (Third Eye Comics Retailer Cover)
Artwork by Chip Zdarsky

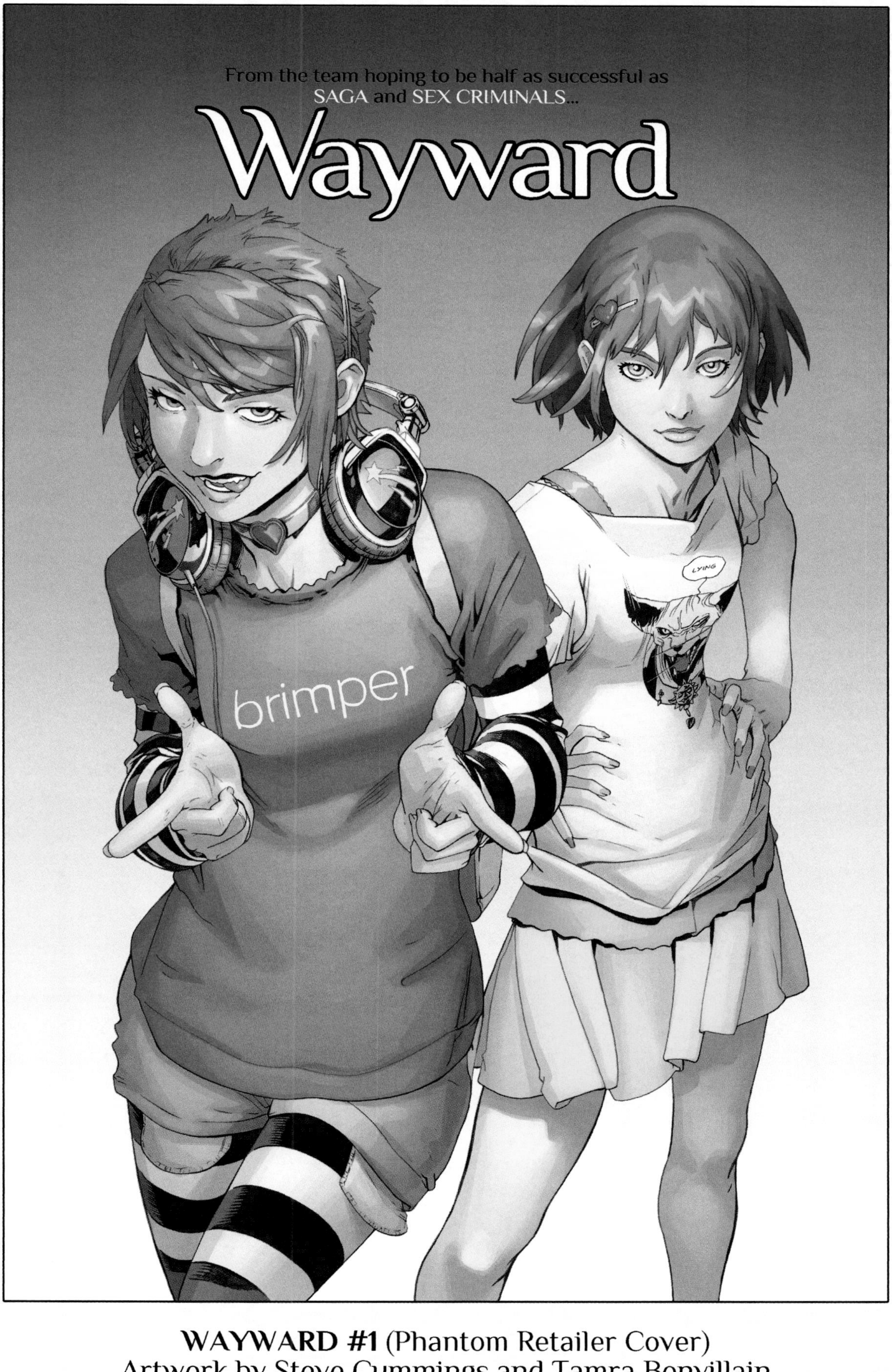
From the team hoping to be half as successful as
SAGA and SEX CRIMINALS...
Wayward
brimper
LYING

WAYWARD #1 (Phantom Retailer Cover)
Artwork by Steve Cummings and Tamra Bonvillain

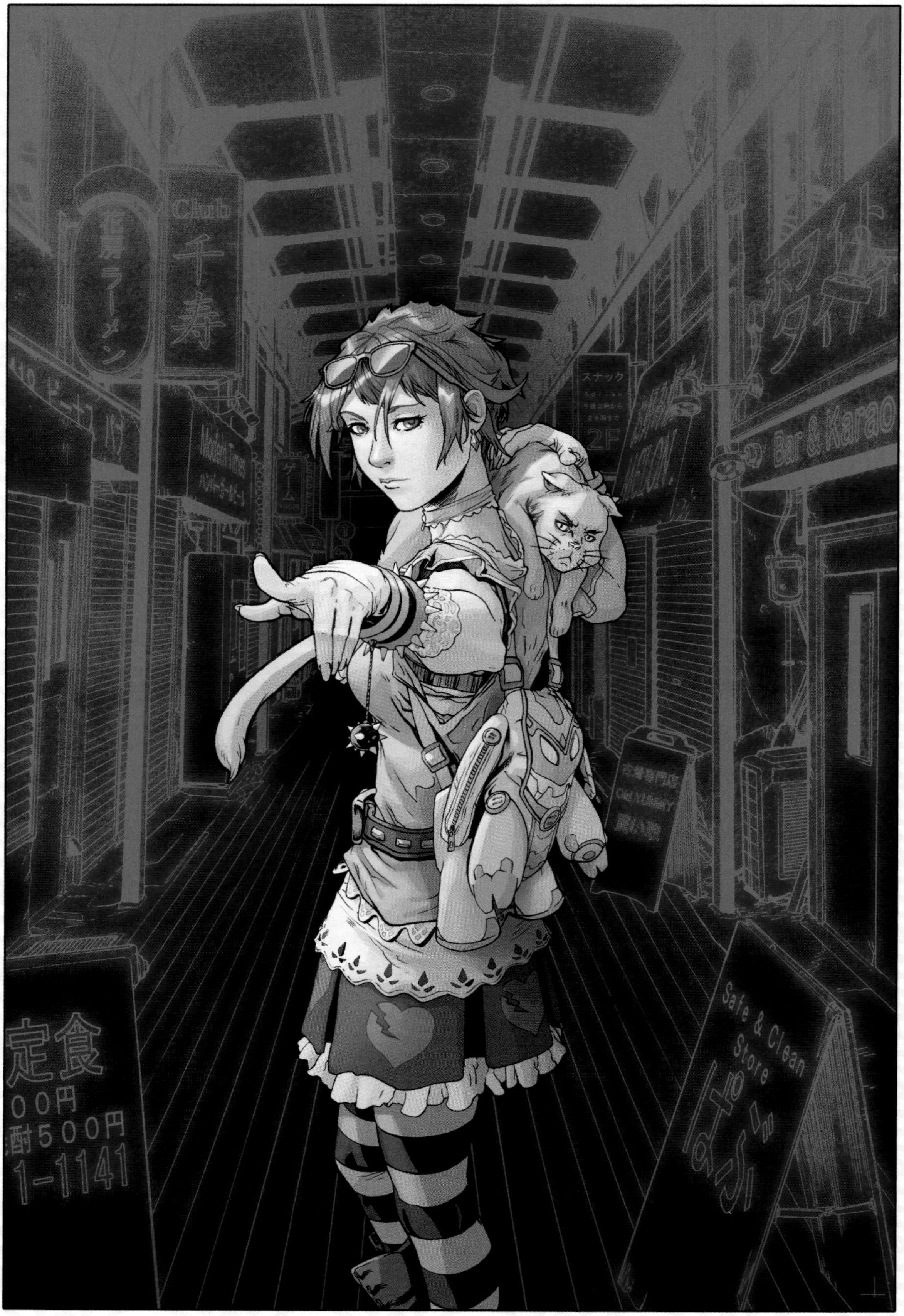
Club
千寿
スナック
2F
ゲーム
Safe & Clean
Store
定食
1-1141

WAYWARD #1 (2nd Print Cover)
Artwork by Steve Cummings and Tamra Bonvillain

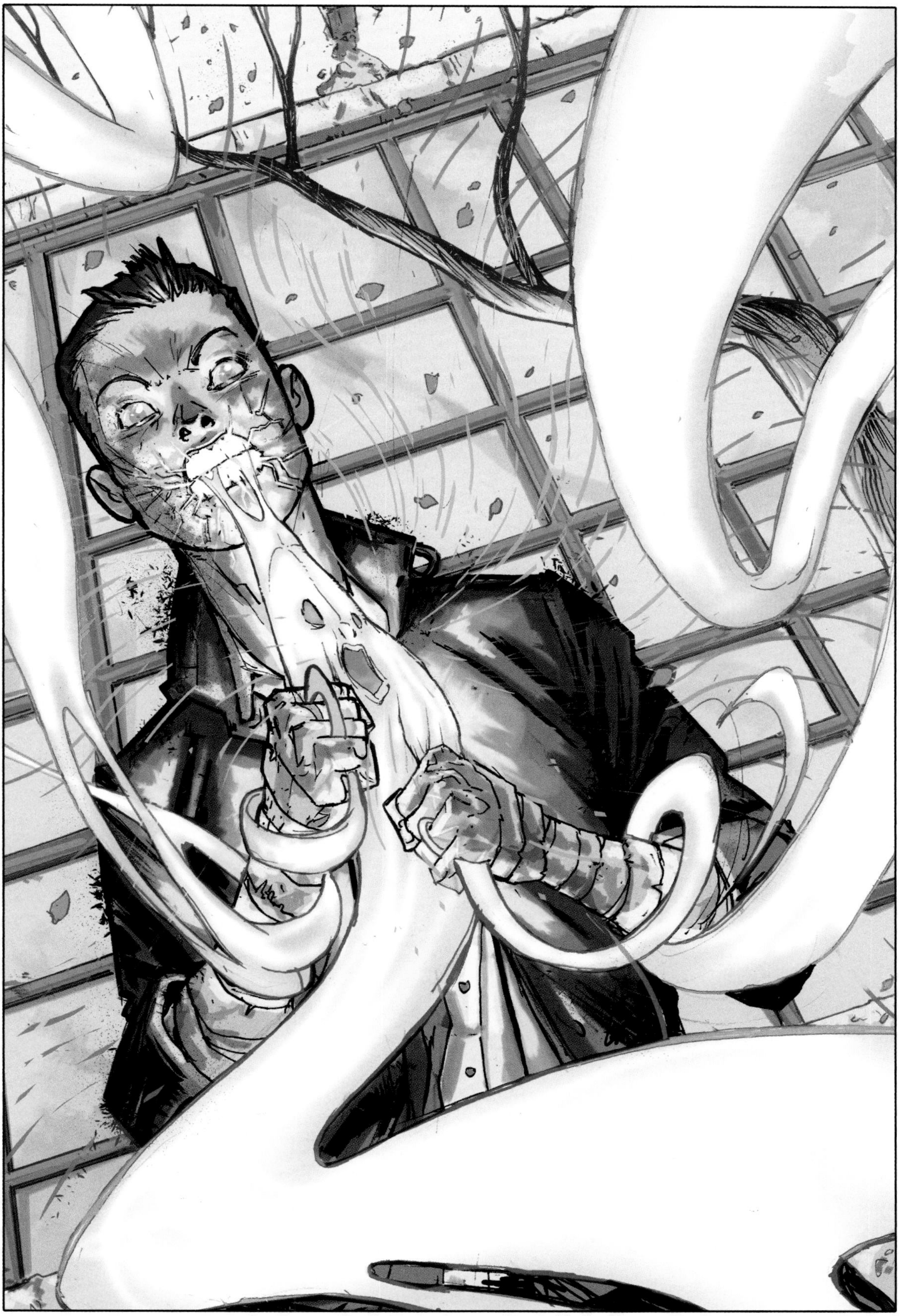

WAYWARD #2 (Cover B)
Artwork by Riley Rossmo

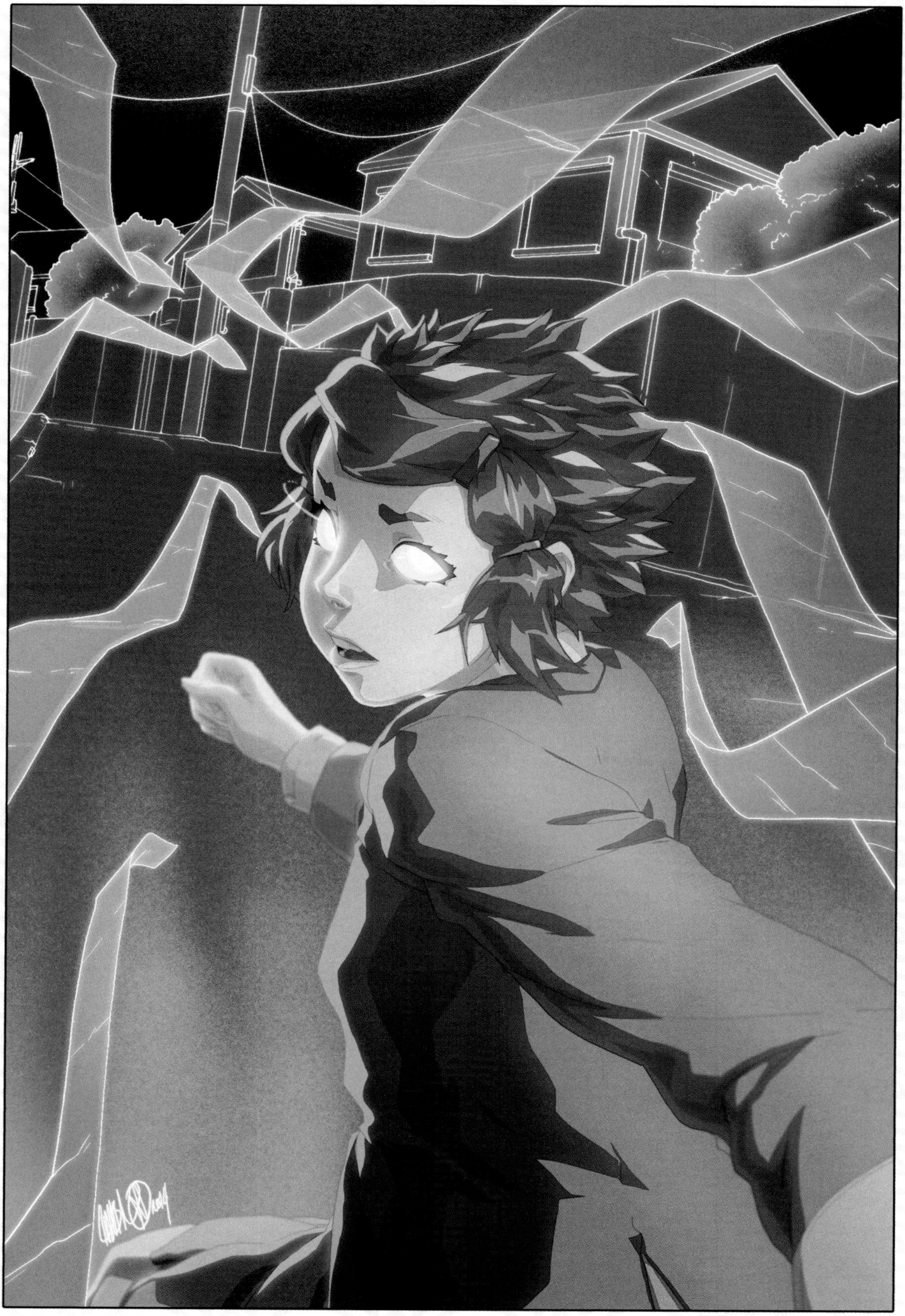

WAYWARD #2 (DCBS Retailer Cover)
Artwork by Jeff "Chamba" Cruz

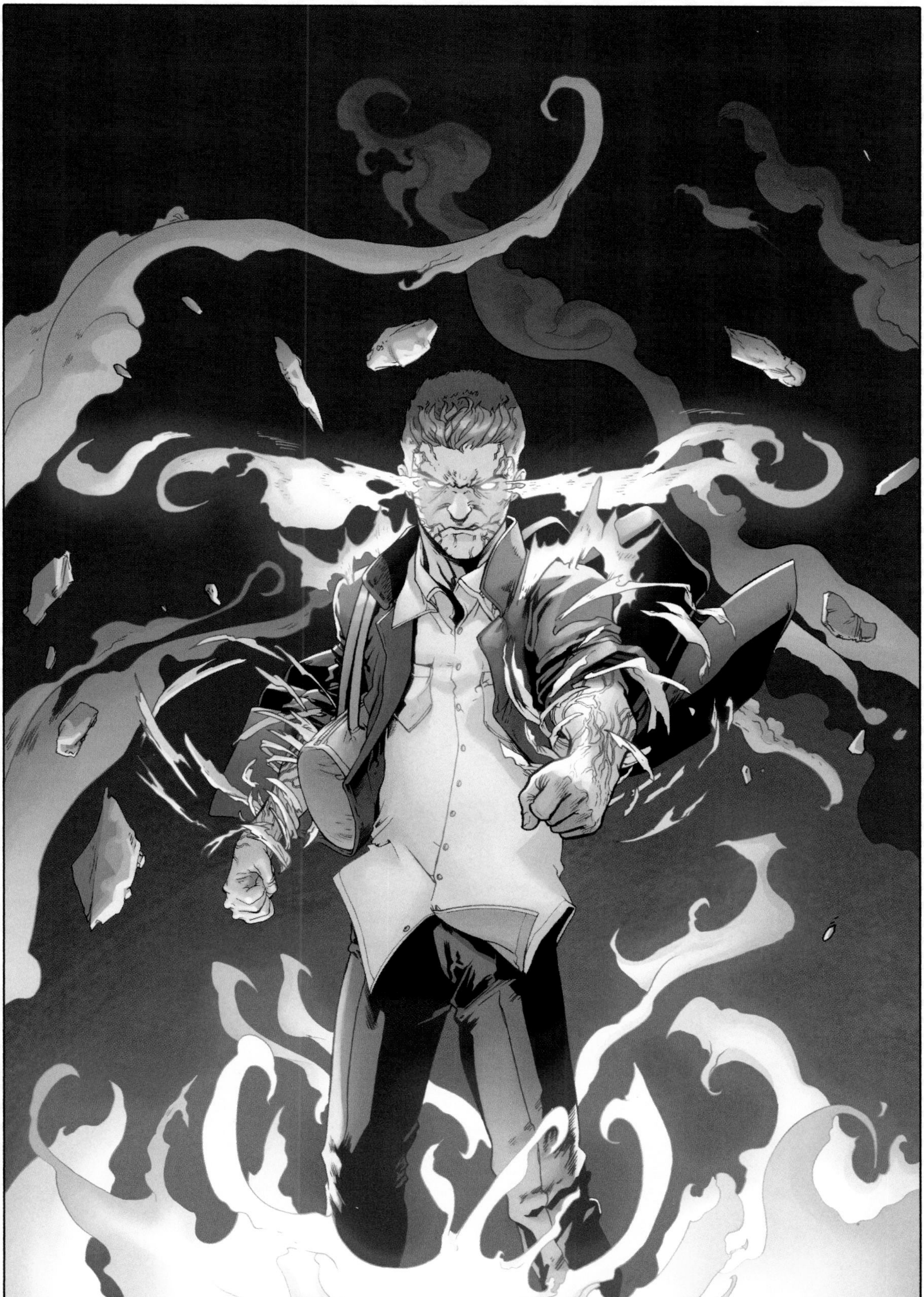

WAYWARD #2 (2nd Print Cover)
Artwork by Steve Cummings and Tamra Bonvillain

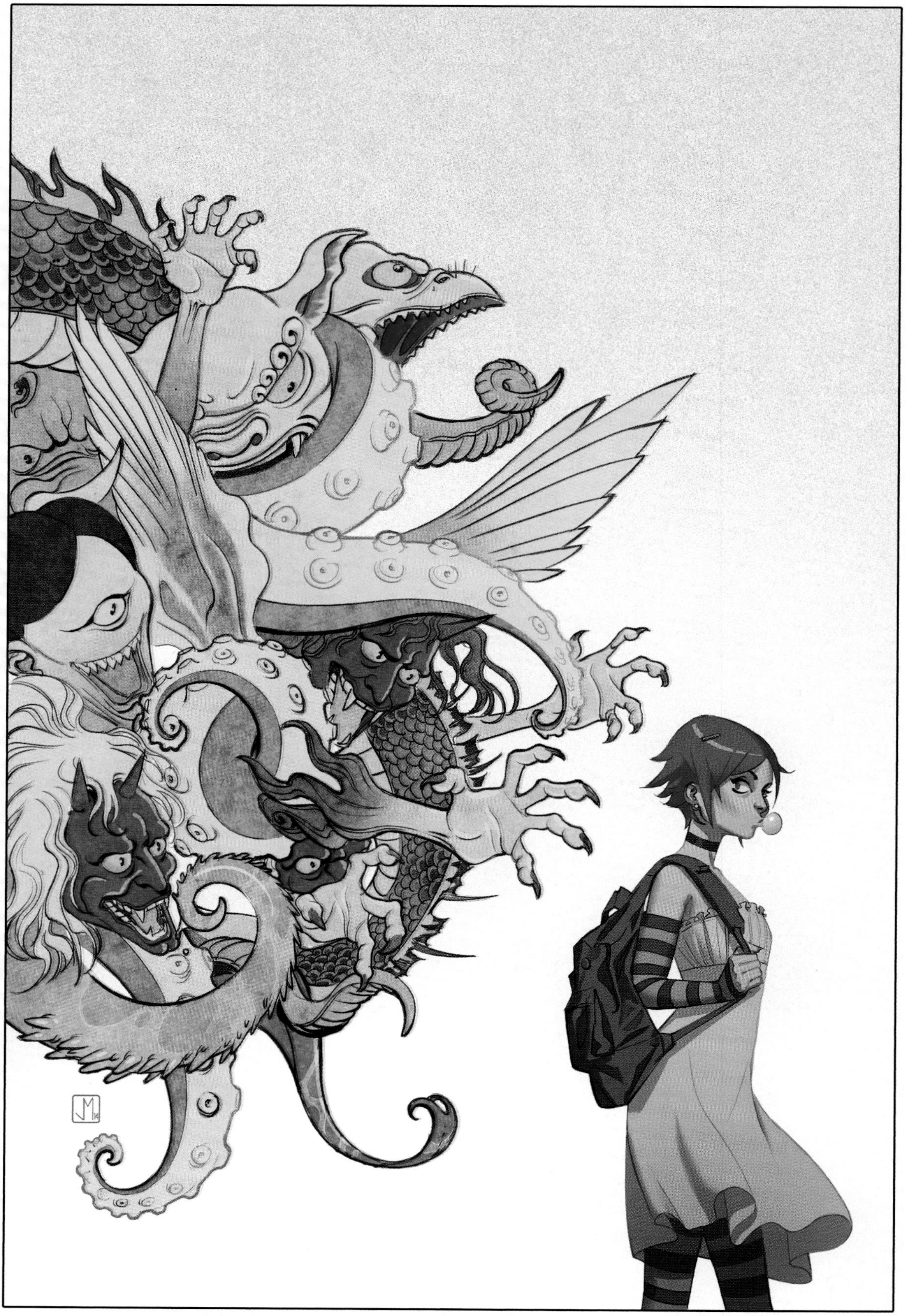

WAYWARD #3 (Cover B)
Artwork by Jorge Molina

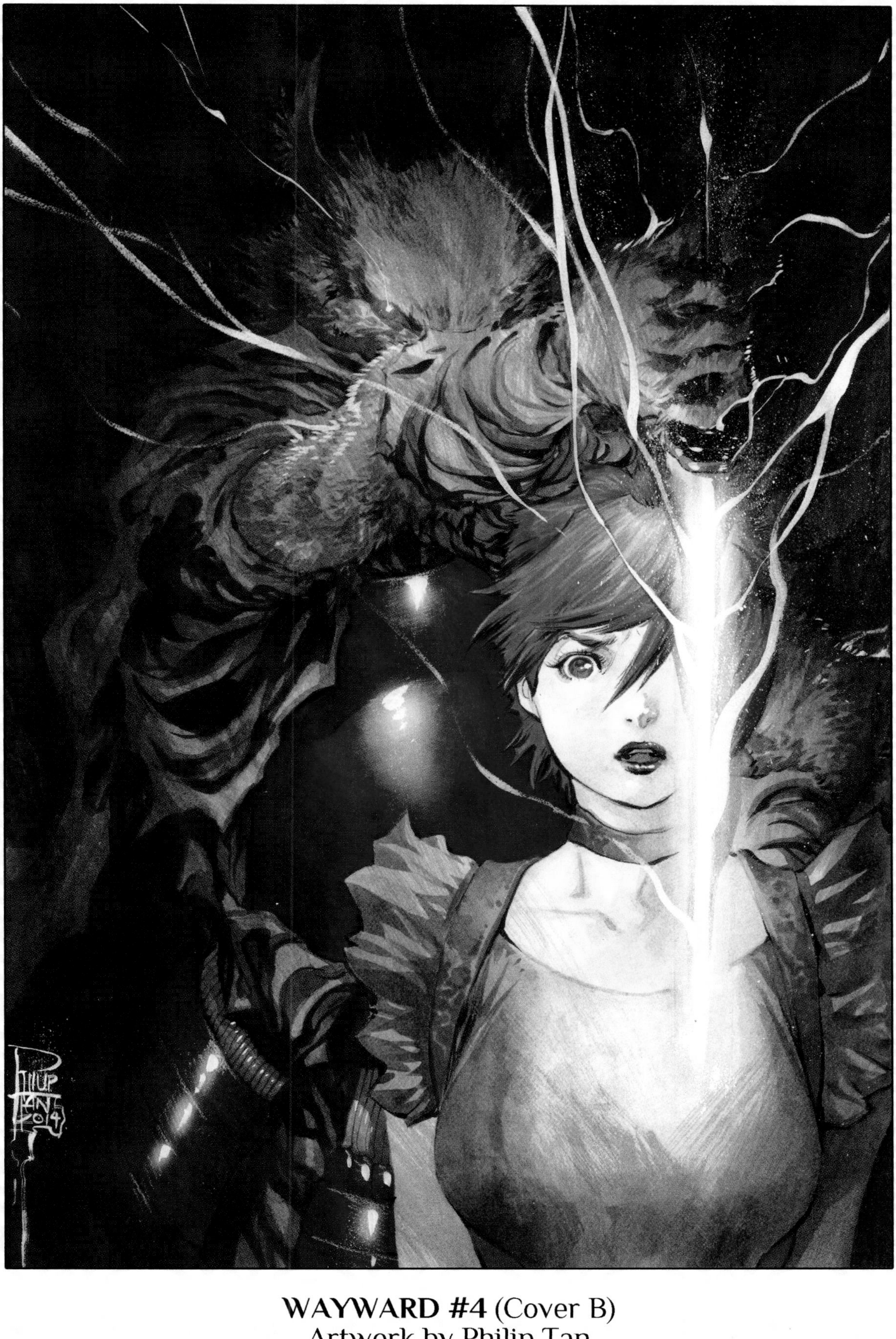
PHILIP TAN 2014

WAYWARD #4 (Cover B)
Artwork by Philip Tan

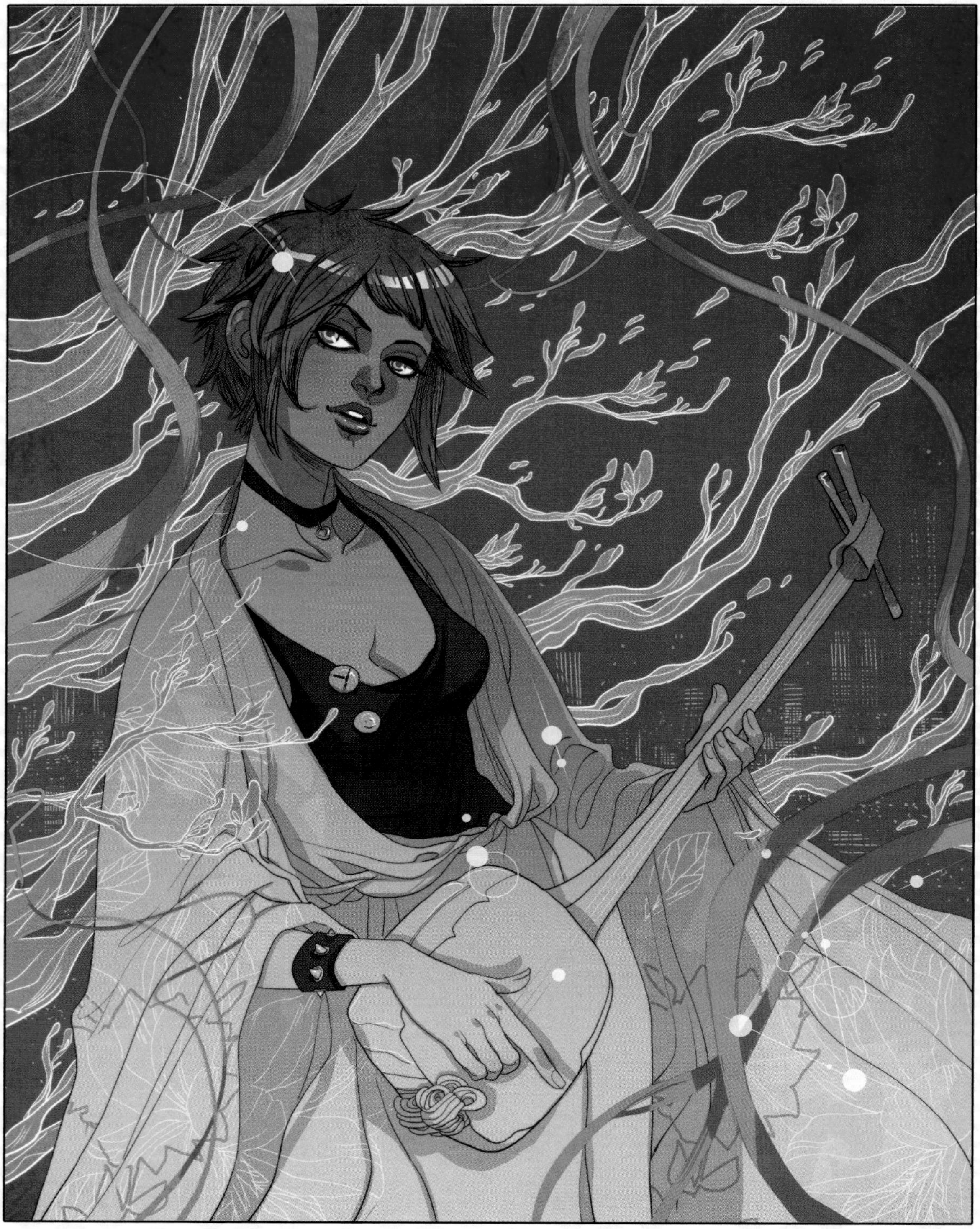

WAYWARD #5 (Cover B)
Artwork by Marguerite Sauvage

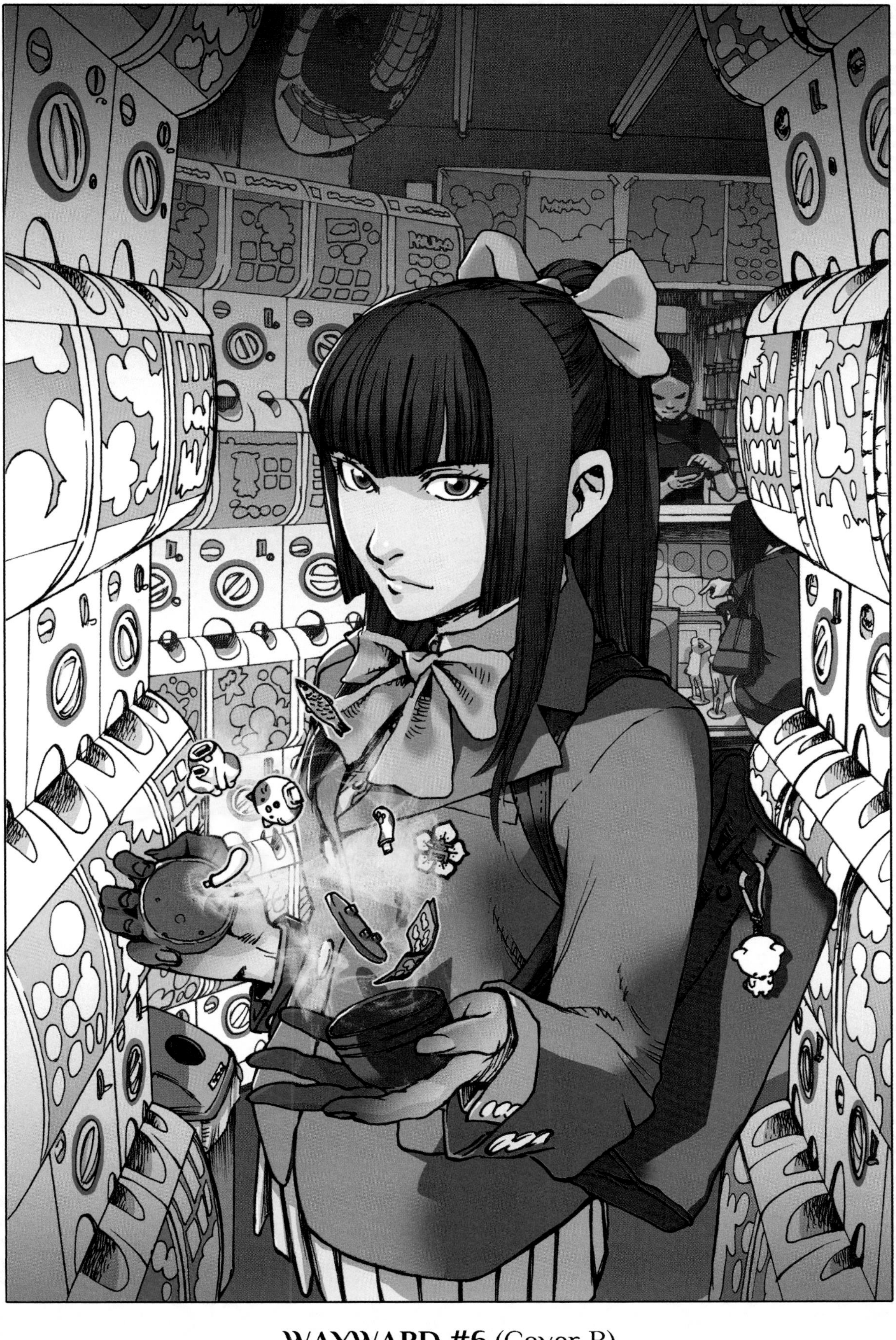

WAYWARD #6 (Cover B)
Artwork by Takeshi Miyazawa

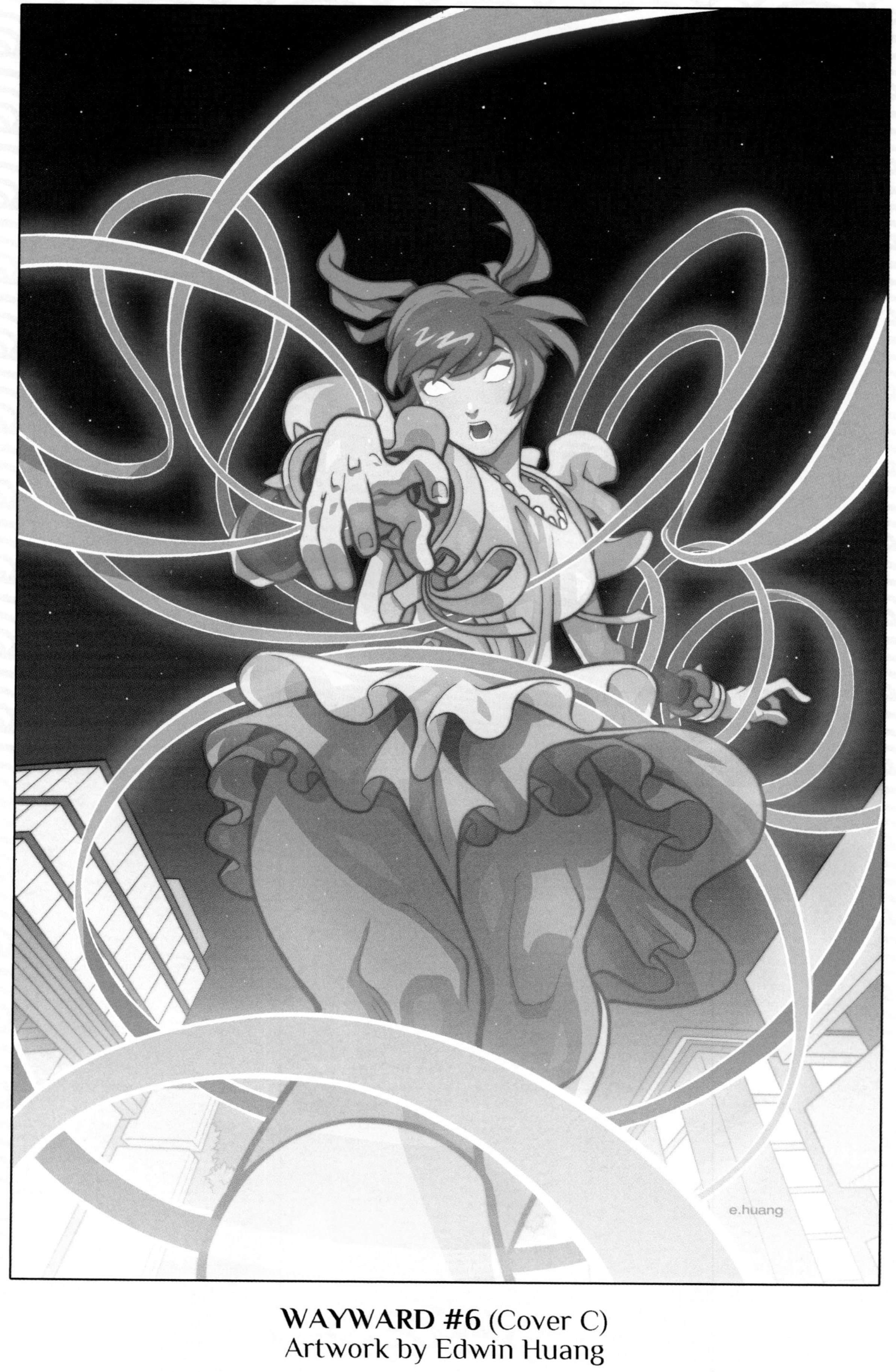
e.huang

WAYWARD #6 (Cover C)
Artwork by Edwin Huang

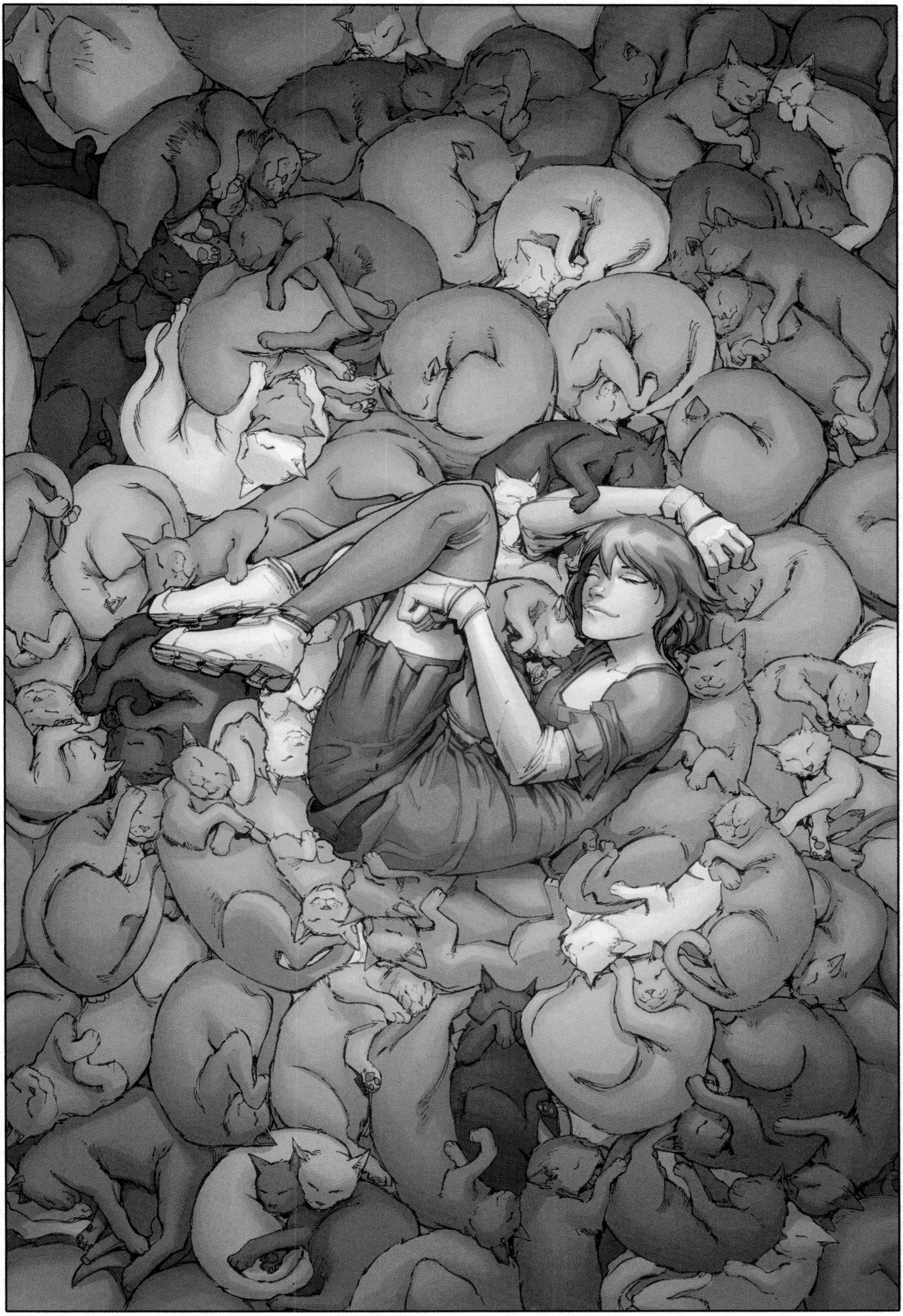

WAYWARD #6 (Calgary Expo Cover)
Artwork by Max Dunbar and Tamra Bonvillain

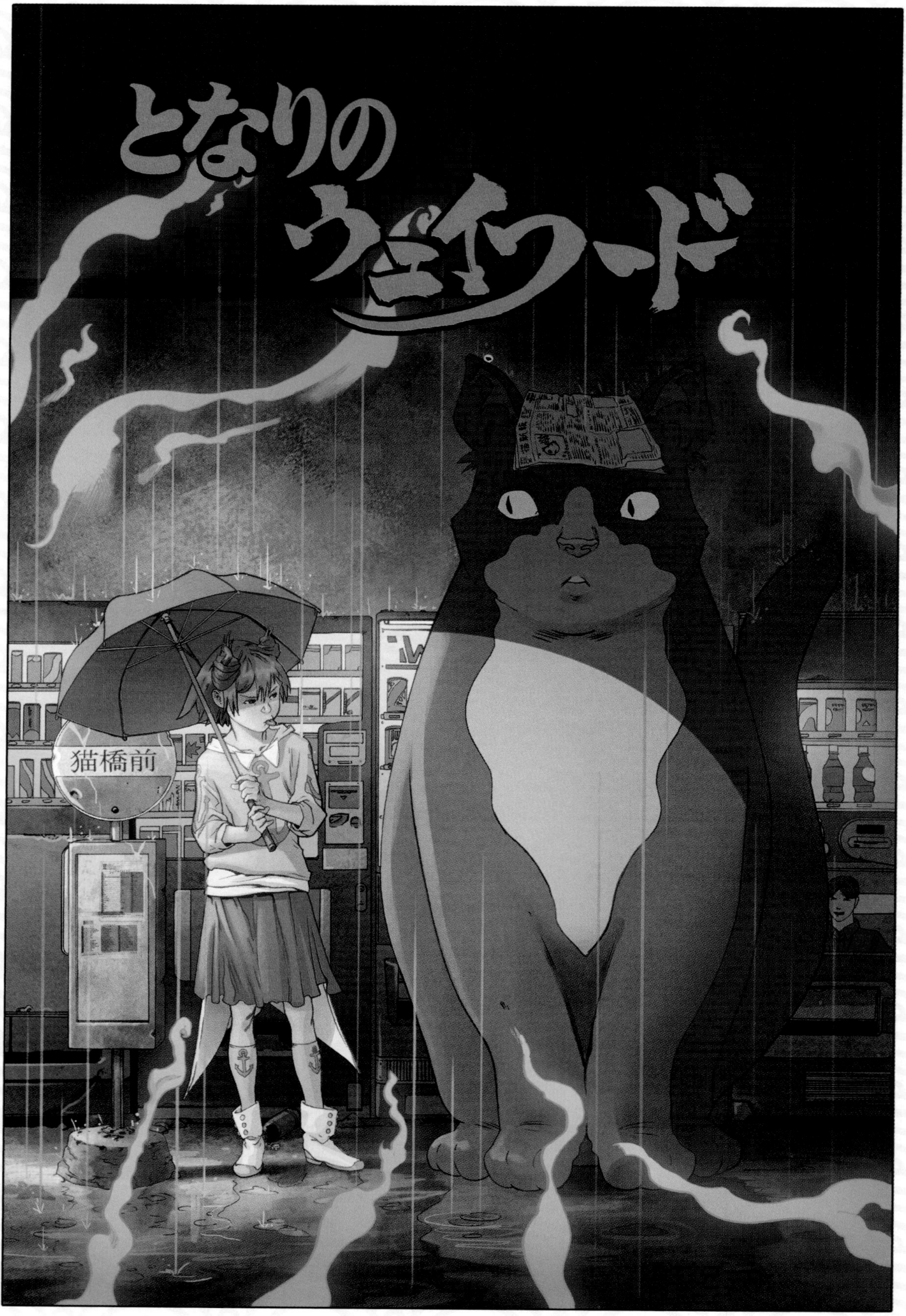
となりのウェイワード
猫橋前

WAYWARD #6 (Third Eye Comics Retailer Cover)
Artwork by Steve Cummings and Tamra Bonvillain
(an homage of '*My Neighbor Totoro*' by Studio Ghibli)

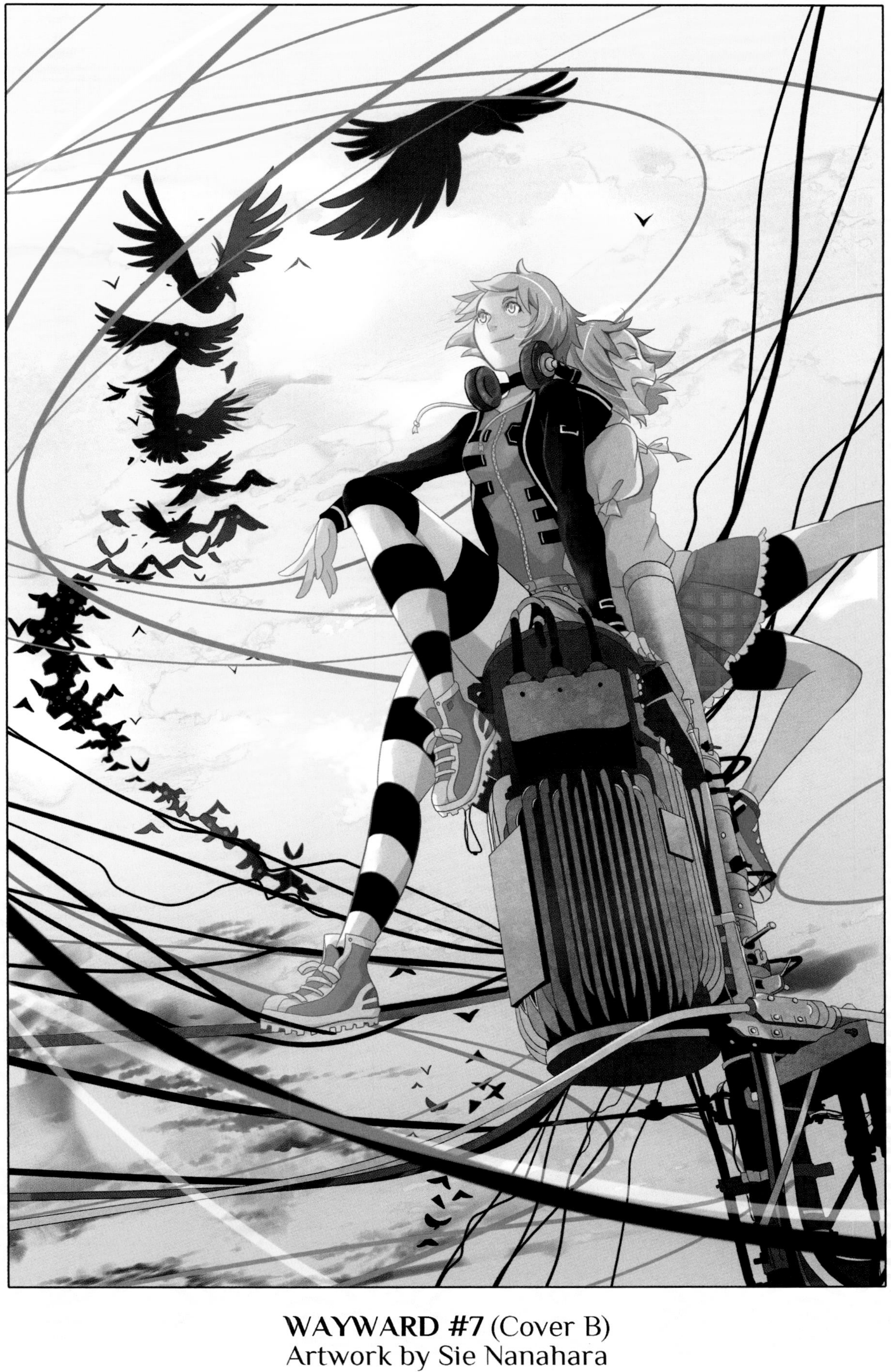

WAYWARD #7 (Cover B)
Artwork by Sie Nanahara

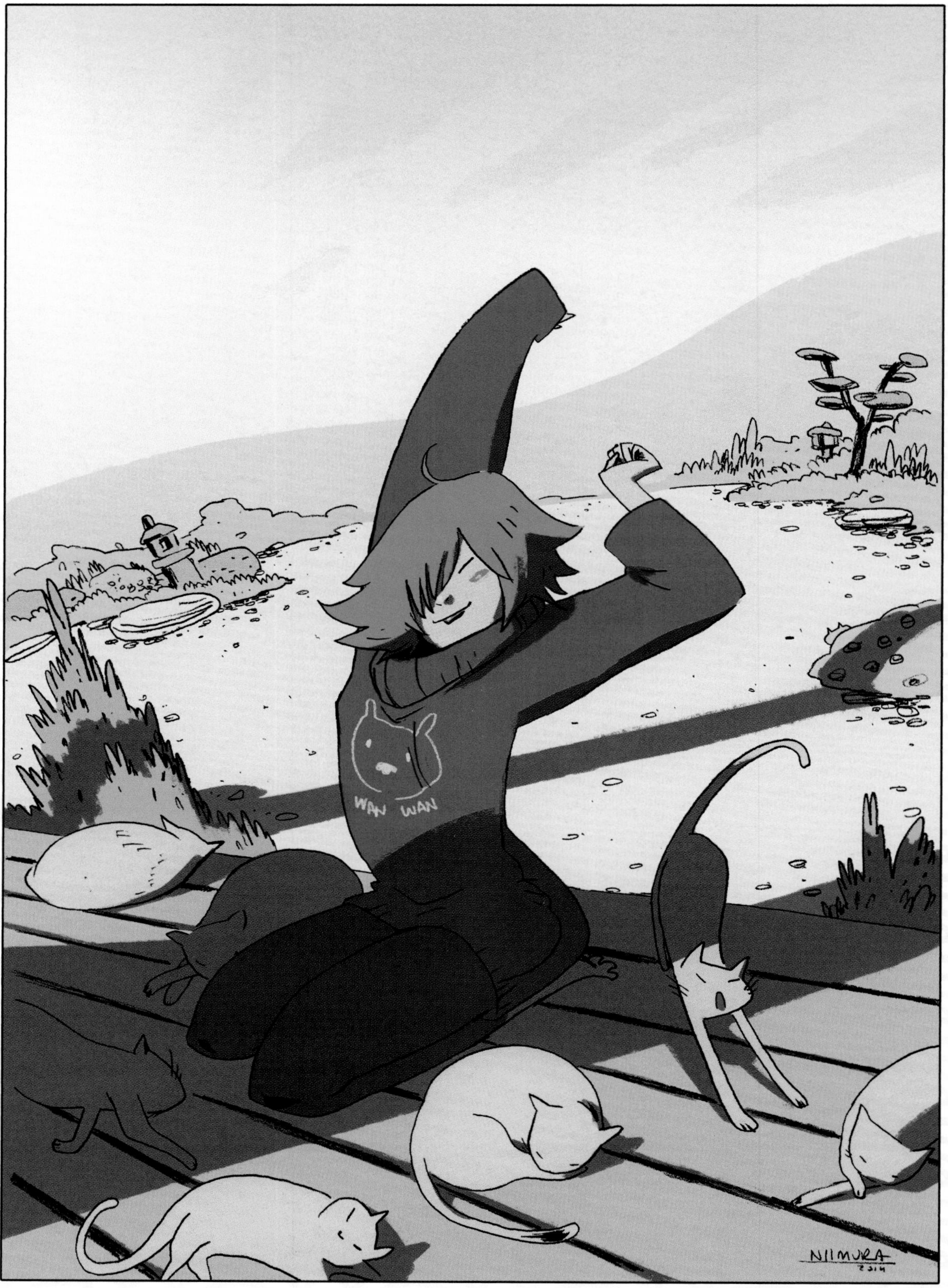
WAN WAN
NIIMURA
2014

WAYWARD #8 (Cover B)
Artwork by Ken Niimura

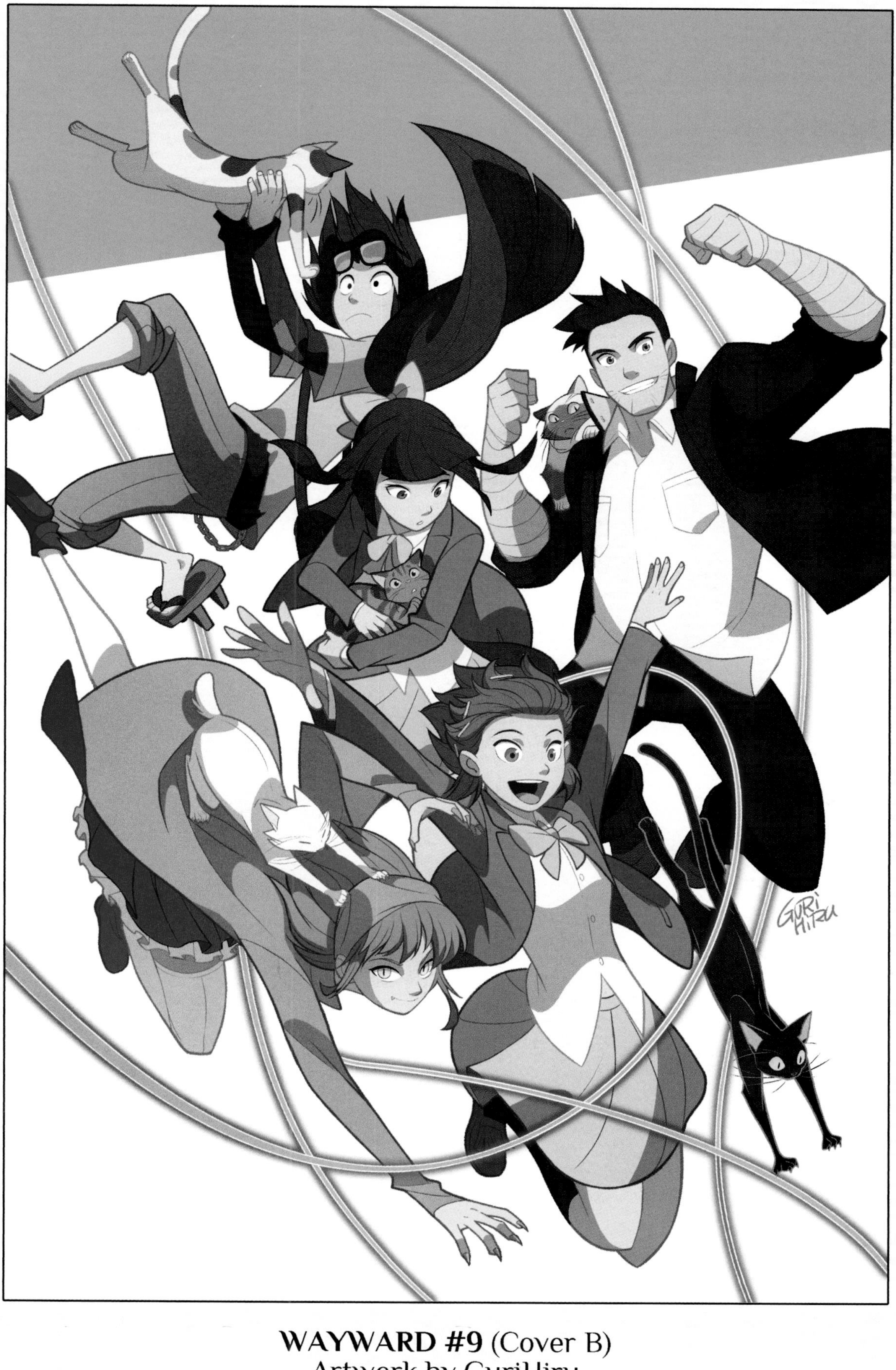
GURI HIRU

WAYWARD #9 (Cover B)
Artwork by GuriHiru

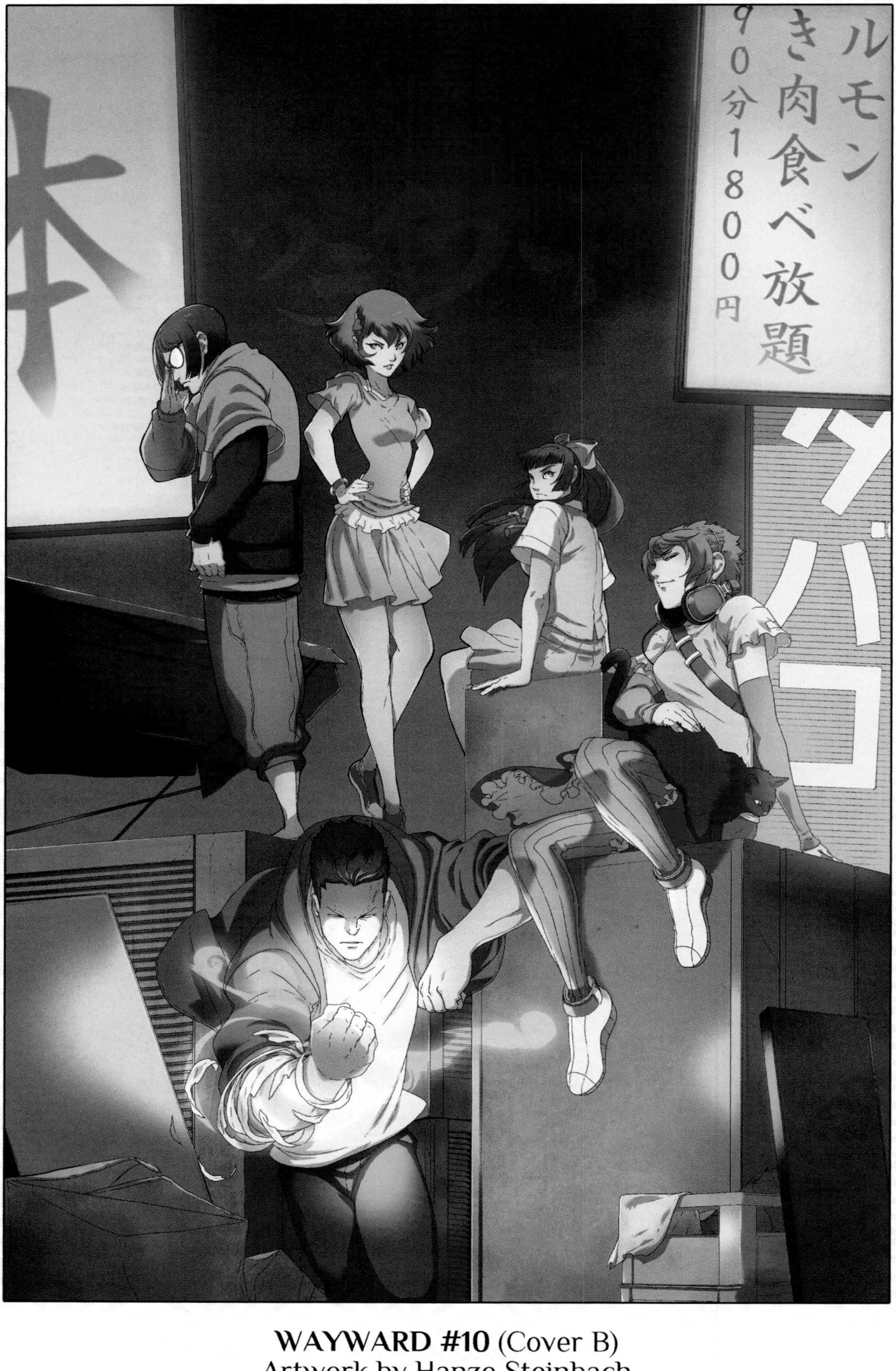
ルモン
き肉食べ放題
90分1800円

WAYWARD #10 (Cover B)
Artwork by Hanzo Steinbach

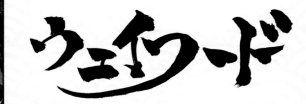

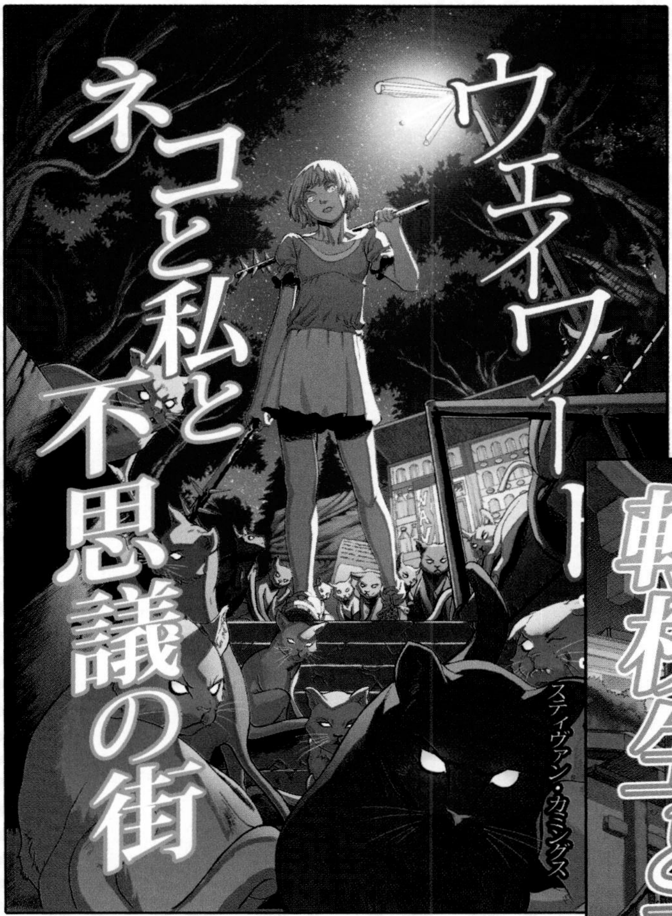
ウェイワード
ネコと私と不思議の街
スティヴァン・カミングス

ウェイワード

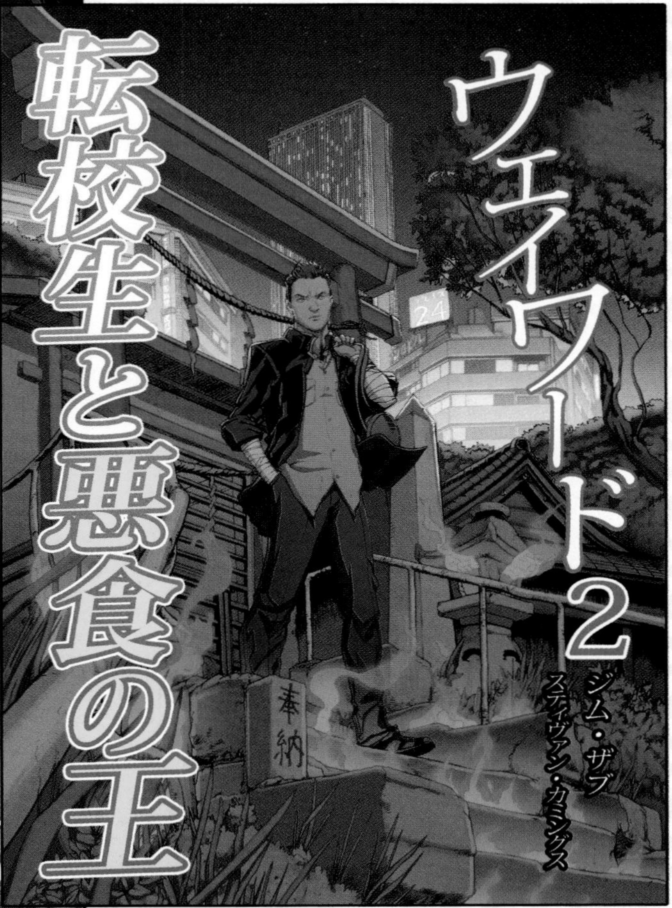
ウェイワード2
転校生と悪食の王
ジム・ザブ
スティヴァン・カミングス

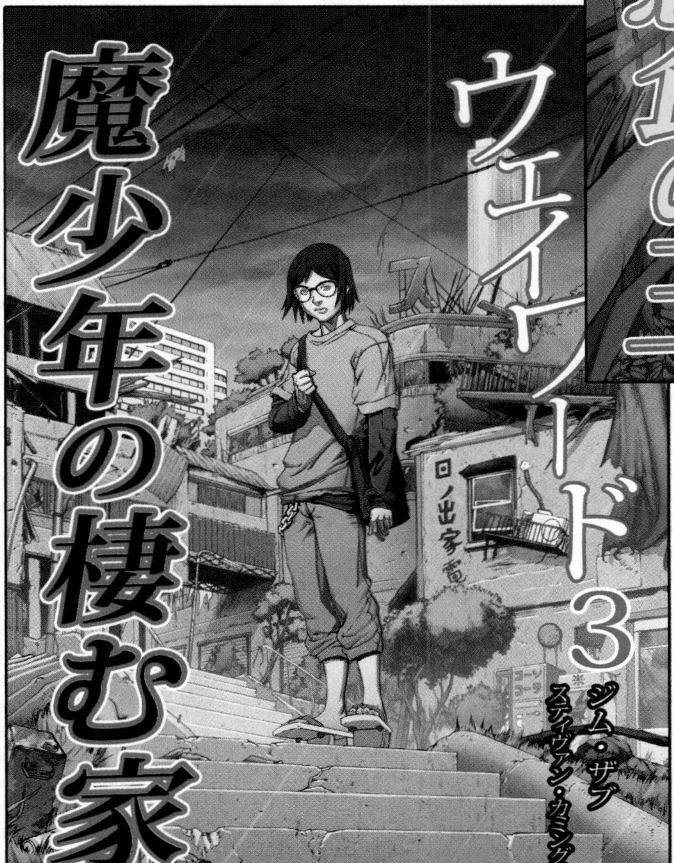
ウェイワード3
魔少年の棲む家
ジム・ザブ
スティヴァン・カミングス

Wayward "Dōjinshi"

Steve Cummings lives in Yokohama, so he and his friend Nishi Makoto decided to put together a limited run of *Wayward* in Japanese with page art taken from Steve's original black & white line art. These limited print run "dōjinshi" versions are some of the rarest *Wayward* comics so far.

Here are the Japanese covers to the first three issues.

Wayward
BEGINNINGS

In 2010 UDON Entertainment was preparing an art book called VENT to celebrate the studio's 10th anniversary. My contribution to the book was a tutorial piece on how to tone by hand.

I live in an area of the Kanto with lots of hills and inclines and there are concrete staircases built into many of them leading to who knows where. I like the spooky feeling from them and wanted this piece in that kind of setting.

To round out the feel I added lots of cats because there's nothing spookier than a small army of feral, hungry cats eyeballing you as walk by like a potential meal. I added a cute girl into the mix to contrast with the creepiness of the surroundings but I'm not sure why I gave her metal pipes covered in spikes. I'm sure some kind of weird inspiration caused me to add that element.

-Cummings

I worked at UDON for quite a few years, starting as an illustrator and eventually moving into more of a project management/editorial role. The VENT book was one I helped put together and Steve's piece really jumped out at me as something cool and atmospheric. That girl looked out at the viewer and seemed to have a story to tell.

Three years later, my freelance comic writing career had built up some momentum. After launching *Skullkickers* at Image I received quite a few other offers for comic writing gigs and it turned into a pretty steady source of work. Steve and I would chat from time to time about the possibility of working together on a creator-owned comic, but it seemed like our schedules would never sync up to make it happen.

Then, in July 2013, Steve let me know that he had time to develop something and we dug in. That original illustration of the cat-girl who would eventually be called 'Ayane' was the inspiration for everything that followed.

-Zub

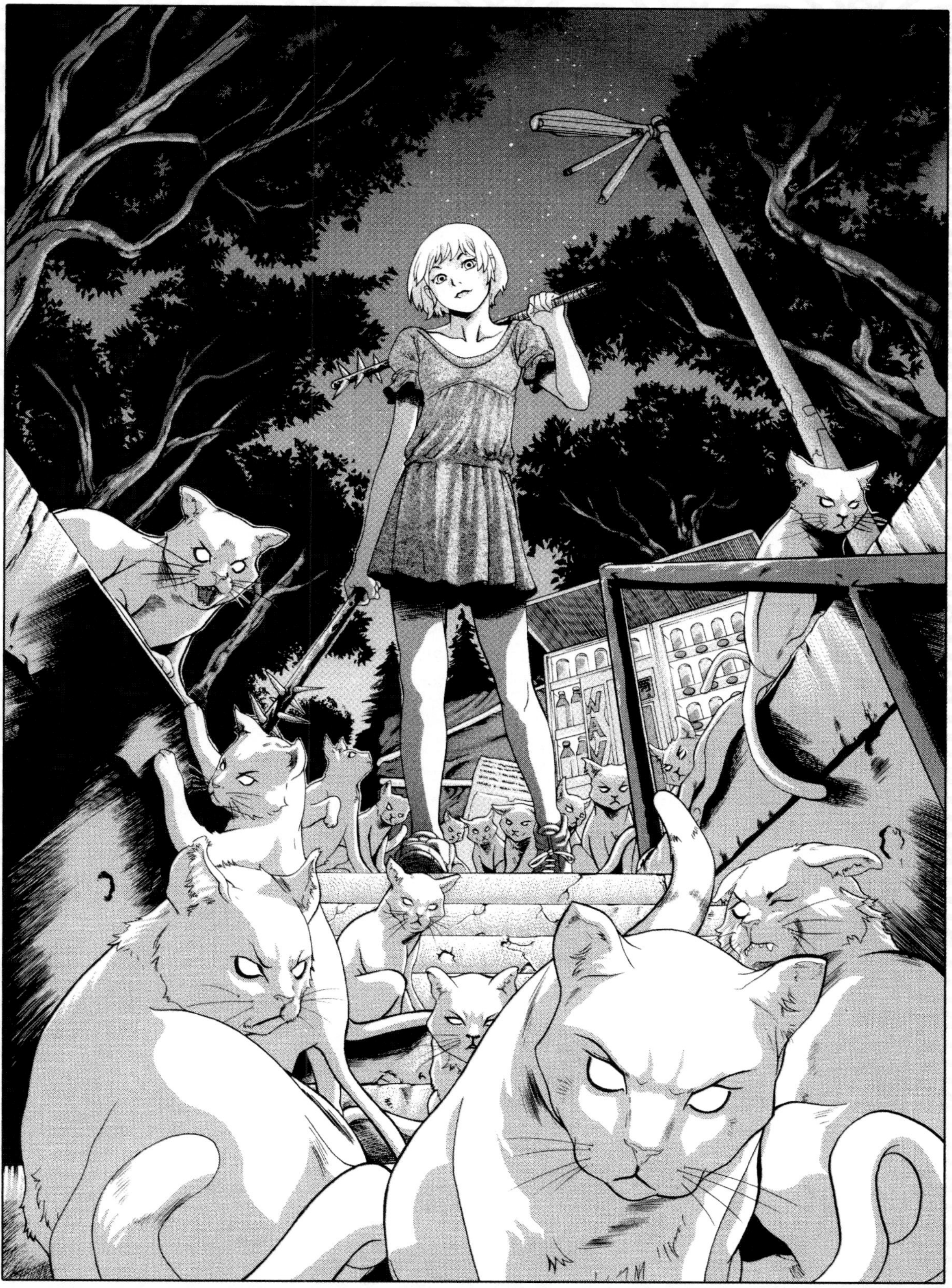

Cat Girl Illustration
Artwork by Steve Cummings

Looking back at the first big brainstorming email I put together, I'm actually really surprised at how much of it was fully formed right from the start.

-Zub

Tokyo Story Concept   2013-07-11   1:49pm

Heya,

Got back yesterday and it's been a whirlwind of SDCC prep and dealing with our bathroom renovations underway. My house is a total mess right now.

Anyway, on to idea stuff:

With a city as historical, dense and populated as Tokyo I think it would be really cool to build an urban supernatural 'mythos' of sorts, centering on a group of teens (and I like the idea that one of those teens is actually a 'cat girl', but not the cliche cat-girl of anime fame but a girl actually formed by the collected aura power of sentient cats living in Tokyo) who juggle dealing with bizarre mystical stuff in weird/wonderful corners of the city alongside growing up.

If that broad concept interests you I can start outlining specific characters and their development.

Character concepts beyond the "cat girl":
• A boy who feeds on ghost energy.
• A boy who traps emotions so he can use them later.
• A girl who uses street/subway routes to 'draw' mystic symbols and cast spells.
• A girl who can control manufactured things (plastic, steel, polymers, polyester, concrete, chemicals) but not natural ones (wood, stone, earth, water, etc.).

It would be great to mix old world/new world elements and give them a twist.

As for a title, that's tough. I tend to just collide word combinations and then double check there are no comics or major properties already with that title.

Some random association title brainstorming:
Wayward
Under Edo
Faded Fires
Missing Heartbeats
Crowded Spaces
Ghosts in the Gutters

If one of those 'clicks' for you, cool. If none do, that's cool too. We can brainstorm a bunch more.

I want to avoid using the word "Tokyo" in the title, as I don't want people to pigeonhole it as a "manga". The art style will give off some of that and that's fine, but I don't want the covers or title to push away people who would make assumptions about the content based on the title. Is that okay?

Let me know what you think.
Jim

With Rori's design I wanted her to feel young and a little punk, but also didn't look like she had much money to work with when putting together her outfits.

I gave her hair a Chelsea cut but to keep with the poor angle I make it look like it had grown out quite a bit since she wouldn't have the money to get a haircut often.

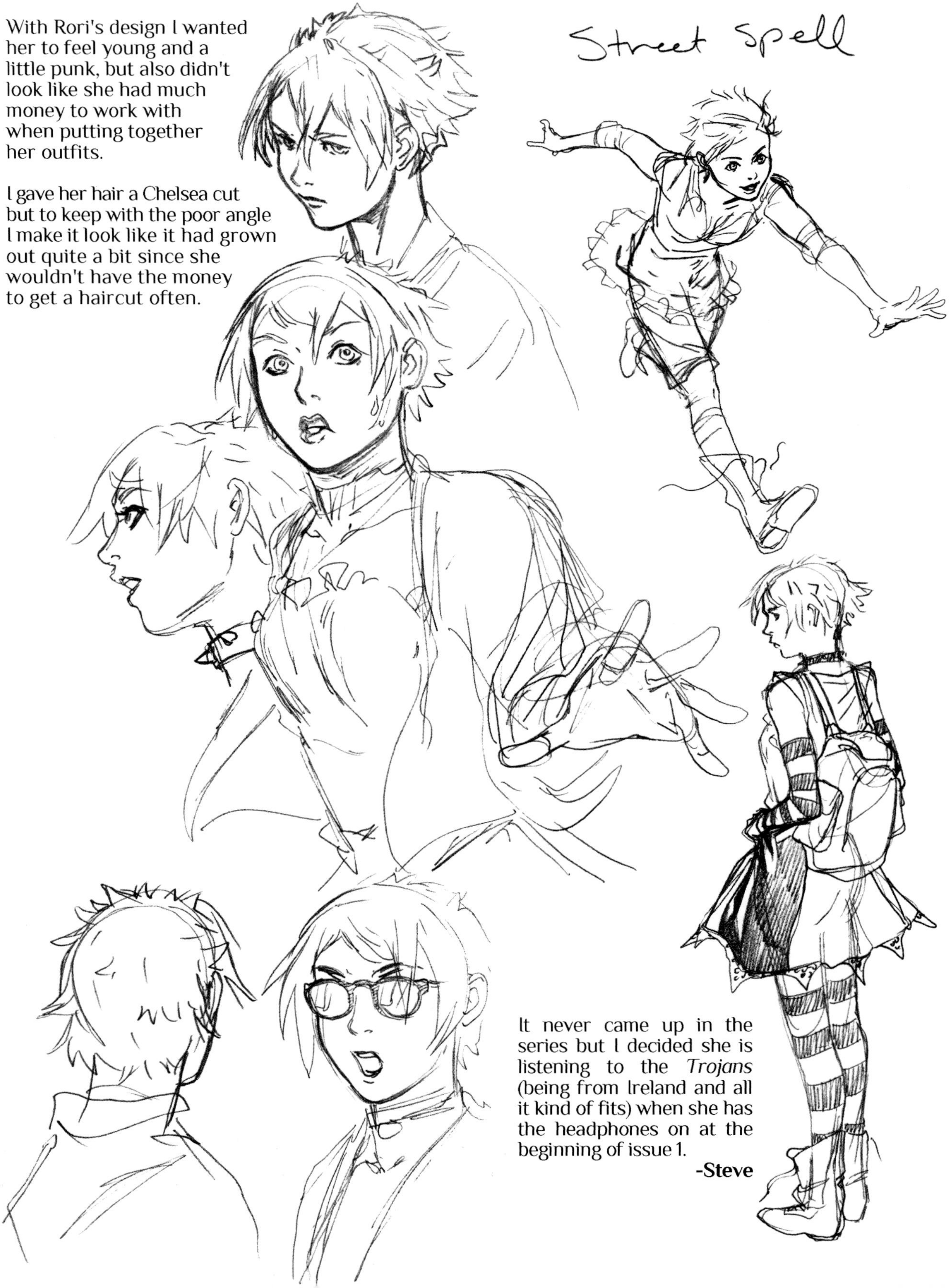
Street Spell

It never came up in the series but I decided she is listening to the *Trojans* (being from Ireland and all it kind of fits) when she has the headphones on at the beginning of issue 1.

-Steve

The Cat, Ayane

謎の猫女子 (綾)

Ayane is based on the girl from my VENT illustration that started all this. In that illo she was a youngish teen in summer clothes with wild hair carrying metal rods with spikes on them.

There was a little tweaking when I did a redesign for the comic version. I made her a little older looking with longer dresses/skirts and the clothes she now wears are more fashionable and up to date. Her weapons stayed in the book though. They've kind of become her symbol.

-Steve

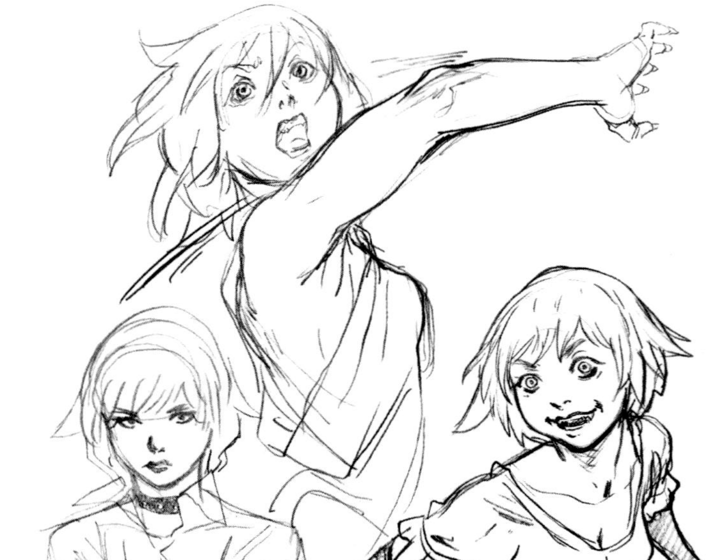

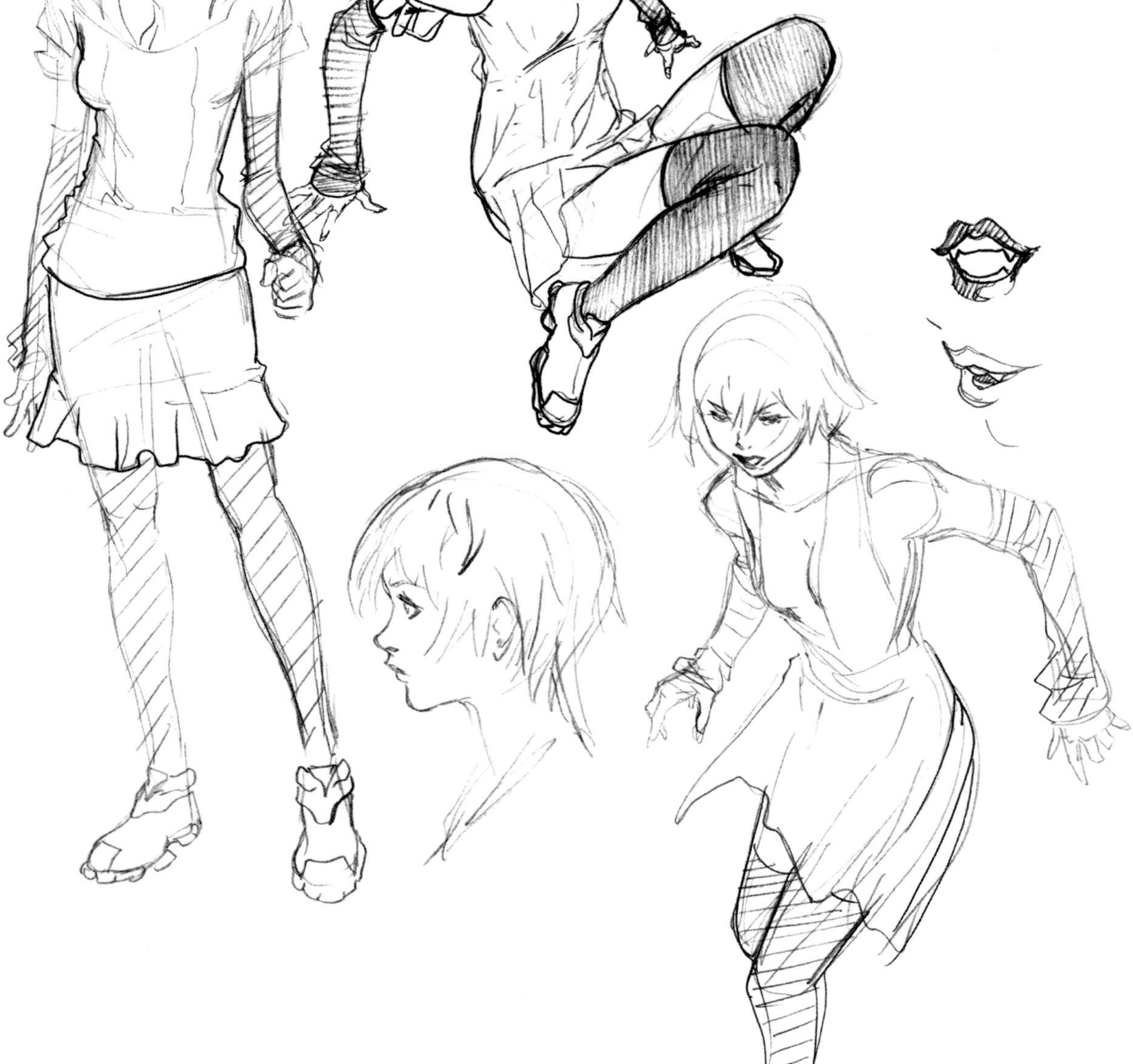

Shirai is kind of the muscle in the group, but I didn't want to go the route of giant superhero physique to show that, so I based his look on baseball players; tall and lean with either shaved heads to the point they are shiny-bald or short on the sides and ever so slightly long on the top.

His clothing style is more or less "if it fits wear it" or school uniform based. When I designed him I intended for him to have a slight slouch with his hands in his pockets as if to show a bit of insecurity.

-Steve

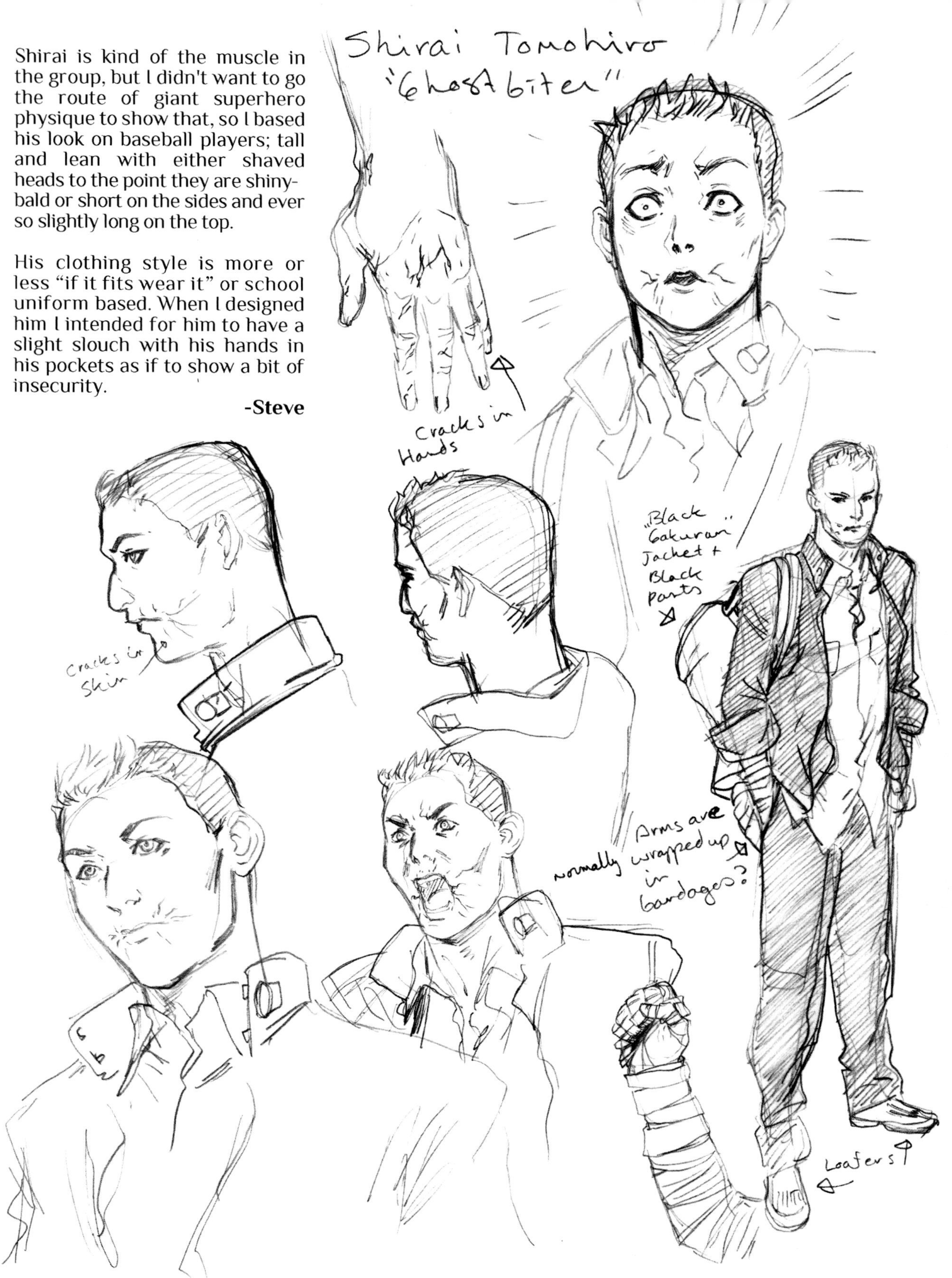
Shirai Tomohiro
"Ghostbiter"
Cracks in Hands
"Black Gakuran" Jacket + Black pants
Cracks in Skin
Arms are normally wrapped up in bandages?
Loafers

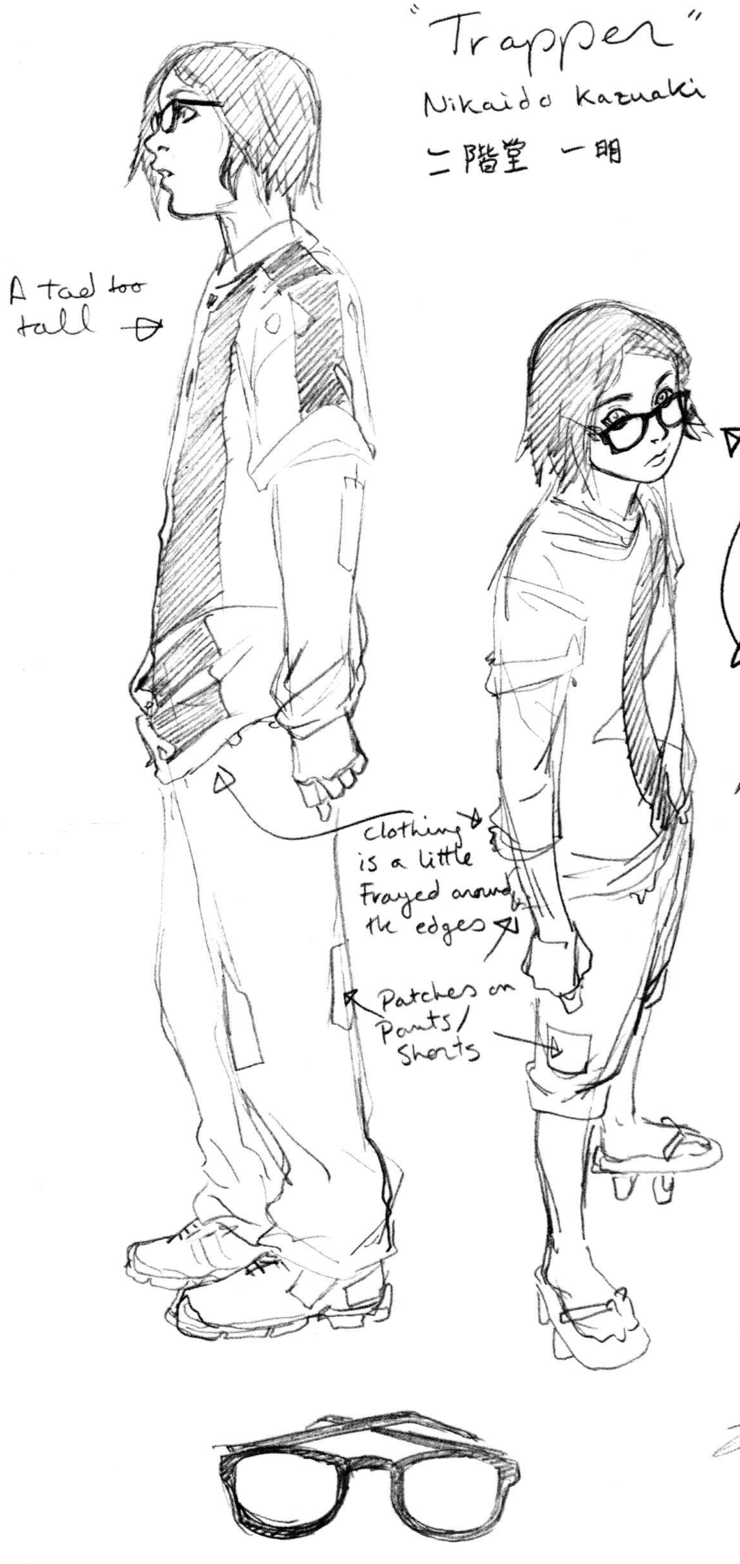
"Trapper"
Nikaido Kazuaki
二階堂 一明
A tad too tall
Clothing is a little Frayed around the edges
Patches on Pants/Shorts

I went with big loose clothes and a floppy hairstyle for Nikaido.

He is really poor and before meeting our other characters he lives on the streets alone. I wanted to show that sort of thing in his outfits, complete with frayed edges on his shirts and smudges of dirt. In order to show how bad off his situation is I didn't even draw him wearing shoes initially.

-Steve

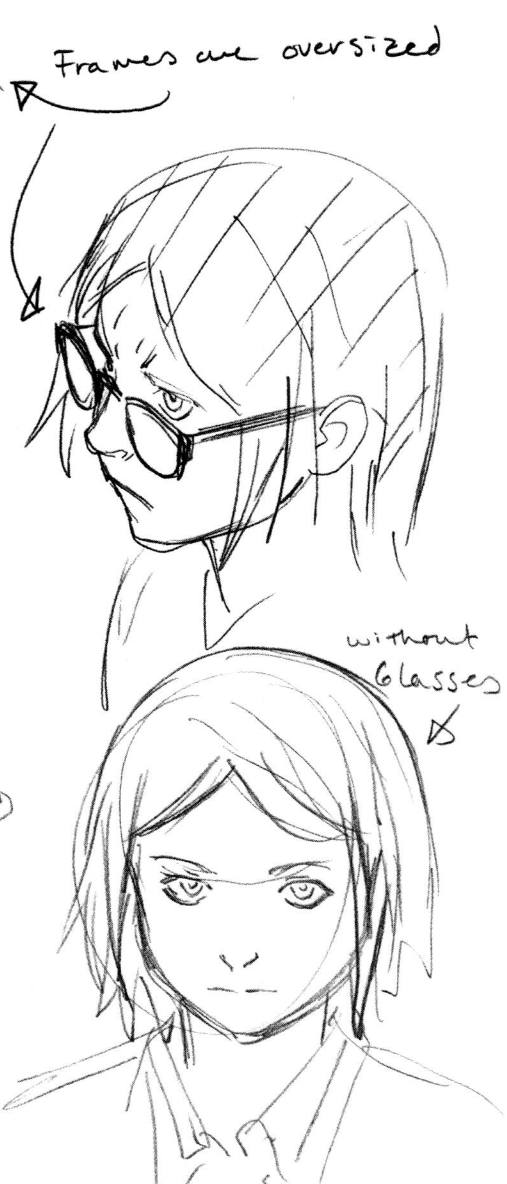
Frames are oversized
without Glasses

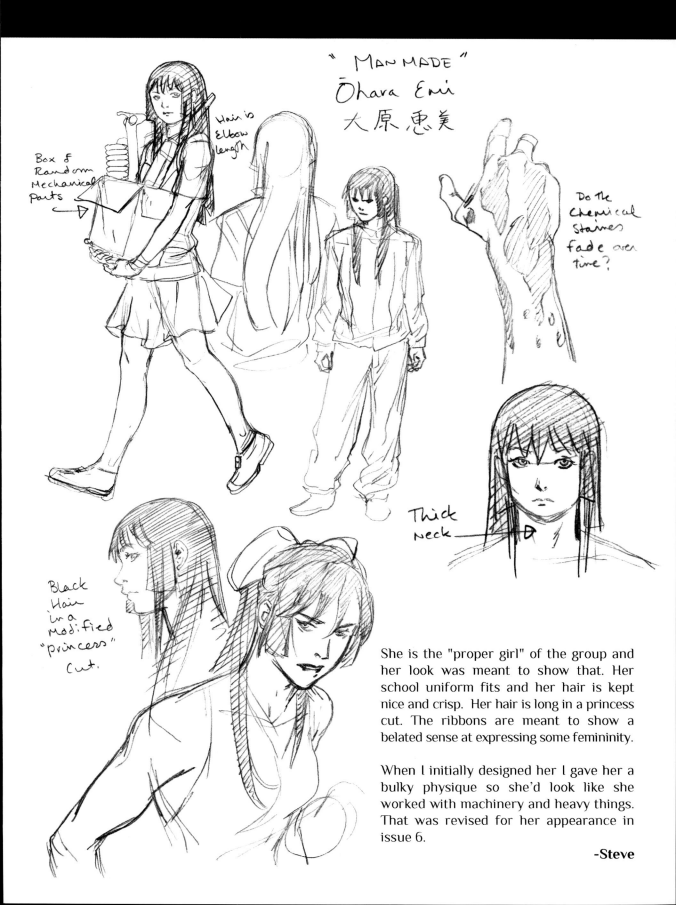

Ohara

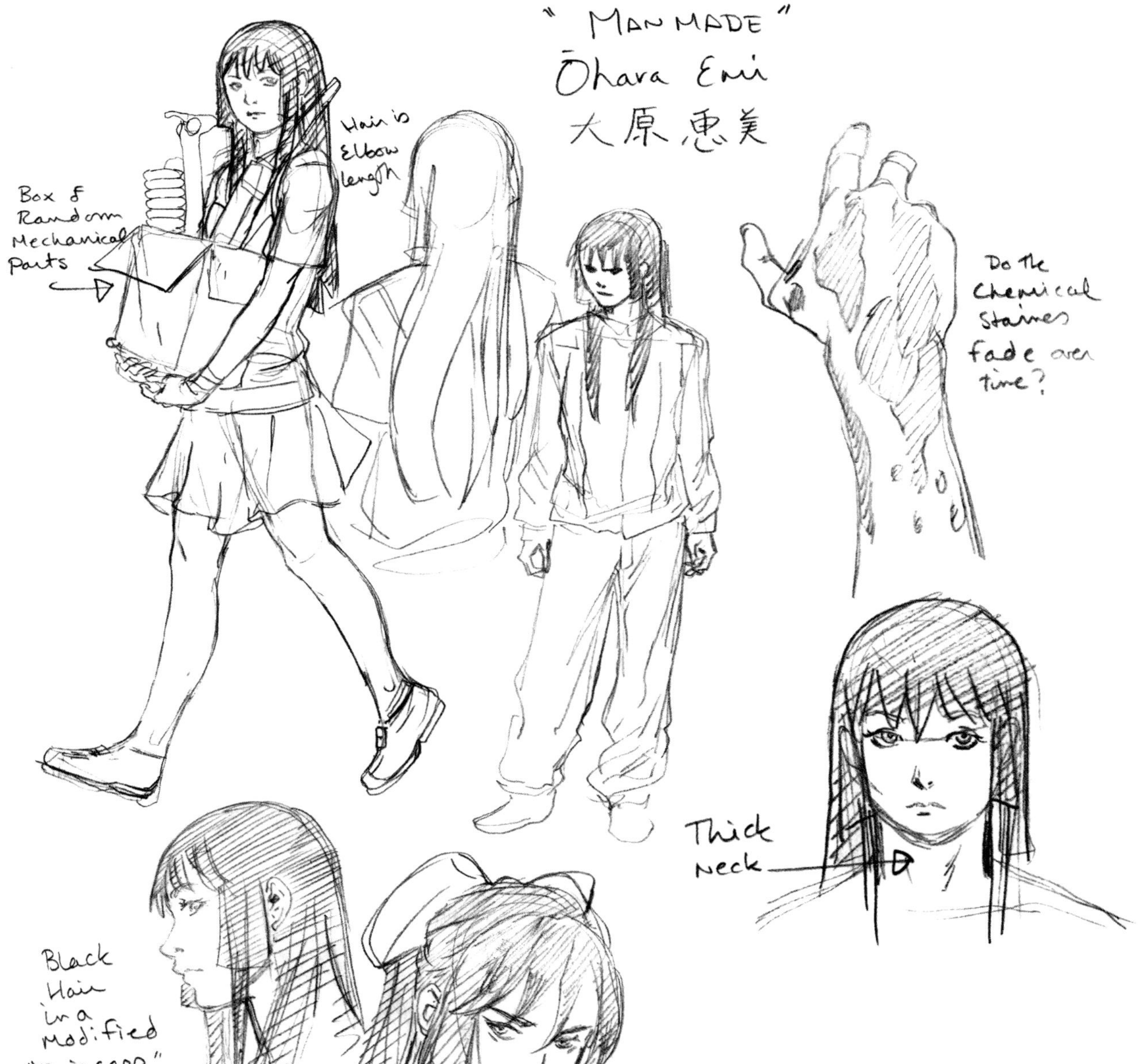
" MAN MADE "
Ōhara Emi
大原恵美
Hair is Elbow length
Box of Random Mechanical Parts
Do the Chemical Staines fade over time?
Thick Neck
Black Hair in a modified "princess" Cut.

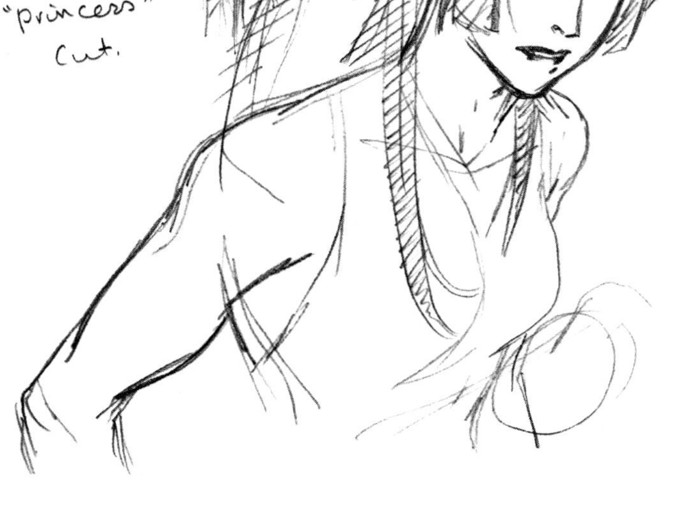

She is the "proper girl" of the group and her look was meant to show that. Her school uniform fits and her hair is kept nice and crisp. Her hair is long in a princess cut. The ribbons are meant to show a belated sense at expressing some femininity.

When I initially designed her I gave her a bulky physique so she'd look like she worked with machinery and heavy things. That was revised for her appearance in issue 6.

-Steve

Coloring *Wayward*

Colorist Tamra Bonvillain walks us through her coloring process on *Wayward* using an example panel from Chapter 6.

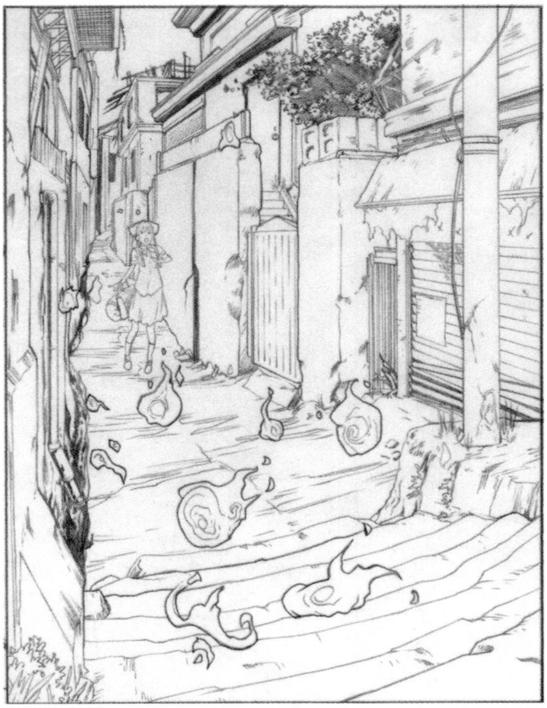

1) This is the raw unadjusted scan of the pencil line work received from Steve Cummings.

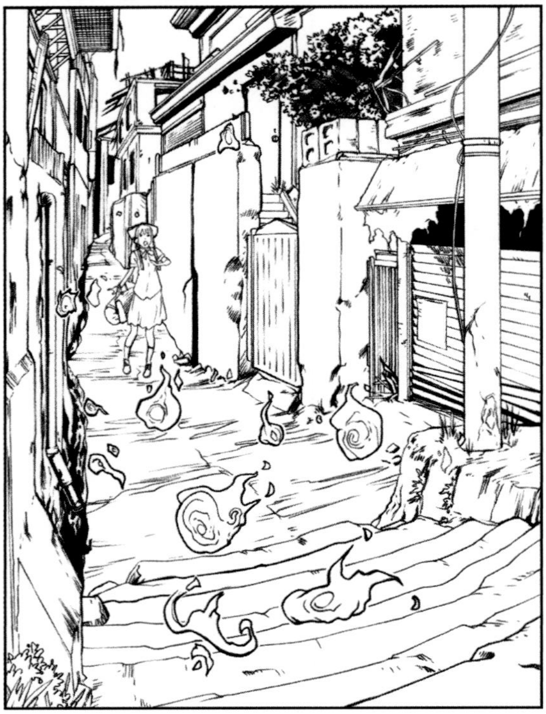

2) After Jim adjusts the levels, touches up smudges or lost lines and fills in large dark areas, this is the line art as I receive it.

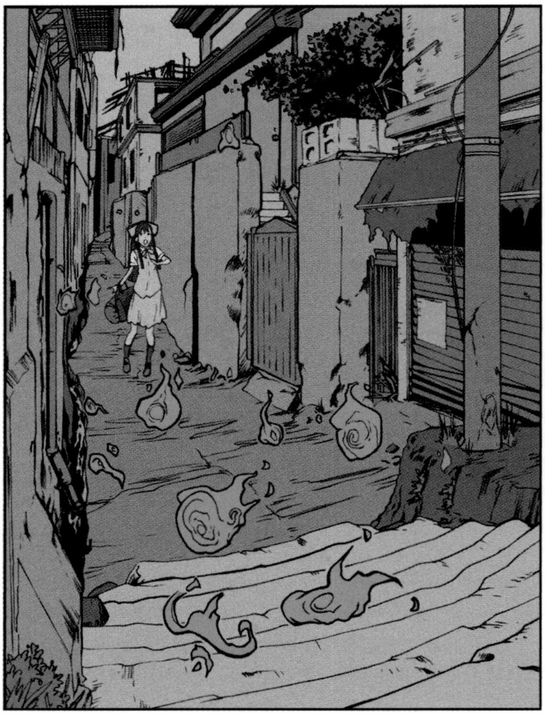

3) Our flatter, Ludwig, separates all the different pieces out on a single layer in Photoshop so it saves me time in the coloring process. This is the adjusted version I color corrected to match my palette for the scene.

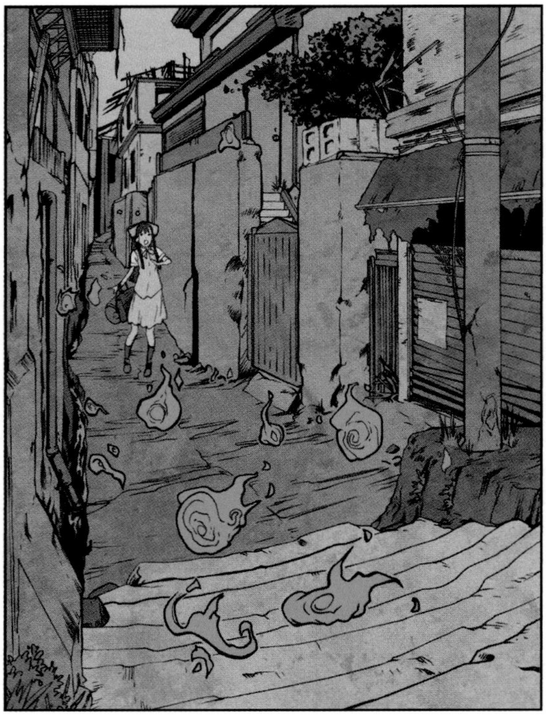

4) Next, I apply texture to the flat colors. Here, I added some rough textures to the worn out and dirty parts of the panel. This is also the stage I would add patterns to clothing, or rosy color to the skin tones.

5) Then, I apply shadows and highlights to the textured flats. I could go into much greater depth on this stage, but I'd need a lot more space!

6) At this stage, I add the finishing touches. I go in and add color to the previously black line art to give it a softer look and to blend certain areas. Then, I'll add in special effects like the glow from the magic energy and some atmospheric perspective around the sky and the buildings in the background.

THERE!

SHE'S ONE OF THEM!

MAYBE...

7) Finally, the complete version that appeared in issue 6 with Marshall's lettering added in.

-Tamra

Zub - Here's that same panel from the script so you can compare the original description and the final printed version:

Panel 5: A line of small green fire 'puffs' are floating just above the ground in front of Ohara. They're *kitsune-bi* (foxfire). She looks up to see where the voice from off panel is coming from.

VOICE (OP) <There!>

VOICE (OP) <She's one of them!>

NARRATION (OHARA) <Maybe...>

Welcome to Weird Japan

Kappa. Kitsune. Oni. Or towering, post-war engines of destruction like Godzilla, Mothra, and Gamera. Even the endless parade of Pokémon—Japan is monster country. They write books about monsters; make movies about monsters; draw comics about monsters. From a young age, Japanese children wean themselves on folklore creatures with *Kitaro*. They graduate to modern, esoteric beasts with *Neon Genesis Evangelion* and *Attack on Titan*. When they head to college, *yōkaigaku* — monsterology —is a serious course of study.

It is a fact undeniable: Japan <u>embraces</u> the weird.

There's a reason why the country is in love with the supernatural. Monsters are a part of Japan's deep magic. They are found as far back as the creation myth and are threaded through all of Japanese history. And as Japan has evolved from a primitive tribal culture to a modern, scientific superpower, the monsters have kept pace.

The birth of Japan's gods and monsters is recorded in the 8th century *Kojiki* (*Record of Ancient Matters*)—the oldest known work of Japanese literature. The *Kojiki* tells of the god Izanagi, creator of the Japanese islands, freshly returned from the land of the dead. He purifies himself in a bath, and as he dries his body each falling drop of water soaks into the soil and imbues the land with latent supernatural potential.

For tens of thousands of years this supernatural potential manifested itself as invisible energy, a nameless, faceless, field that swaddled the islands. It was an elemental force that brought both life and death, in the same way that water both nourished the crops as a gentle rain and pounded villages in the form of typhoons. Like any natural resource, this power could be harvested; shrines were built to contain and focus the energy, and used as spiritual batteries. When this energy was good and beneficial they named it *kami* (神). When it was wild and dangerous they referred to it by the euphemism things of mystery—*mononoke* (物の怪).

Things changed rapidly in the Heian period (794 – 1185), when contact with China brought the ideas of incarnate deities and organized religion. The influence of Buddhism forged that loose collections of folk beliefs and kami worship into the religion called Shinto. Simultaneously, new ideas created new beliefs that blended the ancient and the modern, like the ghost-religion Goryō Shinko and the sorcerous art of geomancy called Onmyōdō.

With this change, the mononoke first gained individual form and identities. Artists were at the forefront of this spiritual revolution, imagining a wild menagerie of thousands of forms and shapes that would shame Hieronymus Bosch with their variety. Heian period artists crafted long scrolls that would be unrolled to slowly reveal new and terrible monsters marching in a celebration of pandemonium called the *Night Parade of 100 Demons*—one of Japan's initial forays into sequential art.

The supernatural took a back seat for the next few centuries as Japan was ripped apart by civil wars and more physical horrors. Finally, peace arrived with conquest, as the shōgun Tokugawa Ieyasu took command and kickstarted modern Japan with the Edo period (1603-1868). Many of the things Japanese —the aristocratic samurai and the artisanal geisha; the elegant theater of bunraku and the wild spectacle of *kabuki*; the floating world of *ukiyo-e* artists-sprouted and flowered during the Edo period. This era of peace and prosperity also gave birth to *yōkai* (妖怪).

The Edo period was marked by a mania for the supernatural. A popular parlor game, called *Hyakumonogatari Kaidankai*, gripped the nation. A hundred candles would be lit in a circle, and players would tell weird tales one after the other, extinguishing a single candle with each story. Players told stories of monsters—now called yōkai—expounding on those same beasts from the picture scrolls of the Heian period. Writers and storytellers filled in the details, giving the grotesqueries names and back stories, creating hierarchies and societies and mythologies. Kitsune and tengu were cast as aristocrats, while kappa and tanuki were earthier —the blue-collar yōkai. Others were just bizarre, like the tenjo-name ceiling licker, or the one-eyed, one-footed umbrella monster called the kasa obake.

This enthusiasm lasted more than two hundred years, until war again silenced the supernatural. Japan's growing pains of the Meiji era (1868-1912) through the early Showa era (1926-1989) saw the militarization and mobilization of the country that lead to WWII. The government made a concentrated effort to suppress yōkai and superstition in favor of the new gods of science and industry.

It wouldn't last.

After Japan's defeat, the yōkai again crawled out of their dark holes, finding a new home and an appreciative audience in film and the emergent art form known as manga. Lead by the artist Shigeru Mizuki and his comic *Kitaro*, Japan underwent a yōkai boom that resurrected the lost monsters of previous generations. And they evolved. Director Ishiro Honda combined science and the supernatural to create monsters for the new generation-*daikaiju*. Giant monsters like Godzilla and Rodan captured and continue to hold the imagination of monster-loving Japanese children. And Americans too.

Even now the monsters of Japan are still there. Wander the streets of Tokyo—or anywhere in Japan—and you will find them. Whether it is the obvious sights like the statue of Godzilla in Ginza and the Kappa Bridge, or in the hidden power spots and energy zones laid out centuries ago by mystical onmyōji. Or even more esoteric wonders like the Sunset 60 ghost building or the shrine to the head of the samurai Taira no Masakado in the Otemachi financial district—one of the most expensive areas of land on Earth, but a place that no one will dare build over.

You just have to scratch the shiny, neon veneer of modern Japan to find the true skin of the country —the ancient soil infused with supernatural potential by the god Izanagi. Supernatural potential waiting to be tapped.

High School Is Different in Japan—Really Different

Love it or hate it, school is a big part of our lives. Just look at the number of popular series based around schools—*X-Men. Harry Potter. Buffy the Vampire Slayer. Morning Glories.* Even with nothing else in common, we can relate to school and its particular battlegrounds. If you read Japanese comics, you know school is a national obsession. School horror comics. School love stories. School kids piloting giant robots. It seems like every other series involves school kids. Some, like *Sailor Moon*, are directly inspired by the ubiquitous sailor suits of Japanese school girls. But the differences between American and Japanese high schools are much greater than uniforms.

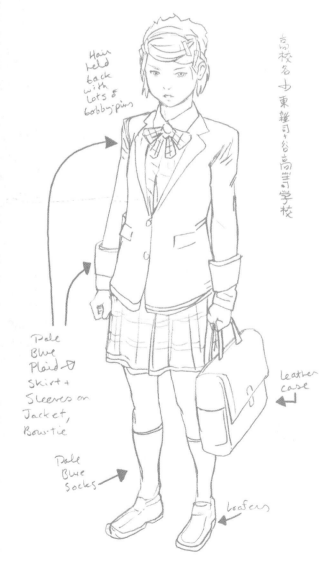

Hair held back with lots of bobby pins
高校名
東雑司ヶ谷高等学校
Pale Blue Plaid Skirt + Sleeves on Jacket, Bow tie
Leather case
Pale Blue Socks
Loafers

Above: Steve's design for Rori's school uniform.

I taught in the Japanese school system for about seven years. During that time I worked everywhere—from a bottom-ranked rural school that expelled 10% of its students every quarter, to the prestigious Osaka University. From my experience, the biggest difference between American and Japanese high schools is variety—Japan has more.

In the U.S., primary education is mandatory and location is determined by zip code. Sure, there are private schools, but these are expensive and rare. You generally go to the schools you are zoned for. With few exceptions, you follow a straight line from elementary school to high school. Your only real decision point comes when you decide where—or if—you will go to college.

In Japan, the path branches three years earlier. Japanese compulsory education runs only to middle school. After that, it is up to the students and their parents to decide if they want to continue education or enter the work force. Granted, almost everyone goes to high school—something like 97% of the population. But they have a choice. And a test.

Japanese high schools are more like American colleges. There are a wide variety, and as different from each other as Harvard is from your local community college. Entrance to a high-academic school puts you on track for a prestigious college, which guarantees a lucrative job. Middle-academic schools (like Rori's school) pump out future project managers and cogs-in-the-machine—the average employees that staff most companies. At vocational high schools you study nursing or applied technology. Commercial schools train you for customer service. There are all-girl schools. Mixed schools. Manga schools. Finally, there are bottom-of-the-barrel agricultural schools that are the dumping ground for all the oddballs and misfits that don't fit into to Japan's structured society.

To get into each school you have to take an entrance exam—and you only get one shot at it. The most prestigious schools are the public schools, where the government supports the education fees. They usually have their entrance exams on the same day so you can only attempt one—no "safety schools" in Japan. As a fall back,

you can pay the higher cost and test into a private school. Unlike the U.S., Japanese private schools are the opposite of elite. They are like for-profit universities, with standards so low anyone who can pay the entrance fee can buy a spot. (I worked at a commercial high school, and a "passing score" was 10%. A single correct question on the 100-question exam earned you a spot. On my first day, my supervisor told me "One thing you must understand about this school: everyone—both the teachers and the students—wants to be somewhere else.")

Once inside the school, depending on what you qualified for, life is going to be very different. High academic schools are strict and regimented. Quiet, serious students line up in straight lines and absorb every word from the respected teacher. Agricultural school students flop over their desks, hang out in the hallways, and ooze a chaotic vibe that is the polar opposite of the rigid order of high academic schools. (I thought agricultural schools were a lot more fun.)

Regardless of type, your school life is dominated by your homeroom. On your first day of school you are assigned a homeroom. Unlike American schools where you reshuffle for every period, Japanese students stay in their homerooms while the teachers come and go. Those classmates are your family for the next three years. About the only exchange you have with students outside of your homeroom is in clubs. Every school has a wealth of clubs—sports clubs; art clubs; chess clubs; martial arts clubs; music clubs. You join a club and that becomes the second circle that identifies you.

Like any close group, your homeroom has its own intrigues and traditions, its own heroes and villains. One of the hardest things is the dreaded transfer student—someone who has the nerve to enter into an already well-established clan. It takes a long time to integrate a transfer student—if they are ever integrated at all. In many cases, the transfer student remains the perpetual outsider. Returnees, Japanese students who have spent considerable time overseas, usually as exchange students, are even further ostracized. They enter at the bottom of the hierarchy.

And the uniforms—oh yes, the famous Japanese school uniforms. It's all true. Kids live in their uniforms for the entirety of their school life. And not just while they are at school. You can see tribes of students wandering the streets on weekends, all in matching school uniforms. Many students rarely wear regular clothes until they graduate high school and suddenly get to pick their own wardrobes. And the uniform extends beyond the clothes. Your hair has to be a prescribed color, and if your hair isn't naturally the right shade of black you might have to die it. Teachers often stand in front of the school doing a uniform check every morning. (At one school I taught at, the teachers had a can of black spray paint to color the hair of any student trying to sneak past the rules.)

For good or ill, uniformity is highly valued. In many ways, the key is to adhere to the role assigned to you. And not rock the boat. Japanese society has certain expectations of you, and that begins with high school. Where you go to high school will affect the rest of your life, and that's a decision you have to make at 15 years old.

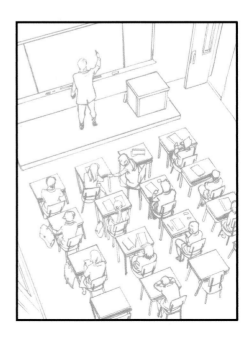

There is the Tokyo you know from movies. A paradise of high technology and strange fashions—gleaming superstructures paneled with massive televisions that stab the sky; bullet trains that whistle by at impossible speeds. This Tokyo is a dream of neon and chrome, as close to science fiction as you can get in real life. Look deeper, and you'll see the real Tokyo where people actually live. Less fantastic, it's a realm of weekly garbage schedules, dirty alleyways, dingy bars, corner stores, commutes, PTA meetings, annoying neighbors—brown and dingy, this Tokyo is stuffed with the boring aspects of everyday life.

Then there is a third Tokyo—the subterranean city that lies below. A maze of shopping arcades, restaurants, car parks, foot paths, and subway tunnels, the true size of underground Tokyo remains unknown. The official survey says it is around 200km of tunnels. Journalist and author Shun Akiba would put that number closer to 2,000km.

You can tour this underground city anytime, simply by buying a subway ticket. The most highly used rapid transit system in the world, the Tokyo subway system greets millions of riders each year. Along the way from Point A to Point B, you can stop at bars, go to high-end restaurants, or sing karaoke. Maybe even catch a nap at a capsule hotel. Brightly lit and bursting with life, removed from the elements and the color of the sky, underground Tokyo always reminds me of Las Vegas—a surreal place separate from reality that keeps its own electric time. Walking along this nightless city you forget you are underneath thousands of tons of rock and skyscrapers, in a city prone to earthquakes.

If you keep your eyes open, you can spot... oddities. There are doors marked B1 and B3, but missing B2. Tunnels lead off to nowhere. Tracks turn to places where nothing exists. Even walking through above-ground Tokyo you can see entrances that are closed off, or locked doors that can lead nowhere but down. In his book *Imperial City Tokyo: Secret of a Hidden Underground Network,* Shun Akiba started comparing old ordinance maps from different eras and found they rarely agreed with each other. Prewar maps show tunnels near major government buildings that disappear from modern maps. Tracking through records, he found

public funds allocated for constructions costs of new tunnels that already existed. Enquiries were met with closed lips and government blacklisting.

Underground complexes are nothing recent in Japan. As far back as the Edo period, the mansions of the rich and famous sat on top of ant hives of dungeons, storehouses, and hidden escape routes. The Imperial Palace was rumored to use tunnels to move the Emperor in order to keep him safe. These were relatively small scale, limited by need and technology. During WWII, however, Japan went tunnel crazy. With the constant threat of Allied bombing, it made sense to put a few layers of rock over your head. The Japanese military and political arms burrowed deep.

An entire secret underground government office was constructed in Nagano—complete with Imperial palace and shrine. Called the Matsushiro Underground Imperial Headquarters, it began construction in 1944 and didn't end until the official war's end on August 15th, 1945. Plans were made to relocate the Emperor, the Imperial Regalia, and the entire war command to this sprawling bunker. It was never used. The complex still exits, although it officially remains closed.

The Allied occupying government made use of the secret tunnels interlinking Tokyo—and some say expanded them. The postwar General Headquarters was one of the most mysterious places in Japan. It was a bulwark of secrets. MacArthur's engineers may have worked to link existing tunnels to the Allied offices, allowing the provisional government to move about the city unseen and unthreatened. When they left, the Japanese government swiftly gathered whatever secrets they left behind. They have been in no hurry to make them public.

Rumors persist of secret train lines used only by the military and the government, of atomic bomb shelters under the diet building, and even an entire secret military base under the Showa Memorial Park. These are probably true. After all, you would be hard-pressed to find a government that *didn't* build an emergency get-away during the terrors of the Cold War, when the threat of nuclear bombs loomed real. The US built an entire government safe-house under a luxury hotel that has only recently been made public.

Certainly not all of these off-map tunnels lead to secret government bases. Some are truly abandoned —train lines no longer needed that serviced depopulated neighborhoods. As in most major cities, these tunnels are occupied by Tokyo's itinerant homeless population. They pry open doors and rip down condemned signs, making their way into the interior of the underground to carve out what existence they may. And something else lurks inside Japan's secret tunnels...

Yōkai—the traditional monsters of Japan—exist in the boundaries. They live in the in-between places, like the surface of the ocean or at the bottom of wells, in places that connect one realm to another. And they live in tunnels, which connect the world above with the world below.

Especially dangerous are tunnels that pass under graveyards, or through places of spiritual power.

The Shirogane tunnel in Meguro, Tokyo, is said to be a direct entrance to the spirit world. The tunnel is travelled by no less that the *shinigami*—the God of Death. When you pass through, it is said that you can catch glimpses of tormented faces lining the walls. The yūrei of the restless dead haunt underground Tokyo as well. The WWII digging craze was accomplished through Korean slave labor, and many hundreds died unburied and un-honored. Events like the 2011 tsunami swept countless corpses into the tunnels via gutters and sinkholes.

Ghosts, monsters, or secret military complexes —it is best to stay on the brightly lit paths of underground Tokyo. It's not safe to venture into the dark.

In the closing years of the Heian period (794-1185), Japan's yōkai did the most peculiar thing. They began to march. On certain nights of the year, they assembled into a cacophonous procession and pranced through the streets of the capital city of Kyoto, in what was known as the *Hyakki Yagyō* (百鬼夜行; *Night Parade of 100 Demons*). And while that may sound like a lot of fun, it was more than just a quaint superstition—it was a yōkai invasion.

No one really knows how the Hyakki Yagyō began. For all of prior history, these mysterious, dangerous, unfathomable beings—known then as *mononoke* (物の怪; *things of mystery*)—had been content to exist in their own sacred realms. They haunted the edges of civilization; the high mountains; the deep forests; the eternal sea. The places humans dared not go. Then suddenly, things changed. Without warning, the spooks came marching in.

Stories of the night parade started to appear around the 1100s, in books like the 1120 *Konjaku Monogatarishū* (*Collected Tales of Times Now Past*) and the 13th century *Uji Shūi Monogatari* (*Tales Gleaned from Uji*). The procession was invisible and undefined; an interruption of pure, elemental chaos into the ordered human civilizations. It was deadly, if you accidently stumbled upon this celebration of madness. The medieval encyclopedia called the *Shūgaishō* (*A Collection of Miscellanea*) predicted when the night parade was likely to appear, and even offered a special chant to protect you. Belief was so strong that official warnings were posted warning people to stay inside their houses on those days.

It wasn't until the Muromachi period (1337-1573) that artists got involved. The earliest known scroll painting of the parade comes from the 16th century, called the *Hyakki Yagyō-zu* (*Illustrated Picture Scroll of the Hyakki Yagyō*). There were many copies, many interpretations. Artists did what no sorcerer or priest had been powerful enough to achieve—they made the invisible visible. They took the formless chaos of the night parade and sculpted characters of the imagination. In his book *Pandemonium and Parade*, Michael Dylan Foster refers to this as "the translation of vague unreasoned fears into carefully individuated monsters."

Artists copied artists, and in a slow process personalities began to emerge. Along with rank and prominence. Creatures began to march in a certain order in the night parade. The long scrolls of the *Hyakki Yagyō-zu* were not meant to be seen at once, but unfolded like a story. You laid out a scroll and slowly unrolled it—the figures revealed themselves along the timeline of the parade. A question began to form in peoples' minds; "Who leads the Hyakki Yagyō? Who leads the yōkai invasion?"

By the Edo period (1603-1868), the invasion was complete. Yōkai had completely occupied the country, and were no longer constrained to the hinterlands. A new breed of urban yōkai arose, like the slippery *nurarihyon*, the faceless *noperabo*, and the long-necked courtesan *rokurokubi*. These human-like yōkai made their homes wherever they chose, and gave rise to a new fear—you could never quite tell if that stranger you met on a shadow-haunted night was human or yōkai.

During the 17th century, an obsession rose of naming and categorizing the monsters. Instead of

scrolls of the Hyakki Yagyō, artists began to produce yōkai encyclopedias that carefully cataloged the strange creatures. The Mikoshi Nyudō was identified as the *Yōkai Sōdaishō* (総大将; *Supreme Commander of Yōkai)*. His wife was a rokurokubi, and their cute little child Tofu Kozō became the first city-bred yōkai (and consequently the first yōkai used by a shop as a mascot.)

Humans struck back against this yōkai invasion in the Meiji period (1868-1912). Contact with the West brought new powers of science. Superstition and magic gave way to technology and industry. A conflict arose between the old and the new. When steam trains first started to chug across the Japanese landscape, drivers told tales of terrifying near-collisions with trains running the opposite way on the tracks, only to disappear the moment before contact. The next day they would inevitably find the body of a kitsune or a tanuki killed near the tracks. These shape-changing yōkai fought the first battles against technology—and lost.

More important was electricity. Even with the urban invasion, yōkai were still creatures of the darkness. Theirs was a night parade, after all. As the dark corners started to blaze with electric lights, the yōkai were repelled, forced to retreat. Manga artist and yōkai scholar Shigeru Mizuki even speculates that electricity may have caused some types of yōkai to go extinct. For the older species of yōkai, electricity was anathema. They learned to adapt, or they went away.

Perhaps the most poignant and beautiful depiction of this clash between yōkai and technology was shown in the Studio Ghibli film *Pom Poko*. In the movie, a group of magical, shape-shifting tanuki are slowly

pushed further and further away, as human civilization encroaches on their habitat. It is a reverse of the Heian period yōkai invasion—the humans now tear down the deep forests and high mountains that were the ancestral realm of the spirits. In a last, desperate defense the tanuki group together and use their magical power to summon the Hyakki Yagyō once again. But instead of inspiring awe and terror, the humans are enchanted by the night parade. The yōkai's power to generate fear is gone forever, a victim to modernity.

But that has always been the secret of the Hyakki Yagyō. When you unraveled the scroll, desperate to see who was leading the parade, who was the most powerful yōkai of all, the final scene was of the dawning sun. And then you knew. No one leads the night parade. Instead, the yōkai flee backwards into the night. Creatures of shadow and imagination, they run from the light that blinds them and renders them powerless.

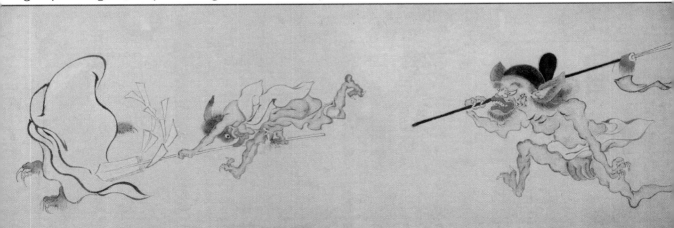

Tradition and Japanese Society

One of the best ways I know to describe Japanese society comes from the musical *Fiddler on the Roof*. In the opening song *Tradition*, Tevye the milkman tromps through his village while the townspeople sing about their lives. Boasting of the stability brought by tradition, Tevye bellows "Because of our traditions, every one of us knows who he is, and what God expects him to do."

So it is with Japan.

If you are born Japanese in Japan, for the most part you know who you are, and what God (society) expects you to do. Fathers are the workhorses, putting in long hours at jobs that demands both office time and social obligation. Mothers command the home, determining the finances and ruling over the development and education of the children. The children—sons and daughters—prepare diligently for their life ahead.

Life is routine. Structured. Ordered. From birth you fall into a groove carved centuries ago. Entrance exams let you change course a little, but once in a job raises and promotions are determined by tenure, not performance. The longer you stay at the same job, the better. In a society of 90% middle class, social climbing is rarely an option.

Inside the home, each family role comes with a proscribed set of tasks and obligations. Family members are often addressed by title instead of name—older brother, father, mother, aunt, etc... You graduate from these roles only by assuming a different title. A daughter becomes a wife. A son becomes a father. A mother becomes a grandmother. Age doesn't come into it. I was startled when a coworker once told me she woke up early and prepared breakfast for her entire family before coming to work. She was a professional in her 30s, but at home she was an unmarried daughter. She had duties to perform.

You might think these traditional roles are ancient, but they only stretch back about 400 years. Prior to the Edo period, Japan was a country tearing itself apart. The centuries of chaos and civil war called the *Sengoku Jidai*—the Warring States period—ended when Tokugawa Ieyasu seized power as the shogun in 1603. One of his great tasks was to enforce order on the country, to create structure and social framework. The tool he used was Neo-Confucianism.

Neo-Confucianism combines the ethical structure of Confucianism with the mystical elements of Dao and Japan's native Shinto religion. The basic idea is that for a wall to maintain, each brick must be individually strong. You begin with a foundation of the family, making a single, stable brick. From there you stack bricks to a slightly larger structure of the town or village, then the state or province, then the nation. The stability of the individual bricks makes the wall strong; too many bricks out of place brings the whole structure tumbling down.

The mortar that holds these bricks together is *giri*—obligation. This is one of the core concepts of Japan; you are born with debt in the way that Christians might think you are born with original

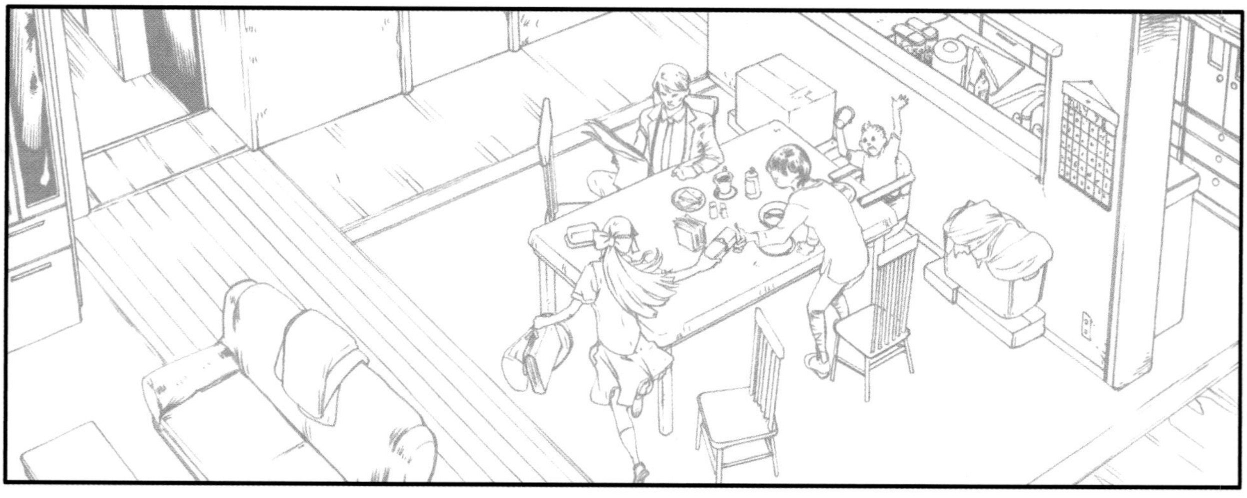

sin. By birth, you *owe* society. You have duties to your parents, to your community, to your nation. You pay back this debt by playing your assigned role; by making your brick stable.

Of course, human beings are not bricks. Opposing giri is *ninjō*—human desires. This is the secret heart of every person. The part that makes you want to chuck the family soba business and try and make it big as an actor. The part that makes you want to reject the nice, stable boy your parents picked out for the flashy jerk. Almost all traditional Japanese theater is based on the conflict between giri and ninjō, between the obligations of society and what you really want to do. There is an unwritten rule to these stories; those who chose ninjō do not get a happy ending. The best they can hope for is the romance of a double-suicide with the non-societal approved love.

Scared yet? Most Westerners see Neo-Confucianism as oppressive and terrifying. I certainly did. Even writing about it sounds terrible, like some flavor of Stalinist Russia. But that is the arrogance of the Western nations, to think our way is the best way.

While some chafe under society's expectations, many Japanese people find these roles comforting and freeing. Like Tevye sings in *Fiddler on the Roof*, each person knows who they are. With the big questions answered—Who Am I? What Does the Future Hold? What is My Place in the Universe?—they are able to focus more on enjoying life. They are at peace with themselves and their surroundings, and not in such constant conflict.

Things in Japan challenged my beliefs. A friend in her 20s asked her parents for an *omiai*—an arranged marriage. She went to "wife classes" once the marriage was arranged, and then proceeded to have children and be very happy for all the years that I knew her.

I laugh at my own cultural blindness when I thought I would liberate my wife from the demands of Japan by bringing her to the US. In fact, she found the ambiguous nature of Western society more stressful, where everybody can be anybody. Nothing was decided. Nothing was clear. Even the simple act of ordering a salad at a restaurant involved an array of options and decisions. She would get angry, saying "Why do I have to choose so much!?" In our own

relationship, she was frustrated at my lack of giri, that I didn't feel like I had obligations based on my gender. I was raised by a single mother, so the concept of "men's work" and "women's work" was a hard pill for me to swallow.

There is no easy answer. In Japan, traditions provide guidelines and safety, but at the cost of less freedom and personal choice. Or as my wife would say, at the benefit of less anxiety. And that too is a choice.

Obon - The Festival of the Dead

I stepped off the plane in Japan during high ghost season. My new home of Nara blazed with lanterns in every shrine and candles in every window. The famous Nara Park—with its tame deer and massive bronze statue of Buddha—was lit with tens of thousands of candles spread out across the dark like a starry sky. People silently wandered the park, carrying paper lanterns and dressed in traditional summer kimonos. It remains one of the most beautiful, most magical sights I have ever seen. I joked at the time that the city had gotten decked out for my birthday. I only found out later that I shared the date with a more ominous occasion—Obon, the Festival of the Dead.

Obon takes place in the summer, during a 3-day window when the walls between the world of the living (*konoyo*) and the world of the dead (*anoyo*) grow thin. Hundreds of millions of yūrei come flying back from anoyo, flooding the country with ghostly energy. This isn't as terrifying as it sounds; in fact, Obon has more in common with Thanksgiving than Halloween. These returning spirits are greeted with open arms and given honored seats at the table. After all, they are coming home for the holidays to spend time with their families.

The roots of the festival are ancient, and shrouded in mystery. Glimpses of the beliefs can be traced as far back as the Jōmon period (12,000 BCE – 300 BCE) and the haniwa grave dolls. These burial mounds and corpse houses eventually evolved into Shinto shrines, but no one really knows when or how or why the Japanese people started celebrating the return of their ancestors in the summer. Even the origins and meaning of the word Obon are unknown.

The kanji for Obon in modern times—盆 (*bon*) —literally translates as *tray*. Most people stop here, saying the name Obon comes from the serving trays and small dishes of food and drink set out to welcome home the returning dead. However, that kanji is most likely an *ateji*, selected for sound rather than meaning. Some follow the etymology along a deeper and murkier path. The Sanskrit word *ullambana*—which means *hanging upside down* and implies the suffering for spirits who have not peacefully re-incarnated—is approximated phonetically in Japanese as *urabon*. It is possible that urabon could have been shorted to read simply Obon. Or not. No one knows for sure.

No matter how you define it, Obon is one of the most important holidays in Japanese life. During those three days in the summer, Japan shows just how much they respect and revere the dead. Business are closed. People generally do not work, and many journey from the urban centers where they live to the rural homes of their ancestors. This echoes the way that the dead themselves return to their ancient homes. These spirits are acknowledged and celebrated, their graves washed clean, and fresh offerings are placed before them. Respect and appreciation are given.

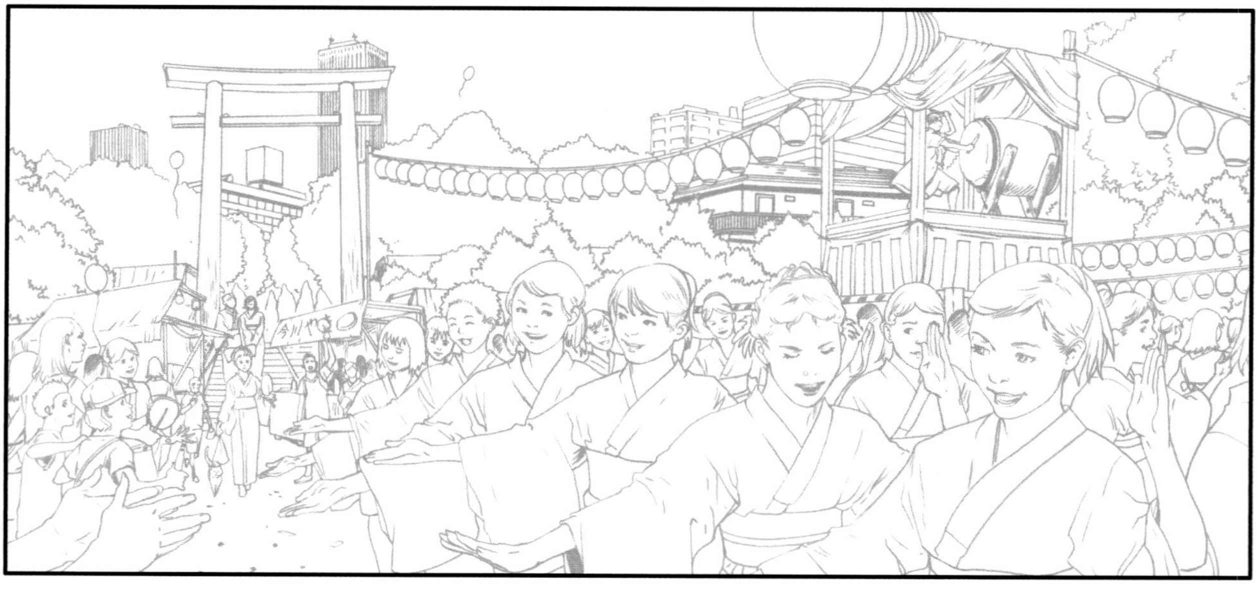

During their festival, yūrei love to be entertained. Obon features a traditional folkdance called the *bon odori*, performed for the spirits' pleasure. There are as many variations of the bon odori as there are towns and villages in Japan. Memorizing the dance begins from school age and is handed down year after year across the centuries. This dance is one of the few traditions that has been exported overseas. Anywhere there is a significant Japanese population, they dance the bon odori to honor and entertain the dead.

Obon is a festival of elements, of fire and water. According to the ancestral religions of Japan, water is a path to anoyo. An island nation, Japan is surrounded by the ocean on all sides. In the days before ocean-going travel, the misty realms that lay across the impassable oceans must have seemed a perfect place to serve as a dwelling for ancestral spirits. For three days out of every year, the wells and waterways of Japan—both the underground aqueducts as well as the visible surface rivers—transform into crowded super highways for the dead. Because of this, during Obon people stay out of the water.

Friendly as these yūrei may be, they are still spirits of the dead. Trying to escape the stifling heat of a Japanese summer, I once planned a camping trip to a mountain river during my birthday. My supervisor at work cautioned me against this quite seriously. I was told not to swim during the three days of Obon—the spirits might mistake me for one of their own and drag me back to anoyo with them.

Lanterns and fire serve as beacons to guide the dead home. Obon is sometimes translated as *The Lantern Festival* because fires are lit to guide the souls to konoyo, where the people of Japan are waiting to welcome and thank them. This can be as simple as a candle on the family altar or as fantastic as the 10,000 lanterns that light Nara Park, or the giant bonfires that glow on the sides of mountains in Kyoto.

While the dead are met with open arms, like any relatives it wouldn't do to have them out-stay their welcome. It would be even worse to have them become lost on their return to anoyo. In order to guide them back, the custom of *toro nagashi*

features candle-lit lanterns floated down the rivers and out to the sea for the spirits to follow home. Toro nagashi is an old custom. Lafcadio Hearn describes it in his book In *Ghostly Japan*, in the story At Yaidzu.

Japan during Obon is one of the world's most beautiful sites, alive with candlelight—so long as one can shake off the sensation that the world is thick with invisible yūrei, traveling up the waterways, guided by fire, and floating freely through the air as they return to the places where once they walked.

Circle of Protection Tokyo! The Goshiki Fudo

The legend goes that in the early 17th century, shogun Tokugawa Ieyasu commissioned the abbot Tenkai to generate a mystical power field surrounding Edo, the new capital of Japan. Tenkai drew a 5-pointed star around the city—the symbol of the onmyōji sorcerers. He consecrated each point of the star with a temple. Inside each temple stood a statue of the god of Fudo, each with a different eye color, facing a different direction.

- **Me-guro** (目黒: Black Eye: North; Water)
  Ryosen-ji (Spring Waterfall Temple)
- **Me-jiro** (目白: White Eye: West; Wind)
  Kornjyo-in (Parliament of the Power of Money)
- **Me-aka** (目赤: Red Eye: South; Fire)
  Nankoku-ji (South Valley Temple)
- **Me-ao** (目青: Blue Eye: East; Wood)
  Saisho-ji (Great Victory Temple)
- **Me-ki** (目黄: Yellow Eye: Center; Earth)
  Eikyu-ji (Eternity Temple)
- **Me-ki** (目黄: Yellow Eye: Center; Earth)
  Saisho-ji (Great Victory Temple)

And then there is Fudo himself. His name translates literally as "unmovable," and he looks like an oni with his fierce visage, proudly upheld sword, seated on his flaming throne. Powerful and terrifying, if you are going to pick a deity to defend your city, Fudo is a good god to gamble on.

The statues bind the power of the five sacred colors with the five elements and five directions to form a *goshiki* (五色)—a circle of protection that ensures the city's prosperity and safety. The Goshiki Fudo—the Five Fudo Temples—protect Tokyo to this day.

Or so the legend goes ...

If you look at a map, the story unravels. The temples don't make a pentagram, except in the most imaginative sense. There aren't even five. On top of that, the Goshiki Fudo are conveniently located along the central Yamanote train line that circles Tokyo.

That's right; the Goshiki Fudo are a tourist trap, with little historical basis.

The oldest known mentions of the Goshiki Fudo supposedly comes from a mystery novel popular in the Meiji period (1868-1912). The novel used the idea of the five-temple circle of protection as a plot device. It was a popular book, and the idea of a magical circle around Edo captured the imagination. Readers assumed the locations were real and went in search of them. The Black Eye and White Eye were easy enough to find. They were probably where the writer got his idea. But the other ones were a bit harder—due to the fact that they didn't exist.

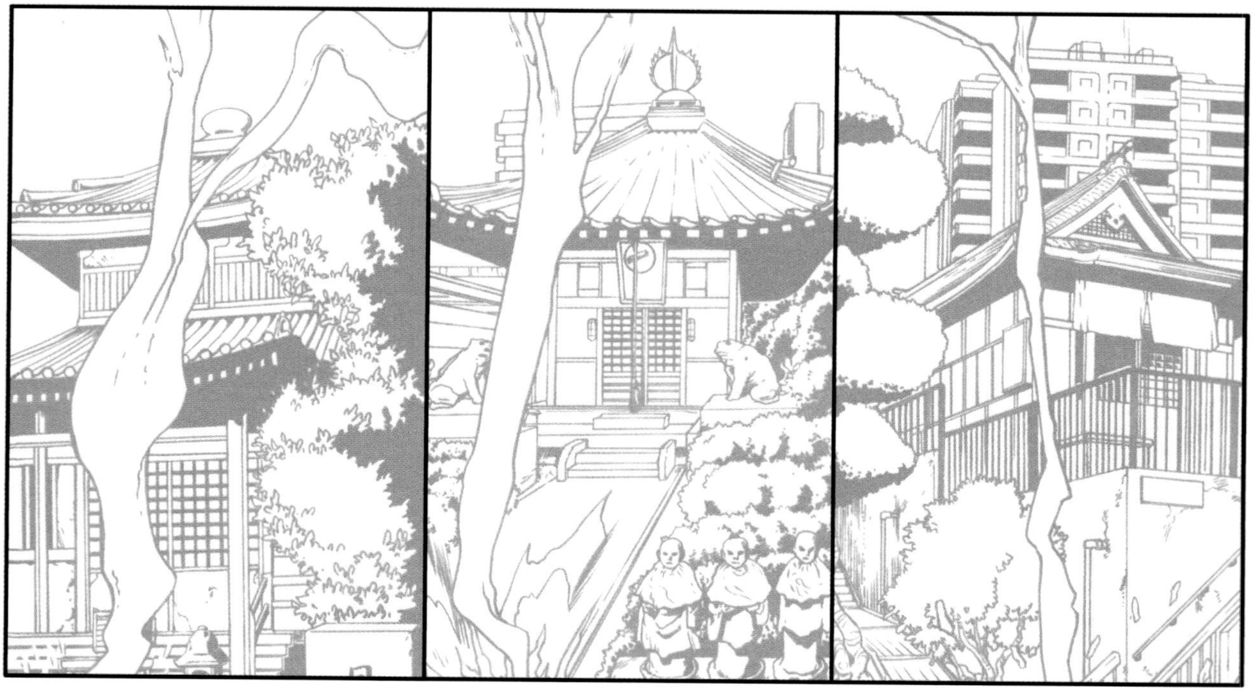

With all those tourist dollars up for grabs, it didn't take long for enterprising priests to turn these fictional locations into reality. They painted the eyes of existing statues to match the legends and declared themselves the home of the missing three Fudo. Multiple temples vied for authenticity. Finally, these settled into the six temples known today, with two still claiming to be the authentic "Yellow Eye." In reality, with the exception of the Black and White Eyes, the Goshiki Fudo can be traced to around the 1800s.

Me-guro (Black Eye) is the oldest, dating from 808 CE. Next comes Me-jiro (White Eye) from 1594, although it was actually named for a type of bird called the Japanese white-eye. Me-aka (Red Eye) dates from 1616. Its Fudo statue suddenly changed eye color in 1788 when it declared itself the authentic Red-Eyed Fudo. The statue and temple were burned to the ground in WWII, then reconstructed in 1985. The temple was relocated in 2011 with the old grounds converted into a parking lot. Me-ao (Blue Eye) is a youngster dating from 1882. It was built over the top of a previously ruined temple, and the blue-eyed Fudo statue was installed as part of construction. Of the two Me-ki (Yellow Eye), Eikyu-ji dates from 1880 with the yellow-eyed Fudo newly installed. The book *Kanto no Fudosan to Shinko* identifies this as the true Me-ki. The rival Me-ki Saisho-ji shares a name with Me-ao but is unrelated. Dating to 860, it was moved to Hirai district in 1912. The exact date of its association with the Goshiki Fudo unknown.

When researching the Goshiki Fudo for *Wayward*, the truth was disappointing. I prefer the magical and mystical. It's more fun. However, the tourist trap truth of the Goshiki Fudo was inescapable. But then I wondered if that even mattered. After all, belief often creates reality, not the other way around. In Japan, the fact that it was originally a tourist trap doesn't stop people from embracing the power of the Goshiki Fudo. The story trumps history. As it does in many cases.

Thousands visit Kinkaku-ji (*Temple of the Golden Pavilion*) in Kyoto every year, even though it was only built in 1955 and finished in 1987. They pay homage to the graves of the 47 Ronin, even though the story owes more to kabuki than history. These sites serve as a focus of belief and cultural heritage–a way to reinforce what it means to be "Japanese"—more than some factual record.

It is no different from Christians going on pilgrimages to see holy icons. They aren't "real." Any amount of research reveals that they were tourist traps too, from the Shroud of Turin to pieces of the True Cross. Or for that matter American pilgrims going to see the Liberty Bell. The fact that it could not possibly have been rung on July 4th, 1776 (as the legend goes) does not mean that the story isn't good, or prevent it from being a powerful symbol of the country. In Scotland, the Wallace Sword on display was mostly likely never held by William Wallace.

I've been to all of these sites, and felt their power. When I was in London, I went to 221b Baker Street to see the home of Sherlock Holmes and swung by Platform 9 ¾ to catch the train to Hogwarts. I knew it was pure fiction, but that didn't dampen the feeling that I was standing in the home of the Great Detective. It was magic.

Every country has similar venerated forgeries. But that doesn't affect the honest emotions they summon up for believers and non-believers alike.

After all, as a wise man once said "When the legend becomes the fact, print the legend."

Sokushinbutsu – Buddhas of the Living World

Hike up Mount Yudono in Yamagata, Japan. It's a long journey, but worth it. Aside from the beautiful scenery, if you stop by Dainichi-Bo temple along the way you might be introduced to one of Japan's most extraordinary citizens. Daijuku Bosatsu Shinnyokai Shonin won't say much; but be polite. When the priests of the temple present you before his mummified form, resplendent in Buddhist robes and seated eternally in a meditative pose, remember he is to be treated as a living person. Address him with the respect owed to one of Japan's most holy humans. That is, if someone who transformed themselves into a living Buddha can be considered human.

Sokushinbutsu (即身仏; Buddha of the Living World) are the most bizarre, gruesome, and holy relics of Japanese Buddhism. Found mostly in the Yamagata region, sokushinbutsu are created when an individual willingly undergoes *nyūjō* (入定), a 3000-day process of self-mummification.

It goes something like this:

After committing to become a sokushinbutsu, you start a 1000-day diet of nuts and seeds combined with rigorous exercise. Often this is combined with completion of holy pilgrimages, such as a thousand circuits of a holy mountain. The goal is to eliminate body fat, the most easily decomposable part of the human body. Then, you switch to a 1000-day diet of bark, roots, and pine needles. This reduces the amount of fluids in your body. Towards the end of this period, you begin drinking what is essentially lacquer—a special tea made from the sap of an urushi tree. This expels remaining bodily fluids, and embalms you from the inside out to repel maggots and decomposing insects.

Having become a living skeleton, you take the final step—you are interred into a tomb, where you assume the lotus position and begin meditation. The tomb is tiny, with just enough room to sit. A small air tube leads outside. In your hand is a bell. You ring the bell daily to signal you remain alive. When the bell rings no more, the monks pull up the air tube and seal the tomb. After a further 1000 days, the tomb is open and your body exhumed.

If your body is decomposed, then you have failed. The attempt is respected, but you are were not holy enough. If your body has mummified—if you sit in the lotus position rigid and intact—then you have proven your worth. You are not dead, but transformed into a manifest Buddha, to be worshipped forever more.

The long, horrific trial is far from guaranteed. In fact, between the 11th and 19th centuries of the hundreds of monks who attempted to become sokushinbutsu less than 30 are known to have succeeded. The last was Bukkai Shonin, who was buried in 1900. By 1903 the practice had been outlawed and he was left in the ground. When he was finally dug up in 1961, it was discovered that he had succeeded in his attempt.

What was the point of this gruesome self-torture?

Sokushinbutsu was the ultimate manifestation of the practice of meditation—*corpus ascensus*. To many Westerners, meditation is thought to be relaxing and contemplative. People practice it to heal their minds and bodies, and feel rejuvenated afterwards. Zen brings up images of flowing saffron robes and ancient temples illuminated by candlelight. But true Japanese Buddhist meditation is far from relaxing. It is an endurance test, where you subject yourself to pain in order to train your spiritual dominance over the demands of your body. In temple Zen meditation, waiting monks beat you

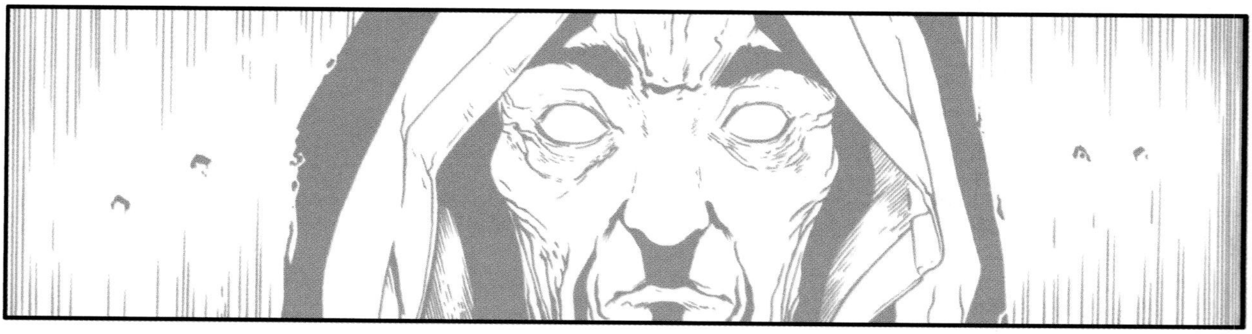

with bamboo rods while you maintain your focus. Some took it further. There is a reason why samurai meditated under ice cold waterfalls; it wasn't because the waterfall delivered a gentle massage.

The practice of sokushinbutsu was thought to have been brought to Japan from Tang China by the miraculous Kobo Daishi. One of the holiest people in Japanese Buddhist history, it is no bad comparison to say Kobo Daishi is as revered as Jesus or Mohammad—although perhaps not with the same fervor. He is the revealer of the Shingon —the "true word" of Japanese Buddhism. Temples founded by Kobo Daishi decorate Japan. Books are filled with records of his miracles.

Towards the end of his life, Kobo Daishi stopped eating and dedicated himself to meditation. At the end, he was entombed on the eastern peak of the holy Mount Kōya. When the tomb was opened much later, Kobo Daishi was found still seated in the lotus position, looking unchanged by death. His followers declared he had not died at all, but was only deep in meditation. He sits there still, awaiting the appearance of Maitreya, the future Buddha

Those happy few who transformed into sokushinbutsu are far more than symbols. Their bodies are pure and incorruptible. They are manifest transcendence, physical vessels of enlightenment. Potent artifacts, sokushinbutsu exude spiritual power. Others may gain the benefit of their purity simply by standing in their presence. Of the 28 known, 16 are on open display. Others were hidden, becoming *hibutsu*-secret Buddhas. And perhaps there are more. In 2015 a statue in China was x-rayed and revealed a 1000-year old sokushinbutsu disguised inside. No one knows how many others remain unrevealed.

Walking through Seattle the other day, I was reminded of the difference between Western and Japanese ideas of meditation. I saw ads for a new condominium building promising "Zen living in the heart of Downtown." Their poster showed a woman in a yoga pose, surrounded by images of relaxation and gentle nature. I wondered how many condos they would sell if they continued the woman's meditative pose to the conclusion favored by Kobo Daishi, slowly starving herself on a diet of berries and pine needles while drinking bowls of

lacquer to harden her insides until she transformed herself into something not quite living but not quite dead—a sokushinbutsu; a Buddha of the Living World.

The Red String of Fate

This story comes from long ago, from Tang dynasty China (618-907 CE):

"A young man named Iko was traveling about the country, when he came upon a waypoint town in southern Souki. In front of the gates to the town there was a mysterious old man. He sat in the middle of an enormous pile of books, all of which were illuminated by a moonbeam. The old man's books concerned themselves with the spiritual worlds. He was diligently reading them.

When Iko approached to ask what he was reading, the man told him that all human marriages were decided when the spirits were still in their raw state. Human beings were created as a pair, and an unbreakable red rope bound two souls together by the ankle. No matter the time or distance that separated them, any two people bound by this red rope would eventually be drawn together. This was their destiny.

Iko said that he had recently proposed marriage, but the old man told him it wouldn't work. He could see the red rope bound him to another. Iko was joined to a 3-year old orphan girl, being raised by a vegetable dealer in that very town. Iko was enraged. He said this was a lie, and told his servant to locate and murder the child. The servant found her, and stabbed her with a knife between her eyes—then ran away in fear.

14 years later, Iko rose in position but was still unmarried. One of his superiors introduced him to a 17-year old woman of astounding beauty, and they were soon wed. Iko was entranced by his new bride, and on their wedding night he noticed a small scar between her eyes. Asking about it, she replied that as a child she was suddenly attacked for no reason, but the knife only cut the skin before her attacker fled. Iko realized it was that same 3-year old girl that he was bound to, and he came to realize that what the old man had said was true."

This is the oldest known story of what is called the unmei no akai ito (運命の赤い糸), the red string of fate. The legend comes from China, and concerns the lunar deity and god of marriage Yue Xia Lao (月下老). According to the stories, Yue Xia Lao binds two souls together with an unbreakable red cord wrapped around their ankles. As they wander through life, this cord may stretch or become tangled with others, but its draw is irresistible. The destined lovers will come together, and recognize each other as soulmates.

It's a romantic legend, and one that has spread across all of East Asia. In Japan the *unmei no akai ito* is found extensively in romance novels and comics aimed at young girls, who dream of their own red cord binding them to some handsome lover as yet unmet. Popular anime and manga like

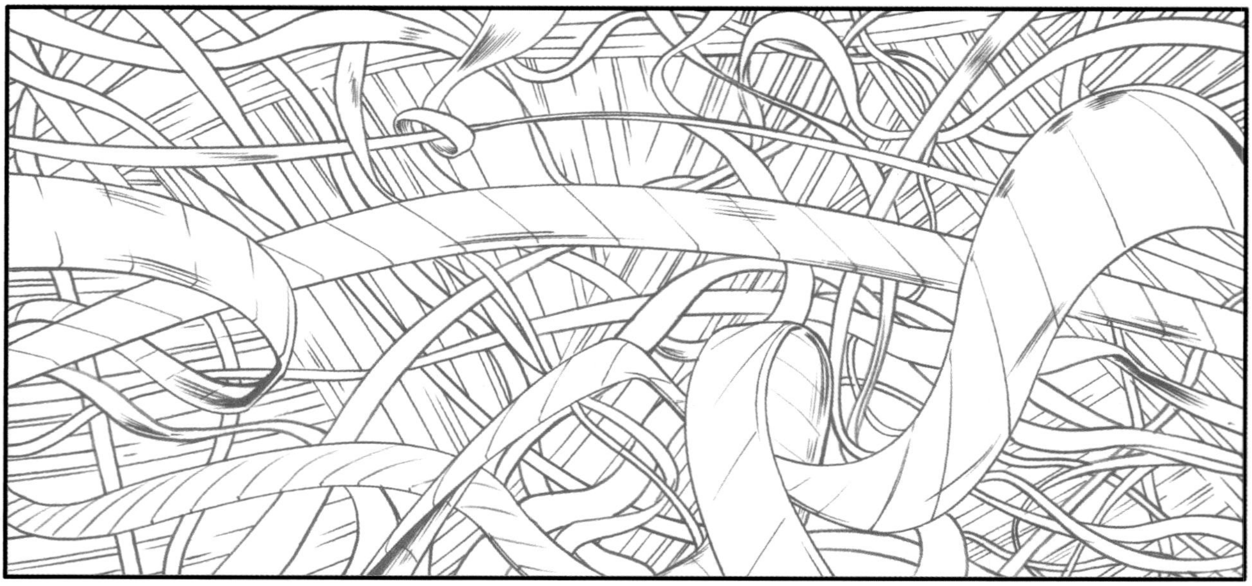

Ai Yori Aoshi, *Free!*, and even *Naruto* are filled with the red cord, showing it tying together the often-convoluted collection of characters that populate the stories. Although in Japan it is usually tied around the pinky finger instead of the ankle as it is in China.

But the magic of the red string goes beyond frivolous romance—if a driving force in human nature can be called frivolous. There is power in red cords. Many cultures have recognized this; like the Jewish *segula* of a red wool bracelet knotted seven times and worn around the left wrist to protect from the evil eye and other calamities; or the knot magic of Celtic and Chinese traditions.

Across many cultures, across many times, weaving has also been seen as magical. The way that individual threads are deftly woven together to create a pattern is a metaphor for human society. We are all threads in the weave. We all combine to create the Great Tapestry of Life. And because we are so tightly woven, none of us has the distance required to see the pattern of the cloth. Or to know whose hand is doing the weaving.

In ancient Greece it was the Moirai who wove the threads. Three crones carefully measured out the thread of each person's life, determining its length and the role it would take in the pattern. Clotho spun the thread from her distaff. Lachesis measured its length with her rod. Finally Atrops chose the manner of each person's death before severing the thread with her sheers. Even the gods of Olympus were subject to their rule. In Norse mythology these women were called the Norns, and their names were Urðr (Wyrd), Verðandi, and Skuld. Other cultures have similar variants.

Japan does not have a mythology of weavers of fate, but acknowledges that act of stitching adds additional power. During the first and second world wars, Japanese soldiers were often equipped with *senninbari* (千人針; thousand-person stitches). These were prepared by mothers, sisters, and wives who would wander through town with a white belt, begging other women to stitch a single red thread on the belt, until a thousand women had given their blessing. Senninbari were worn as protection against bullets and other harm—a

powerful talisman combining the strength of the red thread with the power of binding one thread to another.

Belief in the thread runs deep. There are matchmakers who claim the power to see the thread, and whose services are in high demand. While researching this article, I asked my own wife if she believed we were connected by an *unmei no akai ito*. She looked at me like I was stupid—we met in a bar on New Year's Eve, while going up to order drinks at the bar at the same time. Two weeks later she moved in, and now we have been together ten years. What else could it be, she said, but the power of the red string drawing us together?

Akaname

垢嘗 (Lit: Filth Licker)

Yōkai come in many forms, from devolved deities like the kappa to visual puns like kyōkotsu. Some even play a more traditional role, one found in every culture on earth—that of the bogeyman. Parents use these yōkai to frighten their children into good behavior. In the case of the akaname-the filth licker—they scare children into keeping the bathtub clean. Do your chores, or a monster will come to get you!

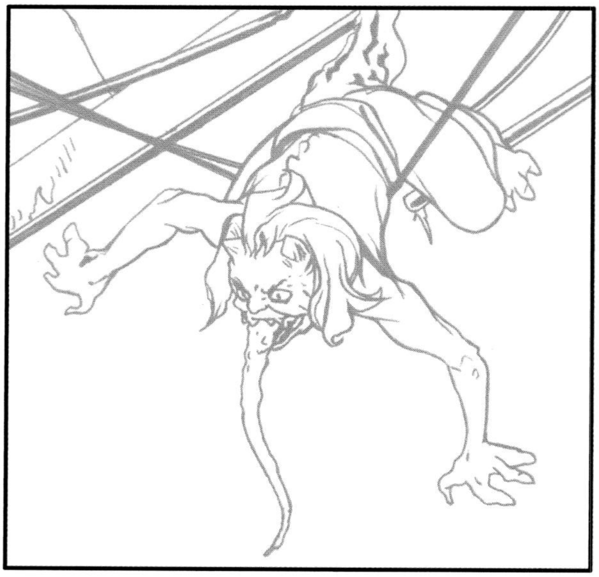

The bath is a venerated space in a Japanese home. More than just a place to get clean, the bath is where you relax and carve out some much-needed privacy in a packed house. Families wash outside of the tub, then climb in to soak. Everyone uses the same bathwater, and the bath is entered by order of Confucian precedence—the father first, then the mother, then the children by birth order. This means the tub gets progressively dirty (and the water more lukewarm) by the time the youngest child climbs in. As insult to injury, the youngest child is often responsible for cleaning the tub.

A dirty tub is a feast for akaname. The cockroaches of yōkai, they scutter in after dark and lick the remaining scum from the bathtub. While this may seem like a free cleaning service, they are pestilence bringers as well as just plain disgusting. Akaname come in an infinite variety; they can be any color from a filthy, moldy green to the bright pink of open sores. They can have one eye or two, and different counts of fingers and toes. The one characteristic all akaname share is their long, sticky tongue that they use to lap up the grease, hair, and filth left behind in the family bath.

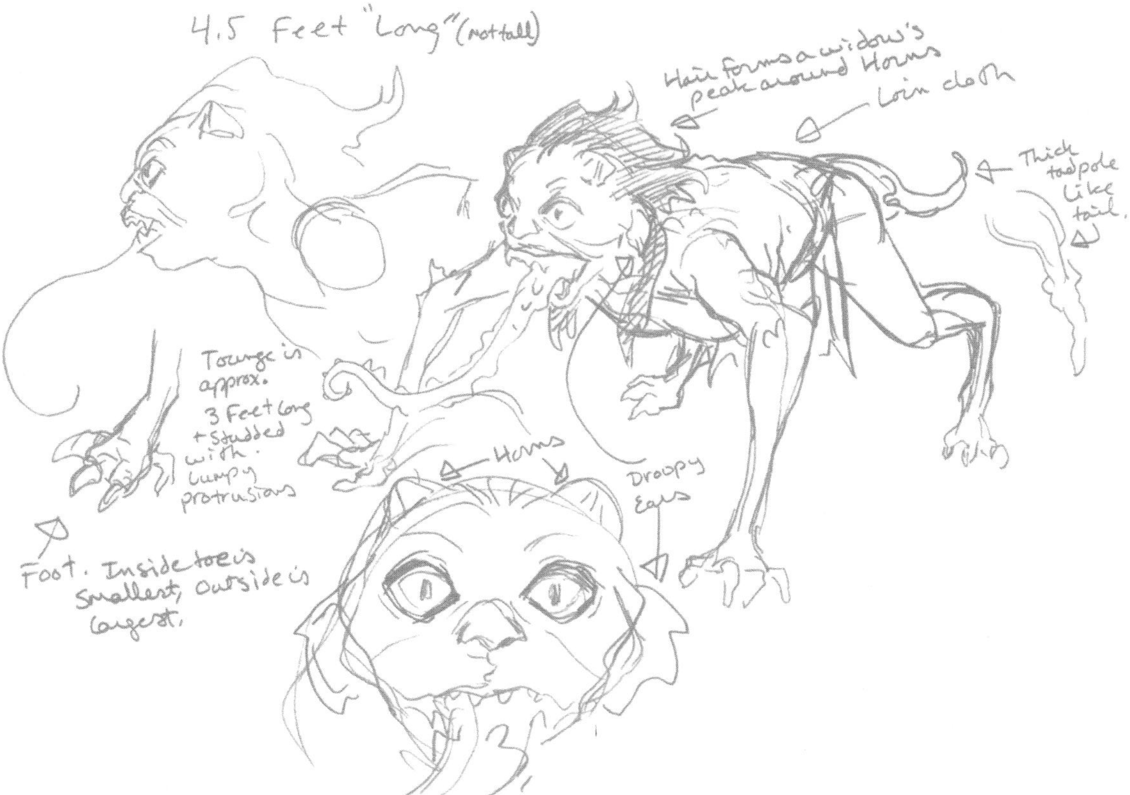
4.5 Feet "Long" (not tall)
Hair forms a widow's peak around Horns
Loin cloth
Thick tadpole like tail.
Tounge is approx. 3 Feet Long + Studded with lumpy protrusions
Horns
Droopy Ears
Foot. Inside toe is smallest, outside is largest,

Will-o'-the-wisp. Foxfire. Corpse candles. There are many names in many cultures for the small balls of ghostly fire that appear during the twilight hours over bogs and swamps and graveyards. Scientists explain them away as the oxidation of hydrogen phosphide and methane gases produced by the decay of organic material—like rotting corpses. But they have long served a dual role in Japan as spirits of the dead as well as mysterious and spectral lanterns accompanying other supernatural creatures.

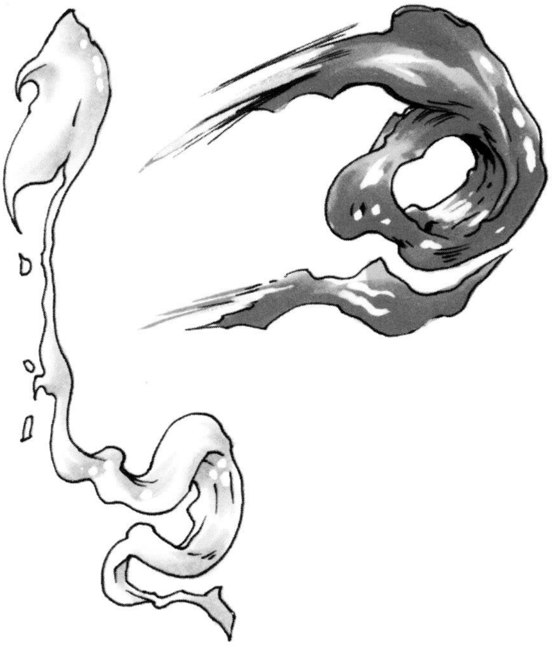

These balls of fire go by various names in Japan, each with its own nuance. *Onibi* (鬼火, demon fire) are dangerous evil spirits that can drain the life force from living things. *Kitsunebi* (狐火, foxfire) are manifestations of fox magic, summoned by magical foxes to light their processions. *Aosagibi* (青鷺火, blue heron fire) is the powdery breath of the magical blue heron, drifting lazily from treetop to treetop in the night. There are many more.

And then there are *hitodama*, which translates as human soul. They usually accompany some sort of spirit, such as *yūrei*—fully manifested ghosts. Alone hitodama pose little danger, serving only as ill omens or to announce the presence of paranormal activity. They are often seen lingering around old shrines and ancient battlefields.

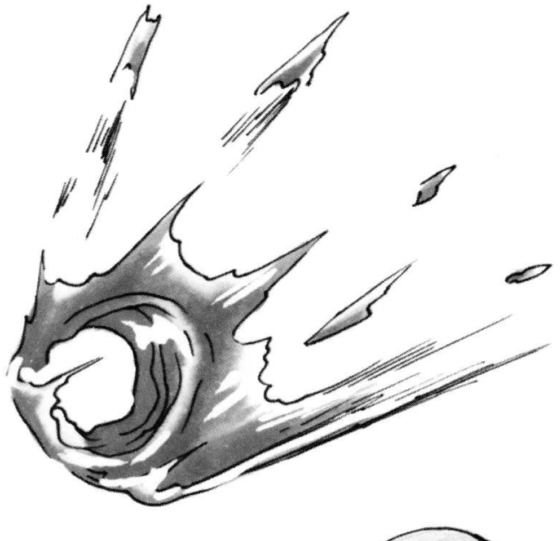

The exact nature of hitodama is a mystery. Are they souls of the dead, as the name implies? Are they lingering pieces of human essence? Are they human souls, as the name implies? Are they some lingering essence, not able to manifest as a full-blown yūrei, yet still not able to pass over complete to anoyo? Perhaps they are little more than whorls in the supernatural ether that surrounds Japan. Nobody knows.

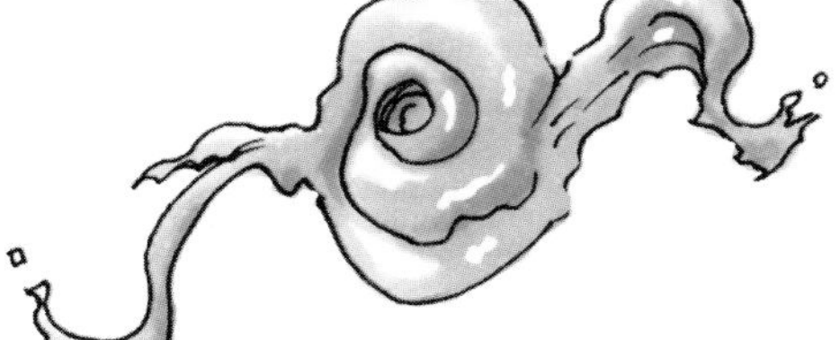

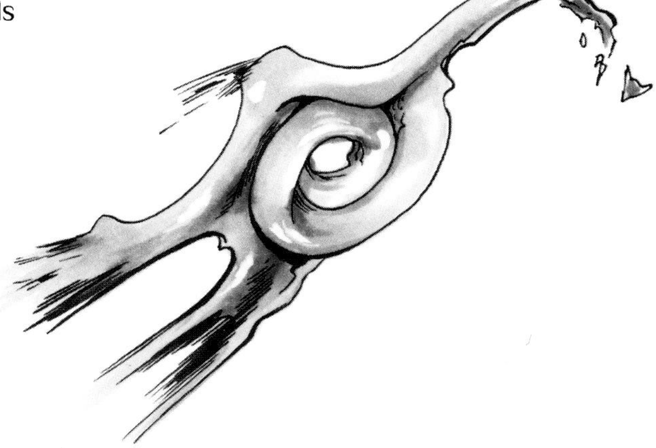

Sometimes a yōkai tells you almost everything you need to know about it in its name. That's the case with hyakume, the 100-eyed yōkai. It's a blobby fellow with a body covered in a hundred eyes. However, hyakume does hold a rare place in the yōkai pantheon by being one of the first to debut on the modern medium of television.

From 1966-67, yōkai grand master Shigeru Mizuki had his first TV hit with a tokusatsu (special effects) adaptation of his comic *Akuma-kun* (*Devil boy*). Tokusatsu shows like *Ultraman* and the various *Sentai Rangers* series (known in English as *Power Rangers*) thrive on weekly oddities and monsters that can be thrown at their heroes. For *Akuma-kun*, Mizuki created a host of weird creatures, including the all-seeing beast hyakume.

Some note that hyakume bears a resemblance to an illustration in Carl Jung's *Symbole der Wandlung* (*Symbols of Transformation*). Well-read and deeply interested in philosophy and symbols, this is most likely the source of Mizuki's design. There is also an Edo period illustration of a hyakubyakume oni (百々眼鬼; *hundreds and hundreds-eyed oni*) that may have been an influence.

As a yōkai, hyakume's strength is also its weakness. They often set up as guards, their all-seeing eyes able to spot thieves in the thickest of darkness. Their eyes can even detach and stick to infiltrators. But their sensitive eyes cannot tolerate sunlight

—nor has the sunglasses been made yet that can shield all hundred eyes.

Mizuki liked hyakume. He later pitted him against his other famous creation *Kitaro*, and even added hyakume to his yōkai encyclopedias that form the foundation of supernatural knowledge for Japan. It wasn't long until hyakume was absorbed into Japan's monster lore, the monster's television origins forgotten.

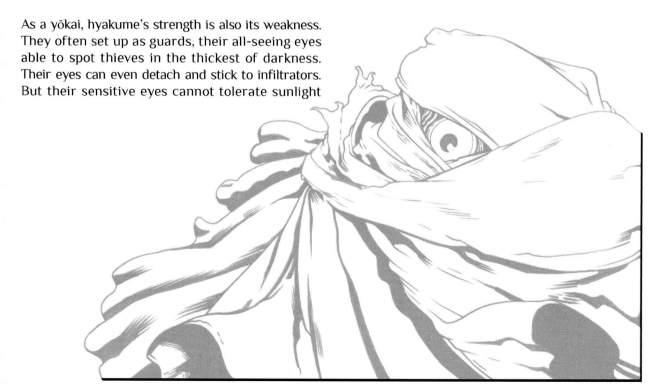

When Tokugawa Ieyasu seized control of Japan as shogun in 1603, he established peace by absolute control. Unable to ban people's desire for pleasure and indulgence, he attempted to contain it. Tokugawa established three great walled pleasure quarters (*yakuko*), in Kyoto, Edo, and Osaka. These pleasure quarters were like Disneyland and Las Vegas combined. Cloaked in fantasy, it was only a short time before urban legends and mythologies arose about their denizens. Many of the prostitutes of the yakuko were rumored to be yōkai—bakeneko or kitsune or other transformed animals. But none were more dangerous than *jorōgumo*—whore spiders.

As you can see by their name, jorōgumo were predatory yōkai prostitutes disguised as beautiful women. They are said to be proficient in biwa music, and strummed their instruments to lure in customers. Once inside, customers would be wrapped in spider silk and slowly consumed by the evil yōkai.

There are several known nests of jorōgumo throughout Japan, such as the Jōren Falls in Shizuoka or Kashikobuch in Sendai. Most of these are near water, relating to legends of hapless lumberjacks who were almost pulled in by the jorōgumo's webs. The lumberjacks managed to survive by fixing her silk to a nearby tree stump. Belief persists in jorōgumo in these locations, and shrines have been created attempting to transform the monsters into guardian spirits who protects people from drowning.

Jorōgumo were included by Toriyama Sekien in his first yōkai encyclopedia, *Gazu Hyakki Yagyō* (*The Illustrated Night Parade of a Hundred Demons*). Their inclusion in this first volume marks her as a legitimate folkloric creature, instead of one of Sekien's own creations. However he wrote nothing more about them than their name.

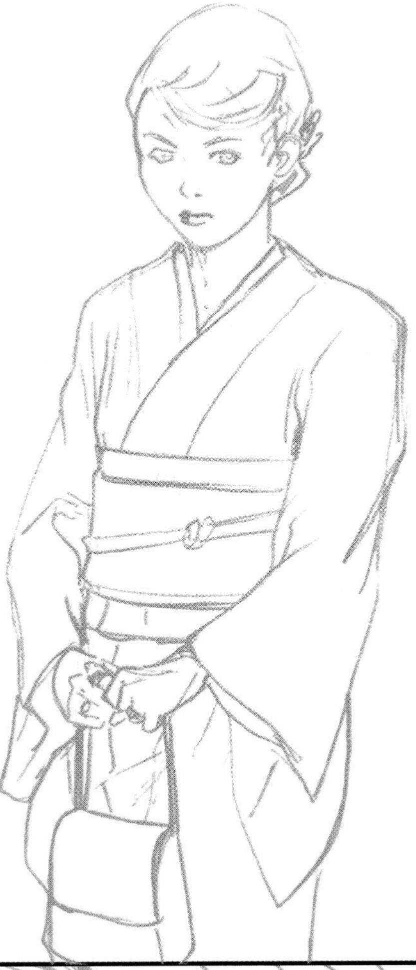

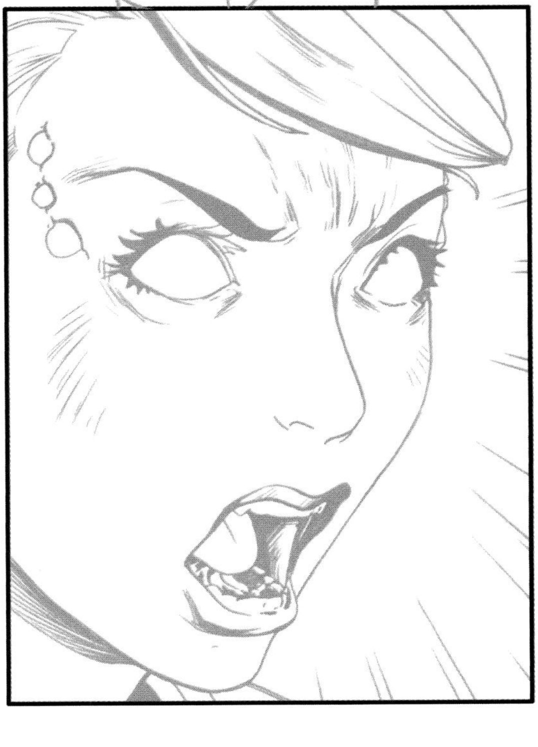

One of the most ubiquitous yōkai in Japan, kappa are found wherever there is fresh water, throughout the Japanese islands. Once worshiped as gods of the rivers (and indeed you can still find shrines dedicated to kappa across Japan), they are now viewed as little more than mischievous imps—albeit dangerous.

Traditionally about the size of a small person, kappa appear as humanized turtles, complete with shell and beak. Even with their small size, they are stronger than normal humans. Their skin is green and mottled, and their hands and feet are webbed and studded with claws. They reek of fish. The kappas' most distinctive feature is the bowl-shaped indentation on their heads. This small bowl holds a reservoir of water that is said to be the source of their powers. If the water is spilled, they have to return to their river or die—although some kappa adapted to wear metal plates over their bowl for protection.

Myths about kappa are myriad, and show their changeable nature. Their arms are detached from their bodies—pulling on one arm shortens the other. Their favorite foods are cucumbers and the elusive *shirikodama* —a magical ball that resides in the human anus which kappa forcibly rip out in brutal attacks.

Their level of civilization is also fluid. The 1910 *Tono Monogatari* portrays kappa as barbarians who raid fishing villages and rape women. Other folklore describes them as civilized and intelligent; they are said to have taught medicine and bone-setting to humans, and are masters of the strategy game *shogi*. In Ryunosuke Akutagawa's 1927 book Kappa, they are portrayed as having a society based on radical capitalism, where poor kappa are slaughtered as food for the wealthy class.

In modern Japan, kappa experienced a renaissance lately, depicted as children's toys or cute, harmless mascots for sushi restaurants. But underneath the plastic smiles and friendly waves lie the brutal monsters of folklore.

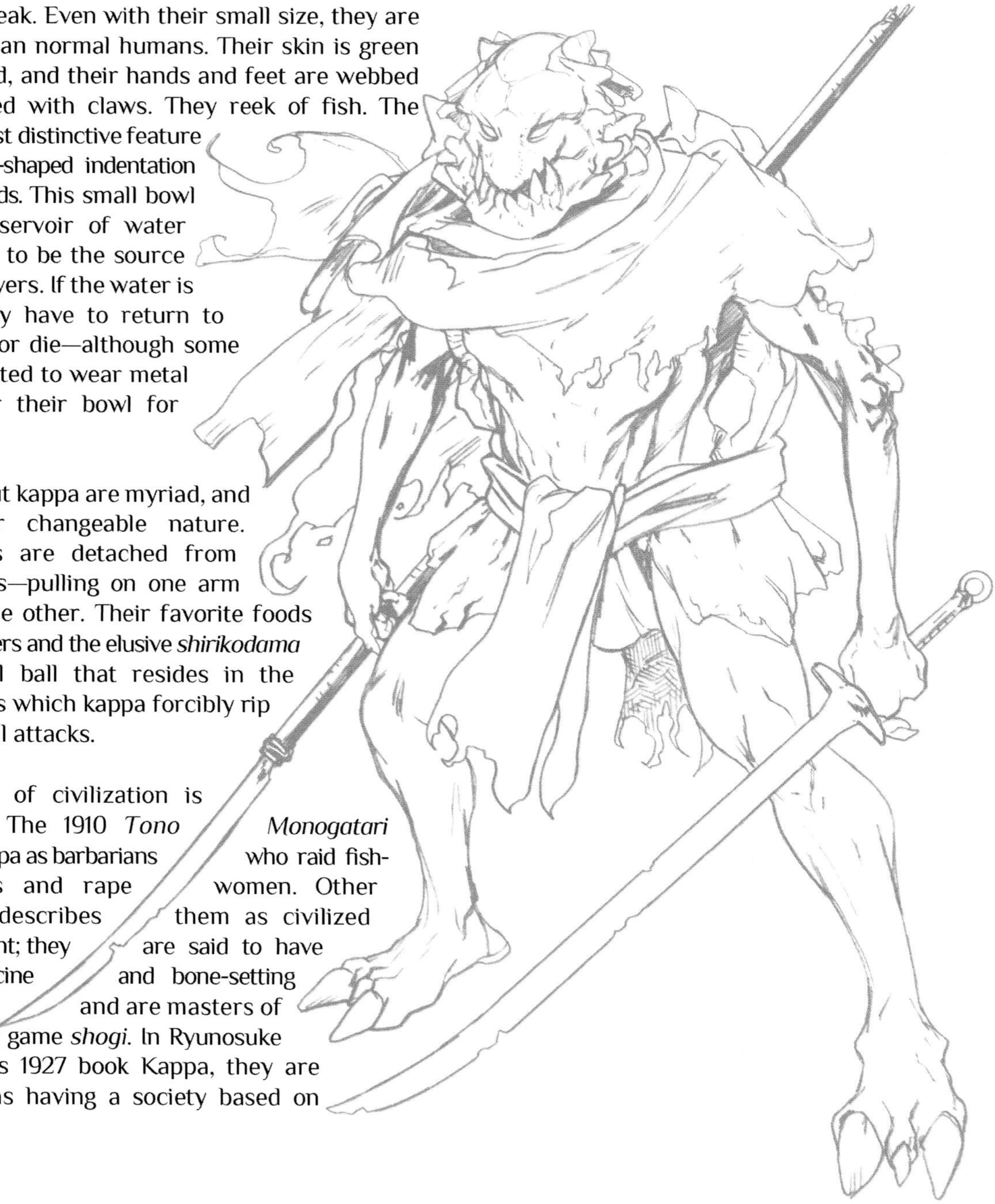

Wander off any beaten path in Japan, towards any shadow-haunted corner, and you will inevitably run into a pair of stone foxes, grim-faced and daunting, standing guard before a sequence of lonely red gates. The atmosphere of these shrines is different from other places—they are not for tourists. These are the fox shrines, dedicated to the kami Inari and her messengers the kitsune, the magical foxes of Japan.

Kitsune (狐) are the most complex and abstruse yōkai in Japan's menagerie. Simultaneously sacred and profane, good and evil, celestial and earth-bound, they are a study in contrasts. Kitsune are the servitors of gods, and worshipped as gods in their own right. They are the husbands and wives of poor farmers, hiding their true natures with their shape-shifting abilities. Kitsune wield vast magical powers, and are sorcerers feared across the land. They are also vermin and trouble-makers who possess humans for no other reason than to get their hands on some tasty fried tofu. On days when rain falls from a blue sky, they hold their wedding ceremonies. On dark nights, balls of fire ignite from their tails. Their stories are as mercurial as the kitsune themselves.

Part of their wayward nature comes from the multiple sources for kitsune legends. While there is some dispute, most scholars agree that stories of magical foxes are not native to Japan. The majority of the oldest known Japanese kitsune stories come from the 12th century collection *Konjaku Monogatarishu* (*Tales of Times Now Past*). This 33-volume series collected the magical tales of China, India, and Japan. It is thought that the kitsune stories were based on Chinese legends of *huli jing*, mischievous, nine-tailed, shape-shifting fox spirits that behave similar to European fairies. Whatever their origin, kitsune were adopted with gusto by Japan, which quickly adapted and expanded on the tales of the huli jing.

In Japan, kitsune belong to a class of yōkai called henge, transformed animals who have gained supernatural powers through long life. The necessary longevity varies legend-by-legend, but in general kitsune must reach 50 years of age before they come into their powers. When they attain 100 years old, they gain an extra tail and more abilities, and then another tail and level-up each subsequent century until they reach their ultimate form, a glorious nine-tailed fox—immortal and immensely powerful—called a *kyubi no kitsune*.

Like almost all transformed animals, kitsune have the ability to shape-shift and cast illusions. While skilled, they are not the most powerful in either of these arts. In a classic tale, a kitsune challenged a tanuki to a contest of illusions, and paid with his life. According to a common saying kitsune are able to take seven forms, while tanuki can take

Mystical Markings on the Head ——▷

In fox form they are very Bulky.

eight, and itachi (weasels) are the most capable, with ten forms to flow between. The seven forms of the kitsune are enough, however. There are myriad tales of kitsune who assume human form, get married and have children, then are betrayed by a fox tail poking out of a kimono on a warm summer's night.

But the true terror of a kitsune was in possession. Just as in old Europe, where mental illness was blamed on demonic possession, in old Japan the finger was pointed at kitsune whenever someone started acting strangely or frothed at the mouth. Many was the story of a mother who murdered her own children in a fit of rage, or a man found wandering naked in the streets, bathed in the blood of his own horse. In cases like this, there could always be a den of foxes found nearby to take the blame. Sometimes this possession was intentional; sorcerers called *kitsunetsukai* (狐使い; fox users) commanded kitsune and used their abilities for nefarious purposes. Percival Lowell detailed cases of fox possession in his 1895 book Occult Japan, as did Lafcadio Hearn for his 1894 *Glimpses of Unfamiliar Japan*. During the Edo period, *kitsunetsuki* (狐憑き; fox possession) was a very real problem.

At the same time that they were considered dark devils, the familiars of foul sorcerers, kitsune were also sacred messengers and avatars of the kami spirit Inari, the goddess of rice and fortune. The origin of the connection with Inari is uncertain; they first appeared as her messengers, and the stone statues of Inari shrines still carry document rolls in their mouths. Eventually, the myths of Inari and her fox guardians merged until the goddess herself was depicted as an immense white fox.

Myths of the white fox are as contradictory as the kitsune themselves. Some see two distinct species of kitsune; the pure white *zenko* (善狐; good foxes) or the base-colored *yako* (野狐; field foxes). However these zenko were not always as pure as their fur. In the 16th century, the warlord Takeda Shingen became obsessed with a 14-year-old girl, the Lady Koi. Rumor had it that Koi was a white fox in disguise, the spirit of the Suwa Shrine bewitching the mighty warlord.

Fox shrines are scattered all across Japan, usually kept apart from the main buildings in some sparse and gloomy place. Worship is conducted by buying a small red gate and placing it before the shrine. There are exceptions to Inari's solitary nature, most especially the famous Fushimi Inari outside of Kyoto city, with literal tunnels of red tori gates placed by petitioners. The spectacular vision of Fushimi Inari has led to its appearance in films like Memoirs of a Geisha. But the pretty scene belies a more sinister nature.

Good or bad, sacred or profane, kitsune are always dangerous and not to be dealt with lightly. They are honorable after their fashion, and will keep their bargains. But a warning at these shrines—kitsune are powerful and can make wishes come true, but they exact a heavy price. More than most people are willing to pay.

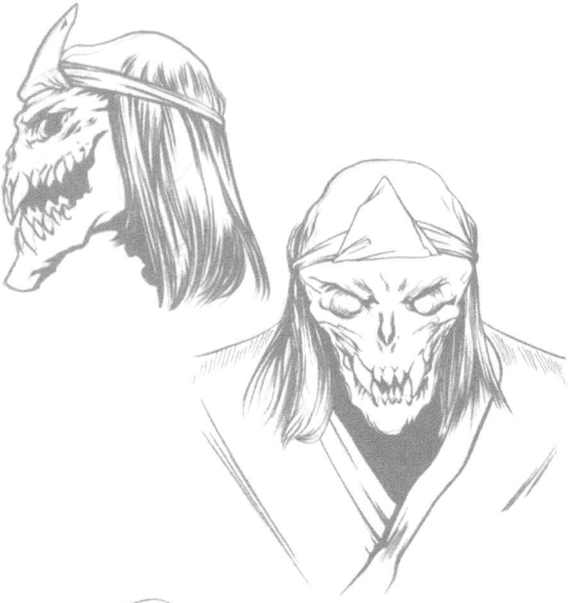

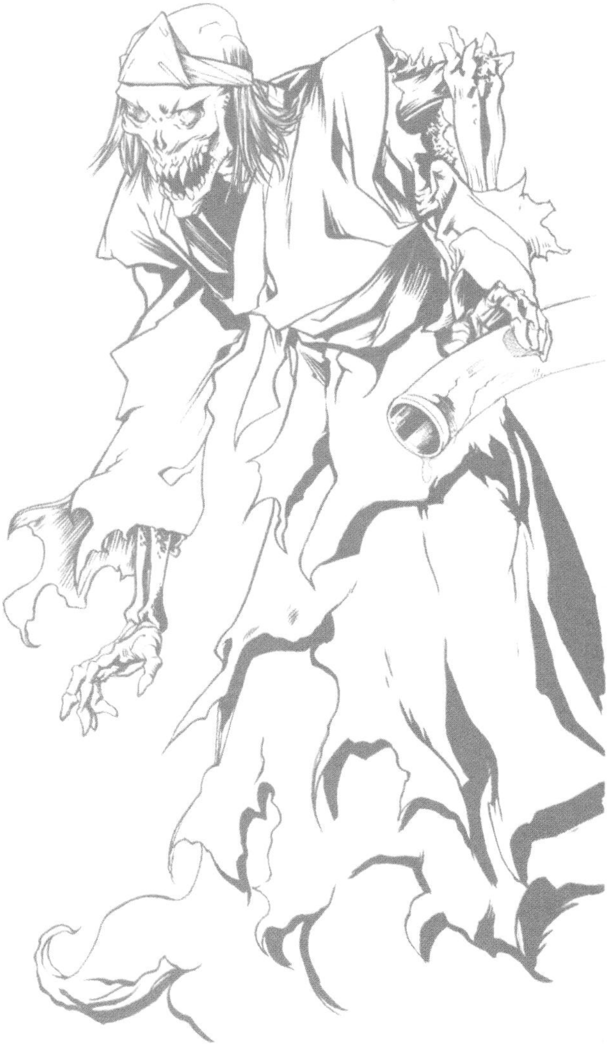

Be careful when you pull up a bucket of water from an ancient, abandoned well—you can get more than you bargained for. Draw from the wrong well and a *kyōkotsu* might come popping up, like some skeletal Jack-in-the-Box eager to deliver its curse.

Clad in a white burial kimono, kyōkotsu appear as little more than bones wrapped in a shroud. Shocks of white hair spring from their bleached-white skulls. They are thought to arise from people who were murdered and had their bodies stuffed into wells to hide the deed. Angry at being undiscovered and unburied, the bones reanimate and attack anyone unfortunate enough to come within their reach.

At least that's the theory. In reality, the kyōkotsu was invented by artist Toriyama Sekien for his Edo period book *Supplement to the Hundred Demons of the Past*. Publishers were desperate for Toriyama to produce sequels to his popular *Hundred Demons* books, but the unfortunate truth was that he had run out of folkloric yōkai to catalogue. So Toriyama did what any good artist would do—he made up new ones. Several of Toriyama's yōkai, like kyōkotsu, are based on puns and turns of phrases. The word "kyōkotsu" literally translates as "crazy bones," which was a slang term for violent or aggressive men. Toriyama's "kyōkotsu" was not unlike a modern monster artist creating his own "lazy bones" character.

Toriyama did have a basis for his creation. In Japanese folklore, water is a channel to the world of the dead, and the bottoms of wells are directly connected. Those who died in wells—by accident, suicide, or murder—were thought to be bound to it. Their curse was indiscriminate, attacking anyone who came too near. With his creation, Toriyama tapped into the old belief of an inexhaustible grudge that can come from water and the bottom of wells.

Japan is full of cats. Not pets; not tame cats quietly curled up at the foot of the bed. Just cats. They slink in alleyways. They haunt Shinto shrines. They lurk in shadows. There is an entire island off the coast of Tokyo where cats have taken over, roaming in and out of human houses as they please, taking what they want, and generally lounging around in what amounts to a cat paradise on earth. And with their nocturnal habits, ability to move silently, and eyes that glitter and change size in the flashing of lights, cats are natural yōkai.

Japan's cat-lore is vast and deep. Known collectively as *kaibyō* (怪猫; *strange cats*), magical cats come in many types—like the split-tailed *nekomata* (猫又; *again cat*), the shape-changing *bakeneko* (化猫; *changing cat*), the cat/human hybrid *neko musume* (猫娘; *cat daughter*), the beckoning *maneki neko* (招猫; *inviting cat*), and the corpse-stealing *kasha* (火車; *fire cart*). Depending on their variety, their magical powers are equally varied. They can predict the weather. They manipulate corpses like puppets. They bring good luck. Only kappa surpass cats for sheer variety of yōkai species.

Along with tanuki and kitsune, cats are one of the primary magical animals of Japanese folklore. Classified as *henge* (変化), these animals are shape-shifters who gain magical powers from long life. All henge have different ages, but cats generally come into their power from 12-13 years old. Just to

be on the safe side, Edo period cat owners were cautioned to kill their cats after 7 years. And while their fellow henge tanuki and kitsune have been pushed from their homes and seen their numbers diminished, cats adapted to modernity and urban environments. In fact, kaibyō are more prevalent now than they were in ancient times.

The oldest actual Japanese cats on record are the monstrous *yamaneko* (山猫; *mountain cat*). Little is known of these ancient wild cats except that they existed from as far back as the Jōmon period (14.000-300 BCE) and seem to have gone extinct sometime during the Yayoi period (300 BCE - 300 CE). Yamaneko were as big as cougars, and supposedly stripped like tigers. Like many cryptids, rumors persist of yamaneko surviving to the modern day, but there is little evidence.

Cat history then jumps ahead by about 700 years. By most accounts, domestic cats arrived in Japan around the year 1000 CE, as a gift to the Emperor from China. Other accounts show cats in the Nara period (710-794), but there is confusion due to the writing system using identical kanji (狸) for both cats and tanuki. From the Nara period comes the oldest known magical cat, the *mikeneko* (三毛猫; *three-colored furry animal*). This was a dangerous beast with fiery eyes, incredibly intelligent but vengeance prone against anyone who betrayed its secrets.

Gift from China or not, it is around the Heian period that magical cats appeared in earnest in Japanese writing and folklore. Exotic animals, incredibly expensive and exclusively the toys of aristocratic ladies of the court, cats appeared in works like *Genji Monogatari*, *The Tale of the Bamboo Cutter*, and *Essays in Idleness*. Sei Shōnagon described the perfect cat as black with a white belly in her late 10th century ode to aesthetics The Pillow Book. These pampered pets were also fond of drinking the fish oil of lanterns. As they stood on their hind legs to reach the tasty oil, their long shadows gave rise to a new fear. Superstitions began of cats walking upright and even dancing. Stories spread of the cat-beast kasha flying from the sky to steal corpses from coffins. In rural Japan, the split-tailed nekomata stalked the forests, large as tigers and hunting and killing humans.

With the Edo period came the rise of cities, and a major change in Japanese cat-lore. As people clustered together in urban environments, cats morphed into alleyway scroungers and ratters. The newly arisen pleasure districts created a new kind of kaibyō—prostitutes that were secretly transformed cats called *bakeneko*. Customers needed to be careful whose affections they were actually buying. These bakeneko prostitutes eventually evolved into the hypersexual cat girls of modern anime and manga.

Magical cats gained something else important in the late Edo period. When the shogun banned images of geisha and kabuki actors for fear of corruption of public morals, artists took to substituting cats in their depictions of libertine society. In the 1840s, images of cats having all night drinking bouts and carrying on affairs and gallivanting around town became the favorites of artists like Utagawa Kuniyoshi. The idea arose of a complex culture of magical cats, using their shape-changing magic to blend with human society.

From this burst, tales of kaibyō spread even further. A ramen maker was walking home one night, when he saw a cat beckoning him from an alley. As he approached the creature, lightning struck behind him. Considering this an omen, he commissioned a statue of the cat and set it in from of his shop, which flourished. Soon all over Japan the image of

a white cat raising a single paw—*the maneki neko*—became a symbol of prosperity, one that is seen in Asian restaurants all over the world today.

Cats performing similar miracles would gain sacred status. On places like the island of Tashirojima, *neko jima* (cat shrines) were built, enshrining cats as kami spirits. Today there are hundreds of cat shrines spread across Japan, each with their own unique story.

In modern Japan, it's difficult to go anywhere without seeing cats—either waving at you from restaurant windows, springing from the pages of manga, or hiding in the shadows at Shinto shrines. Hello Kitty! is beyond ubiquitous. Yet they remain multi-faceted and mysterious creatures. Even the bravest of persons thinks twice about crossing a cat.

Neko Musume

猫娘 (Lit: Cat Daughter)

Half-cat. Half-human. Neko musume—cat daughters—have a unique place in Japan's yōkai lore. They are some of the few *hanyōkai* (half-yōkai) in Japanese folklore, although the cat/human blending is of essence not blood. Neko musume are the result of a curse or magic. There are human/yōkai marriages, but the children are almost always 100% human. Neko musume are something else. They are also perhaps the only yōkai who can be traced back to a single, actual person.

The first neko musume was exhibited in the 1760s in Asakusa, Edo as part of a Misemono Show—the equivalent of 19th century Freak Shows—where she claimed to be a cat/human hybrid. Little is known of this original cat daughter, other than her appearance was startling and that she looked exactly like what she claimed to be. When the Misemono Shows faded, the neko musume disappeared.

She emerged again in 1800 as a story in the kaidan collection *Ehon Sayoshigure* (*Picture Book of a Gentle Rain on a Late Autumn Evening*). The story *Ashu no Kijo* (*Strange Woman of Ashu*) told the tale of a rich merchant whose daughter had the strange habits of licking things. Her tongue was rough like a cats, and she was nicknamed the neko musume. Variations of this story appeared in later kaidan collections, and by the 1850 *Ansei Zakki* she was a full-fledged yōkai, able to scurry along hedges and rented out by her mother as a rat catcher.

Neko musume was revived in 1936 by Shigeo Urata, and later by Shigeru Mizuki in 1958 in his comic *Kaiki Neko Musume* (*Bizarre Tales of the Cat Daughter*). He later included her as a regular character in his popular yōkai comic *Kitaro*, where she became known across all of Japan.

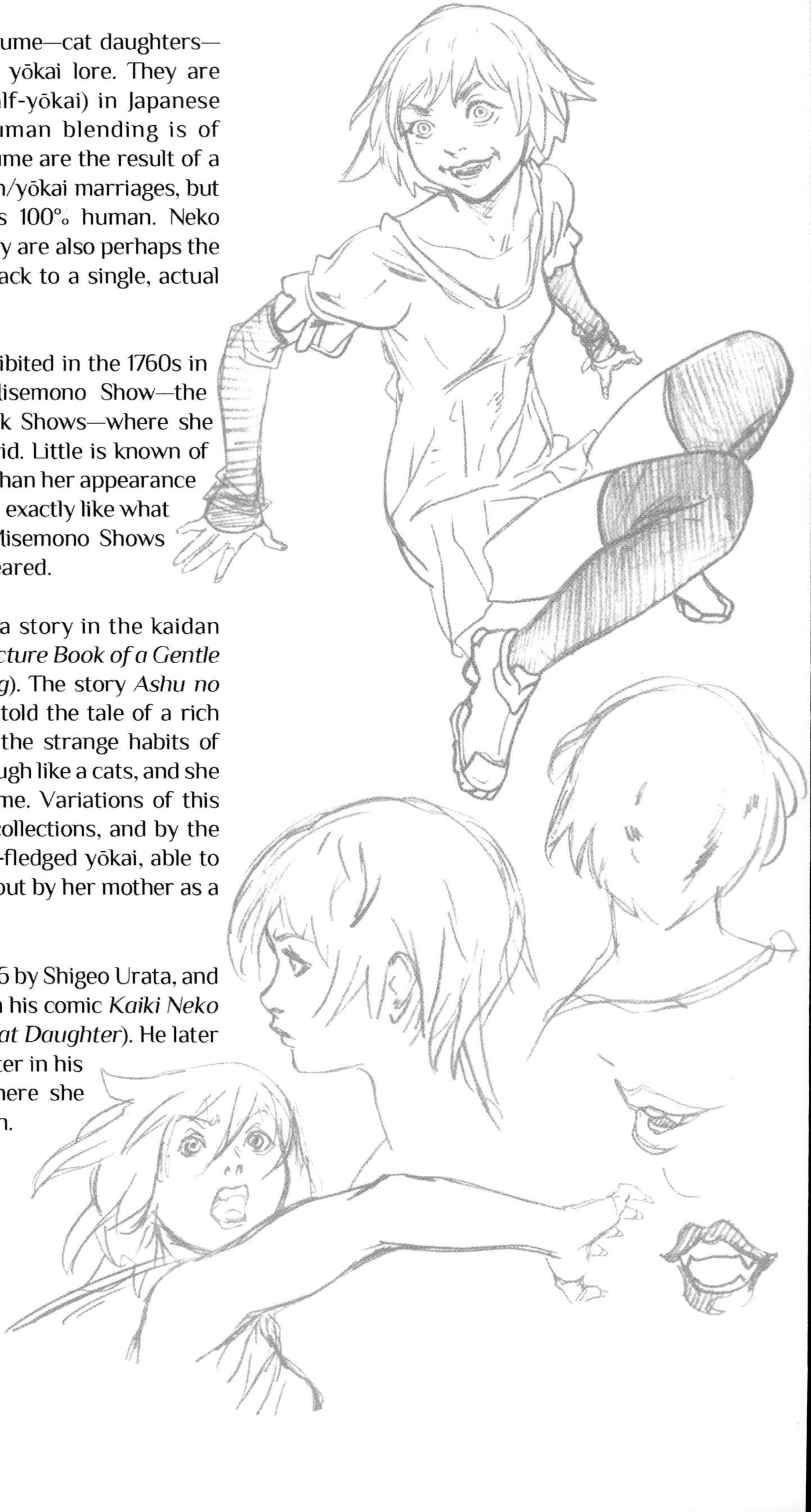

Nurarihyon
ぬらりひょん (Lit: Slippery Gourd)

One of the most elusive of Japan's yōkai menagerie, the slippery spirit called Nurarihyon has evolved far beyond his humble origins.

In the oldest stories of Nurarihyon, he was a sea monster—his blobby head was the personification of the Portuguese man-o-war jellyfish, floating in the Seto Inland Sea. In Okayama prefecture, he was considered an aspect of the massive *umibōzu* sea monk. Yet when artists began illustrating the *Hyakki Yagyō-zu*, an odd man appeared dressed in a simple robe, balancing an enormous, veined, gourd-shaped head on a spindly neck. Somehow, this peculiar character was identified as Nurarihyon.

By the Edo period, Nurarihyon was a prominent member of the urban yōkai. Stories of him described his powers as a mysterious air of authority. Nurarihyon would find prosperous houses, then come in and start giving orders, eating and drinking delicacies, and acting like an important house guest. The people would feel so flustered at his imperious nature they began serving him without question. Only after Nurarihyon left would they realize they had been tricked.

In the late Showa period (1926-1989), Nurarihyon got a promotion. He gained the reputation as a commander of yōkai, leader of the Hyakki Yagyō. (All you have to do is look at the old scrolls to see this isn't true.) His elevated rank can be traced back to Shigeru Mizuki's seminal yōkai comic *Kitaro*, where Nurarihyon showed up and announced himself as the Yōkai Sōdaishō. This position was formerly held by the massive Mikoshi Nyudō. Whether the two fought some Great Yōkai War that saw Nurarihyon as the victor, or whether Nurarihyon used his slippery nature and air of authority to seize command is unknown. Either way, in modern Japan it is accepted that Nurarihyon is a leader of yōkai.

Straw hat?

Slightly out of fashion Showa Era Suit

Suspenders no belt

veins

Top of head is covered in veins

Face and Ears drop

wide mouth

Round nose

Mouth is full of lots of small pointy teeth

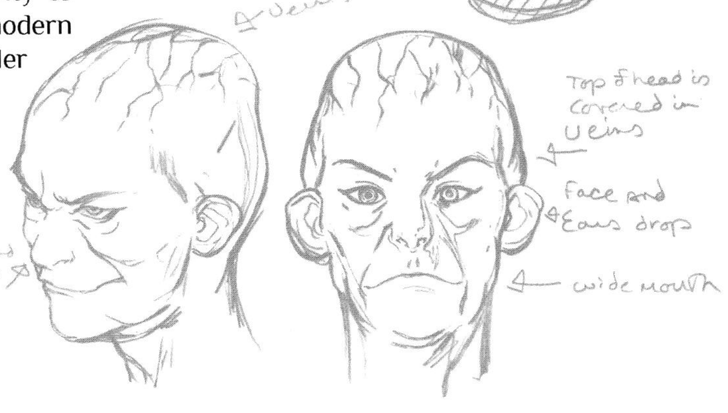

Kappa are the most ubiquitous of Japan's yōkai. While many monsters are found only in a particular region or environment, stories of kappa—or varieties of kappa–can be found almost anywhere across the Japanese archipelago. But this does not mean they are all the same.

The monsters called *suiko*—or water tigers—are massive and dangerous variants of the standard-issue kappa. Like vampires, suiko subsist on human blood. For unknown reasons, they fear scythes, flax seeds, and black-eyed peas. They are giants, covered in scales like a pangolin, and with hooked kneecaps and elbows that resemble a tiger's claws. Their skin is described as being mottled and patterned like a tiger's as well, which is all the more strange when you consider that suiko are invisible.

It is said that suikos' massive, twisted bodies only become visible when they die. They can be trapped by using a dead body they have drained as a lure. Build a straw hut around the body, and the suiko will be inescapably drawn to it. They will run and run in circles around the hut. One trapped, the suiko will continue running as the corpse decays. Exhausted, they will die, and their horrible form will be revealed.

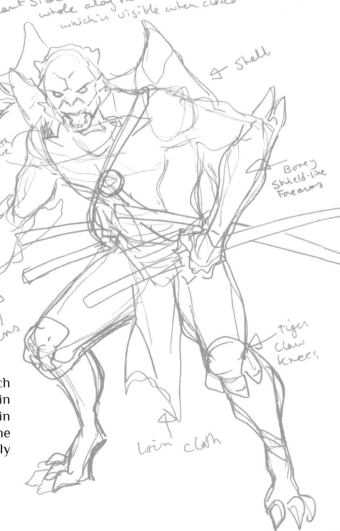

Mouth can open up to a giant size to swallow victims whole along the "Mouth line" which is visible when closed.
Shell
Mouth Line
Boney Shield-like Forearms
Long forearms
Tiger Claw Knees
Loin cloth

There are even some reports that kappa society is organized into gangs like the yakuza or the American Mafia. In these tales, suiko play the role of *oyabun*, meaning something like a capo or lieutenant. Each suiko oversees 48 kappa in its squad. The suiko in turn reports to Ryū-ō, the dragon king, who lives in his magnificent palace Ryū-gū at the bottom of the sea. All water yōkai pay homage to Ryū-ō, but only the kappa have become organized and ranked.

Tengu
天狗 (Lit: Heaven's Dog)

Few yōkai straddle the sacred and the profane like tengu. Perhaps only the demonic oni and the elusive kitsune are as immersed in the triple worlds of Buddhism, Shinto, and folklore superstitions. Disruptors and bringers of war. Impious anti-Buddhas who lead people into temptation and ruin. Mighty warriors who taught the secrets of martial arts to the famed Minamoto no Yoshitsune. Deities and spiritual focus of the mountain ascetics known as Shugendō. Tengu have played many roles over the centuries.

Tengu are one of Japan's most ancient yōkai, first appearing in the 720 CE book *Nihon Shoki* (*Chronicles of Japan*). They are thought to take their name from the Chinese *tiāngou*, a dog-shaped meteor that heralds war and misfortune. Name aside, Japan's tengu have always been more bird-like than dog-like; the earliest depictions are of a kite-like bird person dressed in the sacred garb of a Buddhist priest. There is speculation this appearance comes from the Hindu eagle-beings called *garuda*, identified as one of the major non-human races in early Buddhist scripture. Tengu later became associated with the long-nosed Shinto deity Sarutahiko, altering their appearance into the red-faced, long-nosed, winged goblins you see today.

Accounts of tengu are too numerous to list. The 11th century *Konjaku Monogatari* shows tengu as powerful beings able to carry off dragons under their arms. The 14th century *Genpei Jōsuiki* describes the tengu road, a third path that lies between the roads to Heaven and Hell. Edo period books such as Inoue Enryo's *Tenguron* list and rank tengu in the same way as medieval demonology books ranked demons in Hell.

A further legend tells of the evil emperor Sutoku, who resurrected as the Ō-Tengu, the Great Tengu and Lord of Evil. Along with the nine-tailed kitsune Tamamo-no-Mae and the oni lord Shuten-dōji, Sutoku is one of the Three Great Yōkai of Japan.

The history of the *tsuchigumo*—the dirt spiders—is the history of Japan itself. But it is a secret history. A shameful history. One known by few in the modern era, due to ancient propaganda that buried the truth deep under the earth where the spiders still hide today.

This secret is that the people living in Japan today—the people known as Japanese—are actually invaders. Once there were several distinct tribes native to the islands: To the north, the Ainu, remnants of whom still survive on snowy Hokkaido. On the island of Kyushu were the Kumaso, the bear people, now long extinct. To the south were the Ryukuan people, known today as the ethnic Okinawans. And on the mainland, were the Tsuchigomori, known only as "those who hide in the ground."

The history is sketchy, written by the victors and with archeological evidence still tampered with and tainted to this day. Facts and legends can be pieced together and sifted through as best possible to achieve a general picture. Sometime during the Yayoi period (300 BCE to 300 CE), invaders sailed across the Sea of Japan from China and the Korean peninsula. Landing on populated islands, they started a pattern as old as humanity itself—the technically superior invaders displaced the aboriginal populations, driving them off the mainland and onto the less hospitable islands of the north and south. These invaders took ground and established their own kingdom, identified in 8th century Chinese literature as the Wajin—the People of Wa. They called themselves the Yamato.

Along with technology and civilization, the Yamato wielded the weapon of religion in their battle against the native tribes. They raised their own emperor and declared him divine. In order to cement their divine Right of Rule, they commissioned the books *Kojiki* (*Record of Ancient Matters*) and *Nihon Shiki* (*Chronicles of Japan*) showing how their emperor was a direct descendent of the sun goddess Amaterasu. Along with raising up themselves, they also used the *Kojiki* and the *Nihon Shiki* to demonize their enemy, portraying them as less than human. It should be no surprise that these books contain the first mention of the tsuchigomori.

The reason for the name is unknown. There is speculation that it is literal, that the tsuchigomori were underground dwellers who dug their houses under the earth instead of building them upwards. The word-switch from descriptive (tsuchigomori, 土隠; those who hide in the ground) to the derogatory (tsuchigumo, 土蜘蛛; earth spider or dirt spider) was a short leap. However, more strange is the description of these people. Instead of the multi-limbed spider-people you might imagine, they

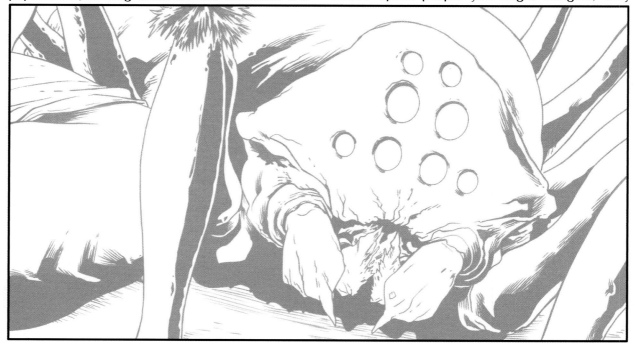

were described as having long glowing tails which they used to push around rocks.

This odd appearance makes a little more sense when you realize that Japan has no native species of tarantula or other large spiders. Referring to their enemies as filthy ground-digging spiders may sound good, but didn't bring up a particularly fierce image. They had to come up with something scarier—apparently stone-shoving glowing tails fit the bill.

Use of the term tsuchigumo spread from these indigenous people to other enemies of the empire. Eventually all who refused to bow down to Yamato authority were branded as tsuchigumo, and dehumanized as monsters. There are several descriptions of the emperor attempting to tame these rogue people. In the *Hizen no Kuni Fudoki*, it states that the Emperor Keiko captured the tsuchigumo Oomimi and Taremimi on a state visit to Shiki Island. Other legends tell of five great tsuchigumo gathering forces in the Katsuragi Mountains to oppose the emperor.

So how did they become spiders? That transformation would not happen until the 14th century.

By the 14th century the Yamato were firmly established as the dominant people. The 12th century Genpei War had been the last serious challenge to their authority, and they were no longer worried about random tribespeople. Commerce with China had brought new and wonderful things, including fabulous animals like the Chinese bird spider, a large, tiger-striped tarantula that burrows into the ground to build its nest.

The monster was almost too perfect; Japan had its true dirt spider at last. The 14th century scroll *Tsuchigumo Soushi* reinvented the historical tsuchigumo as a tribe of monstrous yōkai that invade the capital. The heroic commander Minamoto no Yorimitsu repelled the invasion. Following the trail of skulls, he was led to a cave in the Rendai field, in a mountain north of Kyoto. There he hacked his way through an army of yōkai, fighting through the night until dawn arose.

With the welcoming rays of the sun, a beautiful woman emerged from the cave. Claiming to be held prisoner. Yorimitsu was no fool, and he drew his katana and slashed her. She left a trail of white blood as she fled into the cave. Following her, Yorimitsu confronted her true form, a gigantic spider with the striped body of a tiger. He battled the tsuchigumo for hours, finally cutting off her head. The heads of 1,990 dead people came pouring from her stomach, while countless small spiders—her babies—came flying from her body to seed the country with more tsuchigumo.

The *Tsuchigumo Soushi* was extremely popular, inspiring further legends of Minamoto no Yorimitsu and battles with tsuchigumo. In one story, Yorimitsu fell ill, and only recovered when he followed a dubious monk into the forest where he found he was under the spell of a giant tsuchigumo. Yorimitsu pierced it with an iron spike, that later became the sword *Kumo-kiri* (*Spider Cutter*). For yōkai, the tsuchigumo were unusually crafty and vengeful. They formed alliances with oni, and attacked the Minamoto family including Yorimitsu's father.

In modern Japan, the giant spider legends are all that remain of the aboriginal people who once fought against an invading army and defied their emperor. The Yamato clan was almost successful in striking the tsuchigumo from the record books, leaving them only as half-whispered legends. But still they persist.

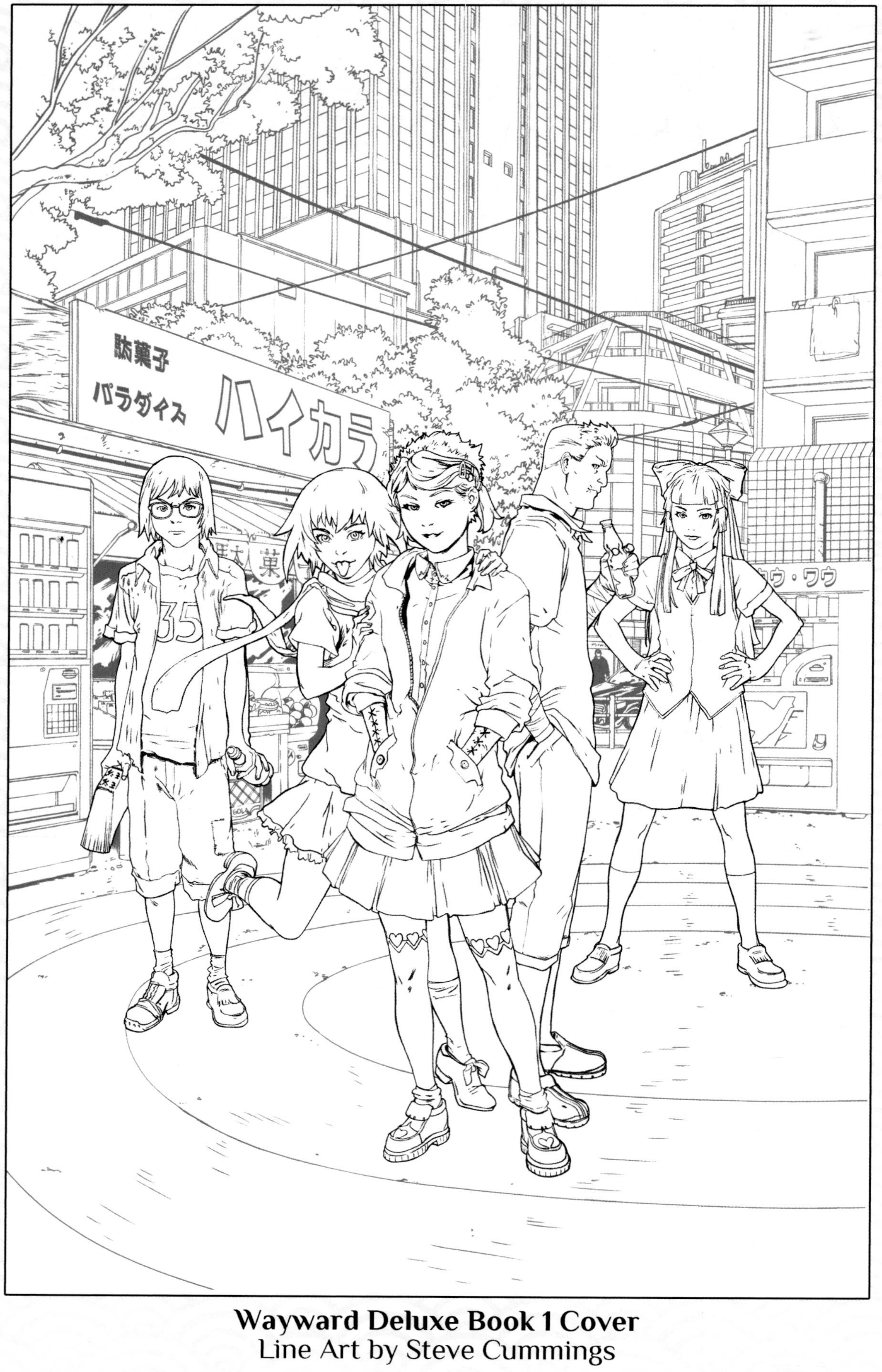
駄菓子
パラダイス
ハイカラ

Wayward Deluxe Book 1 Cover
Line Art by Steve Cummings